ILL WIND

Nevada Barr

G. P. PUTNAM'S SONS   NEW YORK

G. P. Putnam's Sons
Publishers Since 1838
200 Madison Avenue
New York, NY 10016

ISBN 0–399–14015–8

Printed in the United States of America

This book is printed on acid-free paper.

1

N O GRAVEYARDS; that bothered Anna. People died. Unless you ate them, burned them, or mailed them to a friend, the bodies had to go somewhere. In any event, there would at least be bones. A civilization that lived and died for six hundred years should leave a mountain of bones.

No graveyards and then no people. Inhabitants cooking, weaving, farming one day, then, the next, gone. Pots still on cold ashes, doormats rotting in doorways, tools lying beside half-finished jobs.

So: an invading army swooped down and massacred everybody. Then where were the bashed-in skulls? Chipped bone fragments? Teeth sown like corn?

A plague: the American version of the Black Death, an antiquated form of Captain Tripps, killing two out of every three people. The survivors abandoning a desolated community, carting thousands and thousands of dead bodies with them? Not bloody likely. Not in a society without benefit of the wheel.

Once people got factored into an equation all bets were off; still, there ought to be corpses. Anna couldn't think of any civilization that couldn't be counted on to leave corpses and garbage for the next generation.

* * *

A hand smacked down on the Formica and Anna started in her chair.

"Where were you?" hissed Alberta Stinson, head of Interpretation for Chapin Mesa.

"Anywhere but here, Al," Anna whispered back. She dragged a hand down her face to clear it of dreams and looked surreptitiously at her watch. The staff meeting had been dragging on for two hours. The coffee was gone and there never had been any doughnuts.

Stinson poked Anna in the ribs with a blunt forefinger. "Stay awake. The Boys are on a rampage." Al always referred to Mesa Verde's administration rather disdainfully as "The Boys." Stinson was fifteen pounds over what the glossy magazines recommended, with salt-and-pepper hair that looked as if it had been cut with pinking shears. Leading tours, giving programs, wandering the myriad ruins on the mesas, she had a face creased by the weather from forehead to chin, and the skin around her eyes was crinkled from squinting against the sun's glare. Near as Anna could tell, the woman had but two passions in life: discovering why the Old Ones had vanished and seeing to it that any despoilers of their relics did likewise.

Anna pulled Stinson's yellow pad toward her. Beneath Al's sketches of nooses, guillotines, and other means of mayhem, she scribbled: "No help here. I'm a lowly GS-7. No teeth."

Al snorted.

Thirty minutes had elapsed since Anna had mentally checked out and still the debate raged. Money had come down from Congress, scads of the stuff, allocated for the digging up and replacing of the antiquated waterline serving the homes and public buildings of Mesa Verde National Park. Since May heavy machinery and heated arguments had roared over the ancient land. Meetings had been called and called off on a weekly basis. The resultant acrimony clogged the high desert air like dust from the ditcher. As always in small towns, toxins trickled down. When the powers that be waged war, the peasants took sides. Even the seasonals gathered in tight groups, biting assorted backs and sipping righteous indignation with beer chasers.

New to the mesa, Anna'd not been drafted into either army, but the constant dissension wore at her nerves and aggravated her hermit tendencies.

Around a table of metal and Formica—the kind usually reserved for the serving of bad chicken at awards banquets—sat the leading players: a lean and hungry-looking administrative officer with a head for figures and an eye for progress; the chief ranger, a wary whip of a man determined to drag the park out of the dark ages of plumbing and into the more impressive visitation statistics additional water would allow; Ted Greeley, the contractor hired to pull off this feat in a timely manner; and Al Stinson: historian, archaeologist, and defender of the dead. Or at least the sanctity of science's claim on the dead.

When the Anasazi had vanished from the mesa, their twelfth-century secrets had vanished with them. Stinson was determined to stop twentieth-century machinery from destroying any clue before it was studied. Since the entire landscape of Chapin Mesa was a treasure trove of artifacts, the digging of so much as a post hole gave the archaeologist nightmares. The contractor had been brought on board to trench seventeen miles of land six feet deep.

Theodore Roosevelt Greeley of Greeley Construction had a job to do and was being paid handsomely to do it.

Though Greeley had a veneer of bonhomie, he struck Anna as a hard-core capitalist. She suspected that to his modern Manifest Destiny mentality, the only good Indian was a profitable Indian.

Fingers ever-tensed on the purse strings, the chief ranger and the administrative officer leaned toward Greeley's camp.

Anna and Hills Dutton, the district ranger, were the only noncombatants present. Dutton's impressive form was slouched in a folding chair near the end of the table. He'd removed the ammunition from the magazine of his Sig Sauer nine-millimeter and appeared to be inventorying it bullet by bullet.

"Anna?"

As was his want, the chief ranger was mumbling and it took her a second to recognize her name.

"What?"

"Any input?" The chief was just shifting the heat from himself. None of this august body gave two hoots about what she thought. She and Hills were there only because the secretary refused to go for coffee.

"Well, if all nonessential personnel were required to live out of the park the problem would be alleviated considerably." Nonessential included not only seasonal interpreters, but also archaeologists, department heads, the administrative officer, the chief ranger, and the superintendent himself. Anna's suggestion was met with annoyed silence. Satisfied she'd offended everyone at the table and it would be a good long time before they again bothered her for her "input," Anna retreated back into her own world.

When visitors left for the day and evening light replaced noon's scientific glare, she escaped the hubbub.

It soothed her to be where the people weren't. After working backcountry in wilderness parks—Guadalupe Mountains in Texas and Isle Royale in Lake Superior—Mesa Verde, with its quarter million–plus visitors each year, struck her as urban. During the day, when the ruins were open to the public, she couldn't walk far enough to escape the hum of traffic and the sullen growl of buses idling as they disgorged tour groups.

After closing time, on the pretext of a patrol, she would slip down into the new quiet of Cliff Palace, one of the largest of the Anasazi villages ever discovered. Climbing as high as was allowed, she would sit with her back to the still-warm stone of the ancient walls, around her rooms and turrets and towers, sunken chambers connected by tunnels, plazas with stone depressions for grinding.

The pueblo hung above a world that fell away for a hundred miles, mesas, buttes, and green valleys fading to the blue of the distant mountain ranges that drifted into the blue of the sky. The air was crisp and thin. Without moisture to laden it with perfumes, it carried only the sharp scent baked from piñon and ponderosa.

From her perch high in the ruin she would gaze down Cliff Canyon. Dwellings appeared singly, first one, then two, then half a dozen, like the hidden pictures in a child's puzzle.

Tiny jewel cities tucked in natural alcoves beneath the mesa stood sentinel over the twisting valleys. Nearly all faced west or southwest, catching the heat of the winters' sun, providing shade through the summers. The towns were built with fine craftsmanship, the work of practiced masons evident in the hand-chipped and fitted stones. Walls were whitewashed and painted, and decorations of stars and handprints enlivened the sandstone. Doorways were made in the shape of keyholes. Ladders, constructed of juniper and hide, reached rooms built on shelves forty and fifty feet above the slate of the alcove's floor.

These were not tents for folding and slipping away silently into the night. These were edifices, art, architecture. Homes built to last the centuries. If the builders had been driven out, surely the marauders would have taken up residence, enjoyed their spoils?

If the Old Ones had not died and they'd not left of their own volition and they'd not been driven out . . .

Then what? Anna thought.

Food for thought.

Plots for Von Daniken.

Anna's radio crackled to life and everyone at the table, including Al, looked at her as if she'd made a rude noise.

"Excuse me," she murmured.

As she left the room she found herself hoping for something dire: a brawl at the concession dorm, another medical at Cliff Palace, a bus wreck—anything to keep her out of the staff meeting.

"Seven hundred, three-one-two," she answered the call.

"Could you come by the CRO?" the dispatcher asked. Frieda, the chief ranger's secretary and the park dispatcher, was always even-toned and professional. From her voice one could never tell whether a bloody nose or grand-theft auto awaited at the chief ranger's office.

"I'm on my way. And thank you."

"KFC seven hundred, fourteen-eighteen."

The chief ranger's office was built from blocks of native stone and beamed-in logs darkened by time. Like the museum and the upper-echelon permanent employees' houses, the CRO was a historic structure built in the nineteen thirties by the Civilian Conservation Corps when "another day, another dollar" was the literal truth.

Anna banged through the screen door and leaned on the glass-topped counter. In true bureaucratic fashion, the inside of the graceful little building had been cobbled into cramped "work areas" and further vandalized by the addition of indoor-outdoor carpeting and cheap metal desks.

Frieda Dierkz looked up from her computer. In her thirties, with short reddish-brown hair cut in an ear-length wedge, more hips than shoulders and more brains than just about anybody else in the Visitor Protection and Fire Management Division, Frieda was the heart of the office. Or, more correctly, as the computer-generated sign on the bulletin board above her desk announced, Queen of the Office. Anna guessed there'd been a time, maybe not yet quite past, when Frieda had hoped to be Queen of a more intimate realm. But a plain face and, more damaging to matrimonial prospects, an air of absolute competence, had made her a career woman.

Though Frieda might have seen that as a bad thing, Anna didn't. It was always the breadwinner, she'd noticed, who had the adventures. Support staff—whether at work or in the kitchen—seemed ever relegated to keeping the tedious home fires burning.

"So . . ." Anna said for openers.

"Patsy called. Tom's in the park." As ever, Frieda was economical with words.

Patsy Silva was the superintendent's secretary; Tom the estranged husband. Ex-husband. "What this time? Bad guitar music at three A.M.?"

"Suicide notes and chocolates. The chocolates were put through her mail slot. The dog opened them. Half melted on May's bank statement. The dog threw up the other half on a four-hundred-dollar Indian rug." Frieda laughed. In his capacity as two parts joke, one part pathos, Tom Silva had been a thorn in law enforcement's side since Patsy had been hired the previous winter. Had they lived outside the park they would have been the problem of the Colorado police. Inside park boundaries the task fell to the rangers.

Anna hated domestic disputes. The good guys and the bad guys kept switching roles; an outsider didn't stand a chance. "Where's Stacy?" Anna hoped to drag another ranger along for moral support.

"Occupado. Another medical at Cliff Palace. Elderly lady."

"Damn. What does Patsy want us to do about it?"

"Just go talk to her, I guess. She wasn't too specific. 'Do something but don't say I said.' "

Anna nodded. "On my way." Halfway out the door she stopped and turned back. "Frieda, can I come visit Piedmont tonight?"

"Anytime," the dispatcher returned, already back at her computer. "If I'm not there, let yourself in. Door's never locked."

The tower house was the most picturesque, if not the most convenient, of the historical homes. Named for the round tower that housed the master bedroom, the staircase, and a small round living room, it sat on a gentle hill just west of the museum behind the more conventional homes. For one person it would have been perfect. For a woman with two teenage daughters it had proved a nightmare of bathroom scheduling and closet-space allotment.

Rumor had it, because of the girls, Patsy would be moved as soon as a two-bedroom became available, leaving the tower house up for grabs. Due to the housing shortage, when Anna entered on duty eight weeks before, the district ranger had parked her in the seasonal women's dormitory till more suitable quarters could be found, so it was with a more than slightly proprietary eye that she allowed herself to be ushered in.

Patsy Silva was compact, with the voluptuous curves of a woman who has borne children. Her hair was close-cropped and honey-blond, her eyes made impossibly blue by tinted contact lenses. Teeth as straight as an orthodontist's slide rule were shown off by hot-pink lipstick drawn on slightly fuller than her natural lip line.

Patsy smiled and waved distractedly toward the living room with its mess of clothes and magazines littering every flat surface. "Missy and Mindy are over at Frieda's watching the VCR," she said, as if the temptation of video explained a hasty and untidy departure. "She's got quite a movie collection and lets the girls watch almost anytime. It helps."

Anna nodded. Bucolic park living was fine for adults and children but could weigh heavily on adolescents with a long summer on their hands.

"Sit down. Sit." Patsy shooed Anna toward the kitchen. "Coffee or anything?" With the offer, as with most of Patsy's communications, came a tight bright smile. More a habit of placating, Anna suspected, than a genuine show of happiness.

"Coffee'd be fine."

The kitchen, the only square room in the house, was small but efficiently made, with wood cabinets and a restaurant-style booth under one of the two windows. Anna slid into the booth. Patsy busied herself at the counter. Anna wasn't particularly fond of reheated coffee, but people seemed more comfortable after their hospitality had been accepted. Maybe some ancient instinct about breaking bread together. Or maybe it was just the comfort of having something to keep their hands and eyes occupied.

Patsy put the cups on the table along with a sugar bowl and creamer in the shape of ceramic ducks wearing blue calico bonnets.

"Thanks." Anna pulled the cup to her and poured pale bluish milk out of the duck's bill. Patsy's smile clicked on then faded slowly, the effort for once proving too great.

"It's Tom," she said, as if admitting a tiresome fact.

"Chocolates."

"And a note. It's awful. How can you protect yourself from that? The police act like I'm lucky to have such an attentive husband."

"Ex-husband."

"Yes. Thank you. He makes me forget. Ex-husband. Ex, ex, ex as in exit, finito, gone. Except that he's not." She put her fingers to her temples, looking as if she would have run them distractedly through her hair had not each wave been expertly coaxed into place.

"What makes him more than a nuisance?" Anna asked. At a guess, she might have added "other than guilt?" How could a woman not feel guilty for walking out on flowers, candy, and serenades?

"I was afraid you were going to ask that," Patsy replied with an explosive sigh. She slumped back in the booth. "I don't know. I mean, he doesn't really do anything. It's just kind of an increasing sense of weird. Know what I mean? As if my not folding like I always did with the flowery courtship business is pushing him near some edge. This last note seemed, well . . . edgy." Patsy apologized with a particularly bright smile.

Anna would have laid odds that Patsy Silva had apologized a lot in her thirty-seven years; sorries and smiles poured like oil on life's troubled waters. "Can I see the note?"

"Yes. I kept it. At least I've learned that since the divorce. Anything edgy, I keep. You can't imagine how silly this all sounds, even to me, when I try to tell it to some big burly policeman who thinks his wife would die and go straight to pig heaven if he ever paid her this kind of attention. Here it is."

While she talked, Patsy rummaged through a doll-sized bureau complete with miniature vanity mirror. Decals of ducks matching the creamer were centered on each tiny drawer. From the bottom drawer she pinched up a scrap of paper. Holding it by the edge as if she didn't want to smudge incriminating prints, she laid it on the table.

In a childish but legible scrawl, more printing than script, was written: "What do you want, Pats? I've give you everything. A car, nice close, everything. What do you want? Maybe you want me to do like that guy you told me sent somebody his ear. I'll go him one better. I'm not living without you, Pats. I'm not."

"And you think it's a suicide note," Anna said. To her it read more like a threat but she was not privy to the inner workings of Tom Silva's mind. Being the new kid on the block, Anna'd not yet caught up on the gossip.

"I wish it was a suicide note!" Patsy snapped.

Anna liked the anger better than the shiny smiles. At least it rang true.

Patsy, who'd been rereading the note over Anna's shoulder, slid onto the bench beside her. Such proximity made Anna uncomfortable. Before her husband, Zachary, had been killed, when she'd lived in the confines of New York

City, Anna'd fought for personal space on elevators and in subway cars. Since joining the Park Service and moving to less constricting climes, the need had increased, rather than the opposite. An acre per person and bullhorns for communication struck her as about right for socializing.

She turned as if to give Patsy her full attention and put some space between them.

"I told Frieda it was a suicide note because it seemed easiest—you know, made sense for me to be calling." Patsy picked up her coffee but just stared into it without drinking. "It was that ear thing he said—like van Gogh. Besides the chocolates there was an envelope. One of those little square ones that come with florists' arrangements."

Anna waited, sipping coffee made gray and tepid by skim milk. Patsy didn't go on with her story. "And the envelope?" Anna prompted.

"I burned it."

Since silences didn't draw Patsy out the way they did most people—too many years of being a good girl and not speaking till spoken to, Anna guessed—she asked her what was in the envelope.

"A little piece of brown material, soft, like expensive crepe. Tom isn't circumcised. I think it was foreskin."

Anna winced. It seemed a little "edgy" to her as well.

For maybe a minute neither spoke. Whether Patsy sensed Anna's discomfort with her proximity or, once her information was told, no longer needed the closeness, she moved to the sink to dump her untouched coffee. When she returned she resumed her place on the bench opposite.

"What do you want me to do?" Anna asked.

Patsy burst into tears.

While Patsy Silva cried, Anna thought.

"I don't suppose Tom has any outstanding wants or warrants against him?" she asked hopefully.

Patsy shook her head. "I'm sorry."

Anna didn't know if she was apologizing because she still cried or because her ex-husband wasn't a known felon. "I'll run him anyway. You never know." After a moment she said: "Maybe a court restraining order; keep the guy away from you. I'll look into it; see if you have to prove harassment, what it will take to keep him out of Mesa Verde."

"It's too late. He's here," Patsy wailed, sounding like the little girl who saw poltergeists. "He's got a job with the contractor putting in the new pipeline."

The waterline. It was getting so Anna was tempted to blast the thing herself. Perhaps Mesa Verde's staff had been on the outs for decades—living in isolation where dead people were the main natural resource had to have an impact—but since she'd entered on duty the pipeline had been the lightning rod.

"Are you dating anybody?" Anna asked abruptly.

Patsy looked pained. "Not exactly," she said, not meeting Anna's eye.

She was dating somebody. A tidy old-fashioned triangle in the making. "Does Tom know?"

"No! I don't even know for sure." Patsy smiled a shy smile. Inwardly Anna groaned.

"Talk to him," Patsy pleaded.

"Sure," Anna promised.

"Talk to his boss. Mr. Ted something. He seems reasonable."

"Ted Greeley. I can do that."

"But don't get him fired. With Missy and Mindy both in high school next year we're counting on the child support."

Anna repressed a sigh. Domestic stuff. "Gotta go," she said, glancing at the clock over the sink. "Quittin' time."

Patsy laughed for the first time in a while. "Hills blew his overtime money on an all-terrain vehicle. I'm kind of glad he did—he's so cute at budget meetings when he begs."

"Take care," Anna said, setting her Smokey Bear hat squarely on her head and taking a last look around quarters she hoped soon would be hers.

"I'll keep anything else . . . personal . . . Tom sends and give it to you," Patsy promised as she held open the door.

"I can't wait."

Summer was off and running.

2

No REST for the weary—or was it the wicked? Anna couldn't remember. There was definitely no rest for those fated to share dormitory quarters.

Her briefcase, used for carrying citation notices, maps, and brochures, banged against the screen door, jarring her elbow. Simultaneously her ears and nose were assaulted. The first by the Grateful Dead and the second by a kitchen that would daunt even the most hardened health inspector.

Early on in this allegedly temporary housing arrangement Anna realized she had two choices: bite the bullet or play Mom. As she had neither the taste nor the inclination for the latter, she had spent the four and a half weeks since the seasonals entered on duty knee-deep in unwashed dishes and empty beer cans. The mess wasn't as hard to take as the noise. After some sparks had flown she'd been given a room of her own but the walls of the flimsy, prefab structure were so thin, at times she swore they served better to conduct than deflect sound waves.

Clad in a homemade ankle-length sarong of double knit, Jamie Burke was draped across one sofa. Jennifer

Short, the other woman with whom she shared the two-bedroom house, was sprawled in a pajama-party attitude. They were intelligent, funny, interesting women. Left ignorant of their domestic habits, Anna would undoubtedly have found them delightful.

As she tried to slip unnoticed into her bedroom the imperious call of "Stop there!" arrested her progress.

The order came from Jamie, one of the army of seasonal interpreters hired on each summer to lead tours of the cliff dwellings and, for a short time—or so Hills repeatedly promised—Anna's housemate at Far View.

Dutifully, Anna waited, briefcase in hand.

In her late twenties, Jamie had the look of someone who has been athletic all her life. Muscular hips and legs gave her a stocky silhouette that was accentuated by the flat-brimmed hat and cloddy shoes of the NPS uniform she wore on duty.

In contrast to her juggernaut physique, her face was a perfect oval, the skin flawless, setting off pale blue eyes and a sensuous mouth. Jamie's hair, fine and smooth and blue-black, fell to her knees in a single braid thickened by red yarn woven through and bound around, Apache style, at the tail.

Jamie boasted that she inherited the black tresses from a half-blood Cherokee mother but Anna strongly suspected that she dyed it. In a women's dorm there were few secrets. All of Jamie's body hair was not of the same raven hue.

"What's up?" Anna asked, trying to keep the weariness from her voice.

"Stacy had to walk an old lady out of Cliff this morning. Where were you?"

Anna ignored the accusatory tone. "What was the problem?"

"Some kind of pulmonary thing. Wasn't breathing right. There was that old guy last week."

"Yup." Again Anna waited.

"They're pissed. I'm not surprised, either."

Now Anna was lost. The previous week's carry-out had gone well. The man's wife had even sent a glowing thank-you letter. "The man's family is pissed?"

"No-o." Jamie drew out the syllable slightly, as if Anna was too obtuse for words. "The Old Ones. The Anasazi. They should close this park to everybody but native peoples. It's not Frontierland, it's a sacred place. We shouldn't be here."

Jamie Burke leaped from one drama to the next. In the few short weeks Anna had known her she'd been through exposure to AIDS, been engaged to a nameless state senator in Florida, and been involved in an affair with a married man so discreet it had to be imaginary. The pipeline was a bandwagon made for jumping on.

"Ah. Chindi." Anna used the Navajo word for spirit or—she was never quite sure—evil spirit. "Could be. Listen, I've got to slip into something less deadly." She grimaced at her gun and escaped down the hall.

Once divested of the dead weight of her gun and the airtight shoes required by NPS class "A" uniform standards, Anna felt less hostile. By the time she'd poured herself a generous dollop of Mirassou Pinot Blanc, she was civilized enough to join the party in the front room.

The television was on with the volume turned down and Jamie was verbally abusing Vanna White as she turned the letters on "Wheel of Fortune." It was a nightly ritual that seldom failed to amuse.

"Arms like toothpicks! Look at that," Jamie was exclaiming. "I don't think she's pretty. Do you think she's pretty? Who in God's name thinks she's pretty? Little

Miss Toothpick Arms. Little Miss White Bread."

Anna curled her feet under her on the nubby fabric of an armchair. The boxy room was furnished in Early Dentist's Office but it was serviceable. Anna, barefoot, in pink sweatpants and an oversized man's shirt, surrounded by girls with Budweisers—or women that looked like girls from a vantage point of forty—had a sense of being an uncomfortable traveler in time. Even the cheap southwestern print of Jamie's sarong put her in mind of the India-print bedspreads she'd found so many uses for in her college days. In a gush of self-pity she felt her world as dead as that of the Anasazi. She missed Christina and Alison, the woman and her daughter with whom she'd shared a house in Houghton, Michigan, when she worked on Isle Royale.

Chris was a rock: gentle and soft and stronger than Anna ever hoped to be. Alison, at six, was like a kitten with brains—irresistible and a little scary.

Anna'd left on the pretense Mesa Verde was a promotion as well as a return to her beloved southwest. In reality she'd cleared out because she knew Chris was in love but wouldn't move in with her sweetheart if it meant abandoning Anna. So Anna'd abandoned her.

I'm a fucking saint, she thought sourly, watching Vanna turn E's on "Wheel of Fortune."

The job wasn't too bad. Though at times Anna felt more like a nurse than a ranger.

Mesa Verde was an old and staid national park. As early as 1906 it was clear that the ancient cliff dwellings, though already largely looted of artifacts, were a part of America's heritage that must be preserved.

Visitors to Mesa Verde went out of their way to get there and had the money to do so. Consequently, the clientele tended to be older, with gold cards and expensive RVs. Retired folks with bad hearts and tired lungs from San Diego, Florida, and the south coast of Texas found themselves up at altitude for the first time in thirty years. If drug dogs were called in Anna suspected they'd sniff out more nitroglycerin tablets than anything else.

There'd been two fatalities—both elderly visitors with cardiopulmonary problems—and eleven ambulance runs, five of them out of Cliff Palace. And it was only early June.

Swallowing the last of her wine, Anna leaned back and let the alcohol uncoil her mental springs.

Jennifer wandered back to the TV with a fresh beer.

Short was a round-faced woman with good hair, bad skin, and too much makeup. Fresh out of Tennessee State's one-semester course, she was the new law enforcement seasonal in her first national park job. Jennifer was a Memphis belle in what Anna had thought was a bygone tradition: all magnolia blossoms, little-ol'-me's-led-a-sheltered-life, and eek-a-mouse. Proven tactics, guaranteed to turn the boys to putty.

Anna hadn't yet decided whether she was more irritated or intrigued with the femme fatale routine. On the one hand it would be interesting to watch. On the other, given the job, it could get a person killed.

"Jamie, I saw that poor little thing you were talking about," Jennifer was saying. Or, to be more accurate: "Ah saw thet pore lil' thang yew were tawkin' abaht."

"She had the cutest face, but her little body! I just couldn't live like that. High school is going to be pure hell. It'd be a mercy to drown people like that at birth. I don't want to sound mean, I mean for their own sakes. I wouldn't want to live like that. I just wouldn't."

A natural silence fell and they all stared at Vanna. Jennifer had been talking about Stacy and Rose Meyers' daughter, Bella. A sadness threatened Anna and she was glad when loud knocking interrupted her thoughts. She made no move to uncoil herself. Jennifer sprang up, "I'll get it" out of her mouth almost before the knocking ceased. The first week on the mesa she had announced one of her prime motives for choosing law enforcement: a way to meet straight men.

A moment later two seasonal firefighters from the helitack crew followed Jennifer back in. Because of the wealth of ruins and artifacts on the mesa all wildfires were put out in their infancy by a crew of wildland firefighters flown in by helicopter. Dozers and other heavy equipment customarily used to cut fireline would be so destructive to the cultural aspects of the park that fire was never allowed to spread if it could be helped. When nothing was burning, helitack performed the high- and low-angle rescues often needed to evacuate sick and injured people from the less accessible ruins.

Jimmy Russell and Paul Summers had the youth and build of most seasonal firefighters and the living room fairly crackled with sexual energy. Russell's heavily muscled arms and back were shown off in a tight T-shirt emblazoned with a flying insect wearing a yellow shirt of fire-resistant Nomex. A budding good ol' boy from Kentucky, Jimmy chewed his words like tobacco. Summers was a striking blond with a born-again surfer haircut and finely chiseled features. Somehow managing to look sophisticated in worn Levi's and a baggy, wrinkled, oxford shirt, he carried the libations: a six-pack of Coors Light dangled from each hand.

"Hiya, Anna." Paul smiled at her and she was annoyed to find herself flattered.

Popping a Coors, Russell settled cross-legged on the carpet. Jamie pulled herself around on the couch and began kneading the muscles of his neck and shoulders.

Let the mating rituals begin, Anna thought sourly. Unfolding her legs, she levered herself up: time to go visit Piedmont.

On the way through the kitchen she grabbed up what was left of the Mirassou Blanc.

Frieda Dierkz had a house in what was called the Utility Loop. It was near the maintenance yard, about a mile from the Headquarters/Museum Loop. The houses were small, white one- and two-bedroom homes with the charm and inconveniences of 1940s construction. These homes were for lower-level permanents, the GS-4s and -5s and -7s. Higher-ups claimed the beautiful historic homes in the Headquarters Loop. The fire dorm, where helitack was housed, was also on the loop, as were a couple of aging trailers rented out to seasonal interpreters each summer.

Frieda lived in number thirty-four. Most of the front yards were overgrown with weeds and native grasses. Her marigold border and tended lawn looked out of place in piñon-juniper country.

A sad-eyed black lab was resting on some newly dug up and soon to be dead marigolds. He thumped his tail half-heartedly as Anna came up the walk.

"Hi, Taco." She stopped to pat him on the head. The dog yawned widely to show his appreciation. "Where's Piedmont?" Anna demanded, cradling the animal's jowly face between her hands. "Don't tell me you've eaten him?"

"Alive and well." Frieda had come to the door and stood behind the screen. A large yellow tiger cat, so limp it looked dead, was draped across her arm. With her free hand she pushed open the door and let Anna in.

Anna traded the wine bottle for the cat, buried her face in the soft fur of his neck, and breathed deeply. "Ahh. Thanks. I needed that."

"For me?" Frieda eyed the already opened bottle.

"Park Service social motto: Bring something to share."

As Frieda went into the kitchen to get glasses, Anna sat down on a couch identical to the one in the Far View dormitory and spread the cat across her knees.

Seasonals in the Park Service were not allowed the solace of pets. As long as Anna was stuck in the seasonal housing dorm, her cat had to board with a permanent employee fortunate enough to get "real" housing.

Frieda returned with two Kmart wineglasses and poured them each a healthy slug.

"If you're in the middle of something, Piedmont and I can go out in the yard," Anna offered. "I just needed a medicinal cat this evening."

"Don't know what I'd do without Taco," Frieda said by way of agreement. She propped her feet up on the scarred coffee table and took a long drink.

"But Taco is only a *dawg*," Anna confided to the cat in a stage whisper.

The dispatcher laughed. It was a rare sound and surprisingly pleasant, close to what Anna and her sister, Molly, had called "the Princess Laugh" when they were children. A sound that put one in mind of tinkling bells. She and Molly had even spent time practicing it but had never graduated from girlish "tee hee hees." Bells were for princesses. And, evidently, the Mesa Verde dispatcher.

"When I see you with that cat I can hardly believe

you're the same hard-ass who tickets little old ladies in wheelchairs for parking their cars in the handicapped spaces without a permit," Frieda said.

Frieda was just making conversation but still Anna was stung. "I don't," she insisted but felt compelled to add: "How am I to know they're handicapped? For all I know it could be Joe Namath parked there."

"Namath's handicapped," Frieda returned. "Bad knees."

"Gotta have a permit."

Again the dispatcher laughed her silvery laugh and they drank in silence. Tired of being adored, Piedmont leaped off Anna's lap. Moments later they heard feline lappings from the direction of the bathroom bowl.

"What do you know about Tom Silva?" Anna asked, her mind inevitably returning to NPS chores.

Frieda thought for a moment. "Patsy was divorced when the superintendent hired her—last fall, November, I think. She brought the girls up to live with her when school ended in May, so Tom hasn't been around much socially—not where you'd get to know the guy. I've seen him up here. He's good-looking. Younger than Patsy, is my guess, but not by much—maybe thirty-five or so. Maybe just looks young. He's got that kind of perfect olive skin that's practically indestructible."

"Does he come up to visit the girls?"

"More than Patsy would like. She thinks it's just a ruse. I guess his lack of interest in his kids was part of the reason she left him. From hints she's dropped, I gather Tom's thirty-five going on seventeen. She once said she couldn't handle being a single parent to three teenagers. Luckily he's been doing roofing or framing or something for an outfit in Grand Junction. The two-hour commute keeps him down to a dull roar."

"The contractor putting in the new waterline just hired him," Anna said.

"Oops."

"Yeah. Oops." Piedmont came back and settled down on the couch just out of Anna's reach. She contented herself with holding the tip of his tail. Occasionally he twitched it to show his displeasure.

"Sulking," Frieda noted, and Anna nodded. They sat for a while without speaking. It wasn't a comfortable silence, at least not for Anna. She hadn't known Frieda long enough for that.

"Do you think Silva's dangerous?" Anna asked.

"Maybe. No—I don't think so. He seems like a guy more into gestures." Cutting off one's foreskin was a hell of a gesture, Anna thought, but she didn't interrupt. In park society a person's private life seldom was, but as far as she knew Silva's penis had not yet made it into the public domain.

"The one time I met him he did strike me as a bit of an opportunist, though."

"Like a magpie? Won't kill it but doesn't mind eating it if someone else does?"

"Exactly like that. You hit it. He even looks kind of like a magpie, dresses too well, talks too loud, struts."

Silence fell again. It was a little easier this time but after a minute or so the strain began to get to Anna. "I better go," she said, giving Piedmont's tail a last gentle tug. "I want to call my sister tonight and it's already nine-twenty New York time. Thanks for the visit."

"Thanks for the wine," Frieda replied as she followed Anna to the door.

On the four-mile drive back to the dorm Anna found herself once again lonely for Christina and her daughter, missing Molly, missing silences that didn't chafe.

Fending off self-pity, she forced herself to concentrate on the delicate scent of juniper blowing in the Rambler's window, the piles of cumulonimbus the setting sun was painting in glorious shades of peach, the glistening peaks of the La Plata mountains, still wearing a veil of winter snow.

From many places the view was unchanged from when the ancients had inhabited the mesa. A time Anna liked to believe was simpler. Along Chapin Mesa Road were villages, skeletons now, but still imbued with an unmistakable human spirit. If she squinted, let her mind play, Anna could almost see women with bundles on their backs watching thunderheads build as she did, wondering if the rains would come in time for the corn.

The considerable benefit of this environmental therapy was blasted away the moment the Rambler pulled into the dorm parking lot. The nucleus of people she had left had spontaneously combusted into a flaming beer party.

Something that, to rock-and-roll-trained ears, sounded like 33⅓ Muzak played at 78 was audible through the open windows. Half a dozen cars were parked in the lot and at least that many bodies were standing around in the living room. Theatrically, Anna rested her head against the steering wheel and groaned.

With ill-concealed bad grace, she slammed the car into reverse and drove back down the Chapin Mesa Road.

A mile shy of the Museum Loop she turned onto a spur road, parked, and let herself into the Resource Management building. It was small and square, built of the same pink stone blocks as the chief ranger's office. The single room was filled to capacity by two desks, filing cabinets, dead lizards, bones, rocks, and what had to be at least fourteen years' worth of accumulated paperwork.

For those lucky enough to have keys—the people who really needed them and law enforcement—Resource Management had the after-hours attraction of a private phone.

Anna cleared off a chair and, still standing, punched in the twenty-four numbers of her sister's home phone and her AT&T calling card. She suspected if she could clear her brain of all memorized numbers there would be space enough created for housing all of Shakespeare and some of Johnson.

As Molly's smoke-roughened voice growled a characteristic "Dr. Pigeon," Anna dumped herself into the swivel chair.

"I'm too old for this," she said in lieu of a greeting.

"Damn old," Molly agreed.

"Too damned old. If it wasn't politically incorrect, I'd get my eyes done."

"On an NPS salary you could only afford to do one."

"Some psychiatrist you are. Whatever happened to 'You're as young as you feel' and 'Age is just a state of mind'?"

Molly laughed, a chuckle that sounded evil to the uninitiated. "That's what young psychiatrists tell their middle-aged clients. I'm pushing fifty. Take it from me: damn, yes, it's a bitch. Gird up the sagging loins and get on with it. Come to New York. I'll buy you a day at Elizabeth Arden's. 'Behind the Red Door': not quite an erotic fantasy but one that sells just as well. Youth! Men want to buy back the dreams they once had of themselves. Us old bats like the dreams of our middling years, it's our faces we want to buy back.

"So, one foot in the grave, the other on a banana peel. How's the rest of your life?"

Anna laughed. Her face could fall, her hands gnarl, her hair acquire another streak of gray. The camaraderie of women on the wrong side of *Mademoiselle*'s hit list was a joy she'd never been taught to expect.

"Dorm living is a drag. I'm leaning hard on the district ranger."

"Hills Dutton."

"I was trying to avoid the name."

"Got to be an alias."

"Nope. Too imaginative. Forced to think up an alias, I expect Hills would ponder a good long time, read all the Standard Operating Procedures, then settle on John Doe."

"Is he going to get you a house?"

"I don't know. To give the devil his due, he's up against it. They're redoing a waterline laid down a zillion years ago. A whole passel of archaeologists have been brought on board to analyze every foot of the digging. No housing left, everybody's hair in a knot, heavy equipment roaring around."

The waterline put Anna in mind of the afternoon's drama and she was glad to unfold the story of Patsy's Tom and the piece of foreskin.

After she'd finished there was a silence broken by a sighing sound. Molly was lighting up. Camel straights: Anna had heard them sucked into her sister's lungs for twenty years. Molly was an MD, she knew what the cigarettes were doing. She was a psychiatrist, she knew why she smoked them. And Anna was in law enforcement, she knew drugs had a logic of their own. So she said nothing.

"Sounds like the man's in trouble," Molly said finally, and Anna imagined thick smoke coming out with the words. "A construction worker?"

"That's what I gathered."

"Not a likely candidate for voluntary therapy. Any alcohol problems, drugs, things of that sort?"

"Probably," Anna replied, then thought better of her prejudice and added: "I don't know, really. I've heard he goes on a drunk now and then."

"People who cut themselves—hurt themselves—usually have a problem with self-esteem. A healthier attitude is 'Damned if I'm going to hurt anymore over you.' He may be harmless. I'm talking physically here; emotionally he could be devastating to anybody who gets tangled up with him. But now and again it goes beyond self-injury. In extreme cases I've seen the murder/suicide pattern. Shoot the wife then shoot yourself. That's rare but not so rare it doesn't crop up in the case history books and on the front page of the *Post* fairly regularly.

"I'd tell her to watch him, Anna. Watch him and watch herself. Whoops. Got to go," Molly finished in the abrupt manner Anna'd grown accustomed to over the years. "I've got an article due tomorrow for the *Times* on co-dependency. An are-you-or-aren't-you kind of thing. Of course it turns out everybody is. Keep me posted." She rang off, leaving Anna still holding the phone to her ear.

Shoot the wife then shoot yourself. Anna hung up the phone. Before she wrote Mr. Silva off as a magpie she'd do a little digging. It hadn't escaped her notice that more than a third of the women who came to hospital emergency rooms for treatment had been damaged by husbands or boyfriends.

Full darkness had come and she drove slowly back up to Far View. Cottontail bunnies, scarcely bigger than kittens, tried to find their way into the next world under her tires, but she successfully avoided them.

At the dorm, the parking lot was still full, the noise still blaring, and the bodies still in evidence. Anna slumped down in the Rambler's seat, wondering not for the first time if she should have taken the promotion that, along with Chris' defection, had tempted her back to the southwest, whether the seductive sense of smug selflessness and the warm dry climate had been worth the trade-offs.

3

BEFORE SHE'D properly gotten to sleep, Anna's alarm was buzzing like a hornet. She swatted it into silence and lay for a minute staring at the acoustical-tile ceiling above her single bed. The beer party had clanged on well past midnight.

Now that she had to get up the house was finally quiet. Rolling up on one elbow, she looked out into the new day. A breeze blew cold on her naked skin. At eighty-two hundred feet, summer never got a firm foothold. Chapin Mesa, a thousand feet lower than Far View, was often as much as ten degrees warmer.

A family of chipmunks had taken up residence under a scrap of black plastic Maintenance left behind when they finished the rear deck. With much flipping of tails, chattering, and scurrying, they were maintaining their cute Disneyesque image. Anna'd been so inculcated with Chip and Dale that she'd felt betrayed when she'd first seen a chipmunk breakfasting on a luckless brother squashed in the road. Roadkill provided food for a lot of animals. Anna sometimes speculated as to whether or not scavengers looked upon highways as a sort of endless buffet catered by Chrysler.

Squeaks, flusters, and the chipmunks vanished under the plastic. A lone red-tailed hawk spun careful circles over the serviceberry bushes.

A toilet flushed. The dorm was stirring earlier than anticipated. Leaving the chipmunks to their fate, Anna pulled on her robe. This morning she intended not only to get a shower, but also a hot one.

Jennifer shuffled past in the hall. Her eyes were puffy and her cheeks dragged down. " 'Morning," Anna said.

"Unhh."

As Anna lifted the coffeepot down from her kitchen cupboard she heard the thump of a wished-she-were-dead weight falling back into bed.

"Three-one-two in service." Anna made the call around her second cup of coffee. Once the initial insult of regaining consciousness was over, she enjoyed early shifts. Since neither the cliff dwellings nor the museum opened for visitors until nine, the park was quiet.

In the clear morning air a comforting illusion of isolation crept over Anna. Law enforcement at Mesa Verde taxed her energies in a way the hard physical work in the backcountry never had. People's needs were immediate and complex, their wants changing with the hour. Anna suspected mankind descended not from the ape but from the mosquito. In swarms they could bleed one dry.

With morning's peace came the animals: those just coming on diurnal duty, those going off nocturnal shift, and the crepuscular crew with a split shift framing the day. Two does and a fawn still in spots grazed between the white-flowering serviceberry bushes; from a fallen log an Abert squirrel showed off its perfect bushy tail.

At Far View Lodge, a black bear lumbered down from

the direction of the cafeteria, where it had undoubtedly been raiding garbage cans. Anna hit her siren and the bear bolted across the two-lane road into the underbrush below the Visitors' Center.

This year several "problem" bears had been knocking over trash cans. The bureaucratic machinery was beginning to grind at its usual snail's pace, but Anna doubted a solution would be found, agreed upon, funded, and implemented before these particular bears died of old age. Or were shot in the name of visitor protection.

She gave one more blast on the siren for good measure, then headed down toward Chapin Mesa, opening gates to ruins that Stacy Meyers had closed seven hours before. Coyote Village was first. Just a mile south of Far View, it was one of the highest pueblos on Mesa Verde, and Anna's favorite. Though it lacked the drama of the cliff dwellings with their aeries and towers, she loved the maze of intimate rooms and the patterns the ruined walls made against the dun of the earth. Perhaps since it was less alien she could better identify with the people who had once dwelt there, and so wonder at what prosaic magic had caused them to vanish.

Archaeologists hated the word "vanished," with its implication they'd not done their homework. Visitors loved it. In it was carried the mystery they felt walking through the ancient towns, peering in windows dark for seven centuries.

Theories of where the Anasazi had gone proliferated: war, draught, famine, loss of topsoil, overpopulation. No one concept carried the burden of proof. Theories changed with the political weather.

More than once it crossed Anna's mind that the best thing about the Anasazi was that they were gone. Their ruined homes forged chalices into which a jaded modern people could pour their fantasies. Never in dreams were there noisy neighbors in the dwelling next door, the reek of raw sewage, chilblains, or rotting teeth. In memory, especially one so magnificently vague as the lives of the Old Ones, the sun always shone and children didn't talk back.

In a tiny room, not more than five feet square, a cottontail nibbled at grasses prying up through the smooth flooring. Not wishing to disturb the new resident, Anna left quietly.

At Cedar Tree Tower Ruin Anna stopped to watch the sun clear the treetops and pour its liquid gold into the centuries-old kivas. These circular underground rooms, roofless now, were centers for worship or clan gatherings or places of work: the interpretation changed over the years as fads came and went and the science of archaeology grew more exact—or thought it had.

For Anna it was the symmetry and sophisticated simplicity of function that spoke to her of the Old Ones. Air shafts to ventilate fire pits, complex masonry, fitted stones handcrafted by a people who had no metal for tools.

In Europe King Arthur was dreaming his round table. Peasants lived in huts, the Black Plague waited just around the century's turning, and war and starvation were a way of life. Here where Colorado, Utah, New Mexico, and Arizona would one day meet, a people had farmed, traded, worshiped, and worked in peace and prosperity for six hundred years.

Park interpreters stressed the terrible hardships the Anasazi must have faced, the daily battle to wring a livelihood from an ungiving land. To Anna the kivas, the tunnels, the towers, the plaster and paint and pottery, suggested a people with an eye for beauty and at least enough wealth and leisure to pursue it.

The sun higher and the shadow play over, Anna continued to the last gate on her rounds, the one located at the four-way intersection near the museum. It blocked off the roads leading to the mesa top ruins, Cliff Palace and Balcony House. As she had every Tuesday for the last six weeks, she made a mental note to tell Stacy not to twist the chain into a figure eight before latching the padlock on his late shift. Placing the butt of the lock up as it did made the key easier to insert, but the chain was pulled so tight it took a wrestling match to get the lock arm pulled free of the links.

As she was securing the gate, Meyers called into service. Due to a paucity of vehicles, he would patrol with her.

Stacy and his family lived in a one-bedroom bungalow several houses down from Frieda's. With his daughter, Bella, it had to be cramped, but he was lucky to get it. A temporary appointment didn't carry much more in the way of perks than a seasonal.

Anna pulled up in the shade of an apple tree that grew near the wall shoring up an elevated yard. A picnic table sat under the branches. Two plastic milk bottles with the sides cut away lay tipped over near it. Presumably at some point Mrs. Meyers had intended to hang them for bird feeders. The bottles had been in the same place since Anna entered on duty. The lawn was ill kept and, for a home where a child dwelt, surprisingly untrammeled. No one used this yard as a playground.

Anna had seen Bella Meyers only a couple of times. From the waist up she had developed normally. There was no distortion of her facial features or upper body, but her lower limbs were stunted, half the size they should have been. Bella suffered from dwarfism.

Stacy and his wife, Rose, never brought her to any of the endless potlucks Mesa Verde was so fond of. There were two schools of thought in the park about this obvious cloistering. One was that the Meyerses were ashamed of Bella's deformity. The other was that the child suffered from delicate health.

Though the latter was the more charitable of the two rumors, it struck a deep chord of sympathy in Anna. Stacy wasn't a permanent employee. He was on what was called a temporary one-to-four-year appointment: no medical, no dental, no retirement. A GS-5's eighteen thousand–plus a year wouldn't go far to purchase comforts or specialty needs for a delicate child with a physical disability.

The sound of the screen door banging announced Stacy. A tall, slender man, six-foot-two or -three, he had dark hair and eyes, and a neatly trimmed beard. On his narrow hips the gunbelt looked out of place and the long sensitive fingers clasping his briefcase more suited to a surgeon or pianist than an officer of the law.

Rose Meyers followed him out.

Mrs. Meyers kept to herself. Jamie and Jennifer were convinced she felt government employees beneath her socially. Anna'd never spoken to the woman. She'd called Stacy at home on business once or twice but always got the phone machine with Rose's over-sweet message: "Hi! I'm so *glad* you called!"

Mrs. Meyers didn't look glad this morning. Her face was twisted into a mask of contempt. Short dark hair was molded in sleepy spikes. Rose carried quite a bit of excess weight. The pounds didn't form voluptuous curves or wide generous expanses as on more fortunate women, but sagged in lumps like sodden cotton batting in a ruined quilt.

" 'Bye, darling," Stacy said, and Anna smiled. No one

but Cary Grant could call somebody "darling" and not sound stilted. Stacy leaned down to kiss his wife but Rose stiffened as if the kiss had a foul taste. Anna looked away to give Stacy the illusion of privacy.

Moments later he threw his briefcase and hat into the rear seat and slid in beside her.

" 'Morning," she said. Stacy didn't respond. Anna was unoffended. She clicked on the radio for company.

"Where to this morning?" he asked after a while. Wherever his preoccupation had taken him, he was back with her now, the light in his brown eyes lost its inward shadows. His were compelling eyes, as liquid as a doe's, and framed with long lashes that showed black against clear skin. He put Anna in mind of the young dandies from the turn of the century who'd purposely exposed themselves to tuberculosis to attain the pale burning look lent by a fire within.

"We're going out to Wetherill Mesa," she told him. "Patsy's ex-husband Tom's been hired on by the pipeline contractor. He'll be surveying line near mile two. We need to talk with him."

"Has he been bothering Patsy again?"

"More or less. Sending her candy and notes that sound threatening or suicidal, depending on how you look at it. This time he sent her a bit of something that Patsy thinks was foreskin."

"Holy moly," Stacy said, and, "God I hate law enforcement."

Stacy had chosen law enforcement not as an avocation, but as a way in. With crime pouring out of the cities onto the nation's highways, more law enforcers than naturalists were hired in the national parks, more citations given than nature walks.

"You're a born tree hugger," Anna remarked amiably. "I could do without the domestic stuff. One way or another the ranger always comes out with a sore thumb. Matrimony is a dangerous game to referee."

"Were you ever married?"

"Widowed." She could say it now without feeling a hollowness in her chest.

"Lucky."

Anna laughed. "Troubles at home?"

Realizing what he had said, Stacy apologized. And blushed. Anna had never seen a forty-five-year-old man blush before. It charmed her.

"Not Rose. Rose's good to me. I just wish I could do more for her. She's used to better. You should have seen her in high school. God was she beautiful! She didn't even know I was alive. I was just this pencil-necked geek who played trombone in the marching band. She even modeled for *Glamour* magazine once."

Anna knew that. Stacy had dropped it into their first conversation. Evidently he dropped it into most conversations about his wife. One evening after she'd sharpened her tongue on Vanna, Jamie had ranted on about it. "*Glamour!* Give me a break! Maybe for the *Glamour* Don'ts! And a quarter of a century and sixty pounds ago."

Stacy noticed the smile. "She did, you know."

"She's a good-looking woman," Anna agreed politely. "So what did a pencil-necked geek have to do to get a fashion model's heart and keep it?"

Stacy laughed. "Are you kidding? In high school Rose wouldn't give me the time of day. No, we met again about three years ago. I was out on the west coast visiting old friends and there she was."

"Love at first sight?"

"Let's say interest at first sight. I was going through a divorce. Rose saved my life," Stacy added simply. "I'll always owe her for that."

"Your ex the one that made widowerhood seem so desirable?"

"She wasn't a bad woman. There were just too many people she had to meet—without her clothes." Stacy paraphrased Leonard Cohen.

"Ah." Anna wasn't going to touch that remark with the proverbial ten-foot pole.

Past the Far View cafeteria, she turned left onto the Wetherill Mesa. Wetherill was just one of the five mesas, spread out like the fingers of an open hand, that made up the park. The road wound down the mesa's edge for twelve miles. Along the way there were overlooks, most on the west side. The views changed with the hour of the day and with the weather. Sleeping Ute Mountain nearby kept watch over the town of Cortez in the valley. The solitary white mysticism of Lone Cone pierced the horizon to the northwest. The Bears' Ears peeked coyly from behind a distant mountain range. To the south glimpses of Ship Rock in New Mexico tantalized. The craggy volcano neck bore a startling resemblance to a ship in full sail gliding through a sea of haze created by the power plant near Farmington. Farmington, Cortez, and Shiprock were home to most of the nontourist-related industries in the four-corners area; smelting the silver for the jewelry trade, the machinery for the farmers.

"Rose would never leave me," Stacy said quietly.

Since the silence between them had been so long, and he seemed to be speaking only to himself, Anna pretended she hadn't heard. She pulled the patrol car off onto the overlook where Greeley's company pickup was parked and switched off the ignition. "You want to do the talking or shall I?" she asked.

"You do it. Silva's supposed to be quite the ladies' man. Maybe we'll get lucky and he'll underestimate you."

Anna laughed. "I like you, Meyers."

Following the pink plastic tape marking the section of line already surveyed, they started down into the ravine. Mesa Verde's oakbrush grew to the size of small trees—some reaching twenty feet or more—but retained the many branches of a lesser shrub. In places the bushes were virtually impenetrable and provided habitat for quail, rabbits, and other creatures who lived longer if they went unnoticed.

The survey crew had cut a swath through the brush with loppers and chain saws. Suckers, severed just above ground level, stuck up sharp as pungi sticks. Intent on where she put her feet, Anna nearly ran into a man working his way up the hill.

"Whoa there, honey!" He spoke with a slight lisp and he put his arms around her as if she were going to fall. "I do love hugging women packing heat."

Anna extricated herself from his grasp. The man was Ted Greeley. He was not much taller than Anna, maybe five-foot-eight. In his early fifties, he had startlingly blue eyes and snow-white hair that hugged his round head in tight curls. He'd kept himself in good shape. Anna couldn't help but notice the muscular arms when he'd grabbed her. Beginnings of a potbelly attested to the fact that physical fitness was an ongoing struggle.

"Checking up on me, eh?" He reached down and pulled up a blade of grass to chew on.

"Good morning, Ted," Stacy said.

"Ted," Anna echoed the greeting. "We need to talk with Tom Silva. Is he working this stretch of line?"

"You girl rangers really make a difference." Greeley winked at Anna. "In the construction business all I ever see are men's ugly pusses. Say, how's that wife of yours, Stacy? Still eating your cooking?"

Stacy just smiled.

"And how's my little Bella?"

"Bella's fine." Stacy's tone was icy and Anna sensed a sudden hostility. "Dispatch said Tom Silva was working this section. Do you know where we can find him?" Stacy dragged the conversation back to business.

Greeley's smile broadened. "Tom in some kind of trouble? Let me know if any of my boys get out of line. You know what they say: you get in bed with somebody, it pays to stay friendly."

"No trouble," Stacy said stiffly. "We just need to talk with him."

"Help yourself." Greeley gestured down the hill. "He's holding the dumb end of the tape for an overpaid surveyor, so don't keep him too long. Anna." He tipped an imaginary hat as he brushed by her.

The surveyor was at the bottom of the ravine setting up his tripod. "Silva?" Anna asked as they approached.

"Keep walking," the man replied without taking his eyes from his instruments. Ahead, down a fresh-cut line, a second man sat on a boulder smoking a cigarette.

"Tom Silva?" Anna asked when they were close enough to be heard.

"You're looking at him." Silva blew smoke out in a thin stream and looked Anna up and down. The half smile on his lips suggested she should feel complimented.

She didn't.

"I'm Anna Pigeon. This is Stacy Meyers. Can you take a break for a minute? We'd like to talk to you."

"Taking five, Bobby," Silva shouted past them. "Somebody set the law dogs on me." He smiled up at Anna. "Pull up a rock and sit down."

Anna crouched, rocking back on her heels, her forearms resting on her knees. Stacy remained standing, seeming tall as a willow from her new vantage point.

For a moment Silva studied them, and Anna him. The morning's heat was beginning to collect in the canyon, held close by the oakbrush thickets. Shirtless, rivulets of sweat traced trails through the dust on Silva's smooth chest. Stick-straight black hair stuck out from beneath a battered, straw cowboy hat. With his unlined olive skin and dark eyes, he was pretty rather than handsome.

Meeting Anna's eyes, he crushed out his cigarette and pointedly tucked the butt into the rolled cuff of his jeans. "No litter here," he said. "This is a national fucking park."

A challenge: Anna chose to ignore it.

"Patsy asked us to talk with you, Tom," she said evenly.

"What's old Pats up to now?" He shook another Marlboro from the pack that rested beside him on the rock, then made a show of offering one to Anna and Stacy.

Anna declined. Stacy just shook his head.

"Suit yourself. Mind if I do?" The question was rhetorical and neither bothered to reply. Silva didn't light the cigarette but played with it between his fingers. The gesture was so classically phallic that Anna felt tired.

"Patsy's concerned that some of the presents you've been giving her might have more than one meaning," she began. "This latest—attention—has her fairly upset."

"So she screamed for the rangers? God, Pats loves a good scene."

"Your ex-wife—"

"My wife," Tom interrupted.

"—would be more comfortable if you stayed away from her."

"Hey, a man's got a right to work. She's always hollering I don't pay enough goddamn child support, now she's trying to lose me my job. Christ!"

"Patsy's not trying to get you fired, Tom. She mentioned specifically that she didn't want that to happen. She just wants you to stay away from her."

"What grounds, man? She's got my kids, for Christ's sake." Tom quit playing with the cigarette and lit it, striking a wooden match with an expert—and probably much rehearsed—flick of his thumbnail. "There ain't no way she can keep me from going over there. I've never done a damn thing, not one damn thing she can hold up in a court of law to say I can't. Hell, I never even hit her."

"I believe you, Tom," Anna said soothingly. "But there's a thing called harassment. Patsy has pretty strong feelings about some of your gifts."

Tom shook his head. Smoke poured from his nostrils. His eyes were fixed on a point beyond Anna's left shoulder. Behind her she could hear Stacy shifting his weight.

"She's got a scrap of skin in an envelope, Tom. She said it was foreskin. That's a pretty loaded thing to send somebody." Anna was uncomfortably aware of the unintentional humor. She heard Stacy clearing his throat, a small cough that could have been thwarted laughter.

Fortunately Tom seemed not to pick up on it. For a moment he sat smoking and Anna waited, letting the silence soak in, work for her.

"Christ! It was a joke," he finally burst out.

Stacy spoke for the first time. "A joke? It must've hurt like crazy. Where's the funny part?"

Tom looked up at him, his mouth twisted with irritation. "I didn't take a fucking knife to myself, if that's what you mean. The doc did it. Pats had been after me for years. I thought she'd like it."

"You got circumcised in your thirties?" Stacy asked. Anna bit back a laugh at the "oh ouch!" she could hear under the words.

"That's right." Tom smiled; his teeth were square and white. "Barnum and Bailey got a new tent."

Inwardly, Anna sighed. "Here's where we stand, Tom. You, Patsy, me—we've all got to live together on this mesa top. At least for a while. I'd suggest that you steer clear of Patsy. If you've got visiting rights to your kids, you two work that out. I'll ask Patsy to file whatever agreement you reach at the chief ranger's office. You stick to that and you won't have to deal with us, okay?"

"Fuck!" Tom flicked his cigarette butt into the brush. Anna didn't even follow it with her eyes. "Why don't you rangers do your job instead of hassling people that work for a living? You get a fucking free ride from the government and can't even keep the fucking roads safe. Monday night a big goddamn truck nearly ran me off the road. Where the hell were you then? Christ!"

"We'll look into that." Pushing herself to her feet, Anna heard both ankles crack in protest.

"Will that be all, ranger?"

"Almost," Anna returned. "Just find that cigarette you tossed and put it out and we'll be out of your hair. Fire danger's bad this year. Manning Class four yesterday."

"Find it yourself," Silva muttered.

"I got it." Stacy had crushed the life from the butt and now tucked the filter into his pocket.

"Good enough for me," Anna said. "Take it easy, Tom."

"Yeah."

*   *   *

When they'd passed the surveyor and were climbing out of the ravine, Stacy said: "Foreskin is a loaded gift," and the laughter Anna had swallowed came bubbling out.

"The way he was playing with the cigarette . . ." Anna's laughter took over and she had to stop climbing just to breathe. "You'd think he was auditioning for the role of Johnny Wad in *Debbie Does Dallas*."

"You mean that didn't toss your confetti? I kind of thought I might give it a shot. Run it up the flagpole, see if the cat licks it up."

Stacy stopped beside her. Pressed close by the brambles, Anna was aware of the smell of him: freshly laundered cotton and soap. Heat radiated from her, and it wasn't only from the sun and the climb. Anna stifled her basic instincts and shook herself like a dog ridding its fur of water drops.

Abruptly, she turned and pushed up the side of the ravine. In places it was so steep she pulled herself along using the low branches. Her laughter had evaporated.

"You drive," she said as they reached the patrol car. "These seats break my back."

"You're too short. This is a man's machine. A car for Johnny Wad." Stacy slipped behind the wheel and slid the seat back as far as it would go.

"Thanks for picking up that cigarette butt. What was I going to do? Shoot the guy? Never try to out-macho a construction worker."

"Believe it or not, picking up litter is why I went into this business. I don't work for the Park Service. I work for the parks."

Anna settled back into the seat. "The NPS could use a few more fern feelers. I, for one, hope you get on permanent."

"So do I," Stacy said. "So do I."

His tone was so grim, so determined, Anna dropped the subject. Everybody had to contend with their own demons. Some of hers were such old familiars she considered naming them and renting them closet space.

Leaning her head back against the vinyl headrest, she closed her eyes. Zachary was dead eight years come August. She could no longer consistently call his face to mind. Without his memory clear and present, her fortieth might turn out to be a damn lonely year.

4

HOUSEMATES OUT, television off, Anna had been sleeping with glorious abandon. Deep sleep, REM sleep, sleep without nightmares. Of late a good night's sleep had become such a rarity her fantasies about it bordered on the erotic.

Hence the cursing reluctance with which she relinquished it to answer the phone.

"Anna, Frieda. Sorry about this."

Anna turned on her bedside light and snatched up the alarm clock: 2:02 A.M.

"Nobody else to home," Frieda said. All law enforcement on MEVE shared an emergency party line called the '69 line because of the last two digits of the number. Every call rang in quarters on Chapin and at Far View. Anna'd been the unlucky ranger who picked up first.

"What's up—other than me?" Anna was already threading her legs into yesterday's underpants.

"Got a report of lights in the maintenance yard. Somebody needs to check it out."

"I'm headed in that direction." Maintenance was scarcely a hundred yards from the housing loop on Chapin. Stacy would have been the logical one to respond but he never answered the '69. Scuttlebutt was he unplugged it nights. Some said for Bella, others said Rose did the unplugging.

Loss of sleep was a trade-off for money. Every call, short or long, earned two hours' overtime. As she buckled on her duty belt, Anna totaled it up. Two hours at time and a half was close to thirty bucks. She'd've paid nearly that for an uninterrupted night's sleep.

From the patrol car, she called in service. Frieda responded—not because she had to, she wasn't officially on duty. There would be no overtime or base pay for her. Frieda monitored because she took her job more seriously than her employers did. She didn't like rangers out without at least rudimentary backup.

The air was cool and fresh. Anna rolled down the Ford's windows and let the darkness blow in around her. On her first late shifts she'd had a new experience—or if not new, one she hadn't felt for a long time, not since leaving New York City. Anna'd found herself afraid of the dark.

Walking trail in Texas, skirting islands around Isle Royale, she'd worn the night like a star-studded cloak. But Mesa Verde was all about dead people. In the mind—or the collective unconscious—there was a feeling they'd not all left in the twelve hundreds. Or if they had, perhaps whatever it was that drove them out had taken up residence in the abandoned cities. Everywhere there were reminders of another time, another world.

Given the propensity of Jamie and some of the other interpreters to capitalize on New Age voodoo, Anna never admitted her fear but she patrolled with an ear open for voices long gone, footsteps not clothed in mortal flesh.

A half-moon threw bars of silver across the road, enough to see by, and as she turned onto the spur leading to Maintenance, she clicked off her headlights. The Maintenance yard, a paved area with a gas pump in the center, was surrounded by two-story buildings: offices, garages, a carpenter's shop, storage barns. Built in the 1940s, the buildings were of dark wood with small many-paned windows. One remnant remained from the thirties: the fire cache, where helitack stored the gear needed to fight wildland fire. It was of stone with juniper beams supporting a flat roof. Behind the cache a twelve-foot cyclone fence topped with barbed wire enclosed the construction company's equipment behind padlocked gates.

In the inky shadow of a storage barn, the car rolled to a stop. Anna called on scene and received Frieda's reassuring reply. Setting the brake, she listened. Pre-dawn silence, fragile and absolute, settled around her. The pop of her tires as they cooled, the clicking of insects flying against the intruder lights, pattered like dry rain.

Trickling out of the quiet, it came to her why Mesa Verde nights pricked some nerve deep in her psyche. Like New York City, the mesa was comprised of peopled dark, dark that collected in the corners of buildings and under eaves, choked alleys, and narrow streets. A darkness permeated with the baggage of humanity. Dreams and desires haunted the mesa the way they haunted the rooms in old houses. Traces of unfinished lives caught in the ether.

Anna felt her skin begin to creep. "Why don't you just rent a video of *Hill House* and be done with it?" she mocked herself.

Another minute whispered by. Apparently nothing was going to manifest itself in her windshield. She loosed the six-cell flashlight from its charger beneath the dash.

Metal clanked on metal as she opened the car door and she froze. It wasn't the familiar click of door mechanisms, it was what she'd been waiting for: something not right, a sound where silence ought to be.

Noise gave her direction. Leaving the car door open rather than risk a racket, she moved quietly toward the fenced construction yard. Between her car and the fence were three board-and-batten shacks used to store hand tools and pesticides. In the colorless light the short road looked like a scene from Old Tucson's back lot.

Anna followed the line of buildings till she ran out of shadow. Two junipers framed a picnic table where the hazardous-fuel-removal crew cleaned their saws. She slipped into the protective darkness. Closer now, she could see the gates to the yard. A chain hung loose, its padlock broken or unlocked.

Within the confines of the cyclone fence, equipment clustered like prehistoric creatures at a watering hole. Bones of metal linked with hydraulic cable in place of tendons thrust into the night: the skeletal neck of a crane, the scorpion's claw of a backhoe, the rounded back of a water truck—one she'd never seen in use though dust from construction was a constant irritation. Easily a million dollars' worth of machinery brought in to do the work needed for the waterline.

Again came the clank, softer this time and followed by a faint scraping sound. Moving quickly, Anna crossed the tarmac and slipped through the gates. Moonlight caught her, then she was again in shadow, her back against a wheel half again as tall as she.

When heart and breath quit clamoring in her ears, she listened. Concentration revealed sounds always present but seldom noted: the minute scratch of insect feet crossing sand, a whispered avian discussion high in the trees. Nothing unnatural, nothing human. Odd, Anna thought, that "man-made" and "natural" should be considered antithetical.

Time crawled by; the slight adrenaline rush brought on by the act of sneaking faded and she began feeling a bit silly crouched in the darkness chasing what was undoubtedly a wild goose—or at worst a chipmunk who'd decided to build her nest in one of Greeley's engines.

Probably the last guy out had forgotten to lock the gate. Monday nights Stacy had late shift. He should have checked it but something may have distracted him.

Realizing she'd been taking shallow nervous breaths, Anna filled her lungs. Muscles she hadn't known she was clenching relaxed and she felt her shoulders drop. Expelling a sigh to blow away the last of the chindi-borne cobwebs, she switched on her flashlight and stepped out of the shadows.

Weaving through the parked machines, she played the light over each piece of equipment. Nothing stirred, scuttled, or slithered. A backhoe at the end of the enclosure finished the group. Anna shone the light over the yellow paint, up an awkward angle, and into the mud-crusted bucket. Nothing.

The goose could consider itself chased. Anna was going back to bed. Turning to leave, her beam crawled along the oversized tires and across the toe of a boot, a cowboy boot, scuffed and brown like a hundred thousand others in the southwest.

Like a dog chasing cars, she thought. Now what? Indecision passed with a spurt of fear. She stepped into the shadows and moved the flashlight out from her body lest it become a target.

"Come on out and talk to me," she said. "No sense hiding at this point."

There was only one way out of the yard that didn't involve scaling the fence, and Anna waited for the intruder to show himself or bolt for the gate.

The toe twitched. "Come on out," Anna said reasonably. "You're not in too much trouble yet."

Slowly, with a feeble skritching sound, the toe pulled back into darkness. A peculiar shushing followed and Anna realized whoever it was was pulling off the boots.

Little hairs on the back of her neck began to prickle. "Enough's enough, come out of there." She walked toward the backhoe's rear tire, unsnapping the keeper on her .357 as she went.

The intruder was quick. On silent sock feet, he'd retreated into the jungle of blades, tires, and engines. Anna had no intention of following. Backing slowly out of the alley between the metal monoliths, she ducked clear of the moonlight and took her King radio from her belt.

Frieda, bless her, was still monitoring. "We've got an intruder in the construction yard," Anna said clearly. "Get me some backup."

The radio call stirred the stockinged feet. Distinct rustling from a careless move riveted Anna's attention on a ditcher parked one space nearer the open gate. Staying well back in the shadow, she waited. Silence grated on her nerves and she listened as much for the approach of help as she did for the movements of the person she tracked.

Scuffling: the tiny sound made her flinch as if a cannon had gone off near her ear. Behind her now, beyond the backhoe; loath to leave the dark for the glaring moonlight, Anna knelt and turned her light between the wheels. A flick of gray; a tail disappearing through the fence. She turned the flashlight off. Time to move. The rodent had tricked her into giving away her position.

Easing to her feet, she tried for quiet but knees and ankles popped like firecrackers in the stillness.

A foot scrape on concrete and a singing of air: a black line with a hook windmilled out from the rear of the ditcher. Moonbeams were sliced, air whistled through the iron. Someone was swinging a heavy chain with an eight-inch tow hook attached to the end.

Reflexively Anna dropped to her belly and rolled under the backhoe as the weighted chain cut through the air, striking the tire where she'd been standing. Iron links whipped around the hard rubber and struck the back of her neck, the links cracking against her temple. Shock registered but not pain.

Wriggling on elbows and knees, Anna worked her way deeper under the belly of the machine.

Footsteps, soft and running, followed the cacophony of chain falling. Whoever it was ran for the gate. Courage returned and Anna scrambled into the open. She was on her feet in time to hear the gate clang shut. Sprinting the twisted path across the pavement, she caught a glimpse of a figure flitting through the shadows of the utility buildings beyond.

When she reached the gate she stopped. The chain had been strung back through and the lock snapped shut.

"Damn it!" Greeley had his own locks and the rangers had not been given access keys. With a jump she reached halfway up the fence and hung there. A double line of barbed wire slanted away from the fence top. She could probably thread her way through with only a modicum of damage but not in time to catch whoever had locked her in.

Smothering an obscenity, she dropped back to earth and unsheathed her radio. Not even Frieda heard her call this time. Leaning against the wire, she caught her breath and let the nervous energy drain away. Fatigue welled up in its place and her legs began to shake. Where the chain had lashed ached and her head felt full of hot sand.

She crossed the asphalt and rested her back against the tread of a D-14 Cat. Her insides shook and her breath was uneven. What scared her wasn't so much the attack but her lack of readiness to meet it. Like a rookie—or a complacent old-timer—she'd wandered happily into the middle of a crime in progress. And nearly been killed for her stupidity. She'd gotten sloppy, let down her guard.

Mesa Verde was old and slow and visited by the old and slow. Situated on a mesa in the remote southwestern corner of Colorado, approachable only by twenty miles of winding two-lane mountain road, it didn't get the through traffic of a park on a major highway. No accidental tourists on their way from Soledad to Sing Sing.

Mesa Verde's dangers had struck Anna more akin to the pitfalls of Peyton Place. Societies, like other living organisms, sometimes fell ill. But she hadn't expected violence. She had let herself be lulled into a false sense of security.

Scrapes from the chain throbbed and she brought her mind back to the machinery yard. What had the intruder been after? The stuff was too obvious to fence, too big to steal. Something important enough to risk imprisonment. Assault on a federal officer was a felony offense.

The fog in her head was clearing and only a dull ache behind her eyes remained. Anna pushed herself to her feet. Somewhere beneath the backhoe was her flashlight. Before morning's business stomped over the whole place, she would use it to see if Mr. Brown Boots had left anything behind.

Cigarette butts were scattered beneath the ditcher. Sherlock Holmes might have made hay with such an abundance of clues but Anna didn't bother. Half the construction workers smoked and, near as she could tell, all of the maintenance men. Marlboro, Camel Lights, Winston, she noted the brands for the sake of feeling useful but they were too common to draw any conclusions.

In the cab of the Caterpillar she found some battered hand tools. Behind the seat of the water truck were a pair of welding gloves and what looked like a gas mask left over from World War II. Unless they were some brand of rare antiques they didn't look worth stealing.

The D-14 Cat yielded up the answers. Beneath the iron tread Anna found a plastic bag with a trace of white powder in it. She didn't taste it. She didn't have to. It was sugar.

Monkeywrenching was the only thing that made any sense. Someone waging guerrilla warfare against the new waterline. There was no telling how much time the intruder had had before Anna interrupted, how much damage had been done. As soon as she was let out of her pen she'd have to call Greeley. The contractor would not be pleased.

Monkeywrenching—sabotage—was an ancient form of combat. Anna respected it in its purest form: David Environmentalist against Goliath Industries. Whether or not this was the case with the waterline, she'd not decided.

Rogelio, her lover in Texas, had thrived on such night action. She'd met many of the ecotage experts he ran with. They didn't tend to violence against persons. No swinging of chains, crushing of skulls. Brown Boots had a good deal to lose, it would seem. Or a good deal to gain.

Al Stinson cared enough to throw a wrench in the works, a sabot in the machine, but it seemed absurd to risk a twenty-year career when she had legal avenues at her disposal.

Jamie maybe. She had nothing to lose materially and might still be naive enough to believe she wouldn't be thrown in jail if she were caught.

Somehow Anna couldn't see either Al or Jamie swinging a tow chain, but then she'd been wrong about people before. Brown boots: Tom Silva was the consummate drugstore cowboy. He probably had a whole closet full of boots. It wasn't too hard to picture him with a chain. Did he have a grudge against his employer, access to a key?

Again she tried Frieda.

This time there was an answer. "Sorry. I've been trying to raise somebody for you," the dispatcher apologized unnecessarily. "I finally went over to Stacy's. He'll be there shortly."

"Thanks." Anna called 316, Stacy's number. "Wake up Maintenance," she told him. "Find somebody entrusted with Greeley's master key."

Minutes ticked by. Anna didn't mind the wait. The night was dry and not too cold. A slight breeze whispered through the pine trees and she wasn't lonely. Closing her eyes she tried to recall everything she could about the intruder. One boot toe, brown, and a retreating form in dark clothing. She couldn't even say for sure if it was male or female, tall or short.

Outfoxed, outmaneuvered, and left penned up for everyone to see, Anna was beginning to get testy about the whole affair.

Boots ringing on pavement brought her head around. Stacy, in uniform, defensive gear, and flat hat, ran across the maintenance yard following the beam of a flashlight.

"Got the key?" she called.

"Got it."

Anna pushed herself to her feet and waited impatiently while he fumbled with the lock. "Whoever it was had a key," she remarked.

Stacy didn't say anything.

"Did you check it before you went off shift?"

"I honestly can't remember." Stacy was sullen, it was unlike him. The "honestly" bothered Anna.

The lock came open and he pulled the chain from the gates. Once freed, Anna demanded: "Why didn't you answer the six-nine line?"

Stacy turned his back to her and locked the gate. "The phone plug got knocked out somehow," he said flatly.

Rose. Anna didn't pursue it.

Stacy declined a ride home but Anna swung through the housing loop anyway. As she'd hoped, Frieda's light was on.

"Dropped by to say thanks," Anna said when the dispatcher answered the door.

"Likely story. Piedmont thinks you're here to see him."

It gladdened Anna's heart to see the yellow streak that ran to the screen at the sound of her voice. Scooping him up she kissed him between the ears. "Coming home sucks without a cat to meet you at the food dish."

Because all good dispatchers are mind readers, Frieda brought Anna a glass of wine. Out of deference to regulations, Anna removed her gun before taking the first draught. Piedmont spread himself down the length of her lap, his orange-and-white chin draped over her knees.

Anna related the night's tale to the dispatcher. Frieda was genuinely interested and Anna too keyed up to shut up and go home.

"Greeley hasn't made a lot of friends up here," Frieda said. "The interps are making quite a stink about the disturbance of the mesa. Al eggs them on—not on purpose, but most of them are of an age when passion's contagious."

"I'd like to think she'd draw the line at offing a ranger," Anna grumbled.

Frieda laughed. "Hard to picture. Maybe it's not ecotage at all. Just pure meanness. Greeley's own guys aren't that crazy about him either. He's a little on the oily side."

Anna took a long drink of wine and tried to call the construction workers to mind. They all ran together: big men in hard hats. The ache at the base of her skull suggested she pay a little more attention in the future.

"Sorry about the backup screwup. I'm glad you're not dead. Would I ever have felt a fool," Frieda said.

"Did you have trouble prying Stacy out of bed?"

"He was up watching television. I tried everyone else before it dawned on me he might have turned his phone off."

"Got 'accidentally' unplugged," Anna said cattily.

Frieda nodded. This was clearly not a surprise.

It crossed Anna's mind that had Stacy been the saboteur, he would have had time to run from Maintenance to the housing loop in the ten minutes it had taken Frieda to come knocking on his door. Meyers had the right temperament for a monkeywrencher—passion and a sense of his own importance in the scheme of things. Had he found the lock open when he made his last rounds and felt an opportunist urge to strike a blow for conservation?

Anna didn't like to think Stacy would swing an iron hook at her head.

Before she left she presumed on Frieda's hospitality one more time and borrowed her phone. If Greeley was home he wasn't answering.

"I'll try him again first thing in the morning," Frieda promised.

When Anna got back to the dorm it was after three and all the lights were blazing. Laughter and the rattle of voices met her at the door. "You were there, did it happen or not?" Jamie was shouting.

On Mesa Verde, it would seem, no one but Anna had any interest in sleep.

"Jimmy, you saw it—" A thud followed by laughter interrupted.

"Jimmy's had so much he couldn't see past his own nose." Jennifer Short's Memphis drawl.

"The spirit veil, oooooooh." Another voice, probably Jimmy Russell's, wailed like the ghosts in the Saturday morning cartoons. Then laughter shouted down by Jamie's: "Funny, real funny, you guys—"

Anna banged through the kitchen door. Moaning like Casper the Friendly Ghost, Jimmy Russell was traipsing around the living room in a drunken parody of a wraith. His face was flushed and his eyes bright but he was steady on his feet. Anna had known he was a drinker. Noting how well he'd learned to cope, she couldn't but wonder if, at twenty, he was an habitual drunk.

A study in superiority, Jamie was leaning in the entrance to the hall. "Laugh away," she was saying. "They're here. I've seen them before. Are you going to pretend you didn't, Jennifer? You were practically peeing your pants tonight."

"My, my, Jamie. Such a ladylike phrase," Jennifer drawled.

Rolling his eyes and fluttering his hands, Jimmy wailed.

"Keep it up. Keep it up," Jamie said with exaggerated patience.

Sprawled in one of the armchairs, her body limp, Jennifer percolated giggles in support of Jimmy's antics. "Aw, come on, Jamie. He's only teasin' yew."

"It's not me he needs to worry about." Jamie had taken on an air of secret knowledge.

"Excuse me," Anna cut in. "Could you guys take the party elsewhere? I've got to be up at six."

"We're sorry, Anna," Russell said contritely. Head slightly lowered, he looked at her from under thick blond lashes.

Undoubtedly it had been irresistible when he was six.

"Jamie saw the third world or whatever coming through that thing . . . a see-poo-poo—" Dissolving into giggles, Jennifer couldn't go on.

"Sipapu. See. Pah. Pooh." Jamie pronounced the word with the care one might employ when conversing with an imbecilic and not much loved child. "It's too bad law enforcement doesn't require their rangers to learn about the places they are supposedly protecting."

The merriment went out of Jennifer's face and a hardness came into it that Anna had never seen before. "Y'all can piss and moan the rest of the night if you want to. I'm going to bed. 'Night Anna."

The magnolia blossom apparently had a core of good Southern steel.

" 'Night," Anna returned automatically.

"Jamie really did see something. She's got a weird sense like that—you know, ghosts and shit," Jimmy Russell said somberly.

The boy was so transparent, if she'd not been tired and cranky, Anna might have found him amusing. Jennifer gone, Russell was trying to re-ingratiate himself with Jamie. Somebody wants to get laid tonight, she thought without charity but with undoubted accuracy.

Russell fell back on the sofa, his feet splayed out in front of him. Brown cowboy boots. Anna had no trouble picturing him with an implement of destruction. Environmental concerns didn't seem to be the Kentucky boy's mainstay but drunken pranks might be. After a six-pack or two Jamie could probably talk him into almost anything.

Anna began to wonder if all the ghostly theatrics were designed as a cover story for more practical measures taken to protect the Anasazi heritage.

Jamie interrupted Anna's train of thought. Stalking to one of the two refrigerators in the kitchen, she took out a Tupperware container and kicked the refrigerator door shut. "Bonegrinder!" As she spat out the word, she jerked open a drawer. In one continuous motion she fished out a serving spoon and popped the plastic lid off the food container.

"If somebody took one of those huge ditchers and started chewing a trench through Forest Lawn you can bet there'd be an outcry. It just wouldn't happen." Ladling a bite of some pasta concoction into her mouth as if to calm her nerves, Jamie went on. "You can't go around digging up white people's cemeteries. Oh no. Big sacrilege. They won't get away with it." Jamie inhaled another serving-spoonful of pasta. "The whole mesa is sacred ground."

Though it had been in vogue at one time, there wasn't any archaeological evidence to support that theory, but Anna didn't say anything. She dumped her hat and gun on the dinette table and collapsed in one of the straight-backed chairs.

"They're not going to get away with grinding our bones up. Not this time."

Anna noted the "our." She also noted that Jamie's brown roots were just beginning to show at the base of her part. Raising her eyebrows politely, she invited Jamie to continue ranting.

"Solstice is coming," the interpreter said with finality.

June twenty-first; perhaps that was the proposed date of some planned event. Anna let the idea filter through her mind. Why would Jamie divulge that bit of information in the presence of a law enforcement ranger? Unless, as was often the case in publicity stunts, the law was necessary to provide the drama required to lure out the press. It was illegal for government employees to "tattle" to the press on touchy issues. But bringing down the wrath of the six o'clock news was almost the only way to effect any real change. Like any other entrenched bureaucracy, the Park Service was filled with people passing the buck and covering the hindmost parts of their anatomy.

"What happens on solstice?" Anna asked.

"It's a sacred day to the Old Ones," Jamie replied, with the air of an insider who only hands out information in pre-approved sound bites.

"Are they going to hold those Indian dances or something?" Jimmy Russell wanted to know.

"Not likely. 'They' have been dead for seven hundred years," Anna told him.

"They might," Jamie said cryptically.

"Ah. Chindi." Anna was suddenly too tired to play along.

"The spirit veil, ooooo—" Jimmy's wail ended abruptly at the look on her face.

"Are you driving, Jimmy?"

"Yes, ma'am." He dangled his car keys.

Anna took them and slipped them into her pocket. If Russell was her chain-swinging eco-terrorist, he was too far gone to do much damage till morning.

"You're drunk. Sleep on the couch. I'll leave your keys on the table when I go to work. Good night."

A few minutes of murmuring came through the wall as Jamie dragged out bedding for the inebriated helitacker, then the house was blessedly quiet. Anna took two aspirins for her head. For her nerves she recited the only prayer she knew all the way through: "From ghoulies and ghosties and long-leggety beasties/And things that go bump in the night, Good Lord, deliver us!"

5

AT EIGHT A.M., when Stacy pulled up in the patrol car, Jimmy Russell was still curled up on the couch. He didn't even twitch when Anna walked through. Without so much as a twinge of guilt, she let the door bang shut behind her.

Usually Stacy's aesthetic countenance was a welcome sight, but lack of sleep had left Anna surly. Evidently the night's festivities had left their mark on him as well. In lieu of "good morning" he said: "Mind if we stop by my house? Rose's going to Farmington and Bella needs a ride to Maintenance. Drew said he'd keep an eye on her till six."

Anna wanted to ask why Rose didn't take the kid along, but she minded her own business. The radio was tuned to a Navajo station and a language that sounded like Chinese sawed at her nerves. With an abrupt movement, she switched it off.

"Wrong side of the bed?" Stacy asked.

"Tired. My housemates kept me up after our rendezvous in Maintenance. Jamie said she'd seen a veil or some damn thing. Chindi passing from the underworld to this one. They were out at Cliff Palace, drinking and scaring each other is my guess."

"I checked the book." Stacy sounded alarmed. "There were no permits for Cliff Palace last night."

Any employee going anywhere—or anytime—the public was not allowed had to have a backcountry permit signed by the chief ranger. Cliff Palace after hours fell under that restriction.

Anna wondered if Stacy entertained the same suspicions she did about possible monkeywrenching business. "If that's really where they were then I doubt much harm was done."

"When I made my sweep at eleven I didn't see any cars," he said stubbornly.

"Maybe they were on bicycles." Leaning her head back against the seat, she closed her eyes and let the subject drop.

At the housing loop, she fiddled with the radio while Stacy went in to fetch Bella. A little mental arithmetic told Anna that Bella was his stepdaughter. She was a first- or second-grader and he'd met his wife three years ago. Taking on the responsibility, not only of someone else's child, but a child with a disability, spoke of powerful love—or powerful need.

"Hello, my little pine nut," she heard Stacy call when he was halfway up the walk. He disappeared into the house to reappear moments later with Bella. The child's face was a testament to her mother's youthful good looks. A rounded heart set off by a crop of carefully tended curls. Brown hair, several shades lighter than Rose's, caught the morning sun and glinted with blond highlights. Wide-spaced eyes sparkled above a small straight nose. This loveliness made more pathetic the rolling gait and bowed legs, far too short for her upper body.

Hand in hand with Stacy, Bella chattered up at him. For

every glitter of hero worship in her eyes, there was an answering glow of adoration in his. Stacy's slender frame shaped itself into a question mark as he curbed his steps, leaning down to hear her.

What Anna had seen as a burden clearly lightened the load Stacy professed to have carried after his first wife left him.

"You're Anna Pigeon," the child announced when they reached the car.

"You got me there." Anna leaned over the seat-back to shove briefcases and hats out of Bella's way. Fleetingly, she wondered if Stacy had been talking about her.

"I read your name tag," the child explained as she swung herself into the rear seat. "That's in case you thought I might be a psycho or something."

Stacy laughed. "Psychic, pine nut. Psycho is crazy."

"I'm not old enough to be crazy," she said confidently. "Do you have children, Mrs. Pigeon?"

"None to speak of."

"Oh." Bella sounded disappointed.

"I have a cat." Anna tried to exonerate herself.

"Don't you like children?"

"Some of my best friends are children." Anna was thinking of Alison, her Michigan housemate's daughter.

The truth must have rung through the words. Bella brightened immediately. "That's okay then. If the cat has kittens, can I play with them?"

"Your mom's allergic, pine nut," Stacy reminded gently.

"Not have, Stacy. Play with. I'd wash after."

"Piedmont's a boy cat," Anna said. "So no kittens. But he might like it if you'd come play with him. Sometimes I suspect he misses the little girl we used to live with."

"Does he try to hide it?" Bella asked, and Anna sensed she was already adept at hiding hurt and loneliness.

"Yes. Sometimes he goes out and kills mice. Then I think he feels better."

"I like mice."

"So does Piedmont." Anna was losing ground in this conversation. A smile played on Stacy's lips. She was willing to bet it was at her expense.

The maintenance yard was loud with heavy equipment. Stacy pulled up in front of the fire cache. "Stay in the car, honey. Too much traffic. I'll find Drew."

"Are you married?" Bella resumed the interrogation as Stacy disappeared into the cache.

"Used to be," Anna replied.

"Did he divorce you?"

"He died." Anna wished Stacy would come back. "Maybe I'd better go and see what's keeping your dad."

Her cowardly exit was thwarted. "No. Stay. Stacy'll be right back. He never forgets. My first dad divorced us because I wasn't born normal," Bella stated matter-of-factly. "Momma said."

Anna didn't know what to say to that. She was saved by Stacy's reappearance, Drew beside him. Drew Kinder was as close to a "mountain of a man" as Anna'd ever met, made of a core of stone-hard muscle covered with a layer of baby fat a couple of inches deep. Unruly eyebrows and a moth-eaten mustache grew like lichen on his round face.

Next to the helitacker, Stacy's six-foot-two looked average, short even, and his slenderness was accentuated. Seeing the two men together, an image of a bass fiddle and bow flashed through her mind.

"Hiya, Drew," Bella called.

"Hiya, beautiful." Drew leaned down, hands on the door frame. His head filled the window. "I gotta fuel the truck, then we hit the road."

"Hit the road," Bella repeated, as if the phrase had struck a harmonious chord within her.

"I'll help you with the truck," Anna volunteered. She didn't want to be left alone with Bella again. The child's unrelenting forthrightness was unsettling.

"Can't hack it?" Stacy asked over the roof of the patrol car as she climbed out.

Anna just laughed.

While Drew filled the fire truck with diesel, she leaned against the fender. In his huge hands the nozzle looked like a child's water pistol.

"Bella's quite a girl," he said.

"Seems smart enough. Too bad she's . . ." Aware she was giving pity where none was asked, Anna left the sentence unfinished.

Drew straightened up. The sun was behind his head. In silhouette he loomed as solid as the proverbial brick outhouse. "Maybe that's what makes her so strong, so smart. She sees right through people. Maybe she got that from being the way she is. Ever think of that?"

"I will now," Anna promised.

"Her mom wants her to get all these operations on her legs. Pretty painful stuff. Make her more 'normal.' Maybe it's a good idea, maybe it's not. All I know is it's got to hurt. I don't like seeing kids hurt."

"Nobody does," Anna said mildly.

Drew shot her a look that startled her with its venom. "Don't kid yourself," he said, and went back to pumping diesel. "Her folks ought to leave her alone. I'm a giant. She's a dwarf. We're the variety that adds spice."

A blue Ford six-pac carrying five men in orange hard hats pulled up behind them in line for fuel. Ted Greeley was driving.

"Well, if it isn't my own personal ranger," Greeley greeted Anna. "How am I doing? Running afoul of the law?"

"Not yet," she returned.

He looked at his watch. "It's early."

"Did Frieda get ahold of you about last night?"

"She did. Damn near too late. You guessed it. The son of a bitch dumped sugar in the gas tank of my ditcher. If anybody'd fired it up I'd've been proud owner of a piece of shit retailing at close to a hundred grand. I'm none too happy one of my boys left the gate unlocked and I'm none too happy one of your boys didn't catch it. I'd hate to think all my tax dollars are paying for are cute uniforms for pretty little rangers." He winked and Anna managed not to spit in his open eye.

Silva got out of the truck. He had his shirt on this time—a western cut with pearl snaps—but the tails were out, the cuffs not snapped, the collar open. He looked just tumbled out of a woman's bed or ready to tumble into one.

" 'Morning, Ranger Pigeon," he said lazily as he looked Anna up and down. Again she wasn't flattered.

"That ever work for you?" she asked.

He didn't even play coy. "More often than not. Is it going to work on you?" Silva removed his hard hat and ran a hand through his shock of black hair. "Or are rangers' sex drives too low?"

"IQs are too high," Anna retorted.

Everybody laughed but Silva. Anna guessed she'd struck a nerve. A smile broke slowly on Tom's face but it never reached his eyes. She braced herself. She had the sinking feeling the repartee was about to take an ugly turn.

All he said was: "Better watch it. I'm getting more and more eligible every day. By August I ought to be Bachelor of the Year. Ain't that right, Ted?"

Greeley didn't return Silva's smile.

"Got to hop to it," Silva said. "The boss wants to leave early to get in a round of golf. Me, I can't play golf. I'm not over the hill yet."

"Come on," Greeley growled. "I don't pay you to chase—"

Anna was sure he intended to say "pussy" but he saved himself at the last second.

"—your tail," he finished.

"See you around," Silva said to Anna as he put his hard hat back on.

"By the way, I never did find out anything about that truck that ran you off the road," Anna told him.

"Was no truck," Tom said as he turned away. "I was just jerking your chain."

He was wearing brown cowboy boots. But then so were Greeley and two of the others. So was Anna, for that matter.

Drew finished fueling the truck and Stacy brought Bella to the gas shed. As he lifted her onto the high front seat their radios rasped to life.

"Seven hundred, this is Beavens at Cliff Palace."

As one, Drew, Anna, and Stacy turned up the volume on their portables. The interpreters in the ruins seldom called in unless there was a problem.

"Lockout," Drew offered.

"Let's hope," Stacy said.

"Shhh."

"Cliff Palace, this is seven hundred. Go ahead," Frieda's voice came over the air.

"We've got a litle girl here having trouble breathing. She doesn't look too good."

Anna and Stacy began to run for the patrol car. Anna flipped on the vehicle's lights and siren. "Nothing like starting the day off right."

"Jesus. Not another one."

The anguish in Stacy's voice startled a laugh from Anna. "Hey, it's something to do."

The two-way road to Cliff was narrow and twisting with no shoulders. Despite lights and sirens, tourists plodded ahead, refusing to give right-of-way.

Trapped behind an RV, Anna and Stacy crawled along at twenty-three miles an hour. Anna grabbed the public address mike and turned up the volume. "Pull to the right, please. Pull to the right. Pull to the right, please." She repeated the command until the RV's driver came out of his comatose state and began to slow, squeezing the oversized vehicle to the side of the road.

"Damn. Just once I'd like to ride shotgun with a shotgun and permission to use it."

Stacy said nothing. His eyes were fixed on the road as he hunched over the wheel. Above the dark line of beard, his cheek was pale. Tension pulled his shoulders almost to ear level.

Cliff Palace lot was full. They parked in a handicapped space near where the trail started down to the ruin and Anna called in: "Seven hundred, three-one-two, we've arrived on the scene."

Having taken the red trauma pack and an oxygen bottle from the trunk, she led the way down the crowded trail using "excuse me" the way a frustrated motorist uses the horn.

As soon as they climbed the eight-foot ladder that brought them within the cliff dwelling, they saw the knot of people surrounding the sick child.

On the periphery was Jamie Burke. The moment she noticed Anna and Stacy she marched toward them. They met halfway through the alcove and the interpreter started in: "It's not like you weren't warned, for God's sake. Nobody listened. This time it's a child. Solstice—"

"Hold that thought, Jamie," Anna cut her off. "I'll get back with you this evening." Dodging past the other woman, she plowed through the tourists at a fast walk.

Mesa Verde's most famous cliff dwelling, Cliff Palace filled an alcove several hundred feet long. The dwelling itself was composed of two hundred and seventeen rooms, twenty-one kivas, and, at the far end, a four-story tower, the inside room of which boasted intact plaster with discernible paintings. The entrance to the tower was reachable only by ladder that led to a narrow path around yet another roofless kiva.

In this congested part of the ruin was a frail-looking child. She strained for air with the rounded chest of those suffering chronic pulmonary disorders. Dark hair fell forward over her face, and stick-thin arms and legs poked out from beneath an oversized T-shirt. The child was propped in a sitting position against a stone wall built seven centuries before she was born. A man—probably her father—sat on the wall, one leg on either side, supporting her. A hand-lettered sign reading PLEASE DO NOT SIT OR CLIMB ON THE WALLS had tumbled to the path at the foot of the wooden ladder.

The girl braced her hands on her knees and leaned forward. Tendons in her neck pulled like ropes with the effort of breathing, yet only squeaks of air were pushed out.

Anna eased through the crowd and put down her gear. "Hi, I'm Anna," she introduced herself as she removed a nasal cannula from the oxygen kit and fitted it to the cylinder. "What's your name?" The girl hadn't enough breath to spare for an answer.

"Her name's Stephanie," the man seated on the wall answered for her. "Stephanie McFarland. She's got asthma."

An ominous blue tint colored the skin around Stephanie's lips and in her fingernail beds.

"She was doing fine a bit ago, then she started feeling like she might throw up," a thin-faced woman in her early thirties told Anna. "She's been at altitude before and we've never had trouble like this. We're from Denver. It's nearly this high. Steph should be used to it. I'm her mom," the woman finished in a whisper.

"Well, Stephanie, we're going to get you down to a doctor so you can breathe better, okay?" The girl nodded slightly, all her concentration taken by the effort of drawing and expelling air.

"Meyers, hand me the—" Anna broke off as she looked over at Stacy.

Clutching the red trauma bag to his chest as a frightened woman might clutch her baby, he stood at the edge of the circle of concerned onlookers. The blood had drained from his face and he was so pale Anna was afraid he was going to pass out.

"Meyers!" she said sharply.

The brown eyes turned toward her. They were clouded with fear—or shock.

"Hand me the bag. Then give Frieda a call and see if we can't get helitack down here with a litter. We're going to need the ambulance as well."

For a moment it seemed as if he didn't understand, then his eyes focused. Anna watched him for a few seconds more but he began making the calls. She turned down her radio so she could talk with Stephanie and her parents.

Seven minutes and Drew called on scene at Cliff Palace parking. In that time Stephanie had begun to go downhill. By the time Drew arrived with the Stokes, she had lost consciousness.

Keeping up a running commentary to calm the parents and Stephanie if she wasn't beyond hearing, Anna had taken the IV kit from the trauma bag and prepped the child's thin arm. "This is just to get some fluids in her; it may help to break up the congestion. And, too, if she needs medication at the hospital, they can just put it right in."

She swabbed the skin with alcohol and readied a number-sixteen needle. To Drew she said: "We're not wasting time with this. One try; if I don't get in, we're out of here."

"Do it," Drew said.

"Damn," Anna whispered. "This kid has no veins."

"What? Have you got it?" Drew asked.

"No. Load and go. Wait. I'm getting a flashback."

"Too many drugs in college," Drew muttered under his breath.

Anna noted the red of blood in the flashback chamber of the IV catheter with satisfaction. She was in. Carefully, she pulled the catheter off the needle, sliding it into the vein. "Pop the tourniquet." She taped the catheter in place. "Go."

Anna addressed herself to the little girl strapped into the evacuation litter. "Stephanie, we're carrying you out. You're in good hands." Maybe the child's eyelids twitched in response. Maybe it was just the play of the sun.

Drew had taken his place at the head of the litter.

Crouched down, elbows on thighs, he looked solid, like a rock. When he began to rise Anna was put in mind of the unfolding of the stony peak of Bald Mountain in Disney's *Fantasia.*

Stacy knelt at the foot of the Stokes. His lips were pressed in a thin line and his eyes turned inward, unreadable.

"Ready?" Drew asked.

Meyers didn't respond. "Stacy!" Drew raised his voice. Like a man in a trance, Stacy slowly began to lift. "Atta boy," said the helitacker.

The Stokes was of orange plastic hard enough to haul up inclines and drag over rough terrain. Encasing the fragile form of the child, it resembled a medieval instrument of torture rather than the secure embrace of modern emergency evacuation equipment, and Anna felt bad for the parents, already frightened half out of their wits.

Four ladders of juniper wood, polished to a dark gloss by the palms of countless tourists, led up twenty-five feet through the crack in the cliff's face to the mesa.

Stephanie McFarland would not be roped up this incline, but carried back out the entrance trail. The distance was greater but the ascent not so precipitous.

"Coming through," Drew boomed. Curious onlookers parted reluctantly. Drew going first, the procession began to move down the path fronting the cliff dwellings. Tourists shifted, pressing back against stone walls. Bright-hued clothing, cameras, sunglasses, all combined to create a jarring kaleidoscope of color against the serene peach and buff of the ancient village.

Over the centuries roofs had fallen in, paint chipped away, and fiber mats rotted from doorways; the clangor of life leeched away until the structures had taken on the timeless purity of Greek statuary. But, like the ancient Greeks who had painted their pale marble figures vivid colors, the Anasazi had plastered the warm neutrality of their sandstone exteriors, then decorated them in red and black patterns.

Mesa Verde's Old Ones might have been as much at home with the cacophony of neon and spandex as the moderns.

The pathway clear, Drew picked up the pace. Holding the IV bag above shoulder level, Anna walked beside the litter. Stephanie's chest movement was barely perceptible and the tissue-thin eyelids blue and delicately veined. Some of the pallor was probably natural but the faint bluish at lips and fingernails was not.

Anna stroked back the dark hair. The child's skin was cool to the touch, clammy.

"Seven hundred, three-one-four."

"Seven hundred," Anna and Drew's radios bleated as Dispatch responded. Anna turned hers down.

"The ambulance has arrived at Cliff Palace. We're at the entrance. Repeat: the entrance."

"Seven hundred copies. Did you get that, three-one-two?"

Anna pulled her radio from her duty belt. "I got it. We'll be up in ten minutes or so. Two helitacks are standing by at the stairs. There's a narrow spot there. Send somebody down from the overlook to clear the visitors out of it."

"Ten-four. I'll send Claude Beavens." The dispatcher named the seasonal interpreter, who had radioed in the incident.

Anna put her radio back on her belt and watched her footing as she trod the uneven pavement. Like all the park's ruins accessible to tourists, Cliff Palace had a paved path leading to it from the parking lot on the mesa top. When the ruins were first opened there'd been primitive trails that ladies in long dresses and picture hats had picked their way down, carefully placing each buttoned-up boot. In the thirties the Civilian Conservation Corps had come in and earned their Depression dollars with the back-breaking chore of carving staircases from native rock and shoring up trails with stone.

Beauty and grace had gone the way of cheap labor. Now the paths were a hodgepodge of asphalt and rock, patched and repatched.

The trail switched back several times then narrowed to hand-hewn steps leading into a crevice between two boulders. After more than half a century the workmanship of the CCC still held fine. Only the lips of the steps had been fortified with pale scabs of modern concrete.

The stairway, just wide enough to admit people single file, was choked with tourists who'd started down before Claude Beavens had been sent to stop traffic.

"Gonna have to ask you folks to go on back up," Drew called over the low-grade chatter. The hips of the better endowed scraped a patter of sand from the soft rock as they shifted in the confining space. Faces displayed the sheeplike vacancy of vacationers who've come upon the unexpected.

"Ask the guy behind you to turn around," the helitack foreman suggested patiently. He spoke over his shoulder, his thick arms showing no strain at holding Stephanie's little weight.

Attuned to the vital signs of her patient, Anna caught a faint sigh. She laid the palm of her hand on the girl's diaphragm. Through the knit T-shirt, she could feel the bones of the rib cage but not the gentle rise of lungs filling with air.

"What?" Drew pressed.

Anna shook her head, waited. With a sucking sound, like the hiss of a new kitten, the child drew a sudden breath.

"Thanks," Anna said to no one in particular. To Drew she said: "We're in a hurry." Edging past him, she stood at the foot of the stairs.

"Got to move you out. This girl needs medical attention. Up you go. Thanks. Thanks." Anna spoke pleasantly, but she was prodding rounded backs and pudgy shoulders, herding people up the stairway.

As they began retreating, she turned back to Drew. His head was sunk between his massive shoulders. The little braided pigtail he affected poked out incongruously as he stared down into the litter.

Adrenaline spurted into Anna's system. "What? What've you got?"

"Breathing, but way too slow. Assholes," Anna heard him mutter. "Bringing a sick little kid way out here."

Paul Summers, looking as close to a *GQ* model as anyone could in the ill-fitting Nomex, thrust his head over the rock above Anna's head.

"You gonna need ropes?"

Drew shook his head. "It'd take too long. Here, Anna, you hold the front." Stacy's arms had grown slack, his end of the litter close to slipping from his grasp. "Stacy, pay attention," Drew snapped as he handed Anna the litter and eased butt first under the loaded Stokes. "Put the weight on my back."

Taking the head of the litter, Anna looked down at her patient. Even with the oxygen canister, lashed for security between her knees, turned to fifteen liters per minute on a non-rebreather face mask, the blue tinge around Stephanie's mouth remained.

Crouched down, Drew was in place underneath the Stokes. He straightened up, and like a rowboat on the crest of a wave, the litter with its fragile burden was lifted into the air.

Anna's arms were fully extended when he stopped. "Let's do it," she said.

One step at a time, she backed up the stairs. The orange plastic scraped along the sandstone but, balanced on Drew's back, the Stokes was high enough to clear the narrowest part of the crevice. "Keep coming," Anna said. "We'll make it but just barely."

"Barely's good enough," Drew grunted through a kinked esophagus.

Tossed as if on stormy seas, the orange litter wobbled through the crack in the rock. The GQ helitacker peered anxiously down, his blond head bobbing in sympathy as he worked his way along the top of the boulders they crept through.

Arms at full reach, Anna was out of eye contact with Stephanie McFarland. As the seconds ticked by, she could feel her anxiety rising.

"Paul," she called up. "What's she look like?"

"Not good."

"Breathing?"

"Can't tell."

"Get the bag valve." Anna kept her voice calm both for her patient and for the audience of tourists she could hear Claude Beavens organizing twenty feet up the trail behind her.

At last Drew's head and shoulders emerged from be-

tween the walls of stone. Humped over, he carried the litter onto the landing at the foot of a long metal staircase
leading up to a viewing platform cut from the mesa top.

Over her shoulder Anna glimpsed a gauntlet of visitors
yet to be run. Instead of stopping them on the spacious
platform, the interpreter had arranged them all on one
side of the stairs, where they stood like a Busby Berkeley
musical kick line waiting to go into their eleven o'clock
number.

Beavens, all bony elbows and wrists, with a neck so
long and skinny his flat brimmed hat took on the aspect
of a plate balanced on a broom handle, was waving his
arms like an officious dance master. "People, people," he
shouted. "Give them room. Emergency evac. Give the
rangers room."

"Down," Drew said. Slowly he knelt, Anna and Stacy
keeping the litter stable.

Stephanie McFarland came into view. Her face was gray
and her hypoxia had grown more pronounced. Again
Anna laid a hand on the child's diaphragm. Drew and
Stacy repositioned themselves around the Stokes.

"Ten," Anna announced, timing the child's respirations.
"Let's bag her. Paul!"

There was a scuffling sound as he slid down the sandstone to land lightly on his feet. "Okay!" he called back
up the face of the boulder. An unseen person pushed a
green airway kit over the edge and it fell neatly into his
waiting hands. Within seconds he had the Ambu bag—a
soft plastic barrel about the size of a football with a face
mask on one end and a length of plastic tubing trailing
from the other—out of the satchel. With an economy of
movement that in one so young and so pretty always took
Anna by surprise, he hooked the length of tubing to the

green oxygen cylinder, then handed Anna the bag so she could fit the mask over Stephanie's mouth and nose.

"Take the IV, Paul. Ventilating her at twenty-five breaths a minute," she informed them, as she began pumping air into the child. "Go."

Keeping in step with Anna as best they could, they carried the Stokes up the metal stairs. Drew had taken the foot and used his height to keep the litter level.

"In and out and in and out and," Anna chanted under her breath, keeping time as she forced oxygen into the failing lungs. Behind her she could feel the gentle battering of camera cases and shoulder bags as she pushed past the line of people along the stair rail. Occasionally she felt something softer than steel mesh beneath her boots and heard a squawk of pain but she was only dimly aware of these things. Her eyes and mind were fixed on the now deep and regular rise of the little girl's chest.

"Looking good," Drew was saying. "She's pinking up."

Anna glanced at Stephanie's face. The deathlike pallor had abated somewhat. "Paul," she said quietly. "Radio for a patrol car escort. We'll be running hot. I want the road clear."

The firefighter keyed his mike with one hand. Keeping the IV drip high with the other, he began a series of radio calls.

The stairs were behind them. "Clear sailing," Drew said cheerfully.

Anna secured the Stokes to the gurney with webbed belting. Stacy'd gone catatonic and without his help, she banged it ungracefully into the back of the waiting ambulance. Not for the first time, she cursed the antiquated equipment a poverty-stricken Park Service was forced to make do with year after year.

Anna and Stacy rode down in the ambulance. Paul Summers drove, Mrs. McFarland rode in the passenger seat. Anna changed Stephanie to humidified oxygen and rechecked the girl's vital signs. Strapped into the seat near the gurney's head, Stacy held the run sheet on his lap, but it didn't look as if he was writing the numbers as she called them out. He'd not said a word since he'd completed his radio requests half an hour before.

Anna patted the little girl's arm. "You're doing real good, Steph. Hang in there." The child had not regained consciousness and Anna had no way of knowing if she heard. To Stacy she said: "Are you okay?"

Stacy just shook his head.

Two emergency room nurses met them in the ambulance bay at Southwest Memorial. Stacy stayed in the ambulance while Anna replaced the inventory they'd used on the run from the hospital's stock room. Anna then took a couple of minutes to talk with Bill McFarland. Stephanie had had a severe attack once before. Ridiculous as it was, the information comforted Anna, as if the park had been somehow exonerated.

Anna drove the ambulance on the return trip. Paul Summers threw himself on the cot. "These carry-outs are getting to be a bore," he complained. "How many now? One last Tuesday, one the week before that."

"Maybe it's a conspiracy," Anna returned. "Hills gets a healthy chunk of the five hundred dollars paid for each run for his budget."

"Hills'd do it, too," Paul said with a laugh. "Mr. Tightwad. How about you, Stacy, are you getting a cut?"

Stacy's silence remained unbroken. Paul abandoned light conversation with a "G'night."

Meyers had panicked, frozen. Anna wasn't so much angry with him as sympathetic. Everybody had a panic button. The heroes just managed to stumble through life without it being pushed. Two hundred feet beneath the icy waters of Lake Superior Anna had met up with her own cowardice.

But she could avoid deep cold water. If Stacy wanted to be a ranger he'd have to get used to handling sick and injured people. In most national parks the only doctors available were there on vacation.

Writing the report on the McFarland medical fell to Anna. In the crowded back of the CRO, where three desks were crammed into a space where only one should have been, she sat in front of an old IBM Selectric and stared down at the 10-343 threaded around the platen. The form was five thicknesses. Hitting a wrong key meant Wite-Out in quintuplicate.

Putting off the inevitable, she turned to the district ranger. Hills Dutton was a large square-faced man with thinning sandy hair that curled at his collar. From somewhere in the mare's nest that was his desk top, he'd retrieved a pair of calipers. Shirttail in hand, he was measuring the thickness of the excess flesh on his belly.

"Hills, what did you think of the medical today?"

"Nine percent body fat," he announced with satisfaction, and carefully wrote in the numbers on a physical training graph he'd colored with felt-tipped pens. "Bet you can't top that, Anna. You're a woman more or less, right? Maybe eighteen percent? Women can be up to twenty-eight percent before they're considered fat. Men pork out at seventeen. You got it easy."

Unzipping his pants, he tucked the shirt in and gave his flat belly an affectionate pat before putting his gunbelt back on. "Not bad for an old man."

"Seems like there've been an awful lot of carry-outs at Cliff this summer," Anna persisted. "What's usual for June?"

"It happens," Hills admitted vaguely. "Lots of senior citizens up here."

"Today we carried out a third-grader."

"Asthma." Hills fished a tool catalogue off the top of the pile.

Anna gave up and went back to staring at the 10-343, trying to screw her courage to the sticking place and make that first typo.

"Frieda," Hills called over the partition to the front desk. "Call Maintenance and see if they've got any old ratchet sets they can spare. I've got to get some for the vehicles."

"Your credit's no good with Maintenance," Frieda returned. "So tight he squeaks," she muttered.

"I heard that," Hills said. "Maybe I'll order some. Got any DI-ones?" He named the purchase order form.

"Sure you will," came the murmur. Then: "All out." There was no forthcoming offer to run over to Administration and get them. Frieda's territory as the chief ranger's secretary and dispatcher was carefully defined. It didn't include running errands for the lesser rangers.

"I'll get them," Anna offered, glad of an excuse to postpone writing the report a bit longer. "I need to talk to Patsy anyway."

She poked along the twenty feet of path between the buildings, stopping to watch a tarantula make its majestic way across the asphalt. After the tarantulas she'd met in the backcountry of Guadalupe Mountains National Park in Texas, these northern creatures were decidedly non-threatening. Beside their teacup-sized Trans Pecos cousins they seemed almost cute. Still, Anna didn't get too close.

No one had yet dispelled to her satisfaction the myth that they could jump long distances.

"Don't you just love them?"

Anna looked up from her bug to find Al Stinson, hands on knees, studying the tarantula with a look akin to true love. Off duty, Stinson dressed in classic archaeologist style: khaki shorts and a white oxford shirt. Gray hair poked out around her lined face. Chapped knuckles and clipped nails made her hands as ageless and practical-looking as any working man's. "Just beautiful," Stinson said of the spider.

"Maybe to a lady tarantula," Anna hedged.

"This is a female. Lookie." The interpreter reached down and touched the creature gently on one of its legs. "See? No hair. I don't know about European girls, but ours don't have leg hair. Only the males."

"You're kidding."

"No." Stinson laid her hand flat on the asphalt and the tarantula tested it gingerly with a hairless foreleg. Something was evidently amiss. The creature backed away and took another route.

"Too bad," Stinson said. She straightened and rested her hands on prominent pelvic bones. "It feels neat when they walk on you. Little elfin feet."

"It'd take four elves to make that many tracks," Anna returned, not envying Al the experience.

Stinson sniffed the air with a round, slightly squashed nose. "God! I love it."

Politely, Anna sniffed too. Mixed with the smell of bus exhaust and hot tar was a delicate perfume, warmed off the tiny yellow blooms of a bush near the walk. "The bitterbrush?"

"The silence. It was after three-thirty. Construction had stopped for the day. No roaring bonegrinder. Some bones were uncovered. May mean a burial. Wouldn't that be great? We'll get Greeley shut down yet." Al laughed, a nasal but infectious whinny. "The Boys will not be pleased."

One of the many mysteries of Mesa Verde was that so few Anasazi burial sites were found. Some remains had been uncovered in sealed and abandoned rooms in the dwellings and some in the midden heaps below the cliff dwellings, but no burial ground had been discovered and surprisingly few individual sites for a society of near ten thousand souls that had flourished for more than five centuries.

Talk of the pipeline put Anna in mind of her housemate. "Al, Jamie was on duty in Cliff Palace when we had that medical this morning. Lately she's been dropping heavy-handed hints that something's going down on solstice. Is there anything I ought to know?"

Stinson threw back her head like Barbara Stanwyck in *Maverick Queen* and snorted a laugh. "The less law enforcement knows, the better I sleep nights."

Anna laughed with her, partly at the sentiment and partly at a mental image of Al Stinson as Queen of the Cattle Thieves. Amid the merriment she found herself wondering if the maverick queen could swing a chain as well as a lariat.

"If you hear anything that sounds like it could get somebody hurt or fired, let me know and I'll see if I can't fulfill my role as Professional Party Pooper."

"Better you than The Boys."

By the time Anna wandered into Administration it was after four P.M. and people were stirring to leave for the day. The receptionist's desk was tidied and, engrossed in a phone conversation, she barely gave Anna a nod.

Anna fetched the procurement forms from the storage

room in the basement. On her way back she stopped in the doorway of Patsy Silva's office.

The superintendent's secretary kept her office in a state of impressive order. Plants in macramé hangers, pictures, and a stained-glass image of Kokopelli, the flute player, in the window kept the orderliness from being oppressive.

"Hills could use your decorating service," Anna said as she leaned against the door frame.

"Hills could use a bulldozer," Patsy replied with a smile.

"How's it going? I didn't get a list of times and places for paternal visits so I just assumed you and Tom worked it out."

Patsy turned away briefly, fussed with some papers. Anna tried to read the expression on her face but it was too fleeting.

"We're doing okay," Patsy said.

"Any more gifts of the weird persuasion?"

"Only this." Patsy produced an extra bright smile as she held up her left wrist for inspection.

Anna whistled long and low. The watch Patsy wore was—or looked to be—fourteen-carat gold with at least a carat's worth of diamonds sparkling around the face. Even with the union doing its fiscal magic, the watch must have cost Silva a month's wages.

"Tom?"

Patsy nodded and Anna caught the expression again. This time she pegged it: embarrassment. Evidently it wasn't all gifts Patsy took offense to. Only cheap ones.

"Good for you." Anna glanced at her own Wal-Mart special. She'd managed to kill enough time. In six minutes she was off duty. The 10-343 had been effectively avoided for one day.

She called Stacy on the radio and he brought the patrol

car to give her a lift to Far View. He still wore a haunted look and drove through the empty parking lot with the same hunched intensity as when weaving down a narrow road with lights and siren blaring.

"What happened to Bella?" Anna asked to make conversation.

"What do you mean?" Alarmed, Stacy lost his inward look. "Did something happen to Bella?"

"Drew was on the carry-out. Wasn't he baby-sitting today? I just wondered where he'd stashed her."

Visibly, he relaxed. "Bella stayed at the fire dorm watching cartoons with Jimmy. He called in sick. That's all I need, for Bella to catch a dose of something."

"Don't worry. Unless she comes down with a case of Coors, Bella won't get what Jimmy's got."

They rode without speaking till Stacy turned off Chapin Mesa Road toward the Far View dormitories. There was something familiar in the drawn face, the tight voice. Putting it together with the medical, Anna realized where she'd seen it before. He carried himself like a man in pain.

"Take off your gun and I'll buy you a beer," she offered on impulse.

For a moment she was sure he was going to turn her down. "I'll get you home before six," she added, remembering Bella and Drew's baby-sitting schedule.

"A beer would taste good tonight."

The lounge at the Far View Lodge was on the second floor and boasted an open-air veranda to the east side. The view, though somewhat curtailed by an expanse of tarred roof studded with air-conditioning ducts, justified the name of Far View. Mesas receded into mists that melded seamlessly into mountain ranges. In the afternoon light, strong at midsummer, the muted blues and grays were given an iridescence that at some times made the mesas appear as unreal as an artist's conception, and, at others, the only reality worth living.

When Anna arrived Stacy was not there. She took a table that backed on a low adobe wall. The plaster radiated heat collected during the day and deflected a cold wind that had sprung up.

Anna's nerves jangled. She couldn't shake an unwelcome First Date feeling. Possibly because she'd taken the time to comb her hair out of its braids and dab perfume between her breasts. A Carta Blanca took the edge off. By the time she was halfway down it, Stacy arrived.

The edge came back.

He looked as awkward as she felt, and wordlessly she cursed herself for moving their relationship out of the secure arena of work.

Stacy ordered a Moosehead and folded himself into one of the wire garden chairs.

"I hardly recognized you with your clothes on," Anna said.

"Ah. Out of uniform."

"You clean up nice."

"Thanks."

Small talk died. Anna sipped her beer and resisted the urge to glance at her watch. "I thought the medical went well this morning," she said to get the conversation into neutral territory.

"God." Stacy shook his head. Pain was clear in his eyes.

Anna forgot her discomfort. Leaning across the table, she took hold of his arm.

A familiar laugh brought her head up. Ted Greeley had taken a table across the veranda. As he caught her eye, he raised his highball in a salute. Anna smiled automatically then returned to Stacy. "What is getting to you?"

"Stephanie McFarland died. I called the ER before I came."

Anna felt as if he'd slapped her. "That's not right," she said. "Stephanie was just a kid with asthma. They got the name wrong."

Stacy shook his head. "The name wasn't wrong. She died."

"Fuck." Anna took a long pull on the beer. It didn't help. "Third grade. What the hell happened? She didn't have to die."

"Yes she did."

Stacy sounded sure of himself, like a man quoting scripture or baseball scores.

"Why?" Anna demanded.

"Figure it out," Stacy snapped. "You saw me. I couldn't do a thing, not one damn thing."

Anna looked at him for a long moment. Self-pity in the face of the child's death struck her as blind arrogance. "Give it a rest. We did what we did. You were useless, not deadly. Don't make yourself so important."

Stacy stared at his hands. Clearly this was a cross he was determined to bear. Maybe he was Catholic.

"I'm sorry," Anna said.

"Yeah. Me too. Sorrier than you know."

Stacy made circles on the glass tabletop with the beer bottle.

Anna finished her beer and ordered another.

"Bella can get bone grafts in her legs," he said, as if this were part of an ongoing conversation instead of a non sequitur. "She could dance, fall in love, marry, save the world—whatever she wanted."

"Does Bella want the operations?" Anna asked, remembering Drew's sour appraisal of the treatment.

"She's scared. But Rose wants them for her. Rose was so beautiful. She once—"

Anna nodded.

"I've probably told you. But she was, and it meant a lot to her and she wants that for Bella."

"What do you want for Bella?"

"I want her to have a chance at the brass ring, whatever that means." Stacy took a long drink of his beer and let his eyes wander over the panorama that was northern New Mexico. "It's not cheap."

Anna's eyes followed his over the soft blue distance. The beers were taking effect. Words were no longer as necessary.

"Rose's used to better," Stacy said after a while.

"So you've said. Old Number One was rich?"

"A lawyer. Megabucks."

"The vultures always eat better than anyone else on the food chain," Anna said. Meyers barely smiled.

"Rose left him. She says she had a problem with commitment." Stacy made it sound like a compliment.

Remembering Bella's remark about her dad leaving because of her deformity, Anna said nothing.

Stacy folded his hands around his Moosehead in a prayerful attitude and looked across the table at her. She smiled and he smiled back. Something sparked, ignited the rushes of emotion the medical had left strewn about their psyches.

Nature's narcotic: more addicting than crack, harder to find than unadulterated Colombian, and, in the long run, more expensive than cocaine. But, God! did it get you there. Anna's breath gusted out at sudden, unbidden memories of love.

"I've got to go." She stood so abruptly her chair overturned.

"Yes." Both of them pulled out wallets and tossed bills on the table. The waiter would get one hell of a tip, Anna thought as she walked out of the lounge.

"Can I give you a ride?" Stacy called after her. Anna just waved.

Unwilling to return to the cacophony that was home, she walked down the Wetherill Mesa Road till she was out of sight of the lodge, then sat under the protective drapery of a serviceberry bush. She felt like crying but was too long out of practice.

6

ANNA GROPED her way to the kitchen to start her morning coffee. Clad in striped men's pajamas, Jennifer sat at the dining room table eating cereal. Already in uniform, Jamie played with an unlit cigarette.

She held it up as Anna passed. "Trying to decide whether or not to have breakfast," she volunteered.

"Better light up," Jennifer said. "It's going to be a long day."

"The longest." Jamie pulled herself out of the straight-backed chair and took her morning drugs out onto the rear deck.

"Long day," Jennifer repeated.

Since it was obviously expected of her and because early in the morning Anna actually found Jennifer's refined version of the Southern drawl soothing, she asked, "Why long?"

"Longest day of the year. June twenty-first."

"Right: solstice. If something doesn't happen, I'm going to be miffed." Anna spooned coffee into the drip filter.

"Oh, nothin' will. You know Jamie. There's always got to be something. A bunch of the interps got a backcountry permit to go down into Balcony House to watch the moon rise. That's about it."

"I'd think they'd want to watch the sun rise." Coffee was dripping through the filter but too slowly. Balancing the cone to one side, Anna managed to pour what was in the pot into her cup without making too much of a mess. "That's when all the magic is supposed to happen: spears of light through scientifically placed chinks—that sort of thing."

Leaning in the doorway, she sipped and watched Jennifer eating cereal.

She and Jennifer had such disparate schedules they seldom had the opportunity to work together. But bit by bit Anna was getting glimpses that this hair-sprayed and lipsticked magnolia blossom had a penchant for heavy drinking, late nights, and speaking up for herself. Anna found herself warming up to the woman.

"Jamie mentioned something about Old Ones and solstice again last week when we were carrying Stephanie McFarland out of Cliff Palace." Anna threw out the line, not sure what she was fishing for.

"Who knows what Jamie's up to," Jennifer said impatiently. "She says she hears Indian flute music coming out of the ruins at night; she's always seeing some big thing— ghosts and mountain lions and big-horned sheep and cute boys. I never see anything except illegally parked cars."

Jennifer sounded so disgusted that Anna laughed. "What about Paul Summers? He's as cute as they come."

"He's got a girlfriend back home."

"Back home is back home. Going to let it get in your way?"

"No, but it's sure gettin' in his. I just hate fidelity."

"Jimmy Russell?"

"He's ten years younger than I am." Jennifer pronounced "ten" as "tin." She shrugged philosophically. "If things don't start looking up soon, I'm going to have to start poachin'."

Anna's coffee was done. She walked back into the kitchen.

"Stacy's kinda cute," Jennifer mused.

Anna didn't want to get into that.

Running late, she called into service from the shower. At quarter after seven, hair confined in a braid and her teeth brushed, she pulled out of the Far View lot.

Hills was in Durango attending a wildland fire seminar, so Anna had the small four-wheel-drive truck. It was newer than the patrol car and had been built by Mitsubishi. Anna attributed the commercial success of Japanese cars to the fact that they were designed and built by a small people, hence they tended to fit American women far better than the wide-open spaces Buick and Dodge incorporated into their vehicles. At any rate, the seat didn't hurt her back.

Late June marked the peak of the tourist season and there were cars waiting at the locked gates to Far View Ruin and Cedar Tree Tower. The four-way intersection was backed up four cars deep. Anna liked to play hero with the simple act of letting folks go where they wanted to. This morning the kindly ranger routine was turned into a comic interlude while she wrestled with one of Stacy's signature twisted chain locks. Eventually she succeeded and was embarrassed by a round of applause.

Leaving the Four-Way, she drove slowly around the Museum Loop, stopping to check the picnic grounds for illegal campers. It was blessedly empty and she was spared the unsavory task of rousting out people in their night-gowns.

As Anna was passing the Administration Building, Patsy Silva flagged her down. The clerical staff wasn't required to wear uniforms and Patsy was in a flame-orange blouse and close-fitting gray trousers. Her lipstick echoed the color of her top.

Though immaculately dressed and every hair character-istically in place, Patsy looked somehow disheveled, as if she'd had a bad night or bad news.

"What's up?" Anna asked as she rolled down the pickup's window.

"Can you believe it, I lost my keys!" Patsy smiled apolo-getically. "Would you radio one of the Maintenance guys to let me in?"

Anna made the call.

Patsy didn't look relieved. "Are you all right?" Anna asked.

"I need to talk to you."

A slight gray-haired man with a dowager's hump came from the direction of the museum. When he saw them, he jangled a ring of keys.

"The superintendent's having a breakfast meeting. I've got to set it up. Can you come over to the house around twelve?" Patsy pleaded.

"Will do."

Patsy clicked on her smile and started thanking the jani-tor before she'd closed the distance between them.

Anna managed to kill twenty minutes cruising the ruins road. Cliff Palace was about halfway around a six-mile loop. Just before the parking lot the two-lane road became one way. Beyond the ruin a mile or so, at Soda Point, it crossed onto the Ute Indian Reservation. When the road had first been designed it had been incorrectly surveyed and a quarter-mile stretch crossed the park's boundary onto the reservation. A dirt track, never used anymore, ran for several miles into the piñon/juniper forest owned by the Utes. Brush had been piled across it to deter wandering visitors. A plan to barricade it had been in the works for years but nothing had ever been done.

Where the dirt road started into the woods, on a wide graveled turnout, was a curio shop and a trailer selling Navajo tacos and Sno-Kones. Short of rerouting the existing road, Mesa Verde's superintendent had little recourse but to accept this unauthorized invasion of commercialism. Authorized park concessionaires had jacked food prices so high the little stand did a booming business, especially among the rangers.

Past Soda Point, back on park lands, the one-way road widened into a parking lot at the Balcony House ruin. A mile or so farther on, the loop completed, traffic rejoined the two-lane road.

On Isle Royale Anna had patrolled in a boat, in Guadalupe Mountains on horseback. Both were preferable to the automobile. Anna wondered what it was that was so alienating about cars. Somehow, more than any other machine, they seemed to create a world of their own, a mobile pack-rat midden full of personal artifacts that utterly separated man from the natural environment he hurtled through. Maybe, she thought as she crept along in the line of cars trolling for parking spaces at Balcony House, that was why Americans were so enamored of them: power without connection, movement without real direction.

At nine, she returned to Far View, picked up Jennifer, and took her to Maintenance, where the patrol car was

parked. As the seasonal dragged her briefcase from behind
the seat, she volunteered to pick up Stacy when he came
on duty. Anna remembered the poaching threat but forbore comment. If the Catholics were right and the thought
was as bad as the deed, she was in no position to cast any
stones.

With two rangers on duty and nothing happening,
Anna felt lazy. She parked the truck and wandered over to
the fire cache to find someone to amuse her. Helitack was
gone. Physical training, she recalled. Every morning for
PT Drew ran his firefighters two miles down the Spruce
Canyon trail, then back up the steep pathway to the mesa
top.

As she turned to leave, a clattering arrested her attention. Moments later a child's bicycle with pink training
wheels came into view around the corner of the cache. It
wasn't one of the modern plastic monstrosities, but a classic, old-fashioned, metal bicycle. Extensions had been
welded onto the pedals so Bella Meyers could ride.

She rolled to a stop in the shade beside Anna. "Drew's
not here, Mrs. Pigeon. He's supposed to be back by nine
but he's always late. He says it takes him longer to shower
because there's so much of him. I'm always early."

"That's good to know. Does your dad know you're
here?" Anna was thinking of Stacy's concern about traffic
the only other time she'd seen Bella in Maintenance.

"Stacy'd already gone to work. Me and Momma only
got back from Albaturkey this morning."

Stacy didn't come on duty till later and it crossed Anna's
mind that the child was lying. But Bella didn't seem the
type. Life, for her, had to be full of personal triumphs and
grown-up dramas. She had no need to fabricate.

"I thought Stacy was on project shift," Anna probed

gently. Project days were scheduled from nine-thirty till six.

"Sometimes he goes early. He likes to go off by himself and look at birds and things. Sometimes he takes me. I like being by myself with Stacy."

Anna leaned back against a workbench set up outside the cache.

"That's where they clean their chain saws," Bella warned. "You'll get grease on your behind."

"Too late now."

"Glad I'm not your mom."

"Doesn't your mom approve of greasy behinds?"

"Hates 'em," Bella returned. "You know why Stacy always looks so good?"

Anna shook her head.

"Momma dresses him. Stacy'd just put on whatever was laying closest on the floor. Never iron it or anything. When we got him he was a mess."

Anna smiled. "Like a stray dog brought home from the pound?"

"Not that bad," Bella answered seriously. "He didn't have fleas or anything. But he was pretty scruffy."

Anna glanced at her watch more out of habit than anything. There was no place she had to be, nothing she had to do. In parks with backcountry her days had been spent walking, looking for people in—or causing—trouble. In the automobile-oriented front country of Mesa Verde the days were spent waiting for Dispatch to send her on an emergency or visitor assist.

"You're too old to have anyone dress you," Bella said, giving Anna a frank appraisal. "You do pretty good."

"Not as good as your mom?"

"No," the child answered honestly. "Mom's going to

buy her and me all new stuff when she gets thin again and I get my legs fixed."

Bella seemed disinterested and Anna suspected the new clothes promised a greater delight to Mrs. Meyers than to her daughter.

"I got to go," Bella announced. "Drew comes walking over now." Having carefully looked both ways, she rode across the maintenance yard toward the asphalt path that wound down to the housing loop several hundred yards away and invisible behind a fragrant curtain of evergreens.

No one left to play with, Anna decided to head for the chief ranger's office to fill out a few forms and pester Frieda. As she crossed the tarmac to where she'd parked, Greeley's six-pac rolled in. The contractor wasn't in evidence and a man she recognized but had never met was driving. Tom Silva rode shotgun. The pickup pulled in close to her truck. Since there wasn't room for both vehicle doors to open at once, Anna waited while they got out.

Silva was completely dressed; everything buttoned, belted, and tucked in. " 'Morning," he said as he slammed the door. He didn't meet her eye and, for once, there was nothing bantering in the way he spoke.

"Good morning, Tom. Have you gotten any closer to Bachelor of the Year?"

His head jerked up as if she poked him with a cattle prod. There was something different about his face as well as his demeanor. He struck Anna as older, less alive.

"I was just messing around," he said sullenly. "I didn't mean anything by that. 'Scuse me." He pushed by her and disappeared into the shop where the soda-pop machine was housed.

Anna speculated as to whether this new subdued Tom

had anything to do with Patsy's lunch invitation. The day was definitely getting more interesting.

Anna reached the tower house before Patsy and sat in the sun on a stone wall by the front door fantasizing about how she'd arrange the furniture if she inherited the house. She'd just gotten around to hanging curtains when Patsy hurried up the walk.

"Sorry I'm late," she panted. "You could have let yourself in!"

"I've only been here a minute," Anna assured her. "I was early."

"You didn't have to sit out here all that time."

Anna gave up and let herself be apologized to.

Patsy bustled around the kitchen making bologna sandwiches and small talk. Anna kept up her end of the conversation. Perhaps they were to follow formal rules of dining: no business discussed until brandy and cigars were served.

After every condiment and chip had been taken out of cupboards and put on the table, Patsy sat down. Anna noticed she no longer wore the expensive wristwatch. A Timex with Pluto's face on the dial had taken its place.

Anna bit into her sandwich. Patsy pushed her untouched plate away as if she'd already eaten. "It's about Tom," she said.

Anna nodded encouragement.

"He's been so full of himself lately. He was bragging and giving the girls school money. You saw the watch he gave me. I guess he thought he'd bought his way back in. When I said no, he got sore."

Anna waited but Patsy showed no inclination to finish the story unprompted. "What happened to the watch?" she asked to get the wheels turning again.

"I threw it in his face. He made a lot of noise about the money having nothing to do with anything, but I noticed he took it with him when he left."

Anna washed the sandwich down with Diet Pepsi. "I saw Tom this morning. He didn't seem like his old self."

"He's not." Patsy picked up a potato chip and began breaking it into small pieces. "Or else he's so much more like his old self it's scary. He gave me a gun."

"Did he say what the gun was for?"

Patsy shook her head. "I didn't see him. He left it sometime last night. A couple of times I woke up thinking I heard something—the girls are in Gunnison with their grandma. When I'm alone I don't sleep well. I hear things—you know: branches scraping and the wind. I scare myself silly thinking it's an escaped murderer or a crazy person."

"With a hook instead of a hand?"

Patsy laughed. "You know him?"

"I first heard of him at a pajama party at Mercy High School. When I moved to Manhattan I swear he had a sublet under my bed."

"Campfire Girls," Patsy explained her arcane knowledge.

"Anyway . . ." Anna brought the subject back to Tom and his gun.

"Anyway last night I woke up a couple of times but I never came downstairs. I scare myself more if I start peeking in closets and under beds. For once it wasn't all my imagination. This morning there was a gun in the middle of the kitchen table."

Patsy got up and opened a cupboard door. Bundled onto a high shelf was a blue apron with white eyelet ruffling. She took it down and unwrapped the apron from around the gun.

"It's a derringer," Anna told her. "A twenty-two." The

flashy little gun seemed in keeping with Tom Silva. "Do you know for sure it was Tom who left it?"

"I recognize it. He won it in a stock-car race. And there was a note." Patsy had tucked the note in the pocket of the apron. She unfolded it and handed it to Anna.

"'Pats, see how easy it is to get into this place? Get yourself new locks,'" Anna read aloud. "Definitely edgy."

"I thought so."

"I'll look into it," Anna promised. "Meanwhile I'd do what he suggests: get new locks. Give Maintenance a call, okay?"

Patsy said she would. As Anna was leaving, she stopped her. "Do you want to take the gun?"

Anna thought about it for a moment, thought of Tom, of the girls. "Do you know how to use it?" she asked. Patsy nodded. "Then why don't you keep it for a while."

Anna went off duty at three-thirty. Ninety minutes before tradition allowed cocktails. She peeled off her uniform and, sitting on her bed, opened the top drawer of the dresser. Expensive lace underwear, a legacy of more intimate times, mingled with cordovan-colored uniform socks, hollow-point bullets, and half a dozen ragged handkerchiefs.

In the back, lying on its side, was a metal container. With its fitted lid and wire handle, it was much like a paint can sans label.

Jamie Burke professed singular discomfort living in a house tainted by the presence of a firearm. Anna wondered what the interpreter would think if she knew that the remains of Anna's husband rested amid her underwear.

"You were always happiest when you were in my pants, Zach." Anna smiled as she closed the drawer.

The clock on the dresser read 3:47.

The hell with tradition. Anna went into the kitchen to pour herself a drink. Glass in hand, she wandered out onto the rear deck. Four miles away, on Chapin, it was warm enough for shorts. At Far View, a thousand feet higher, Anna was slightly chilled in long pants and a sweatshirt.

The serviceberry bushes were in full bloom and the valley between Far View and Wetherill Mesa looked as if it had been decorated for a wedding. Glittering emerald-green hummingbirds with ruby-colored throats were busy at the blossoms. Mating, showing off, or just celebrating the day, they flew up thirty or forty feet then dove down in a buzz of wings.

Leaning against the wall of the dormitory, Anna let her legs rest on the sun-warmed planking and closed her eyes.

Tom Silva wasn't the only one who wasn't acting like his old self. Till she'd left Michigan for the southwest, Anna hadn't realized how big a part of her life Christina and Alison had become. The gentle, clear-thinking woman and her spirited daughter had kept her on an even keel. Kept her looking ahead instead of back.

Banging of the kitchen door announced the end of solitude. Jennifer was off shift. Anna took a long drink and held it in her mouth, savoring the rich bite of the alcohol and trying to shut out the muffled thumps from within as the seasonal law enforcement ranger noisily divested herself of briefcase and gunbelt.

Moments later the sanctity of the rear deck was invaded. Wearing a T-shirt and faded jeans, Jennifer came out to share the last of the afternoon's warmth. She folded down, crossing her legs tailor-fashion, then popped the top of a Bud Light.

"You devil, you!" She shook an admonitory finger at Anna. "You snatched old Stacy right out from under my nose."

For a brief instant Anna wondered if Stacy had stated some preference for patrolling with her. She couldn't decide whether she was more flattered or alarmed.

Jennifer laughed. "Still waters and all that. When I went to pick him up, his wife said he'd already left."

"Not with me he didn't," Anna defended herself.

As if in counterpoint to their conversation, Anna's radio, clearly audible through the open bedroom window, crackled to life.

Three times, seven hundred called Meyers' number. Finally came Frieda's voice saying: "No contact. Seven hundred clear. Sixteen-forty-five."

This was followed by three attempts to reach "Any Chapin Mesa patrol ranger" and "No contact."

"I thought Stacy was on till six," Jennifer said.

"He is." Anna waited for an uneasy feeling to pass but it didn't. "I guess I'd better make a few calls." She looked longingly at the wine in her glass, righteously considering pouring it over the deck railing. Instead, she took it all in one gulp. Something told her she might need it.

7

STACY DIDN'T turn up that night or the next or the night after that. Though Hills Dutton, in his capacity as district ranger and resident scrooge, had grumbled about paying her overtime for working on her lieu days, Anna had been on duty. She was needed to cover Meyers' shifts. And to search.

Investigation indicated that at the end of Stacy's late shift on Monday night, all the ruins' gates had been locked, and the patrol car he'd been driving was parked in the maintenance yard. Apparently, somewhere on the hundred yards of paved path between Maintenance and the housing loop, he had simply disappeared.

Tuesday Hills spoke with Mrs. Meyers. Coming home late from Albuquerque, she and her daughter had chosen to spend Monday night in Farmington where they could take in a movie and do some shopping rather than continue the two hours on to the park. Around seven—the time Stacy customarily took his meal break when he was on late shift—Rose phoned him from the motel. He had answered and they spoke for several minutes. Rose said Stacy had seemed calm and cheerful.

AT&T long distance corroborated the call.

Just after eight Monday night, while she was taking her evening walk, Al Stinson said she saw Stacy locking the Cedar Tree Tower Ruin gate. After that Stacy had been neither seen nor spoken to by anyone. At least not anyone willing to come forward.

On arriving back in the park Tuesday morning, Mrs. Meyers found the bed made and the sink free of dishes. As her husband was a man of tidy domestic habits, she couldn't say if this indicated whether or not he had slept at home.

Wednesday Anna saw Bella on her bike riding back from Maintenance. Nine-thirty A.M.: Anna guessed she'd been escorting Drew to work after his physical training.

Pulling the car to the side of the narrow lane, Anna called the girl's name. For a moment the green eyes looked at her without recognition. When a spark did dawn it was feeble and suddenly gone as if very little held the child's interest anymore.

Bella rode up to the Ford and Anna climbed from behind the wheel. Wordlessly the girl looked up. Anna could read the question as clearly as if it had been written in felt marker across the unlined brow. "No," she said gently. "We haven't found Stacy yet."

Bella didn't change expression but it was as if her soft cheeks froze. Anna ached to see so adult a reaction on a six-year-old's face.

"We're looking real hard everywhere," Anna told her.

Sadly, Bella shook her head. The curls, as carefully tended as always, glimmered in the sunlight. "Not everywhere. Not where he's at."

"No," Anna conceded. "Not there."

"I wish Aunt Hattie would come," Bella said, and propped her chin in her hands, her elbows resting on the handlebar. "She knows things."

"How to find things?" Anna asked.

"No. Just things."

"Like what?" Anna leaned against the fender of the patrol car, enjoying the warmth of the metal through her trousers.

Bella screwed up her face with the effort of thought and Anna was glad to see, for a moment at least, she was distracted from her worry over Stacy.

"Not *knowing* knowing exactly. But Hattie plays with you. Not like she's a grown-up who's playing with a little kid. Like she's *there*. Sometimes we'll be witches. We turned Timmy Johnson into a toad."

Bella looked pleased. Anna was careful not to look anything.

"Why a toad? So you could kiss him back to handsome princehood?"

"Yuck-oh!" Bella stuck out her tongue as if she were gagging on something foul. "He said mean things about me."

Anna could guess what.

"We didn't exactly turn him into a real toad," Bella said after a moment's thought. "I mean to other people he still looked like a piggy little boy. But Hattie said he'd turn his own self into a toad if he kept doing toady things so we just helped a little. I could see the toad parts though, after that. He'd say stuff and I'd squint and laugh at the greeny warts just ready to pop out on his pig face. But that was a long time ago when I was little."

Anna laughed. "Do you think the transformation's done by now? Is he all toad?"

"Maybe not," Bella said kindly. "He stopped being so toady after a while. He may have saved himself. Aunt Hattie thinks so."

Bella laid her chin on the handlebars of her bike and pushed back and forth, rocking herself absently. "Aunt Hattie's like those big colored balloons, the ones with the little baskets for the people to ride in. She just lifts you up, zoop, zoop, zoop."

Bella accompanied the words with floating gestures, small white hands like leaves blowing upward.

"We could all use some of that," Anna said.

"Maybe she'll come. Sometimes she does," Bella said hopefully. "I have to go." She stood up on the pedals of the bike and wobbled past Anna.

" 'Bye." Anna felt slightly abandoned. "I have to go too," she added childishly.

Bella pedaled faster and never looked back. Worry was back in the hunch of the little shoulders.

That evening Anna spent an hour with Rose going over Stacy's routines and the times of the phone call and her return to the park. Rose mixed vicious snipes at Hills, Ted Greeley, Drew Kinder, the superintendent, and the National Park Service with seemingly heartfelt pleas that no stone be left unturned in the search for her husband.

Bella crept about like a tortured spirit. White-faced and silent, she hid herself behind coloring books that she didn't color in, dolls that she didn't enliven with imagination. Twice the child curled up at her mother's feet the way a dog might, her knees pulled up, her chin on hands fisted like paws. The only time Anna saw her play was when Bella dressed up in Stacy's class "A" uniform jacket and winter hat. On the child's stunted frame the jacket brushed the floor.

Anna had to look away, aware for the first time how terribly costly Stacy's abdication would be. His wife had an edge; she would cut her way through life regardless. Bella truly loved.

In the end it was the interpreter Claude Beavens who found Stacy. Or, more accurately, a family of canyon wrens that had made their home high in the ancient ramparts of Cliff Palace.

Early the Thursday morning after Stacy's disappearance, Beavens was down in the ruins. He climbed into the back reaches of the dwelling in hopes of finding a vantage point from which he might see the wrens' nest. Clambering around the fragile site was forbidden to all but officially permitted archaeologists and NPS brass. But, finding himself with a quarter of an hour till visitors would be allowed down, Beavens had decided to take a few liberties.

Given the nature of his discovery, admitting his transgression seemed the lesser of two evils.

Anna was at Navajo Overlook on the Ruins Road Loop with binoculars pressed to her eyes. Jennifer Short, back to the canyon, stood at her elbow.

"It's not like every damn inch of those trails you keep lookin' at haven't been looked at before," Jennifer was saying. She leaned against the chest-high cyclone fence. Endless civil suits designed to dig money out of Uncle Sam's "deep pocket" had forced the government to mar every precipitous view with safety devices. Jennifer's flat-brimmed hat was pushed back to protect her hairdo. It gave her a Rebecca-of-Sunnybrook-Farm look that Anna found annoying.

"If y'all ask me, he just took a powder," the seasonal drawled, rehashing a theory that had been voiced by a number of people in the park as the search wore on. "Found himself a woman who hasn't let herself go, kept her figure. Can't blame him. If they ever strayed from the missionary position he'd be squashed flatter'n a bug. Uh-uhg-lee!"

"Reubens wouldn't agree with you," Anna said mildly. "I doubt Stacy would either." Again she traced the fragment of trail visible in the canyon below. Worn bare of vegetation over the centuries by feet and paws and hooves, it showed white, a ribbon in the canyon bottom. Brush and scrub grew to either side, becoming taller toward the cliffs. Finally, at the base, where walls sheered up toward the mesa and the strata of sandstone met a strata of slate, natural seep springs nourished the grander ponderosa pines.

Anna didn't expect to see the straggling—or fallen—form of Stacy Meyers. It had not escaped her notice, nor Hills', that Meyers had vanished in full defensive gear with his radio. If he wanted to be found or still had strength and voice, he would have called for help. Looking was just something to do. And Anna needed something to do.

Had anyone dared to suggest she was falling in love with Rose Meyers' husband, Anna would have denied it. When she chose to consider her loss, she could not but see the wraithlike face of Bella and know that the vague emptiness she felt was of no importance. Still, the days of seeking without finding, of work and worry and waiting, had worn her down in a way that was more than professional frustration or budding friendship.

"And that poor little thing!" Jennifer sighed gustily. "What man'd want to deal with that when it wasn't even his?"

"Bella," Anna corrected, finding "it" offensive. In saying the child's name something she had sensed from the onset became crystal clear: "Stacy wouldn't leave Bella. No way. No how."

"I don't know—" Jennifer began again.

"I do," Anna said flatly. Maybe Rose, maybe. But never Bella, never his pine nut. With that realization came another: Stacy Meyers was dead or close enough it wouldn't matter unless they found him soon.

Anna lowered her binoculars. "You drive," she said. "My back is killing me."

That was when Claude Beavens made his call.

The transmission was garbled. In the patrol car, Anna fiddled with the radio's volume as Frieda said: "Unit calling seven hundred, you are broken." Scratches and crackles came over the air a second time.

"Head toward Cliff Palace Loop," Anna told Jennifer. From within the Cliff Palace and Balcony House ruins radio transmissions were frequently too broken to understand.

Frieda repeated Anna's thought over the air: "Unit calling seven hundred, you are still unreadable. Try again from higher ground."

Silence followed. "Pick up the pace," Anna said. The patrol car smoothly picked up speed, Jennifer conning the boxy vehicle neatly around the meandering RVs and rental cars.

" 'Nother carry-out?" she asked.

"Maybe," Anna said.

"Good. I keep missin' out. Everything seems to happen on Tuesdays, when I'm off."

They were heading up the straightaway toward the intersection with Cliff Palace Road when the radio crackled to life again.

"Seven hundred, can you hear me now?" was bleated out in breathy tones.

"Loud and clear."

"This is Beavens at Cliff Palace. You better send somebody down here right away."

There was a short silence. The entire park waited for particulars. "What's the nature of the incident?" Seven hundred asked evenly.

"I—uh—I found Stacy Meyers. He's up in one of the back kivas." Another silence followed, longer than the first. Then in a sudden blurt of sound Beavens said: "I think he's dead. There were flies."

"Holy shit!" Jennifer whispered. She flipped on the lights and siren.

Anna thought to switch them off again. No sense going code three to a body recovery. Speed meant nothing to the dead, and the commotion could startle the living into having accidents. In the end she let Jennifer call the shots. Somehow the outward shrieking was in keeping with the small cries trapped in her skull.

And, she told herself, there was a slim chance Beavens was mistaken and Meyers was alive. Slim.

Hills' 4X4 was already there when Anna and Jennifer screamed into the Cliff Palace lot. The district ranger was fumbling with the lock on the tool box in the bed of the truck.

He handed Anna the green oxygen kit. "Might as well," he said, echoing her pessimism. Shouldering the trauma bag, he started down the path at a fast walk. Anna and Jennifer had to run to keep up with his long-legged stride. In an unconscious parody of Scarlet O'Hara, Short was clutching the top of her flat hat to keep it from flying off.

Tourists drew aside as they passed, curiosity enlivening their stares. Revolver hammering one thigh and the O_2 bottle the other, it crossed Anna's mind that they—or she and Jennifer at any rate—looked like idiots. With his trim bulk and square face, Hills was protected by the inviolate image of John Wayne To The Rescue. Guilt followed: guilt that she could harbor such petty thoughts en route to what was most likely the death of a fellow ranger.

Armed with cameras, visitors were already fanned out along the low wall that surrounded the overlook platform. Dimly, Anna was aware of the clicking of shutters as photographers tried to capture the ruin below.

At the foot of the long metal staircase leading from the platform, Jamie Burke had just finished unlocking the barred gate, opening Cliff Palace for the day.

"Lock it behind us," Hills said as he brushed past.

Burke pulled the gate closed so abruptly that Anna had to turn sideways to fit through. As she pressed by, she noticed Jamie's pale eyes narrow as she muttered: "Claude saw."

Still holding on to her hat, Jennifer clattered after and Anna was pushed into the stone stairway that formed the first part of the descent to the ruin.

Claude Beavens was waiting for them at the top of the ladder where the alcove began. A green NPS windbreaker was zipped up tightly under his Adam's apple. Bony wrists protruded from sleeves an inch too short. Long knobby fingers danced an uncomfortable jig on his thighs. "It's about time," he snapped, and his Adam's apple vanished momentarily behind the windbreaker's collar.

Beavens was a skinny, busy man, not well liked by Anna's housemates. He tended to officiousness and factual-sounding declarations that had little basis. Jamie had once grumbled that he seemed incapable of uttering the one true answer to many of the questions about the Anasazi: "We don't know."

"Show us what you've got." Hills could have been asking to see baseball cards or a skinned knee. In the face of his unflappable calm, hysteria was almost impossible.

Beavens settled down perceptibly. His fingers still fidgeted, but now they plucked at the fabric of his trousers instead of simply twitching.

"Yeah. Okay." He turned and began leading the way down the asphalt path in front of the ruin. At a small wooden sign bearing the number three, he leaped up onto a retaining wall that served both to reinforce the ancient structures and to keep tourists from climbing on the ruins.

"Watch where you step," he said, panic gone and officiousness returned. "These dwellings are fragile."

Hills grunted. Behind her, Anna heard Jennifer mutter: "Crimeny, we're not from Mars."

With sureness bred of familiarity, the interpreter guided them up the slope above the public pathway. Claude was quick and light on his feet. For all his size and strength, Hills had trouble keeping up with him. To their left the alcove dug deep into the side of the mesa. To the right was Cliff Canyon, filling now with early sunlight. They passed a terrace, then a crumbling wall pierced by a single high window.

Beavens turned into an alleyway formed by two buildings, roofless now but still more than a story tall. To keep her mind from their mission and because the magic of these suddenly deserted and long-empty villages never palled for her, Anna took note of this, her first venture into the closed part of Cliff Palace.

Much of the masonry was intact even after seven hundred desert winters. The stones still bore the signature of their architects in the many fine chips where harder stones had sculpted them to fit. Rubble, fallen between the walls, harbored dozens of pot sherds: pieces of white pottery, some the size of half dollars, marked with black geometric shapes.

The short alley dead-ended at another masonry wall. With a bit of scrambling, Beavens was on top of it. Catlike he walked along the stonework. Hills followed, then Anna. Last, Jennifer handed up the O_2 kit then climbed. Her boots dislodged a stone. When the sound reached Beavens' ear, he turned as if he'd been stung.

"Careful!" he hissed.

The whisper bothered Anna. People whisper in secret, in church, and around the dead.

The wall Claude led them down widened out into an abbreviated terrace. A sheer, circular wall dropped off to the right forming a kiva, one of the round subterranean rooms favored by the ancient people.

"Not this one," Beavens said, and stopped. "There." He pointed. At the end of the flat area where they stood was a low wall, a moon-shaped shadow suggesting another kiva, then a tower of stone with a high window.

Rapunzel, Rapunzel, let down your hair, Anna thought idiotically.

Ever pragmatic, Hills stepped past Beavens then over the parapet. "Let's get to it."

Anna didn't move.

Hills looked down into the kiva gaping at his feet, then turned back. His square face was devoid of expression. "Yup. This is it," he said.

8

AN INVISIBLE switch was thrown in Anna's head. She ceased being a shocked spectator and again became a ranger. Stepping over the wall, she stood next to Dutton. A miniature hail of gravel dislodged by her boots pattered into the kiva below. The skittery sound thickened the silence, fixed it hard in her ears.

At their feet stone and mortar walls curved away then became one again, forming a circle twenty-five feet in diameter. Approximately four feet down, halfway to the floor, the wall widened abruptly into a bench called a "banquette" by the archaeologists. Built up from the bench were six stone pilasters. When the kiva was still in use, the pilasters had supported a roof. Like many others, this kiva roof had long since been destroyed by fire. When Cliff Palace had been excavated the debris had been cleared away, leaving an open pit.

On the south side of the circle, at banquette level, was a recessed stagelike area that graced most of the Mesa Verde kivas. A hundred theories and ten times that many guesses had been put forth as to its use, but none had ever been validated by archaeological data.

Below the recess a rectangular opening large enough for

a small child to crawl through led back into the masonry to connect with a ventilator shaft that kept air flowing into the underground room to feed the fire and the occupants. Directly in front of the shaft was a section of wall several feet long and a couple of feet high. This deflector wall was a yard or so from a shallow depression ringed with blackened stone: the fire pit. Forming a south-to-north line with the fire ring and deflector wall was a pottery-lined opening the size of a coffee cup. Taken from the Navajo language, it was called a "sipapu" and was assumed to be symbolic of the opening through which the ancients had been said to move from the destroyed underworld to this one.

Within the kiva only two things were out of place. A flat-brimmed NPS hat had been placed carefully in the center of the deflector wall and, curled into the fetal position, face tucked against his knees, Stacy Meyers lay on his side within the tight circle of stones around the fire pit. His right arm was stretched over his head, partially concealing his face. His fingers were spread. It looked as if he was reaching for—or attempting to ward off—something that had come out of the sipapu.

Protected by the deep alcove, the kiva was perennially in shadow. Even in December the sun did not sink low enough to touch the back wall of Cliff Palace. The temperature remained relatively constant throughout the year. Consequently the deterioration of Stacy's body had progressed in a stately fashion, leaving out none of the classic steps of decomposition.

From where Anna stood, ten feet above and fifteen feet away from the remains, she could smell the sickly sweet odor of decay. Flesh had made the inexorable change from living tissue to inert matter. From the cuff of Stacy's summer uniform shirt to the tips of his patrician fingers, the skin was deathly pale and dimpled. Blood, stopped from flowing when the muscle of the heart could no longer function, had settled to its lowest point. A shadow of postmortem lividity showed on the underside of the arm where it stretched toward the sipapu.

Curled on his side, only Stacy's left eye was visible. It was open, the brown iris partly obscured by the upper eyelid, as if Meyers' last glance had been in the direction of the fabled underworld.

A black fly dug at the tear duct, searching for any trace of moisture. Flies clustered around the nares of the nose. In death Stacy's mouth had fallen open, or was frozen in a final cry. His beard and mustache camouflaged the flies and maggots around his lips but the tiny all-encompassing movement was more repellent than obvious incursions.

Two days. Stacy had been missing since Tuesday morning. Two and a half, if he had died on Monday night. By now his every orifice would be infested with flies and, therefore, maggots.

The bitter sting of bile backed up in Anna's throat and her vision tunneled. She had been expecting a corpse—expecting Stacy Meyers' corpse. She had steeled herself for it. But in her desert-trained mind, she had seen a desert corpse. A person dead seventy-two hours under the relentless sun of the Trans Pecos. A body jerked like prime beef, baked red then brown, then black; peeling, seared, dehumanized. Purified by the arid desert winds. The bulk of the human body that was water purloined by the sun. Moisture, blood, the stuff of life, sucked away, a mummy created. A thing so elemental soul and memory had no handhold where grief could cling.

This was immediate demanding death. Death not yet

turned back to the earth. This corpse would be hard to make peace with. There was no indication the soul had found its way free.

And it was the death of a friend.

Shaking her head clear of ghosts, Anna schooled her mind. "Want me to call for the Polaroid?" she asked Hills. Her voice had a quaver she didn't like.

"Somebody better." The district ranger turned and stared out across the sun-drenched canyon. A wren called its characteristic dying fall of song. "Yeah. The Polaroid, chalk—ah, Jesus!" he interrupted himself. "If we chalk the outline of the body on the floor of this kiva we'll have every archaeologist in the southwest jumping down our throats. Hell. Where was I?"

Glad to rest her eyes on the living, Anna glanced up at him. Something had kept her from following his example and turning her back on Stacy. A perverse puritanical lust to punish herself? A desire to bid Meyers good-bye? She made a mental note to ask her sister. "You were at chalk," she answered Dutton's question.

Hills ran his tongue along his upper teeth as if clearing them of spinach particles. "Yeah. Hell. Get chalk, a body bag. Bring down an accident kit from one of the vehicles—it's got chalk, tape. You got that, Jennifer?"

As was his habit, Hills had been talking in a low monotone. Its usual effect was to dissipate panic and reduce trauma. This time he seemed to have outdone himself. Both Jennifer and the interpreter looked as if they had fallen into a trance.

Hills snapped his fingers. "Jennifer, got that?"

Short came awake with a comic, "Huh?"

"Here, let me." Anna pulled a notebook from her hip pocket and hastily scribbled down a list of the items Hills had asked for. Adding a couple of requests of her own, she spoke aloud to clear them with Dutton. "Get helitack over here for a carry-out. Tell Jamie to keep the ruin closed till we're out of here, and get the ambulance up top."

"Ambulance? Then he's not—" Jennifer began. She'd kept close to Beavens, the crumbling wall blocking her view down into the kiva.

"He is," Hills said shortly.

"It's the ambulance or we toss him in the back of the four-by-four," Anna said.

"Logistics," Jennifer said firmly, as if that one word explained away the messy business of transporting the dead. In a way it did.

Anna stepped over the wall and handed Jennifer the list.

"What do you want me to do?" Claude Beavens sounded alarmingly eager, and there was an avidity in his face that made Anna uncomfortable.

"Uh . . ." Hills looked to Anna but she gave him no help. Making the hard decisions was what he was paid the big bucks for. "You go with Jennifer, I guess. You can fill out a witness statement. Frieda'll explain."

Beavens shrugged—a definite pearls-before-swine shrug—then hurried past Jennifer so that he would be the one leading the way out.

"Watch your big feet," Anna heard him say as he dropped down the wall into the blind alleyway.

"Yew watch yer big mouth," Jennifer snapped back.

Hills laughed, a high-pitched giggle. Hysteria would have been Anna's guess had she not known the big block of a man always laughed that way.

"Guy gives me the heebie-jeebies." Dutton shuddered. On so large an individual the gesture seemed out of place.

"Kind of like a Jim Jones wannabe?" Anna asked.

"I guess." Hills had turned his attention back to the kiva and its contents. "Shee-it." His East Texas heritage showed briefly. "Everybody ever died on me was fresh. Did CPR all the way to the hospital and let 'em die for sure there. What the hell do we do now?"

Anna didn't know. Three times in her career there'd been bodies to deal with, but the crime scenes had been so unstable, they'd needed to be moved. "Secure the scene, collect evidence, maintain the chain of evidence," she said, parroting a list from her federal law enforcement training.

"Right," Hills said. "We'll stay out of the kiva and call the feds. Stay here," he ordered. "I got to make some calls."

He scrambled down the wall into the alley and headed for a place open enough he could radio Dispatch. Anna felt abandoned. "Shee-it," she echoed.

For a moment she just stared out through the junipers, watching a scrub jay scolding an invisible companion. Scenes from old movies and books came to mind: wives, mothers, grandmothers, dressed in widows' weeds, sitting in darkened rooms knitting or crying with no company but one another and death personified in the body of the man they'd bathed and dressed and powdered, lying in state on the bier. Unbidden a picture from Dickens' *Great Expectations* took over: the moldering wedding feast, mice and maggots the only partakers.

"Not your bridegroom," Anna said aloud, narrowed her mind to the task at hand, and turned to face the deceased.

There were a few tracks and scuffs on the stones around the kiva: hers, Hills', probably Claude Beavens' or the stabilization crew's. The surface was too hard to make any inferences. No buttons, threads, dropped wallets, white powder, semen, or anything readily identifiable as a bona-fide *clue* was in evidence.

Keeping to the stones topping the kiva wall, she walked around till she stood over the ventilator hole, looking down into the southern recess, then to the deflector wall, then the fire ring with its cold tinder.

No obvious signs of violence were apparent, at least not on the side of the body that was exposed. The soft layers of dust that had accumulated on the floor of the kiva were freshly raked.

It was customary for interpreters to rake out human tracks made in closed areas. Both so the footprints wouldn't entice others to trespass and to retain an illusion of freshness, of the first time, for those who would come next.

One line of footprints crossed the raked dirt. It led from below the banquette on the west side of the kiva to the fire pit.

Stacy reached away from her with one long bony arm that was looking more spectral every moment she was left alone with it. With him, she corrected herself. The flesh was pale, life's blood pooled on the underside of his arm. Near his sleeve, on the upper side, was an old bruise, a reminder that once this flesh could feel.

"Wait," Anna whispered. Stacy's shoes were off, lying untied very near where his feet were tucked up by his hip pockets as if he'd kicked them off to get more comfortable. Something about the stockinged feet was so vulnerable, so human, Anna felt an unaccustomed pricking behind her eyes.

She forced herself to continue the study. Except for the shoes and the hat on the deflector wall, Stacy was immaculately dressed. If, as Bella said, Rose dressed him, she would find nothing to be ashamed of. His shirt was crisply ironed, his trousers neatly creased, his duty belt firmly buckled on with gun and speedloader visible.

Anna continued her circuit, viewing the scene from every angle. Nothing more of interest turned up. She was relieved when Hills finally hauled himself out of the alleyway and crossed to join her.

"Frieda got the federal marshal out of Durango on the line. They'll send somebody up. This won't keep." He waved a hand toward what had once been a man. "We got to get what we can, bag it, and take it down to the morgue. I've got Drew's boys coming."

Hills crossed his arms and stared down into the kiva. "What'd he do? Just walk in, curl up in the fireplace, make hisself comfy, and die?"

"Looks that way."

"Jesus." The district ranger blew a sigh out through loose lips. "This is a hell of a note. Solstice. Some of the seasonal interps are going to make hay with this."

Remembering the strange spark in Jamie's eyes as they passed her by the gate, Anna didn't doubt it one bit.

9

THE GLASS had started getting in the way so she'd left it behind and drank straight from the bottle. Never had the Rambler driven so smoothly. Green eyes of a deer or a coyote flickered in Anna's peripheral vision as the headlights picked them out of the night. A vague and uninteresting idea that she was driving too fast crossed her mind. The proof of it, the squealing of tires as she made the ninety-degree turn into the Resource Management area, made her laugh out loud.

When she'd recovered control of the car, she felt between her legs. The wine bottle was still upright, its contents unspilled.

"All present and accounted for, officer," she said. "No casualties." The Rambler rolled to a stop in front of the square stone building. "Car in gear, brake set," Anna said. Then: "Whoops. Key *off*. Too late!" As she took her foot off the clutch, the car hopped and the engine died.

For a time she leaned back against the seat, glad to be still. "Nights in White Satin" played on the oldies station out of Durango. Through the open window the air blew cool, smelling of juniper and dust. Overhead, without the pollution of the glaring intruder lights that had become epidemic even in remote areas during the last decade, the stars were fixed in an utterly black sky. Small night sounds kept the dark from being lonely. Anna could hear scufflings of some nocturnal creature digging in the pine needles, the sigh of a breeze approaching through the forest's crown, clicking and snapping as tiny twigs or bones were broken.

Only humans, cursed with the knowledge of their own mortality and that of those whom they loved, were truly alone; each trapped in an ivory tower of skull and bone peeking out through the windows of the soul.

The body recovery, as sanitized language would phrase it, had gone on till afternoon. The packaging of the meat that had once called itself Stacy Meyers had taken only a few minutes, but the attendant crime-scene recording and preservation had worn on so long even Hills' deep-seated nerve endings had become frayed.

Hills had even less experience than Anna with foul play in the form of park corpses, and his plodding methodicalness took a definite turn toward the anal retentive. Pictures were taken and retaken from every angle.

"Don't know when somebody's going to pop up out of the woodwork saying how you should've done it," he explained. "So by God we're going to do it all. Hell of a note. Where are the feds when you need 'em? We forget something and our tit's in the wringer."

This and more of the same was muttered in an ongoing monotone as he directed the investigation. After the photographs, stones around the kiva were examined, swept, and the leavings collected in a plastic bag that Anna dutifully marked KIVA DUST with the date and her initials.

"Maintain the chain of evidence," Hills said.

"It's dirt," Anna returned.

"You never know . . ."

The kiva floor was photographed, re-raked, all items bagged and marked. Then, finally, Stacy was photographed and zipped into the body bag. His hat and shoes wouldn't fit in the narrow plastic shroud. Anna threw them in the trunk of her car to return to Rose.

The entire "dog and pony show," as Hills termed it, had taken several hours. During most of it Stacy lay curled absurdly in the fire pit, reaching toward something the living couldn't see, his beard growing ever blacker with flies.

It was odd how the human mind switched off an unpleasant reality. Moose slept seconds at a time, their brains clicking on and off like binary computers, allowing them to rest yet never be long out of a dangerous world in need of watching. Anna, Jimmy, Drew, Paul, Jennifer, they'd all clicked in and out of the reality of death in the kiva. Jokes were told, people laughed, measurements were taken, even mild flirting between Jennifer and Paul.

Interspersed with this flow of life were chalky looks, strained silences, and equally strained conversations as someone saw again Stacy's face, remembered his wife, his child, recalled him as he had been in life, and woke to the realization that this fly-blown corpse was all that remained.

The schizophrenia wore Anna down. She had already needed a drink in the worst way when Hills dragged her to Meyers' house to give condolences to the widow.

Blessedly he had foisted off the chore of informing Rose onto Frieda. Their visit was mere formality—courtesy, the East Texan said. "Leave any questions to the feds."

"The feds" Hills relied on so heavily was a federal investigator the superintendent had called in. Mesa Verde was under exclusive jurisdiction, which placed it off local law enforcement's turf.

The Meyerses' house was shut up. Windows closed, blinds drawn like a Victorian house of mourning.

Hills knocked tentatively then stepped back, leaving Anna marooned on the welcome mat as Rose opened the door. She was neatly dressed in dark blue polyester pants and a white blouse with a Peter Pan collar. Her short dark hair was combed and she wore pearl earrings, but her face was in disarray; dry eyes rimmed with red, her cheeks drawn and pale.

Anna looked to Hills but he was studying a crack in the sidewalk. "We just stopped by to tell you how terribly sorry we are, Mrs. Meyers," Anna managed. "Your husband's body is being taken to Durango."

Rose waited. When Anna could find no more words, Rose closed the door. In the curtailed view of the living room there'd been no sign of Bella. For that Anna was grateful. The child would have been hard to face. She turned to Hills.

He shrugged. "That about does it," he said, and: "You're off the clock."

"Overtime. You're a real sensitive guy," Anna groused as they walked back to the patrol car.

"Gotta be thinking of something," he said philosophically.

Anna raised the bottle from between her thighs and peered at it, measuring the level against the dull glow of the dashboard lights. One third left. Of how many bottles? she wondered. Surely this was only the second. Maybe the third.

She took a mouthful and speculated on any possible

New Age numerological significance that one third of the third might have. "Got to ask Jamie," she said. "Warthog." This last descriptive was triggered at the memory of her housemate.

Jamie had been hovering at the dormitory door when Hills dropped Anna off. Burke was decked out in the sarong, her hair, free of its braid, fanned into a crimped black curtain that fell past her butt. Kohl—or some modern equivalent—ringed her eyes and she wore a single gold earring beaten into the stylized shape of a lizard. Her face was somber but excitement radiated from her in tangible waves.

"Like a bitch in heat," Anna told the wine bottle.

"We've got to talk," Jamie had said grimly.

"Not now." Anna had tried to squeeze by but Jamie'd laid hold of her briefcase.

"Now."

Anna dropped her hat and gunbelt on the nearest chair. "So talk."

Jamie ignored her rudeness, or was too caught up in her own drama to notice it. With a sigh, she spread herself on the sofa. "Stacy and I were very close. Very."

Anna doubted that, but the declaration in no way surprised her. The dead had more friends than the living. Especially those meeting an untimely end. It was as if knowing a murder victim invested one with some sort of celebrity. Jamie had wanted something to happen on solstice. Murder must've been beyond her wildest dreams.

Murder: Anna hadn't said it to herself so bluntly. Suicide, accident, incident, those were the words Hills had resolutely stuck with all day. In thinking it, Anna believed it to be true. Stacy was too much a conservationist to defile the ruins with his twentieth-century corpse.

"We all know dead people, Jamie," Anna said unkindly. Then: "Sorry. I'm beat." She picked up her duty belt and turned to go. Again the interpreter stopped her.

"Claude saw," she repeated her cryptic phrase of the morning, playing it like a trump card in her bid for attention.

Anna was almost too tired to ante up but she managed a mild show of interest. "Saw what?"

"The night Stacy was taken. He saw it."

The spark of interest flickered and died. Anna was too tired to play. "Get him to write 'it' up on his witness report." She dragged herself to the questionable sanctuary of her room.

The evening continued to unravel from there. Through the thin walls of the Far View dorm, Jamie could be heard holding court. Once—or maybe twice—Anna slunk from her lair to return with reinforcements in the form of alcohol. Finally, needing air, but unable to again run the gauntlet of avid faces greedy for details, she opened her window, popped off the screen, and climbed out, taking the last undead soldier with her.

She poured wine into her mouth and a bit on her chin. "Quick," she said as she closed her eyes and rested her head on the Rambler's seat. "Red or white?" Could've been either. "Some palate." She pushed open the car door. For a moment it was impossible to make any headway. Then she remembered to undo her seatbelt and tumbled out.

Molly picked up on the seventh ring. "What? What is it?" she demanded.

"It's just me." Anna was mildly offended.

"Where are you? What's going on? Talk to me." Molly rattled out the words.

"Can't," Anna replied. "Can't get a word in edgewise. Just called to chat."

There was a long silence devoid, for once, of the poisonous note of tobacco smoke sliding into dying lungs. Then Molly spoke very deliberately. "I don't know what time zone you're in, but here in the civilized world it's three twenty-seven in the morning. If you're okay, you'd better lie to me. Tell me something dire enough to warrant this rude awakening."

Three twenty-seven. Anna pushed the tiny silver button on her watch and squinted at the lighted dial. It was hopeless. The numbers were small and furry. "That can't be right," she said.

"Trust me on this one." A sigh: the cigarette. "Begin at the beginning, Anna. Before your first drink."

Anna started to cry, great whooping sobs that hurt her throat. Tears poured down her face, dripped from her jaw. "Zach's dead," she barked when she was able. Her sister said nothing, choosing not to try and override the storm of grief.

When finally she quieted, Molly said, "That's right, Zach's dead. Been dead a long time. Kids born the day he died are old enough to rob liquor stores. What's going on, Anna?"

"Zach?" Anna was confused.

"You said Zach was dead."

Anna digested that for a moment, taking a little wine and letting it burn under her tongue. "No I didn't," she said at last. "Stacy's dead. Stacy Meyers."

"Who is Stacy Meyers?"

"Goddamn it, listen to me!" Anna screamed.

"You're drunk, Anna," her sister said reasonably. "I love you—Lord knows why—and I want to help you. But you're beyond me. I'll call you tomorrow."

The line went dead. Anna laid her head on the desk and wept.

10

CONSCIOUSNESS DAWNED like a foggy day. Anna opened her eyes. She was facedown on a rough brown surface, her cheek wet from drool, and she was terribly cold. Thin gray light filtered from somewhere. Through the static in her head she could hear the fussy chatter of scrub jays.

Without moving, as though to do so might prove dangerous, she took stock of the situation. She was lying on the front seat of the Rambler, her clothes rumpled and damp. Pins and needles prickled through her right arm and leg where they were pinned under her. Graying hair, clumped and sticky-looking on the vinyl, fell around her face.

Slowly she raised her head. Her first instinct had been right: to move was dangerous. Even her eyeballs ached. Her mouth was so dry her tongue rattled between her teeth like the clapper in a bell.

She pushed herself to a sitting position. The sun was not yet up. The Rambler was still parked in front of the Resource Management Office. The car and her hair reeked of stale wine. Anna checked her wristwatch: five thirty-five.

She shoved her stinking locks back with both hands. "What the fuck happened to me?"

The keys were in the ignition. She slid over behind the wheel and tried the starter. There wasn't even a whimper of life. When she'd stumbled out the night before, she had left the ignition on as well as the radio and the lights. "Lucky for me and God knows who else." Her head dropped back against the seat and she grunted with the ache of it.

The last thing she remembered was dialing Molly's number in New York. She wondered what she had said.

Tires humming on the pavement brought her back into the present. Soon the park would begin to stir, archaeologists on their way to the lab, the tree kids toting chain saws into the woods to remove hazardous fuels, helitack jogging by on physical training, maintenance men, trail crew, tourists.

Panic tore the fog of alcohol clouding her mind. This was no way to greet the public. Balancing her head carefully on her shoulders, she retraced her steps to the Resource Management Office. The door was unlocked and open. Inside, on one of the desks, was a bottle with half an inch of red wine in the bottom. Mercifully it was upright and the resource management specialist's nest of papers unbesmirched by her night's debauchery. The bookcase had not fared so well. It was overturned and the books hurled around the room. Memory, like a snapshot, flashed in Anna's mind: her hands pulling the shelves toward her, books and periodicals cascading down over her feet.

Why she had done it, what she'd been looking for or trying to prove, remained a mystery.

She dropped to her knees, righted the bookcase, then crawled after its contents and restored them in what she hoped was relative order. Having finger-combed her matted hair and braided it off her face, she tied it with a piece of pink plastic surveyor's tape she'd found in the office.

Putting on the best face—and the best lie on it—she could, she walked the mile through the woods to the heli-tack dorm. Paul Summers drove her back in the fire truck and jump-started the Rambler.

Driving back to Far View, Anna felt weak-kneed and queasy. A strong sense of God not being in Her heaven and all's wrong with the world pervaded every cell of her body. Not only the hangover shook her, but the hours in blackout. A chunk of time she'd been active, talking, walking, evidently hurling research manuals, was utterly alien to her. A black hole she'd fallen into and, but for a dead battery, might never have crawled out of.

A hot shower steamed the booze from her pores and rinsed it from her hair but not even hot coffee could burn the fumes from her brain. As she pulled on her uniform, she hoped no great feats of kindness, courage, or intellect would be required of her for a few days. She longed to call Molly, but embarrassment combined with the need to sort things out on her own stayed her hand.

Purposely avoiding the Museum Loop, the chief rang-er's office, and most of the visitors, Anna patrolled the tra-ditionally uneventful four and a half miles from Far View Lodge to Park Point, the highest place in the park at 8,571 feet. The twisting road to the mesa cut through the flanks of mountains in two places, Bravo Cut and Delta Cut. Rocks falling from the unstable hillsides littered the road-way and were a constant headache. After rains the rocks were numerous and sizable enough to present a hazard to motorists. Delta Cut, the higher of the two, presented a slashed hillside to the town of Cortez far below. Held in by a metal railing, the road ran along a ragged drop edged with thickets of oakbrush. Today Anna found nothing but pebbles, none even as big as a woman's fist. Still she parked the car and meticulously began kicking each little rock off the asphalt.

It felt good to be quiet and alone and in the sunlight.

Bit by bit her mind cleared and she thought of Stacy Meyers. Not of Stacy Meyers the man, with his intellectual charm and heartfelt commitment to the land—that would have led her back to those lost hours in the Resource Management building. Anna thought of the "Meyers Incident," reducing it to a puzzle, a mystery that, unlike mysteries of the heart, might prove solvable.

On the grounds of woman's intuition she'd been quick to discount suicide but it was a real possibility and one that would have to be explored. Stephanie McFarland came to mind and Anna remembered Stacy's anguish at panicking. Could he have decided he no longer deserved to live? To a sane mind, it seemed excessive, but Anna knew from experience depression could breathe an insane logic into the most bizarre courses of action.

Anna knew very little of Stacy's inner life, or, as Molly would say, his real life. It was clear that he had financial problems. Short of a generous trust fund, any temporary GS-5 with grown-up responsibilities would have money problems. Stacy's were exacerbated by Bella's needs and Rose's wants.

Would he fake his own murder to provide for them? Anna took out the yellow notebook she carried in her hip pocket and wrote "Life Insurance?" on the first clean page. She had worked a couple of suicide investigations in the past and dreaded them. In many ways they were more destructive to those left living than homicide. Always, with unnatural death, came anger. Homicides had a healthy target, a suitable bad guy, a foe worthy of hatred. Suicide carried the same furious baggage but it fed on the bearer. As widowhood was said to be easier than divorce, so murder was easier than suicide. At least no one chose to leave.

The other possibilities were accident, natural causes, murder, and, if Jamie had her way, vengeful intervention of spirits. Hills was overwhelmingly in favor of the first idea but even he, faced with the neatly placed hat and doffed shoes, had to admit that: "If it was an accident it sure was a lulu."

Anna harbored a secret preference for the Revenge of the Anasazi. Paranormal foul play would be a nice diversion from man's daily inhumanity to man.

Foul Play: Anna smiled at the phrase and flicked a stone off the roadway with the side of her foot. It sounded so English, so Old School, implying subtle distaste for something not quite cricket, not entirely sporting. Homicide had an American feel, a businesslike violence-as-usual ring to it. Anna preferred Foul Play. She said it once aloud. In the gentle silence of a summer's day spoken words grated and she didn't try it again.

The sun was warm on her back, and a breeze, blowing across from the snow-covered peaks of the Abajos a hundred miles away in Utah, smelled gloriously of nothing. Up high there was only air in the air and Anna took a moment to fill her lungs to capacity.

If one must think of murder, this was the kind of day to do it: a pure day, one without guile.

Murder, then; the motives were usually predictable. Somebody got mad, got greedy, or got even. The pathologically neat arrangement of the scene seemed to rule out a crime of passion. Those killed in sudden heat were customarily found sprawled and bloody in bedrooms, barrooms, on kitchen floors, and in parking lots.

Getting even seemed a possibility. By leaving the corpse in such an odd place perhaps the avenger had hoped to pay back not only the dead but, in some way, the living—the widow, a friend, or even the National Park Service. Again Anna pulled out the notebook. "Enemies?" went under "Life Insurance."

Greed was Anna's favorite. Greed seemed to motivate a goodly number of human behaviors, murder among them. But, if greed were the motivating factor, the grandstand play of laying the corpse in the fire ring of a kiva struck her as out of place.

Why wouldn't the body be buried, hidden, disposed of somehow? Only the very naive would think Stacy's remains would go undiscovered in Cliff Palace. Even if the archaeologists or the stabilization crew didn't stumble across it, eventually the odor or the vultures would have given the location away.

Stacy was meant to be found. To prove something? To frighten someone? To stop the search before too many noses were poked into too many places? Beneath "Enemies" Anna scribbled "Where Else Should We Have Looked?" and "Greed/Rose" with an arrow drawn back up to "Life Insurance."

She'd run out of stones. The stretch of road through the cut was clean. Disappointed to have completed so pleasantly mindless a task, she began to walk back along the highway to where she'd left her patrol car.

A gold Honda Accord was stopped fifty yards or so from her vehicle. The hood was up in the international symbol for motorist in distress. Anna perked up, walked a little faster. Citizen assists were good clean ranger work, the equivalent of firemen rescuing kittens from trees.

A generous behind covered in rich plum fabric was

swaying rhythmically to the left of the front fender. Anna approached the far side of the vehicle and looked under the hood. An exceedingly round woman with a froth of chestnut curls shot with gray and held off her face by a yellow plastic banana was chanting "drat, drat, drat" and shaking small dimpled fists at an unresponsive engine. Her face was as round as the rest of her and showed no signs of age. Earrings of green-and-yellow parrots dangled to her shoulders, the birds looking at home against the print of a Hawaiian shirt.

"Trouble?" Anna said by way of greeting.

The woman looked up, bright blue eyes sharp-focused behind glasses nearly half an inch thick. "Oh, hello. Do you know anything about these horrid things?"

Her voice was high and had a singsong quality about it that was exquisitely comforting. Anna, who usually disliked voices in the upper registers, placed it instantly. In her mind she heard Billie Burke in *The Wizard of Oz* asking Dorothy, "Are you a good witch or a bad witch?" The resemblance didn't end there. This woman was big, two hundred pounds or so, but seemingly as light and translucent as the bubble in which the Good Witch of the North traveled.

She shook her fists again and Anna half expected her to float with the effort.

"I only know about six things to poke," Anna apologized. "If that doesn't work, I call a tow truck."

"Ooooh." The woman sounded wickedly delighted. "Let's poke."

Anna laughed and took a hard look at her companion. The familiarity wasn't born just of fairy tales. "You're Aunt Hattie!" she declared. Bella hadn't described her aunt in physical terms but she had painted such a clear picture of her spirit, Anna was certain. Hattie bore a slight resemblance to her sister, Rose, but her features were more refined and looked to have been sculpted by laughter where Rose's were etched by discontent. Rose carried less weight, but she seemed cursed by gravity. The pounds dragged her down. Hattie was buoyant, uplifting.

While Bella's aunt tried the starter, Anna pushed butterfly valves and rattled air filters. Finally, noting a depressing lack of fuel squirting into the carburetor, she gave it up as a lost cause and radioed Dispatch to call a tow truck from Cortez.

The Honda disposed of, Anna gave Hattie a lift to the mesa top. Hattie appeared completely at her ease, simply sitting, riding, watching the scenery. Hattie had seemed at ease shaking her fists over a dead engine and Anna was surprised to find herself at an unaccustomed comfort level as well.

"You came because of Stacy?" Anna asked.

"For Bella."

"Rose call you?"

"Bella," Hattie said again, and laughed. "This is a bit of a surprise visit, I'm afraid. But I don't think Rose'll mind. She'll have so much on her mind. And I do think she will have a hard time of it without Stacy. He was a good man and Rose isn't used to that."

"Her first husband?" Anna prodded.

"A pig face. Rose was besotted." Hattie shrugged soft graceful shoulders. "Where's the fun? I liked Stacy. And Bella liked Stacy."

This last was clearly the most heavily weighted factor in the equation and Anna let it sit without comment for a while. Remembering the conversation she'd had with Bella about her aunt and how she "lifts you up, zoop, zoop, zoop," Anna said: "Bella will be glad you've come."

"Bella's a magical spirit," Hattie said. "Till I got to

know her I'd pretty much forgotten how the world looks when you're new."

Not new anymore. After a murder the newness got lost. Even at six—perhaps especially at six. This would rob Bella's world of a lot of magic.

Hattie scrunched down in the passenger seat and leaned her head back. The breeze through the open window ruffled her hair, teasing it into a froth around the banana clip. The parrots danced gaily. Life cloaked Bella's aunt so vibrantly; coupled with the scent of pine and the warmth of the sun, made it infinitely precious. Anna could remember a time, the years after Zach died, when it was a tremendous burden. One she might have shucked if it hadn't been for Molly and a good healthy dose of cowardice.

"Do you think Stacy could have committed suicide?" she asked impulsively.

Hattie straightened up, the languor gone, the blue eyes sharp. "Rose said he was killed."

Anna sensed a question behind the statement and waited, hoping the silence would draw it out. On the radio a country-western artist began singing "When I say no I mean maybe." Anna switched it off.

Conning the car around the last in a series of hairpin curves, she started up the last climb to the mesa top where Far View Lodge looked down over the southwest. An oversized RV plodded ahead at twenty-six miles an hour. Anna was glad of the delay. Once the buildings came in sight, tour-guide questions would distract them both.

"That would be the worst possible thing for Bella," Hattie said at last. "The worst kind of abandonment. The most awful rejection. God, I hope not."

"But maybe . . . ?"

"Bella, in a little kid's way, thinks maybe. She never said

so much but Rose and Stacy had a shouting match on the phone the night he disappeared. Bella thinks about that. Rose wouldn't've bothered to hide it from her. Rose is a tad self-centered. She believes anything she says or thinks is worthy of publication. God forbid one of her emotions should go unvented."

The acid touch cut through what Anna had perceived as an almost too-sweet soul and she delighted in it. A few snakes and snails made the sugar and spice more interesting.

"What was the fight about? Did Bella say?"

"She thinks it was about her. A six-year-old's view of the world is limited. My guess is it was about money. Rose always argued about money—even when she had it."

Rose hadn't mentioned a fight. That didn't surprise Anna. Couples were often embarrassed they quarreled, never quite believing it was as common as dandruff in most marriages. If the fight had been over money, Rose might have had more than one reason for not mentioning it. Insurance companies didn't pay off on suicides.

They crested the hill and the mesa spread south; a green tabletop. The RV turned on its blinker and lumbered off the road into the Visitors' Center parking lot. Talk turned to other things.

By the time they reached the housing loop it was midday and the place was deserted. Anna let the patrol car roll to a stop under the tree in the Meyerses' yard, then got out to retrieve Hattie's luggage from the trunk.

The screen door banged open and Rose cried, "Hattie!"

As the women embraced in the middle of the walk, Anna dragged the heavy bags from the back of the car. On Hattie's side the hug appeared to be heartfelt, but Rose was kissing air. "What a surprise," she said. And: "I hope you packed a lunch. Stacy left us with nothing to live on. Nothing."

Anna slammed the trunk a bit harder than necessary.

"Are those yours?" Rose eyed the size of the suitcases.

"All mine," Hattie said cheerfully.

"You can put them in the front room," Rose directed Anna.

As her younger sister turned to reenter the house, Hattie put her fists on her ample hips and cocked one eyebrow at Anna in a perfect parody of a disapproving schoolmarm. Anna laughed and hefted the bags. Bella had been right. Zoop, zoop, zoop.

As she dumped the luggage and turned to go, Rose issued a last directive.

"Bella took her sandwich over to eat with that Drew. Tell her her aunt's paying us a visit."

Anna resisted the urge to pull a forelock and back humbly out the door.

Irritation short-circuited her brain till she'd driven out of the housing loop. As she was turning right at the stop sign to backtrack around the island of piñons separating the houses from the maintenance yard, the short exchange between the sisters sprang back into her thoughts with sudden clarity.

"Stacy left us with nothing to live on. Nothing."

No insurance; no insurance, no suicide-dressed-as-murder. At least not for monetary reasons. That was one item Anna could cross off her list.

Bella was just leaving the fire cache. She walked her bike, laboriously pushing it ahead of her as if the machine were as heavy as her heart.

Anna pulled up beside her, letting the Ford creep along at idle, keeping pace with the child. "I've got some good news for you," she said.

Bella didn't even look up. There was no more good news to be had in the world.

"Your aunt Hattie's here," Anna said quickly.

"Aunt Hattie?" Something, maybe two parts relief and three parts joy, enlivened Bella's face. "That's okay then." She pulled herself astride the bike and began pedaling.

"Wait," Anna called as she cruised up beside the girl again. "What did your mama and Stacy fight about on the telephone?"

Bella stopped, shot Anna a cold look.

Anna couldn't back down. "It might be important," she said.

Whatever Bella weighed in her mind evidently came out in Anna's favor. "Some man," she said, and rode down the path into the trees.

Suicide was back. Because Rose, like the infamous ex, had "too many people she just had to meet"? Or murder by the jealous boyfriend? Both solutions were too mundane and melodramatic for Anna's taste. But if people died only for good reasons, a lot of mortuaries would go begging.

11

ANNA HAD barricaded herself in her room. Etta James singing "Stop the Wedding" on the boom box served to block the tinny sounds of "Wheel of Fortune" coming from the other room. Anna wasn't in the mood for Jamie, even if she was abusing Vanna White. A glass of chardonnay waited on the dresser by the bed. Anna sat cross-legged in the middle of a Mexican blanket bought when she'd worked in Texas. The phone was in her lap.

As the wine worked its way down into the muscles of her neck, she let her head rest against the wall. Tonight she would go easy. There must be no more black holes.

Molly answered on the third ring. "Yes?" she said peremptorily.

For an instant Anna felt like slamming down the receiver, hiding in silence. The prospect was too lonely. "It's just me," she said, sounding unnecessarily cheerful.

"How are you feeling?" Molly asked, and Anna knew she would not be allowed to pretend last night had never happened.

"Better than I was," she admitted.

"A little hair of the dog?"

"No," Anna lied. "Anyway, that's not what I called to talk about."

"Better me now than the entire staff at Hazelden in a couple of years. You've got a problem, Anna."

Anna took a long sip of the chardonnay in a lame gesture of rebellion. "No. I've got a solution."

There was a sucking silence, then Molly mumbling: "Ten, fifteen, twenty, twenty-five . . ."

"What're you doing?"

"Trying to count up how many times in my umpteen years' practice I've heard that one. It's no go, Anna. Normal people—at least people over the age of seventeen—don't drink until they black out."

"I didn't black out." Second lie in as many minutes. Anna was beginning to worry herself.

"What did we talk about the third time you called me?" Molly demanded.

"Oh shit." Anna vaguely remembered the one call. "Okay. I blacked out."

"Hah."

"'Hah'? Is that substance-abuse parlance? One blackout does not an alcoholic make."

"What's the magic number? Three? Ten?"

Anna chose not to answer.

"Okay, talk about Stacy Meyers."

"Maybe I don't want to." Anna felt peevish.

"That's not the idea I got during call number three at four-ten A.M. this morning."

Anna sighed, fortified herself with another draught of wine. "How many times did I call?"

"I don't have the foggiest. After number three I unplugged my phone."

Depression settled like coal dust across Anna's mind. "Tough love? Or are you just in a very bad mood?"

"I want you to take this seriously, not to weasel, charm, or rationalize your way out of it."

"It won't happen again," Anna snapped.

"It happened."

"A friend of mine was murdered."

"Stacy Meyers."

The conversation had come full circle. Anna told Molly about Stacy, his wit and intense brown eyes, his undeserving wife and high ideals.

When she had finished, Molly said: "You kept calling him Zach last night."

"Caught the girl in the Freudian slip?" Anna teased.

"Freud was a deeply troubled man," Molly returned.

"In vino veritas, then?"

"Hardly. Maybe in mucho vino mega confusion. You had the two men mixed up in your mind last night. There was a physical resemblance?"

"Slight."

"A similar intensity?"

Anna said nothing.

"Confusion, Anna. That's what I heard. Lots of it. Psychological wounds are like soft-tissue injuries. You get hurt in the same place twice and they may never heal. You need clarity right now, not oblivion. The time for that, if there ever was one, is long past. No sense playing that scene out again. This time you might not survive, and boy would I be pissed.

"Gotta go," Molly finished. "Stay alert."

"What's a 'lert'?" Anna whispered the childhood joke into a dead phone line.

She finished the glass of wine but didn't pour herself a second. Clarity: she thought about that for a while. There were times reality didn't have all that much to recommend it. "Like now," she said to the face in the mirror, then, thinking of Bella, was shamed out of her self-pity. "Clarity," she repeated aloud, and slipped on her moccasins. At least she could do what she was good at: aggravating people into telling her more than they wanted to.

Down on Chapin it was significantly warmer. The difference between summer and fall, shorts and long pants.

Anna slowed the Rambler to an idle and crept past the houses trying to organize her thoughts. Day's end; it was warm and the light would last till nine o'clock or later. People were out walking dogs, sitting at picnic tables gossiping while dinners cooked on outdoor grills. Several members of the helitack crew sat on the steps of the fire dorm drinking beer. Drew waved her over, pointing at the bottle of Colt 45 in his hand.

"The devil is at mine elbow," Anna muttered. She pulled the Rambler in and parked in front of the dorm. Drew, Jimmy, and Paul sat on the steps looking for all the world like fraternity boys on a Saturday afternoon.

"How goes the hunt?" Drew asked.

"An arrest is imminent," Anna said, and declined another offer of a beer.

"It won't help Bella," Drew said. "She's breaking my heart, poor little kid. Who'd've thought she'd take it so hard? Stacy wasn't even her real dad. With all that threat of cutting her legs up, I'd've thought she might be relieved. She hid it pretty good, but it scared her a lot. What a waste." Drew sucked down half a Colt at one gulp and crushed the can into a wad of tinfoil.

"Sure you won't have a brewski?" Jimmy asked as he popped another for Drew and one for himself. Anna wasn't at all sure she wouldn't so she took her leave.

By the time she parked under the tree in front of the

Meyerses' bungalow, her plan still hadn't taken on any real form. She toyed with the idea of returning to Far View but the need to keep busy forced her out of the car.

The door was open. She peered through the screen. The front room was a mess of magazines and newspapers. The couch, desk, and much of the floor were littered with them. No toys, she noted. A television, a *TV Guide* open on top of it, stared with a blank eye from a small table in the corner. Familiar sounds of an evening game show came from elsewhere in the house.

A TV in the kitchen or bedroom, Anna guessed. "Hello, anybody home?" She rapped lightly on the door frame.

Clattering from the kitchen answered her query. A moment later Rose Meyers appeared on the other side of the screen. "Yes?" she said when she saw Anna on the doorstep.

"In the neighborhood," Anna said. "Just thought I'd drop by."

"No one is here. Hattie and Bella went for a walk."

"That's okay."

Rose looked nonplussed. Several seconds ticked by during which she evidently remembered her manners. "Would you like to come in for a minute?" she offered.

"Thanks. That would be nice."

Rose stood aside, holding the door, while Anna slunk by. "I hope I'm not interrupting anything. . . ." Anna began, and waited for the usual reassurances but none were offered.

Shoving aside several days' worth of coupons in the midst of the clipping and sorting process, Anna settled on the couch. "I've always liked these little houses," she said, looking around the room with its wooden floor and wood-burning stove. She'd seen the homes redone for permanent employees. They had wall-to-wall carpeting and more recent paint jobs—more comfortable but less picturesque.

"It's cramped," Rose said.

"After dorm living, a doghouse would look like a mansion to me if I had it all to myself."

Rose gave up her post at the door and went so far as to perch on the edge of a chair but she didn't get comfortable. That this was not to be a long visit was made abundantly clear.

"I can't stay long," Anna said to put her at her ease. "Only an hour or two," she added, just for the fun of watching Rose flinch.

Mrs. Meyers looked as if she were ill and Anna, remembering widowhood, softened. "How are you doing?" she asked. "That's really all I came by for. This is a hard time."

"Yes." The rigid cast of Rose's features trembled and for a moment it looked as if her control might crack but she recovered herself. "Hard."

"Was Stacy depressed over anything?" Anna ventured. "Poor health, family problems, finances—anything like that?"

Rose's head jerked up, her face so full of anger Anna was half surprised her hair didn't catch on fire. "Stacy was in perfect health," Rose said coldly. "And, not that it's any of your business, but, no, there were no 'family problems,' as you put it. If you're implying my husband killed himself, you can put a stop to that line of thinking right now. This minute. Stacy wouldn't do that to me."

Anna waited a minute, letting Rose cool off. She searched her mind for a way of connecting with the woman, breaking through the wall of fury. "My husband was killed,"

Anna told her. "I had a real bad time for a while." Still have, she thought, but didn't say it.

"How was he killed?" Rose asked without interest.

Anna hated this part. More than once she wished Zach had had the good taste to die rescuing a child from a burning building, or skiing in avalanche country. "Crossing Ninth Avenue against the light, he was hit by a cab."

Another silence began. Anna watched Rose's drawn face and downcast eyes. Her need for information seemed petty in the face of this grief and she made up her mind to quit badgering. "Are you going to be all right?" she asked impulsively.

"All right?" Rose laughed. "Now that's relative, isn't it? I have no job, no income, a child with special needs. All right?" Rose's voice was becoming shrill. The dam was breaking and Anna wasn't altogether sure she wanted to be there when it gave way. "No, I'm not going to be all right. Maybe if the Park Service would stop piddling around and find out who did this, I could be all right. You can bet your cozy little government job I'm going to sue for everything I have coming to me. No health insurance, no retirement, no death benefits. Like Stacy was a migrant worker, no better than a strawberry picker. Temporary appointment!" She spat out the words. "We can't even stay here much longer. Not that that's a big loss but it is a roof over our heads.

"Oh, yes," she continued, as if Anna had argued. "I'm going to sue all right. Tell that to Mr. Hills Dutton. And tell him to stop writing parking tickets and talk to Ted Greeley."

"Ted Greeley?" Anna probed.

"Money can buy anything, anybody," Rose said, then snapped her mouth shut so hard her jowls quivered. Anna doubted she would get another word out of Rose with anything short of a crowbar.

"Well . . ." She levered herself up out of the nest of papers. "I'll sure tell him. We can use any help you can give us. Let me know if you need anything." With that and other platitudes, Anna paved her way to the front door and escaped down the walk.

She'd gotten what she wanted, a flood of unedited words. Out of which "Ted Greeley" and "Money can buy anything, anybody" merited consideration. Rose seemed to be suggesting Greeley had bought off Hills, paid him to steer the investigation away from him or his. If he had, Greeley was a fool. Hills wasn't the head of this incident, the Federal Bureau of Investigation was. Their man was due in in the morning.

That left the possibility that Rose believed the contractor had something to do with her husband's murder. Coupling Rose's finger-pointing with Bella's admission that the fight on the phone between her mom and Stacy was over some man made for interesting hypotheses. Was "some man" Greeley? Was Greeley jealous of Stacy, in love with his wife?

Anna made a mental note to mention this interview when she met with the federal investigator.

She dropped the Rambler in gear and pulled around Rose's Oldsmobile. Her mind flashed back to the day she and Stacy had confronted Tom Silva about the foreskin note. Greeley had said something that chilled or angered Stacy. Anna remembered: "How's my little Bella?"

Could Greeley be Rose's rich first husband? No, Anna remembered, Number One was a lawyer. Greeley as Rose's lover? Worth pondering. Uncharitable as it was, Anna thought it unlikely any man would kill for the pleasure of Mrs. Meyers' company but she knew that was pure prejudice on her part. On like occasions her father used to say: "Perhaps she has talents we are not privy to." The human heart, though often predictable, remained unfathomable. People loved who they loved and killed who they killed. Rhyme and reason, when they entered in, were often so skewed as to be meaningless to an outside observer.

Anna shoved these new ingredients to the back burner of her mind to stew awhile.

Killing time, she drove down to the Museum Loop and through the picnic grounds. Snuggled down in the evergreens, the picnic area seemed common, if charming, but a few steps carried one to the lip of Spruce Canyon. There the mesa fell away in staggered steps of fawn-colored sandstone, before a sheer drop to the wooded ground below. Like many canyons cut into the mesa, Spruce was small. For Anna there was always a sense of Shangri-la about these hidden places. Each had its own dwellings, long since abandoned by their owners and bleached back to the color of the earth.

Since Mesa Verde's cliffs had first been inhabited the Anasazi, the Utes, the Navajo, cowboys, hunters, and tourists had all tramped the trails. Yet there remained a tremendous sense of discovery. In that lay much of the park's allure.

Anna parked the Rambler and walked out toward the canyon rim. The sun was just setting, casting golden light that made the trees greener and the sandstone seem to glow from within. Blue-and-black-winged butterflies settled on the milkweed as if trapped in the amber light.

Since there was no camping on the mesa top, the picnic grounds were gloriously deserted in the evenings. Anna breathed in the solitude.

Not wanting to break the peace, she made her way through the band of junipers between the picnic area and the canyon with great care, placing each moccasined foot on bare ground to avoid snapping needles and twigs.

Such stealth had paid off several times since she'd moved to Colorado. Once she had seen a mother lion with two speckled cubs behind Coyote Village and once a bull elk looking fat and fine and full of himself at Park Point.

This evening she crept up on a much stranger game.

Out on the canyon's lip the sandstone had been worn into a shallow trough sixty feet wide. Over the centuries summer rains had scoured it smooth. In the middle of the pour-over a stone block the size of a sofa and relatively the same shape had come to rest. Lying on the rock, dyed red by the setting sun, was the body of Bella Meyers. Her hands were crossed on her breast in the classic pose of the deceased. Aunt Hattie, her hair a frizz of sun-drenched brown, bent over the child. The woman's small, perfect hands were doubled under her chin. She was murmuring or singing.

Anna stopped at the edge of the trees. The little scene played on; the child motionless, Hattie moving occasionally as if exclaiming or weaving spells. After a time, Anna ventured out into the dying light, her footfalls soundless on the stone.

When she was eight or ten feet away she heard Hattie asking in her high, pleasant voice: "Shall I kiss you awake now?" and was relieved to see a small shake of Bella's head. The child had not been slaughtered in some bizarre ritual.

"Oh my, but she was such a beautiful girl, beloved of all in the kingdom." Hattie sighed over the little body.

Hattie glanced up then and saw Anna. "Someone else has come to pay their last respects to the lovely Bella," she said in her storybook voice. To Anna she whispered: "We're playing Dead Princess."

Anna cocked an eyebrow.

"It's a game Bella made up when she was little," Hattie explained in a whisper, careful not to break the spell. "The princess lies in state and is admired by all and sundry until she is awakened by the magic kiss."

"Sounds like my kind of game," Anna returned.

"The princess has been dead a very long time today," Hattie said sadly. "She doesn't seem to want to be kissed back to life."

"Aunt Hattie!" came a remonstrance from the side of Bella's mouth. Her eyes were still squeezed shut.

"Yes, Royal One?"

"Okay. Now."

Hattie leaned down and placed a gentle kiss in the middle of the child's forehead. Slowly Bella opened one eye, then the other, and looked around as if she were in a strange place.

"Welcome back, little one," Hattie said. "The crowds are cheering your return to the world of the living. You have been sorely missed."

Bella smiled a little. "Okay. I'm done." She sat up abruptly and swung her short legs over the side of the boulder.

Hattie sat beside her and both of them looked at Anna. "We're done," the aunt said.

Anna squatted on her heels. The sun threw their shadows a dozen feet, shading her eyes. "I didn't mean to interrupt your game," she apologized.

"That's all right," Bella assured her. "I was about to come to life anyway. My behind was getting tired of the rock. Being dead isn't as easy as it looks."

"I guess not."

"Do you want to play?" Bella offered. "My behind's waking up some."

"I don't know how," Anna told her, and Bella looked disappointed. "Maybe your aunt Hattie could teach me," Anna relented, and won one of Bella's smiles.

"It's a good game," Bella promised as she lay back down and folded her hands over her chest.

Anna stood and looked down at the little girl with her angel's face and stunted legs, so peaceful in her pretended and admired state of suspended animation. Anna was glad Hattie had come. Everybody needed someone to kiss her back to life.

"Does the kiss always work?" Anna teased the other woman.

"It does if you do it right."

12

FIRST THING the following morning, Anna received a secondhand message by way of Jennifer Short that she was to meet Hills at the CRO. Unable to sleep, she came down early and sat on the bench opposite the office door, enjoying the freshness of the day. Soon buses and cars would begin puffing the park full of carbon monoxide and noise. The first hours after sunrise were new made, hinting of wilderness, of what the world was once and, in dreams, might be again.

Across the walkway, amid the knife-point leaves of the agave, a yellow-and-black bull snake uncoiled himself into the warmth of the sun. The snake lived in a hole in the stonework of the superintendent's porch. At least that's where Anna'd seen him flee other mornings when the first foot traffic of the day began.

She stretched her shirt against her shoulder blades and took primal pleasure in the sun's rays. "I think I'm an exotherm," she said. The snake didn't even blink.

An unnatural sound, high heels clacking on paved ground, got a better response. Anna looked in the direction of the racket and when she turned back her narrow fellow had gone.

"You scared away my snake," she complained as Patsy Silva came down the walk.

"Good. Nasty things." Patsy was dressed in a colorful Mexican skirt with a turquoise blouse and sandals. She looked chipper. But she always looked chipper so Anna deduced nothing from that.

"You look chipper," she said to see if it were so.

"Found my keys." Patsy dangled a ring with a neon-pink rabbit's foot on it. "Good omen."

" 'Bout time. What with chindis and"—she almost said "dead guys" but realized to those not in law enforcement it might seem unnecessarily cavalier—"what not," she finished safely. "Find them in the last place you looked?"

Patsy laughed. "Usually. Not this time. They were in my purse all along. They'd fallen down among the used Kleenex and dead lipsticks—the bottom-feeders."

"Speaking of: how goes it with Tom? Since I haven't heard, I've assumed no news is good news."

"I suppose so." Patsy sat down beside Anna, deciding to take time for a proper chat. "He's not around. I mean he's here and I see him and the girls see him, but it's like he's sneaking. Lurking, sort of."

"Spying?"

"Not spying, I don't think. I'd've reported that for sure. No, it's sort of like a storm cloud always on the horizon. Not really threatening you, but you know it's raining on somebody somewhere."

Anna shook her head. "I'm still not getting the picture. Does he come over and moon at you or leave notes or what?"

"No. I'd've called you for that too, I think. He's just around, in our peripheral vision, sort of. Like the girls'll be waiting for the bus and he'll drive by at a time he should be working. Or I'll come home after dark from somewhere and he'll just be walking by my house. Mindy and Missy and I came out of the movies in Cortez and he was across the street having coffee at that little lunch place."

"Following you?"

"Maybe—but from a big distance."

"Does it scare you or the girls?"

Patsy laughed again. "I suppose it should but it doesn't. It's sort of comforting, like that old song 'Someone to Watch Over Me.'"

Tom's behavior struck Anna more in the stalker than the guardian-angel mode. "He doesn't talk to you or the girls, he just sort of skulks?"

"Doesn't talk. In fact he seems to be avoiding us. A couple of times we've responded, you know—like friends—and Tom acted like he wanted to get away."

"Well, holler if he starts scaring you," Anna said, because she could think of nothing else to say. She looked at her watch: seven fifty-seven.

Adept at taking hints of dismissal, Patsy stood and arranged her purse on her shoulder. "Waiting for Hills," Anna explained. "I've been summoned for God knows what."

"Oh." Patsy brightened. "I bet it's to go to Durango. The FBI man is arriving on the ten-eleven from Albuquerque. The superintendent had me book it."

"That's it then. Pigeon's taxi service."

Patsy picked up on her annoyance. "Hills thought you'd want to go. It turns out the investigator is an old friend of yours, a Frederick Stanton."

"You're kidding! Frederick the Fed? I'll be damned."

"He's not an old friend?" Patsy had such a practiced look of concern Anna would've pegged her as a mom even if she hadn't known of the girls.

"We worked together once," Anna said. "We're more like old acquaintances."

Hills strode up looking lean and marvelously rangerlike with his blond bulk and tight pants. Her assignment was, indeed, to fetch Frederick Stanton from the Durango airport ninety miles to the east.

The drive between the park and Durango wound down off the mesa and through the Mancos Valley nestled between the snow-topped La Plata mountains to the north and the red mesas to the south. Fields were carpeted with dandelions, and blue irises lined the streams. Several hundred sheep, herded by men and boys on horseback, stopped traffic for twenty minutes, making Anna late to the airport. Fortunately, the flight was even later.

Abandoning the terminal for the out of doors, she sat on the concrete with her back against the warm brick of the building and passed the time remembering Frederick the Fed.

Isle Royale had been a while ago but she still remembered the gory details. The FBI agent was a tall gangling man with well-cut features a size too large for his face. Anna estimated his age at thirty-five. Dark hair, cut in the inimitable style of a third-grader, class of fifty-eight, flopped over his forehead; skin showed white around the ears where the clippers had cut too close.

Stanton had a vague and bumbling manner but was usually a step or two ahead at the end of every heat. Too much Columbo, too much Lord Peter Wimsey, Anna thought. Or, perhaps, *Revenge of the Nerds* and "Saturday Night Live." Stanton didn't fit the mold. It made him hard to type and impossible to predict. Which was, Anna guessed, exactly why he did it.

He used people. He'd used Anna and he'd done it effortlessly; that was the part that rankled.

A twin-engine prop plane, the commuter out of Albuquerque, roared in from the taxiway and came to a stop on the ramp beyond the chain-link fence.

Anna eased herself up.

The fourth passenger off was Stanton. Anna laughed at how like himself he looked. Same haircut, even the same clothes. He wore a short-sleeved madras shirt he must have unearthed from a vintage clothing store, rumpled khaki shorts, white socks, and brown lace-up shoes. As he came down the metal steps that folded out from the fuselage, he kept looking behind him, swatting at his posterior.

Absorbed in this activity, he ambled across the ramp. When he reached the fence he looked up. If he was surprised to see Anna, he didn't show it. "I think I sat in something ooky," he said, wrinkling his long nose. "Anything there?" He turned to give her an unobscured view of his backside.

There was perhaps a speck of something on his right hip pocket but Anna wasn't in the mood to enter into a discussion of it. "Looks fine to me."

Stanton craned his neck and looked down over his shoulder. "Okay then," he said. "I'll have to trust you on this one. Sure felt sticky for a minute."

"Luggage?" Anna said to get things moving.

"Got it." He shook the strap of an oversized leather shoulder bag he carried.

"You must be planning on wrapping this one up in record time."

"I heard you were on the case so I only brought one change of underdrawers."

There wasn't much to say to that so Anna merely nodded.

With what seemed a maximum of fuss and fiddling

around, she got the federal agent buckled into the passenger seat of the patrol car and started the trip back to the park.

As they drove to the main highway, Stanton waved graciously at passing traffic. "Boy, I love riding in cars with lights and sirens," he said. "Everybody waves back. They think they did something and you're not stopping them for it. Kind of makes you pals."

Anna laughed. "I wondered what it was."

Stanton made idle conversation, the kind she'd grown used to working with him on the island. During the weeks of that investigation she'd come to look upon it as his personal music, the kind designed to soothe the savage beasts; charming in its whimsy, disarmingly inane. When one became complacent, convinced he was a complete boob, he'd pounce.

"Okay," he said as she pulled out onto highway 160. "Tell me the good-parts version."

Anna switched off the radio and pulled her thoughts together. As succinctly as possible, she recounted the disappearance, the discovery of the body, the widow's whereabouts the night of the murder, and Rose's casting blame in the general direction of the pipeline contractor.

Stanton sat for a while humming "I Heard It Through the Grapevine" under his breath. The patrol car crawled up the long slope out of Durango. Anna unfettered her mind and let it wander over the now-green ski slopes of Hesperus and the fresh new-leaved poplar trees skirting the mountain ravines. The sky was an impossible blue, a blue seen only on hot midwestern summer days and high in the mountains. Cornflower blue—the phrase flickered through her mind, though she'd never seen a cornflower.

"That's no fun," Frederick said finally. He twisted

around in his seat till the shoulder strap pushed his collar up under his right ear and his bony knees pointed in Anna's direction. "Tell me the gossip, innuendo, lies, suppositions, weird happenstance. Dead guys are pretty dull without some good dirt. Do dish me."

"The dead guy was a friend of mine," Anna replied irritably.

"Oops." Stanton looked genuinely contrite and she was sorry for such a cheap shot. She'd thought of Stacy as the dead guy not three hours earlier. She's almost made up her mind to apologize when Stanton spoke again.

"Callous, that's me all over. How about this: Deceased individuals, however meritorious in life, lack the essential spontaneity to generate interest. So those left living must keep their spirits alive through the practice of the oral tradition."

Anna snorted. "Callous is right. The dirt." Out of spite—or self-defense—she told Stanton everything she could think of that occurred in the park, or in anyone's imagination in the park, around the time of the murder: Jamie's chindi, the pipeline, medicals, evacuations, the superintendent's secretary's marital problems, the monkey-wrenching, the dorm, Piedmont's foster home, Bella's dwarfism. She got bored before he did, running out of words as they passed through the tiny town of Mancos.

"And the meritorious deceased?" Stanton pushed.

Anna was torn between a desire to snub the fed for his flippancy and a need to talk of Stacy. The need to talk won. She'd used that need a dozen times to pull information from people. Mildly, she cursed herself for giving in to it now. To retain some vestige of self-respect, she culled all emotion from her tone. Dispassionately, she recounted Stacy's sensitivity, love of the parks, his attachment to Bella and addiction to Rose.

At the word "addiction," Anna realized she was being catty. Hoping it had slipped by Stanton, she made a mental note to talk to Molly about it.

"Rats," he summed up when she'd done. "Sounds messy and domestic. Widows and orphans and who's divorced and who's dead. Any drug dealings, you think?"

He sounded so hopeful Anna laughed as she shook her head. "Doesn't seem like it."

"Too bad." Stanton screwed himself around in the seat, draping one long arm over the back and looking down into the valley as the car climbed the winding road cut in the side of the mesa. "Drug dealers make such satisfying bad guys. Not so good as Nazis or Hell's Angels, but then who is? Hate doing the widows, especially when they're all fresh and weepy."

Hills Dutton was waiting for them in the CRO. In the past Anna had often found rangers loath to turn an investigation over to an outside agency. Some hated surrendering the power, others suffered a natural discomfort at letting anyone not a member of the family paw through the dirty laundry. Lord knew what they might choose to air.

Dutton was the exception; he couldn't wait to dump this one in somebody else's lap. Statements, paperwork, the photographs, and the autopsy—unopened and dated two days previously, Anna noted—had been stuffed into a manila envelope. Hills thrust it into Stanton's hands the instant the introductions were over. Lest the abdication appear incomplete, he added: "This is our busy season and I've got a park to run so I'm giving you Anna for whatever while you're here."

"My very own ranger," Stanton gloated as he and Anna walked back to her patrol car. "Just what I always wanted . . . well, next to a pony."

Anna grumbled because it was expected of her but she was pleased with the assignment. Parking tickets and medical evacuations had begun to pall, replaced by an undoubtedly unhealthy obsession with Stacy Meyers, living and now dead.

She took Stanton, the envelope still clamped under his arm, to Cliff Palace and played tour guide as she led him down the steep path into the alcove where the village was built. During the descent a metamorphosis took place. By the time they stood before the ruin, Stanton had lost his puppyish ways. Even his physical appearance was altered. The angles of his bones had sharpened, his stride was no longer gangling but purposeful, and his step had softened till the leather soles fell with scarcely a sound. Anna was put in mind of the time they had sat on a rock overlooking Lake Richie on Isle Royale waiting for a murder suspect; the sense she'd gotten then of the wolf shedding its sheep's clothing.

The ruin was packed with tourists moving through the ancient pueblo in a sluggish stream. At the base of the tower where Anna and Stacy had found the asthmatic child, people were backed up twenty deep waiting to stick their heads through the window to see the paintings.

"Like the Matterhorn at Disneyland," a voice from above and behind Anna sneered.

Jamie Burke was seated high on a boulder in the shade. A silver counter rested in her right hand and she clicked off tourists as they came by. The usual questions: when? who? how? and where did they go? were all answered in the same way: "It's in the brochure."

Anna was not impressed. Unlike the wilderness parks, which she staunchly believed were for the animals and plants dwelling therein, Mesa Verde was for the visitors.

Humans paying tribute with curiosity and awe to human ancestry. On Isle Royale and in Guadalupe, law enforcement was there to protect and preserve. The main function of rangers on the mesa was to keep the flow of traffic orderly so the interpreters could bring this history to life.

"Hi, Jamie," Anna said neutrally.

Ignoring her, Jamie slid down from the rock to land on legs strong as shock absorbers. "Are you the FBI guy?" she demanded of Stanton.

The agent stuck out his hand. The unhinged, bumbling look had returned, donned like a disguise. "Yes indeedy."

Jamie didn't shake his hand. Putting fists on hips, she squinted up at the walls filling niches high above the dwelling. "You're too late. Too bad Stacy had to die. He was my closest friend," Jamie said. "Maybe he'd still be alive if you'd listened to me."

"You" was generic, as in "they," and Anna didn't bother to challenge it.

"How so?" Stanton asked politely.

"Al said this strip-mining was killing the sacred land. They've got to be given their home, their peace. Are you going up into the ruin?" she asked suddenly.

"That's what us FBI guys do."

"It's a sacred place. Fragile. People aren't allowed to go stomping around up there and for good reason."

Annoyance was nibbling away at Anna's already strained patience. She drew breath to speak. Stanton heard and shot her a look that shut her up.

"What's the good reason?" he asked.

"Death."

He didn't react to the melodrama. "Wow," he said with seeming sincerity. "Whose?"

"Stacy was not the first. You want him to be the last, then stop intruding."

Stanton was mystified. Jamie was enjoying her part in this homemade theatrical and would play it out as long as she could.

Anna jumped in with the punch line. "Old Ones, Anasazi, chindi, ghosts, spirits," she told Stanton. "Jamie believes—"

"Along with a lot of other people," the interpreter stuck in.

"—that the ghosts or spirits of the original inhabitants of the mesa are popping up out of the underworld now and then, showing their displeasure at the modern tourism industry by striking down a select handful of the hundreds of thousands of people who pass through here every year."

"Not exactly!" Jamie snapped.

"Girls, girls," Frederick chided, and Anna quelled an impulse to bite him.

"We'd best get moving," she said, glancing at her watch as if time was of the essence.

Jamie puffed out an exaggerated sigh. "I'd better go with you. That's an easily impacted area."

"Stay," Anna ordered.

Jamie bristled but stayed. Anna didn't add "Sit!" but she thought about it.

"Will you be here for a while?" Stanton asked the interpreter. "I'd like to talk with somebody who really has a feel for this place."

Jamie's bristles lay back down. She tossed her braid over her shoulder and almost smiled. "I'll be here."

"More flies with honey, Anna. Got to get them flies," Stanton said as they walked down the path.

The kiva had not been disturbed since the body was carried out. Yellow tape marked POLICE LINE DO NOT CROSS and held down with stones was placed in an "X" over the top of the kiva. Once Stanton had examined the scene the tape would be removed and the floor raked smooth.

The FBI agent sat down on the edge where the roof had once been and dangled his legs over the side. "Other folks find bodies in dumpsters, storm drains, vacant lots. Yours turn up in bizarre places. Your karma must be very strange," he said to Anna.

"Out in the sticks you've got to take what you can get." She sat down next to him.

He took the envelope he'd been carrying under his arm for the last forty minutes and pulled out the photographs of the crime scene. Pictures of the body had been blown up into 8x10 color prints.

Looking at the photos, Anna knew memories of Stacy in life would be hard to come by. This was how she would remember him: a banquet for flies. She'd never viewed Zach's body really, just the barest of glimpses to ID it. Studying pictures of Stacy, the value of open-casket funerals, the laying out of the body, night watches—rituals that cut across religious and cultural lines—became clear. To let the living see the dead were most certainly dead and so to let them go. Ghosts were not the spirits of the dead returning but the memories of the living not yet laid to rest.

"The man is dead." Frederick startled her with an echo of her thoughts. "He's curled himself up—"

"Or been curled up by somebody."

"In a what . . . a fire pit?"

"Yes."

"Gun on, radio on, no marks of violence, no tracks but his, the ground all raked neatly and his little hat tidy on that wall thing."

"And his shoes off. See." Anna pointed to the cordovan shoes tucked up near the brown-stockinged feet.

"You know what I like? I like big old bullet holes and somebody standing a few feet away with a smoking gun screaming, 'My God, I killed him! I killed him!'"

"That happen often?"

"All the time. How do you think we catch as many as we do?"

Anna stared down at the trampled kiva floor. "At least this gives us job security."

Stanton laughed and she realized how rare that occurrence was. Too bad, it was a good wholesome sound.

He put the photographs back and took out the autopsy report. "The envelope, please," he said as he ripped it open. "And the winners are . . ." His voice trailed off as he looked over the three single-spaced typed pages.

Anna couldn't read the small type without all but sitting in his lap so she possessed her soul in patience, passing the time by imagining how the village would have looked with cook fires burning, people hauling water, weaving cloth, children playing on the kiva roofs.

"Time of death."

Her attention snapped back to the twentieth century.

"Somewhere between eight P.M. and three A.M. Monday night, the twenty-first of June. Had rice and chicken for dinner and red licorice for dessert. Cause of death, heart failure."

"Can't be!"

"Right there." Stanton pointed a big-knuckled finger at the bottom of the second page.

Anna took the report and read the offending sentence. "Natural causes?" she ventured, then read on. "Doesn't say."

"Could be a lot of things. Did he have a history of heart disease?"

"His wife said he was in perfect health. Perfect. And that's a quote."

Stanton pondered the underground room. "Shock, fear, drug overdose, respiratory failure, what causes the heart muscle to stop?"

"Electrical current, lightning, blunt trauma." Anna couldn't think of anything else.

"I opt for one of those," Stanton said. "Even if he had a bad heart, I can't see a guy with chest pain, nausea, having trouble breathing, climbing up, crawling down, kicking his shoes off and the bucket."

"Callous."

"Sorry."

"Neither can I."

"Read me that third paragraph on page two—after all the chemical breakdown gobbledygook," Stanton said.

"There was no sign of drug or alcohol in the blood or muscle tissue."

"There goes drug overdose," Stanton said sadly.

"No bruising of the soft tissue."

"There goes blunt trauma."

"No sign of ingested poison. No entrance or exit wounds. No occluded arteries or symptoms of arteriosclerosis."

"Damn. So much for natural causes. That pretty much leaves us with your Miss Burke's spirits. Fear and shock. Guy lays down for a nap in the fireplace, up pops a sipapu and *wham!* scares him to death. Case closed."

"A sipapu's a place, not a thing." Anna pointed to the crockery-lined hole. "Your bogeyman had to come out of there. Pretty tight squeeze for a truly terrifying critter."

"Bad things come in small packages."

Anna went back to the autopsy report. "'Oval burn marks approximately one inch by an inch and a half, first degree, on the right arm between the elbow and the shoulder. Similar mark on the left upper arm two inches above the antecubital space.'

"I saw that. That mark. I thought it was a bruise. I get bruises there sometimes from the butt of my gun banging my arm."

Stanton pulled a pair of half glasses out of the breast pocket of his madras shirt and shoved them up onto his nose. They were the kind with heavy black frames sold by drugstores. A children's show host Anna had watched as a child wore those same glasses. Uncle Happy, she remembered.

The agent held the photo they'd been discussing under his chin and stared down at it through the magnifying lenses. "Oval burn marks. That smells clue-y to me. What did they look like?"

Anna took her eyes from the picture, rested them on the stone of the kiva floor, and let Stacy's corpse rematerialize. "I didn't inspect them closely at the time. Like I said, maybe bruises from the gun or being grabbed too hard. Thinking back, they were brownish—no purples, greens, blues, or yellows you might find with a healing bruise. And scaly. I touched one and it felt the way sunburned skin does when it's just beginning to peel."

Stanton whistled "An Actor's Life for Me," from *Pinocchio*. Lost in thought, he waggled his feet over the open air. "Leaning against something hot," he suggested. "Like a motorcycle manifold."

"Both arms and both on the inside? Odd."

"True. He'd have to be hugging the Harley. Pretty silly he'd look too, if you ask me. Sorry," he apologized automatically.

They thought awhile longer. "Something dripped?" Anna ventured. "Hot wax. He was reaching up to take a candle off the mantel or something."

"Could be. Kinky sex stuff? I've seen wax used in S and M movies—strictly Bureau research, of course."

"Of course."

"Stacy didn't seem the type."

"Still waters?"

"Maybe." But Anna didn't think so.

They fell into silence again. The steady hum of the tourists below provided white noise, the occasional call of a canyon bird a pleasing counterpoint.

Grating sounds cut through and Anna pulled her thoughts up out of Stacy's grave. Jamie Burke marched toward them along the wall that accessed the kiva where they sat, her heavy tread designed more to garner attention than to protect an "easily impacted area." Claude Beavens was behind her. There was no tow rope visible but he moved with the reluctant hitching motion of a vehicle not under its own power.

"That's him." Jamie pointed an accusatory finger at Frederick Stanton. "The FBI guy."

Stanton scrambled to his feet and stuck out his hand. "How do you do?" he asked formally.

Beavens looked around for someplace else to be. Not finding one, he took the proffered hand and mumbled, "Pleased to meet you," the way children are taught to in grade school.

"Look," Beavens began. "This isn't my idea. I just—"

"Tell him," Jamie insisted.

Looking annoyed but beaten, he shrugged. Beavens had been so anxious to be a part of the murder investigation the day the body had been found, Anna wondered what held him back now.

"Claude was here the night Stacy died," Jamie said for him, and Anna understood. Few people wanted to participate quite that intimately in the investigative process.

"Not *here* here," Beavens defended himself.

"But here," Jamie said. "Tell him."

Frederick folded himself back down onto the lip of the kiva and stared expectantly up at the interpreter.

"I was out on the loop Monday night—that's when Jamie says Stacy was . . . was here. That's all. No big deal."

Stanton seemed less interested in Beavens than in Jamie. She stood with her profile to them, her long black hair trailing down her back. Her arms were crossed and her feet were planted wide apart in what, for good taste's sake, Anna hoped was an unconscious parody of Hiawatha.

"Monday night. You hit it right on the nose, Ms. Burke." Stanton flapped the papers from the autopsy. "The coroner says that's the date."

Not willing to break the pose, Jamie shot him a scornful look from the sides of her eyes. "Summer solstice."

Stanton waited. Beavens fidgeted and Anna watched. Claude was clearly uncomfortable about something but there was no way of telling what sort of ants were inhabiting his mental trousers. Guilt, embarrassment at being dragged into Jamie's little drama, nervousness at being questioned by the FBI—all were possible, as were a dozen things that didn't come readily to mind.

Jamie was basking in the limelight, dragging the interview out with cryptic sentences and pregnant pauses.

Anna was sorely tempted to spoil the show, but Stanton was satisfied to let the scene play out.

"It's when things tend to happen," Jamie said after a

moment. "Some people have a feel for these things. A kinship. I felt it. Ask Anna. Something was coming down on the twenty-first."

"Or up," Anna said, pointing at the sipapu.

"Go ahead. Investigate me, Mr. FBI." If one could judge by the glint in Jamie's pale eyes, the prospect wasn't unwelcome. "You'll have to look in your paranormal films for this one," she finished.

"The X Files," Stanton said gravely.

Jamie liked that. She turned on Beavens, now with hands deep in pockets, poking at a dung beetle with the toe of his shoe. "Tell him," she ordered.

"Better tell me," Stanton said. "Just the facts, like Joe Friday says. Nobody'll interrupt you." He didn't glance at Jamie when he said it. Somehow he didn't need to.

"Doggone it, Jamie!" Beavens exploded, then took a deep breath. "It really is no big deal. I was out here that night—Monday. I didn't go to Balcony House with everybody. That New Age stuff—crystals and mantra-ing at the moon—is crud." His hand went to his throat and he nervously fingered a tiny gold cross Anna hadn't noticed before. "I just rode my bike out here. Sat on the rocks over the canyon till the moon was up. Later I guess, two or two-thirty, maybe. Then I rode home. No big deal. I didn't see Stacy or anything." He stopped, waited a moment, then shrugged. "That's it. No biggie."

"God, I hate invertebrates masquerading as men," Jamie sighed. Turning her back on Claude, she said to Stanton: "Claude saw."

Anna remembered the phrase; the words she had used the morning the body was discovered. She'd hissed it as Anna squeezed through the gate above Cliff Palace.

"Just spit it out," Anna growled.

Stanton deadpanned in her direction. "You're such a people person, Anna."

"Claude saw what?" she pressed.

"Where they come through, the veil," Jamie said triumphantly. "He told me Tuesday morning, before anybody'd even thought to look for Stacy. He said he'd seen the shimmer in the light of the solstice moon as if the spirits were passing through."

"Not exactly," Claude complained.

"Exactly," Jamie countered.

"Exactly in your own words." Stanton stopped the argument.

"What's the time?" Beavens asked.

All three of them glanced at their watches. "One-ten," Anna said before anyone else could.

"Gotta go. Balcony House tour in twenty minutes."

"The veil?" Anna asked again.

Beavens pulled his hands out of his pockets. Again the shrug Anna was beginning to think was a nervous habit. "I was just kidding around. Jamie's always on about this spirit garbage. I was kidding. Ask the other interps. I heard some of them leaving the loop in their truck later than I did."

They watched Beavens trot off, surefooted, down the balcony to disappear into the ancient alleyway.

"He is a lying little weasel," Jamie stated.

It was the first thing she'd said all day that had the ring of truth.

13

ANNA AND Stanton followed Jamie out of the closed part of the ruin and left her at the entrance clicking visitor statistics into the metal counter.

Rather than go against the flow of traffic, they climbed the four ladders at the western end of the alcove and regained the mesa top. The climb always winded Anna but she forced herself to breathe silently through her nose, enjoying the sound of Stanton's puffing. "Want to rest?" she asked solicitously as they walked back toward the parking lot.

"Yes, please," he said humbly, and threw himself down on half a log round smoothed to make a bench. Gratefully, Anna sat beside him and refilled her hungry lungs with the thin air. Her childishness made her laugh.

"I hope you're duly impressed," she said. "It's damn hard to hold your breath after that climb."

"Tell me about it. I do it to impress the young agents. Nearly did myself in last training session. Gets harder every year."

They sat for a while just breathing and feeling the sun on their faces. Anna made small talk with the visitors who came panting up from the ruin. The uniform made it mandatory and it was a part of the job she took pleasure in. Sharing beauty with total strangers made the world seem a friendlier place. In a culture dominated, if not by violence, then certainly by the overheated reports of it dished out by a ratings-starved news media, it reassured her that the love of peace and natural order was still extant in the human soul.

"Let's do lists," Stanton suggested after a while. "Pretend we're organized."

Anna reached in her hip pocket and fished out the yellow notebook. She'd already written "Life Insurance," "Enemies," "Where Else Should We Have Looked," and "Greed/Rose." "Life Insurance" was crossed out since she'd overheard Rose telling Hattie that Stacy had left her and Bella with nothing.

"I'll be the secretary." Stanton lifted the notebook from Anna's hands and the government-issue ballpoint from her shirt pocket.

"No life insurance?" he asked.

"Apparently not."

He wrote "Check" beside the crossed-out words. "Greed, always good. Was there an inheritance? That's a good one for Greed."

"No. Stacy wasn't rich."

"'Where Else Should We Have Looked'?"

"It's my guess we were meant to find the body and be mystified by it. Too coy, too precious, to be an accident. The only reasons not to hide the corpse are to prove death to get insurance or something or to stop people from looking for it in embarrassing places."

"Good point." Frederick underlined it. Beneath he wrote, speaking the words aloud as he did so: "'C. Beavens on scene. Interpreters in truck. J. Burke knew date. Spirit Veil.' Anything else?"

"Put down Greeley. The widow wants us to talk to him. It's worth finding out why."

Dutifully he wrote the name at the bottom of the list, then tapped the pen against his teeth. The top row was white and even but his bottom teeth were crowded, one pushed forward. As he tapped he hummed a tune Anna didn't recognize.

"So," he said finally. "We've got the wife because—who knows? Because there's always a good reason to kill your husband. Beavens because he was in the neighborhood. Burke because she knew the time of death and hates the white man's depredation of sacred grounds. Stacy was a white guy?"

Anna nodded.

"I remember." Stanton shook the autopsy envelope. "Said so. And we've got Greeley because the wife says he might know something. What else?"

"There's always us," Anna stated the obvious. "A ranger. We've all got what it takes."

"Oooh." Stanton looked impressed. Anna chose not to be amused.

"Keys to the ruin, to the Four-Way, knowledge of the upper kiva. Stacy would trust one of us. We could get him up here. All we'd have to say is we'd found some archaeological crime—graffiti, digging, theft, whatever."

"Any ranger got a motive?"

Other than her own story of unrequited bullshit, Anna couldn't think of any. She shook her head. "He was a temporary employee so he wasn't a threat to anybody promotion- or job-wise. He should have been—he was one of the best rangers we had. But without permanent status he couldn't get promoted. He wasn't even eligible for pay raises, and I don't think he had anything worth stealing. Unless you count his wife, and I'd question that one. Sorry," she apologized for the nasty remark. "Personal taste. Count her. Nobody seemed to hate him, and if he was blackmailing anyone or selling drugs he was good at it. No rumors."

"Somebody offed a nice, poor, unthreatening park ranger. Not promising."

"Nope."

Stanton closed the notebook and pocketed it along with Anna's pen. "Let's do Greeley first since nothing else makes a whole lot of sense.

"Want to have lunch first?" he asked as they drove past the Navajo taco stand.

"Not hungry."

Stanton looked pitiful but Anna didn't notice.

Ted Greeley was sitting at the break table in the maintenance shop along with Tom Silva and several other construction workers. Tom and two of the others were smoking. Ashtrays, already full, and soda pop cans cluttered the scarred Formica.

Greeley's feet, crossed at the ankles, were propped up amid the debris. Even in heavy Red Wing boots his feet looked small. His white curls were stuck to his forehead with sweat and he sucked on a Diet 7-Up.

"Hey, Ted," Anna announced herself. "Don't you guys have to work for a living?"

"Not much longer if *Ms.* Stinson has her way. We can sit right here in the shade drinking sodie pops and whistle for our paychecks. The old witch—spelled with a 'b'—is still trying to get the pipeline shut down till they dig up some beads and bones. A shitload of money to keep a handful of eggheads employed, if you ask me."

"Ain't nobody ever asks you, Ted," one of the men said.

"Boy, you got that right."

Anna would have expected the smart remark to come from Tom Silva but he sat a little apart from the others quietly smoking his Marlboros. He showed no interest in the banter. To Anna he looked thinner than when she'd last seen him, and paler—not as if he'd been out of the sun for a while—it wasn't so much a lack of color as a lack of energy, vividness. Somehow he'd turned in on himself, faded.

She remembered Patsy talking of his haunting her and the girls and hoped he wasn't winding up to a psychotic break of some kind.

"Howdy, fellas, Tom," Anna said to check his social reflexes. There were none. The others nodded or grunted, said "hi" or cracked jokes. Absorbed in his own thoughts, Silva gave no sign he'd even heard her.

"What's with him?" she asked Greeley.

"Time of month."

The men laughed and Anna knew there was no use pursuing that line of questioning.

"This is Special Agent Stanton of the FBI. Agent Stanton's here to investigate the death of Stacy Meyers. I'd appreciate it if you could give him all the help you can." Her little speech given, Anna was happy to step out of the spotlight. As Stanton shook hands all around, she slipped back to the refrigerator, put a dollar in the coffee can, and took out two Cokes. One she put in front of Stanton, the other she kept. Not only was she thirsty, but the role of waitress rendered her comfortably invisible.

The construction workers, with the exception of Silva,

were taken by the romance of the FBI. They clustered as happily as scouts in a den.

Opening her Coke, Anna leaned back against the tool bench and watched.

For a few minutes they chatted about the shutting down of work on the pipeline. Ted held forth on the financial burden of running a construction company. Stanton got an unedited earful about Al Stinson. The nicest thing she was called was a fruitcake. Occasionally, when the language grew rough, one of the men would remember Anna and mumble "Excuse my French, but it's true" or "I'm no sexist, but . . ." and then, conscience salved, dive back into the conversational fray.

Stanton listened, made all the right noises, and looked as solemnly interested as a priest taking confession. Once the political landscape had been colorfully painted, he moved the talk around to the investigation.

To Anna's surprise, the construction workers didn't hold her high opinion of Stacy. "Full of himself," "A little light in his loafers" were some of their comments.

Greeley summed it up. "Meyers was a nineties kind of guy. Sensitive, caring, proud of his feminine side."

"Yeah, what's that cologne he used?" a man still wearing his hard hat asked.

"Jasmine Dick," a short block of muscle replied, and spit tobacco juice in an empty Pepsi can.

By the practiced laughter, Anna knew it was an old joke and no doubt what they called Stacy behind his back.

Buoyed along on the Old Boy laughter, Stanton managed to get the whereabouts at the time of the murder of everybody but Greeley and Tom before they caught on.

"Alibis?" Ted asked finally, and raised his eyebrows. "Hey, we're suspects!" This amused them nearly as much as Jasmine Dick. Still, the men who'd cleared themselves looked relieved. "How 'bout it, Tom," Greeley took over for Frederick. "Where were you the night Stacy was tagged?"

"Nowhere," Silva snapped.

"I guess that lets Tom off the hook," Greeley laughed. "Me too. At least nowhere I can say and keep in the lady's good graces."

"Better to keep in mine," Stanton said with a half smile that sobered Ted instantly.

"When I gotta say, I'll say. Not till then," Ted returned sharply. "Break's over." Greeley fixed Anna with a cold look. "You want to make yourself useful? Catch the s.o.b. who's been screwing with my equipment." The men gathered up their cigarettes and left Anna and Frederick in possession of the battered lunch table.

"Well, that was certainly productive," Stanton said. "All non-suspects were in jail with seven nuns at the time of the murder; the two suspects were 'nowhere' and 'nowhere with a lady.'"

"Is Silva a suspect? I don't think he even knew Stacy to say hello to."

"It may end up being a choice between Silva and the chindi," Stanton cautioned.

"Now that you mention it, Silva looked guilty as hell," Anna said.

"If you ever quit rangering, you might try the FBI. I think you've got a flair for this sort of work."

Anna glanced at her watch. "It's three-thirty. Do you want to drop by the Widow Meyers before we quit for the day?"

"Is she all sad-eyed and teary?"

"Nope."

"Looks guilty as hell?"

"I don't think she was in the park that night."

"Too bad."

"She could have made it," Anna said hopefully. "There's a phone call placing her in Farmington at seven P.M. That's only two hours from here. She could have driven up and back in one night easily."

"Well, that is good news," Stanton mocked her amiably.

"Beats chindi."

"Could we have something to eat first?" he asked plaintively. "I'm faint."

"Sorry. I forget."

"Probably how you keep your boyish figure."

Rose was at home. When not shopping in Durango or Farmington, Rose was usually at home. Nature apparently held little allure. The front windows of the bungalow were closed and the shades drawn to shut it firmly out of doors. All the interior lights were ablaze. Rose was on the sofa opposite the wood stove. Magazines—*Self, Money, House Beautiful*—littered the floor. The remains of an iced tea and a plate covered in crumbs held down a pile of like literature on the coffee table.

A single bed, the kind on wheels that folds in half to be rolled into storage, was made up in one corner beneath the window. It was the brightest spot in the room. A cotton coverlet in rich red, green, and blue paisley covered the mattress. Throw pillows in similar colors—some prints, some solids—were tumbled in organized chaos, giving the bed the look of a gay and welcoming nest.

The window above was the only one in the room open, the shade up. Hattie sat cross-legged amid the kaleidoscope of color, holding a sketch pad. Bella had a pad of newsprint propped up against her aunt's thigh. She lay on her belly with her legs bent at the knee, little bare feet in the air. They stopped their work long enough to be introduced to Frederick Stanton.

Rose fussed with the magazines, moving them from one place to another without creating any real order. She was more on edge than Anna had seen her in the past week or so. Though the death was tragic, Anna would have thought the wait would have been worse on the nerves and the conclusion harder on the heart. Short, controlled movements as she stabbed at the clutter and tight muscles around her mouth spoke of something more than anxiety or irritation. Rose was furious.

There was bound to be some anger at Stacy for having had the bad judgment to die—if Rose had not profited by the death—but it was more specific than that. It was directed at Anna.

Frederick was offered a chair and a glass of tea. Anna was snubbed. She was not even invited to sit. Indeed there was no place left to do so. But for Hattie's bed and the couch, Stanton had been given the only chair in the room, an office swivel tucked in the kneehole of an old wooden desk.

Sensing this production of "good cop, bad cop" had already been cast, Anna left the federal agent to question Rose and wandered over to the sunlit bed.

Obligingly, Bella scooted over and Anna sat down, happy in the cheerful disarray. "What are you guys drawing?" she asked to make conversation.

"We're doing landscapes," Bella told her. "Here." She tore off a sheet of newsprint and handed it to Anna. "You can do it too. Put a coloring book under it so you can write on it. You can share my pens."

Obediently, Anna put the paper on the hard cardboard cover of a *Birds of the Southwest* coloring book and selected a pink felt-tipped pen from the pile. "Aren't we supposed to have a landscape to draw from? Or are we just drawing the living room?"

"We're doing *inner* landscapes," Bella said importantly. "Tell her, Aunt Hattie." The little girl dropped the black pen she was drawing with, picked up a dark purple one, and promptly forgot them in her concentration.

Anna looked expectantly at Hattie. The woman stopped sketching and thought for a second. Her hair was pulled up in a knot, curled wisps escaping in all directions from where she'd stored and plucked colored pencils. Seven or eight still resided in her bun, poking out like the spines of a rainbow porcupine.

"We-ell," Hattie said, dragging the word out. "You close your eyes."

Anna waited.

Hattie waited.

Anna realized this was for real and closed her eyes.

"You go down your esophagus."

"That's your throat," Bella volunteered helpfully.

"Turn left at your breastbone."

Anna snuck a peek. Hattie's face was serious.

"Go into your heart."

"Cree-aa-eek." Bella provided the sound of a heavy door opening on rusted hinges.

Maybe because I haven't opened it in a while, Anna thought, caught up in the game.

"Look around you," Hattie continued. "What do you see? Don't tell it, draw it."

Anna wasn't about to tell it. Or draw it. In her mind's heart she'd seen a lot of furniture covered with drop cloths. Molly would have a field day with that one.

To keep her credit good, she drew a picture that was supposed to be of Piedmont. A great orange blob with four legs and a tail. The eyes she made emerald green because Bella didn't have a bronze pen.

Hattie stopped drawing, a frown creasing her otherwise smooth brow. She was looking down at Bella's picture.

The child had made black-and-purple concentric circles filling the page. It looked like the top view of a tornado or a giant whirlpool. In comparison, shrouded furniture seemed perfectly okay for decorating a heart.

"What is that, Bella?" Hattie asked easily, but the worry was still on her face.

"Just colors," Bella replied. "Like in a flower."

More like a bruise, Anna thought.

Stanton and Rose emerged from the kitchen where they'd vanished a while before. Stanton was just finishing a tall iced drink and Anna realized with some annoyance how thirsty she was. After her time on a damp island in Lake Superior, she had forgotten how the arid climate of the southwest could suck the moisture from the human body.

Stanton looked at her lumpy pumpkin-colored drawing. "Are you done?" he asked politely.

"All done."

"Can I see?" Bella asked.

Anna showed the child. "You forgot his whiskers," Bella told her. "If you don't draw him whiskers, he'll run into things. That's how cats know how big the world is. They feel it with their whiskers."

Anna picked up a black pen and began to fill in the missing items. "I'm making them extra long," she said. "In case Piedmont wants to explore the galaxy."

"Good idea," Bella agreed.

"Honey, come here," Rose said to her daughter as Anna

and Frederick let themselves out. "Momma needs to talk to you."

The sun was still high but the angle had changed. Light streamed between the trees in long fingers filled with golden dust. The cicadas had hushed and the bulk of tourists gone from the mesa top.

Loath to confine themselves inside the patrol car after the claustrophobia of Rose Meyers' living room, Anna and Frederick leaned against the Ford, their backs to the bungalow. In front of them a fringe of trees separated the houses and Spruce Canyon. From where they stood the piñon-juniper forest, not a hundred yards wide, seemed to stretch on forever.

"I had fun," Anna said.

"Bully for you. I didn't. The good news is I did get some iced tea."

"Rub it in."

"What's she got against you?" Stanton asked. "The claws were definitely unsheathed whenever your name came up."

"Beats me. Today's hostility is a new development."

"The bad news is we're back to Silva and chindi as far as suspects go—unless Burke or Beavens show some spunk."

"How so?"

"Rose was in Farmington with Ted Greeley."

Anna thought about that for a moment. It fit none of her preconceived notions. "I thought Rose hated Greeley."

"She does. Not only did she say she'd had no inter-course—her word, not mine—with that 'little, little man' since Farmington, but she alibied him through clenched teeth. I got the feeling she'd've rather put him in the gas chamber than admit she'd been with him in Farmington. But she swore to it."

"All night?"

"Most of it."

"Go figure." Anna shook her head, remembering Bella saying the argument her mom had had on the phone with Stacy that Monday night had been over some man. "Maybe we're back to suicide, maybe Stacy couldn't hack another wife cheating on him."

"It's been known to happen." Stanton didn't sound convinced. "No gunshot wound, no knife cuts, no pills, no poison—'it is a good day to die'? Meyers just lay down and willed his life away?"

"Not likely." After Zach died Anna'd tried it enough times to know it didn't work.

"Frederick!" Rose was calling from the front steps. "Do you have Stacy's things? Hills said Anna had taken them."

She made it sound like petty theft. It took Anna a minute to realize what she was referring to.

"His shoes and hat," she said. "I'd forgotten. They're in the trunk," she hollered to Rose as she walked around to the rear of the Ford.

They were still where she'd tossed them the day of the body recovery. The hat was a little the worse for wear, crushed by the toolbox. Anna pushed the dent out. She had to dig under traffic cones, shotgun, and shovel for the shoes.

"Got 'em," she called, and pulled them out. As the clear afternoon light hit them, she sucked in her breath. "Hey, Frederick, come here for a minute."

Reacting to something in her voice, the FBI agent was beside her in seconds.

"Look familiar?" Anna showed him the low-cut cordovan shoes. On the heel of the right and the instep of the left shoe were the same oval burn marks the coroner had described on Stacy's arms.

*   *   *

Sipping the Beaujolais, Anna was careful not to let the wineglass clink against the telephone receiver. She was in no mood for another lecture from her sister on the evils of worshiping Bacchus.

She'd just finished an acerbic account of the interview with Mrs. Meyers. "The green-eyed monster," she said. "One of us is acting like a jealous woman."

"Gee, yah think?" Molly returned sarcastically. "Obviously you had a proprietary interest in her husband, for whatever reasons. Maybe because he had some of the same characteristics as Zach?"

"Maybe because he had a brain. Rare in these backwoods."

Molly laughed. "Your jealousy is obviously rooted deep in childhood trauma and will require umpteen thousand dollars' worth of therapy to root out. What's more interesting is why she's jealous of you—if the anger was inspired by jealousy."

"I sure don't know. Maybe Stacy said something."

"It started before the murder?"

Anna thought about that. "No. After. Way after. I mean she was never My Friend Flicka but the outright hatred is new."

"Something since? She could have found a torrid entry in his diary or an unmailed love letter."

The idea thrilled Anna in a morbid sort of way. She sighed deeply and sucked down some of the red wine.

"Somebody telling tales out of school?" Molly suggested.

"Stacy and I were never together except professionally," Anna said. "It could be all in her head, a way to justify a less than ideal marriage. Looking at it from the outside, it didn't seem to be based on the principles of wellness.

More mutual need than mutual respect and admiration, if you know what I mean."

Molly chortled her evil-sounding chortle. "Why do you think I never married? Nothing like an internship in family counseling to put the fear of matrimony in one's soul."

"I hate feeling jealous!" Anna said with sudden vehemence. She pulled in another draught of wine and felt comforted. "It makes me feel like such a *girl*."

"Ah, yes. Such helpless, emotional creatures. Given to anorexia and fainting fits. Run like a girl, throw like a girl, whistle like a girl."

"My point exactly."

"Stacy's gone on two counts," Molly reasoned. "He's dead and he wasn't yours. I'd recommend you grieve like a girl. Let it run its course. It's not cancer or frostbite, it's just pain."

"Like the phantom pain in an amputated limb?"

"Very like. Not much you can do with a feeling till you give in and feel the damn thing. As long as you mask emotions, anesthetize yourself, the confusion will only get worse."

Anna had the irritating sense that Molly wasn't talking only about jealousy.

"You know, Anna, you don't have to do everything alone. Even out there in the back of beyond there are bound to be support groups." Molly cut the inevitable argument short: "Just think about it. It works. Lord knows why. It's not profitable to us honest shrinks. If there weren't plenty of nuts around to keep me in pin money, I'd keep mum about it."

After that Molly let Anna change the subject and they talked on for a while but it failed to eradicate the hollow feeling behind Anna's breastbone.

When she'd hung up, she sat awhile on her twin bed playing with the fringe of the Mexican blanket that served as a spread.

To the lamp, she said: "I could sure use a good game of Dead Princess long about now."

14

WINTER WAS never far from the high country, and Anna woke into a day cold and dreary enough to remind her how fragile the warmth of summer could be.

Thunderheads pressed low on the mesa but didn't obscure the view. Beneath the lowering gray, black piles of cumulonimbus rolled like billiard balls from the mountains of Arizona to the Colorado buttes. Through the thin walls of the dormitory, Anna heard the grind of thunder.

Helitack crew would be delighted; good fire weather. Lightning could bury itself deep in a juniper and smolder for days. When the weather let up and the fuels dried there might be hazard pay all around.

Throwing back the covers, Anna leaped out of bed. In the lowlands around Lake Superior weather fronts, with their attendant changes in pressure, gave her headaches. Not so the mountain storms. Cracking thunder and flashing lightning filled the air with ozone till it tingled in the lungs, rejuvenating body and spirit much the same as the air at the seaside or near waterfalls.

Having braided her hair off her face, she jammed herself into uniform and, catlike to avoid getting wet, ran from the dorm to her patrol car. Thunderstorms made for good thinking weather: the tourists were chased safely indoors and the brass wouldn't venture out and so catch one cogitating.

Anna drove the short distance to the Far View cafeteria parking lot and pointed the nose of the Ford toward the panorama of northern New Mexico. Many-tined forks of lightning in the grand tradition of Frankenstein movies shattered a slate sky. Virga fell in curtains, now obscuring, now lifting to reveal a distant butte or valley. Colors were muted, the greens almost black, the reds of the earth somber.

The car radio was tuned to National Public Radio and something vaguely high-toned was being played on a harpsichord. The ordered gentility of the music and the wild vagaries of the weather suited Anna, and she rolled down the window to better enjoy the concert.

Special Agent Stanton had taken Stacy's shoes with their odd marks to Durango so they could be sent to the lab in Hobbs, New Mexico, for analysis. Since she'd been assigned to him for the duration, she wasn't on Hills' schedule. The day was pretty much hers to do with as she pleased.

She took the lid off her plastic coffee mug and took a sip. Once she'd had a severe coffee habit but luxury had cured it. After she'd begun fresh-grinding beans and using heavy whipping cream, the brew with nondairy powders found in most offices didn't tempt her in the least. However, two cups of the good stuff each morning was a ritual she never missed.

Anna unbuckled her seat belt, rearranged the .357 and cuffs, and settled in for some serious thinking. Humanity, thus examined, struck her as sordid. Rose and Ted Greeley

having their affair—or whatever it was they were having—in a motel in Farmington with little Bella . . . where?
Left in the car? Packed off to a movie? Anger and disrespect—at least from Rose's side—the hallmark of the en-
counter.

Drew's love of Bella seemed a bright spot in this dreary
landscape but it too was tinged with anger. For reasons of
his own he was tilting at what Anna hoped was a wind-
mill: the abuse of that lovely child. To Anna's way of
thinking the operations might cause less pain in the long
run than fighting the good fight against prejudice.

Tom and Patsy Silva held together even after divorce by
greed on Patsy's side and some as yet inexplicable obsession on Tom's. A fixation that had gone from an alarming
but active harassment phase to an even more alarming but
passive stalker phase.

Jamie and her posthumous affair with Stacy—in the
past two days it had gone from "dear friend" to "dearest
friend." A bizarre form of psychological necrophilia, rare
but, according to Anna's sister, not unheard of. Molly
lamented the loss of the melodrama that had been such a
part of American life before the turn of the century. A time
when people took themselves more seriously, were less
bored, less sophisticated. A time when widows wore black
veils, the occasional duel was fought, and, though there
were no documented incidents of it, people were believed
to die of shame and of love.

The human animal needed its dramas, the psychiatrist
believed. Denied, it sought them in unhealthy ways. Like
imagined romances with dead married men. This last
thought struck too close to home. Made physically uncomfortable by the parallel between her and Burke, Anna
literally squirmed in her seat.

An affair with a dead married man. "That's got to be it," she exclaimed. Taken back to her nonexistent romance with Stacy, she flashed on their one rendezvous: the curtailed cocktail hour at Far View Lounge. Ted Greeley had been there. Anna remembered him making a mock toast as she grabbed Stacy's arm, remembered the leer he was passing off as a smile.

That's why Rose was so hostile. In the last couple of days Greeley must have told her, or led her to believe, Anna had been having an affair with her husband.

"Damn!" Anna struck the steering wheel with an open palm. Everything seemed so sordid. Everything.

Lightning struck through the looping black clouds, the wide fork straddling the valley between Chapin and Park mesas. Automatically Anna began to count "one Mississippi, two—" Thunder drowned out the thought. The strike had been less than a mile away.

She took another sip of excellent coffee and leaned back, letting past conversations with and about Rose drift through her mind. Why hadn't Rose said right off the bat that she was with Greeley in Farmington? It certainly got her off the hook more effectively than one seventeen-minute phone call several hours before the murder. Embarrassment over being caught in a compromising position? Possibly, but had she been up front about it, no one need have known. It was the nineties. No one believed dinner— even a late dinner—with a member of the opposite sex doomed a woman to wear the scarlet "A."

Earlier in the investigation Rose had been pointing the finger at Greeley. A lovers' quarrel now patched up? Love me or go to the gas chamber? Anna shook her head. The facts, if such a hodgepodge of information and instincts could be labeled that, didn't support the theory. Stanton said Rose was loath to let the contractor off the hook, said she hadn't seen or spoken to "that little, little man" since Farmington.

Rain came down more heavily, blowing in sheets against the windshield, and Anna was forced to roll up her window or drown.

Rose's hostility had sprung full blown less than an hour after Stanton had questioned Greeley in the maintenance shop. Ergo, whatever had turned Rose against Anna had occurred recently, within the last couple of days. If Anna was right, and Rose's ire stemmed from jealousy, and that jealousy was ignited by Greeley, then Rose had lied. She had "had intercourse" with that "little, little man" since Farmington.

Did Greeley invent Stacy's infidelity so Rose would be less reticent to expose hers, thus giving them both an alibi?

Surely Greeley was aware it also gave them both a motive.

Sharp rapping at the window startled Anna out of her reverie. She yelped in a decidedly unrangerlike fashion and slopped coffee on her knee. Adding insult to injury, a kindly-looking elderly woman under an enormous black-and-white umbrella said, "Sorry to wake you up," as Anna rolled down the window. "Could you tell me how far it is to the cliff dwellings?"

After the information was disseminated, Anna opted to move her brown study to a less accessible locale. More because it was secluded than for its ghoulish ambience, she chose the closed section of Cliff Palace. In her exalted capacity as the FBI guy's chauffeur, the ruin was still open to her.

Weather had driven the tourists from the lesser-known

sites but Cliff was doing a booming, if soggy, business. It was one of the most famous cliff dwellings in the world. Visitors, some on the mesa for only a day, had traveled from as far away as Japan, Germany, Australia. Come hell or high water, they would see Cliff Palace.

Tucked up in the ruin, out of sight lest she stir envy in lesser beings, Anna felt her privilege. Deep within the alcove she was completely dry and out of the wind, yet privy to the wondrous perfume the rain struck from a desert land. One hundred feet below the mesa top, Cliff Palace was still several hundred feet above the bottom of Cliff Canyon. Anna had a lovely view out past ruined walls and turrets. Along the canyon rims rainwater had begun to pour over the sandstone, cascading down in thin ribbons of silver.

Near Jug House, a closed ruin on Wetherill Mesa, there was a stone reservoir built at the bottom of such a pourover. The archaeologists surmised it could have been a tank to save the water. Anna was surprised there wasn't one at every ruin, but then the Anasazi were such accomplished potters, perhaps they had caught and stored rainwater in earthenware vessels.

Impromptu waterfalls delighted the tourists as much as they did Anna. From her hiding place she could hear the occasional squeal of pleasure. Leaning back on her hands, Anna let the sounds wash over her. She couldn't identify with Jamie's need to invent supernatural phenomena. As far as Anna was concerned these were the spirit veils. Common miracles that never lost their power to stir the human soul.

Just for the hell of it, she said a vague, nondenominational prayer for the spirit of Stacy Meyers.

Feet dangling into the abandoned kiva, the white noise

of running water and muted voices to still her mind, she let the world settle around her. Details came sharply into focus: a small handprint in black on the alcove overhead, the stark slash of a vulture's feather fallen in the center of an ancient building block, concentric circles marking the butt of a centuries-dead juniper hacked down by stone axes.

Half an hour melted away. No earth-shaking realizations came to her, no revelations as to why Greeley might have told Rose she and Stacy were having an affair. No guesses as to why Rose lied about having communicated with Greeley after the night of the murder; whether Beavens lied to Jamie when he said he saw the veil or lied to Anna when he said he didn't.

Hunger and cold overcame pastoral beauty and her thoughts began to turn materialistic. She stood and slapped some life into her rear end, then surreptitiously made her way back to the populated areas of the ruin.

A tall gray-haired interpreter, a retired philosophy professor from San Francisco State, was talking to a group of people near the tower. His long arms, encased in NPS green, semaphored information and enthusiasm.

Claude Beavens held down the post at the mouth of the alcove. Not only was he not speaking to the visitors but he also didn't seem interested in them even as statistics. Anna could see the silver counter dangling from an elastic band around his wrist. Binoculars obscured the upper half of his face. Because of the rain, birds were roosting, deer tucked up somewhere dry, and Anna wondered what he stared at so intently. She followed the direction of his gaze down Cliff Canyon toward Ute reservation lands. Without the assistance of field glasses, she couldn't see anything out of the ordinary.

"What've you got?" she asked. Beavens jumped as if she'd goosed him with a cattle prod.

"Nothing!" he snapped, pulling the binoculars from around his neck as if they could testify against him.

"No law against looking," Anna reassured him.

A visitor stopped beside them and asked what the Anasazi used for bathrooms. Beavens escaped into an earnest discussion of waste disposal in thirteen hundred A.D.

Anna stepped up to the rock where he'd been holding his vigil and looked down the canyon. All seemed to be as it always was. Then it came to her. "Somewhere out there Jamie's spirit veil does its elusive thing, doesn't it?" she asked as the visitor moved on.

"Who knows?" he said with his signature shrug. Whatever it was, it had ceased to interest him and, so, to be of much interest to Anna.

She was not sorry to reach her patrol car. Not only was it warm, dry, and upholstered, but a moving vehicle was one of the few places in the modern world a person had some semblance of privacy. Cellular phones were an abomination. Along with bullet-proof vests and panty hose, it was a piece of equipment she'd never submit to. The radio was intrusion enough.

Driving back to the chief ranger's office, she went as slowly as the traffic would allow. There was something about rain that opened the doors to dreaming. The steady beat, a softening of the edges of things, promoted a meditative state that unraveled the threads of linear thought. The drift was restful and Anna found herself glad to be freed from Stanton's sharp mind for the day.

Through the CRO's windows she saw enough gray and green to color a medium-sized swamp. The office was clogged with rangers holing up till the rain stopped. Not quite ready to rejoin the real world, she ducked around the building to the balcony in back. Set as it was into the side of Spruce Canyon, the front of the chief's office was only one story high, its door opening directly onto the walk to the museum. The rear of the building was comprised of two stories. A heavy wooden balcony framed in the blocky saw-cut gingerbread of the southwest provided a picture-perfect view down into the canyon. On the far rim three silvery ribbons fell from pour-overs smoothed into troughs edging the cliff top. Through a screen of huge pine trees, black now with turkey vultures sitting out the storm, was Spruce Tree House; one hundred and fourteen rooms and eight kivas tucked neatly into a natural alcove.

The timbers framing the balcony were dark with water. A sand-filled standing ashtray and a bench built in the same massive style as the framing were the only furnishings.

To Anna's relief there was only one visitor seeking sanctuary there. A woman in an ankle-length cranberry slicker and a canary yellow nor'easter hat stood near the far corner looking at the sky where the storm was darkest. Clouds hung down in bruised mammalia. Lightning was generated not only between heaven and earth but from cloud to cloud, as if the gods fought among themselves.

The woman turned slightly and bent her head. Anna amended her earlier census: there were two seekers of sanctuary. A child sat on the wide railing, enfolded securely in an ample cranberry embrace.

It was Hattie and Bella. Somehow they didn't qualify as destroyers of solitude and Anna was surprised to find she was glad to see them. Lest she be the one to shatter the peace, she slipped quietly onto the bench and watched the lightning play against curtains of rain.

Thunder's grumbling was foreshadowed and echoed by faint feral sounds closer to home. Soon Anna lost interest in the meteorological show and watched Bella and her aunt with rapt attention.

They were growling.

Because of the innocence that blessed both faces, the sight was not frightening but it was disturbing. Bella Meyers' perfect little mouth was pulled back into a square, exposing small white teeth. Her cheeks pushed up till they made slits of her eyes, and her hands—at least the one Anna could see clutching the sleeve of Hattie's raincoat—were curled into a caricature of a claw.

The growls, nearly soft as purrs, were not amusing. There was too much anger for that. Bella snarled and clawed at something very real—at least to her. What kept the scene from being alarming or, worse, pathetic, was the power. A definite force, even in so small a girl, commanded respect. It was not the desperate anger of helplessness. It had focus. And, too, the child was safe in the loving arms of her aunt.

Growling at the universe isn't half scary when you know you're loved, Anna thought.

Hattie was snapping and snarling too, but her fury was diluted. Maturity and understanding had undermined the purity of her attack. Hers was more of a supportive growl, giving Bella's anger confirmation.

The minutes passed. The storm moved to the south. Bella's growls and snarls grew less ferocious. Hattie rested her chin on top of the child's head and hugged her tightly. Finally the last little "grrr" was squeezed out and they stood still as statues. The rain stopped.

"Well. I guess that's that," Hattie said.

"Sure is," Bella returned with satisfaction. Using her

bottom as a fulcrum and her aunt's arms as a brace, the little girl levered her legs over the rail and slid to the balcony floor.

"Hi, Anna," she said, apparently unsurprised. "Aunt Hattie and me were making it storm. But mostly me because I'm the maddest."

"You sure cooked up a doozy," Anna said. "I practically got drowned."

"Everybody did," Bella said, unrepentant. "Even the vultures."

"How did you make it storm?"

Bella pulled herself up on the bench beside Anna and patted the seat, inviting her aunt to join them. "Aunt Hattie taught me. First you have to be really, really, *really* mad. Then you screw it all up into a ball and put it right here." She reached up and tapped the middle of Anna's brow where the Hindus often drew the mystical third eye. "Then you just point it at some clouds and order them to do it."

"Ah," Anna said.

"It helps if they're the black piley-up ones."

The three of them were quiet for a minute, just sitting in a row listening to the pine needles drip. "Do you say something like 'Rain, rain, don't go away, come and stay today'?" Anna asked after a while.

"No." Bella sounded as if that was an exceedingly stupid question and Anna felt as if she'd asked Willard Scott what he meant by partly cloudy. "You talk cloud language," Bella explained, and growled for Anna—but not too loudly lest it unleash another deluge.

"You must have been really, really, *really* mad," Anna said. "That was one of the best storms I've ever seen."

"I was pretty mad," Bella conceded.

"What were you mad at?"

Bella looked at her aunt.

"You can be mad at anybody you want to, honey. It's okay. Sometimes I even get mad at your uncle Edwin."

"Really, *really* mad?"

"Yup. Sometimes I get really mad at God."

Bella looked impressed.

"She doesn't mind one bit," Hattie said. "She probably gets mad at the angels sometimes."

"When would anybody get mad at an angel?" Bella asked skeptically.

"Maybe when they're molting," Anna offered. "Dropping feathers all over heaven."

That seemed to make sense. "Okay." Bella dropped her voice to a whisper. "I'm really, really mad at Momma." She waited. No stray lightning bolt struck. With greater confidence, she added: "Rose is a thorny, thorny, morny, dorny, thorny old Rose."

Anna laughed and Bella was offended. "What're you mad at your mom about," Anna asked to win the child back but it was too late.

"Can't tell you," Bella said, and jumped down from the bench.

"Why not?" Now Anna was offended.

"Because Momma said blood's sicker than water."

"I can't argue with that."

"Nope."

The sun was beginning to peek through. Hattie and Bella left. Anna waited a few more minutes to allow the newly clement weather time to lure the crowd out of the office, then walked around to the front door. Jennifer Short sat on the table behind the counter swinging her legs and eating candy out of a jar Frieda kept stocked. Her hair was squashed flat against her head from crown to ears, then stuck out at right angles.

"Idn't it awful," she was complaining to Frieda. "Ah feel like something out of a horror flick. The one that goes crazy and hacks everybody up at the slumber party."

"Terminal Hat Head," Frieda contributed. "Occupational hazard." The dispatcher sat behind her desk, her computer for once dark, the radio mike near her right hand.

"Hey," Jennifer greeted Anna.

"Howdy." Anna leaned her elbows on the counter. Beneath the sheet of glass that topped it were maps of the park and surrounding areas. "Talked to Patsy lately?" she asked Frieda when it became obvious she'd killed the conversation in progress.

"Matter of fact." Frieda laughed her delicious laugh. "She's doing okay but Tom's got her and the girls all atwitter."

"She'd better be careful," Anna said. "Stalking is stalking, not flattery. This guardian-angel-in-a-Chevy-truck routine strikes me as a bubble or two off plumb. I think Tom is one weird guy."

"I think Tom Silva's cute," Jennifer said. "Kee-ee-yoot."

"Better watch out," Anna kidded her. "Remember what happened to the last guy you thought was cute."

"Serves Stacy right for bein' married," Jennifer retorted. "All the good ones are married."

"All the good ones are dead," Anna said before she thought.

She was rewarded with an awkward silence and averted eyes.

"Guess I better look like I'm doing something constructive." Jennifer smashed her hat down over the ruined hairdo and swaggered toward the door. It wasn't braggadocio, Anna knew from experience. For a short woman there was no place left for the arms once the gunbelt was strapped in place.

"I should too," Anna said. Grabbing a handful of Frieda's butterscotch candies, she made her way back to the eight-by-six-foot cubbyhole that served as an office for Hills, the fire management officer, Anna, half a dozen seasonals, and the Xerox machine.

Her desk was nearly as bad a rat's nest as Hills', and most of the rubble wasn't of her making. Space shared—shared with Homo sapiens who'd not yet attained their thirtieth birthdays—was reduced to chaos. Anna preferred order and knew herself to have entered upon that stage of the game Molly dubbed the Pre-Curmudgeon Warm-ups.

Everything that wasn't hers she scraped into an accordion envelope, marked it "The Poltergeist File," and stowed it in the kneehole under Hills' desk. Before anyone dared to dig that deep the stuff would be transmogrified into historical artifacts by the sheer passage of time.

To impose some semblance of organization, she unearthed all the 10-343 Case Incident and 10-344 Criminal Incident reports that had been turned in since the beginning of the tourist season in April. Thanks to Frieda, they had all been neatly filed in chronological order. Hills hadn't yet found the time to stir them into his ongoing stew of papers.

Anna separated out all the incidents that had occurred in or around Cliff Palace and ordered them again according to date. The last was the report she had written on the discovery and evacuation of Stacy Meyers' body.

Reading through it, the day was re-created in her mind but no new details or connections were generated.

Slouching down in the chair, she put her feet up. More blood to the brain. Again she read the report. Words on a page: no leaps of logic, no sparks of genius.

Putting the 344 aside, she picked up the sheaf of 343s and thumbed through them. Most were medicals: broken wrist, respiratory failure, anxiety attack, tachycardia w/confusion, asthma, fractured C-spine from a kiva diver—the local parlance for tourists who tumbled into the underground rooms.

Anna selected out all the evacuations. But for the wrist and the C-spine, each carry-out was in some way, shape, or form a heart, brain, or breathing difficulty. Not unusual at seven thousand feet with a high percentage of elderly visitors. She set the two fractures aside and looked through the remaining reports.

Pretty standard stuff; the only thing peculiar was the number of them. Anna carried the file into an ex–coat closet now pressed into service as a computer room and called up all the 343s for six summers past. Even accounting for the steady increase in tourism, medical evacuations had quadrupled at Cliff Palace this season. She checked reports for Balcony House and Spruce Tree House. They had remained more or less constant.

"Frieda, are you busy?" she hollered.

"Always."

"Too busy?"

"What do you want?"

"Computer-nerd stuff."

"Come here then, I can't leave the front desk."

With Anna breathing down her neck, Frieda used D-Base to cross-reference all the evacuations by the patients' point of origin, age, sex, race, and primary complaint. "Looks like a normal group," Frieda said. "Old people and sick people. You were expecting somebody else?"

"I don't know what I was expecting." Anna sat down on Frieda's desk and looked through the reports again: ten-thirty, eleven o'clock, eleven-eighteen, April twelfth, twenty-sixth, May third, twenty-fourth, and thirty-first, June seventh, June fourteenth. "Try by time."

Frieda complied. "All but two were in the morning."

That was something. The usual time for rescue excitement was midafternoon, when the day's heat was setting in. "Try by date."

"Hey ho." Frieda clicked the keys. "Well, lookie there!"

"What?" Anna demanded.

"All but two—the afternoon ones—fell on Tuesday. And I thought Mondays were tough . . . Coincidence?"

"Got to be," Anna said. "Thanks, Frieda."

Back at her own desk Anna fanned out the reports now reduced by two, the two neither in the morning nor on a Tuesday. "What do I know now?" she whispered to herself.

"What?" Frieda called.

"Nothing," Anna answered both her own question and the dispatcher's. She pored over the paltry bits of information she had gathered. Rose lied about when and where she'd seen Greeley both the night of the murder and since.

Greeley was still grousing about the sugar in his D-14 Cat's fuel tank. The murder had so overshadowed it there'd been no further investigation to speak of.

"Hey, Frieda," Anna interrupted herself. "Do private vendors like Greeley have to show proof of insurance before they're hired?"

"Yes. Too much liability otherwise. Why?"

"Just wondering." Even if Stacy had been the sugar-slinging chain swinger, his ecotage had been aborted. Had he succeeded, all Greeley would have suffered was a fat

check from the insurance company—not even much in the
way of inconvenience or delay. Greeley killing Meyers to
avenge the Caterpillar was absurd.

Tom Silva was sullen and scared or angry—Anna couldn't
tell which. Beavens was lying to somebody, either to her or
to Jamie about his veil sighting. His report of leaving before the other interpreters had yet to be checked out.
Jamie was claiming a closer kinship with the deceased
than Anna believed existed and riding the revenge of the
Anasazi theory pretty hard. She had even filed a backcountry permit to hold a vigil all night in the fatal kiva.
The request had been denied.

How any of that tied in with seven evacuations from
Cliff, all cardiopulmonary or central nervous system problems, all early in the day on a Tuesday, Anna couldn't
fathom.

An unpleasant thought wandered through her tired
mind. "No," she breathed as she dragged a calendar from
the middle of a pile. On it she marked all the days of the
evacuations with a tiny, faint "X" in pencil. Forgetting her
gun and radio, she took the calendar over to the museum.

Jamie Burke was working the front desk. Several visitors clustered around a single brochure arguing over the
drawing of Mesa Verde's road system. Jamie stood behind
the counter, her elbows resting on the glass, reading Louis
L'Amour's *Haunted Mesa*.

"Got a minute?" Anna asked.

Jamie raised her head with a practiced look of long-
suffering patience. When she saw it was Anna, she relaxed. "I'm stuck here till five-thirty."

Anna pushed the calendar over the glass. "Could you
mark the veil sightings for me, if you remember when they
were?"

Jamie studied the calendar for a minute, then borrowed Anna's pen. "April the eleventh, May twenty-third, the thirteenth of June, and, no matter what he says now, Claude saw one on the twenty-first." As she counted each day she made a big black check mark on the page.

"Thanks." Anna gathered up the calendar without looking at it and tucked her pen back in her shirt pocket.

"Aren't you going to tell me what this is all about?" Jamie asked.

"When it gels," Anna lied easily.

Back at her desk in the CRO, she took out the calendar and studied it. All alleged veil sightings were on Monday nights before the Tuesday morning medical evacuations.

"Damn."

"What?" Frieda hollered.

"I said I'm calling it a day, giving up the ghost, so to speak."

Chindi.

"Pshaw!" Anna used her sister's word for "expletive deleted."

15

"YOU SHOW me yours, I'll show you mine," Stanton said.

"No dice. Yours first."

Stanton hummed the first few bars of "Getting to Know You" from *The King and I* and Anna laughed. There'd been too many times on Isle Royale when he'd gotten her to share more than she intended, then failed to return the favor.

"I got the marks on the shoes analyzed," he said. "You know what amazed me the most?"

Anna waited.

"That the NPS actually makes you wear them. They're symptomatic of a severe fashion disorder."

"The marks . . ." Anna prompted.

"Yes. The marks. They were spaced right for finger-prints." She and Stanton were sitting on the ledge above the Cliff Palace ruin, a wide chunk of sandstone tucked up in the shadows under the trees. In front of them stone fanned out in an apron to the cliff's edge, then there was darkness; the gulf of Cliff Canyon. Beyond the black was another pale ribbon where the far side of the canyon cut down through reservation lands. Even without a moon the sandstone picked up illumination from the night sky, reflecting back the dim glow of starlight. The soft down-canyon wind brought on by cooling air settling had died and the air was absolutely still.

Stanton scrunched his legs up more tightly, hugging his knees to his chest, and sucked air through an architecturally generous nose.

"Sitting on a cold rock in the dark is so much more fun than crawling into bed after a long day. Wish I'd thought of this years ago."

"You were showing me yours."

"You've no romance in your soul, Anna. Too many years hobnobbing with Mother Nature. Too pragmatic a lady for my money. In south Chicago we know what moonlight's all about."

"Moon's not up."

"In Chicago we have glorious streetlights and we can turn them on whenever we want. But have it your way. Showing you mine." He dropped a long arm down and snatched off his shoe without untying it. The white sock was pulled partway off and dangled trunklike over the rock. "The marks were here, here, and here on the right shoe." He placed his thumb and two fingers so the thumb was on the inside of the shoe and the index and middle fingers on the outside, his palm cupping the heel, as if the shoe walked on his hand.

"They weren't smudges so much as burns. Something reacted with the leather and caused the discolorations."

"Funny I never noticed them till the other day," Anna said.

"They may not have shown up right away."

"Any idea what made them?"

"Acid—what kind he didn't know." Stanton studied the

shoe. "But looky." He held it up at eye level, still grasping it with his palm beneath the heel. "We can figure Meyers didn't pull it off himself. It wouldn't be impossible to take your own shoe off with your hand in this position, but highly unlikely."

"So something with caustic digits removed his shoes after he was dead?" Anna teased.

"That seems to about sum it up."

"That fits hand in glove with what I've come up with."

"Goody." He stretched his legs out in front of him and waggled his feet. His bare shins gleamed in the starlight. "Now do I get to find out why I'm sitting on a rock in the middle of the night instead of curled snug in my little bed?"

"We're on chindi patrol."

Stanton groaned.

"I'm getting overtime," Anna added helpfully.

"I'm exempt."

"Too bad. This promises to be a long one." Anna told him her story of carry-outs and spirit veil sightings, Monday nights and Tuesday mornings, and left him to flounder with cause and effect.

He continued wagging his feet as if transfixed by the metronomic motion. "Ms. Burke lying?" he suggested after a minute or two. "Putting her paranormal next to the normal to lend it credence?"

"I wouldn't put it past her, but I didn't tell her when the medicals were or why I wanted the sighting dates."

"Could she have gotten the dates of the medicals out of the files?"

"I suppose. She doesn't have a key to the CRO and it would cause comment if she came in and looked through the files. They're no guarded secret or anything, interps just never look at them, so it'd be something to gossip about when who's sleeping with whom grew thin."

"Could she get into the office at night, when no gossips were about?"

"Sure. Somebody'd probably let her in if she asked. Security—except for the administration building—is pretty lax. It seems a stretch though. Why bother? She never bothers to substantiate any of her other stories. Anyway, at least one Monday night I heard her talking about the veil and then the next day we had that medical. There's no way she could've planned to have all the cardiopulmonary and central nervous system problems occur on Tuesday mornings."

"Was she on duty each time there was a carry-out?"

Anna thought about it. Near as she could remember, she was.

"Jamie Burke, Medicine Woman." Stanton bounced his eyebrows suggestively. Light and shadow dappled his fair skin, and Anna realized the moon had risen.

"Wouldn't Jamie love that," she said. "She's an opportunistic actor. Takes every chance to dash out on stage. But I doubt she has the tenacity to write the script to that extent."

"If she didn't set it up and she's not lying, then we really are out here waiting for the dead to walk."

"When you've ruled out the impossible, whatever's left . . ."

They sat awhile without speaking. Anna was enjoying herself. A smear of lights over Farmington, fifty miles distant, was the only flaw in a perfect sky. Deep in the canyon an owl called and was answered.

"So write me your autobiography and we'll get this life-long friendship rolling," Stanton dropped into the stillness.

Anna would have laughed but, remembering how sound carried in these natural amphitheaters, settled for a smile.

"Aw, come on," Stanton pleaded. "Since we can't have cheeseburgers and coffee out of paper cups, that's the next best thing for making this feel like a real stakeout."

If an expectant stare indicated anything, he was serious. Suddenly Anna felt shy.

"Just start any old where," he encouraged.

"Well, I was born naked—"

"Not the ishy parts! I don't want to know you that well."

"I thought you should know the worst if we're to be lifelong friends."

"Okay then. Ever married?"

"You consider that the worst?"

"My ex-wives did."

It was Anna's turn for raised eyebrows, metaphorically if not literally. *"Wives?"*

"Two."

"Children?"

"Several."

"Ages?"

"Oooh, that's a toughie. Thirteen going on fourteen—second marriage. Nineteen and twenty-three—introductory marriage. Girl, girl, boy, respectively."

Anna revised her estimate of Stanton's age from late thirties to mid forties. She didn't ask what had happened. Once or twice in the past, when she was feeling excessively polite or nosy, she'd asked that question. Nothing new happened under the sun and certainly not before the altar.

"You ever married?" Stanton asked again.

"Yes."

"Died?"

"How'd you guess?"

"A lady who finds corpses on sunken ships and in kivas wouldn't be so bourgeois as to be divorced. No glamour, no drama."

A pang of embarrassment let Anna know he was right. Like other widows, especially young widows, she was prone to wearing her weeds like a badge of honor. Widowhood conferred a mystery and status divorce lacked. The difference between returning World War II and Vietnam veterans. Both had been through a war, but a judgmental public conferred glory only on those who had been victimized in a socially acceptable manner. In divorce, as in a police action, nobody truly won and everybody got wounded.

"You know the only reason Romeo and Juliet didn't get a divorce is because they died first," Stanton said.

A rustling stirred the pine needles behind them. "Are there snakes?" he demanded abruptly.

"Snakes don't tend to be nocturnal. They're too cold-blooded."

"Most of the cold-blooded creatures in Chicago are exclusively nocturnal."

"Our tarantulas come out at night," Anna offered.

"Stop that!" He pulled his legs up again. "Don't tell me that. You're such a bully."

"So tell me about the dead guy," he said after he'd gotten himself arranged in a defensive posture.

"I already told you all I know and then some."

"Not the kiva dead guy, the dead guy you're married to."

Anna noticed he didn't use the past tense and wondered if he'd tapped into her idiosyncrasies. "Neurosis," she heard her sister's voice in her mind. "Spade for spade." All at once she felt terribly tired. A middle-aged lady up past her bedtime sitting on a rock in the dark.

Stanton was still looking at her, his face open and interested. Briefly, Anna thought of what she might tell him, wondered if it would have the cathartic effect of confession. Or if she'd merely paint the old pattern of the perfect marriage. Romeo and Juliet Go To New York.

"Nothing's perfect," she said finally. "It was a long time ago."

Stanton laid a hand on her arm. At first she resented his pity, then realized that wasn't inherent in the gesture. He was shutting her up, pointing to the west where a quarter mile distant the walls of an ancient ruin appeared in a flicker of light then vanished again into darkness. The effect was unsettling, as if, like Brigadoon, the pueblo had appeared momentarily in the twentieth century.

"Headlights," Anna shattered the illusion. "That's Sun Temple. It's on another part of the mesa but your headlights rake across it when you come around the bend before the Cliff Palace parking lot."

"The last ranger sweeping out leftover tourists?" Stanton ventured.

Anna shook her head. "Too late. Jennifer went out of service at midnight." She squeezed the tiny button on the left side of her watch and squinted at the barely illuminated numbers. "It's after one. Probably interps. Maybe Jennifer gave them the key. They may be out for the same reason we are." Levering herself up, she stomped some blood back into her feet. "Might as well go after them. We're legal; they're not: in a closed area without a permit."

"A firing offense?"

"Definitely a calling-on-the-carpet offense."

The roar of an engine followed after the lights. "Sounds like a truck." Following the deer trail they'd taken to the mesa's edge, Anna began threading her way quickly through the junipers.

"You must have eyes like a cat," Stanton complained.

She stopped, took the mag light off her duty belt, and shone it back down the trail for him. He wasn't far behind. When he chose he could move quietly.

The sound of an engine being gunned stopped them both. "Saw the patrol car," Anna said. She began to run and heard Stanton follow. In less than three minutes they reached the parking lot but the truck was gone. "Rats."

"No lights and sirens?" he asked as she backed the patrol car out.

"They have no place to go," Anna reminded him. "We'll catch them at the gate unless they left it open." Still, she drove as fast as the winding road permitted. Partly to catch the offending vehicle and partly for the sheer fun of it.

"Whee!" Stanton said, and pulled his lap belt tighter.

"Three-one-two, three-zero-one." The radio commanded their attention.

"That's you," Stanton said. "Boy, you've got an exciting job. Wish I were a park ranger."

"Stick with me. You may get to see a dog off leash." Anna picked up the mike and responded with her call number. Three-zero-one was Frieda's personal number.

"Are you still on duty, Anna?"

"Yes. I'm on Cliff Palace loop with Agent Stanton. We've a vehicle in a closed area."

"You may have to leave it. There's a disturbance at Patsy Silva's residence. It sounds serious. Al called. She said she's heard shouting and what she thinks might be gunshots."

"I'm headed that direction. See if you can't get some-body else out of bed to lend me moral support."

"Ten-four. Three-zero-one, zero-one-thirty-four."

Anna made an educated guess that the instigator of this particular melee was Tom Silva and refreshed Stanton on the Silvas' post-matrimonial relationship.

"Bet you're glad I'm along," he said smugly.

"And why would that be?"

"You'll need somebody to calm the hysterical wife while you're disarming and subduing the enraged husband."

Anna laughed. "You've got the more dangerous of the two jobs."

"I wish you were kidding."

She took the turn at the Three-Way too fast and scared herself into taking her foot out of the carburetor. By the time they reached the four-way intersection she'd slowed to a safer speed.

The gate was closed and the chain in place.

"We couldn't have been far behind. Where's the truck?" Stanton demanded.

"They hid out somewhere along the way. Looped back around or ducked up a fire road. We won't catch them tonight."

In the headlights she could see the padlock's arm was through the chain links but not clicked closed. "The gate is false-locked," she told Stanton. "Get it for me, would you?"

Stanton complied, relocking the chain behind him. "Maybe we'll get lucky, lock 'em in."

Anna's thoughts had moved ahead to the upcoming fes-tivities. Shortly before reaching the tower house, she told Frieda she had arrived on scene, then opened the car win-dow and turned off the headlights. Moonlight was enough to see by.

"Stealth ranger?" Stanton whispered as the car crept up the short drive.

"The dark is my friend," Anna quoted a self-defense instructor from the Federal Law Enforcement Training Center in Georgia.

The Silvas' residence was dark and, at the moment, quiet. Anna grabbed her flashlight from the recharger and pushed open the car door. Stanton folded himself out his side. "This is the creepy part," he whispered.

For a moment they stood in silence not softened even by the hum of night insects or the rustling of predators and prey. Just when they'd come to count on it, the stillness was destroyed by the sound of shattering glass and shouting. "Goddamn you, Pats! Let me in. Jesus, Mary, an' Joseph, listen to me, for Crissake!" Fierce pounding followed.

"Ahh. Better," Stanton said. "Now we know where he is and his church of choice."

"It's Tom." Quietly, Anna led the way up the flagstone walk curling around the building. Behind the jut of the square kitchen, set into the curved wall of the tower, was the front and only door. It and the small porch protecting it were wooden. The rest of the dwelling was stone.

"You're a dead woman if you don't let me in!" came a cry so slurred it hardly sounded like Silva.

Anna switched on the flashlight. In her peripheral vision she saw Stanton melt out of the moonlight into the shadows as the beam spotlighted the man on the doorstep.

Looking like a refugee from the movie set of *Bus Stop*, Tom Silva, in Levi's, boots, an open white shirt, and battered straw cowboy hat, leaned on the front door. Both arms were raised, fists balled, propping him up. He rested his forehead against the wood. The hat was pushed to the back of his head.

"Tom," Anna said softly.

"Gun," Stanton said just as quietly, his voice penetrating from the shadows.

Almost swallowed up in Silva's right fist was a derringer. Anna took her .357 from its holster and trained it on him. "Tom," she said again. "Put the gun down. It's Anna."

Silva turned. The act unbalanced him and he stumbled backward, his shoulders crashing into the planks. The derringer sparked in the light as his arm swung up. Anna's stomach lurched and her finger tensed on the trigger but he was only shading his eyes with the weapon, squinting to see past the glare.

"Fucking idiot." Shaken by the anger adrenaline leaves behind, Anna said: "You just nearly scared me into shooting you, you know that? Put that gun down. Slow! Don't you dare scare me like that again."

"Anna?" Tom staggered half a step forward then fell back once more against the support of the door. "*Ranger* Anna? No shit?"

"The gun," Anna reminded him. "Put it down."

Tom brought the derringer in front of his face and studied it. Anna's breath caught at the movement. She was becoming uncomfortably aware of the strain of holding the revolver at arm's length in one hand and the six-cell flashlight in the other.

"This is my door knocker," Tom said. It looked a match to the one he'd given Patsy.

"Drop the damn thing," Anna snapped.

"Jeez-Louise," he mumbled. "Keep your pants on."

"Now," Anna ordered, trying to cut through the alcohol shrouding his mind.

"I'm not dropping it," he said petulantly. "It's got a pearl handle. How 'bout I set it down real nice like? Okay?"

"Okay. Just do it."

Silva bent down to lay the little pistol on the cement, lost equilibrium, and fell against a post supporting the porch roof. The derringer clattered to the concrete. "Fuck," Silva growled. "If you've busted it . . ." He reached for the pistol but a hand shot out of the shadows and snatched it away.

"I'll go ahead and take care of this for you, Mr. Silva," Anna heard Stanton saying politely.

Flashing blue lights and a screaming siren made Anna jump. She squeaked as well but fortunately the clangor drowned her out. Silva screamed outright. "Sheesh!" He collapsed on the welcome mat, his back to the door, and hid his face in his hands. "Pats is a dead woman. Missy and Mindy: dead. Fuck." In slow motion, he rolled to his side and vomited into the petunias.

Anna holstered her weapon and took a deep breath to steady her nerves. Stanton materialized out of the shadows and began patting the incapacitated Silva down for weapons. "Now you've done it, Anna," Stanton said.

"Don't I know it. I took 'it' out," Anna said, referring to her revolver.

"Gonna be paperwork to atone for that."

Loud bootfalls on the flagstone announced Jennifer Short's arrival. "The pitter-patter of little feet," Anna muttered unkindly. "Hey ya, Jennifer," she said as the other woman came up beside her. "You might want to call 'in service' when you go out and 'on scene' when you arrive. It's okay to spoil the surprise."

"Sorry. Damnation. I'm always forgettin' that."

The porch light came on, giving Stanton light to work by, and Anna switched off her flashlight.

Jennifer's face was flushed and her eyes bright. Clearly she was scared, but excited too. Maybe she'd arrived a bit like Wyatt Earp into Dodge but she'd made a quick response from Far View and she hadn't hung back. "Good to see you. Come to join the fun?" Anna asked.

"Looks like it's all been had. Ol' Tom the only perpetrator?" Jennifer asked, disappointed. "Frieda made it sound like a riot."

"He had a gun," Anna tried to sweeten the pot. Jennifer perked up a little. "Why don't you go work with Special Agent Stanton," Anna suggested. "I need to check on Patsy and the girls."

Tom Silva was still retching, Agent Stanton standing beside him looking mildly ill. Jennifer strode up, jammed her hat more tightly down on her head, then fumbled out her handcuffs. "You have the right . . . Oh shit." She pulled her Stetson off and tugged a bit of paper from inside the hatband. "Hold this." She handed the hat unceremoniously to Stanton and finished reading Tom his rights from the paper. When she'd done, she turned to Anna. "What now? Cuff him?"

Anna nodded. "There's a belt in the trunk of my car. A leather one with some metal rings on it. Put it around his waist and cuff his hands in front of him and to the belt. Frederick will assist. You're looking good."

"It's my first," Jennifer said, and grinned. "Y'all be gentle with me," she said to Silva. He threw up again.

Anna waited till Jennifer and Stanton had helped Tom to his feet and led him away, then she knocked on the tower house door. "Patsy, it's me, Anna. Tom's gone. Are you okay?" There was a scraping sound from within, as if something heavy was being dragged away, then the door opened a crack. Looking terribly young with her short hair and pink pajamas, Patsy stuck her head out and looked around to discern the truth of Anna's statement.

"Are you all right?" Anna repeated her question.

"I guess. Mindy! Missy!" The girls came up from the living area and stood on the landing looking wide awake and confused. "Yes, we're okay," Patsy said, comforted by having her girls around her. "He never got in or anything."

"He wouldn't have hurt us," Mindy complained. At thirteen or fourteen, she was the younger of the two daughters. "You don't have to take him anywhere. He was drunk," she added, as if this exonerated him.

"Maybe you could make me a cup of coffee," Anna said to Patsy. "Instant would be fine."

The girls settled in the little booth in the kitchen. The domesticity of Mother putting the kettle on seemed to soothe all of them. Patsy poured the water over the coffee crystals when it was barely warm and handed Anna skim milk from the refrigerator.

Anna leaned against the counter and forced down a swallow. "What happened?" she asked now that a semblance of normalcy had been restored.

"It was Tom," Patsy said unnecessarily. "He came over earlier. I could tell he'd been drinking and I wouldn't see him. He went away again but came back about half an hour ago. He was pretty drunk."

"Blotto," Missy said.

"Not blotto," Mindy contradicted her.

"Blotto."

The girls were so close in age and so alike in blond good

looks, Anna often got them confused, which didn't endear her to either one of them. Both wore their hair long and straight, framing round scrubbed faces marked with a scattering of pimples. Mindy wore a nightshirt with Bart Simpson's likeness on it, and Missy an oversized T-shirt and boxer shorts, both the worse for wear.

"Go on," Anna said to their mother.

"That's about it. He was drunk. Blotto," she added, giving Mindy a yes-he-was-too look. "He tried to get in. That's when I locked the door."

"What did he want?"

"I don't know." Patsy started to cry.

"He kept yelling he was going to kill us," Missy said.

"He did not!" Mindy punched her sister in the arm.

"He did too, you little creep."

"Girls, that's enough!" Patsy slapped the tabletop with the flat of her hand and the girls were quiet.

"He didn't say he was going to kill us," Patsy said. "He just said things like 'You're dead if you don't listen to me' and 'You're a dead woman, Pats.' Things like that. He did not threaten to kill us, Missy. Don't you go saying things like that."

"Like that's not a threat." Missy tossed her hair and started French-braiding it back off her face.

The comments struck Anna as threatening as well, but Patsy and her daughters, even Missy, didn't seem particularly terrified by the incident, so maybe they weren't. Maybe it was a fairly standard family interaction. "Is that all you can remember?" she asked Patsy.

"That's about it. I think he maybe shot that little gun off once or twice. He was mad that I gave it back to him. I left it in his pickup the other day. With the girls, I didn't want it around the house."

Anna waited a moment but no more information was forthcoming. "Okay. We're going to arrest him and take him down to Cortez. What do you want to charge him with?"

"Arrest him?" Patsy looked alarmed. "You don't have to do that. Can't you just take him somewhere till he sobers up? You don't have to arrest him."

"I already did."

Now she looked aggrieved. "I won't press charges."

"I will." Anna rinsed her cup and put it in the sink. "Drunk and disorderly, disturbing the peace, unlawful possession of a firearm in a national park, refusing to obey a lawful order, obstructing a federal officer in the execution of her duty, public intoxication, DUI if he drove here, noise after quiet hours, and brain off leash. If I were you, I'd think it over before I let him off the hook. His behavior is unacceptable, illegal, and unsafe. You let me know if you change your mind."

Anna left the three of them sitting at the table giving her and each other dirty looks.

Tom was cuffed and belted into the back of the patrol car. Jennifer and Frederick stood by the open door, waiting without talking. As Anna walked up, Frederick stepped away from the vehicle and addressed her in hushed tones. "Can you and Ranger Short take Mr. Silva in by yourselves?"

"I think we can manage that," Anna said dryly.

"Oh whew. You don't have to give me a ride home even. I can walk back to my quarters from here easy."

"Tired of my company?" Anna asked as he turned to go.

Stanton looked over his shoulder. "He's going to throw up in your car. All the way down the hill. Ish."

"Coward."

"Hypersensitive gag reflex," he called back cheerily.

Blue lights still blazing, Jennifer had parked the 4X4 truck behind the patrol car. She was leaning against the fender, apparently enjoying the evening.

"Agent Stanton opted out," Anna told her. "Follow me to Maintenance. You can leave your vehicle there and ride down to Cortez with me."

"Guess I gotta turn out the overheads," Jennifer sighed. "Too bad. They're kinda pretty."

As Anna pulled into Maintenance, the patrol car's headlights shone on the gate to the locked yard where the pipeline contractor kept his equipment. In the beams Anna could see the red water truck and the ubiquitous yellow of heavy machinery. A man in dark clothes, welding gloves stuck in his hip pocket, was fiddling with the lock to the enclosed area. Anna flipped on her high beams and drove up to him. Shielding his eyes, he turned. It was Ted Greeley. She glanced at the dashboard clock: two-nineteen. Greeley didn't stay on the mesa top nights; he rented a place in Mancos.

" 'Morning, Ted." She stepped from her vehicle and stood behind the open door. "You're up early."

"So're you. But I knew that. Running my little buddy out of town?"

"Something like that. What're you doing up here at this hour?" It was late, and she was too tired for prolonged pleasantries.

"Why, Anna, I didn't know you cared. As it happens, I was visiting a sick friend. I heard on the radio that my boy Thomas was on the rampage and I got to wondering if he'd borrowed a cup of sugar from any of the neighbor ladies. That boy's one butt short of a pack and he's got a key to the yard. His kind of help I don't need."

"I didn't know you had a radio."

"I don't." Greeley winked and said good night.

For a moment Anna was nonplussed. Then she remembered: neither she nor Hills had gotten Stacy's personal protective gear from the widow. Rose still had his revolver and his radio. But a lot of people had radios: Drew, Jimmy, Paul, Jennifer, Al, Frieda. Though most of the seasonal interpreters didn't carry them, they all had access to those kept in the museum for use in the ruins.

Anna let the thought go. Something else had been triggered by Greeley but she was at a loss as to what it was. She let her brain empty and the thought floated up: Tom Silva had a key to the equipment yard. Had his sudden increase in cash flow that washed Patsy's new watch into the picture come from pilfering parts? Tools?

Stanton was right, of course. Silva vomited half a dozen times on the way down. Jennifer, riding beside him in the backseat, swore every time he threw up. "These're my Class A's, damn you," she snarled at one point. Anna rolled down her window and turned the air-conditioning on to clear the air. By the time they reached the Cortez sheriff's office Silva was nearly comatose. During the car trip he'd been too far gone to question; now it would have to wait till morning.

Anna turned him over to the booking officer and wrote him up for drunk and disorderly and illegal possession of a firearm, knowing without Patsy's corroboration not much else would stick.

She and Jennifer took the car over to an all-night Shell station on Main Street and swamped out the backseat.

It was after four A.M. when they started the long drive

back up to Far View. Anna'd never been comfortable in the cold predawn hours, that waiting time from after midnight till sunrise. As a child she could remember standing shivering watching her parents load suitcases into the trunk of the old Thunderbird. On their rare vacations, the importance of getting an early start was paramount. Upon reaching adulthood she'd expanded the concept of "vacation" to include sleeping in, and seldom booked a flight before noon if she could help it.

Now those unholy hours were allocated for pacing the floor on bad nights.

At Anna's request, Jennifer was driving. The late hour and the abandoned road had awakened the Indy 500 driver lurking just under the surface of every American, and Short was taking the curves with expert and nauseating speed. The two swallows of instant coffee Anna'd choked down in Patsy's kitchen felt like they'd lodged behind her breastbone and were trying to burn their way out.

"Slow down," she griped, "or we'll be mopping out the front seat."

"Sorry." Jennifer didn't sound it.

Events of the night had pushed the truck Anna and Stanton had heard on the loop out of her mind. In her irritation it resurfaced.

"You had late shift?" she asked, knowing the answer.

"I got two lates now Stacy's kaput."

"What time did you lock Cliff Palace loop?"

Jennifer thought a moment. "Maybe ten or thereabouts."

"Did you have to go back out later? Get a call or anything?"

"No. Why?" Jennifer's voice changed slightly, that touch of wariness that signaled the end of conversation and the beginning of interrogation.

"Around one-thirty a truck of some sort drove through

the Cliff Palace parking lot," Anna told her. "About then I got the call to come rescue Patsy. We were right behind the truck—not close enough to see it, but we had to be close. Somehow they hid out. Nobody was at the Four-Way when we got there. The gate was false-locked, so whoever was in there had access to a key. I wondered if Jamie'd talked you out of yours so she could go play with her little dead friends."

"That's against the rules," Jennifer said piously.

"Everybody bends the rules once in a while," Anna tempted confession.

"Not everybody." Jennifer put her in her place.

"Did anybody have a backcountry permit for tonight?"

"No. I checked. I always check."

"Who of the interps owns a good-sized truck?"

Jennifer was more comfortable with this line of questioning. It didn't cast aspersions on her merits as a ranger. "Nobody I know of," she said after a minute. "Interps have subcompact minds—you know; no extra irreplaceable fossil fuels and shit."

Claude Beavens had said the "interp's truck" left after he did the night of the murder. Offhand Anna couldn't remember if he'd seen or only heard of it. She made a mental note to ask.

"Jimmy Russell's got a truck," Jennifer volunteered. "He'd've took 'em. Jimmy's always looking to get his horns clipped or at least a couple of free beers. If it was a party, he'd've been there."

"Have you been locking the Four-Way funny? Like Stacy used to, all twisted and tight and hard to undo?" Anna asked abruptly.

Jennifer hooted. "Ranger Pigeon, what is the matter with you? You're as fussy as a cat with new kittens. You on the rag?"

"Past my bedtime," Anna grumbled. "Have you?"

"My locks aren't twisty and tight," Jennifer said primly, and turned on the radio to drown out any further assaults on her character.

Anna didn't push it, but promised herself she would do some serious checking of stories when the world opened for business: Jamie, Beavens, Jennifer, Russell. She had a feeling if rangers were puppets, the mesa would have more long noses than trees.

16

"I'M NOT LOOKING forward to this." Anna switched off the ignition. She and Frederick sat in the patrol car under the shade tree in Rose Meyers' front yard. "What I'm looking forward to is a nap." By the time she and Jennifer had returned to the mesa it had been close to five. She'd had less than two hours' sleep before she went on duty at seven A.M.

"Getting old?" Stanton teased.

"I'm too tired even to yawn."

"Want me to do it?"

For a second Anna thought he was offering to yawn for her. Then she focused on the task at hand. "It's bound to be tedious, personal, and unpleasant. Of course I want you to do it."

"Generous to a fault."

Anna twisted in her seat till the bones in her lower back popped. "I'll do it, but you'd better come with me in your capacity as Hysterical Wife Sedative."

Hattie answered the door in her nightgown, a knee-length poet's shirt in burgundy with the sheen of satin and the wrinkle-free texture of good polyester. Graying hair was wild around her face. She looked the embodiment of an elemental force. Whether of earth or sky, for good or evil, Anna couldn't hazard a guess. Greek mythology had never been big in Catholic school.

"You're just in time for a cup of tea," Hattie said. Much of her usual spark was banked beneath fatigue or worry, though still she sounded genuinely welcoming. "C'mon in, Anna. Agent Stanton."

"Fred," Stanton said, and Anna shot him a startled look. In the years she'd been acquainted with him "Frederick" was the only accepted form of address. She looked back at Hattie. The elemental force: the quintessential aunt with all the rights and privileges conferred therein. One's aunt would scarcely call one "Frederick" unless some formal trouble were in the air.

"Fred," Hattie said warmly. "I've never known a weak or dishonest Fred."

"Or a pretty one, I bet," Stanton said.

Hattie laughed as she opened the screen and waved them in. "Maybe to a Fredericka."

"The only one who finds a papa moose handsome is a momma moose."

The banter carried them indoors, where they pooled in front of the archway leading to a small built-in eating nook that separated the living area from the kitchen. Rose and her daughter sat in their nightgowns over breakfast. Rose had two plastic curlers clipped on the crown of her head, just enough to give her coif that rounded pouf short hairdos seem to require. A definite chill radiated from the woman as she looked at Anna.

Bella, in a sleeveless white nightie covered with little blue sailboats, huddled on the bench opposite her mother. Knees tucked up and arms pulled inside the armholes, she hid her face in the open neck of the gown; a personal fallout shelter.

Anna guessed discussion over this morning's bananas and Grape-Nuts had been somewhat strained.

"Yes?" Rose said in lieu of a greeting. She opened her hands to encompass the food-littered table. "As you can see, it is a bit early for receiving callers."

It was after ten o'clock. Anna resisted the urge to glance at her watch. In true coward's fashion, she stepped aside and drew Stanton into the line of fire.

"Agent Stanton and I are just tying up a few loose ends," she said. "Did Hills happen to collect Stacy's duty belt?"

Rose looked blank but she knew exactly what was referred to, Anna would have laid money on it.

"C'mon, punkin," Hattie said. "Let's get dressed and go for a walk."

Eyes full of alarm, Bella glanced at Stanton.

"We'll change in your mom's room," Hattie assured her. Modesty met, Bella climbed from the bench.

"Hiya, Bella," Anna said.

"Hello." Bella was merely being polite, she didn't meet Anna's eyes.

While Bella slid to the floor, Rose managed to pluck the rollers from her hair and secret them away somewhere. "Would you care for a cup of coffee?" She was talking to Stanton.

"No thanks," Anna replied just as he said: "That'd really hit the spot."

Accordingly, Rose went to the kitchen and returned with a mug of coffee for the FBI agent. Anna wondered if she would have gotten one even if she'd said yes.

"Any progress finding Stacy's murderer?" Rose asked as she regained her seat.

Stanton sat down across from her. "Not as much as we'd like. But Ranger Pigeon and I are still chipping away at it."

Rose didn't look up at Anna leaning coffeeless in the archway.

Amid the breakfast debris on the table were papers that had an official fill-in-the-boxes look to them. "Looks like we've caught you at a bad time," Stanton said apologetically.

"Yes, rather." This time Rose did look at Anna.

Disrespect, verbal and sometimes physical abuse was often directed at the uniform, the badge. Anna'd become practiced at not letting it get under her skin. But this was personal and it felt personal. She found herself becoming irked and began to count to ten in Spanish.

"Death and taxes?" Stanton asked solicitously.

"Medical forms for Bella," Rose said.

Anna'd just gotten to *cinco, seis*. She quit counting. The conversation was getting interesting. "Is Bella sick?" she asked.

Rose ignored her. "Bella's getting an operation," she told Stanton. Excitement was clear in her voice. "It's been something I've been wanting for a long time. She can't have it yet, but in a few years. They think they can fix her legs, make her normal."

"That's wonderful," Stanton said.

Anna was undecided. "We're the variety that adds spice," she remembered Drew saying.

"Stacy's insurance left us with enough money to cover medical expenses." Rose volunteered the information and Anna wondered why.

"Stacy had a life insurance policy?" she asked.

Rose took a second to respond. In that second the silence shouted "Not that it's any of your business but— yes, he did, Miss Pigeon. Stacy was a good husband."

Good was emphasized, and logically or not, Anna found herself wanting to defend Zach for dying broke and unprepared. She chose not to rise to the bait—real or imagined.

"You're welcome to see the policy, if you want, Miss Pigeon."

"Sure, why not."

Rose rolled her eyes for Stanton's benefit and left the table to get the form.

There was a murmured exchange in the bedroom, then Hattie and Bella emerged and slipped out the back door with exaggerated sneakiness. Anna suspected some Hattie-led game was afoot.

Rose returned. Her hair was combed and Anna's female eye detected a discreet layer of blush brushed on the high cheekbones.

"Miss Pigeon?" Rose held out the insurance policy then, dismissing Anna with a look, sat again. "All that's of no interest to the Federal Bureau of Investigation, I imagine," she said sweetly to Stanton. "Is there anything I can help you with this morning, Agent Stanton?"

"Coffee's all I need," he said. "Anna?"

She laid the two-hundred-thousand-dollar life insurance policy on the table. "Just Stacy's duty belt—gun, radio, leather gear."

"I have no idea where I put it," Rose said disinterestedly. "I'll drop it by the CRO later this afternoon if it turns up."

In a house the size of a postage stamp, inhabited by a six-year-old child, it was unlikely she'd mislaid her recently deceased spouse's gunbelt. Whether she lied to hide something or just for spite, Anna hadn't a clue. Admitting defeat she said: "Thanks, Mrs. Meyers. That'd be a big help. We won't take up any more of your time."

"Thanks for the coffee," Stanton chimed in.

"Anytime, Fred. It was so sweet of you to come by."
Rose blessed him with a Pepsodent-perfect smile.

"Watch out," Anna said ungraciously as they climbed
back into the patrol car. "You've got Husband Number
Three written all over you.

"First there's insurance, then there isn't, then there is.
There's chindi, then they're gone, then they're back. Gates
are locked, unlocked, locked. Silva's a thug, a guardian
angel, then presto chango, a thug," she ranted.

Stanton rolled up the windows of the car and cranked
up the air conditioner.

"Everybody's got a radio, then there's not a radio to be
found. Interps have trucks, then they have subcompacts.
The truth is getting to be such a variable. New realities to
be announced as needed." Anna turned the air conditioner
off and rolled down her window. "What now? You're
choreographing this show."

"Gee, thanks." The radio cut off anything further.
Jamie Burke at Cliff Palace was reporting a medical. Unceremoniously, Anna shushed Stanton and turned up the
radio. A boy, fourteen, was complaining of faintness and
shortness of breath. He insisted he could walk out, his
parents demanded he have medical attention.

"Do you need to go?" Stanton asked.

Anna shook her head. "Hills and Jennifer are both on
today. They can do it." For a second she stared at the
radio thinking. "Damn," she said finally. "Let's go anyway. I've got some questions to ask."

Cliff Palace parking lot was full and a line of cars extending a hundred yards back up the one-way road followed those creeping slowly through the lot looking for
nonexistent parking places. Anna turned on her blue lights
and, driving on the shoulder, nudged past the sluggish

stream. She parked with two wheels in the dirt and two in the "motorcycles only" zone.

The sun burned through the thin atmosphere, touching the skin ungently. Anna loved its rough kiss and had the wrinkles and age spots to prove it. Red-faced tourists queued up at the drinking fountains.

Down in the Palace the heat and the crowding would be exacerbated. To keep from adding to the congestion, Anna and Stanton stayed on the mesa top monitoring events over the radio.

In the fifteen minutes it had taken them to get to Cliff, the boy's condition had deteriorated sufficiently. Burke's voice had gone from self-important to mildly panicky. Hills had called in on scene. From the two patrol vehicles parked in the lot, Anna guessed in all the excitement Jennifer had forgotten again.

Stanton found a bench in the shade at the trail head. Two German women, both in their seventies or early eighties, wearing print dresses and straw hats, moved over to make room for him.

Anna leaned on the split-rail fence behind the bench and tilted her head back to catch the sun on her face. The heat drew wind up the canyons and she reveled in its touch.

"Some questions to ask, you said. Let me in on your secret?" Stanton asked.

"I wish I had a secret. It'd make me feel superior. This doesn't even qualify as a hunch." Since she didn't choose to add to that, Stanton made small talk with his bench companions in German and Anna was duly impressed. She would have been more so had the ladies not laughed so much as they tried to puzzle out what he was saying.

The ambulance arrived, Drew driving, Jimmy riding shotgun. They came to wait with Anna.

"They're walking him out," Drew said. "A kid again. Asthma, up at seven thousand feet. His parents ought to be shot."

Hills' voice, phlegmatic as ever, came into the conversation via the airwaves. "Seven hundred, three-eleven. We're going to need some help. Fella's collapsed on us. If the Stokes isn't already up top, don't wait on it. We're to the metal stairs. Send me some big boys 'n' we'll hand-carry the kid out."

"Lifting heavy objects, that's you, Drew," Anna said. The helitack foreman and Agent Stanton followed her toward the overlook at a trot.

Looking disgustingly heroic, Hills was halfway up the metal stairs, in his arms a pale young man in khaki shorts and a blue T-shirt. Oversized unlaced sneakers—the fashion that summer—made the boy's legs look even skinnier than they were.

Walking beside and behind, Jennifer carried an oxygen bottle, the mask affixed to the patient's face, plastic tubing connecting him to the cylinder. Following so closely they trod on Short's heels were the boy's parents.

A panting woman with permed reddish hair and an overheated complexion held on to one of her son's feet to comfort him or herself. The father was lost in testosterone hysterics. Fear masquerading as anger, he berated the stolid Dutton even as Hills carried his boy. Behind them walked an older couple, grandparents, Anna guessed.

Drew came alongside Hills. They propped the young man, still conscious but barely so, against Anna and interlaced their arms. The boy's breathing was labored, the wheezing audible without a stethoscope. His lips pursed with effort and he sipped at the air, sucking it into his lungs a bit at a time, working to push it through shrunken bronchial tubes. Anna eased him into the chair the men had made of their arms. "You're almost there," she said encouragingly. He nodded and made a valiant attempt to smile.

Her part in the process completed, Anna stepped back, letting Hills and Drew carry their patient to the waiting ambulance. She fell into step with the elderly couple. They seemed the sanest of the group. Both wore wide-brimmed hats, baggy shorts, and the comfortable walking shoes of experienced tourists.

"Grandson?" Anna asked.

"Our first," the woman said.

"And probably last," the man snarled. Obviously this was an old bone of contention in the family.

"Not now, Harold. He has had asthma ever since he was a baby," the grandmother told Anna.

"It's usually not bad," Harold argued. "I told Eli not to bring him up this high."

"Okay, Harold. I don't think it's the altitude," she whispered conspiratorially, though her husband could easily hear. "Dane has been up to seven thousand feet half a dozen times and been just fine. It's radon. Like in caves. Last time Dane was taken this bad it was something like that."

"Irma! Leave the lady alone. It wasn't radon. He was sniffing that glue like the kids all got crazy about."

"Nonsense."

The party reached the parking lot and the grandparents were lost in an organizational shuffle.

As the ambulance drove away, Stanton came to stand by Anna.

"All your questions answered?" he asked.

"Oh, yeah. The pattern's crystal clear. I have no idea what it's of, but it's clear." She twisted the watchband around on her wrist and showed the face to Frederick. "Tuesday, eleven twenty-eight A.M. Another collapse, another carry-out, right on schedule."

"Whose?" Stanton asked.

"You tell me."

17

A PRETTY LITTLE mouse with ears Disneyesque in their cuteness and whiskers Gus-Gus would have been proud of poked her nose out of the kitchen and contemplated crossing the risky expanse of carpet in the living area.

"You're getting fat," Anna warned. "One day you won't be able to squeeze under the door."

The mouse looked up at the sound of her voice but was otherwise unmoved. When Anna had first arrived at Far View there'd been no mice. With the largesse left on countertops and on dirty dishes by her roommates, the little creatures had come to stay. This one was so plump Anna was put in mind of an ink drawing in her childhood copy of *Charlotte's Web*; a very round Templeton the rat lying on his back at the country fair saying: "What a gorge!"

Early on Jennifer and Jamie had set out d-CON. Dying mice had staggered out with such regularity the living room began to resemble the stage after the final act of *Hamlet*. Disgusted, Anna'd thrown the poison out. "Not cricket," she told her housemates. "You can feed them or kill them. Not both."

Since then they'd all come to terms with one another

and the dorm no longer had pests but, as Jennifer had dubbed them, politically correct pets.

Anna's wristwatch beeped. The mouse squeaked on the same frequency and ran behind the refrigerator. Three A.M. on the nose: Anna tried a combination of invisible-to-the-naked-eye buttons on the watch to turn off the hourly alarm. The beeping stopped but she had no idea whether it was of natural causes or if she'd won. "Man against Nature: Woman against Technology," she mumbled.

Half a glass of burgundy sat before her on the table. Her third, but since the first two were downed six hours earlier, she figured they didn't count. Hopefully, this one would help her to sleep and without the usual cost: waking with the jitters just before dawn.

Jack of diamonds: she put it on a black queen in the solitaire game she'd been playing since one-thirty. A space was freed up and two more moves revealed a second ace. She enjoyed a vague sense of triumph. Her mind wasn't on the game, merely in free-fall, unloosed by solitaire's mantra of boredom. This game had many of the earmarks of the one she and Stanton had spent the day pursuing. One by one they'd peeled away lies in hopes of uncovering a truth they could play, one that would start the game moving again.

Another of Frederick the Fed's infernal lists cluttered up her notebook. While Jennifer and Hills attended to the medical at Cliff Palace, the two of them had divided up all the stories in need of checking. "The lie detector part," Stanton had called it. A line cut down the middle of the yellow notepaper. On Anna's side was "Policy, Truck, Rose/Radio" and "Beavens/Veil." In her own handwriting was added "Stephanie/Dane." On Stanton's side was "Silva/Gun/Threats."

Stanton's day had been a complete washout. Before he could question him, Silva had been let out on bail, paid not by Patsy but by Ted Greeley. Neither Greeley nor Silva could be found.

Anna's half of the investigation had gone well. One phone call proved Rose Meyers a member of the liars' club. The two-hundred-thousand-dollar life insurance policy she'd shown Anna had been canceled six months previously for lack of payment.

Knowing the truth without knowing the rationale behind it was fairly useless. Maybe Rose was not yet aware the policy had been canceled—or knew but wasn't ready to admit it to herself or anyone else. Maybe she'd been trying to impress Stanton. An underpaid public servant might find a lady a wee bit more enticing if she had two hundred grand. Money was a proven aphrodisiac.

Whatever the reason, Mutual Casualty and Life told Anna there was no policy, no payoff. Rose had said Stacy'd left them with nothing, then changed her tune when the truth was nothing.

Red seven on black eight; nothing revealed. She turned over another three cards.

It seemed unlikely Rose would be lying to Bella and Hattie about the operation. That would be cruel, and despite her dislike of the woman, Anna believed that in her own way Rose loved her daughter. Therefore logic would suggest Rose did have money. Fact indicated it did not come from where she'd claimed.

Anna was too old to believe that people always lied for a reason. Mostly they lied because it was easy, felt good, or was habit. However, this particular lie was complex, suggesting a more focused motive. If Rose wanted to hide the source of the money, it was probably illegal or embarrassing.

Greeley as a potential new stepdaddy might have that kind of capital. Would Rose want to admit she and Ted were that intimate? Sharing a bed meant nothing but sharing a checkbook was a real commitment. And money was a stronger motive for murder than love.

Anna put a red four on a red five, woke up to her game, and took it back. Things just weren't adding up: murdering one's spouse was passé. Stacy had no inheritance, no insurance, and though in a divorce he might sue for custody of Bella, he had the proverbial snowball's chance in hell of winning. Rose could be intimate with whomever's checkbook she pleased without much in the way of adverse consequences.

If there was a good reason for Rose to kill her husband, Anna was missing it. A woman scorned crossed her mind but she dismissed it. Her own presumed affair with Stacy might possibly foment a woman miffed, but hardly scorned.

Twenty-four-carat motive or not, Rose had a lot of money and was lying about where she'd gotten it. That qualified her as a suspect.

"Truck," the next item on Stanton's hit list, referred to the elusive truck Beavens reported hearing and Anna and Stanton had chased. A tour of the housing areas revealed the whereabouts of thirteen trucks. Trucks were in vogue even for suburbanites. In parks they were de rigueur. Without exception they were teensy little Toyotas, Ford Rangers—toy trucks. Only Tom Silva owned a good old-fashioned bubba truck complete with shovel and gun rack. But even Silva's Chevy couldn't grind out the kind of racket that had pulled Anna and Stanton from their chindi vigil.

The thought of Silva jogged something in the back of Anna's tired mind. She set down the playing cards and stared into her wine as if waiting for a vision. Trucks and Tom and noise and trucks and Tom . . . It was coming to her. Back in June, before all the fuss, Tom had complained a "big goddamn truck" almost ran him off the road. Anna remembered following up on his complaint just to prove she was fair-minded and finding nothing. She'd even written a case incident report to keep her credit good. Later Silva'd said he was just "jerking her chain."

Tom drove a real pickup and wore cowboy shirts with the sleeves ripped out. What would he consider big? Surely not a snubby-nosed little Mitsubishi. To a construction worker, "big truck" would mean a Kenmore, a Peterbilt, a Mac.

First a truck, then no truck, now a truck. Another lie. Anna swallowed the medium through which the oracle had revealed this truth.

Next on the list was "Rose/Radio." That had been a worthless line of inquiry. Rose had returned belt, gun, and radio to the CRO around two o'clock. When Anna'd dared ask if she'd lent or used the radio, Rose had climbed into an uncommunicative huff and departed.

Feeling spiteful, Anna had taken the radio out of its leather holster and dusted the hard plastic case for fingerprints. There wasn't a print on it. Either Rose was an anal-retentive housekeeper or it had been wiped clean so the last user could go undetected.

"Beavens/Veil" had proved a bit easier. At least Beavens was still speaking to Anna, that was a start. She'd found him down in Spruce Tree House just as he was being relieved for a meal break. He'd brought a bag lunch and they sat together in the cool of the alcove at the rear of the ancient pueblo amid the prosaic needs of a modern-day Park Service: oxygen bottle, backboard, first-aid kit, and white helium-filled balloons. The last interpreter out of the ruin in the evening affixed these to the upper ramparts. Al Stinson's brainchild, the balloons kept the vultures from roosting and whitewashing the national historic treasure with bird droppings.

Beavens had been his usual self: shrugging, replying to everything with "no big deal." Halfway through his bag of Doritos—that and a ruin-temperature Dr Pepper constituted lunch—Anna noticed he was nervously fingering a gold chain around his neck. At an earlier meeting she remembered him holding on to a small gold cross suspended from it as Stanton had questioned him about the veil.

On a hunch, she turned the conversation along more spiritual lines. After a moment's silence, she said, "One thing I don't like about living in the park is it's so far to church."

Beavens' face, pasty despite the best efforts of the high desert sun, lit up for the first time in Anna's short acquaintance with him. Animation lent him youth and even a certain charm. "Have you accepted Jesus as your personal savior?" he asked.

Such was the hope in his voice, Anna might have felt guilty had she not been fairly sure she'd stumbled on the key that would unlock his confidence. "Washed in the blood of the lamb a year ago next month," she said.

A boyish smile curved up the corners of his mouth and transformed his face. "You!" he exclaimed. "I never would have guessed."

"The Lord works in mysterious ways."

"Amen. Which church do you go to?" He was leaning forward, defenses down. Anna didn't want to lose him with a wrong answer.

"I've only been here a couple months. So far I haven't

found anything that really works for me," she equivo-
cated.

Beavens nodded sympathetically. "I can't find anything
either. This New Age stuff is like a cancer. It's eaten away
a lot of real belief. Maybe we could get together a Bible
study group up on the mesa?"

Anna had a sinking feeling she was going to pay dearly
for this particular deception. "The park is kind of a mag-
net for the New Agers," she said. "What with crystals and
the American Indian thing that's caught on."

Beavens' face continued to look receptive, so she pressed
on. "All this sitting around in kivas waiting for spirits, I
don't know . . . ." She trailed off, hoping he would fill in
with his own ideas. She wasn't disappointed.

"It's just an invitation to Satan, that's all it amounts to,"
he said eagerly. "The Bible warns us that there'll be stum-
bling blocks on the road to heaven. These people are just
providing the Devil with tools—or maybe I should say
fools—to do his work. It's like holding séances or messing
with Ouija boards. You can't go calling up this kind of
stuff. You've got to turn away from it, turn to the Bible."

"Prayer," Anna said.

"Yes!" Beavens looked relieved beyond measure; someone understood him.

Anna ignored a mild pang of remorse. "What with all
that's been happening, I kind of think the demons have
been called up already."

In the middle of a sip of Dr Pepper, Beavens nodded his
agreement and nearly choked himself to death. When he'd
recovered somewhat, he managed to squeak out: "Burke,
the spirit veil."

Now Anna leaned forward. "Summer solstice—the
night you saw the interp's truck—"

"Heard it."

"Heard it, then. Did you really see the veil?" she asked as one conspirator might ask another.

"I saw something," Beavens replied in the same tone. "But we can't give it credence, can't spread the bad word. I say get thee behind me, Satan!" He laughed, but Anna could see he was serious, nervous and serious. He was fiddling with the cross again.

An instinct to pounce welled up strongly. Forcing it down, she leaned back and crossed her ankles. "That kind of thing spreads like wildfire," she agreed. "People want to believe in signs and portents."

"Original sin," Beavens said.

Anna didn't know where that fit in or exactly what it was. Sister Mary Judette had explained it in religion class but that was close to thirty years before. To say something, she threw in a cliché from her own formative years and hoped it was general enough to fit any conversational requirement: "If you're not part of the solution, you're part of the problem."

"Exactly."

"What was it like, the something you saw?"

"Weird," Beavens confided. "'Spirit veil' is a pretty good description. It's Jamie Burke, she'd better cut it out, too. She's got no idea who she's messing with."

Anna looked interested.

"She's got half the interps in the park watching and thinking and waiting. So it shows up. You call up the Devil, he comes."

Anna nodded sagely. "Was it like a kind of curtain?" She brought the conversation back to where she wanted it.

"Kind of. An iridescent shimmer. Maybe a hundred feet long. It was really neat-looking," he said, then thinking better of it added, "But then it would be, wouldn't it?"

Another interpreter, a frosted blonde art teacher from

Oklahoma, came into the shade of the alcove. "They're all yours, Claude," she said as she took a Flintstones lunch box out of the first-aid cabinet and sat down cross-legged on the smooth stone floor.

Anna walked Beavens out into the sunlight. "You didn't want to admit seeing the veil because it'd just give the Devil his due? Recruiting for him, sort of?"

"No sense being Lucifer's patsy."

As Anna turned to go, he followed her a couple of steps. "Let's do that Bible study, okay?"

"Anytime." Anna escaped into a knot of visitors.

So there had been something—a spirit veil or the Devil's shirttail, but definitely something.

Anna stared at the cards on the table. Nothing left to play. Miss Mouse was back, poking her little gray nose around the door frame from the direction of the kitchen. "I've got a cat," Anna threatened. The mouse twitched her whiskers but didn't run away.

Eyes down at the tabletop with its scattered playing cards, Anna rested her head in her hands. Three choices: finish her wine and try to get some sleep, deal another hand of solitaire, or cheat. Cheating seemed the most profitable course.

Shuffling the remaining cards into what she hoped would prove a more cooperative order, she eyed the last item on the list, the one she had written: "Stephanie/Dane."

Hills would have a few choice words to say about the phone bill she'd run up tracking them down. Stephanie McFarland was the asthmatic girl she and Stacy had carried out of Cliff Palace. The child who had died. Dane was the boy helitack had evacuated earlier in the day. Both were young and, other than asthma, in good condition. Both sets of parents had insisted the children had been up at seven thousand feet before without ill effects.

Fourteen long-distance calls had gathered the information Anna'd been looking for. Both children had had
previous attacks of like severity. Stephanie's had been triggered by fumes when as a child she'd locked herself in a
broom closet and shattered a bottle of cleaning solution in
her attempts to dislodge the door. By the time her mother
had found her she was suffering statis asthmaticus and she
very nearly lost her life.

After a bit of cajoling, the ER nurse at Southwest
Memorial in Cortez told Anna Dane's parents, Eli and
Dina Bjornson, were staying at the Aneth Lodge. Immediate danger to their son past, they'd been fairly commu-
nicative. Dane had had one serious attack before, brought
on not by radon or sniffing glue but by exposure to chemical Mace some boys at his junior high school had been
playing with.

One explanation of the Cliff Palace incidents was that
the ruin was exhaling poisonous vapors, perhaps the
dying breath of the fabled underworld blowing through
the sipapus. Stacy had been reaching toward the entrance
to that world with his last dying gasp. Or so the corpse
had appeared. Anna put no credence in the underworld as
a mythical entity but there had been cases of poisonous
gas, naturally generated, escaping to the detriment of humankind. Could that be the rationale behind the sudden
and complete departure of the Old Ones? A phenomenon
that for some geological reason was just now reasserting
itself?

Another solution was coincidence. Two asthmatic kids
with similar medical histories collapse within a few weeks
of one another on a Tuesday morning. Not really much of
a coincidence. It wouldn't have raised an eyebrow with
Anna had it not been for Stacy and the rest of the Tuesday
Morning Club.

Anna was stuck with the facts: something or someone was causing people to collapse in Cliff Palace on Tuesday mornings. Not random, not coincidental, not paranormal, but cause and effect. Anna figured the culprit or culprits were individuals with greater material desires than your average ghost.

She turned her mind back to her solitaire game. Reshuffling hadn't broken a single space loose. She gathered up the playing cards and reboxed them. Miss Mouse had gone to bed. Anna would follow suit.

She'd just swallowed the last of the dry red sleeping draught when the phone rang. In the dead of night it was always a sickening sound, though at Mesa Verde nine times out of ten it was a false alarm from the concessions facility. The new motion detectors were so sensitive, the least vibration set them off, sometimes two or three times in a night. Anna often wondered how much money the hapless taxpayers had forked out in overtime so fully armed rangers could shoo mice out of the Hostess Twinkies. With the monies concessions pulled in they could easily afford Pinkertons.

Again the phone rang. Anna threw herself on it as if it were a hand grenade. Half the night she'd been up, and if there was any overtime to be had she was damned if she'd let anyone else get it.

"Mesa Verde."

A short silence followed, punctuated by a sharp intake of breath. "What?" came a faltering voice.

"Mesa Verde National Park," Anna elaborated. "You've reached our emergency number."

"This is an emergency?" the voice said uncertainly. It was either a very timid woman or a small child.

"What can I help you with?"

"A car's gone off the road down here. I think somebody's still inside."

Anna felt her stomach tighten and her mind clear. "Where are you calling from?"

"A phone by the road."

There were only two, one at Delta Cut and one at Bravo Cut, two places where the road to the mesa top sliced through the side of a hill. "Are you closer to the bottom of the mesa or the top?"

"The top, I think."

"Are you hurt?"

"I don't think so, I mean no, I'm not. We . . . I was out on the point looking at the lights when we . . . I saw the headlights go over. They're way down. Somebody drove off. That's all I know." There was a click and the interview was over. Whoever had called had been out frolicking under the stars, Anna guessed, with an inappropriate "we" and, now that the altruism brought on by shock had worn thin, had thought better of involvement.

Delta Cut was sheer on one side, a dirt-and-stone bank rising vertically from the roadbed. The other side dropped off precipitously in a jungle of serviceberry and oakbrush. Unless traveling at impossible speeds, a passenger car wouldn't have the clout to break through the iron and concrete. A vehicle over the edge would've had to run past the railing on one end or the other.

Anna changed phones and put in a call to Frieda from the bedroom as she pulled on her uniform trousers. Frieda would wake up someone to bring the ambulance and call out helitack in case a low-angle rescue was needed.

The call completed, Anna banged on Jennifer Short's bedroom door. No one grunted. Jennifer slept like the dead. Anna pushed open the door but the room was empty. Either Jennifer was partying late or had gotten lucky and found a more entertaining bed for the night.

Stars hung close to the mesa, not dulled by moisture or atmosphere. A half-moon spilled enough light to see by. Garbage was strewn over the walk, and as she walked to the car Anna saw a big brown rump vanishing into the underbrush. When she returned she'd clean up the mess and not mention the marauder to the brass. At Mesa Verde the solution to problem bears might be to shoot first and justify later.

As she backed the patrol car out of the lot and started down the main road the three miles to Delta Cut, she ran through her EMS checklist. Rehearsing emergency medical procedures and inventorying available equipment calmed and centered her.

With no traffic to slow her, she reached Delta Cut before she'd played out more than a few possible scenarios. Not surprisingly, no car waited at the pull-out. The phone box hung open as if deserted in haste. Anna pulled the Ford into the left lane, switched on her spot light, and cruised slowly along the guardrail.

Serviceberry grew thickly down the bank, camouflaging drops and ravines. Late blooms glowed white. Beyond, the thickets were impenetrable in their darkness. Anna rolled down the car's windows and listened but nothing was audible over the hum of the engine.

A crank call? It hadn't sounded it. Crank calls were usually accompanied by a background of party-animal noises. A trap? The thought made the little hairs on the back of her neck crawl. Could someone have lured her out in the dead of night for sinister purposes? Highly unlikely, she soothed herself. For one thing, there was no guarantee she'd be the one to answer the '69 line, for another, who could've guessed she'd come alone other than Jennifer and whomever she was with? The only reason for making her a target was the Meyers investigation and she hadn't exactly been burning up the turf in that department.

Reassured by her own sense of inadequacy, she left the patrol car to walk the same ground. Free from the distraction of machinery, she found what she was looking for. Eighty or a hundred feet down the bank, almost hidden by the thick foliage, was the yellow glow of automobile headlights. To the left of the lights she could just make out the pale shape of a vehicle's body and adjusted her thoughts: not a car, a pickup truck, white or yellow in color.

Having radioed in the exact location of the wreck, she collected the jump kit and a flashlight, backtracked to the end of the barricade, and shone the light into the brush. A barely discernible trail of broken branches and scarred earth showed where the truck had left the pavement. There were no skid marks, no deep cuts in the sod indicating the brakes had been applied.

Hunching up like a woman in a windstorm, she forced her way through the brush, following the broken trail. Four or five yards down the steep bank the ground fell away. A cliff, maybe thirty feet high, was cut into the hillside where the undergrowth had let go of unstable soil during the previous winter's snows. Dirt and scree dropped down to a rubble of boulders scattered on a shoulder of land. Past that was a sheer drop to the valley floor, where the lights of Cortez twinkled invitingly.

The pickup had cut through the brush at the point where she stood, then hurtled over the embankment. Boulders stopped its fall. The nose of the truck was crushed, the windshield and both side windows smashed. Either time was of the essence or all the time in the world would not be enough. Whoever was inside would be lucky to be alive.

Anna'd been carrying the orange jump kit in front of her like a shield. Now she strapped it on her back. Eroded soil made the bank soft enough she could work her way down crablike, heels and butt breaking the descent. Prickly pear sank disinterested fangs into the palm of her right hand and she swore softly. Tomorrow, without adrenaline for an anesthetic, the barbs would itch and burn.

From above, she heard the whooping cry of the ambulance approaching and was glad of the company.

At the bottom of the broken bank, the ground leveled out in a litter of rocks from fist- to house-size. Anna leaped from one to another, her balance made uncertain by the moving flashlight beam.

The truck was wedged between two rocks. One beneath the front axle, the other crumpling back the hood and holding the vehicle at an angle almost on its right side. Both rear wheels and the front left tire were free of the ground. The front tire still turned slowly. The crash had been recent and Anna felt a spark of hope that she was not too late.

"Anna!" It was Hills on her radio.

"Down here," she responded, flashing her light up to the road till she got an answering flash.

"What've we got?" Hills asked.

"Stand by."

Between her and the cab were two boulders roughly the size of Volkswagens and woven together by a tangle of oak brush. For lack of a better place, Anna shoved the flashlight down the front of her shirt, then, hands free, scrambled to the top of the first boulder and jumped the crevice to the second.

The tilted cab was on a level with the rock, the driver's door parallel with the top of the stone where she stood. Heat radiated from beneath the hood; the engine was still running. Anna rescued her flash and surveyed the scene. Broken and hanging in fragments, the safety glass of the side window fell in ragged sheets. Isolated pieces sparkled in the beam. From the interior came strains of country-western music. A faint green glow emanated from the dashboard lights. All else was lost in a darkness fractured by moonlight through fragmented glass.

Anna unstrapped the jump kit. Cursing her slick-soled Wellington boots, she inched down the boulder where it sloped to within eighteen inches of the truck. Spinning gently, the pickup's front tire, along with the broken angles of metal and stone, gave her an unsettling sense of vertigo, as if she might topple into the window as into a bottomless well.

At the boulder's edge she stopped, recovered her equilibrium, and peered inside. From her new vantage point, the cab and a small slice of the passenger door were visible. On the far window, where it had been forced inward, drops of ruby mixed with the glittering diamonds of glass.

Fresh blood was startlingly red—too red for paintings or movies. Comic-book red; believable only in fantasy and real life.

Gingerly, Anna pushed at the truck's exposed undercarriage with a foot. It held steady. Apparently the truck was wedged firmly between the rocks. How firmly, she was about to find out.

Getting down on her knees, she restored the flashlight to its bruising hammock between buttons and breasts and crawled her hands out onto the door. Bit by bit she transferred her weight from the rock. The truck remained stable. Emboldened, she brought one knee onto the door. catching hold of the handle to keep herself steady.

Moonlight reflected off the white paint. Details, overwhelmed by the hard light of day, were surrealistically clear: a pencil-thin scratch beneath the side mirror, a square patch where a sticker had been inexpertly removed, fading black stenciled lettering, once showy flourishes almost obliterated by time, spelling the initials T. S.

Tom Silva, Anna realized. It was his truck. Better a stranger; no psychological buttons pushed interfering with efficiency.

Pulling herself up to her knees on the slanting metal, she braced butt on heels and took the flashlight from inside her shirt. Silva was crushed down on the far side of the cab, his back to her. One leg trailed behind him, wedged beneath the driver's pedals. His left arm, the palm turned up, rested on the hump between the seats. She couldn't see his face. "Tom," she called clearly. "Can you hear me?" No response.

Having wrested the King from her duty belt she made her assessment out loud, sharing it with Hills. "One individual, white male," she began, avoiding Silva's name lest Patsy or the girls should hear in such a manner. "About thirty-five. Unconscious, no seat belt. He's half on the floor at the far side of the cab nearest the ground. He submarined," she added, taking note of where the operator's pedals had bent and the floor mat ripped when Silva's unrestrained body was hurled beneath the steering wheel. "His right leg's broken. The foot caught beneath the clutch and twisted a hundred and eighty degrees from anatomical position. I can't see his face but there's a lot of blood on the dash and windows."

In the minute the climb and assessment had taken, the

rubies had pooled into a puddle of crimson. As she spoke it spread, a bright beautiful stream dripping from dash to windshield. "Bring the Stokes, backboard, oxygen, and jaws of life. I'm off radio now, I'm going to try and get to him." She heard the ubiquitous "ten-four" as she doffed her gunbelt and tossed it back onto the boulder. The radio she kept, using its heavy leather case to knock the remaining glass from the window frame.

"Sorry about that," she muttered as fragments rained down on Silva's back, caught shining in his hair.

One hand on either side of the window, she lowered her legs into the cab until she straddled the body of the man inside. Her left foot was on top of the passenger door above the shattered glass. Her right foot she wedged in the angle made by the windshield and the dash inches from where Silva's head rested.

Hanging on tightly to the outside door handle lest her precarious perch give way, she stretched down and switched off the ignition. Blessedly, the tinny sounds of country pop were silenced and the bizarre party feeling quenched. A click of the headlight button turned on the interior light and she freed up the hand she used to hold the flashlight.

Edging down till her knees rested along the upper edge of the passenger door, she slipped two fingers between Silva's jaw and shoulder, seeking by touch his carotid artery. Blood, warm and slippery, reminded her she'd forgotten to put on rubber gloves. Rangers with emergency response duties were required to be given hepatitis B vaccinations, but at a hundred and fifty bucks for each ranger, Hills couldn't bring himself to comply. AIDS, there was no shot for.

"You better be clean, Tom," Anna said as she pressed down. No pulse. Holding on to the rearview mirror for support, she crouched lower and repositioned her fingers in the hollow of Silva's neck beside his trachea.

"Bingo," she breathed as she felt the faint and thrilling thread of life. Given the mechanism of injury—a headlong flight off a cliff—and the absence of a seat belt, there was a good chance Silva had suffered damage to his spine and she was loath to move him without at least a short backboard. "Hills," she barked into the radio. "Where are you guys?"

"Just starting down."

"Jesus," she whispered. Since she'd dropped into the truck it seemed as if half an hour must have passed but she knew in reality it had been minutes. "It's bad," she said. "Bring a short spineboard. He's all crunched down on the passenger side and the truck's tipped. We'll have to haul him straight up through the driver's door."

Hills undoubtedly responded but Anna'd quit listening. Silva had made a sound. She crouched as low as she could, the man's dark head between her knees. Cupping his chin in her left hand, she supported his head and neck in the position she'd found it. "Tom, Tom, it's Anna."

A gurgle, half felt through her fingers, half heard, came from the injured man. Liquid trickled over her fingers where they curled around his chin. "Hang in there, Tom, help's here. Stay with me. We'll get you out."

"No," came out with more blood. "Killed Pats."

The adrenaline rush in Anna turned to cold horror. With her free hand she fumbled the radio from where it rested on the drunken tilt of the dash and held it to her mouth. Her right leg had begun to shake uncontrollably. "Hills, send somebody to check on Patsy Silva."

He asked something but Anna'd dropped her radio. The fragile beat of life beneath her fingers had stopped. "Fuck."

Silva was wearing a denim jacket, the collar turned up. Grasping collar and shoulder seams in her fists, she pulled the dead weight upward, straightening her legs to take some of the strain off her back. Silva's head fell against her forearm. In the uncompromising light of the dome she could see the gash in his forehead. White bone gleamed through the torn flesh.

Grunting with the effort, she pulled him chest high and wedged her right knee under his rump. Locking him in her arms, she looked up at the driver's window a couple of inches above her head. Impossibly far. Silva was a slight man, not more than one hundred and thirty-five or forty pounds, but she doubted she could push that much weight over her head.

"Come on, Tom, don't wimp out on me, damn you, come on," she murmured in his ear. Blood dropped onto her neck. "On three, ready, Tom. Jesus!" Anna coiled the strength she had into her legs and back. "One, two, three!" With all the power she could muster she pushed Tom up toward the night sky. Her back creaked in protest and she felt the muscles burn and grow watery in her shoulders.

Eyes squeezed shut, she tried to force him beyond her strength, but the soft weight of him was slipping from her. Then, miraculously, he went, his body light as air. Anna's eyes sprang open and the air exploded from her lungs. Her hands fell away and still Silva rose like Christ on Easter. As his feet drew level with her face, Anna heard voices. For an instant, Drew's face was visible in the glare of someone's light. He held Silva by the shirtfront, supporting him with one arm.

"Get him flat," Anna shouted. With shaking arms, she tried to lever herself out of the cab. Drew grabbed her wrists, lifted her clear of the truck, and set her on the rock near Tom. "Get me an airway," Anna said. "He had breath and pulse not a minute ago."

Crawling, she positioned herself over Silva's chest, placed two fingers on his carotid and her ear an inch from his mouth. "Damn."

"Nothing?" Drew asked.

"Nothing. Airway," she snapped. Behind her she could hear Hills pawing through the jump kit. She tilted Silva's jaw, pinched his nose, and blew two slow breaths into his lungs. "Compressions, Drew."

The big man leaned over Silva and, elbows locked, depressed the man's chest for five counts, forcing blood through the now quiet heart and into the dying organs. Anna breathed for Silva. Five more compressions and another breath.

Sour vomit from Silva's stomach filled Anna's mouth and she spat it out, refusing to let her own bile rise in its wake. "Airway," she barked as Drew compressed the chest.

A curved plastic oropharyngeal airway was pressed into her palm and she took a second to work the plastic into Silva's throat to keep his airway patent.

Drew compressed and Anna performed rescue breathing while the backboard was moved into place. The time for delicacy was past. Emergency personnel often referred to the Golden Hour, those first sixty minutes in which quick transport to a medical facility can still save a life. Time for Silva was running out, if, indeed, not already gone.

Unceremoniously, Silva was slid onto the board and strapped in the Stokes. Paul Summers took one end, Hills the other and lifted. Anna breathed, Drew compressed.

"Can't do it," Paul cried, shame and anger hot in his voice. The downward pressure of the compressions were too strong for him to support.

"Switch," Anna called.

Drew moved to the head of the Stokes and Paul took over compressions. "Breathe," she said, and blew into Silva's lungs.

"And one, and two . . ." Paul counted off as they crabbed awkwardly along the two boulders.

"Stop," Drew ordered when they reached the edge of the second rock. Anna and Paul stepped back. Drew set the litter down, Hills knelt still holding his end. The hell-tack foreman jumped from the rock then took up the Stokes again.

Hills scrambled down and they moved with startling speed over the river of boulders. Paul and Anna ran after. The big men, the litter, the moonlight, the rocking and rocky passage, gave the scene a jerky, keystone-cops look and Anna felt inappropriate laughter pushing up in her throat.

It came out in gasps as they reached the foot of the steep incline.

"Now," Drew said.

Anna felt for pulse, listened for breathing. Nothing. Again she gave two slow rescue breaths, then Paul began compressions. Bones broke—Silva's ribs—another rescue breath, five compressions.

Jimmy appeared from somewhere with ropes. Stanton's voice behind Anna said, "Can I spell you?" Anna blew oxygen into Silva's lungs, then shook her head. Five more compressions, more ribs snapping.

"Stop," Drew commanded.

Gratefully, Anna stepped back and wiped her mouth on

the back of her hand. The Stokes was roped up. Jimmy and Stanton had regained the top of the dirt slope and on a three count began to haul Silva upward.

CPR couldn't be interrupted for more than a minute. Without bothering to catch her breath, Anna began to claw her way up the incline. On the other side of the Stokes, she could see Paul bounding up the hill and envied him his youth.

The Stokes bumped to a halt on the cliff top. Anna was there waiting. "Now," Drew ordered. No breath, no pulse: Anna blew into the lungs. Paul did compressions. Bile spewed up, the acid burning Anna's lips. She spit it out and heard gagging. For a second she thought it was Silva breathing on his own, but it was Stanton.

The agent pushed ahead, trying to keep the oakbrush from scraping the rescuers away from their patient. Branches scratched Anna's face and hands but she was aware of them only peripherally, she didn't feel the sting or cut.

Finally they broke free of the brush. In minutes the Stokes was loaded into the ambulance. "Jimmy drives. Me, Drew, Paul, here in back. You guys see if you can figure out what happened." Hills slammed the door on the last of his words and the ambulance drove off, leaving Anna and Frederick standing in the middle of the road.

Darkness and stillness returned. The moon, temporarily eclipsed by the ambulance lights, reasserted its dominion. Shadows softened. Night creatures began timid explorations. Anna noticed she was cold and her back hurt like the dickens.

Pressing her hands into the small of her sacrum, she stretched in an attempt to ease it. "I've lost my strength of ten men," she said to Stanton.

The FBI agent was looking at her oddly and pawing at the side of his mouth. Moonlight gave his face a ghoulish cast. Primitive fear of the dark pricked Anna's sensitized nerves.

"What?" she demanded. "What is it?"

"You've . . . um . . . got something . . ." Tentatively he reached toward her but pulled back short of actually touching her. "It's . . . ah . . . vomit."

Anna wiped her mouth. Sour-smelling chunks came off in her hand. "I hate CPR. They're dead. If they don't sit up and take notice in the first sixty seconds, they're going to stay dead. But we've got to pound and poke and blow just like it made sense. Got a hankie?"

Stanton fished an enormous white handkerchief from his hip pocket and handed it to her. She scrubbed her mouth and cheeks, then pocketed it out of deference to his hypersensitive gag reflex.

"So, what happened?" Stanton turned and looked down the hill. Oakbrush and serviceberry had closed ranks, creating a wall impervious to the moonlight. Beyond, down the sharp slope, the pickup's carcass showed as a paler boulder in the boulder field.

"Drunk, I would guess. The cab reeked of alcohol, among other things." Anna, too, stared down the slope. The excitement over, fatigue weighed heavily and the thought of climbing back down the hill wasn't pleasant.

"Got a flashlight?" Stanton asked.

"It's down there. You?"

"Not me. Got a spare in your car?"

"Of course. Doesn't work though." The dark grew darker. Prickly pear spines lodged in Anna's hand were making themselves felt.

"The blind leading the blind?" Stanton asked.

"I'll go first."

"Good. Snakes and things, you know."

"First person just wakes them up and makes them mad. They always bite the second person. That's a proven statistic."

"Where'd you read it?" Stanton demanded as he hurried after her into the arms of the oakbrush.

"*U.S. News and World Report.*" Anna gave him the standard comeback of the 1968 Mercy High School debate team.

Without lights, music, and Silva, the wreck looked old, all life gone, metal bleached like bones. Anna appreciated its peacefulness. Lowering herself back down into the cab, she felt a kinship with Tom. It had less to do with ghosts than with the now all-pervasive odor of alcohol.

"Here but for the grace of God" crossed her mind like a prayer as she remembered the night she'd lost to booze and self-pity.

By the dome light, she retrieved her flashlight from where it had fallen down next to the door and passed it up to Agent Stanton.

Searching the cab was a job for a contortionist. Anna squatted over the broken passenger window and poked through the debris that had been shaken from under the seat and floor mats. A pack of Marlboros, two cigarettes remaining that would go unsmoked; five empty cans of Budweiser and one full, still cold to the touch; a McDonald's bag, the contents so old they no longer smelled; bits of paper, maps, and registration from the glove box; a pencil with a chewed eraser and broken lead; and a golf ball completed the inventory. But for the golf ball, it was more or less what she had expected to find. Silva didn't strike her as a golf sort of guy. A bowling ball or squirrel rifle would have been more in keeping with the image she had of him.

Hoisting herself out of the cab, she sat on the door with her feet still inside. The effort cost her a wrenching pain in her lower back, muscles protesting the lifting of one hundred and forty pounds.

"Ooof!" Stanton dragged himself up on the boulder nearby. "Find anything?"

"Just what you'd expect: beer, cigarettes, fast food. The detritus of a misspent youth."

"I didn't find anything revelatory outside the truck," Stanton said. "We ought to come back by the light of day but it looks like what it is: DUI with fatality. Back on the hill the truck left the ground and was airborne till it struck here. What I want to know is where Silva was between getting bailed out of jail and getting killed."

"Killed. Patsy!" Anna remembered with a fresh sense of horror. "Tom said he'd killed her."

18

PATSY WAS fine, at least until they told her about Tom. "Seriously injured" was how Anna put it. One of the great contributions of cardiopulmonary resuscitation was that nobody ever died on a carry-out, or in an ambulance, for that matter. Through the vomit and the cracking bones and the blood, the body was kept pumped up with oxygen, the organs pantomiming life till a doctor pronounced it officially dead.

Patsy wept like a shattered bride. Regardless of divorce, this had apparently been a till-death-do-you-part kind of relationship. "There's always hope, Mom," Missy said, holding her mother's shoulders in an odd moment of role reversal.

Anna had ambivalent feelings about hope. Just because artists depicting the last refugee from Pandora's box always dressed the horrid little bugger like Tinkerbell, people tended to think hope was a good thing. Often it was the worst of the evils let loose to plague humankind.

"Is there hope?" Patsy pleaded.

"It was pretty bad," Anna told her. "He was still talking when I got to him. He said your name."

Patsy cried harder but it was different and Anna was glad she'd kept the context of Tom's remark to herself.

The sun was rising when she and Agent Stanton left the tower house. Too tired to sleep, Anna sat for a moment behind the wheel of the patrol car, staring stupidly in front of her. "My back is killing me," she said to no one in particular though Frederick was in the seat next to her.

"Want me to drive?"

The offer sounded so halfhearted, Anna realized she'd never seen Stanton behind the wheel of a car. "Have you got a license?" she asked abruptly.

He laughed, a sound that soothed her frayed nerves. "Almost like new, only use it on Sundays."

"Don't like to drive?"

"I'd rather look out the window."

"It's not far." Anna referred to the tent frame Frederick was bivouacked in. "I'll drive."

"Goody. I'll give you a back rub. My first wife—or was it my second? Anyway, I come highly recommended in the back rub department."

Leaving the tower house, Anna turned right and drove three hundred yards the wrong way on the one-way to the tent colony where VIPs and stabilization crew were housed.

Like the other service areas in Mesa Verde, this was on a loop. Communal showers, toilets, washer/dryer, and pay phone occupied the island created by the gravel drive.

Some of the dwellings were charming. Of native stone, they were built in the round style of Navajo hogans, but the majority were single-room plywood shacks called tent frames. Sixteen by sixteen feet square, they had just room for a bed, stove, and refrigerator. There was no running water. At one time they'd been wooden platforms with canvas forming the walls and roof. When housing became short, they'd been walled in and wood-burning stoves added to give them a longer season of use.

Though cramped and primitive, Anna saw in them

blessed privacy and a home for Piedmont. When Stanton left, she would lean on Hills to give her his tent frame till permanent housing became available.

She pulled the Ford into the graveled spot in front of number seventeen. A picnic table under the junipers provided a platform for two scrub jays squabbling over a bit of orange peel. A fire pit with grill was near the table. "I could live here," Anna said.

"Come in. I'll give you the fifty-cent tour. Make some decaf."

Not ready yet to go home, Anna accepted. The tour consisted of "Honey, I'm home," called to imaginary scorpions. Anna sat on the single bed. It was made up so neatly it worried her. What kind of man made his bed when called out on a motor vehicle accident at three A.M.?

Apparently reading her mind, Stanton said: "Not anal retentive." He pointed to the long wooden table that occupied the wall between the wood stove and the foot of the bed. It was covered with papers and sketches, some in tidy piles, some scattered about where he'd been working into the wee hours.

Anna got up and looked to keep herself occupied while Stanton busied himself with coffee, drawing the water from a five-gallon plastic container with a spigot.

Photos of Stacy in the kiva, of the shoes with burn marks, were laid out neatly. Drawings of the kiva, of Cliff Palace—quite good drawings—with entrance and exits marked, were placed like maps above the autopsy and 10-344 report. Lists were everywhere; lists of clues and suspects, lists of things done and things left to do, lists of lists.

"Not anal retentive, you say?"

"Well, not about housework anyway. Although my second ex-wife—or was it my first—thought I should be."

"You don't think much of marriage, I take it?"

"Are you kidding? It's my favorite hobby. Spend every spare penny on it. I'm completely in favor of it, wish both ladies would remarry today."

Anna laughed. "No doubt about it, widowhood has its upside." She took the coffee he offered and sat in the straight-backed wooden chair. There being no others, Stanton perched on the foot of his bed.

"Come up with any bright ideas?" Anna indicated the desk. The hasty report she'd written on her previous day's findings was lying above a legal pad where yet another list was forming. A pair of half glasses served as a paperweight.

"Nothing brilliant. I'm getting slow," he said. "Can't solve them in record time anymore. I used to do it with one victim. 'One-corpse Stanton' they called me. Now it takes two or three before I catch on."

He was poking fun at himself but Anna understood. There was no solving a crime till it happened. By then the damage was done. What kept the chase worth the effort was the hope a second could be prevented.

"Pushing forty-five," Stanton said. "Headed over the proverbial hill."

"Over the hill," Anna echoed.

"You aren't supposed to agree with me," he complained. "For a park ranger you sure don't know anything about fishing."

"No," Anna said absently. She put down her coffee and took the golf ball from her shirt pocket. "This was in Silva's truck."

"And?" Stanton looked at the little ball with interest. His instant attention was gratifying. He trusted Anna not to waste his time.

"Over the hill," Anna repeated. "In a conversation once,

Tom said he couldn't play golf because he wasn't over the hill yet."

"Not his ball."

"What do you figure would happen if you wedged a golf ball in the linkage over a gas pedal?"

"When the car crashed the ball would roll out."

"When the pickup crashed." Anna swiveled in her seat to set the ball down amidst Stanton's case work. Twisting tore the damaged muscles and she groaned.

"Ready for that back rub?" Stanton asked.

"No thanks." Anna had been given a goodly number of back rubs over the years. They'd been anything but relaxing and healthful. Most had degenerated fairly quickly into wrestling matches. She was too tired to defend her virtue.

"You'll like it. It'll be good for you. Really." Stanton was bustling: setting down coffee, grabbing up pillows and blankets. "I've been to school. I'm certified and everything." He carried the bedding out through the screen door.

He was shaking an army blanket out on the picnic table. The jays had fled to the branches of a nearby juniper and watched with interest. "Soft is no good," he was saying as Anna came up behind him. "You can't really do much with soft. Padded is best but this'll do." He plumped a pillow down on one end of the table. "Climb on up," he said. "Office hours have commenced."

More out of curiosity than anything else, Anna complied, lying belly-down on the tabletop.

"I'm a Rolfer," Stanton said, climbing up and straddling her. "A proponent and practitioner of the art of Rolfing." With that he pushed his knuckles into her back.

What followed was the least sexual and most healing

experience Anna had ever had. His strong fingers seemed to knead and pry the pain from between her muscles and realign her much maligned vertebrae.

When he'd finished, she lay quiet for another minute or so, enjoying the heat radiating through her back. "That's the first honest-to-God back rub I've ever had," she said truthfully.

By mutual agreement she and Stanton put the investigation on hold till they'd rested. Anna suffered from the pleasant but frustrating sense that things were just about to come clear, words on the tip of the tongue, connections about to be made. She doubted she'd be able to sleep but natural fatigue and the continuing warmth Stanton's fingers had worked into her back conspired to shut down her brain and she slept without dreaming.

Around two-thirty that afternoon she awoke. Even that late in the day she was doomed to a cold shower. "Sorry," Jennifer said when she stalked into the kitchen to make coffee. "I didn't figure anybody else'd be showering so late. I was steaming me out a hangover. A doozy. Alcohol poisoning of the worst kind. Have some of my coffee as a peace offerin' whilst yours does its thing."

Anna accepted a mugful and dressed it with a dollop of heavy whipping cream.

"How do you stay so skinny?" Jennifer demanded. "I get fat on NutraSweet and water."

"Are you on late today?" Anna asked.

"Yes ma'am. Till forever. I can't wait till you stop messin' with that FBI guy. With both you'n Stacy off the schedule, seems all I do is work night shifts."

Anna tried to look sympathetic out of gratitude for the coffee. "Where'd you get your hangover?"

Jennifer laughed, then clutched her head. "Jamie and I

did Durango. She's still in bed. You should've seen her. She got to arm-wrestling boys for drinks. She's just too strong for her own good. We like to drowned."

"Sounds like fun," Anna fed the conversation. Not yet through her first cup of coffee and already prying suspiciously into other people's lives; she'd be glad when the investigation was over and she could resume the life of a disinterested third party. "Who drove you home?"

"The bartender at Flannigan's took Jamie's car keys. We had to crash in her station wagon till he opened up around ten this morning."

Jennifer buckled on her gun and left Anna to finish the coffee.

By four-thirty Stanton still hadn't called. Anna left word with Dispatch to radio her if he checked in, and drove down to the CRO. The events of the previous night were settling in her mind and she needed to sort them out. Laying out facts in the no-nonsense format demanded by government form 10-343 seemed to help. As senior person on the scene, Hills should have written the report but Anna had no worries that he'd beaten her to the punch. Like a lot of district rangers, Hills had joined the NPS because of a love of hiking, canoeing, shooting, backpacking, climbing—challenging himself physically. When he climbed up into management he was forced to confront his worst fear: paperwork. Brawling drunks he could handle. The sight of a computer lit up the yellow streak down his broad back.

As she banged into the CRO, she asked Frieda, "Has Stanton called?"

"Not yet."

"Silva?"

"DOA. Massive cerebral hemorrhage."

"Too bad."

"Yes indeedy. You, Hills, and the guys are scheduled to

do a fatality debriefing with Dr. Whitcomb Friday morning. Write it down."

Successfully resisting the urge to unload the night's pressures on Frieda, Anna slipped around the partition to her desk. As usual it was piled with clutter not of her making. Evidently Hills had dumped Stacy's personal defensive equipment there after inventorying it. Anna scooped it up to dump back on the district ranger's desk. The radio's leather case tumbled out of her clutches. "Whoa!"

"What?" Frieda called over the room divider.

"Nothing." Anna dropped the gunbelt back where she'd found it and pinched up the radio case between thumb and forefinger. Burnt into the leather were two prints, etched marks such as had manifested on Stacy's shoes. The prints on the case hadn't been there when Rose had returned it. Anna was sure of that. In her fingerprinting frenzy she would have noticed.

The prints on Stacy's shoes had taken between one and three days to appear. Lost as they'd been in her trunk, Anna couldn't be more precise.

If these marks came from the same hand, and it was hard to imagine they hadn't, they'd been made not more than one to three days previously, considerably after Stacy had died and before Rose had returned the radio.

Anna closed her eyes and ears and marshaled her thoughts. Whoever removed Stacy's shoes had used the radio. Whoever used the radio had access to Rose's house. Did Stacy's murder have anything to do with Silva's death? Probably. Two murders in one sleepy park were highly unlikely. Rose might have killed Stacy for some matrimonial crime as yet unpublished, but why Tom? Greeley killing Silva for pilfering, monkeywrenching? Overkill to say the least. *Strangers on a Train?* You kill mine, I'll kill yours.

There weren't enough players for a really good game of

detection, Anna thought. Drew was in and out of the picture. Clearly he felt Stacy and Rose were making the wrong choices for Bella. Did his protectiveness over children extend to Silva's? Did he believe Tom was abusing Missy and Mindy in some way? Anna thought back to the wreck. Drew's efforts to salvage Silva's life seemed genuine enough.

Rousing herself, Anna called over the wall. "Frieda, Stanton call yet?"

"You're sitting on the phone back there. Did it ring?"

"I guess not," Anna conceded. Taking the radio case, she again gave Frieda the message to let her know when Stanton woke up. Frieda rolled her eyes but Anna was wrapped up in her own thoughts and missed it.

There was one last thing to check, then she would go stir Stanton up whether he was rested or not.

The maintenance yard was empty when she drove in. Maintenance and Construction worked seven A.M. to three-thirty Monday through Friday. By three thirty-one there was never any sign of them.

As she'd expected, the chain-link gate to the fenced-off area where Ted Greeley kept his heavy equipment was locked, the chain and padlock as she had thought they would be.

Frieda called then and Anna abandoned her train of thought. Stanton was awake. She found him sitting on the picnic table with his feet on the bench nursing a cup of coffee.

"Good morning." She sat down beside him, adjusting her gun so the butt wouldn't pry against her ribs. "Get a good nap?"

"Yes indeedy. Is it still Monday?"

"All day."

Anna told Stanton about chains and locks and their connection with Stacy Meyers, Monday nights, and the Cliff Palace loop. "What I can't figure out is why and how. Without those, 'who' is pretty worthless."

Stanton took another sip of coffee. Anna wished he'd offer her some. Not because it looked particularly good, but because it was something to do with her hands. In lieu of the coffee, she picked up a twig and began methodically snapping it in small pieces.

They sat in silence for a time. The sun was low in the sky and bathed them in amber light. To the west, Anna could just see the tops of thunderheads. It was probably raining in Dove Creek. A small doe wandered out from behind the tent frame. The air was so still they could hear the tearing sound as she cropped the grass.

Stanton seemed transfixed by the nearness of the graceful animal.

"Missing Chicago?" Anna ribbed him.

"In Chicago we have rats bigger than that."

"Her."

"How can you tell?"

"No antlers."

"I thought they fell off."

"They grow back."

"No kidding!"

Anna felt her leg being gently pulled and laughed. "You're such a rube, Frederick."

The doe's head came up at the sound of laughter but the deer was looking not at them but down the footpath leading along the canyon's edge to the housing loop. Frederick and Anna watched with her. Moments later Bella and her aunt came into view. Bella was in the lead. In her arms she carried a basket woven of pastel strips, a relic of a previous Easter. If the care she took not to let the basket bump or tip was any indication of contents, Anna would've guessed nitroglycerin or at least goldfish. Hattie followed with a plastic spatula, the kind cooks use to scrape the last of the cake batter from the bowl.

"Howdy, Bella, Hattie," Frederick called.

"Fred and Anna!" To Bella, Hattie said: "I told you this was going to be a good walk. So far we've seen three deer, a chipmunk, a park ranger, and an FBI agent."

"An' a Abert squirrel," Bella added, clearly more impressed with the long-eared rodent than the last two sightings on her aunt's list.

Hattie left the footpath and forged through the high grass toward the picnic table. Ryegrass was beginning to plume and bright yellow mustard flowers dipped gracefully in her wake. Bella followed a few steps then stopped, hanging back.

"There's no snakes," Frederick assured her. "I made Ranger Pigeon check."

"Only babies are afraid of snakes," Bella returned. Anna forbore comment but bumped Stanton's knee with her own. "I don't want to get any stuff on you." Bella held the party-colored basket up like a dangerous offering.

"Is it full of nitroglycerin?" Anna asked.

"I don't know," Bella replied. "But probably not."

"Nitro's a liquid but it explodes like dynamite," Anna told her.

Clearly Bella didn't believe a word. "That'd be silly."

"You're right," Anna conceded.

"Battery acid," Frederick guessed.

"This is a basket," Bella said with a touch of impatience. "It'd leak out."

"Spiders," Anna tried.

Bella looked like that wasn't a bad idea but she shook her head. "It's sad thoughts. *Really* sad thoughts. Me and Aunt Hattie thought up all the saddest thoughts and we put them in the basket and we're going to dump 'em in the canyon when the winds go down."

"The winds aren't up," Anna remarked, noting the stillness of the evening.

"They are. Drew said. The winds go up in the morning and down at night."

Anna grabbed Frederick's arm. "Bella's right. You're right," she said to the child.

Slightly mollified, "Up at day, down at night," Bella reiterated. "We gotta go," she told her aunt.

"Gotta go," Hattie echoed, and, "Take care."

"Out of the mouths of babes," Anna said to Frederick as they watched the woman and girl pass out of sight behind a stand of piñons. "Firefighters always watch the winds. When the sun warms the air in the mornings it begins to rise and a wind blows up canyon. In the evening, as the cool air settles the wind shifts, blows down canyon. In the still of night it settles in the low areas. That's pounded into your head with a Pulaski in every fire class.

"You dump the sad thoughts at night, they blow down canyon, away, out to the wide valleys, and are dispersed. You dump them in the morning, when the sun rises, they blow up canyon, into the alcoves, settle into the ruins."

"Holy smoke," Stanton said. "A blinding flash of the obvious."

19

CLIFF PALACE loop was closed; the gate at the Four-Way closed the road and the starless night closed down the world. Clouds obscured a fledgling moon. Trees, crowding close to the road, seemed impervious even to headlights. Shadows were sudden, long, and unnatural.

"This whole place is one big graveyard. Doesn't that give you the willies?" Stanton asked.

"Only when I think about it." The Ford's beams were on low. If Anna'd had her druthers she'd've driven without lights but the night was too dark for that.

When the road widened into Cliff Palace parking lot, she switched them off.

"Yikes! What have we here?"

From the dim glow of the dashboard Anna could see where Stanton pointed. Along the split-rail fence separating the parking area from the trees were dozens of tiny glowing eyes, as if a herd of rats or other small night predators waited for the unwary.

"Glowworms," she told him. "Want to catch one?"

"No thanks. Wow. As in 'Glow, little glowworm, glow'? I'm disappointed. Not a 'glimmer glimmer' in the lot."

"Poetic license."

Again the road was enclosed by darkness. Anna slowed but didn't switch the headlights back on. From here to the Ute reservation the road ran along the canyon's rim. Though in most places there was a fringe of trees between the road and the canyon, any stray light could give them away.

At the Navajo taco stand on the tiny piece of reservation land accidently surveyed into the park, Anna pulled off.

Around the souvenir and taco stand the land had been leveled and graveled in. Beyond, a dirt road led back into the brush and trees. There'd once been a barrier across it to keep out adventuresome tourists but it had long since fallen into disrepair. For several years no one had been caught camping back there so there had been no impetus to get it fixed. Brush made a quick and dirty barrier, a solution often employed to make a track or trail less desirable.

Anna loosed her flashlight from beneath the dash and climbed out of the car. Hands deep in pockets, Stanton followed. "The mesa runs out there in a big finger of land with cliffs on all sides."

"You can see where the brush has been dragged back and forth." Anna shone the light on the bottom of the makeshift barricade. Twigs were snapped and dusty. "Not much in the way of tracks but we've not had rain for a while. Dry, this soil's like concrete."

"Here." Stanton had walked around the pile and poked a toe into the spill of her light. "Truck track. Old but still pretty clear."

Together they moved the brush aside. It took only a minute; the barricade had been culled down to three good-sized bitterbrush bushes so dry they weighed next to nothing.

"A real deterrent," Anna said dryly. "I'm surprised we haven't had wild packs of Bluebirds and Brownies rampaging around back here."

She drove the patrol car through, then they carefully replaced the brush the way they had found it.

The one-lane dirt road was rutted and, though she drove at a footpace, the car jounced from side to side. Without headlights, the trip put Anna in mind of Mr. Toad's Wild Ride in Disneyland. Three quarters of a mile and it ended in a wide turnaround where dirt and rock had been scraped away to help build roads in the park. On the far side of the tree-shrouded clearing was a pile of slash fifteen or twenty feet high.

Anna eased the Ford around behind it, forcing the car over the rubble of limbs. "I feel like a cat hiding behind a blade of grass, like there's bits of me sticking out," she said as she turned off the ignition.

Stanton laughed. He was at the same time more relaxed and more alive than she'd ever seen him. "You love this, don't you," she said.

"So do you, Anna, admit it. Cops and robbers."

Anna wasn't admitting anything.

Stanton tapped the long-lensed camera on the seat between them. "The Colorado Highway Patrol is on standby. We watch, we take pictures for the judge. We call Frieda. Frieda alerts the Highway Patrol. They nab our perpetrator at the entrance station. We're heroes. What's not to like?"

Anna thought of Stacy with his warm brown eyes and passionate love of the natural world. "I'd rather beat a confession out with a rubber hose," she said.

"You may get your chance. Odds are our sniffing around has set the alarm off and we won't get a thing. So far our evidence is pretty thin."

"It's Monday. For whatever reasons the veil was always on Mondays," she insisted. "If it was worth killing for twice, it'll be worth a last run or two. My guess is this particular chindi doesn't scare off easily." She turned off both her belt and the car radios. "It's got to happen because basically we've got zip."

"We know zip but we can't prove zip," Stanton corrected. "I hate these last-minute assignations."

"It's Monday night," Anna defended herself. "Maybe the last Monday night load." Clicking free of her seat belt, she let herself out of the car, taking the flashlight with her. A yellow circle of light joined hers as Stanton walked around the back of the vehicle. Familiarizing themselves with the area, they played their lights over the slash heap and around the car. The slash pile was comprised of the limbs and rounds of trees cleared from near the buildings by the hazardous fuel removal crew. The idea was that, should a wildfire break out on the mesa—a common occurrence during the thunderstorm season—there wouldn't be enough dead and down wood to carry it to any of the historic structures, a theory as yet not tested and not inspiring of much faith among firefighters. But it kept the stoves supplied all winter and a crew of high school and college students busy all summer.

Anna walked one way and Stanton the other till they'd circumnavigated the pile and satisfied themselves that the settled weave of pine and juniper branches was dense enough to hide the patrol car. Then Anna turned her attention to the clearing. Red soil, garish in the flashlight beam, was torn up by the tracks of heavy equipment.

Most were run over so many times the tread was indecipherable.

"There's enough for some good casts," Stanton said. He was down on hands and knees examining the dried mud.

"I'll take your word for it."

"Flunked plaster casts?"

"I don't remember being taught that. I thought it was a Sherlock Holmes kind of thing."

"*Au contraire.* We still do it. It's getting to be a lost art, though. Crime has come out of the closet. They do it right out in the open, then we just arrest 'em. Don't have to finesse much these days. Or else they do it all with computers and mirrors and we never know what hit us until we read about in the *Tribune.*"

Anna traced the mishmash of tracks toward the mesa's edge. They formed a broken fan narrowing to a drop-off point where an opening about forty feet wide made the canyon accessible. To either side trees and sandstone slabs closed in.

Careful not to walk on any salvageable tracks, she made her way to the cliff. Blackness swallowed the feeble beam of her six-cell. Instead of vertigo, it gave her a false sense of security, as if the drop wasn't there at all, as if it were solid and soft: black velvet.

"Don't stand so near the edge." Stanton's voice at her elbow made her flinch.

"Don't creep," she retorted.

"Don't shout."

"Don't snap."

"Nerves shot?"

"Yours too?"

He laughed easily. "A little moonlight would help. Stars. Streetlights. Neon signs. Anything. It is way too dark out here."

"The dark is my friend." Anna flipped off her light. "The invisible woman."

Stanton turned his off as well and they stood in the darkness and the silence. As her eyes adjusted, Anna began to see the faint light that lives in all but deep caves: a blush of peach on the underside of the clouds to the south over the town of Shiprock, a trailing edge of silver where a thunderhead thinned near the moon, a barely discernible difference in the quality of dark between earth and sky, cliff and treeline.

A cold breath of air, just enough to tickle the hair on her arms, was inhaled into the depths of the canyon; air settling as it cooled. Anna closed her eyes and breathed deeply.

"Almonds," she said.

Stanton sniffed, seeming to taste the air in nasal sips. "Could be." He turned on his flash and, in contrast, the night became impossibly dark again. The finger of light stirred in the dirt at their feet. Here the soil was more black than red and the truck tracks amorphous, as if made in soft mud. "Whatever it is, we're standing in it." With the light, he traced the discolored soil to where the canyon claimed it. "Whatever is being dumped goes over right here."

Anna took a plastic evidence bag from her hip pocket and scraped a sample of the dirt into it with the blade of her pocketknife. Not anxious to get a snootful of anything unfriendly, she sniffed it delicately, then offered it to Stanton. "Almonds," he confirmed.

Having rolled the dirt into a package reminiscent of a lid of marijuana, Anna stowed it in her shirt pocket. "Tomorrow we'll get down into the canyon bottom. Cliff Palace is up there at the head of the canyon. From the top of it this spot's clearly visible. If every veil sighting was in reality a Monday night drop, that'd be at least four dumps. At least—on a night like this nobody would see a thing."

"Upcanyon winds when the sun begins to warm and whatever gases this muck gives off drift to the Palace and pool in the alcove. Them what's got weak hearts and lungs fall by the wayside," Stanton said. "If the stuff's heavy it'd settle in the lowest spots. Maybe it filled the kiva Stacy was in, overcame him. That'd account for the single set of tracks."

"Burning prints from the flaming digits on Stacy's arms," Anna reminded him. "Marks like we found on his shoes and appeared on the radio case. I doubt Stacy's murder was quite so second degree."

For a minute longer they stood on the lip of the canyon, Anna feeling there was something more she ought to be doing but uncertain of just what.

"All we're going to do tonight is mess up what evidence there is," Stanton said finally. "Let's find a front-row seat and wait for the curtain to go up."

On the eastern edge of the clearing, they found a flat slab of sandstone partially screened by a thicket of juniper. Their rock was several yards above where the dirt road entered the clearing. Headlights of approaching vehicles wouldn't find them.

For a while Frederick tried to keep the conversation afloat. When he'd exhausted stories about his kids, Anna's pets, and ascertained that she had seen none of the recent movies, he fell silent.

Anna enjoyed the quiet. In complete darkness there was no awkwardness. Alone but not lonely; Stanton was there but invisible and, now, inaudible. Small stirrings as he shifted position, the crack of a joint as he straightened a knee, were comfortable, comforting. Sounds a man made in the bed as he slept beside you, Anna realized. It had been a while since those living human sounds had been there to lull her back to sleep when the nightmares woke her.

Within a couple of hours the meager heat the stone had collected during the day was gone. Beside her, Frederick's deep, even breathing suggested he'd fallen asleep. She didn't begrudge him a nap. Could she have slept, she would've had no qualms about waking him to watch while she caught forty winks.

Cold was settling into the low places and Anna's spirits settled with it. In the wee small hours of the morning, as the song went, was when she missed him most of all. The long and most thoroughly dead Zachary, the husband of her heart—or as Molly caustically put it when Anna waxed maudlin—the husband of her youth, back when all things were possible, all dreams unfolding.

Stacy's haunting brown eyes had a ghost of Zachary's intensity, a shadow of his remembered wit. Unfortunate as Meyers' death was, Anna knew it saved her from making a complete ass of herself. Had the affair become full blown, her life would have disintegrated into that morass of guilt, deceit, and recrimination even the most carefully orchestrated adultery engenders.

Despite Stacy's avowals of dedication to Rose, Anna had little doubt that the affair would have blossomed. Lust leveraged by memory was a powerful force. Ultimately it must have disappointed them both. The Hindus preached that there were three thousand six hundred gates into heaven. Anna doubted adultery was one of them. Like alcohol, it was just a short vacation from life-as-we-know-it.

Stanton's long fingers closed around her knee and Anna was startled into thinking a short vacation might be just what the doctor ordered.

"Listen," he whispered.

She strained her ears but heard nothing. "Sorry, too much loud rock-and-roll music in my youth."

"Shhh. Listen."

An engine growled in the distance. "I hear it now." They fell quiet again, tracking the sound. Anna frisked herself, loosened the baton in its holster, unclipped her keys from her belt, and put them in her shirt pocket where they wouldn't jingle when she moved.

"If the tracks are any indication, the truck will pull in, headlights on the slash pile, turn perpendicular to the canyon, headlights pointed somewhere south of us, then back as close to the rim as possible to make the dump." Stanton went over ground they'd covered in earlier discussions. "I'll stay here. Maybe work my way further around where I can get some clear pictures of the truck, the license plate, and, if we're lucky, the driver actually unstoppering the tank."

"Nothing like a smoking gun," Anna said. Then, because it was safer than assuming, she spoke her part: "I go behind the car, get the shotgun, stay put, shut up, and hope your career as a photographer is long and uneventful."

"Let's do it."

Anna felt Stanton squeeze her knee, then he was gone without a sound, like the mythical Indian scouts in children's books. Moving as quietly as she could, Anna was still aware of the crack and scuffle of her footfalls. She comforted herself with the thought that it was like chewing carrots, more audible to the doer of the deed than any accidental audience members.

In less than two minutes, she'd popped the trunk, unsheathed the shotgun, and was in place by the left rear fender of the car, trying to regain the night vision the trunk light had robbed her of. "Damn," she cursed herself. It was those details that got one killed. If the flash of light from the trunk had been seen, they'd either be in for a fight or the truck would simply keep going, taking all the good, hard courtroom proof of malfeasance with it.

Prying her mind from this treadmill of extraneous thought, Anna slowed her breathing and opened her senses. A feeling of clean emptiness filled her, body and mind receptive to the physical world: the earth firm beneath her feet, the smooth wood of the shotgun stock against her palms, the breeze on her right cheek, the weight of her duty belt, the smell of pine, the sounds of the night and the engine.

Fragments of light began filtering through the trees. She closed her eyes and turned her head away as the truck grew close. Spots of orange danced across her eyelids. The drone became a roar and she felt a moment's panic that she would be run down.

Lights moved, the roar grew louder. She opened her eyes. Headlights stabbed into the woods on the east side of the clearing. Confident the din would cover any sound, she moved to the end of the slash pile and took a stand behind a dead pine branch.

Racket and exhaust filled the clearing, then the sound of clanging as a big red water truck backed toward the canyon. When it was less than a yard from the cliff edge, the roar settled to an idle and the clanging stopped. Placing her feet as much from memory as sight, Anna moved to the rim of the canyon. Twin sandstone blocks, each the size of a small room, were at her back. To the left, between her and the cliff, were three stunted piñon trees.

They were scarcely taller than she but, on this harsh mesa, could've been a hundred years old or more. A bitterbrush bush eight or ten feet tall screened her from the water truck with spiny brown arms.

Headlights were switched off. The night drew close. Far to the west heat lightning flickered from cloud to cloud. If there was distant thunder the truck drowned it out. Engine noise filled all available space, creating confusion where stillness and clarity had reigned.

Tingling in her fingers let Anna know she'd tensed, her grip was too tight. Again she opened her mind, rocked on the balls of her feet, and moved her hands slightly on the shotgun. Over the idle of the engine she heard the slamming of a door. In her mind she heard the click of the camera shutter as Stanton captured the driver on film, the door, the truck, the license plate.

A shadow came around the back of the water truck, bent down, and began pulling or pushing at something. Envying Stanton his infrared scope, she strained her eyes, opening them so wide tears started, but there was no more ambient light to be gathered and she could see nothing more.

Metal clanked on metal and a liquid hiss followed as something cascaded onto the packed earth. Anna smelled almonds. Memories from old movies and Agatha Christie novels flooded sickeningly through her mind. Cyanide gas was said to smell of almonds. She stopped breathing—a temporary solution at best and one not conducive to clear thinking. Shrinking back toward the slash pile, she hoped the down-canyon winds would carry the fumes in the opposite direction. From all reports these night dumps lasted only minutes.

Sudden light flooded the clearing. The figure was spotlighted and Anna sucked in a lungful of almond scent. Not a man but a creature with a human body, the head of an insect, and one long, clawed arm hunkered there.

In an instant her mind recoiled from appearance to reality: a human wearing the self-contained breathing apparatus found on fire trucks stood in the spill of light brandishing a pipe wrench. Liquid, rainbow bright in the headlights, gushed from a line of sprinklers on the rear of the water truck in a fine, even rain. It would take only a beam of moonlight to turn it into a spirit veil.

Like an afterthought, blue overheads and the ululating wail of a siren added to the confusion. Someone shouted. A door banged.

"Goddamn it!" Anna whispered as Jennifer Short, fumbling her .357 from its holster, ran into the light. Once again the woman had neglected to call into service or Frieda would have headed her off.

"Freeze! Freeze!" Short was shouting like a cop in a TV movie. The insect head turned slowly, the pipe wrench fell from sight, hidden behind a trousered leg.

Anna stepped clear of the sheltering brush and chambered a round of double-ought buck. The unmistakable sound cut through the low-grade rumble of the engine and the siren's whine. Insect eyes swiveled toward her. She shouldered the gun. "Drop the wrench," she shouted. "Drop the wrench."

The pipe wrench was moved away, held out to the side, the eye plates of the mask black, unreadable.

"Drop it." Anna leaned forward, flexing her knee, ready to take the recoil if she had to pull the trigger. A cold vibrating in her stomach and the feel of the butt of the shotgun against her shoulder were all she was aware of. The world had shrunk, her vision tunneled till all that existed was the creature with the pipe wrench, clear and contained as a figure viewed through the wrong end of binoculars.

Movement pried open her field of vision. Jennifer, her pistol worked free of the holster, circled to the west, putting the insect directly between herself and Anna's shotgun.

"Jennifer, stop!" Anna cried. Either deaf from noise or adrenaline, Short ran the last yard, completing the line. Now she and Anna stood less than forty feet apart, guns pointing at one another.

The insect realized it as Anna did. Glittering eyes turned from her to Jennifer. The wrench disappeared behind a leg. Slowly, mesmerizing, with the gauntleted hands and inhuman head, it walked toward Short. Jennifer was shifting her weight, her feet dancing in the dirt. Even from a distance Anna could see her hands shaking. "Stop where you are," Anna shouted. Nausea churned in her stomach and she wondered if it was nerves or whatever she was breathing.

Aware that if she pulled the trigger, when the smoke cleared Jennifer might be dead as well, the insect ignored her.

To Anna's left was the canyon. If she shifted right the water truck would block her target. "Jennifer, move!" she yelled. "Move, damn you."

"Stop. Stop now. Don't come any closer," Jennifer was shouting. Shrieking like a banshee, the masked figure dodged right and charged. Anna saw the flash from the barrel of Short's .357 and hurled herself to the ground. High-pitched and ringing, a bullet struck stone. Sparks flew and Anna felt the sting of rock splinters hitting the back of her leg. Two more wild shots rang out, then a scream. Anna looked up to see Jennifer clubbed to the ground by the pipe wrench. The monster-headed figure leaped from sight behind the far side of the truck.

Head and torso behind the right rear wheel, Short lay without moving.

Another fracture of sound and a muzzle flash came from the boulder beyond where Jennifer lay. Stanton. Like Anna, he'd ended up their fools' chorus line.

Flickering blue lights lent his body the fast-forward movement of early films as he ran.

Anna was on her feet running, the shotgun clutched to her chest. Siren and engine roar clouded her brain, clogged her thoughts. Cacophony or cyanide was eroding her synapses. A car door slammed. The ground was uneven and becoming slippery. A stabbing pain, muscles outraged by sudden movement, nearly tripped her.

Stanton was shouting. Then a loud regular clanging cut through the engine's throb. The water truck had been thrown into reverse, the warning bell ringing the intention to back up. Through the shimmering curtain of toxic waste, Anna saw the rear wheels begin to tear free of the mud, crush the strip of ground between themselves and Jennifer Short.

No time to think. Anna threw the shotgun from her, guaranteeing the canyon would be the first to claim it, and hurled herself backward, clear of the moving vehicle.

The tire, silhouetted by garish blue light, filled her field of vision. A couple feet away, in its path, Short lay on her side, an arm thrown above her head reaching toward Anna. A glistening line of blood ran down her temple, over her closed eyelid and onto the bridge of her nose.

In a heartbeat the water truck would roll over her, cut her in two. Scrambling till her butt was on the ground and her feet splayed to either side of the unconscious ranger, Anna grasped Short under the arms and dragged her back, pulling her up like a blanket. Digging heels into the ground Anna shoved both of them back. Something gouged deep into her side, raking the flesh from her ribs: a stick from the slash pile. Ignoring the pain, Anna pushed hard with her feet. The broken end of a branch had caught where the butt of her .357 hooked up and back, and push as she might, she could go no farther.

The gap between the tire and Jennifer's legs was gone. No time: Anna unsnapped the leather keeper that held her gun in the holster. Again she dug heels into earth and shoved back with all the strength in her legs. A tearing at her hip slowed her, then the gun broke free of the break-front holster and with it the stick. Loosed like an arrow from a bow, Anna shot back several feet, dragging Jennifer with her.

Light was eclipsed, noise crushed down. The truck with its burden of poison rolled toward the cliff's edge. Trees snapped like gunshots as the rear axle crashed over the lip of sandstone. Blue lights scratched across Anna's vision. She was seeing them from beneath the chassis of the truck. Tons of metal levered into the air, headlights stabbing wildly into the sky to rake the bottom of the low clouds.

Screeching wrenched the night and the underbelly of the truck scraped down, pulled backward by the weight of the load. A moment of shocked silence followed, broken only by the oddly peaceful sound of small rocks pattering after. Then a rending crash and stillness so absolute the faint oscillating whine of the patrol car's overheads was clearly audible.

Jennifer's head was on Anna's shoulder, her weight pinning her to the ground. "Hope I got your feet out in time," Anna whispered into the stiff web of sprayed hair that fell over her mouth and nose. She worked her right arm from beneath Jennifer's and found the seasonal's throat with her fingers. A pulse beat reassuringly in the hollow of the woman's neck.

"Hallelujah." Anna's voice rang loud in the new-made quiet and she wished she'd not spoken. As gently as possible, she eased herself from under Short and pushed up to her knees.

"Anna!" Stanton's voice.

"Here."

"Anna!"

Stanton was beginning to annoy her. "What the fuck . . ."

"Behind you!"

Anna dropped and rolled as a metal bar crashed into the ground where she'd been kneeling. White light flashed off the sightless eyes of the insect head. A heavily gloved hand raised again, the pipe wrench swung in a deadly arc.

Anna scuttled backward, fell to her left shoulder, and rolled again, grappling for her revolver.

The branch had torn it free of the holster. It lay somewhere in the dirt between her and her attacker.

Crouched, pipe wrench on shoulder like a ball player at bat, the insect ran toward her. Bent low and pressed close to the slash heap, the gamble was Stanton wouldn't shoot for fear of hitting one of the women.

Apparently it was going to pay off. "Shoot," Anna screamed, and kept rolling. Iron glanced off her upper arm followed by numbing pain, then smashed into the ground with such force she felt it through the earth.

Then Anna's collapsible baton was in her hands. In one desperate motion she rolled to her feet and whipped the weighted rod out to its full length.

The pipe wrench struck her shoulder. For a sickening instant she felt her fingers loosen on the baton but no bones had been broken and strength flooded back.

"Shoot!" she yelled as she lunged at her attacker swinging the baton. It connected somewhere between the gauntleted elbow and shoulder with a bone-cracking jar that pleased Anna to her toes.

The insect grunted but didn't fall down or back. The wrench was tossed from right to left hand and slashed at Anna's face.

Jerking the baton up, she braced the tip across her left palm and blocked the blow. The force shot angry pains down her wrists and left her hands tingling. Before her attacker recovered balance she kicked out, hoping to connect with a kneecap. Her boot cut along the inside of the assailant's ankle.

A scream was ripped loose. The wrench chopped down. Again Anna blocked it but this time her baton was forced to within an inch of her face. Her assailant was stronger and more heavily armed.

"Shoot!" she screamed.

"Get out of the way!"

"Jesus." Anna jerked the baton back. Overbalancing, the insect stumbled forward a step. She stepped into the opening and rammed the tip of the baton into the exposed gut with all her strength and weight.

Her attacker bent double. Both hands on the baton, she swung the butt down toward the back of the canvas-covered neck. The pipe wrench caught her across the shins. Her blow fell wild, glancing off the breathing apparatus.

A shoulder slammed into her chest and she fell back. Mud softened the landing but breath was knocked from her and her head snapped back, splashing muck into her hair and face. Curling up like a spring, Anna held the baton perpendicular to her body to ward blows from her face and upper body. With her feet she kicked out, keeping the pipe wrench at a distance.

"Shoot, goddamn it!"

The wrench arced up. Anna kicked but the cloying mud hampered her, adding to the nightmare feeling. Bracing her arms to absorb another strike, she yelled, "Look out!" in the slim hope of unsettling her assailant.

The insect should have heeded her unwitting advice. A gun's report hit Anna's ears at the same time the bullet struck. The force of the shot pushed her attacker upright.

For a bizarre moment the insect head hung over her, the wrench halfway down its arc, as if deciding whether to complete the strike or not. A second shot rang out and the fingers gripped so tightly around the wrench sprang open. The wrench fell, cracking Anna's knuckles against the baton, then slithered heavily into the mud at her side.

The masked figure stepped back stiff-legged, then crumpled, muscles and ligaments no longer receiving orders from the central nervous system. The strings that moved the puppet had been cut.

Anna felt as if the second shot had cut her strings as well. Her head dropped into the sludge, the baton fell from her hands, her legs were rubbery, useless. Confusion clouded her mind, her heart pounded, and she felt as if she were going to vomit.

Sirens and sucking sounds took over but she had little interest. A face formed over hers and she yelled.

"Take it easy," Stanton said. "Are you okay?" Taking her hand, he pulled her to her feet. Disoriented, nauseated, Anna shook her head to clear it. Nothing cleared. She tried to remember if she'd taken a blow to the head and couldn't. Cyanide gas: she remembered the almond smell.

Sirens closed in and the clearing was filled with chaos. "I called the cavalry," Stanton said.

Anna dragged her hand across her eyes trying to gather her wits. Her eyes began to burn viciously. Tears blinded her and she couldn't force her eyes open. Wherever the sludge had come in contact, her skin burned.

"My eyes," Anna said. "My eyes . . ."

"Holy smoke," Stanton said softly as she reached blindly for him. "Let's get you out of here."

Anna held tight to his arm and stumbled over the uneven ground. "Did you kill him?" she shouted over the sound of the sirens.

"I'm afraid so."

"Was it Greeley?"

"Yes."

"Good. What a son of a bitch."

"You're going to be all right," Stanton said.

20

"**D**OES IT HAVE to be so fucking cold?" Anna barked.

"'Flush with copious amounts of cool water,'" Stanton quoted sententiously.

"Cool, damn it, not cold."

Anna heard the protest of antique plumbing as Frederick turned the shower knob. "That better?"

"No."

"Well, think about something else, like July in Georgia."

"Shit. My eyes!" Water cascading down from her hair washed more acid into her eyes. The burning made her whimper. It felt as if the jelly of her eye was being eaten away.

"Keep flushing," Stanton said. "Tilt your head back." Anna felt his hand on the back of her head and tried to do as he said. "Try and open your eyes so clean water gets in them."

"Can't. Hurts." Anna heard the whine in her voice and shut up. She was shivering and not only with the cold. Blindness: now there was a bogeyman to put the fear of God into one. Blindness, paralysis, and small closed spaces.

"You'll see. We got it in time," Frederick reassured her. "I drove like the wind. You would've been proud. A regular Parnelli Andretti. Open now. Come on. A teensy-weensy little peek," he coaxed, and Anna was able to laugh away a bit of her terror.

His fingers were plucking at the buttons of her uniform shirt, peeling it off her back as gently as if he feared he might peel the skin off with it. His very care scared her and she tried to help, jerking blindly at her shirttail.

He pulled it free for her. "Yowch! You've got an ugly gouge down your ribs. Greeley get you with the wrench?"

For a moment Anna couldn't remember. Her brain was fogged and that, too, scared her. The answer came in flashback. "Stick took my gun," she said. "Scraped me."

"You're burnt," Stanton said.

"What does it look like?" Anna strove for a conversational tone but missed.

"Not bad. Not bad at all. Looks like a sunburn but not blistering or anything. Here."

Cold water was deflected to stream down her back. Keeping her face tilted so the dirty water would run away from her eyes, Anna gathered her hair and held it out from her body.

"Let me get your shoes off," Stanton said. "We don't want this pooling in 'em and dissolving your toes."

"That's a soothing picture," Anna mumbled. She kicked off one shoe and felt him pull the other off as she lifted her foot.

"I'm going to cut your trousers off, okay?"

"Cut. And warm up the water. I'm getting hypothermic."

"Just a tad." The aged metal creaked in protest and the edge went off the cold.

Anna pushed her face into the stream and pried her eyes open with her fingers. She must have cried out because Stanton was asking what was the matter and she could feel the warmth of his hand on her bare shoulder.

"Don't touch me," she said. "You'll get this shit on you."

"Right. Are you okay?"

Anna shook her head. She couldn't hold her eyelids open for even a second. The fact that she could see light beyond her eyelids seemed a good sign, but the fluorescent light over the stall in the women's communal shower at the tent frames where Stanton had brought her was so bright even a blind woman could see it. The thought sent another stab of fear into her and Anna tried harder to get fresh water under her lids.

Stanton slit her pantlegs and Anna gasped with the cold and the relief. Her skin burned and itched where the acid-drenched mud had soaked through. As he cut away her underpants he said, "Oooh. Black lace. A collector's item. I shall have them stuffed."

Anna was grateful for the banter. Pain and panic had destroyed any vestige of modesty but she appreciated the thought. "As I recall, you never wanted to know me this well."

He didn't reply.

"How much more time have I got?"

"Thirteen minutes. 'Flush with copious amounts for twenty minutes,' the doctor said. You've done seven."

During the wild and, for Anna, sightless ride from the cliff's edge, Stanton had radioed Frieda to call the emergency room in Cortez. The doctor on call had given instructions for treatment. Stanton was carrying them out with kindness and precision. For the first time in more years than she cared to count, Anna felt taken care of. It made her weak and she was afraid she would cry.

Hoping Stanton would attribute the gesture to modesty, she turned her back on him. "Distract me," she said when she could trust her voice. "What do you figure? What happened?"

"The obvious: Greeley had the water truck rigged to smuggle toxic waste into the park to dump it. It shouldn't be too hard to trace where the stuff was from."

"Cyanide gas," Anna said. "Almonds, remember? And acid. Some kind of acid wash used in industrial manufacturing, maybe. Stacy stumbles onto the scheme. Greeley kills Stacy."

"Maybe."

The doubt in his voice irritated her. She ignored it. At present the topic held little interest for her, but it was the only thing she could think of besides her eyes and she didn't care to think about that. "Greeley must've made Stacy breathe the fumes," she went on. Fleeting sadness darkened her mind. "The prints on his arms and shoes were etched with whatever it is I've been rolling in."

"Think Greeley dumped him in the kiva just to be mysterious?" Stanton asked.

"We'll never know, but probably. Jamie'd been babbling on to everybody about the solstice and angry spirits. He might have been taking advantage of Jamie's ghostly brouhaha."

"So he carries him into the kiva, folds him up in the fire pit, rakes it all smooth, puts on Meyers' shoes, backs out, and tosses the shoes back where he got 'em."

"Mysteries are like magic," Anna said. "Once you know how the trick is done, it's obvious to the point of stupidity. I'll bet dollars to doughnuts Silva was blackmailing Greeley," Anna said, suddenly remembering the short-lived spate of expensive gifts he'd poured into Patsy's lap. "He reported seeing a truck at night once. He was out at all hours harassing Patsy. Maybe he saw something else. Put two and two together." Anna pressed her face near the shower head, hoping the water pressure would force it beneath her lids.

"Tom must have gotten greedy," Stanton said. "Ted probably started threatening the wife and kids to shut him up."

So Tom had been guardian angel and not stalker after all, looking after his girls the only way he knew how. "Killed Pats" wasn't a confession of firsthand homicide but guilt at putting her in danger. "Threats against his family would shut him up all right," Anna said. "Tom was obsessed with his ex."

"But you can't trust a drunk."

"Nope. And nothing easier than getting a drunk to take a drink. Point the truck in the right direction and wedge a golf ball in the linkage. Greeley was a golfer. Tom mentioned it one day."

Silence. "Are you still there?" she demanded. Panic rose in her chest and a sour taste poured into the back of her throat.

Something heavy slammed into the tile near her head. Covering her face and neck, Anna collapsed to the floor of the shower. "I can't see, goddamn it! I can't see!" she was screaming.

"Sorry, sorry, sorry, I'm so sorry. It was me, Frederick the idiot." Stanton's voice was in her ear, his hands on her shoulders. "A spider. A black widow. No kidding. As big as a Ping-Pong ball. Huge. It looked ready to pounce. I hit it with your shoe. Sorry."

"Fuck you. Fuck you." Anna began to cry. Stanton crouched down in the shower and held her. The slick fabric of his windbreaker stuck to her cheek and his arms were warm around her. Water dripped from his hair to her face. He held her as she would hold a frightened kitten, tightly, carefully so it wouldn't hurt and couldn't fall.

When she could finally stop, he helped her to her feet.

"Four more minutes," he said.

"Thanks," was all she could manage.

When Anna had only a minute left to go, Frieda took over. She and Frederick discussed Anna's disposal in hushed tones till she couldn't stand it anymore and shouted at them.

Frieda shut the shower off and wrapped a shivering Anna in clean towels. "Can you see?" she asked.

Anna forced her eyes open a slit. "I guess. No. Sort of." The pain was there but not so intense and she could make out shapes, light and dark.

"Keep your eyes shut," Frederick said, and Anna felt him winding soft gauze around her head. "I'm going to bandage them both closed. You know the routine. Don't want you looking hither and yon scratching things about." The bandaging done, he kissed her on top of the head and left to return to the crime scene.

As Frieda wrapped Anna's hair in dry terry cloth, she said: "I'm going to drive you to Cortez. Hills is out at the scene. Paul and Drew took Jennifer down soon as they got there. She'd come around. She got a hell of a wallop on the head, but it looks like a concussion and a good story's all she's going to come away with. Short's lucky."

"If I weren't so glad she weren't dead, I'd kill her."

"C'mon, you were young once," Frieda chided.

"No, I wasn't." With her aching muscles and acid-etched body, Anna felt as if it were true.

*   *   *

Dr. Dooley kept Anna overnight for observation but released her the next morning with eye salve and a cheap pair of sunglasses. The world was still a little fuzzy around the edges but it looked good to Anna.

She pulled on a pair of mechanic's overalls and rubber shower thongs Frieda'd dug out of her trunk and left for her. Her own clothes were ruined. Hopefully the duty nurse hadn't thrown them away. They were evidence.

On the way out, she stopped by Jennifer Short's room. Jennifer's head was swathed in bandages and both her eyes were swollen shut. She was so contrite Anna's anger, never heartfelt, evaporated entirely. It had taken a good deal of courage to go up against Greeley all alone in the dead of night. Tombstone courage that needed leavening with common sense, but courage all the same, and Anna respected that.

To her surprise, Short was determined to keep on being a ranger. "I'm going to get on permanent," the woman lisped through swollen lips. "Get me some trainin' and get damn good."

"I'll hire you," Anna said, and was pretty sure she meant it.

Hills was waiting near the emergency room desk when Anna walked out. "Where's Frederick?" she asked.

"Glad to see you too," he returned. "Get your stuff. We're gonna have paperwork up the wazoo over this thing."

"I'm wearing my stuff. And I'm on sick leave for a week. Doctor's orders."

"Doggone it. You gotta be more careful."

"You're glad I'm alive, admit it."

Hills grunted. Anna took it for an affirmative. The

depths of his feeling were revealed on the drive back up to the mesa top. He'd found Patsy and the girls lodging. The tower house was hers.

"When?" The question was so abrupt, Anna laughed at herself.

"If you was a tomcat I do believe you'd be up there peein' in every corner," Hills retorted. "It's yours today, I guess, if you want. Patsy had the movers there this morning. I'd think you'd want to let the sheets cool off before you went hopping in."

"Nope."

"Need help?"

"Nope. Thanks though," Anna added belatedly. What she had was in storage in Cortez. Her estate consisted of little more than a futon and frame, a rocking chair, and a few good Indian rugs.

The movers were late, and as it turned out Anna had to spend one more night in the dormitory. A little after eight the next morning she had her belongings stuffed into boxes and paper sacks and piled into the Rambler.

Zach's ashes were last to be loaded. As she carried the tin out through the living room she took a last look around.

"Find anything to miss?" Jamie asked.

"Not much. The company," Anna lied.

"Hah!" Jamie was unoffended. "You forgot your wine cellar."

Anna paused for a second in the kitchen and looked at the five bottles lined up on the counter beneath the shelves she'd claimed as her own. "Share it with Jennifer," Anna said. "Sort of a good-bye toast."

"My, my." Jamie clucked her tongue. "And they told me it was Jennifer who got hit on the head."

On her way down to Chapin, Anna stopped by Frieda's and gathered Piedmont into the canvas satchel that served as his travel carrier.

By two o'clock she'd brought all of her worldly goods up from storage. Her boom box had pride of place on the mantel and Louis Armstrong poured out "It's a Wonderful World" like honey-laced bourbon. Anna amused herself dragging rugs and pictures from place to place, then standing back to discuss the effect with a disinterested cat.

The only furniture she'd arranged so far was a rocking chair and, beside it, a small marble-topped table where the phone sat in solitary splendor. Soon she'd call her sister. Anna'd been promising herself that for three hours but had yet to drum up the nerve. There were things needing to be said, confessions to be made.

Rapping at the front door interrupted both her nesting and her dithering. With less than good humor, she went to the door.

Stanton waved at her through the screen. Despite a flash of awkwardness engendered by their unscheduled intimacy in the shower, Anna was glad to see him. Because it seemed less stilted than leaving him on the doorstep, she invited him into the kitchen and sat down in the booth. The little vinyl benches and polished tongue of Formica were too small to accommodate his lanky frame.

"Kitchens are made for girls," he complained, turning sideways to stretch his long legs. "Just to reach the sink without bending double I've got to stand with my feet so far apart I'm almost doing the splits."

"Sounds like an excuse to get out of doing the dishes to me."

"How're you doing?" he asked when he'd gotten himself arranged.

"Fine. Can't offer you anything. The cupboard is bare."

"I've been tying up loose ends," he said. "Rose is willing to turn state's evidence in return for clemency."

"For the false alibi?"

Stanton nodded. Anna shoved three carpet tacks the movers had managed to leave on the kitchen table into a pinwheel shape. "The woman's husband gives his life to stop the dumping, Greeley kills him, and Rose is still willing to alibi him. Go figure."

Stanton looked uncomfortable—miserable, in fact. He looked like Anna's dad when he had bad news about Fluffy or Bootsie or Pinky-winky—whichever of their multitude of pets had succumbed to the inevitable.

Anna waited. Everyone she knew was safe. Still, there was a hollow place in her belly.

"Stacy was on the take," Frederick said apologetically. "Greeley paid him to unlock the Four-Way and make sure the coast was clear. That's why Greeley did it Monday nights; Stacy was on the late shift. Greeley'd lock up when he was done.

"That funky twisty way with the chain," Anna said, remembering how the same lock configuration at the maintenance yard had tipped her off.

Stanton went on: "After he was killed Rose gave Greeley Stacy's radio so he could keep tabs on the rangers. Without Stacy's keys, Rose says she doesn't know how he unlocked the Four-Way. Presumably at some point Stacy made him a copy."

Anna looked at the table, her mind playing with something as her fingers played with the tacks. Patsy'd said the night Tom broke in and left the derringer, she'd been awakened twice. The next day she mentioned she'd "lost" her keys. "Greeley stole Patsy Silva's keys, copied them, then put them back," Anna said. "I can't prove it, but that's what happened."

Stanton nodded. "Rose said Stacy'd decided to turn Greeley and himself in after a little girl you carried out of Cliff Palace died."

"Stephanie McFarland."

"He and Rose argued about it over the phone the night she was in Farmington, the night Stacy was killed. Up till then he was in collaboration with Greeley to dump the toxic waste." The FBI agent seemed to be repeating the news in case Anna hadn't quite been able to grasp it first time around.

Anna had understood just fine. The devil buys on the installment plan. People are always shocked when he shows up to collect his merchandise.

"Everybody's got their price," Frederick said.

"Stacy's wasn't money."

"But money could buy it."

"And money bought Rose's alibi."

Stanton shook his head. "Matrimony. She hated Ted but he said he'd marry her and put Bella on his health insurance plan. Strictly business. He told her you and Stacy were having an affair to lower any sentimental inhibitions she might have had."

Anna pushed the carpet tacks around till they formed a jagged line, like a bolt of lightning, and she remembered the storm Bella had made with Hattie because her mad was so big. Rose had made her lie, say Greeley was in Farmington. At six telling a lie is still a great burden.

"What was Greeley dumping?" Anna changed the subject.

"There's electroplating plants in the area. One in Cortez, one near Shiprock, and a couple around Farmington. They use an acid for the wash and cyanide in the brass plating process. Greeley was contracted to dump it. I haven't got the particulars yet but evidently Greeley Construction was in financial trouble. Greeley couldn't finish the pipeline, he'd already spent the money. By dumping illegally he hoped to fix his cash flow problems long enough to avoid the penalties."

"Worth killing for?"

"One hundred thousand dollars a day for every day over schedule. Greeley didn't do his homework—or didn't care. He dumped the acid and cyanide in the same place. Mixed, it creates cyanide gas. Sometimes it mixed, sometimes it missed. But the gas was what was drifting up the canyon. Nausea, palpitations, confusion, tachycardia, hyperventilation, hypoxia."

"A smorgasbord of ills."

"Unless it was suspected for some reason, no doctor would even think to test for it."

For several minutes they sat without speaking. Piedmont, alerted by the silence, came and jumped onto the table between them. "Remember the monkeywrenching I told you about? Brown boots, insurance, key to the yard: my bet it was Greeley. A little self-sabotage to claim the insurance money, keep himself afloat awhile longer."

Stanton nodded.

"Case closed?" Anna asked.

"Fun part's over. The lawyer part will drag on till neither one of us can remember who did it." Stanton tweaked up Piedmont's long yellow tail and absently tickled his cheek with the tip of it. Murder might make for strange bedfellows but that wasn't always such a bad thing.

"We're not co-workers anymore, Anna. Want to go out to dinner? Maybe a movie?"

"A date?" Anna sounded appalled and Stanton laughed.

"A date. I come pick you up at the door at seven sharp. You wear lipstick, can't touch the check, and have to call the women's toilet the 'powder room.' How about it?"

"I have to make a phone call," Anna hedged.

Stanton glanced at his watch. "Okay, you've got just under five hours. Then the date."

"I guess. Sure."

Anna would have felt awkward but he didn't give her time. With startling grace he sprang from the cramped booth. "Got to figure out what to wear," he said, and: "Seven."

He was gone, the screen door banging behind him.

Anna stood up. Then sat down. All at once she didn't know what to do with herself. Scooping up Piedmont for support, she went into the living room and to the phone.

It was Wednesday. Maybe her sister wouldn't be at the office.

Molly picked up on the fourth ring. "Dr. Pigeon," she snapped.

"Hi," Anna said. "My name's Anna and I'm an alcoholic."

"Hi, Anna," Molly droned in parody of the group response, but her voice was warmer than Anna'd heard it in a while.

Ten Key Customer Insights

Unlocking the Mind of the Market

Robert Schieffer

THOMSON
™

Australia · Canada · Mexico · Singapore · Spain · United Kingdom · United States

For more information about our products, contact us at:

Thomson Learning Academic Resource Center 1-800-423-0563

Thomson Higher Education
5191 Natorp Boulevard
Mason, OH 45040
USA

Library of Congress Cataloging-in-Publication Data

Schieffer, Robert.
    Ten key customer insights : unlocking the mind of the market / Robert Schieffer.
        p. cm.
    Includes bibliographical references and index.
    ISBN 1-58799-206-X (alk. paper)
    1. Consumers' preferences. 2. Marketing. I. Title.
    HF5415.32.S33 2005
    658.8'343—dc22

                                                    2005017708

CONTENTS

Acknowledgments   v

Introduction   vii

1   Macro Trends   1

2   Unmet Needs   31

3   Emotional and Rational Motivations   51

4   Segmentation and Targeting   69

5   Perceptions and Differentiation   103

6   Critical Features   121

7   Marketing Communications   143

8   Price Sensitivity   165

9   Satisfaction and Loyalty   185

10   New Products   207

Action Plans and Metrics   227

Index   243

This book is dedicated to Phil Kotler, whose ideas on marketing ignited a fire within me 30 years ago that still burns strongly today.

ACKNOWLEDGMENTS

This book began at the encouragement of my students at the Kellogg School of Management at Northwestern University. These students were stimulated by the class discussion of marketing techniques to uncover customer insights, but the book that I had been using in my Marketing class challenged them. While discussing this lack of fit between existing books and my class focus, one student suggested that I should write "the book." After weeks of reflection, I decided to take on the challenge posed by my Kellogg student. Thus, the first group that needs to be recognized is my Kellogg students, who continually challenge me to keep my thinking on marketing ideas cogent and current.

I would like to thank my colleague at Kellogg, Philip Kotler, for his ideas and guidance as this book moved from an idea to completion. Despite his hectic speaking schedule and the great books he continues to write, Phil always found the time to provide guidance to a first time author.

Many whom I consider experts in obtaining customer insight were kind enough to review this book and provided numerous jewels of wisdom from their experiences. Larry Chandler, former Vice-President of Business Research at McDonald's, provided outstanding thoughts that improved this book immensely. Chris Debrauw of Fieldwork, Inc., provided great input, especially in the qualitative approaches to gathering customer insight. Dick Chay of C & R Research was extremely helpful in assisting to clarify the ideas in this book. Dick also provided great suggestions on titling the chapters in the book. Don Hughes, former Director of Marketing Research with Sears, provided many fine thoughts on customer insights from a retailer's perspective. John Klebba, President of Geomation, provided excellent input from a small company's perspective.

I'd like to thank my editor at Thomson, Steve Momper, for his valuable suggestions, especially those on structure and context. Thanks also go to reviewers Sandy Adams of Fieldwork, Inc., John Rust of Rust and Associates, Tim Key of Scotts Corporation, and Ed Wolkenmuth of Ipsos-Vantis for their valuable comments. And thank you to Greg Benz, of the Kellogg class of 2005, for taking the time to provide fine thoughts from a student's perspective.

Last but not least, I need to thank my wife of thirty-four years, Betty Schieffer, for her support of my work on this book. Without her nurturing and understanding, this book would not have been completed.

INTRODUCTION

*"Carefully listening to what customers say and interpreting the information in an imaginative way allows us to do a good job. The trick is to really listen to customers and turn what they say into something actionable. If we can get that **imaginative understanding,** we can almost always figure out how to meet a customer's needs or even go beyond."*

Lewis Platt, former CEO of Hewlett-Packard

Figuring out customer needs, or even going beyond those needs, helped Lewis Platt build Hewlett-Packard (H-P) into one of the most successful corporations in America. Really listening to customers, and turning what they say into something actionable, is the H-P way driving their product development process with both the voice of the customer and the knowledge of their technological capabilities. The evidence is consistently strong that firms that focus externally on their customers, rather than internally on their products and technologies, outperform their competitors in the market. Top managers that focus on gaining **customer insight** to provide superior value to their customers find that customer attraction and customer retention are major problems for their competitors.

What is Customer Insight?

Customer insight is best defined as the **intimate, shared understanding of the spoken and latent, current and future needs of your target customers.** This definition includes five key points:

1. Firms that drive their business strategy based on customer insight have an intimate relationship with their target customers and understand the rational and emotional reasons customers buy from them.

2. Firms share this understanding of customer needs with all their employees, so that everyone in the firm is working toward the mission of providing superior value to customers.

3. Many customer needs are easy to ascertain directly, while other customer needs are latent, or not consciously accessible by your customers.

4. Current needs are usually easy to ascertain. But in many industries with long product development cycles, those firms that can understand where customer needs are headed in the future will have a significant competitive advantage over those who see customer needs as static.

5. Contemporary marketers avoid mass marketing and succeed by focusing on a segment of the market that they can satisfy more fully than competitors can.

What are Customer Needs?

Many view the range of customer needs very narrowly, seeing only survival and safety as important needs to human beings. They view other so-called needs, such as belonging and prestige, as **wants,** stirring up the philosophical debate of needs versus wants.

The famous psychologist, Abraham Maslow, believed that all humans have certain common needs and developed his famous "hierarchy of needs," which captured basic physiological needs, as well as social and psychological needs of human beings. The five levels is his hierarchy are:

1. Physiological needs, such as food, water and air
2. Safety needs, such as protection from threats
3. Love and social needs, such as feelings of affection and belonging
4. Self-esteem needs, such as the need for respect from others
5. Self-actualization needs, such as seeking self-fulfillment

Marketers need to understand that their product offerings are likely to satisfy more than one level of customer needs in this hierarchy. This book is all about developing that intimate understanding of target customer needs at all of these five levels, but especially at the higher levels. Understanding how your product offering addresses the social, self-esteem, and self-actualization needs of target customers can provide the marketer with powerful opportunities to differentiate the product offering from competitive offerings meaningfully. Take beer, for example. Many beer marketers have effectively positioned their brands as meeting the social needs of beer drinkers, especially the need of "male bonding" among male heavy beer drinkers. This need to be accepted by fellow beer drinkers is a very powerful determinant of brand choice in the beer category.

Building a market strategy based on deep **customer insight** can give a brand a powerful competitive advantage. Investing marketing dollars in advertising for the brand that benefits from deep customer insight can upset the competitive structure of markets. The best example to illustrate these two bold statements on the power of marketing can be found in the rise of the Miller Brewing Company in the 1970s in the United States. Many people refer to this period in the development of the beer industry as the **"Beer Wars."**

The Beer Wars

The year was 1972, and the leaders of the major brewing companies in the United States were quite happy with their businesses. Total beer consumption had continued to grow nicely over the past decade, fueled mostly by the post-war baby boomers reaching their prime beer-drinking years: their early twenties. This powerful demographic tidal wave would continue to boost beer sales throughout the decade of the 1970s.

Most of the beer baron families were very friendly with each other, and they socialized frequently during meetings of their trade association, the United States Brewers Association (USBA). The U.S.B.A. had played a key role in ending

Prohibition forty years earlier and continued to be active in portraying beer as the "beverage of moderation" to the government and to the public.

With beer consumption growing in the late 1960s and early 1970s at about 5 percent per year, most of these leaders at the major brewers were comfortable to accept their share of this growth and not rock the boat. Their marketing efforts relied mostly on **push** marketing, which involved aggressive management and training of their wholesalers, the next link in the three-tiered beer distribution system. (The three tiers included the brewers, beer wholesalers, and retail outlets). Most brewers felt there was little need to spend aggressively on marketing and advertising to gain market share from their competitors. Why spend more on marketing and reduce healthy profit margins? A rising tide lifts all boats. Brewers in the early 1970s focused on **push** marketing and on building newer, larger, and more efficient breweries. This healthy, growing industry with low competition lulled many brewery leaders into complacency.

The alarm went off in 1970, when tobacco giant Philip Morris acquired the Miller Brewing Company. Philip Morris was looking to diversify their tobacco business, and beer seemed like a natural companion. Philip Morris was expert at **pull** marketing, which involved gaining insight into customer needs, perceptions, and preferences and then developing and aggressively marketing brands that uniquely addressed these customer needs.

Philip Morris had successfully repositioned the Marlboro brand of cigarettes, using the rugged imagery of cowboys, and grabbed the top position in the cigarette market. The Marlboro brand had previously been marketed primarily to women, with the slogan "mild as May." Ross Millhiser, then president of Philip Morris USA who had worked his way up the ladder from Marlboro brand manager, redesigned the packaging to a rugged, flip-top box, and hired the Leo Burnett advertising agency to create the new advertising for the brand that would appeal to men. Leo Burnett created the "Marlboro Man," the rugged cowboy whose lifestyle represented freedom and independence, which were strong latent needs among the new target segment of cigarette smokers. The Marlboro Man can be described as a tattooed outdoorsman, who is cool and relaxed, and in calm control of his spirit. In short, he was a man that target consumers could identify with and aspire to be like. Marlboro moved into the number one spot in cigarette sales in 1975.

Philip Morris felt that the beer industry was in slumber and that its consumer marketing expertise, as well as aggressive marketing investments, could lead to significant growth for current and new Miller brands.

Many brewers didn't hear the alarm; other brewers ignored it. Marketing leaders at the Joseph Schlitz Brewing Company, a strong number two to Anheuser-Busch in 1972, laughed at the folly of a cigarette company buying a brewing company. "Why would they do something that stupid? Just because you know how to sell cigarettes doesn't mean you know how to sell beer!" were comments made by a vice president in the Schlitz Marketing Department.[1] The leaders at

---

[1] Personal communication with the author.

Schlitz were arrogant and talked frequently about passing up Anheuser-Busch in the next year or two to become the largest brewer in the United States. Why should they worry about some second-rate brewery just because a large tobacco corporation with deep pockets bought it?

Leaders at Anheuser-Busch in St. Louis, the number one brewer, took notice and closely monitored developments at the small Miller Brewing Company in Milwaukee, which just barely made it into the top ten brewers in the United States. The Anheuser-Busch management team was concerned about what tricks the cigarette marketing whizzes might try at Miller.

Philip Morris moved many of their brightest marketing people from their headquarters in New York to the Miller Brewery offices in Milwaukee. Old-line Miller **push** marketers were mostly retained, if they were willing to learn **pull** marketing. The old-line marketers at Miller who resisted the new marketing approach were put in smaller roles or were let go.

It didn't take long for these new marketing whizzes to gain insight into the world of the beer drinker. Within five years, they accomplished the two greatest marketing coups in beer industry history (up to that time): the repositioning of the Miller High Life brand and the introduction of Miller Lite.

Repositioning of Miller High Life

Miller's flagship brand in 1970 was Miller High Life, also known as "The Champagne of Bottle Beer." While this slogan helped the brand achieve a quality, upscale, premium-priced positioning, it hardly appealed to the blue-collar, heavy beer drinker, who felt that champagne was a fine drink for New Year's Eve and weddings. But the champagne positioning overshot the majority of beer drinkers, who felt that Miller High Life was a beer for the tuxedo crowd and not for people like my friends or me.

The marketing whizzes at Miller went to work in 1971, digging into the rational and emotional reasons for beer consumption. Clearly, the rational reason for drinking beer was to quench your thirst, and the rational reason for picking a specific brand was because "I prefer the taste of this brand." While some might stop there, Miller was just beginning. Digging below these "rational" reasons, Miller uncovered a gold mine of emotional reasons driving beer consumption.

Because beer satisfies different emotional needs on different consumption occasions, Miller segmented the beer market by these "need states." They found that the needs present in the largest need state (about 15 percent of beer drinking occasions) was **"relaxation/reward."** On these occasions, blue-collar beer drinkers had just finished a hard day of work and headed to the bar for a few cold ones with their friends to relax and reward themselves. The slogan that captured this need state perfectly became synonymous with it: **"It's Miller Time!"** The television commercials began with relaxing music and the lyrics "When it's time to relax. . ." Spending on television commercials more than doubled, and Miller Time became part of the American culture.

The effectiveness of this "need state" segmentation approach was dramatic. More and more beer drinkers were ordering Miller with their buddies in the bar after work. While these "relaxation/reward" occasions represented only 15 percent of all beer-drinking occasions, almost one-fourth of all beer volume was consumed during these occasions. Sales at the Miller Brewery, which had been fairly flat for five years at about 5 million barrels, **doubled** to 10 million barrels within **two years** of the start of the new advertising campaign.

Anheuser-Busch Responds

Leaders at Anheuser-Busch (A-B) had kept a careful eye on the Philip Morris marketing experiment in Milwaukee. When Miller sales doubled, A-B went into action and dramatically staffed up in their marketing department, hiring many MBAs from the Wharton School at the University of Pennsylvania and other prestigious institutions. These marketing employees were charged with understanding what was happening up at Miller and what A-B should do to avoid the loss of market share. After months of marketing research and study, the marketers of "The King of Beers" had a strategy.

It has been said that imitation is the sincerest form of flattery. If that is true, Miller should have been flattered by the new "**For All You Do, This Bud's For You**" advertising campaign. It positioned Bud (a much friendlier name than the formal Budweiser) as the beer to have to reward oneself after a hard day's work.

A-B had found that Miller had staked out the "high ground," targeting the largest beer-drinking occasion segment. Since Budweiser was the largest brand in America, A-B felt that this relaxation/reward segment was the rightful place for the king of beers, and they decided to take a frontal attack on Miller. It was **This Bud's For You** versus **Miller Time.** When A-B more than doubled advertising spending behind this new campaign, the beer wars intensified.

The heavy advertising behind the Budweiser campaign slowed the dramatic growth in the Miller High Life brand. Growth in Budweiser began to pick up. The marketing staff at Anheuser-Busch was proud of their success and congratulated themselves on stopping the success of this reenergized Miller Brewing Company. But the folks up at Miller still had an ace up their sleeve that would catch everyone by surprise: **Miller Lite.**

Launch of Miller Lite in 1974

Many marketing scholars consider the launch of Miller Lite to be one of the most successful brand introductions in history. It launched a new product category in the beer market that would represent over 40 percent of all beer sales in the United States by 2002. Some background will provide insight into the challenges Miller faced in launching a "low-calorie" beer into a beer market characterized by "indulgent" beer drinkers.

Many brewers had attempted to launch low-calorie beers, targeting beer drinkers who were on a diet. One of the more infamous "diet" beers was Gablinger's beer, complete with a picture of Dr. Gablinger on the label to reinforce the lower calorie feature. Given the focus on product features and the lack of customer insight by these diet brewers, these brands of beer had no success during the 1960s and early 1970s.

The marketers at Miller felt that there may be a market opportunity for a lighter-tasting, low-calorie beer, if it was positioned properly and did not have too much of a taste deficit versus "regular" beer. The strong growth of the lighter Coors beer in the Western United States demonstrated that there was a macro trend occurring among Americans toward lighter beverages. They noticed that Peter Hand Brewing Company, a Chicago brewery, had a struggling diet brand named Meister Brau Lite and acquired the rights to the brand name at a very low cost.

Miller tested many different brews as it developed Miller Lite, with the target to match the taste profile and preference of the successful Coors brand from the Rocky Mountains. It found out early in market research with beer drinkers that a "lower calories" positioning did not excite too many beer drinkers. In fact, a focus on fewer calories was a negative cue to some, who remembered tasting "some of those awful diet beers" in the past.

So what customer benefit could be claimed by Miller Lite and supported by the fewer calorie attribute? And how could Miller reassure drinkers that Miller Lite tastes just as good as regular beer? And how could Miller Lite overcome the stigma that diet beers are for overweight nerds or for women on a diet?

The **"Tastes Great, Less Filling"** advertising campaign created by Miller's advertising agency, McCann-Erickson, was a positioning masterpiece, and addressed all of these issues. The television ads used macho, ex-athletes to reinforce that this brand was for real beer drinkers. The "less-filling" claim offered a **strong benefit** to beer drinkers who hated to get filled up and now could enjoy a few extra beers. The "tastes great" claim strongly tied Miller Lite to the regular beer category and disassociated it from those terrible diet beers viewers may have tried in the past. The slogan was equally clever: **"Everything you always wanted in a beer. And less."** Miller then tripled advertising spending for its brands.

This successful Miller Lite positioning was maintained for seventeen years, and over eighty commercials were produced during that time. A further examination of this highly successful **"Tastes Great, Less Filling"** positioning will be covered in Chapter 5.

Miller Brewing Company's sales doubled again! By 1976, sales were over 20 million barrels. By 1978, sales would reach over 31 million barrels. In the six-year period between 1972 and 1978, Miller sales had exploded from 7 million barrels to over 31 million barrels, the most dramatic growth spurt in the history of the beer industry. Anheuser-Busch, the industry leader, was very uncomfortable with the Miller Brewing Company at two-thirds of its size and gaining. Five years earlier, Anheuser-Busch was four times the size of Miller.

A-B pulled out all stops, and the beer wars further intensified. A-B was not about to give up their position as "King of the Beer Industry," regardless of the

cost. It again added many new marketing employees and boosted marketing spending dramatically. It looked to sponsor every sporting event possible, from baseball to football to rodeos to speedboat racing. It invested heavily in understanding beer drinkers' needs, perceptions, and preferences to gain the **customer insights** that had allowed Miller to close the sales gap so quickly. Miller, with the help of the deep pockets of parent Philip Morris, partly matched the spending increases of A–B. Other brewers struggled in this new marketing-intensive industry, which was no longer "quarter ante poker" but now required substantial investments in marketing and advertising to survive.

Between 1976 and 1980, A–B grew their sales dramatically, from 30 million barrels to 50 million barrels. During the same period, Miller grew their sales from 20 million barrels to 37 million barrels. Since the beer industry grew about 20 million barrels during this period, it meant that the brewers below the top two lost a combined 17 million barrels between 1976 and 1980.

Sales of Leading U. S. Brewers
1970–1980

Sales in Millions of Barrels

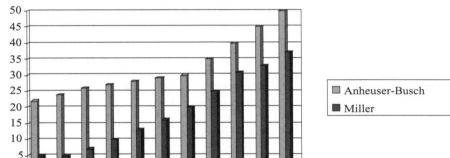

This case history reflects a marketplace that was ripe for customer-focused marketers to capitalize upon, as few companies were addressing the emotional needs of beer drinkers well prior to the repositioning of Miller High Life. Larry Chandler has described this industry opportunity as follows: "As capitalism and consumer learning interplay, a dynamic market situation is created that requires aggressive ongoing listening, learning and leading."[2] This case history also demonstrates that brands not linked to consumer need states are likely to fall by the wayside as stronger marketers spend heavily on advertising and consolidate market share.

The success of Anheuser-Busch has continued, driven by an ongoing focus on the customer and heavy spending on marketing. By 2002, Anheuser-Busch

---

[2] Personal communication with the author.

reached a 49 percent share of the U.S. beer market. Philip Morris was unable to maintain the heavy spending levels that A–B established, but Miller has maintained the number two position in the beer industry, with a market share of about 19 percent.

Thus, these two brewers, who represented just 22 percent of the U.S. beer industry in 1970, now command 68 percent of the market. What went wrong at the other brewers, many of which ranked well ahead of Miller in 1970?

Coors has slowly become more of a customer-focused organization, and recently brought in high-powered marketers from Frito-Lay to lead the brewery. Their market share, which stood at 6 percent in 1970, has grown to 10 percent in 2002.

But where are Schlitz, Pabst, Schaefer, Falstaff, Carling, and Hamms, all members of the Top Ten in 1970? While Schlitz was hurt by product quality problems, the others had very good products. These other brewers felt that a strong focus on "brewing the best beer we know how" and hiring enough salespeople would be sufficient for survival in the Beer Wars of the 1970s.

They were wrong.

The revolution in beer industry marketing was not only driven by dramatic increases in marketing expenditures but also from a shift in management focus from products and distribution channels to customers. Digging deep for **customer insight** into the emotional needs of beer drinkers, and then positioning their brands as those that best satisfy the rational **and** emotional needs was the success formula. A high-quality, good-tasting beer is a necessary, but not sufficient, condition for success in the highly competitive beer industry.

Thus, **Superior Listening** to understand the need states of customers often leads to **Superior Branding** and **Positioning,** which often leads to **Significant Market Share Growth** and **Category Realignment.**

The Need to Focus on Customer Insight

The earlier successes of Miller and the ongoing success of Anheuser-Busch are just two cases of companies and industries that were transformed by a dedication to the marketing concept. Putting the needs of the customer first, and focusing the efforts of all the employees of the company on meeting the expressed as well as latent needs of customers better than any competitor is the Marketing Success Formula. But there are many other success stories that will be discussed in this book, including:

> **How has Oreo cookies maintained its number one position in the U.S. cookie market for over 90 years?**
>
> **How did Harley-Davidson turn its failing motorcycle business around to the point where waiting lists for a new Harley hog reached over one year?**
>
> **How did Corona beer pass up Heineken to become the number one-selling import beer in America?**
>
> **How did the PT Cruiser create the "white-hot" excitement among its target customers at launch?**

Each of these brands benefited from the commitment of management to develop deep insights into the needs and perceptions of target customers and to utilize these insights to drive the strategy of the firm. While many of the examples in this book are consumer product examples, the process of gaining customer insights and developing winning marketing strategies applies equally well to consumer services, Business-to-Business (B-to-B) Products, and B-to-B Services. That process can best be illustrated through the Customer Insight Pyramid.

THE CUSTOMER INSIGHT PYRAMID

The structure of this book can be viewed as a pyramid, which starts with a broad, strong base and builds upward. Understanding the macro trends occurring in the external environment that will impact your market opportunities is the first step in the customer insight process. Understanding the unmet needs of target customers and the reasons they purchase are the next critical steps, which involve developing deep insights into the motivations and needs of customers. Only then can a firm successfully segment customers and select the best segments to target with their positioning strategy.

Customer Insight Pyramid

Once the target segments have been selected, customer perceptions need to be understood to allow the company to position the company effectively and to differentiate it from competitors on benefits that are meaningful to the target customer segments. Tactical marketing then requires insight into the critical product/service features that drive customer behavior, into the most effective communication messages for an integrated advertising program, and into the price sensitivity of target consumers.

As the company grows, insights are required to understand how to keep current customers fully satisfied and loyal to the company. Last, these insights will culminate in the firm having a high degree of success in developing and launching new products that meet the changing needs of a dynamic market.

The structure of this book works up the Customer Insight Pyramid, with each of the next ten chapters covering one building block. These ten building blocks will put the firm in a strong position to provide superior value to target customers in a profitable manner. The last chapter of the book offers insight into actions plans and metrics to ensure that customer insights become the driving force behind the success of the organization. These action plans start with top management dedication to and leadership on providing superior value to customers. Senior marketing positions in the organization need to be the voice of the customer within the firm to ensure that customer insights are heard and understood by all in the organization. Interfunctional cooperation, driven by market-based incentives, can provide the organizational focus to help attract and retain target customers. Dedicated marketing research expertise within the firm is the last piece of the winning formula, as these internal consultants can often uncover customer segments and unmet customer needs more effectively than outside consultants.

WHAT "CUSTOMER DRIVEN" ISN'T

The terms "customer-focused, customer-centric and customer-driven" have become a frequent part of the American business vernacular. Annual reports talk about how the *Customer is King,* but in many firms, this is lip service rather than a business philosophy. Many firms have hired marketing people to collect the voice of the customer, but routinely ignore their insights because their ideas add cost to the firm's product offering or because the insights do not fit their preconceptions. They use their past experience and intuition to make marketing decisions, acting as though the marketplace is static. They fail to act upon an insightful and imaginative understanding of the needs of their customers.

Other firms go overboard and become "customer-compelled." They try to respond to everything their customer's desire, bending over backwards to do whatever any customer wants. The *customer-compelled* companies fundamentally misunderstand the market-driven concept and fail to exercise discipline in their strategy. They try to be all things to everyone, and fail to set priorities for which markets to serve with which benefits and features. Instead of a clear focus, the energies of these organizations are diluted by the uncoordinated efforts of different parts of their organizations.[3]

Being customer-driven does not mean listening to the exact words of customers and blindly giving them what they ask for. This will usually result in incremental improvements to current products rather than breakthrough innovations.

---

[3] George S. Day, "Misconceptions about Market Orientation," *Journal of Market-Focused Management* 4, 1999, 5–16.

Customers should not be the only source for new product ideas, since they spend so little time thinking about your product. Customers are better used to react to new product ideas generated from a number of sources. These customer reactions can be used to identify promising ideas for further development and to "kill the dogs" early; that is, kill bad ideas before they consume an unfair share of the marketing resources. Methods to develop and test breakthrough innovations will be covered in Chapter 10.

Asking customers about their ideal product can often lead to an over-designed product that is too expensive for most target customers. Rather, obtaining customer insight into which product features are critical and which product features are "nice to have" is essential to providing a product offering that is both attractive and affordable to target customers. Trade-off techniques will be covered in Chapter 6.

Other organizations act as if they feel they are smart enough to figure out what is best for the customer without involving the customer in the new product development process. Take the example of the Susan B. Anthony dollar coin, launched by the U.S. government because of the high cost of continuously replacing one-dollar bills. Hundreds of millions of the coins were minted and distributed to banks, but U.S. customers disdained the new coins. One of the reasons for the lack of adoption of the new dollar coin was the continued existence of the one-dollar paper currency in the United States. Other countries withdraw the paper currency to force conversion to coins.

The bigger reason consumers disliked the new Susan B. Anthony dollar coin was confusion: it was the same size and color as the U.S. twenty-five cent coin! Many consumers found themselves putting the dollar coin into parking meters and vending machines, instead of the twenty-five cent coin. Had the government made a small investment in marketing research to understand customers' reactions to the new coin, they would have quickly learned that one of the key attributes of coins that customers value is the ability to differentiate between pennies, nickels, dimes, etc. quickly based on size and color.

Some major companies have been vocal about their success despite the lack of insight into their customers. Sony of Japan has put its focus on knowing what is possible rather than upon knowing the needs and wants of their customers. Their founder, Akio Morita, has stated: "Our plan is to lead the public to new products rather than ask them what they want. The public does not know what is possible, but we do." The Sony Walkman has been cited repeatedly as a highly successful new product that was developed without studying the needs of the customer. Vincent P. Barabba and Gerald Zaltman ask an interesting question, however, about another well-known Sony product that was not a market success:[4]

> Would Sony have been better off if it had listened to the market – which at the time knew little of transistors and magnetic tape technology – and

---

[4] Vincent P. Barabba and Gerald Zaltman, *Hearing the Voice of the Market: Competitive Advantage through Creative Use of Market Information* (Boston: Harvard Business School Press, 1991), 31.

found out whether the market was willing to trade off the attributes of the Sony Beta format for those of the VHS format?

WHAT CUSTOMER-DRIVEN MEANS

One of the thought leaders on customer-driven organizations is George S. Day, a marketing professor at the prestigious Wharton School of the University of Pennsylvania. He has written two of the best books on the topic, entitled: *Market Driven Strategy* and *The Market Driven Organization*.[5] His definition of what it means to be market/customer driven is classic marketing thought:

> To be market-driven means seeing past the short-sighted and superficial inputs of customers, to gain a deep-down understanding that gives managers the confidence that their judgments are right.
>
> Management insight and conviction that a market exists for a new product or service must be grounded in intimate understanding of customer behavior, latent needs, changing requirements and deep-seated dissatisfactions with current alternatives. Such deep insight comes from having the key decision makers literally living with customers, observing them in their natural habitat, and seeking out lead users who have needs well in advance of the rest of the market.
>
> Managers recognize early the potential for delivering new forms of value from technology development or the emergence of complementary products because they have deep insights into the latent needs of customers and can anticipate their responses.[6]

If this describes your management team, you are fortunate indeed. Aligning your organization more closely with the customer can give you sustainable competitive advantages, provide insight into new opportunities, and help avoid costly marketing blunders.

If the previous statements describe your management team, your firm can be described as **customer-centric,** best described by Harvard Marketing Professor Gerald Zaltman:[7]

> Customer-centricity is the degree to which a firm focuses on latent as well as obvious needs of current and potential customers. A customer-centric firm avoids technological arrogance – the notion that customers are passive and must be aggressively sold to rather than skillfully heard.

---

[5] George S. Day, *Market Driven Strategy: Processes for Creating Value* (New York: Free Press, 1990); George S. Day, *The Market Driven Organization: Understanding, Attracting, and Keeping Valuable Customers* (New York: Free Press, 1999).

[6] Day, "Misconceptions about Market Orientation," 12.

[7] Gerald Zaltman, *How Customers Think: Essential Insights into the Mind of the Market* (Boston: Harvard Business School Press, 2003), 21.

If these statements describe your management team, your leaders believe in and have implemented the **marketing concept**, best described by Philip Kotler, the "father" of modern marketing:[8]

> The key to achieving organizational goals consists of being more effective than competitors in integrating marketing activities toward determining and satisfying the needs and wants of target markets.

Are Customer-Driven Firms More Profitable?

Perhaps the strongest argument for adopting a customer orientation is its impact on the financial performance of the firm. Studies have shown that customer-focused companies tend to be more profitable on average than their competitors.[9] One study showed that market-driven businesses were **31 percent more profitable** than self-centered firms.[10]

Truly customer-driven companies are still too rare. If yours is, you're among the fortunate few. If you're not, this book can help in the transformation of your company from an "inside-out" focus, concerned mostly with producing your products, to an "outside-in" focus, concerned mainly with sensing the needs of target customers. This book can help in that transformation by outlining steps to gain deep, culture-changing customer insights. One of the first places to look to see if your firm is "inside-out" focused or "outside-in" focused is to listen to the language used by your management team.

The Battle of Success

A major battle that many companies face is the **"Battle of Success."** As firms become successful in the marketplace, many tend to begin to focus inward because they feel they understand enough about their customers. They continue to follow older methods religiously that had been successful in the past. Their success leads them to underestimate their competition. They tend to focus on safe marketing decisions, such as brand line extensions that are very similar to the parent brand, for sales growth. These employees often focus internally on advancing their own careers rather than focusing externally on anticipating changes in the market and among their target consumers.

An example of success leading to complacency is Sears, which was the leading retailer in America in the 1980s. Sears dominated the value-driven mass retail

---

[8] Philip Kotler, *Marketing Management: Analysis, Planning, Implementation, and Control*, 9th ed. (Upper Saddle River, NJ: Prentice Hall, 1997), 19.

[9] Rohit Deshpande and John Farley, "Measuring Market Orientation: Generalization and Synthesis," *Journal of Market-Focused Management* 2, no. 6, 1998.

[10] George S. Day and Prakesh Nedungadi, "Managerial Representations of Competitive Advantage," *Journal of Marketing* 58, 1994.

market, achieving success with a product-driven branding strategy of strong private labels in tools and garden (Craftsman), appliances (Kenmore), and batteries (DieHard). As competitors began to understand customer segments not fully satisfied by Sears and target them, Sears was attacked on many fronts. But because of their past success, Sears had stopped listening to customers and continued to follow the outdated marketing practices that had created that success. This allowed competitors, such as Wal-Mart, Target, Kohl's, Best Buy, and Home Depot, to target segments of the retail market and serve them better than Sears could, thereby attracting many Sears customers to their stores.

When Arthur Martinez, the former CEO of Sears, first joined the company, he observed that customers had flocked to the competition and identified three things that he felt Sears had done to turn off customers:

- Sears had **ignored** the customer.
- Sears had **underestimated** the competition.
- Sears had focused almost all of its energy on the construction of a magnificent, frustrating **bureaucracy.**

During his tenure at Sears, Martinez was able to break down some of the bureaucracy and make Sears more responsive to customer needs, but the opportunity that Sears provided for competitors to establish themselves was seized. While mid-tier retailers such as Sears and JCPenney have survived the enormous popularity of new retail formats, Montgomery Wards has not.

Some companies fall into the "we're superior to our customers" trap, underestimating the abilities of their customers to help them develop new products. They argue that customers are unable to envision breakthrough products and services, and seldom ask for new products that they eventually come to value.[11] This valid but misleading observation fails to recognize the difference between: 1) asking customers to describe their problems and dissatisfaction with current products, which they can do easily, and 2) expecting customers to generate solutions and new products. Customers are very happy to do the former but often respond with blank stares when asked, "What new products would you like to see us develop in the future?" Methods to uncover and understand the unmet needs of target customers are covered in Chapter 2.

Market Sensing

A key element to becoming customer driven is a firm's skills in market sensing. The ability of a firm to create value for target customers depends on this capability. Market sensing has been defined as **"the ability to understand customers' current and emerging needs and wants, competitors' capabilities, offerings and strategies, and the technological, social and demographic trends that are shaping the future market and competitive landscape."**[12]

---

[11] Gary Hamel and C.K. Prahalad, *Competing for the Future* (Boston: Harvard Business School Press, 1994).

[12] Sean Meehan and Patrick Barwise, "Do You Value Customer Value?" in *Mastering Marketing*, exec. ed. Tim Dickson (London: FT Pitman, 1999), 23.

It is not enough for senior management to rely on their marketing and marketing research staffs for market sensing and for bringing the voice of the customer to them. While this is important and necessary, it is not sufficient. Market sensing expertise also requires executives to have firsthand customer contact. Many firms achieve this by bringing customers in to corporate headquarters and having customers speak on panels where management is required to listen and question the target customers. It is often best to select some demanding and unhappy customers for these internal panels, otherwise management may be lulled into the false impression that all customers love us and everything in the market is fine. However, as powerful as these panels can be, they do lack a critical element: the customer environment.

Visiting customers in their environment can provide this critical context to the understanding of the customer. In the diagnostic testing industry, visiting a hospital laboratory manager in his own environment at the start of the morning shift can provide key insight into the stress and the pressure of the job. Hundreds of blood samples are arriving by the rack to be tested; laboratory technicians are calling in sick for work; angry doctors are calling on the phone and demanding test results for ill patients; and their automated blood testing instrument your company makes is unavailable because of its long, monthly maintenance requirement. Seeing this customer context firsthand can provide a whole new level of insight into customer needs and wants and can often inspire ideas for new product features that solve unspoken customer needs. The customer visit will be covered in Chapter 2.

Market sensing in a (B-to-B) context is somewhat more challenging compared to the established methods in the Business-to-Consumer (B-to-C) context. For the B-to-B manager, customer populations tend to be smaller, more difficult to interview, more expensive to interview, and often involve multiple decision makers in one buying unit that may take months to make a decision. Further, it is often difficult to obtain information in a B-to-B context without revealing the sponsor of the research to the respondent. Despite these additional challenges, customer insight gained from B-to-B customers often provides immediate benefits versus the competition, since some B-to-B competitors find it easier to skip the work of listening to customers.

Are There Only Two Sources of Competitive Advantage?

Jack Welch, retired CEO of General Electric, has said that there are only two sources of competitive advantage:

1. The ability to learn more about our customers faster than our competition.
2. The ability to turn that learning into action faster than the competition.[13]

With the ability of firms to match competitive products and marketing tactics within months, implementing actions based on deep customer insight is the only

---

[13] Jack Welch (lecture, Kellogg School of Management, Evanston, IL, October 16, 2001).

source of competitive advantage today. The advantage is not based on **how much** information is collected, but on the **insights drawn** from that information and how well these insights are **integrated** into the organization.

Philip Kotler has similar thoughts: "If companies don't want to be left behind, they must anticipate change and lead change. The ability to change faster than your competitors amounts to a competitive advantage."[14]

Customer Insight: Fast and Deep

This book will go into depth on both of the points identified by Jack Welch, with particular emphasis on **learning about customers faster and with more insight** than your competitors. Gaining these deep insights and acting on them quickly and with the conviction of all involved in your company can transform the average performing firm into the star of its industry.

---

[14] Philip Kotler, *Marketing Insights From A to Z: 80 Concepts Every Manager Needs to Know,* (Hoboken, NJ: John Wiley and Sons, 2003), 17.

MACRO TRENDS

INSIGHT 1: Your customers are constantly changing in subtle ways that impact their purchasing behavior.

There is no reason anyone would want a computer in their home.
Chairman of Digital Equipment Corp., 1977

Customer Insight Pyramid

The basis for any successful marketing program is a strong foundation: a sound understanding of the macro trends occurring in the marketplace that will impact the behavior of your target customers in the future. The chairman of Digital Equipment was not able to foresee in 1977 the widespread use of home computers, perhaps due to the lack of attention to consumer and technological trends just beginning to develop. This chapter will address the need to continually monitor these macro trends and tools to imagine how these trends could affect your business.

The Boiled Frog Analogy

Bill Coors, the grandson of Adolph Coors, who founded the brewery in Golden, Colorado, likes to tell his employees the story of the boiled frog to stress the importance of monitoring and responding to changes in the environment. He says

that if you tried to put a frog in boiling water, it would feel the heat and quickly jump out of the pot. However, if you put the frog in a pot of cool water, and slowly raised the heat, you would soon have boiled frog, because the frog would not recognize and respond to the gradual increase in temperature.

Bill goes on to say that the same is true for environmental changes and corporations. Most macro environmental changes happen gradually, and many corporations don't recognize the changes. They wind up as boiled frogs.

It is ironic for Bill Coors to tell this story, since he was one of the last brewers to recognize the lifestyle trend toward consuming lighter-tasting beverages and the growth of the light beer segment. Bill did not understand the emotional benefits provided by light beers and was totally focused on the rational product benefits. Bill was fond of saying "The Coors Brewery doesn't need a light beer! Coors (brand) is light enough!" Only after Miller Lite had demonstrated its continued vitality did Bill reluctantly acquiesce to "those marketing people" and allow a light beer to be brewed in Golden, Colorado. Coors Light has been a runaway success, and was the third largest-selling brand of beer in the United States in 2002. It is fortunate for Coors that Bill changed his mind, for now Coors Light represents almost 80 percent of sales at the Coors Brewing Company. Without Coors Light, the Coors Brewing Company would have been a boiled frog.

Macro Trends

Mining for **Customer Insight** is analogous to drilling for oil. Not all drilling will result in a gusher. You will hit many dry wells in the effort to find the gusher that yields millions of barrels of crude oil. Oil companies do not randomly drill for oil but take many core samples and carefully survey the surrounding environment to understand the potential of the site for a gusher. The surrounding environment can provide strong clues as to the chances of finding a rich well.

The same is true with understanding the market environment before "drilling" for customer insights. Companies need to understand the macro trends occurring in the external environment thoroughly to maximize their chances of finding the customer insights that will make the firm more successful. They need to know which segments of the market to focus on before developing a deep knowledge of the needs of customers in that segment.

Macro trends are trends that occur in the environment external to the firm that, over time, can have a significant impact on the firm's customers and their purchasing behavior. Because they are external to the firm, they are easy to neglect, as overworked executives often focus on dealing with internal issues and today's crisis. However, like the frog in the slowly boiling water, shifting macro trends can eventually overwhelm the firm and lead to corporate bankruptcy.

Larry Chandler, former vice president of business research for McDonald's, suggests that the careful study of macro trends "allows management to understand when change is coming, to measure change, to understand whether the change is positive or negative, to understand how to respond to the change, and most

importantly, **how they can drive needed change.**"[1] Capitalizing on the right macro trends can lead to extraordinary performance, evidenced by Hallmark's greeting card **experience.**

Companies such as Hallmark Cards, Inc., employ resident experts like Marita Wesely-Clough in a quest to keep on top of the macro trends impacting the greeting card business. Marita leads a staff of three whose daily tasks include browsing in stores, eavesdropping on conversations, reading social tomes, traveling, or just generally observing American culture. Demographic and attitudinal trends can greatly impact product lines in the greeting card business.

The increasing ethnic and racial diversity in the United States has translated into Wesely-Clough's idea for Common Threads, a line of multicultural Hallmark greeting cards that was launched in 1994. The obsession of some customers with bargains led to the introduction of Warm Wishes, a line of 99-cent cards launched in 1999.[2]

Macro Trend Typology

The five major types of macro trends covered in this chapter are:

- demographic
- psychographic
- economic
- technology adoption
- competitive

Each of these areas needs to be studied carefully to provide the best chances of drilling in the right place for customer insights. For example, the growth in single-person households in the United States over the past twenty years could suggest a new target segment for a firm to pursue.

Firms need to study how these macro trends have impacted their firm in the past, how they are currently impacting the firm, and develop scenarios as to how these macro trends may impact the firm in the future. A simple demographic example is the impact of the shifts in age groups on the total sales of beer in the United States.

Models developed to forecast beer industry sales have found that one variable continues to be highly critical to predicting growth or decline in beer industry sales: the size of the 21-27-year-old age segment. As this segment grows, brewers are happy to see a concomitant growth in their industry's sales. The industry leader, Anheuser-Busch, is especially happy when this age group is growing, given its large 49 percent share of the U.S. beer market.

The following chart shows the trend in the size of this age group over the past twenty years, as well as the U.S. Census Bureau's projections for the next ten years.

---

[1] Larry Chandler, personal communication with author.
[2] Marita Wesely-Clough, quoted in "25 Years of American Demographics," *American Demographics*, April 2003, p. 40.

U.S. Population Aged 21–27
1983–2013
Source: U. S. Census Bureau

Millions of Adults

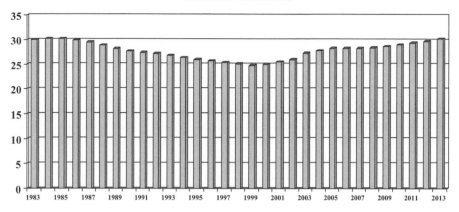

You can see that the size of this age group peaked in 1985 and proceeded to decline for fourteen years. Couples having fewer children in the 1960s drove this decline, as "zero population growth" became a popular sociological trend. Sales of beer "went flat" as the key demographic group shrank. As the new millennium began, this trend reversed and the group grew rapidly for five years. Beer industry sales also grew nicely during this time period.

Another way to look at this key age group is to examine the percent of all beer volume that they consume. This group, while representing 13 percent of the drinking age population, represents 23 percent of beer consumption. Thus, this age group has a Category Development Index (CDI) of 172 (23/13 × 100). Further, the beer market is very dynamic, in that, every seven years, one-fourth of the beer market is represented by new, different beer drinkers that weren't there seven years earlier. This makes it critical for breweries that hope to keep their brands relevant to the young market to keep in close contact with the lifestyles, needs, preferences, and behaviors of this new generation.

Demographic Trends

Without question, the most significant demographic trend impacting businesses is the aging of America. In 2000, the median age in the United States was 35.3 years, the highest in the nation's history. In 1950, the median age was 30.2 years. This change in median age was due to the growth in the proportion of Americans aged 45–54, which increased 49 percent between 1990 and 2000. This boom has had a major impact on many industries, including retirement communities, health care suppliers, and leisure travel providers.

Let's look at historical growth trends and projections by age group between 1980 and 2020.

U.S. Population by Age Groups
1980–2020 in Thousands

Source: U.S. Census Bureau

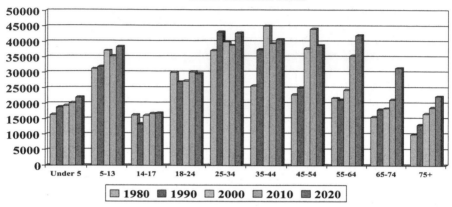

Note from the chart that in 1980, the largest age group was the late baby boomers, those aged 25-34, with 37 million Americans. The median age of Americans in 1980 was 30. By 2000, the largest age group was those aged 35-44, with 45 million Americans in this age group. The median age of Americans in 2000 was 35. Projections for the year 2020 show that those aged 25-34 (43 million) and those aged 55-64 (42 million) will become the largest age groups. The median age of Americans in 2020 is projected to reach 38.

Let's look at the growth dynamics across age groups a little more closely, focusing on the changes between 2000 and 2010. The following graph shows the percent share of the American population that the 45-54 and 55-64 age groups represented in 2000 (lower bars). It also shows the percent share these age groups represent of the **net growth** in the American population between 2000 and 2010. Thus, these baby boomer age groups will account for a remarkable 95 percent of the **net** change in the U.S. population between 2000 and 2010.

Note the dramatic changes occurring in this decade among those aged 45 and older. The group aged 55-64 represented about 9 percent of the population in 2000, but **will represent 60 percent of the net population growth** in this decade! Those aged 45-54 represented about 13 percent of the population, but **will represent 35 percent of the net population growth** in this decade. Advertising and other marketing tactics will change dramatically this decade as more marketers target these older consumers.

The combination of the aging population and the rising number of college-educated adults has resulted in a surge in the number of informed health care consumers, which in turn drove demand for alternative medical care. Wellness clinics have sprung up like dandelions, and herbal medicines are used by one-third

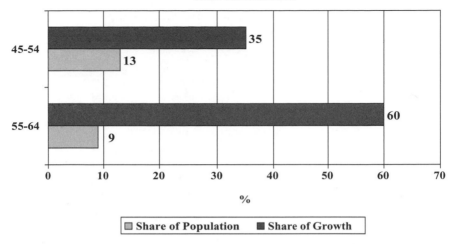

Age Group Dynamics–2010 vs. 2000
Share of Population vs. Share of Net Population Growth
Source: U.S. Census Bureau

☐ Share of Population   ■ Share of Growth

of Americans. These educated, upscale consumers are less likely than their parents to place absolute authority in one doctor.[3]

A second demographic macro trend that is changing consumer behavior is dramatic growth in the participation of women in the workforce, which has greatly increased the productive capacity of the United States. As more women have started careers instead of families, they have delayed childbearing and lowered the birthrate.

In 1970, 40 percent of households were comprised of a married couple with children. By 2000, this proportion would be almost cut in half to only 24 percent. "Working wives change the power structure of the family by equalizing the resources of husband and wife. This results in the working wife having more power in such family decisions as how money will be spent."[4] Working women create growing markets for many companies, such as carryout restaurants and day care centers, and shrinking markets for others, such as marketing research firms that conduct telephone interviews during the day.

A third demographic macro trend that is impacting many industries is the growth in single-person households. The following graph shows the dramatic growth in both male and female single-person households over the past twenty years.

This growth of single-person households has had a major impact on the number of package sizes (SKU = Stock Keeping Units) that package goods manufacturers need to offer their customers, as more companies offer single-serving packages. It has also impacted the real estate market; demand for condos in or near many large cities has boomed as these young singles set up residence.

---

[3] Peter Francese, "Consumers Today," *American Demographics*, April 2003.
[4] Robert Skrabenek, "The Growing Power of Women," quoted in Peter Francese, "Consumers Today," *American Demographics*, April 2003, p. 28.

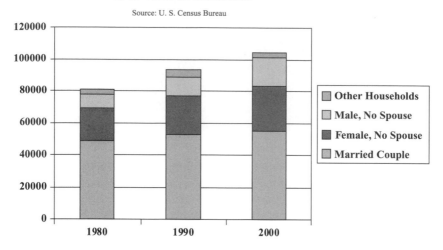

U.S. Household Trends by Type
1980–2000 in Thousands

Source: U. S. Census Bureau

A fourth demographic macro trend that is creating many new niche markets is the continued growth of immigration into the United States, but from very different parts of the world than in the past. During most of the last century, immigration was largely from countries in Western Europe. In the latter part of the twentieth century, immigration from Asia and Latin America became a larger share of the total. In fact, during the 1990s, over 9 million people immigrated to the United States, but **no European country made it into the top ten ranking of countries of birth for immigrants.** Although most of us would have been able to guess that Mexico and China would be in the top ten countries of immigrant origin, few of us would have known that the Philippines and Vietnam ranked among the top four.

These shifts are introducing additional heterogeneity into the U.S. "melting pot of cultures," creating unique niche markets for the astute marketer and diluting the effectiveness of mass-marketing tactics. Over the next twenty-five years, the number of immigrants living in the United States is expected to grow from 31 million to almost 50 million, reaching over 13 percent of the population. Walgreen's stores have been proactive with this macro trend and now offer eight languages on their prescription medicine labels, including Vietnamese.

Ethnic media, such as newspapers, magazines, television, and radio, will experience phenomenal growth. Advertisers will have to do more than just translate their advertising into more languages; they will have to develop advertising messages that resonate with these niche segments. "Companies will not be able to keep swimming in the mainstream, because there is no mainstream. Instead, it's a series of parallel creeks, some constantly filling, and some drying up a little."[5]

---

[5] Dan McGinn, quoted in Alison Stein Wellner, "The Next 25 Years," *American Demographics*, April, 2003.

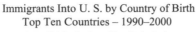

Immigrants Into U. S. by Country of Birth
Top Ten Countries – 1990–2000
Source: U. S. Immigration and Naturalization Service

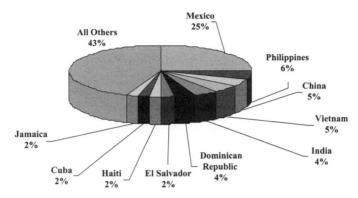

These are just four of many demographic trends that could shape your market in the future. Having a dedicated marketing research staff to continually monitor the possible impact of these demographic trends can keep a firm from becoming a boiled frog.

Psychographic/Lifestyle Trends

The second type of macro trend is **psychographic**, or **lifestyle** trends. Psychographics refer to the lifestyles people live, represented by their activities, interests and opinions. Psychographic research develops quantitative profiles of customers, using batteries of questions to capture Activities, Interests, and Opinions (AIO) information. Examples of components of psychographic questionnaires are:

- **Activities** – work, hobbies, vacation, sports, and social events
- **Interests** – family, community, food, fashion, and recreation
- **Opinions** – politics, business, culture, future, and social issues

Psychographic research reached its peak in popularity in the 1970s, as many advertising agencies developed psychographic profiles of consumers to help them develop better advertising for the changing world. An early example of psychographic segmentation appeared in a marketing journal in 1977. This study grouped women of similar lifestyles into groups based upon their activities, interests, and opinions. Five fairly homogeneous groups were identified by Mehotra and Wells[6], and were given the following names based upon their AIOs:

- **Thelma** – the old-fashioned traditionalist (25 percent of women)
- **Mildred** – the militant mother (20 percent of women)

---

[6] Sunil Mehotra and William Wells, "Psychographics and Buyer Behavior: Theory and Recent Empirical Findings," in *Consumer and Industrial Buying Behavior*, ed. Arch G. Woodside, Jagdish N. Sheth, and Peter D. Bennett (New York: North-Holland, 1977).

- **Candice** – the chic suburbanite (20 percent of women)
- **Cathy** – the contented housewife (18 percent of women)
- **Eleanor** – the elegant socialite (17 percent of women)

These psychographic groups were then used to develop market segmentation strategies for advertising clients. For example, a cake mix product might be aimed at Thelma, the old-fashioned traditionalist, while a new brand of champagne might be positioned at Eleanor, the elegant socialite. The mantra of the advertising world in the 1970s was: "The better you understand your target customer, the better you can communicate with them."

Although tracking these psychographic segments was useful for many advertising agencies in developing advertising, most marketers found that other segmentation approaches were more valuable for strategic marketing. Psychographic segmentation will be explored in more depth in Chapter 4.

Consumers are often grouped into age cohorts and named to describe their vastly different **lifestyles.** Baby boomers, Generation X, and Millennials are popular rubrics for these age cohorts. As Millennials move into young adulthood over the next twenty years, major transformations are expected relative to the previous generation. "We foresee higher standards, improving behavior, more social cohesion (even conformity), closer attachments to parents, more institutional trust, longer-term life planning and greater collective optimism about the future. Millennial young adults will vote more heavily and be far more engaged in mainstream politics than Gen Xers were at that age. In careers, they will take fewer risks, display more teamwork and usher in a new wave of union organizing. They will marry and have children at a younger age .... As consumers, Millennials will be attracted to big brands, friendlier and safer products, more middle-class messages and a quest for a balanced life."[7]

Popcorn Anyone?

One of the gurus of lifestyle trends is Faith Popcorn, who has written a number of books on the topic. Some of her lifestyle trends have received national publicity, such as:[8]

- **Cocooning** – People are spending less time in the outside world and more time in the security of their homes.
- **Down-aging** – Older people don't want to feel old and are working out and having plastic surgery in record numbers.
- **Cashing Out** – Many people have left high-paying, stressful jobs to have the lower-paying career they love.

---

[7] Neil Howe and William Strauss, *Millennials Rising* (New York: Vintage, 2000).
[8] Faith Popcorn, *The Popcorn Report: Faith Popcorn on the Future of Your Company, Your World, Your Life* (New York: Doubleday, 1991).

These insights into current and future lifestyle trends have made Popcorn a highly sought-after consultant.

How Hallmark Cards Anticipates Lifestyle Trends

Hallmark Cards manager of the Trends Group, Marita Wesely-Clough, spoke at a conference called "Future Trends: Visionary Information for Business Now" in Los Angeles in May of 2002. The Institute for International Research sponsored the conference, with highlights reported in the Research Conference Report published by Robert F. Lederer of RFL Communications. Wesely-Clough believes people are searching for solutions to help them assimilate change, add meaning, personalize their existence, and connect with others. Among the trends she identified were:[9]

- **Hunkering Down** – New attitudes, such as Americans' uncertainty about vulnerability, are taking hold. Americans seek comfort in family and friends and renewed focus on what is important in life.
- **Resilience** – Expect more people to rise above difficult situations— personal, professional, or political – and choose to make a positive difference.
- **"Be There Now" Addiction** – Americans expect "be there now" TV, an immediacy fostering "a milieu where speed over accuracy, sensationalism and syndication over dependence can result."
- **Longing for Bygone Days** – There is an emerging nostalgia to go home again, a longing for the past and for simpler times.
- **Refusing to Age** – Baby boomers are making use of every spiritual, physical, medical, and genetic modification in their ongoing pursuit of energy and vitality.
- **Confidence** – Look for an expansiveness of spirit, a warmth and confidence as Americans return to comfort and coziness, enjoying nature and more time in their homes.

Wesely-Clough stated that Hallmark is intensifying its efforts in researching lifestyle trends and is not satisfied producing greeting cards that merely reflect current tastes. She stressed that Hallmark feels an obligation to anticipate what people will want to say next and wants to give them the words to communicate thoughts and emotions that are just now forming in their collective consciousness.

The Yankelovich Social Monitor

In 1958, Daniel Yankelovich founded the research firm Yankelovich, Skelly and White in New York City to track social trends on a continuous basis. His longitudinal study, the "Yankelovich Social Monitor," was launched in 1969 and clearly and comprehensively tracks shifting customer values and social trends. "In the 1950s, the American ideal was uniform and homogeneous: a suburban nuclear

---

[9] Marita Wesely-Clough, (paper presented at "Future Trends: Visionary Information for Business Now" Los Angeles, CA, May 2002), cited in RFL Communications, Inc. *Research Conference Report*, June 2002.

family with a breadwinner father, a homemaker mother, two or more children and a pet. Over the last 25 to 30 years, however, a dizzying array of other lifestyles have gained mainstream acceptance, and this trend shows no sign of abating. While this freedom has enlarged individual choice, autonomy and diversity, it is also linked to a very assertive form of individualism, a sense that my needs come first."[10]

In her 2001 book, *The Mirrored Window: Focus Groups from a Moderator's Point of View,* Judith Langer identified several interesting lifestyle trends that are impacting marketing to customers in the new millennium:[11]

- **Nostalgia** – for many of us, childhood is a period in our lives that we romanticize. Baby boomers are nostalgic for the 1950s, a time of prosperity when families stayed together and things were simpler. This nostalgia makes boomers feel youthful, and the music of the decade continues to have great vitality.
- **Flexible life stages** – The life schedule people were expected to follow in the 1950s was clear:
  - Get married following school
  - Have children, starting in your 20s
  - Become an empty nester in your 40s
  - Retire in your 60s

  Nowadays, this predictable series of life stages is scrambled. More couples are living together and getting married later (if at all), postponing parenthood, and then finding the nest does not always remain empty.
- **Zigzagging women** – More available choices available for women have put greater pressure upon those choices – pressure from society, from family, and from women themselves. Because the rules have loosened, it can be more confusing than ever deciding on what's the right thing to do. The dilemma of choice replaces no choice. On both sides of the mother's-career decision versus the stay-at-home decision, many women feel torn and criticized. Homemakers worry about being viewed as women who "just watch soap operas and eat bonbons" rather than bringing in income and developing their work talents.
- **Not the old 9-to-5** – The rise of in-home offices and career switching has dramatically changed the American work life. Longer hours, global connections at all hours, and expanded work scope have contributed to a time famine for many. These time-starved consumers highly value, and will pay for, products and services that will save them time.

Understanding values that consumers hold dear is critical to discerning why they purchase what they do. The things that their culture holds dear, the roles that

---

[10] Daniel Yankelovich in "25 Years of American Demographics," *American Demographics,* April 2003, p. 35.

[11] Judith Langer, *The Mirrored Window: Focus Groups from a Moderator's Point of View* (Ithaca, NY: PMP, 2001).

they play, and what their culture expects of them are all part of their value system. Roper Starch Worldwide, Inc., a marketing research and consulting firm, has conducted values research on a global basis, interviewing 30,000 respondents age 13 to 65 in thirty countries across the globe.[12] The World's Top Ten Values, according to Roper Starch, are, in order:

- Protecting the Family
- Honesty
- Health and Fitness
- Self-esteem
- Self-reliance
- Justice
- Freedom
- Friendship
- Knowledge
- Learning

Among the better educated, values that are of more importance are: **self-esteem, self-reliance, knowledge,** and **learning**.

Among the young 13-19 age group, values that are of more importance are: **friendship, knowledge,** and **learning**.

Among those aged 20-29, the value of **enduring love** jumps into the top ten listing of values.

Economic Trends

The third major type of macro trend to be covered is **economic trends**. Perhaps the major economic trend impacting American industry today is the rapid growth in the number of higher income households. In 1971, 28 percent of American households earned more than $50,000 (in 2001 dollars). By 2001, 43 percent of American households earned more than $50,000. In fact, the share of households earning more than $100,000 more than tripled during that period, from 4 percent to 14 percent. This increasing household income was driven primarily by the growth in multiple wage earners within a household over that time period. While American households have more income, they have less leisure time than they had thirty years ago. This leads to more spending on luxury goods, expensive vacations, and second homes. Cruise ships are being built in record numbers to cater to these wealthy families.

The level of household income is strongly correlated to demographics. Data from the Federal Reserve Board's Survey of Consumer Finances in January of 2003 show mean and median incomes tend to be higher among:

- households where the family head has a college degree
- white non-Hispanic households

---

[12] Roper Starch Worldwide, "Remapping the World of Consumers," in "The World of Consumers," special advertising section of *American Demographics*, October 2000.

Trends in Composition of U. S. Households
by Total Money Income, in Constant 2001 Dollars

Source: U. S. Census Bureau

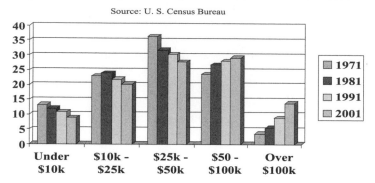

- households headed by self-employed workers
- households that own their home
- households located in the Northeast and West regions of the United States
- households headed by a person in the 45-54 age group.

Borrowing on credit cards seems to be the American way of life, with 44 percent of American families using this type of borrowing. The use of credit card borrowing is notably **lower** among the highest and lowest income groups and among families headed by a person aged 65 or older.

The share of American families owning publicly traded corporate equities (stocks, mutual funds) exceeded 50 percent in 2001. Between 1998 and 2001, the median dollar holding of American families with equities rose more than one-fourth, driven by the growth in stock prices during the first two years of that three-year period.

The number of Americans that bank online has been growing steadily, from 4 million in 1998 to 24 million in 2002, according to Jupiter Research. This is expected to grow to 35 million Americans by 2004, or roughly 16 percent of U. S. adults. Bank of America has the most heavily used online banking service, with almost 9 million customers in 2002, and does not charge customers a fee to use the online banking service.

A major concern among customers who have not begun online banking is **security,** which outweighs the convenience benefit that is offered by online banking. Banks will need to make a proactive effort to educate customers on the security of online banking. Banks had to undertake similar efforts in the past to educate customers on the security of Automated Teller Machines. However, the payback of converting a customer to electronic bill payment through their bank is significant: the customer becomes **more loyal and more profitable.** When a customer is dependent on a bank for electronic bill payment, it is a hassle for them to change their accounts to another bank. Most customers won't change, barring an unsatisfactory service experience or a significant promotional incentive by a competitor.

Roughly half of the community banks in the United States currently offer electronic bill payment, but over 90 percent plan to make it available to customers

in the next three years. What is their incentive? Cost savings. It is estimated that the use of the Internet by customers to pay bills may save banks billions of dollars in making and processing paper checks.[13]

Marketers need to pay close attention to these economic trends, especially changes in the distribution of income across households and the willingness and ability of consumers to take on debt to finance discretionary purchases.

Technology Adoption Trends

The fourth type of macro trend to be discussed is **technology adoption trends**. Ten years ago, it was quite unusual to observe anyone speaking on a "cellular" phone. Today, it is quite unusual to drive the freeways of Chicago, for example, and find someone **not** talking on a cell phone. This adoption of mobile communications has been rapid, as prices and phone sizes have shrunk, and ease of use has improved and reach has increased. This technology has created huge new markets for new companies and is shrinking markets for old-line communication companies. An interesting phenomenon is that the author's parents do not own a cell phone and probably never will, while the author's two children voice-communicate exclusively by cell phone and do not have "landline" phones in their residences. The author is caught in technology-transition, having both a cell phone and a landline.

Motorola was caught in a technology dilemma in the cellular phone market, believing that analog technology would remain viable in light of growth in digital technology. Motorola had made huge investments in plants and products based on analog technology and would have had to commit billions of dollars to move to the newer digital technology. The signals were loud that the market was moving to digital technology, but Motorola delayed acting on these signals. Between 1994 and 1998, Motorola lost its leadership position in the cellular phone market to Nokia, as its share dropped from 60 percent to 34 percent. George S. Day has described the boiling frog syndrome occurring at Motorola well:

> In the early 1990s executives from McCaw Cellular (now AT&T Wireless Services) decided the future of cellular was **digital.** Over the next few years, they met repeatedly with Motorola managers who said they would work on it. Yet in 1996, just as AT&T was rolling out its digital network, Motorola unveiled its Star TAC phone – a design marvel, light, smaller than a cigarette pack, and **analog!** AT&T had no choice but to turn to Nokia and Ericsson for digital handsets.
>
> Why did Motorola miss or ignore the signals from its customers and rivals? Some argue it was hubris: that the company was blinded by its success in creating the cellular phone market. However, Christopher Galvin, the CEO, also attributed the problems to a culture that was engineering and product-driven and distracted by internal rivalries.

---

[13] Karen Hoffman, "Electronic Bill Payment Comes of Age," *Community Banker*, July 2002.

Markets eventually punish firms with arrogant and unresponsive cultures. When this happens, the shock to the system is so great that the dysfunctional values and beliefs can finally be challenged and displaced. Motorola was forced to attack its problems by consolidating its feuding fiefdoms under a common umbrella.[14]

Motorola has seen its stock price drop from $60 a share in 2000 to $8 a share in 2002. Between 2000 and 2003, Motorola reduced its workforce by over one-third as nearly 60,000 jobs were eliminated.

Five Factors Inhibiting New Technology Acceptance

Five factors have been identified that slow the market penetration of new, emerging consumer technologies.[15] Examples of emerging consumer technologies are High-Definition Television (HDTV), digital television, video on demand, smart cards, desktop videoconferencing, network computers, digital cameras, and digital video discs. Customers **defer** technology adoption on products such as these when:

- *The product is of value only if other people also have it.* Economists refer to this as "network externalities." Examples include video systems and many telecommunication services.
- *The technology needs a common standard.* Prior to Matsushita's VHS format for video cassette recorders (VCRs) gaining industry acceptance as the dominant standard, customers were reluctant to make a decision between this format and Sony's Betamax format. Markets where a dominant standard fails to emerge are characterized by low penetration.
- *The product's value depends upon complementary products.* VCR sales only accelerated after movie producers made titles available for rent on videotapes.
- *The switching costs of the product are high.* These costs include not only purchasing costs but the greater costs incurred in learning new systems, as in a change in computer software.
- *It is difficult for consumers to engage in product trial.* While trial opportunities are relatively easy to provide for grocery products, in technology markets it is relatively difficult.

Key strategies suggested by Sabine Kuester, Elisa Montaguti, and Thomas S. Robertson to accelerate the technology takeoff include: aggressive market penetration, ensuring product comparability, preannouncement of new products, and marketing alliances.

---

[14] George S. Day, *The Market Driven Organization: Understanding, Attracting, and Keeping Valuable Customers* (New York: Free Press, 1999).

[15] Sabine Kuester, Elisa Montaguti, and Thomas S. Robertson, "How New Technologies Can Take Off Fast," in *Mastering Marketing: A Comprehensive MBA Companion*, ed. Sabine Kuester, Elisa Montaguti, and Thomas S. Robertson (Harlow, U.K.: Pearson Education Limited, 1999).

Typology of Technological Innovations

Technological innovations can be classified into one of three groups: **continuous innovations, dynamically continuous innovations,** and **discontinuous innovations.** Continuous innovations tend to be most rapidly adopted, while discontinuous innovations tend to be the slowest to be adopted. Let's examine the differences between these three types of innovations.

> *Continuous innovations* are minor modifications of existing products and cause the least disruptions to consumers' established behavior patterns. Continuous innovation is incremental, characterized by progressive refinements, and builds on existing knowledge in existing markets. An example is faster computer-processing speeds caused by the development of improved silicon microchips.
>
> *Dynamically continuous innovations* are the creation of new types of existing products and are sufficiently innovative to have some disruptive effects on established consumers' behavior patterns. An example is HDTV, which required consumers to buy a new television but did not require any new learning to operate it.
>
> *Discontinuous innovations* are totally new products that cause consumers to establish new behavior patterns. Examples are the Internet, videoconferencing, home computers, and the electric car.

An examination of successful firms that have emerged over the past thirty years in technology-intensive industries reveals a pattern of innovations by the firm into new product lines, few of which were continuous innovations. These firms also then worked hard to stay ahead of their competitors, and often would obsolete their own products. The safe, cautious approach of continuous improvement is easier to undertake, because it draws on the existing market framework, infrastructure, and tacit knowledge of customers. The strategy focused on risky, discontinuous innovation is more difficult to implement because people in corporations tend to focus on technologies and products that they are most comfortable with and then work them to death. "Companies that have been successful in redefining their industries have created new discontinuities, by focusing on the future needs of their customers. An effective way to understand the future needs of target customers is to **allow customers to participate in the innovation process**. Only when researchers work jointly with customers can this hidden knowledge be exposed, and only after tacit needs are exposed and understood is it effective to consider the role that technology should play in fulfilling them. Therefore, the discontinuous innovation process is a mutually dependent learning process in which customers must experience what is possible in order to determine what may be of value for the future. The process is driven not by technology itself, but by *how technology is used.*"[16]

The adoption of digital photography is an excellent example of how technology can change entire markets and can lead to major decisions for companies. Consumers are increasingly seeing their camera as an extension of their computer rather than as

---

[16] See "Fourth Generation R & D" summary on publications page of www.innovations.com (accessed April 2003).

a separate device to capture images on film. What strategy should Kodak adopt to deal with this macro trend? Ignoring it and hoping it goes away is clearly a poor strategy. It would be like Coors Brewing ignoring the trend to light beers and hoping they go away. The fundamental macro trend is simply too powerful to ignore.

As recently as 2000, film cameras outsold digital cameras by a ratio of four-to-one (20 million to 5 million). The gap narrowed by 2002, with film cameras only slightly outselling digital cameras (14 million to 10 million). In 2003, sales of digital cameras surpassed sales of film cameras for the first time. In 2004, digital cameras are projected to outsell film cameras by a significant margin.

Sales of Digital and Traditional Cameras
United States – Millions of Units

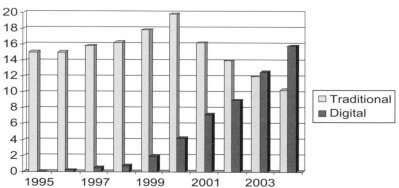

Kodak decided in October of 2003 to move away from the traditional film business, its core competency for 122 years, and to spend over $3 billion on digital technology purchases. It dramatically slashed its shareholder dividend to provide the funding for the acquisitions. Investors were surprised and shocked by the radical nature of this shift in strategy and began to sell Kodak stock. Kodak shares hit a fifteen-year low. One shareholder group met and is encouraging Kodak to roll back its plans to focus on digital cameras and ink printers.

Did Kodak wait too long to adapt to the digital revolution? When it did decide to adapt to this trend, did it do so too rapidly? Are the shareholders confident in Kodak's strategy for dealing with this macro trend?

Product Characteristics that Influence Diffusion

In the classic book *Diffusion of Innovations*, Everett M. Rogers identified five characteristics of products that impact the rate of diffusion, or consumer adoption:[17]

- **Relative Advantage** – the degree to which potential customers perceive the innovation to be better than currently available alternatives

---

[17] Everett M. Rogers, *Diffusion of Innovations* (New York: Free Press of Glencoe, 1962).

- **Compatibility** – the degree of consistency with existing values, practices, past experiences, and needs of potential customers
- **Complexity** – how difficult the innovation is to understand, learn, and use
- **Trial ability** – the degree to which the innovation can be experienced on a limited, cost-effective basis
- **Observability** – the degree to which the benefits of the innovation are visible to others

Thus, as progressive firms pursue discontinuous innovations, these characteristics need to be addressed to increase the rate of customer adoption. Tactics to address these characteristics include:

- Using mass media to **inform** potential customers about the innovation
- Utilizing interpersonal communication channels to **persuade** customers to **adopt** the innovation
- Developing innovations that reduce hassles for customers and make it easier for them to purchase; the Internet is becoming a major distribution channel for many firms
- Developing trial sizes
- Offering free trials and samples where feasible

WI-FI – WIRELESS FIDELITY ADOPTION

Wireless networks have been developed to allow more applications to be conducted on mobile devices. Many restaurants, including McDonald's and Starbucks, offer their customers fast wireless access to the Internet to enable them to read e-mail and check stock quotes while eating and sipping. To understand the rate that consumers will adopt wireless technology for their laptop computers, let's look at how this innovation stacks up on Rogers's five product characteristics.

- Relative Advantage – a recent survey has shown that a majority of Americans perceive WI-FI to be faster to access than broadband and to be easy to install in a home. However, most potential customers had concerns about the **security** of WI-FI networks as well as the cost to install them in their homes.
- Compatibility – given that most potential customers are comfortable using cellular telephones for voice communications, it would seem that WI-FI is highly compatible with the existing values, practices, past experiences, and needs of potential customers. However, market research needs to be conducted to explore other compatibility issues.
- Complexity – WI-FI would not appear to be difficult to understand, learn, and use, although product testing with potential customers should be done to examine complexity issues further.
- Trial ability – sellers of WI-FI hardware for the home may have to offer free trial periods to encourage at-home adoption. WI-FI "hot spot" providers, such as Starbucks, may encourage widespread trial ability by providing the service at no charge to lure customers. By the year 2004,

half of all laptop computers produced had WI-FI capability. Half of all PDAs (Personal Digital Assistants) are forecasted to be WI-FI enabled by 2006.[18]

• Observability – the use of WI-FI could become highly observable in public places, such as Starbucks, thereby encouraging rapid consumer adoption.

Thus, as WI-FI providers address the issue of **security** with customers, it would seem that this innovation has reached the "tipping point" and will be adopted rapidly by the American consumer. But hopefully, not while driving on the freeway.

Monitoring technology adoption trends and understanding how they will impact your business over a five-year planning horizon is a critical element in avoiding becoming a boiled frog. This can be accomplished through scenario planning, which involves thinking through the impact of technology changes on your business in the best-case scenario, the worst-case scenario, and the expected-case scenario. Establishing "trigger points" to indicate which scenario is developing is a key part of the scenario-planning process. For Kodak, a trigger point could have been "more than 10 percent of the target market has adopted digital cameras." This trigger point could have led Kodak to a rational, well-thought-out strategy to enter the digital camera market without causing their shareholders to revolt. Scenario planning will be discussed later in this chapter.

Competitive Trends

The fifth and last type of macro trend to be discussed is **competitive** trends. The cautious monitoring of the marketing tactics of the Miller Brewing Company by Anheuser-Busch in the 1970s allowed them to understand the success Miller was having and to see how Miller was positioning their brands. Their reactions involved substantially increasing their own marketing staff and their marketing investments. This increased investment allowed them to blunt the rapid growth of their competitor and maintain their number one position in the beer industry.

Understanding who your key competitors are, as well as their strategies, objectives, strengths, weaknesses, and reaction patterns, is critical to effective marketing planning.[19] Simple methods that can yield a wealth of information are reading the annual reports of your competitors, regularly reading their web page, and reviewing industry presentations given by your competitors, which are often included in the investor section of corporate web pages. Observing their help wanted advertising and the people your competitors are hiring can also tip you off to future strategies. For example, a competitor who is hiring marketing people regularly from Procter & Gamble is likely to place a lot of emphasis and resources on marketing in the future.

---

[18] Allied Business Intelligence, Oyster Bay, N.Y.

[19] Philip Kotler, *Marketing Management: Analysis, Planning, Implementation, and Control*, 9th ed. (Upper Saddle River, NJ: Prentice Hall, 1997).

For those seeking more thorough insight into competitors, many firms exist that specialize in Competitive Intelligence. Many of these firms utilize highly effective methods to obtain valuable competitive intelligence, such as interviewing employees who have recently left the employment of the competitor, monitoring large databases, tracking patent applications, and interviewing industry experts. Most of these firms avoid illegal and unethical methods, such as calling into a firm under the guise of a student doing research for a thesis, or digging through the garbage of a competitor. When selecting a consultant for Competitive Intelligence, it is wise to request bids from multiple firms and to interview the firms personally to ensure that value is received for the high price charged by most Competitive Intelligence consultants.

Macro Trends upon which to Focus

Thus far, numerous macro trends have been presented, and the reader may feel overwhelmed. Is there a way for a firm to narrow the range and focus their attention on just a few areas?

For many large, global consumer businesses, such as Motorola's cell phone business, the answer is unfortunately **no**, as all of these macro trends have a significant impact on their future success in this business. Demographic trends impact the number of cell phone users globally. Lifestyle trends impact market growth rates by country. Economic trends impact cell phone usage rates. Technology adoption trends impact consumer adoption rates across countries. Competitive trends impact the ability of Motorola to gain market share in a profitable manner.

Business-to-Business (B-to-B) marketers have a somewhat easier time with macro trends, as demographic trends and lifestyle trends usually have less impact than economic, technology adoption, and competitive trends. Thus, a manufacturer of concrete in the Southeastern United States can focus on economic trends (commercial building trends), technology adoption trends (new types of concrete used in different buildings), and competitive trends (new product strategies of key regional competitors). However, focusing on these three macro trends should not lead B-to-B marketers to ignore demographic and lifestyle trends completely, as these could have a significant impact on the concrete market as well. For example, the increasing lifestyle trend of online purchasing on retail goods could lead to slow growth in the construction of shopping centers in the future.

Macro Trend Tools

The major tools that are used for continually monitoring macro trends are:

- environmental scanning
- secondary data acquisition
- SWOT analysis
- scenario planning
- data mining

Let's discuss how these tools can keep a firm on top of the macro trends impacting its market and its consumers.

Macro Trend Tools

	Demographic Trends	Psychographic Trends	Economic Trends	Technology Adoption Trends	Competitive Trends
Environmental Scanning	+	++	+	++	+
Secondary Data Acquisition					
SWOT Analysis (TOWS Analysis)					
Scenario Planning					
Data Mining					

Environmental Scanning

Monitoring the environment systematically to learn of technological and competitive developments is an excellent way to generate ideas for new product concepts. Mentioned earlier in this chapter was Hallmark Cards, which employs methods such as browsing in stores, eavesdropping on conversations, reading social tomes, traveling, or just generally observing American culture.

As part of its annual strategic planning process, the Ritz-Carlton Hotel Company, LLC, a division of Marriott International, Inc., hotels, performs an extensive "macroenvironment analysis" and distributes the results to senior leaders before the first planning session. This analysis considers factors ranging from the world economic outlook and global supply of hotel rooms to specific measures of customer and employee satisfaction. The Ritz-Carlton is focused on the details. Managers are then expected to come to these strategic planning meetings prepared to develop strategic objectives for the next three years. This focus on the environment has had very positive benefits for Ritz-Carlton; besides winning the prestigious Malcolm Baldrige National Quality Award in 1999, earnings and return on investment have nearly doubled in just four years.[20]

All firms need to encourage their executives to be continually scanning the environment for macro trends as well as clues to the future. Hunting for and gathering external information should be a top priority for all managers in the firm. *The Economist* and the *Wall Street Journal* are excellent sources of what is happening in the world. *Scientific American, Discover,* and *Science* are excellent sources of what is

---

[20] "News from NIST: Malcolm Baldrige National Quality Award, 1999 Award Recipient, Service Category; The Ritz-Carlton Hotel Company L.L.C." *National Institute of Standards and Technology,* www.nist.gov/public_affairs/bald99/ritz.htm (accessed May 2003).

happening in the world of science. *The Futurist* magazine, a publication of the World Future Society, is an excellent source of ideas for how the future may unfold and what those futures mean for businesses, governments, and other organizations.

Firms may also decide to formalize the process and establish an ongoing environmental scanning function. This function would not replace the work of executives continuously monitoring the environment but would complement it with full-time experts, such as the futurists employed by many larger firms. This function's charter is to explore continuously the complex relationships between **consumer behavior** and demographic, psychographic, economic, and technology adoption trends. The information gathered will be critical as the firm creates alternative scenarios about the future, a process described later in this chapter.

Environmental scanning is an especially effective tool for keeping on top of psychographic and technology adoption macro trends, as shown in the previous table.

Macro Trend Tools

	Demographic Trends	Psychographic Trends	Economic Trends	Technology Adoption Trends	Competitive Trends
Environmental Scanning	+	++	+	++	+
Secondary Data Acquisition	++	+	++	+	+
SWOT Analysis (TOWS Analysis)					
Scenario Planning					
Data Mining					

Secondary Data Acquisition

The acquisition of secondary information can be broadly classified into two types: *free* secondary information, and *commercial* secondary information. Free secondary information of high quality and utility can often be obtained over the World Wide Web from government sources (http://www.census.gov, Statistical Abstract of the United States, CIA), from industry and trade associations, from financial reports, from competitors web pages, from patent filings, and through the use of search engines.

The U.S. Census Bureau is a gold mine of demographic and economic information. The U.S. CIA (Central Intelligence Agency) updates a fascinating publication annually called "The World Factbook." The factbook provides information on

267 countries on 124 key topics, including population, median age, population growth rate, birth and death rates, life expectancy, religions, languages, literacy rate, overview of the economy, Gross Domestic Product (GDP), GDP growth rate, inflation rate, unemployment rate, currency, number of telephones, number of radio and TV stations, internet country code and the number of internet users.

Internet search engines have dramatically multiplied the amount of secondary information that can be accessed in a given time period. The search engine of choice for many is **Google** (http://www.google.com), because of the more than 600 million pages that it indexes and its ease of use. Companies looking for competitive intelligence can use Google to find a wealth of free public information available on the web. Competitive intelligence professionals find gold mines of insights on corporate websites, with the following areas often yielding the largest "nuggets."[21]

- **Investor relations sites,** which lay out the company's financial performance in a summarized fashion. These sites also may include presentations given to investor groups, which give an overview of the company's strategies, new products in development, market shares for key products, and outlook for the future of the industry.
- **Management profiles** are very helpful to understand the backgrounds of the key executives running the firm, which may help you anticipate their actions in the future.
- **Speeches** given by senior executives are often included on the corporate website or can be found in the trade press and sometimes give insight into strategies and plans.
- **Press releases** are valuable in providing information on new products, ventures, and executive promotions.
- **Employment opportunities** listed on the website can provide insight into future competitive activities. For example, a competitor who is actively seeking new salespeople may be preparing to launch a new product.

In addition to competitor websites, message boards and chat rooms dedicated to the company or industry you're interested in can occasionally provide valuable information. While there is a lot of garbage to wade through, you may find valuable tidbits from exchanges between disgruntled employees sharing information with industry experts who also frequent the sites.

However, Google can often overwhelm the user with results, even when the search criteria are carefully defined. David Pring, former president and general manager of Protocol Research Solutions, current senior vice president and general manager at Ipsos-Insight, has given high praise to an alternative search engine called **Vivísimo** (http://vivisimo.com). Vivísimo takes a different approach based on "document clustering." The result is that the search automatically organizes query results into meaningful hierarchical folders. The folders comprise categories

---

[21] Susan Warren, "Corporate Intelligence – I-Spy: Getting the Lowdown on your Competition is Just a Few Clicks Away," The *Wall Street Journal*, 14 Jan. 2002.

that are selected from the words and phrases contained in the search results themselves. A search run by Pring on "data privacy" resulted in 167 results, divided into ten basic categories ranging from "protection" to "management." The identical search performed on Google yielded 19,500,000 basically unsorted references, unless a detailed advanced sort was specified. While there is some risk that Vivísimo may miss an important website, the benefit of 99 percent reduction in clutter is compelling.

Valuable information on a competitor's future product strategy can be obtained by searching for patents registered by your competitors. The United States Patent and Trademark Office website can be accessed at http://www.uspto.gov.

Free secondary information should always be the first step in any **Customer Insight** endeavor. The breadth of free secondary data available through the Internet, much of it timely and accurate, often makes this an information gold mine and broadens your perspective as you move forward with other customer insight tools. It frequently allows you to better define the problems and opportunities facing the company. Free secondary information is easy to collect in a rapid manner.

However, free secondary information does have some significant negatives:

- Free secondary information may not address the specific question or issue facing the firm.
- If it exists, it may not be current, accurate or objective.
- Searching through the enormous amount of secondary data available often is like looking for a needle in a haystack.

Commercial secondary information is widely available for almost any industry (at a price) from many marketing information companies. A comprehensive listing of published research reports can be found at http://www.marketresearch. com. ACNielsen Company and Information Resources, Inc., provide standardized information on weekly consumer purchases of thousands of SKUs of packaged goods through retail outlets. LexisNexis is an online source that allows the rapid searching of newspapers, business periodicals, and other publications. Mediamark Research and Simmons Market Research Bureau provide marketers and advertising agencies with large databases to understand product usage and media behavior by almost any demographic characteristic imaginable.

Secondary data acquisition tools are especially effective in staying on top of demographic and economic macro trends.

SWOT Analysis or TOWS Analysis?

Understanding these macro trends thoroughly will allow the firm to develop a comprehensive SWOT (Strengths, Weaknesses, Opportunities, and Threats) analysis for their Marketing plan. The SWOT analysis will uncover *internal* **Strengths and Weaknesses,** as well as *external* **Opportunities and Threats.**

Macro Trend Tools

	Demographic Trends	Psychographic Trends	Economic Trends	Technology Adoption Trends	Competitive Trends
Environmental Scanning	+	++	+	++	+
Secondary Data Acquisition	++	+	++	+	+
SWOT Analysis (TOWS Analysis)					++
Scenario Planning					
Data Mining					

But Philip Kotler advocates that the **SWOT** acronym can result in too much of an internal focus and recommends that firms conduct a **TOWS** analysis instead. "It should really be called a TOWS analysis (threats, opportunities, weaknesses and strengths) because the ordering should be from the outside in rather than the inside out. SWOT may place an undue influence on internal factors and limit the identification of threats and opportunities to only those that fit the company's strengths."[22]

This author has participated in many SWOT analyses in the corporate world and agrees with Kotler; many firms pay too little attention to the external environment and subsequently overestimate their strengths and exaggerate opportunities, while at the same time underestimating their weaknesses and minimizing potential threats. These firms are headed for some nasty surprises that could have been anticipated with an objective, thorough **TOWS** analysis. Thus, a major challenge for many firms is to "unlearn" the SWOT acronym and start practicing the TOWS acronym. TOWS analysis is especially useful in staying on top of competitive trends.

Scenario Planning

Scenario planning is a process that allows managers to consider alternative futures and to think through the ramifications of these possible futures on their business strategy. It allows them to escape the blinders of the firm's "official future," which is usually an optimistic, best-case scenario. *The Art of the Long View* is an excellent

---

[22] Philip Kotler, *Marketing Insights From A to Z: 80 Concepts Every Manager Needs to Know* (Hoboken, NJ: John Wiley and Sons, 2003).

Macro Trend Tools

	Demographic Trends	Psychographic Trends	Economic Trends	Technology Adoption Trends	Competitive Trends
Environmental Scanning	+	++	+	++	+
Secondary Data Acquisition	++	+	++	+	+
SWOT Analysis (TOWS Analysis)					++
Scenario Planning	++	++	+	++	+
Data Mining					

book on scenario planning.[23] The author, Peter Schwartz, successfully implemented the process at Royal Dutch Shell in the 1980s.

The scenario-planning process involves managers inventing, and then considering, in depth, varied stories of equally plausible futures. The purpose is to allow management to make strategic decisions that will be sound for all plausible futures. Schwartz goes on to say:

> "No matter what future takes place, you are much more likely to be ready for it, and influential in it, if you have thought seriously about scenarios. Scenarios are a tool for helping us to take a long view in a world of great uncertainty. Scenarios are *not* predictions. It is simply not possible to predict the future with certainty. Rather, scenarios are vehicles for helping people learn. Unlike traditional business forecasting or market research, they present alternative images of the future; they do not merely extrapolate the trends of the present. *The end result, however, is not an accurate picture of tomorrow, but better decisions about the future.*"[24]

Schwartz prescribes an eight-step process for scenario planning in the appendix of his book, paraphrased here:

1. Identify a focal issue or decision – ask top management what keeps them awake at night.
2. List key factors in the local environment – facts about customers, suppliers, and competitors.

---

[23] Peter Schwartz, *The Art of the Long View* (New York: Doubleday/Currency, 1991).
[24] Schwartz, *Art of the Long View*, 9.

3. List driving forces in the macroenvironment – search for major trends and trend breaks.
4. Rank key factors and driving forces by importance and uncertainty – the point is to identify the two or three factors or trends that are most important *and* most uncertain.
5. Select scenarios and logic – the goal is to end up with just a few scenarios whose differences make an impact on decision makers.
6. Flesh out the scenarios – this can be done by returning to the list of key factors and trends identified in steps 2 and 3.
7. Develop implications for each scenario – how does the decision look in each scenario?
8. Identify leading indicators and signposts to identify which scenario is unfolding – it is important to know as soon as possible which of the scenarios is unfolding. Leading indicators and signposts will allow the company to gain a jump on competitors in knowing what that future means to decision makers in that industry and how that future is likely to affect strategies and decisions in the industry.

Those interested in pursuing this fascinating field should read *The Art of the Long View*, or contact Peter Schwartz at the Global Business Network in Emeryville, California.

Scenario planning can be especially powerful when driven by a deep understanding of key driving forces (demographic, psychographic, and technology adoption macro trends) and **Customer Insights.**

Macro Trend Tools

	Demographic Trends	Psychographic Trends	Economic Trends	Technology Adoption Trends	Competitive Trends
Environmental Scanning	+	++	+	++	+
Secondary Data Acquisition	++	+	++	+	+
SWOT Analysis (TOWS Analysis)					++
Scenario Planning	++	++	+	++	+
Data Mining	++			+	

Data Mining

Most firms have a wealth of data on their customers but are not utilizing it effectively to acquire and retain customers. Data warehouses often contain useful information that can be "mined" through powerful statistical and pattern detection techniques. These data-mining techniques can often unearth interesting findings about customers that provide a competitive edge in marketing to them.

Best customers can be identified easily, using the recency/frequency/monetary formula, popularized by database marketing expert Arthur Hughes:[25]

- **Recency of purchase** – how long has it been since the customer last purchased from your company?
- **Frequency of purchase** – how often does the customer purchase from your company?
- **Monetary value of purchase** – how much does the customer spend on a typical purchase?

The lifetime value of each customer can then be easily calculated, utilizing the last two of these three measures combined with the average number of years that a customer could be expected to remain with the firm. Let's assume that the data mining of our customer database reveals that the average customer makes six purchases per year, with each purchase averaging $40,000. Further, let's assume that our database reveals that the average customer remains with our company for fifteen years. Therefore, the lifetime value of one of our customers can be calculated as follows:

6 purchases per year × $40,000 per purchase × 15 years
= LIFETIME VALUE OF $3,600,000

To be more accurate, one should calculate the net present lifetime value, discounting purchases in future years by the appropriate interest rate. One should also calculate the net present lifetime value of customers in different segments to compare the "worth" of customers in different segments to the company. This will help the firm focus its customer care resources on those customer segments that will provide the best financial returns.

Sophisticated tools have been developed to "mine" valuable information from a firm's internal database, looking for hidden patterns that can yield customer insight. Pattern analysis and neural networks are some of the tools used to mine databases effectively. An excellent example of an insight that could only be found through data mining involves credit card fraud.

In looking for ways to identify stolen credit cards and stop expensive fraudulent purchases, a major credit card company identified an interesting pattern. It found that purchases of expensive jewelry using a stolen credit card were very often preceded by a gasoline purchase on the same card in the two hours prior. What was happening was that credit card thieves were "testing" the credit card at the gas pump

---

[25] Arthur M. Hughes, *The Complete Database Marketer: Second-Generation Strategies and Techniques for Tapping the Power of Your Customer Database* (Chicago: Irwin Professional Pub., 1996).

to see if it was still being accepted! If it was accepted, the thieves would rush to the jewelry store for an expensive purchase before the card was reported missing.

Using this insight, the credit card company was able to implement a new policy wherein all credit authorization requests for purchases of expensive items were held to see if gasoline was bought in the two hours prior. If so, a telephone call was placed to the cardholder to determine if his or her credit card was missing. This new policy saved the company millions of dollars in bad debts.

Enlightened companies have utilized their customer database for database-marketing purposes. This requires merging everything a firm knows about a customer into one database and then periodically collecting additional information from each customer during ordering or service transactions. This additional data can include "softer" information on each customer, such as attitudes, pets, and birthdays. An excellent resource on database marketing is the Arthur Hughes book, *Strategic Database Marketing* (1994).

Data mining can be very useful in understanding the relationship between demographic trends and purchasing behavior in the database of the company.

Strategic Planning and Market Intelligence

Two functions that need to be in place to scan the environment and translate market signals effectively into usable intelligence are Strategic Planning and Market Intelligence. While smaller companies may combine these functions under one manager, large companies need to invest personnel resources in each function.

Strategic planning departments are most effective when comprised of experts from various departments across the company, including engineering, R and D, manufacturing, finance, and marketing. Educational backgrounds that include technical training coupled with an MBA are beneficial. The strategic planning department should focus on anticipated trends in technology and their impact on the company over the next five years as well as competitive trends. Members of this department should be highly skilled in the tools of scenario planning, SWOT analysis, and environmental scanning.

Market intelligence departments are most effective when comprised of experts who have had close contact with customers. Some companies hire former customers to add to this department; many companies use this department as a developmental position for analytical salespeople; and many will staff this function with former government intelligence experts. The market intelligence department should focus on demographic, psychographic, and economic trends and their impact on the company over the next five years. Members of this department should be highly skilled in the tools of secondary data acquisition, data mining, and environmental scanning.

Investment Cost

Much useful secondary information can be obtained at no cost, either from published sources or through the Internet.

Published studies on markets, such as those found on http://www.marketresearch. com, can be purchased for as little as $4,000 and will usually provide recent, accurate information. More comprehensive market studies can cost $20,000 and up.

Many firms, such as McDonald's and Abbott Laboratories, have invested in a strong library information system, staffed by information experts who can retrieve valuable secondary information in a timely, cost-effective manner.

Competitive Intelligence consultants will usually charge $5,000 to track down several specific pieces of information (for example, "How many sales reps does my major competitor have throughout Europe?") For more comprehensive strategic analyses of a competitor, expect to pay $20,000–$50,000.

Data mining is an expensive undertaking, often involving significant upfront costs to prepare, clean, and merge databases.

Macro Trend Checklist

- Does your company suffer from what George S. Day calls "Market Blindness"? The symptoms are the weak ability to capture market signals, a product-focused organization, and a focus on costs and the short run.
- Does your company have access to internal or external trend anticipation resources, such as demographers and futurists, engaged in an ongoing program of environmental scanning of macro trends that are impacting your markets and customers?
- Does your firm engage in an ongoing process of scenario planning to allow management to develop strategies that are sound for numerous plausible futures, or have you "bet the ranch" on one "official future"?
- Does your entire management team have a clear understanding of how your business strategy addresses the macro trends that your company has identified?
- The U.S. government created a federal office on nanotechnology in November of 2003. How will nanotechnology change your markets? How can you use nanotechnology to provide more value to customers?
- Has your company developed a marketing strategy to capitalize on the large number of non-European immigrants arriving in America each year?
- Has your company developed a marketing strategy based on a clear understanding of the psychographic trends that are occurring among your target customers?
- Does your firm have a clear understanding of the rate of technology adoption among your target customers? Are they innovators or laggards?
- Does your firm have a strong competitive intelligence function with sufficient resources to understand the objectives and strategies of your key competitors?
- Does your marketing department have easy access to library information specialists who can retrieve needed secondary information quickly?
- Does your market intelligence staff have expertise in obtaining quality secondary information in a rapid, cost-effective manner?
- Have you invested in data-mining tools to understand your customers fully on a one-to-one basis?

Unmet Needs

INSIGHT 2: Your customers can't tell you about their unmet needs, but you can uncover them.

The ability to anticipate consumers' responses based on deep knowledge about them lies at the heart of skillful marketing. A deep understanding of customers is the only sound basis for developing marketing strategy for discontinuous innovations.

Gerald Zaltman, Harvard Business School

Customer Insight Pyramid

Imagination is critical to successful marketing. But imagination is not just day-dreaming about which new products will meet the unmet needs of customers in the future. Imagination combined with **customer insight** is a powerful, winning combination to satisfy the unmet needs of your target customers.

Can Unmet Needs Be Uncovered?

Critics of marketing and marketing research feel that talking to customers about their unmet needs is a waste of time. They point to successful products that were

developed with no input from customers at all, like the Sony Walkman. They may point to earlier unsuccessful attempts at generating ideas for new products by asking customers direct questions. They disdain listening to customers, sometimes out of arrogance, and feel that if you can just build a better mousetrap, the world will beat a path to your door.

Motorola fell into this trap when it was convinced that the world needed a global communication system, and it was a major investor in the $5 billion Iridium global satellite communication system begun in 1987. Upon commercial launch in November of 1998, Iridium had high hopes for the system and had committed to its bankers in loan covenants that it would have a minimum of 52,000 subscribers to the Iridium global communications system by March of 1999. Due to a number of significant changes in the competitive landscape and numerous marketing missteps, Iridium missed the target subscriber level badly, signing up just over 10,000 customers five months into the launch. Five months later, Iridium filed for bankruptcy.

There is no question that it is possible, with a little luck, to hit a home run with a new product without involving customers at all. It is also possible to strike out with a new product, even with heavy involvement of customers. However, many studies have shown that these patterns are the exceptions, rather than the rule. Involving customers in the new product development process can increase the likelihood of success of those products, but more importantly, can help firms to "kill the dogs early." New products in search of a market that few customers want need to be killed early in the new product development process before these marginal new products consume an unfair share of the scarce new product development resources available to the company.

Technical experts in research and development (R and D) and engineering often have a strong understanding of where technology is going and what technology may enable in the future, but without insight into customer problems and dissatisfactions, this technology expertise lacks focus and direction. Successful new products have been developed without the benefit of customer insight, but the odds tend to be stacked against the "dreamers." The author has witnessed successful new product ideas emerge from behind the mirror during focus groups, as technical experts listen carefully to the problems and dissatisfactions of customers and exclaim, "I know of a technology that can solve that problem!"

Overt Needs versus Latent Needs

Customer needs can be expressed/overt, or unspoken/latent. For products where customer needs are easily seen and can be easily expressed, the market research task is fairly straightforward. Focus groups using direct questioning methods will prove to be quite successful. For products where customer needs are not easily seen and are very difficult for customers to get in touch with, **indirect** techniques, such as observation, ethnography, and archetype research, are usually more effective.

Exploratory Approaches

Six exploratory approaches are commonly used to attempt to discover unmet customer needs. These six approaches are:

- **observation**
- **ethnography**
- **focus groups**
- **depth interviews**
- **archetype research**
- **customer visits**

Let's examine how leading companies use these approaches to yield customer insights.

Observation

In July of 2001, Procter & Gamble (P&G) launched a program to videotape customers in eighty households around the world. They hoped to capture the daily household routines and habits of their target customers across the globe, with the objective of coming up with new products that solve problems that customers don't even know they have.

Crews spent four days with the families around the world and videotaped virtually all activities. (Certain bathroom and bedroom activities were excluded!) Videos were edited, and highlights are regularly reviewed by P&G managers and product designers.

P&G hopes that this videotaped observation of customers will yield valuable insights into consumer behavior. P&G feels that more traditional methods, such as focus groups, surveys, and home visits, may miss some of the insights that videotaped observation can reveal. People tend to have selective and inaccurate memories when interviewed by market researchers.

P&G is utilizing this technique in the hope of solving problems that customers don't realize they have. "The behaviors that customers don't talk about – such as multitasking while feeding a baby – could inspire product and package design in ways that give the company a real edge over rivals."[1]

The observation of customers is a highly effective technique that can often provide insights into customer behavior that are not accessible through direct questioning. MTV executives, often in their 30s and 40s, spend time in the homes of their target customers, young teenagers, to understand their world and what is in and what is out. Teenagers are videotaped, and highlights are regularly reviewed by MTV management. The attitudes and behaviors captured through this structured observation process provide insights that would be difficult to obtain through other marketing research methods.

---

[1] Emily Nelson, "P&G Checks Out Real Life – Giant Marketer Plans to Visit People's Homes to Record (Almost) All Their Habits," The *Wall Street Journal*, 17 May 2001.

In the world of Business-to-Business, observing customers using your product at their place of work has often been referred to as **"contextual inquiry."** Edward McQuarrie describes the distinction of contextual inquiry from other qualitative research techniques: "The distinguishing feature of contextual inquiry is that product designers watch customers using a product *at the customer's place of work.* Designers discuss with users what they just did or what just happened. The basic idea is that so much of a user's product experience is *tacit* or taken for granted that it cannot be effectively vocalized or discussed unless the user is placed *in context* – that is, examined while doing their job. Contextual inquiry gets beyond the limitations of customers self-report that occur with other qualitative research methods and gets designers out of their laboratories and into the world of their customers."[2]

The Medical Products Division of Hewlett-Packard (HP) has used direct observational methods, including contextual inquiry, to uncover unmet needs of many of their customers, including surgeons. Surgeons can now perform laparoscopic surgery, using a small video camera attached to the end of a probe that is inserted inside the patient as surgery is performed. The surgeon observes the surgery on a TV monitor in the operating room. This surgery involves a smaller incision for the patient, and is less stressful on patients and results in quicker recovery times.

While observing surgeons perform laparoscopic surgery, HP managers noticed that surgeons were occasionally interrupted as nurses walked in front of the TV monitor that the surgeon watched as the procedure was performed. Surgeons did not complain about this interruption but rather viewed it as a necessary part of this wonderful, new surgical process. Observing this surgical procedure made HP managers imagine how the process could be improved if the monitor were not occasionally blocked in the operating room. The result was a very successful new product developed by HP: a surgical helmet with goggles that cast images right in front of the surgeon's eyes.[3] This latent need was not identified through customer complaints or through interviews with customers; rather, it was uncovered by observing the customer in action.

Firms should also carefully observe and study **internal** sources of customer information. Important sources that companies can use to discover unmet needs include customer requests, customer comments, and customer complaints, received via letters, e-mails, face-to-face, or phone calls. Recently, a major hotel chain was interested in making a financial investment to improve customer satisfaction among its hotel guests. A review of its customer satisfaction survey responses was not helpful in identifying specific investment opportunities. However, it had a brilliant idea and decided to review its internal records to identify the most requested item from room service. Its review of internal records, at no cost, revealed that one item stood well above the rest in terms of frequency of customer requests: an iron for

---

[2] Edward F. McQuarrie, *The Market Research Toolbox: A Concise Guide for Beginners* (Thousand Oaks, Calif.: Sage Publications, 1996), 136.

[3] Bob Becker, "Take the Direct Route when Data Gathering," *Marketing News*, 27 Sept. 1999.

pressing wrinkled clothes. The hotel chain invested in an iron and ironing board in each of its rooms and has found the investment had paid rich returns in increased customer satisfaction and loyalty.

Ethnography

Ethnography is an approach borrowed and adapted from cultural anthropology and involves immersing yourself in the world of your target customer. It is distinguished from other qualitative research techniques by the intensity of the engagement with a small number of customers, with designers and marketers often spending a number of days physically immersed in the lives of their target customers. Ethnography allows marketers to understand consumers whose cultures are very different from their own through experiencing firsthand subtle differences in communication styles, lifestyles, and behavior patterns. The marketer joins the subject in mundane activities in the natural environment – shopping, eating, driving, and going into a bar with friends – and observes, videotapes, and asks questions. While videotaping can be obtrusive at times, its ability to capture the customer experience fully for viewing later is critical. Ethnographers dive right into the population they are studying, becoming "participant observers," and use the intimacy they develop with their subjects to gain richer, deeper insights into their culture and their behavior.

Ethnography is especially useful as a **customer insight** tool when you need to understand experiences that customers cannot recall in sufficient detail, or when you need to understand the components of your customer's purchase and usage behavior thoroughly.

Unilever utilizes ethnography to obtain a greater level of intimacy with their target customers of home and personal care products around the world. Vice President of Consumer and Market Insight John Kastenholz feels that marketers have become more distant from the ultimate customer over the years. "We need to get back in touch, so we are spending a lot more time in consumers' homes, bathrooms, in Laundromats, and shopping with them. We've had great success in markets like Thailand and India. Our marketers and market research managers go and live in peoples' homes – and for weeks in rural villages that may not have running water or electricity. We replicate that around the world because our marketers often come from dramatically different socio-economic classes than the bulk of consuming marketplaces."[4]

General Motors (GM) has established a process to allow designers and marketers to get to know target customers deeply, through repeated, direct interactions. Customer panels have been created by Dr. Jeffrey Hartley, who is the manager of Brand Character and Theme Research at GM. Hartley feels that important insights are missed with traditional marketing research tools, such as focus groups,

---

[4] John Kastenholz, quoted in "Research Department Report," May 2003, RFL Communications, Inc.

where someone else asks the questions. "Through repeated interactions between our personnel and our customers, we build trust and understanding – not possible in focus groups, especially for tacit information. We just don't try to find out what customers want; we try to impress upon them what our world is like, and what decisions we must make. Then they are better equipped to help us delight them."[5]

Recently, GM paired customer panelists up with Saturn design and marketing people and sent them to an auto show to talk about which vehicles they were attracted to and why. "This was informal, and the dialogue was fluid and two-way," noted Hartley. The designers and marketers who work with panel members in this ongoing manner become privy to Saturn customers' most emotional memories. The more they get to know these customers by listening to their recollections, the more committed they are to serving customer needs.[6]

Kitchen in a Box

Target, the Minneapolis-based discount retailer, has recently used ethnography to develop successful products for the 15 million students who leave home for college each year. These first-time dorm denizens, along with their college peers, spend an estimated $200 billion on everything from microwave ovens to shower loofahs, representing an attractive market opportunity for Target.

To help their retail-product designers, who were well past their college years, to gain insight into these young customers, Target hired Jump Associates of San Mateo, California. Jump Associates decided to take an unusual approach to elicit deep insights, emotions, and motivations about life away from home in the dorm. The firm sponsored a series of "game nights" at high school graduates' homes, inviting incoming college freshmen as well as students with a year of dorm living under their belts to participate.

To get teens to talk about dorm life, Jump devised a board game that involved issues associated with going to college. The game led to valuable informal conversations about life in the dorm – conversations that were carefully observed and recorded by Jump researchers.

The insights generated from the board game research paid off for Target. In 2002, Target launched the Todd Oldham Dorm Room product line designed for college freshmen. Among the new offerings were **Kitchen in a Box**, which provided basic accoutrements for a budding college cook, and **Bath in a Box**, which included an extra large bath towel to preserve modesty on the trek to and from the dorm shower, as well as a laundry bag with instructions on how to actually do the laundry printed on the bag. These products were highly successful and led to a 12 percent increase in revenues in Target stores in the third quarter of 2002, to $8.4 billion. Sales among competitor's stores increased only 1 percent during the same period.[7]

---

[5] Gerald Zaltman, *How Customers Think: Essential Insights into the Mind of the Market* (Boston, Mass.: Harvard Business School Press, 2003), 250.

[6] Zaltman, *How Customers Think,* 251.

[7] Alison Stein Wellner, "The New Science of Focus Groups," *American Demographics*, March 2003.

The Spouse Acceptance Factor

Cambridge SoundWorks, a manufacturer and retailer of stereo equipment based in Andover, Massachusetts, was puzzled by the low number of male customers who purchased their large, powerful speakers after visiting their retail outlets. These male shoppers were very enthusiastic about the powerful sound coming from these large speakers, but few came back to purchase the high-end equipment. Cambridge hired Design Continuum to follow a dozen prospective customers over the course of two weeks to see if they could gain insight into this sales conversion problem using **ethnography.**

Observing these consumers in their homes as well as shopping for stereo equipment, Design Continuum discovered that the high-end stereo speaker market was characterized by something they called the "**spouse acceptance factor.**" While men adored the big, black boxes, women hated their unsightly appearance. Concerned about how the speakers would look in their living rooms, many women would talk their spouse out of buying the cool but hideous stereo system. The solution was to provide a system that would meet the needs of both partners: a great sound system that looks like furniture so you don't have to hide it.

Armed with this **customer insight**, Cambridge launched the furniture-like Newton line of speakers and home theater systems in an array of colors and finishes. The Newton series is the fastest-growing and best-selling product line in the history of the firm.[8]

Netnography

A valuable **external** source of customer information that should not be overlooked is the communication that takes place between customers online, on message boards and in chat rooms. John Sherry and Robert Kozinets have named this art of lurking in online fields **"netnography,"** which "holds online participation to be a beneficial investigative movement. Like its offline counterpart, it seeks immersion, a profound experiencing of digital sociality."[9] An easy way to experience digital sociality is to read the "gossip" on the message board of your company on sites such as Yahoo Finance or AOL. Marketers should devote at least two hours each month to this environmental scanning at the fringe of the market. While the sample of consumers is self-selected and not representative of the target market, this cyberspace communication can provide interesting perspectives from customers that can usually not be obtained with traditional methods.

Focus Groups

Focus groups are without doubt the most widely used marketing research tool in the United States. Focus groups can often provide powerful customer insights, under the direction of a qualified focus group moderator. MTV conducts over

---

[8] Alison Stein Wellner, "Watch Me Now," *American Demographics*, October 2002.
[9] John Sherry and Robert Kozinets, "Qualitative Inquiry in Marketing and Consumer Research," in *Kellogg on Marketing*, ed. Dawn Iacobucci (New York: John Wiley and Sons, 2001).

500 focus groups per year to keep abreast of "what's hot and what's not" among the coveted 12-24-year-old age group.[10]

Focus groups are popular because they can very quickly and easily allow marketers to get qualitative input from and insight into their target customers. Focus groups are enjoyable to observe, since observers can sit comfortably behind a one-way mirror in comfortable chairs while they eagerly listen to their target customers talk about companies, brands, new product ideas, or advertising ideas.

One of the pioneers of focus group research in the field of marketing, Dr. Alfred Goldman, clearly described the advantages of the focus group method over individual depth interviewing.[11]

1. The interaction among group members *stimulates new ideas* regarding the topic under discussion that may never be mentioned in individual interviewing.
2. In the group interview, respondents react to the attitudes and behaviors of each other; this phenomenon mirrors the social process of adopting new products, and the marketer can *directly observe that group process.*
3. The group interview *provides some idea of the dynamics of attitudes and opinions;* the flexibility or rigidity with which an attitude is held is better exposed in a group setting.
4. Discussion in a peer group often *provokes considerably greater spontaneity and candor than can be expected in an individual interview.*
5. The group setting is *emotionally provocative in a way that an individual interview cannot be;* members of the group can provoke reactions that elicit interesting and useful insights into the motives of the group members.

Kellogg School of Management Marketing Professor Bob Calder wrote perhaps the most seminal article of the 1970s on focus group research, which clearly articulated the three major approaches to focus group research: **exploratory, clinical, and phenomenological.**[12] These approaches can be summarized as follows:

Exploratory – used to generate ideas and hypotheses and to validate them against everyday experience; heterogeneity of group members is useful to yield rich information

Clinical – used when the objective is to seek information or develop constructs that cannot be ascertained through self-report or direct inference, for example motivation research; some homogeneity of group members may facilitate rapport; clinical judgment and expertise of moderator is critical to success

Phenomenological – used when the management goal is to experience the consumer; homogeneity of group members is preferred for clarity of findings; observation of group sessions by management is critical for experiential benefits

---

[10] RFL Communications, Inc., "Research Department Report," April 2004.

[11] Alfred E. Goldman, "The Group Depth Interview," *Journal of Marketing,* July 1962.

[12] Bob Calder, "Focus Groups and the Nature of Qualitative Marketing Research," *Journal of Marketing Research*, August 1977.

In addition to exploring the unmet needs of customers, focus groups are often used to understand consumer behavior in new markets, to get reactions to new product concepts, to get reactions to advertising in rough, storyboard form, and to understand the most important product and service features to target customers. Bonnie Goebert, a leading authority on focus group research, has identified seven marketing tasks where focus groups can provide insight:

- To explore customers' purchasing habits
- To understand more about the customer in the product category
- To learn more about consumers' attitudes
- To examine a brand's image
- To discern consumers' emotional bonds with a product
- To develop an effective advertising campaign
- To feed an educated hunch

"Focus groups don't provide solutions. They help you form a picture that reveals your possibilities and limits."[13]

Appropriate Business Issues for Focus Groups

Another leading authority on focus group research, Susan Lazar of The Lazar Group, has found qualitative research to be appropriate for a wide variety of business and marketing issues:

- New product development
- Product and concept optimization
- Strategy formation
- Positioning
- Hypothesis testing
- Brand equity and imagery management
- Analysis of acquisitions
- Learning customer language
- Assessing co-branding partnerships
- Optimization of customer insight pre and post quantitative research
- Product placement plus usage satisfaction
- Visual appeal of a product/concept
- Advertising development
- Emergent category trends
- Understanding changes in category trends/usage patterns

Focus groups are a qualitative technique, meaning that they are exploratory in nature, rarely use a random sampling to draw respondents, use unstructured data collection tools (called topic guides), have small samples of customers, and do not allow quantitative conclusions to be drawn. Focus groups should only be used to gain

[13] Bonnie Goebert, with Herma Rosenthal, *Beyond Listening: Learning the Secret Language of Focus Groups* (New York: John Wiley and Sons, 2002), 106.

an in-depth understanding of customers and to develop hypotheses for further quantitative measurement; they should not be used to draw conclusions on major marketing decisions.

Focus groups typically involve eight to ten target consumers, recruited based upon their demographics, psychographics, and product usage behavior. Trained moderators are usually hired to conduct the focus group, which typically lasts for two hours. The moderator uses a topic guide, usually covering about ten topics, and is free to probe deeply into those topics that yield consumer insights. Virtually all focus group facilities have a viewing room with a one-way mirror to allow marketers and product developers to observe the respondents without being seen.

Important Skills of the Moderator

The selection of a skilled focus group moderator is critical, not just to the successful conduct of the focus group session, but also for depth analysis of the patterns from the focus groups that will yield customer insight. According to Susan Lazar, the characteristics to look for in a trained, experienced focus group moderator are:

- Good communicator, in the focus group room AND in the viewing room
- Strong people and client skills
- Excellent listener with solid memory
- Great presenter; enthusiastic, empathetic, articulate
- Strong marketing acumen – high marketing IQ
- Creative thinker and problem solver
- Flexible, adaptable to change and unexpected curveballs
- Learns and understands your business

Focus Group Advantages

A major advantage of focus groups over other exploratory methods is the **group interaction** that occurs in most well-conducted focus groups. Ideas from one respondent can often lead to creative ideas from other respondents, often uncovering serendipitous thoughts that are very valuable to marketers. The second advantage of focus groups is their **experiential** benefit, allowing marketers to experience their target customers easily and quickly while relaxing in a comfortable viewing room. Often, product developers and marketers find these sessions together at the focus group to be a great opportunity to brainstorm about future new products and marketing strategies.

Focus Group Disadvantages

Focus groups have some disadvantages, however. Occasionally, a loud, outspoken member of the group can dominate and actually influence the opinions of others. Often, depth of insight is sacrificed to cover a topic guide that is too long. If there are fifteen topics and twelve respondents in a two-hour focus group, this means that, on average, each respondent will spend forty seconds expressing an opinion on each topic. Sometimes group facilities keep going back to the same consumers for their focus groups, creating "research experts" whose opinions can

hardly be considered representative of the target market. But the largest disadvantage of focus groups is the temptation by marketers to make major marketing decisions after sitting through several focus groups. Major decisions need to be supported with large research studies, with randomly drawn samples of target market consumers.

Two critics of the overuse of focus groups are members or former members of the Marketing faculty at the Kellogg School of Management at Northwestern University: Sherry and Kozinets. They argue that focus groups are "the most overused and misused arrow in the qualitative quiver. Focus groups often provide the illusion of human contact and the occasion of pyrotechnics that efficiently satisfy the prematurely narrowed imagination of clients and researchers behind the one-way glass."[14]

While profound insights into consumer needs can come from exploratory research, they aren't likely to emerge through a poorly conducted, shallow focus group, according to Andrew Arken. "Big insights aren't likely to emerge through the stereotypical, shallow focus group, with observers behind the one-way mirror discussing dinner plans or calling about another project back at the office. The key is running well-designed, in-depth qualitative research with active project team involvement, followed by facilitated creative synthesis and insight-mining sessions. You can't just put someone else to stand between you and your customers."[15] Thus, the brainstorming sessions that usually follow the focus group are often as valuable as the group session itself.

Observers should look for patterns across a number of focus groups to mine for insight and avoid the frequent mistake of quoting one respondent who supported the person's preconceived ideas about the market. The worst danger is for an executive to attend and observe only one of eight focus groups, where the patterns of behavior were consistent in all of the groups except for the one the executive attended. But because of the experiential effects of seeing the one group of atypical customers, the executive now has a distorted picture of the target customer.

Do Focus Groups Work in B-to-B Markets?

While focus groups can work well in most B-to-C markets, they tend to be problematic in many B-to-B markets. Often, business customers are geographically dispersed and difficult to assemble in one location. But the bigger problem is that often your B-to-B customers are competitors and are reluctant to open up in a focus group in front of others who could use the insight to gain a competitive advantage. Therefore, customer visits are usually used in place of focus groups by B-to-B companies.

---

[14] Kevin J. Clancy and Peter C. Krieg, "Surviving Death Wish Research," *Marketing Research*, Winter 2002.

[15] Andrew Arken, "The Long Road to Customer Understanding," *Marketing Research*, Summer 2002.

Some B-to-B companies have attempted to solve the geographic dispersion issue by conducting telephone focus groups using conference call technology available from many communication companies. While this approach can work well to collect general information on behavior, its lack of nonverbal communication severely limits its ability to gain depth into many attitudinal issues.

Focus groups can often be a helpful first step in a serious marketing research process, but they should never be the only step. Follow-up quantitative research should always be conducted on major marketing decisions to minimize the risk of making a wrong marketing move.

Depth Interviews

Depth interviews, also called one-on-one interviews, involve the interviewing of target consumers one at a time by a trained moderator. Like focus groups, the moderator uses a topic guide to guide the discussion but is free to go into depth on issues that are fruitful in addressing the marketing questions at hand. Like focus groups, depth interviews should only be used for developing hypotheses and insights and not for drawing conclusions or quantifying marketing issues.

Depth interviews are useful for sensitive product categories that do not lend themselves to a group discussion. Incontinence and sexual dysfunction are topics of high interest to health care marketers; depth interviews will be more effective than focus groups because few respondents suffering from these conditions will be open and candid in front of a group of nine strangers. Depth interviews are also more useful than focus groups when much information is required from each respondent.

Depth interviews have been a valuable tool for MTV to understand the emotional value of the MTV brand to the target consumer. Heavy MTV viewers were recruited for a "deprivation" study, wherein MTV, MTV2, and MTV.com were taken away from them for a thirty-day period. These deprived respondents were given audio recorders to capture their life without it. Depth interviews were conducted with each respondent at the end of the thirty-day deprivation period. MTV Senior Vice President of Strategy and Planning Todd Cunningham found that "when people are without something they are accustomed to, they really emote. We gained amazing insights from this deprivation study. We learned about the social value and nature of MTV and also how much viewers treasure, celebrate and even desire the advertising."[16] Research efforts such as these have led to a recent ratings surge by MTV, which ended 2003 in the number one position in basic cable among the 12 to 34-year-old age group.

Archetype Research

Many customer memories are *archetypes,* defined as images that capture essential, universal commonalities across a variety of experiences. An archetype is an idea, character, action, object, situation, event, or setting containing essential characteristics

---

[16] RFL Communications, Inc., "Research Department Report," April 2004.

that are primitive, general, and universal, rather than sophisticated and unique. All societies share many archetypes; they are deeply embedded in every culture's social memory.[17] Some have described archetypes as being the human instinct, which plays a dominant role in human behavior, including purchase decisions.

The theory of archetypes was developed by the famous Swiss psychologist Carl Gustav Jung and can help marketers see how certain meanings are constructed in the human psyche and understand how *meaning is associated with emotions*. Jung discovered that a person's fantasy life, like the instincts, has a certain structure, with imperceptible energetic centers in the unconscious mind that regulate instinctual behavior and spontaneous imagination. Thus emerge the dominants of the collective unconscious, or the archetypes. Modern civilized man has built a rational superstructure and repressed his dependence on his archetypal nature.[18]

According to Jung, archetypes per se are not visible.

What we see are their symbols and images; what we hear and read are the myths or themes they inspire. *When confronted with an archetypal symbol or a myth,* we feel an emotional pull, a drive. [19]

Archetype analysis goes to the roots of *why* and *how much* a symbol or a theme impacts consumers emotionally, *why* a symbol is *culturally significant*, and explains *why* a symbol is *motivational*.

The Mother Archetype

One of the most important archetypes is the Mother Archetype. Among the positive characteristics of the Mother Archetype are sympathy, the longing to be loved and cared for, forgiveness, nurturing, and wisdom. This Mother Archetype has been especially useful in advertising directed at the Hispanic market.[20]

A nontraditional but often effective technique for uncovering unmet needs and discovering motivations for consumer behavior is **archetype research,** which has been used by almost half of the companies in the Fortune 100. The leading proponent of this technique is the French-born medical anthropologist Dr. Clotaire Rapaille, who disdains surveys of customers as "prehistoric." Rather, Rapaille feels that long-time members of the same culture share cultural imprints and probes for this "cultural unconscious," or the *reptilian instinct*, in three-hour sessions with consumers. These consumers lie on the floor, some under blankets, some under pillows, and often in the dark. While soft relaxing music plays, respondents are encouraged to think back to their earliest memories of cheese, coffee, barbecue sauce, or paper towels. The latter product apparently appeals to moms, for whom cleanliness plays into a "reptilian" desire to make sure their genes survive. "You're not just cleaning the table," says Rapaille, "You are saving the whole family."[21]

---

[17] Zaltman, *How Customers Think,* 213-219.

[18] *Encyclopedia of World Biography,* 2nd ed., Paula Byers Senior Editor (Detroit: Gale Research, 1998).

[19] *Encyclopedia of World Biography.*

[20] Roberta Maso-Fleischman, "Archetype Research for Advertising: A Spanish-language Example," *Journal of Advertising Research* 37, no. 5 (1997).

[21] Melanie Wells, "Mind Games," *Forbes,* September 2003.

The PT Cruiser and Archetype Research

One of the more successful products whose design was impacted by archetype research was the **PT Cruiser,** Daimler-Chrysler's highly successful sport-utility vehicle (SUV) that was launched in 2000. The PT Cruiser was the first Daimler-Chrysler vehicle designed using archetype research. Rapaille worked with Chrysler at every stage of the car's design to ensure that the target segment would love the SUV. To allow access to unconscious thoughts, respondents were exposed to prototypes while lying on mats in a dimly lit room, to recreate the same brain wave activity you have when you first wake up from a dream.

Two **customer insights** that emerged from this archetype were the target customers' "reptilian hot buttons" for **nostalgia** and **safety and security.** The "retro" design of the PT Cruiser was enhanced to increase its nostalgic appeal to those seeking to return to simpler times. Designers changed the prototype to incorporate bulbous, protruding fenders and big headlights.[22] Some described the PT Cruiser as looking like a "Wurlitzer jukebox" from the 1950s, but with today's modern technology.[23]

When probed during archetype research, Americans like to describe where they live as the wilderness, and they speak of a dangerous outside world as a jungle from which they need protection. These **safety and security** needs were communicated to the PT Cruiser designers, and changes were made to the early prototype – fenders were designed to appear more protective, the hatchback window was made smaller to increase the feeling of security, and the windshield was made more upright to give the vehicle more of a truck-like look.

Did these customer insights from archetype research help the PT Cruiser achieve success in the marketplace? Initial consumer demand was so strong at launch in the spring of 2000 that some buyers were willing to wait nearly a year to get one. Almost half of the first-year buyers added the vehicle to their family, rather than the usual pattern of replacing another vehicle. When these buyers were asked why they bought this additional vehicle, many reflected their unconscious desires (or reptilian instinct) with the conscious response of: "I just had to have one!"

In 2001, the PT Cruiser was voted North American Car of the Year. Dealers were able to charge full list price for the PT Cruiser, while at the same time offering large rebates and no interest loans on most of their other vehicles to move them. Waiting lists were common as Daimler-Chrysler geared up more production capability to build more of their archetype-research-driven PT Cruisers.

Procter & Gamble has used archetype research for over thirteen years on products such as coffee, toilet tissue, pain medications, cough medications, colds, and oral care. Procter & Gamble Research Fellow Jim Donovan was first exposed to cultural archetypes over twenty years ago and began investigating the use of this approach to understand the deeper meaning of things, like the deeper meaning of your breath, your teeth, or your hair.

---

[22] Ruth Shalit, "The Return of the Hidden Persuaders," www.salon.com/media, 27 Sept. 1999.
[23] Joseph Rydholm, "Personal Transportation Indeed," *Quirk's Marketing Research Review*, December 2000.

"Cultural archetypes are not our opinions, our personality, or our biology. Cultural archetypes are something that we have learned within our culture, such as cultural attitudes, beliefs and behaviors. From a business standpoint, we have been able to convert the knowledge from the cultural learnings to help our scientists invent new products and our marketers do an outstanding job of understanding how to communicate the products we offer."[24]

Ritz-Carlton has also used archetype research to meet the expressed and unexpressed needs of their customers, whom they refer to as "guests." "Meeting expressed needs is easy," according to Leonardo Inghilleri of Ritz-Carlton, "but meeting unexpressed is more challenging." Guests frequently say they want to feel "at home" when staying at a hotel, but deeper, archetype research revealed that what they really wanted was a home like their mother's, where everything is taken care of for them and where everything is clean and you don't have to pick up after yourself.

Inghilleri stresses that for a company to be successful, it must have a strong hold on their customers' needs, which requires a deep understanding of the words they use to communicate these needs.[25] A simple need like "feeling at home" can be misunderstood if not probed in depth, using methods like archetype research.

Customer Visits

Experiencing the world of the customer through an organized program of customer visits can transform how decision makers think. A customer visit program is without a doubt one of the most valuable exploratory market research techniques available to Business-to-Business marketers.

Philip Kotler has described close contact with customers as a key element of leadership. "The best leaders don't spend too much time poring over numbers. They devote a lot of time to major customers. Jack Welch of GE spent 100 days a year talking with major customers. So did Lou Gerstner of IBM."[26]

A test to assess how customer focused an organization is is to determine how often the top managers from various functions have contact with customers. "For senior executives to get out of their offices and meet customers directly has long been perceived as best practice among large companies in the B to B sector. Now it is also common to find top managers of consumer goods and services companies spending time with end-users and hearing about their own and their competitors' performance. The best programs bring senior executives from all functions into contact with both major customers and end-users in a formal business setting, not socially."[27]

---

[24] Jim Donovan, quoted on the website of Archetype Discoveries Worldwide, http://www.archetypediscoveriesworldwide.com (accessed August 2003).

[25] Leonardo Inghilleri, quoted on the website of Archetype Discoveries Worldwide, http://www.archetypediscoveriesworldwide.com (accessed August 2003).

[26] Philip Kotler, *Marketing Insights from A to Z: 80 Concepts Every Manager Needs to Know* (Hoboken: John Wiley and Sons, 2003), 96.

[27] Patrick Barwise and Sean Meehan, "Do You Value Customer Value?" in *Mastering Marketing*, exec. ed. Tim Dickson (London: FT Pitman, 1999).

Dr. Edward F. McQuarrie is a leading authority on customer visits, and his book, *Customer Visits: Building Better Market Focus*,[28] is a highly practical guide to planning and executing a successful program of customer visits. In this outstanding book, McQuarrie offers the following sage advice:

- **Why are customer visits needed?** – "The fundamental argument in favor of customer visits is precisely the need to escape from the blinders of one's own experience of the product category and marketplace and grasp the very different experiences of customers."[29]
- **Who benefits most?** – "The prime targets for participation in customer visit programs are, first, engineers and scientists and, second, production and manufacturing personnel. It is individuals such as these, who are typically shielded or prevented from encountering the customer firsthand, who have the greatest need to increase their level of face-to-face contact."[30]
- **What is a "thought world?"** – "Each of us lives in a thought world shaped by our own background, membership in social groups, and current task demands. A thought world consists of tacit and taken-for-granted assumptions about what is important, relevant, or necessary. Vendor engineers tend to live in *Lab World*, whereas the customer's technical people tend to live in *Task World*. In *Lab World,* bits, bytes and baud rate are a source of fascination and the focus of attention. In *Task World*, the priority is to accomplish some job, and the product is merely a means to that end."[31]
- **What is the function of marketing in technology firms?** – "More and more marketers in technology firms will come to understand that their proper function is not to interpose themselves between technical staff and customers, but to facilitate the appropriate amount and kind of direct customer contact between engineers and customers."[32]
- **What is the procedure for planning a customer visit program?** – "The procedure for planning a customer visit program involves seven steps: 1) Set objectives, 2) Select a sample, 3) Compose the visit teams, 4) Develop the discussion guide, 5) Conduct the interviews, 6) Debrief after each interview, and 7) Analyze, report, and store visit data."[33]

It is highly recommended that cross-functional teams participate in customer visits, due to the high degree of functional interdependence that departments like marketing and research and development (R and D) have in B-to-B firms. Often, marketing is a weak (or nonexistent) function in B-to-B firms. In other B-to-B firms, moderate to severe disharmony has been found to exist between

---

[28] Edward F. McQuarrie, *Customer Visits: Building a Better Market Focus* (Newbury Park: Sage Publications, 1993).

[29] McQuarrie, *Customer Visits*, 13.

[30] McQuarrie, *Customer Visits*, 6.

[31] McQuarrie, *Customer Visits*, 11-12.

[32] McQuarrie, *Customer Visits*, 19.

[33] McQuarrie, *Customer Visits*, 43.

the marketing and R and D functions. In firms like this and in firms with highly technical products, it is better for R and D personnel to hear the customer directly, and be able to ask technical follow-up questions. Using marketing as a conduit of information from the customer to R and D in these cases simply doesn't work; R and D suspects that Marketing is inventing difficult-to-develop customer requirements so that their products will be easier to sell.

Customer Visits and the Success of Hewlett-Packard

McQuarrie has worked closely with Hewlett-Packard (HP) on implementing customer visit programs to drive new product development programs and has found very positive response among R&D project managers to the process. A study among more than 200 HP employees who had participated in the customer visit program within a twelve-month period found that 47 percent described the process as **extremely valuable,** while another 49 percent described it as **fairly valuable.** Over 90 percent stated that the customer visits had a direct impact on the products and services offered to customers. A high proportion (76 percent) stated that they had gained some unexpected or surprising information as a result of the visits. Hearing customer problems, dissatisfaction, and how a customer describes a "stressful day" firsthand is an experience that should be required of all decision makers in every company.

Which Exploratory Approaches to Use When

Each of these six exploratory approaches can provide rich insight into unmet needs of your target customers. But which approach will yield the most insight for a specific company?

That depends on the nature of the business and the motivations driving consumer purchase decisions. If the purchase decision involves B-to-B products with predominantly rational attributes driving the purchase decision, the following chart shows that customer visits will be the best exploratory approach to pursue. An example is the decision by a hospital laboratory director as to which automated diagnostic testing instrument to purchase to perform their blood testing on. Rational reasons such as accuracy, precision, test throughput, downtime, maintenance requirements and operator training requirements will highly influence the instrument selection. These rational requirements are best understood by visiting the customer in their environment, in the context where decisions are made that influence patient care.

On the other hand, if the purchase decision involves B-to-C products with predominantly emotional attributes driving the purchase decision, archetype research, ethnography, or focus groups will be the best approaches to pursue.

Each approach has its unique strengths and weaknesses, and the following chart is meant to provide general guidance on exploratory approaches. Marketers should request multiple proposals from external marketing research firms to assess which approach best addresses their marketing issues. An excellent global directory of qualitative research specialists can be found at the website of The World Association of Opinion and Marketing Research Professionals, known as ESO-MAR (http://www.esomar.org).

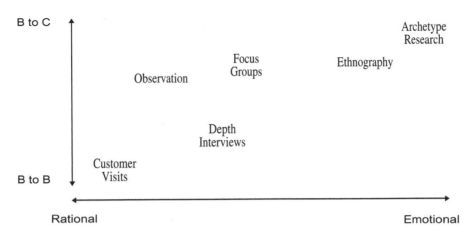

Application of Exploratory Approaches

Investment Cost

The following estimates are from a variety of sources, including the ESOMAR 2003 Prices Survey. Costs will vary depending on the incidence of target customers in the market (their percentage representation among potential respondents contacted) and the cost of incentives to get them to participate in the marketing research study.

- Observational research at its simplest involves just the marketers' time and the cost to travel to the customers' place of business. A large global observational program, like that conducted by Procter & Gamble, can cost $150,000 - $200,000.
- Ethnography at its simplest involves the time of the development team in immersing themselves in the lives of their customers, as well as the cost of travel. At the other extreme, firms can expect to pay $100,000 or more for an ethnography consulting firm to complete a study.
- Four focus groups, conducted by a skilled moderator, with target customers requiring a moderate incentive to participate, and including analysis and report, will cost:
    - $20,000 - $25,000 in the United States
    - $20,000 - $22,000 in France and Japan
    - $17,000 - $19,000 in the U.K. and Germany
    - $4,000 - $6,000 in China and India
- Focus groups with respondents requiring large incentives, such as cardiologists and CEOs, can cost 50 to 100 percent more than the costs shown above.
- Twenty depth interviews conducted by a skilled moderator, including analysis and report, will cost approximately $15,000 - $20,000 in the United States and Japan and $12,000 - $15,000 in major European countries.

- Archetype research studies, such as those conducted by Rapaille of Archetype Discoveries Worldwide, based in Boca Raton, Florida, cost approximately $200,000 - $225,000.
- Customer visits by their nature involve a lot of time and effort by cross-functional teams within the firm. A point person should be named to help organize the teams and to schedule visits with customers. An outside research firm can be used to "recruit" customers and schedule times and dates, which is a time-intensive process. Expect to pay an outside research firm $10,000 - $20,000 per year to coordinate a successful customer visit program between your customers and your management team.

Unmet Need Checklist

- Do your technology experts feel that listening to customers is a worthwhile endeavor?
- Does your management team utilize customer feedback early in the new product development process to "kill the dogs" that can use up valuable time and resources?
- Does your management team understand the difference between "expressed" customer needs and "latent" customer needs?
- How often in the past year has your product development team observed customers using products in your category?
- Has your product development team ever immersed themselves in the world of the customer and walked in the customers' shoes for several days?
- Does your marketing team regularly use focus groups to get qualitative feedback from customers on new product concepts, advertising, and product features?
- When focus groups are conducted, are they observed closely by cross-functional teams or just the marketing people?
- Does your management team brainstorm immediately after focus groups, while everyone's mind is full of the customer's perspectives and needs?
- Has your firm ever used a series of depth interviews with customers to drill down deeply into the needs and motivations of target customers?
- Would archetype research be a worthwhile investment for your firm?
- If your firm is Business-to-Business, how frequently do cross-functional teams, including managers, visit customers?
- Is your customer visit program structured to deliver value to your new product developers, or are your visits social in nature?
- Is your customer visit program limited to sales and marketing personnel, or do cross-functional teams participate?

Emotional and Rational Motivations

Insight 3: Emotional motivations play a greater role than rational motivations in most consumer purchase decisions.

About 95 percent of thought, emotion, and learning occur in the unconscious mind, without our awareness.

Gerald Zaltman, Harvard University

Customer Insight Pyramid

Emotional and Rational Reasons for Consumer Behavior

Some economists theorize that consumers behave rationally in their purchase decisions, making conscious deliberations in their choices and fully weighing the utility of features versus the price. Further, they theorize that consumers make these decisions with complete information about the product in question, as well as available alternatives, and use this complete information to make a decision that maximizes their "utility." For some products, such as automobile insurance and expensive cameras, these conditions may apply, but for most purchase decisions, consumers make decisions involving emotional motivations with limited information.

While these economists believe that consumers make decisions rationally with complete information, marketers think differently. Marketers tend to have a more realistic perspective called *bounded rationality*.[1] H. A. Simon argues that consumer decision makers have limitations on their abilities for information processing and attempt to do as well as they can given the time and attention limitations to which they are subject.

For many products, little information has been processed and emotional motivations far outweigh rational factors in the purchase decision. The Coca-Cola Company failed to recognize the powerful emotional attachment of their customers to Classic Coke and blundered badly when it pulled it from the market and launched New Coke in 1985.

Indeed, decision making hinges upon the simultaneous functioning of reason and emotion. People's emotions are closely interwoven with reasoning processes. Although our brains have separate structures for processing emotions and logical reasoning, the two systems communicate with each other and *jointly* affect our behavior. Even more important, the emotional system – the older of the two in terms of evolution – typically exerts the *first* force on our thinking and behavior. More important still, emotions contribute to, and are essential for, sound decision making.[2]

Recent research by neuroscientists has identified the sections of the brain involved in rational decision making. "The prefrontal cortex, an area that plays a key role in levelheaded decision making and long term goals, takes years to develop and then starts to lose some of its swagger when we're in our late 50s. That means kids under 12 and older people are more susceptible to urges that come from the amygdale, the emotional hot button in our heads. It responds to threats, emotional communication and sexual imagery – some of the stuff we see or hear in ads and other marketing ploys."[3]

These emotional motivations are usually difficult to obtain from consumers by asking them directly; in most cases they are not consciously aware of these motivations and usually respond with rational reasons for their purchase behavior. "Consumers share only the logical aspects of their decision-making process because marketers ask for those aspects – and conscious, logical thoughts are much easier to articulate than emotions. The managerial tendency to focus on conscious consumer thought, while understandable and natural, also blocks managers' access to the world of unconscious consumer thought and feeling that drives most consumer behavior. Marketers assume that consumers can readily inspect and easily

[1] Herbert A. Simon, "A Behavioral Model of Rational Choice," *Quarterly Journal of Economics* 69, 1955.

[2] Gerald Zaltman, *How Customers Think: Essential Insights into the Mind of the Market* (Boston: Harvard Business School Press, 2003); Antonio R. Damasio, *Descartes' Error: Emotion, Reason and the Human Brain* (New York: Putnam, 1994); Jon Elster, *Alchemies of the Mind: Rationality and the Emotions* (Cambridge: Cambridge University Press, 1999).

[3] Melanie Wells, "In Search of the Buy Button," *Forbes,* September 2003, 70.

describe their own emotions. In fact, emotions are by definition unconscious. To surface them, skilled researchers must use special probing techniques."[4]

Beer Brand Choice – Is It Rational or Emotional?

Let's take beer, for example. Beer is a low involvement product category where brand preferences and purchase behavior are driven more by unconscious emotional motivations than by conscious rational reasons. However, when asked why they prefer their favorite brand, most beer drinkers respond with the logical, rational reason of "I like the taste." They were next asked about the relevance of emotionally laden attributes, such as:

- A brand that is popular with my friends
- A brand for people like me
- A brand I would be proud to serve to guests
- A brand that has advertising I like
- A brand I would buy for friends in a bar

In response to these attributes, beer drinkers scoff and claim that these peer-acceptance and self-image attributes have no impact on their preferences. (Many beer drinkers in focus groups also proudly boast that advertising does not affect them!)

However, quantitative analysis of brand ratings on these attributes versus beer brand preferences reveals a very different story. Regression analysis of the ratings given to brands on these five attributes shows that the higher a brand is rated, the higher the preference is for that brand. This indirect approach to assessing the importance of emotional motivations to beer preferences and behavior underlines the importance of not stopping at the rational level when trying to understand consumer motivations. Bud Light has achieved success by consistently reinforcing the brand's core values of "fun, young, and social," according to Bob Lachky of Anheuser-Busch.[5]

It is difficult to think of any consumer purchase decision that involves only rational reasons. Fortunately, many good techniques have been developed to allow marketers to circumvent the conscious, rational mind and tap into the unconscious mind and understand emotional motivations for product preferences and purchases.

The focus of this chapter will be on tools to uncover the **emotional** reasons for consumers' purchases, since these reasons are often buried in the unconscious mind and difficult to access with direct questioning methods. Uncovering **rational** reasons for consumers' purchases is more straightforward, since most consumers can more easily access rational reasons when interviewed with direct questioning methods. These direct questioning methods are the focus of Chapters 4 through 10.

Understanding the emotional reasons driving purchase of brands in your product category can provide insights that can give you a competitive advantage. Oreo cookies, Harley-Davidson, PT Cruiser, and others have benefited greatly from a

---

[4] Zaltman, *How Customers Think,* 10, 39, 51.
[5] Mark Scheffler, "Bud's Greatest Hits," *Chicago Tribune Magazine,* 20 July 2003.

deep understanding of **customer insights** on an emotional level, as will be illustrated in this chapter.

Oreo Cookies

Oreo cookies, made by Nabisco, have been the best-selling cookies in the United States for over ninety years. A large part of the success of Oreo cookies is due to the commitment of Nabisco to truly understand their target consumer and establish an emotional tie between that consumer and Oreo cookies.

Nabisco decided to create a new advertising strategy to reach the growing adult segment in 1988 and began with a situational analysis of all existing strategic and tactical marketing research. This valuable synthesis of past research efforts helped put everyone on the strategy team on the same page. They then proceeded to conduct exploratory qualitative research (seven focus groups) to understand the emotional components of Oreo's imagery and brand personality.

Based on the insights obtained, rough storyboards were developed for several advertising ideas, which they then proceeded to pretest using the ASI Recall Plus Technique. Their success with this marketing research program resulted in their team winning the 1994 David Ogilvy Award from the Advertising Research Foundation.[6]

A variety of projective techniques were employed during the qualitative research to uncover consumers' deeper feelings and emotions about Oreo cookies:

- **Verbal Exercises** – exercises such as projective storytelling, where respondents were asked to tell someone who had never had an Oreo what it was like to eat an Oreo.
- **Psycho-drawings** – respondents drew pictures using crayons to illustrate the experience of eating Oreos and other cookies.
- **Collages** – respondents were asked to cut pictures out of magazines and then paste them into a collage to express how they feel about eating Oreo cookies. The respondents would then explain their collages to others.
- **Photo Sort** – Respondents were given a variety of photographs of people and asked to select which photographs personified Oreo cookies and explain why.
- **Obituaries** – Respondents were then told that the "personified" Oreo cookies had died and were asked to write an obituary, explaining the good things about Oreo when it was alive.

These projective techniques provided the Nabisco team with fascinating and surprising results. A most surprising finding was that many Oreo customers regarded Oreo cookies as almost **"magical."** Oreo cookies recaptured childhood/family experiences and helped adults relive childhood memories. More than evoking a feeling of nostalgia, eating an Oreo made respondents **feel all the "good things"**

---

[6] Larry Percy, ed., *Marketing Research that Pays Off: Case Histories of Marketing Research Leading to Success in the Marketplace* (New York: Haworth Press, 1997).

about being a kid again. The identification of these powerful emotions that consumers attached to the Oreo experience provided the opportunity to develop very motivating and persuasive advertising strategies. The following positioning statement was developed to guide the development of future Oreo advertising:

> Generations can twist open and unlock the possibilities and wonder of childhood experiences, teenage times, or hopes and dreams that have since been forgotten. An Oreo is a magical door, which can transport us into a dimension of youth. Within seconds, we can reflect back on our own childhood when a simple pleasure like eating an Oreo was part of every fun-filled day.[7]

The new campaign that was developed tested strongly in the ASI pretest, and went on the air shortly thereafter. Sales responded dramatically, as the new advertising "unlocked the magic of Oreos" for the "kids" in their target market.

Harley-Davidson Motorcycles

In the early 1980s, Harley-Davidson was struggling to avoid bankruptcy. They faced heavy competition from Japanese motorcycle companies that produced quality motorcycles and sold them at competitive prices. Harley-Davidson motorcycles did not enjoy a quality reputation at the time, and the company had lost touch with its customers.

By launching new product development programs with the emphasis on delivering value to the customer, Harley engineered a total turnaround. Through 2002, Harley has experienced seventeen consecutive years of record sales revenues and earnings. Harley now commands a 45 percent share of the big cruiser bike segment, the most lucrative segment of the market. Second place Honda has a market share of 23 percent.

Harley management knows that one of the best ways to understand the world of the customer is to experience it themselves. Senior management rides motorcycles with the Harley Owners Group across the U. S. to experience their culture and lifestyle fully. Since everyone at Harley, from the CEO down, understands the customer at a deep level, the company can envision and develop products that consistently bring value to customers and profit to Harley.[8]

In addition to riding with their customers, Harley has conducted exhaustive marketing research with its target customers. Early qualitative research in the 1980s involved focus groups with loyal Harley customers, where they were asked to go through magazines to find pictures that captured the Harley experience. These bearded, tattooed customers, many wearing leather jackets and vests, eagerly used scissors and paste as they prepared their collages. They then spent the remainder of the focus groups discussing their collages.

---

[7] Percy, ed., *Marketing Research that Pays Off;* and Norma Larkin, Director of Business Insights for Nabisco, 12-13.

[8] Sheila Mello, *Customer-Centric Product Definition: The Key to Great Product Development* (New York: AMACOM, 2002), 159.

Regardless of the demographics of the Harley riders, two key customer values emerged as **universal** Harley appeals:

- INDEPENDENCE – owning and riding a Harley provides an escape from the everyday world and a sense of freedom
- INDIVIDUALITY – being able to customize my Harley allows me to express my personality perfectly

These **customer insights** allowed Harley-Davidson to develop marketing strategies that focused on these customer values of independence and individuality. Now, Harley-Davidson enjoys a fanatical following. Waiting lists have reached to more than a year. Harley-Davidson is the only brand name in the world that customers regularly tattoo on their bodies.

The Placebo Effect

Researchers have been studying the fascinating "Placebo Effect" for years. It is defined as the measurable, observable, or felt improvement in health not attributable to treatment, and as "the nonspecific, psychological, or psycho-physiologic therapeutic effect produced by a placebo."[9] It was first referenced in the 1955 research paper of H. K. Beecher titled "The Powerful Placebo," in which he concluded that across twenty-six drug clinical studies analyzed, an average of 325 of patients in the control group actually responded to the placebo (a dummy pill). The placebo effect occurs frequently in drug clinical studies; in some pain relief studies, more than half of the control group, taking a sugar pill, improved as quickly as the test group, which was taking the new medication.

The placebo effect demonstrates that the beliefs and expectations of both the patient and the physician can have remarkable effects on patient outcome. In a carefully controlled study reported in the *New England Journal of Medicine* and conducted by a team of orthopedic surgeons in Houston, patients with arthritis of the knee underwent a placebo operation: three incisions were made into the arthritic knee but then closed without any of the standard procedures that orthopedic specialists recommend. Surprisingly, the sixty patients who underwent these phony operations reported a significant improvement in their knee pain and flexibility. Moreover, the 180 patients who had the standard procedure reported no better results than the patients who got the placebo surgery![10]

This placebo effect "demonstrates the power of the unconscious mind to produce very powerful and beneficial experiences over and above those expected from the technical merits of the product. Although the technical quality of goods

---

[9] Jeremy Donovan, "More on the Placebo Effect," Sustained Action, http://www.sustainedaction.org/Explorations/more_on_the_placebo_effect.htm (accessed August 2003).
[10] John M. Kelley, "Lessons for Branding and Marketing," *ABInsight,* IBM Executive Business Institute, January 2003, http://www-03.ibm.com/ibm/palisades/abinsight/issues/2003-Jan/article-2-print.pdf (accessed July 2003).

and services is crucial in providing satisfying consumption experiences, an important part of the consumers' total experience with the firm's offering results from what consumers believe and expect these offerings to deliver."[11]

The placebo effect has **profound** implications for marketers. It is not enough to develop a "killer product"; in many cases, customer expectations must be raised to match or slightly exceed the experience delivered by the product. For example, consumers are willing to pay a significant price premium for Bayer aspirin over generic aspirin, despite the fact that they are chemically equivalent.

"Physical, social and psychological settings and a consumer's emotional state – all of which comprise what researchers call *context* – profoundly shape consumers' interpretation of images, as well as sounds, smells and other incoming sensory information."[12] Thus, many men and women remember the song that was playing when they fell in love with their spouse. Many beer drinkers form strong preferences for the brand they happen to be drinking during positive social situations with close friends. It follows that even though Coca-Cola knew that their drinkers preferred the taste of New Coke over Classic Coke from hundreds of thousands of blind taste tests in 1985, Coca-Cola drinkers rejected the new brand because they did not believe Coca-Cola could improve on their total experience of enjoying **their Coca-Cola.**

Three Marketing Tools for Uncovering Emotional Motivations

Three major marketing tools covered in this chapter are very powerful in circumventing the conscious mind and probing deeper into the emotions and feelings in the unconscious mind. These three tools are: **projective interviewing techniques**, the **Zaltman Metaphor Elicitation Technique** and **laddering.**

Projective Interviewing Techniques

Projective techniques are often incorporated into depth interviews and attempt to tap into the respondent's deepest feelings by having them "project" those feelings into an unstructured situation. A central feature of all projective techniques is the presentation of an ambiguous, unstructured object, activity, or person that the respondent is asked to interpret and explain.[13] Because the subjects are not directly talking about themselves, defense mechanisms are purportedly bypassed. The respondent is talking about something else or someone else, yet revealing his or her inner feelings.[14]

---

[11] Zaltman, *How Customers Think,* 60, 63.

[12] Zaltman, *How Customers Think,* 67.

[13] Harold H. Kassarjian, "Projective Methods," in *Handbook of Marketing Research,* ed. R. Ferber, (New York: McGraw-Hill, 1974); Sidney Levy, "Dreams, Fairy Tales, Animals, and Cars," *Psychology and Marketing,* Summer 1985.

[14] Carl McDaniel, Jr., and Roger Gates, *Marketing Research Essentials,* 2nd ed. (Cincinnati: South-Western College Publishing, 1998), 86.

The more ambiguous the stimulus, the more respondents have to project themselves into the task, thereby revealing hidden feelings and opinions. Projective techniques are useful when it is believed that respondents will not, or can not, respond meaningfully to direct questions about the reasons for certain behaviors or attitudes or what the act of buying, owning, or using a product or service means to them. The underlying assumption is that people often cannot or will not verbalize their true motivations and attitudes.[15] Projective techniques are used to avoid "socially desirable" responses that do not accurately describe the individual's attitudes and behavior.

Ten major projective techniques will be discussed here: **word association, sentence completion, story completion, third person techniques, picture interpretation, consumer drawings, cartoon caption completion, role-playing, brand analogies, and photo sorts.**

In **word association,** the interviewer reads a list of words and the respondent must mention the first thing that comes to mind. It is important that the respondent answer quickly to avoid giving the conscious mind time to think of a "socially desirable" answer. The word list should include words relevant to the product category of interest as well as neutral words. In a word association study conducted for McDonald's, respondents were read a series of words and asked to respond with the first word that came to their mind. Among the words generated from the word association task, the strongest associations were with the words Big Macs, Golden Arches, Ronald, Chicken McNugget, and Egg McMuffin. Words associated strongly with the McDonald's brand were: everywhere, familiar, greasy, clean, food, cheap, kids, well-known, French fries, fast, hamburgers, and fat. In the same study, Jack-in-the-Box had much lower associations with the words everywhere, familiar, greasy, and clean, and much higher associations with tacos, variety, fun, and nutritious.[16] Word association often used in testing brand names and advertising slogans as well.

In **sentence** and **story completion,** the respondent is read a series of incomplete sentences or given incomplete stories and asked to complete them. By creating their own endings, respondents are projecting their unconscious thoughts and feelings into the stories. Some researchers consider sentence completion and story completion to be the most useful and reliable of all of the projective techniques.

In **third person techniques,** respondents are not asked directly what he or she thinks; questions are couched in terms of "your neighbor" or "most people" or some other third party. This technique is often used to avoid issues that might be embarrassing or evoke hostility if answered directly by a

---

[15] David A. Aaker, V. Kumar, and George S. Day, *Marketing Research* (New York: John Wiley and Sons, 2001), 197.

[16] David A. Aaker, *Managing Brand Equity: Capitalizing on the Value of a Brand Name* (New York: Macmillan, 1991).

respondent. Direct questioning tends to be confounded by socially desirable responses.[17] An interesting variation on this technique is to provide respondents with shopping lists and ask the respondent to describe the shopper. One list might contain Budweiser beer, while a second list would be identical, except that Bud Light would be on the list instead of Budweiser. In giving these lists to two different matched groups of beer drinkers, interesting insights can be obtained about the differences in user imagery between the two brands.

In **picture interpretation,** the respondent is shown an ambiguous picture and asked to describe it. The pictures can be line drawings, illustrations, or photographs. This technique is very flexible and can be easily adapted for use to many kinds of marketing issues.

In **consumer drawings,** respondents are asked to draw what they are feeling about a brand or how they perceive a brand. A classic use of consumer drawings was by the McCann-Erickson advertising agency, which wanted to understand why Raid Roach Spray outsold Combat Insecticide Disks by a wide margin in certain markets. In interviews, respondents usually agreed that Combat was the better of the two products because it killed roaches with little effort on the users' part. To get to their underlying feelings and emotions, McCann researchers asked target market respondents (lower-income women in the Southern United States) to draw pictures of their prey, the cockroaches. The researchers were amazed when all 100 women in this study portrayed roaches as men! Upon discussing these drawings, it was discovered that the feelings of these customers about roaches were similar to their feelings about the men in their lives. With many of these women in common-law relationships, they felt that the roach, like the man in their life, only comes around when he wants food. The act of spraying the roach and watching it die was satisfying to this frustrated, powerless group. These customers used the spray instead of the easier disk because it allowed them to "participate in the kill."[18]

In **cartoon caption completion,** the respondent is shown a cartoon, often with two characters with dialogue balloons above their heads, one balloon filled with dialogue and the other blank. The respondent is asked to fill in the blank balloon with dialogue for the second character. For example, the two characters could be standing in front of a Best Buy store, and the first character could be saying, "Bill, I'm thinking about buying a new wide screen television here." The respondent would then fill in the response for the second character, thereby revealing his or her feelings about shopping for televisions at Best Buy.

In **role-playing,** the respondent assumes the role of another person, such as a salesperson in the store. The respondent is asked to attempt to sell the

---

[17] McDaniel and Gates, *Marketing Research Essentials,* 90; Aaker, Kumar, and Day, *Marketing Research,* 200.
[18] McDaniel and Gates, *Marketing Research Essentials,* 88-89.

product to a consumer, thereby revealing their attitudes and feelings about the brand in question. This technique is powerful in revealing the salient attributes and benefits the brand has imprinted on the mind of the respondent.

Products, like people, have personalities. Probing for the brand personality using **brand analogies** can reveal strengths and weaknesses of the brand that can be addressed in future advertising. Brand analogy research asks questions like "If Budweiser were a person, what would he be like?" or "Which animal best describes your feelings about BMW?" An excellent example of the use of this projective technique is given by Bonnie Goebert, who asked TV viewers to describe who *TV Guide* magazine would be if it were a person.[19]

The prevailing image of *TV Guide* that everyone loved was that of a Sherpa. The Sherpa is more than a safari guide; the Sherpa is the guy who has some inside knowledge that you need. This person is going to get you there. You just trust him and you rely on him. In this same way, users trust and rely on *TV Guide*. There's an inherent honesty in *TV Guide*.

These powerful insights are almost always unavailable when direct questioning techniques are utilized.

In **photo sorts,** customers select pictures from a specifically selected photo deck to personify a brand or a company, or to characterize users of different brands. When the New York-based BBDO advertising agency interviewed consumers and asked them to select photos of people that would be attracted to General Electric products, pictures of very conservative, older business types were selected. To address this image problem, General Electric and its advertising agency developed an advertising campaign with the slogan "We bring good things to life," targeted at younger, active consumers.

Zaltman Metaphor Elicitation Technique

Dr. Gerald Zaltman is professor of marketing at the Harvard Business School and a Fellow at Harvard's Interdisciplinary Mind, Brain, and Behavior Initiative. His classic book, *How Customers Think: Essential Insights into the Mind of the Market,* has two central themes:

- Most of the thoughts and feelings that influence consumers' behavior occur in the unconscious mind.
- Insightful analysis of consumer thought and behavior requires an understanding of how mental activity occurs.

"Consumer decision making and buying behavior are driven more by unconscious thoughts and feelings than by conscious ones. These unconscious forces

---

[19] Bonnie Goebert, with Herma Rosenthal, *Beyond Listening: Learning the Secret Language of Focus Groups* (New York: John Wiley and Sons, 2002), 106.

include ever-changing memories, metaphors, images, sensations and stories that all interact with one another in complex ways to shape decisions and behavior."[20]

Thus, direct questioning of consumers about their purchase decisions often leads to shallow, surface, rational reasons that have little to do with their real purchase motivations.

"Metaphors both invoke and express images of all types – visual, tactile, and olfactory – in a nonverbal form. Metaphors are so basic to the representation of thought and emotion that communicators and their audiences alike are largely unaware of their use and significance in the expression of ideas and feelings. Understanding the diversity and importance of deep metaphors in human expression helps marketers tap into consumers' unconscious minds and offer more effective communications and products that meet customers' needs. Market researchers can use innovative interviewing techniques to help consumers express their thinking through metaphors."[21]

Zaltman challenged marketing researchers to rethink their methods in a 1997 article in a leading marketing journal, because many current techniques were failing to develop a sound understanding of consumer thoughts, feelings, and behavior.[22] Zaltman identified nine premises about thought and language that presented significant challenges to marketing researchers:

1. Thought is image-based.
2. Most communication is nonverbal.
3. Metaphors are essential units for thought and feelings, and for understanding behavior.
4. Metaphors are important in eliciting human knowledge.
5. Cognition is embodied.
6. Emotion and reason are equally important and commingle in decision making.
7. Most thought, emotion and learning occur without awareness.
8. Mental models guide the selection and processing of stimuli.
9. Different mental models may interact.

These premises presented serious challenges to many market researchers. Marketing research firms that were selling advertising testing services based on recall of commercials and messages were disconcerted by the seventh premise, which stated that most thought and learning occurs without our awareness. This challenged their theory on how to assess the effectiveness of advertising.

One of the most powerful and frequently used methods to elicit metaphors and tap into the unconscious mind of consumers is the patented Zaltman Metaphor Elicitation Technique (ZMET). This patented technique involves asking consumers to take photographs, as well as gather pictures from magazines, that capture

---

[20] Zaltman, *How Customers Think,* 14–15.

[21] Zaltman, *How Customers Think,* 99.

[22] Gerald Zaltman, "Rethinking Market Research: Putting People Back In," *Journal of Marketing Research* 34, 1997.

the feelings and emotions involved in using a product. The purpose of ZMET is to "elicit metaphors and constructs and establish relationships among the constructs using both verbal and nonverbal stimuli." According to Zaltman, a metaphor is a "definition of one thing in terms of another."

"While ZMET does not represent human thought, it surfaces basic constructs or ideas and the connections among them and does so in a way that is user-friendly."[23] ZMET adds value over other marketing research techniques because it surfaces unique metaphor-based insights that marketers have found to be important and very useful.

In a typical ZMET study, twenty to twenty-five respondents are recruited and asked to take photographs and to collect pictures from magazines, newspapers, or books that reflect their thoughts and feelings about the brand or product category. Personal depth interviews, typically lasting two hours each, are scheduled for about one week later, where the photographs and pictures will be used to create visual stories and collages. This depth interview includes ten ZMET steps:

1. Storytelling, which involves describing the content of each picture,
2. Missed issues and images, where the respondent describes pictures that he or she was unable to obtain
3. Sorting of pictures into meaningful groups
4. Construct elicitation and laddering
5. The selection of the most representative image
6. The description of pictures that would represent opposite images of those in the task
7. Sensory images, where the respondent describes what does and does not capture the taste, touch, smell, sound, color, and emotion of the concept being explored
8. The creation of the mental map, connecting the constructs that have been elicited
9. The summary image, which is constructed on a computer using digital imaging techniques
10. The consensus map, which summarizes the most important constructs found in the mental maps of the respondents in the study

A good illustration of these steps can be found in "Seeing the Voice of the Customer: Metaphor-Based Advertising Research," by Gerald Zaltman.[24]

The goal of this technique is to uncover consumers' hidden thoughts and feelings. This engagement of the language of visual imagery enables the marketer to obtain richer verbal descriptions of the consumers' inner feelings. By evoking and analyzing metaphors from consumers, marketers can draw back the curtains on consumers' tacit knowledge, encourage consumers to look in, and then share what

---

[23] Gwendolyn Catchings-Castello, "The ZMET Alternative," *Marketing Research,* Summer 2000.

[24] Gerald Zaltman and Robin Higie Coulter, "Seeing the Voice of the Customer: Metaphor-based Advertising Research," *Journal of Advertising Research* 35, July/August 1995.

they see so that managers can create enduring value for customers in response to the insights revealed. Consumer researchers around the world have found the use of metaphors to be effective in helping people to bring their unconscious experiences into their awareness and then to communicate those experiences.[25]

Upon completing the ZMET with multiple respondents in the target market segments, the research team reviews each interview to identify key themes or constructs, and **consensus maps** can then be developed to understand the commonalities across respondents in their individual mental models. Consensus maps are visual displays of circles connected by lines, showing how the thoughts and feelings a group of consumers share are connected. Consensus maps represent bundles of thoughts that many target consumers share regarding products, services, and companies. These deeper, shared thoughts tend to drive consumer behavior most strongly and change little over time and can yield very valuable insights for marketing strategy development.[26]

Consensus maps depict the essential thoughts and feelings in a story and how they are stitched together in memory. These common elements represent the *archetypal* story of a brand. Consensus maps allow managers to shine a light into the unconscious thoughts held deep in the memory of the customer. Managers and researchers in several companies have reported independently that twelve to fifteen two-hour interviews with representative consumers can yield a consensus map that accurately represents the larger population of that market segment. Many marketers feel that these consensus maps are the **single most important set of consumer insights** that a marketer can have to win in the marketplace.[27]

Motorola utilized ZMET in developing its marketing strategy for a new home security system. When probing customers on their feelings on home security, many customers used their photographs and pictures of dogs and connected the images of dogs to comfort and feeling secure at home. Dogs gave many respondents a feeling of protection. These **customer insights** from the use of ZMET had implications for how Motorola positioned the product and even impacted the selection of the name for the product: "The Watchdog."

Leo Burnett Advertising used this collage technique to understand the meaning of Altoids, the strong breath mint, to its users. Respondents were given ten magazines and asked to find pictures that represented their feelings about Altoids, use them in a collage, and then describe their collage to the researcher. An analysis of the collages revealed three dimensions to their feelings about the brand. One was the notion of **freshness**, which was depicted by open space and waterfalls. The second dimension was **British**, which was depicted by pictures of Prince

---

[25] Zaltman, *How Customers Think.*

[26] Glenn L. Christensen and Jerry C. Olsen, "Mapping Consumers' Mental Models with ZMET," *Psychology and Marketing* 19, no. 6, June 2002; Giep Franzen and Margot Bouwman, *The Mental World of Brands: Mind, Memory, and Brand Success* (Henley-on-Thames, Oxfordshire, U.K.: World Advertising Research Centre, 2001).

[27] Zaltman, *How Customers Think.*

Charles and Princess Diana. The third dimension was **sex appeal,** represented by "hot" women dressed in red (from male respondents) and romantic embraces (among female respondents). These insights helped Altoids clearly position their brand, associating it with empowerment in social situations and as an old and traditional British brand. Despite a modest advertising budget of $7 million, Altoid sales results were outstanding, with sales growing from $23 million in 1996 to over $80 million in 1999. Market share grew from 10 percent in 1996 to 25 percent in 1999, as Altoids pushed Tic Tac for category leadership.[28]

Laddering and Means-End Theory

Many marketers have successfully discovered strong emotional reasons for consumer behavior, as well as determined customer values satisfied by products, using **means-end theory** and the **laddering** interviewing methodology. Means-end theory states that a means-end chain exists between the attributes of a product or service and a person's values. This **acv** chain identifies associations between three "levels of abstraction," starting with **attributes** (physical features and characteristics), progressing to functional **consequences** (results or benefits of the attribute), and ending with the more abstract customer **values** (the "real" reason why a person uses the product, that is, how it helps him or her accomplish goals).[29]

Laddering is a structured interviewing process that seeks to get to the heart of the reasons for a consumer's purchase behavior. Laddering is used to uncover the means-end chain for a particular respondent and attempts to identify how product attributes are linked to consequences, and how consequences are linked to customer values. Laddering elicits the personal reasons why a discriminating attribute is important to the respondent's decision structure.

The interview starts by identifying the attributes that the respondent considered when making the brand decision. For each attribute, the interview will "climb up the ladder" to consequences and then to values by continually asked questions like "Why is that important to you?" and "How does that make you feel?" The underlying customer values can emerge after as few as two questions or may require as many as twenty questions. Laddering up for a given attribute should terminate when the respondent is at a loss to answer further on that attribute or when the customer value level is reached. A leading authority has proposed that there are only nine values relevant to consumer behavior.[30] These nine terminal customer values are:

- Being well respected
- Excitement

---

[28] Brian Sternthal and Alice Tybout, "Segmentation and Targeting," in *Kellogg on Marketing,* ed. Dawn Iacobucci (New York: John Wiley and Sons, 2001), 21–22.

[29] James H. Myers, *Segmentation and Positioning for Strategic Marketing Decisions* (Chicago: American Marketing Association, 1996).

[30] Lynn R. Kahle, ed., *Social Values and Social Change: Adaptation to Life in America* (New York: Praeger, 1983).

- Fun and enjoyment in life
- Security
- Self-fulfillment
- Self-respect
- Sense of accomplishment
- Sense of belonging
- Warm relationship with others

Other customer goals and values that have been uncovered by laddering interviews with consumers include **self-esteem, peace of mind, independence, self-reliance, power, freedom, and tradition.** Let's consider an example, the purchase of an exercise treadmill. Initial questions may reveal that durability, availability of different exercise programs, and price were the three attributes involved in the purchase decision. Upon probing the availability of different exercise programs, consequences of "I won't get bored" and "I won't quit" can emerge. Upon climbing further up the ladder and probing as to why these consequences are important, abstract customer values dealing with self-respect and warm relationship can emerge ("I want to stay in shape," "I want to look good," and "I want my spouse to stay in love with me"). Understanding these values can provide powerful positioning ideas to the astute marketer of exercise treadmills.

Once the interview is completed, a hierarchical value map can be constructed to show the links between the attributes, usually shown along the bottom, and the consequences, usually shown in the middle of the map. The consequences are then linked to the higher-order customer values, typically shown at the top of the map. An excellent example of a hierarchical value map constructed by a former Kellogg School of Management student follows.

Hierarchical Value Map for Mitsubishi Eclipse Automobile
(Developed based on one interview by Anthony Lee, former Kellogg student.)

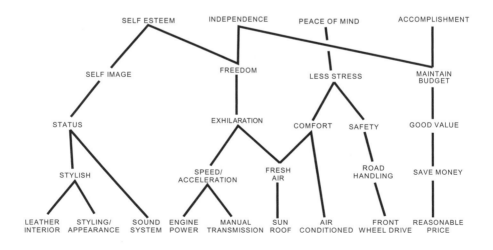

In this automobile map, it can be seen that the **sunroof** *attribute* leads to **fresh air** and **exhilaration** *consequences*, which address the *customer values* of **freedom** and **independence.**

After laddering interviews have been conducted with multiple respondents, a consensus hierarchical map can be constructed, which can accurately reflect the links between attributes, consequences, and values for that market segment. Consensus hierarchical maps should be developed for each target market segment, since subtle but important differences are usually found in consequences and values across market segments.

The linkage of a brand's attributes to important consequences and then to key customer values can provide a powerful positioning space for the brand in the customer's mind. "It is well known that once a brand's positioning is claimed at the benefit and value level, it becomes nearly impossible for competitors to copy or claim that position. Think of the Volvo brand name that has successfully claimed the 'safety' (benefit) and 'security' (value) positioning. Claiming a position explicitly and forcefully through advertising is needed. By being the first to explicitly claim a positioning, it's possible to preempt this positioning for the competition. Brand managers know that such positioning requires continuous investment in marketing communications."[31]

Which Tool to Use When?

Kellogg marketing students at Northwestern University enrolled in my course are required to use all three of these tools in a depth interview assignment. They are required to identify a purchaser of a high-priced item (over $250) and uncover the rational and emotional needs satisfied by the item purchased. Most of these students are amazed by their ability to uncover the difficult emotional reasons using these tools and have a great time with the assignment. When asked which of these tools were most useful to them in uncovering purchase motivations, most students report that one tool worked very well, while the other two were of marginal utility.

More interesting, however, is that the most effective tool is not the same across these student projects. After over 500 projects, students report the following:

- About 45 percent report that the Zaltman Metaphor Elicitation Technique, where the respondents collect images from magazines to create a collage, was the most useful technique. When probed, it was found that most of the products involved were highly emotional purchases, and many of the respondents were creative, right-brain dominant people.
- About 40 percent report that laddering (means-end theory) was the most useful technique. When probed, it was found that most of the products

---

[31] Marco Vriens and Frenkel Ter Hofstede, "Linking Attributes, Benefits and Consumer Values: A Powerful Approach to Market Segmentation, Brand Positioning, and Advertising Strategy," *Marketing Research* 12, no. 3, Fall 2000.

involved were dominated by rational reasons for purchase, and that many of the respondents were logical, left-brain dominant people.

- About 15 percent report that the projective techniques were the most useful to them. No product or respondent pattern was evident.

Thus, it appears that companies with products that have mostly emotional reasons driving brand purchase (perfume, beer) are likely to have more success with ZMET and projective techniques. Companies with products that have mostly rational reasons driving brand purchase (such as digital cameras) are likely to have more success with laddering and projective techniques. It is important to remember, however, that all products have both rational AND emotional reasons driving their purchase, and that the mix of rational and emotional reasons will vary widely across different product categories.

Investment Cost

- Twenty depth interviews, conducted by a skilled moderator utilizing projective techniques, including analysis and report, will cost approximately $20,000–$25,000 in the United States and Japan and $17,000–$20,000 in major European countries.
- Twenty depth interviews, conducted by a skilled moderator using ZMET or similar techniques, will cost approximately $30,000–$40,000, including analysis and report.
- Twenty depth interviews, conducted by a skilled moderator using the laddering technique, including analysis and report, will cost approximately $20,000–$25,000 in the United States and Japan and $17,000–$20,000 in major European countries.

Emotional and Rational Motivation Checklist

- What emotional motivations can you use to make your brand "magical"?
- What do customers believe about your brand and expect it to deliver?
- How many of the ten effective projective techniques have your company used to understand the emotional attachments your customers have to your brand and competitive brands?
- Have you elicited metaphors from your target customers to probe their unconscious minds?
- Has your marketing team developed consensus maps to capture the essential thoughts and feelings of your target consumer segment?
- Have you used laddering interviews to understand how product attributes are related to consequences, and how consequences are related to critical customer values?
- Are your brands strongly connected to critical customer values, such as excitement, fun, security or self-fulfillment?

SEGMENTATION AND TARGETING

INSIGHT 4: It is usually a better marketing strategy to target a segment of customers and get them to love you, than to attempt to get all customers to like you.

If you're not thinking segments, you're not thinking marketing.
Philip Kotler

Customer Insight Pyramid

Markets are composed of customers with very different perceptions, needs, and preferences. No consumer or business market has customers with identical needs. Customers differ in their attitudes, needs, benefits sought, price sensitivity, and product usage rate. Heterogeneity exists in every market, and marketers are well advised to see markets as composed of multiple segments rather than one homogeneous group of consumers.

Marketers today will not do well with a "one size fits all" marketing strategy. While this worked for Henry Ford and the Model T for a short time in the first twenty years of the last century, Ford had no strong competitors prior to General

Motors (GM) entering the market. When GM entered the market and adopted a product differentiation strategy, designing a car "for every purse, purpose, and personality," Ford was headed for trouble. The GM "product differentiation" strategy proved to be highly successful. Ford's market share declined dramatically, from 55 percent in 1920 to 12 percent in 1923![1]

Product line strategies can range from an undifferentiated, mass-marketing strategy, where the market is seen as composed of consumers with highly similar needs, to a mass customization strategy, where each consumer is treated as having unique needs. Dell Computer is a good example of a company successfully using a mass customization strategy. In between these two extremes are the product differentiation strategy and the market segmentation strategy options, as shown in the following chart.

Alternative Strategies for Product Line Development

	Mass Marketing	Product Differentiation	Market Segmentation	Mass Customization
Number of Segments	1	Unknown	Typically 3-8	Each customer is a segment
Philosophy	"One size fits all"	"Several different products may work better than one"	"Identify segments of customers and focus on delighting one or two"	"One size fits one"
Focus	Unfocused	Product	Market	Individual Customers
Begins With:	Production	Products	Customers	Customer Database
Example	Henry Ford (1910)	General Motors (1920)	Marriott Hotels	Dell Computer

The middle two strategies are often seen as highly similar, since they both begin by recognizing that there may be different needs and preferences among customers in the market, and they both often result in several different products being offered to the market. However, the subtle but critical difference between these two strategies is the focus. Is the focus on the product inside the firm, or is the focus on the customer outside the firm? An inside-out focus hopes that the product variety offered will meet the needs of different segments in the market. This approach is similar to shooting arrows at an archery range in the moonlight with no other lighting. Occasionally you hit a target, but a lot of arrows are wasted. An outside-in approach, which seeks to identify one or two target customer segments and focus carefully on their needs, is like shooting arrows with the lights on at the

---

[1] Philip Kotler, *Kotler on Marketing: How to Create, Win, and Dominate Markets* (New York: Free Press, 1999).

archery range. More of your arrows are hitting the targets, and some of them are bull's-eyes.

Market segmentation is the critical first step in developing a strategy for the firm. Many companies consider the pursuit of **operational excellence** to be their strategy for success. Unfortunately, most of their competitors may be pursuing the same strategy, resulting in little competitive advantage. Market segmentation is fundamental to the development of a successful, focused strategy for long-term success in the market, Kotler has stated. "Companies that target a specific group of customers and needs and deliver a different bundle of benefits *can be said to have a strategy* [emphasis added]. It is hard to make a product that everyone will want. It is easier to make a product that some will love."[2]

The essence of marketing strategy, like military strategy, is **"divide and conquer."** Dividing a market into segments, each having similar customers, and identifying a segment to focus on and dominate is the key to a successful marketing strategy. Targeting a segment that places high value on your strengths, while not placing much value on your weaknesses, is a powerful marketing strategy. Devoting the limited marketing resources a firm has available to winning in one segment is usually a more effective strategy than spending those same resources on the broader market.

Large companies with sufficient resources may decide to serve several segments but should develop a separate marketing mix for each of the target segments. For example, Anheuser-Busch has the resources to serve multiple segments of beer drinkers but has developed different marketing mix strategies for Budweiser, Bud Light, Busch, and Michelob. Each has a distinct product, price, promotional, and distribution strategy to allow each brand to win in its target segment while minimizing competition with the other A-B family brands.

The idea behind successful market segmentation strategies is that it is almost always better to be highly preferred by a segment of customers than to be liked by everybody. This is especially true in highly competitive consumer markets, where there are many brands that most customers find acceptable. The brand that goes beyond being liked and that gives a segment of customers a compelling reason to prefer it will win most of the time.

Some firms are afraid to focus on one or two segments, fearful that they are excluding large segments of the market from the marketing efforts. However, many firms have found that it is easier to achieve a 20 percent market share in a segment that represents 25 percent of the market than it is to achieve a 5 percent share of the total market. Once this first segment has been successfully penetrated and secured, the firm can then proceed to develop a new product and marketing mix to achieve a 20 percent share of a second market segment. Trying a "one size fits all" marketing strategy against the entire market to move your market share from 4 percent to 5 percent, then to 6 percent, and so on is a very difficult task,

[2] Philip Kotler, *Marketing Insights from A to Z: 80 Concepts Every Manager Needs to Know* (Hoboken, NJ: Wiley and Sons, 2003), 171.

especially if your competitors are practicing the Segmentation, Targeting, and Positioning (STP) success formula.

Kotler has identified the benefits of focusing on serving customers in a niche compared to mass marketing:[3]

- The company can get to know each customer more personally.
- The company may face far fewer competitors in the niche.
- The company can earn a higher margin in a niche market, since customers are quite willing to pay more because the niching company is so expert in meeting their needs.

The Strategic Marketing Process: STP

Market segmentation is the first step in the strategic marketing process, also known as STP.

> **Segmentation:** groups customers with similar needs, benefits sought, price sensitivity, or other variables
> **Targeting:** the selection of one or more of the segments that the firm chooses to serve
> **Positioning:** making your product stand for something different from your competitors' products to your target customers

Segmentation and targeting will be covered in this chapter; positioning will be covered in the next chapter.

Market Segmentation in the Beer Industry

Major brewers, such as Coors of Golden, Colorado, have many options when it comes to segmenting U. S. beer drinkers. Some of the major ways that breweries segment consumers are:

- **User status** – beer drinker versus non-beer drinker.
- **Usage rate** – light, medium, and heavy beer drinkers. Heavy drinkers are defined as those who drink more than twelve beers per week. These heavy beer drinkers represent about one-fourth of the 84 million American beer drinkers but consume about two-thirds of the beer volume.
- **Brand Loyalty** – do they buy Coors Light regularly, or do they select the light beer that is on price special?
- **Demographics** – the key demographics that drive beer consumption are: young, single males. Once young men get married, the frequency of their beer drinking occasions declines significantly. Instead of a night out with his buddies shooting pool and drinking a few beers, he is now taking his wife out to dinner and a movie. Attempts to target a beer at female beer

---

[3] Kotler, *Kotler on Marketing.*

drinkers, which was successful for Virginia Slims cigarettes, has not yet proven successful for a major brand of beer.

- **Psychographics** – beer drinkers can be grouped based on their personality characteristics, lifestyles, activities, interests, and opinions. The target beer drinker for Coors beer may be an outgoing, optimistic outdoors person who enjoys drinking with his male friends in bars.
- **Usage occasions** – beer satisfies different needs for an individual beer drinker on different consumption occasions, and different brands may be selected based on the needs at that occasion. For example, one Coors Light may be consumed on a Saturday afternoon after cutting the grass. This could be described as thirst/refreshment occasion. The same beer drinker may consume three Budweiser beers while watching college football later that day at the neighbor's house. This could be described as a male-bonding occasion. The following Monday, the same beer drinker may consume three Miller Lite beers with his coworkers after a tough day at work. This could be described as a relaxation/reward occasion. Successful beer marketers have used this mode of segmentation to strongly associate their brand with the needs of the specific occasion-based segment.

What are Market Segments?

Market segments consist of groups of actual or potential customers that are similar in terms of how they respond to a particular marketing mix. For example, high income, older car buyers may respond well to a high priced automobile, positioned on snob appeal, sold only through exclusive dealerships. Younger car buyers just out of college may respond well to a smaller, fuel-efficient automobile positioned on environmental benefits and sold through dealers that offer a low-pressure selling environment.

Why Segment Markets?

In today's competitive markets, it is difficult to survive by trying to serve all customers in the market. Companies that try to serve the entire market often end up being preferred by no one in the market. Abbott Laboratories, the tenth largest pharmaceutical company in the United States, realized that they couldn't go head-to-head with giants like Pfizer and Merck in all segments of the pharmaceutical market. So Abbott decided to focus their limited research and development resources on several disease states, such as diabetes, cancer, AIDS, and pain management. Abbott has decided to limit its battlefield to these areas where it has strong products and scientific core competencies and not to try to compete in fifteen disease state areas. This focus has helped Abbott maintain strong sales and earnings growth.

Few markets have customers with homogeneous needs, where all customers would be happy with the identical product and marketing mix. Most markets are composed of customers with heterogeneous needs, where astute marketers can

succeed by developing offerings that delight a target segment of the market. Alfred Sloan understood this diversity existed in America when he launched his successful product differentiation strategy at General Motors in 1920. However, a product differentiation strategy is unlikely to be successful in today's marketplace, since it is an "inside-out" view of the company relative to its customers. It looks first inside at the products the company could make, and then hopes the market segments exist to buy them. A strategy likely to be more successful is an "outside-in" market segmentation strategy, where the customers in a market are closely studied and segmented, and then products and marketing mixes are developed to closely meet the needs of target segments.

Effective market segmentation can provide the following benefits:

- Identification of a new market opportunity for current products in segments that are poorly served by the competitors in the market – underserved segments may be found that can be quickly captured by a firm's current products
- Positioning of products effectively to win in a key segment – needs of customers in a key segment may be better met by more effectively communicating the benefits delivered by your product
- Identification of opportunities for new product development – an attractive segment may be found that is not served well by any product offering available in the marketplace
- Identification of highly profitable market segments – smaller, overlooked segments may be uncovered that are not price sensitive and are highly profitable to target

Product Segments – Are They Market Segments?

Many marketers mistakenly refer to **segments of products** as market segments. "Extra strength pain relievers," "light beers," and "luxury automobiles" are sometimes called market segments by business professionals. This focus on the **product** rather than on the **customer** reflects backward, inside-out thinking. That is, it focuses on "what we have" and tries to "sell it to those customers out there."

In the early 1990s, General Motors (GM) made the transition from product-based segmentation to customer-based segmentation. They found that "GM had way too many overlapping products targeting the same consumers and that we weren't doing a very good job of targeting consumers."[4] GM basically redesigned itself to focus products on targeted consumer markets and minimize the cannibalization within the GM product line. GM surveys a panel of over 500,000 car and truck buyers annually over the Internet to understand requirements of each market segment and to track which vehicles buyers in each segment have bought.

---

[4] "Research Department Report," RFL Communications, Inc., August 2002, 1.

Masterful marketers focus on the **customer,** and have adopted outside-in thinking, focusing on the needs and benefits sought by target customer segments.

Ways to Segment Consumer Markets

There are many ways to segment consumer markets, depending on your marketing objective and your financial resources. If your marketing objective is to obtain a more comprehensive understanding of your market, you may decide to segment customers on **benefits sought, needs,** and **usage occasions.** If your marketing objective is primarily product optimization, you may find the most powerful way to segment customers is by the **product and service features** most valued in your product offering. If your marketing objective is advertising strategy development, the most powerful segmentation approach may be on **benefits sought, brand preferences, lifestyles,** and **media usage** of the target customers. If your marketing objective is new product development, you may find that the customer's **reactions to new concepts** and **price sensitivity** is the most effective way to segment customers. Market segmentation is as much of an art as it is a science, and an in-depth understanding of the market and customers is critical prior to undertaking a major quantitative segmentation study.

Many companies segment customers using data that is already available to them, at a very low cost. Perhaps the most common approach is to segment customers by their usage rate (light, medium, and heavy users). Many companies find that 20 percent of their customers represent 80 percent of their sales. Thus, focusing marketing efforts on the heavy users is usually a sound marketing strategy. These **a priori** segmentation approaches have provided effective market segmentation strategies in some cases, but they suffer from the disadvantage that all of your competitors can easily segment the market in a similar way, resulting in fierce marketing battles for the same customers with little differentiation between the companies' offerings. The result is often price warfare.

The alternative approach to segment customers is to invest in a quantitative market segmentation study, involving a survey of customers, to measure attitudes, unmet needs, benefits sought, usage occasions, brand preferences, price sensitivity, and reactions to new concepts. This **post hoc** segmentation approach requires a substantial marketing investment but can often yield powerful and surprising insights into segments of the market. The company can then develop a targeted marketing mix for and delight the customers in the target segment far better than any competitor can.

The following table shows some of the common variables used to segment consumer markets and the four major groupings of these variables. In addition to the a priori and post hoc distinction, market segmentation variables can be **general variables,** which don't directly involve the product category involved, or **customer and product interaction variables,** which are based on attitudes toward brands, usage of brands, benefits sought in brands, and needs satisfied by brands.

Key Decision:
Selecting Segmentation Variables

	GENERAL CUSTOMER VARIABLES	CUSTOMER and PRODUCT INTERACTION VARIABLES
DIRECTLY OBSERVABLE (a priori)	Demographics Geographic Social Class Family Life Cycle	Usage Rate User Status Usage Frequency Stage of Adoption
MEASURABLE THROUGH MARKETING RESEARCH (post hoc)	Values Lifestyle (Psychographics) Attitudes about Product Category Media Usage	Needs Benefits Sought Loyalty Status Usage Occasions Attitudes about Brands Brand Preferences Price Sensitivity Reactions to New Concepts

We will now discuss some of these segmentation approaches and provide examples to illustrate their application to marketing strategy and tactics. We'll begin with a priori segmentation approaches, and then proceed to the post hoc approaches.

A Priori Segmentation – General Variables

Key Decision:
Selecting Segmentation Variables

	GENERAL CUSTOMER VARIABLES	CUSTOMER and PRODUCT INTERACTION VARIABLES
DIRECTLY OBSERVABLE (a priori)	Demographics Geographic Social Class Family Life Cycle	
MEASURABLE THROUGH MARKETING RESEARCH (post hoc)		

Segmentation of customers on easily observed or easily obtained information from customers is called **a priori** segmentation, since customers are segmented **prior** to any formal marketing research information being collected. These approaches to segmentation are a good starting point for understanding your market but should not be your only approach to segmenting customers, since you can expect most or all of your competitors to have the same basic insight.

Demographic Segmentation

Virtually all beer companies are aware of and focus on the demographics of the heavy beer drinker:

Single males aged 21 to 27

This demographic group, without a spouse to keep him out of the bars with his buddies, consumes a disproportionately large amount of suds. Many major brands are targeting this segment with their youthful, "let's party!" advertising, and it is getting difficult to tell one beer ad from another.

While of some utility to beer marketers, demographic segmentation has been extremely powerful recently in the cable TV channel market. Carole Black, president and CEO of Lifetime Entertainment Services, has successfully positioned the Lifetime TV Network as "television for women" and broken away from the pack to become *the most popular cable-television network in prime time* in 2002. Carole tripled the program budget to produce original programs and movies targeted clearly at women, with women often portrayed as heroes achieving against the odds. Roles for women include doctors, police, midwives, or politicians.

The success of Lifetime, the number one cable network, has been noticed by competitors, and imitators have already sprung up: Oxygen and Women's Entertainment (WE). While demographic segmentation was successful for Lifetime for several years, market segmentation strategies based on demographics alone are easily imitated by competitors, such is the case here. These three networks may have to explore more sophisticated segmentation approach (attitudes, needs, benefits sought) to differentiate themselves from the others to compete effectively in the future.

Besides gender, age, and marital status, other demographics that can be useful in market segmentation are income, race, occupation, education level, household income, and size of household.

Geographic Segmentation

Geographic segmentation can be as broad as some multinational corporations dividing the world into four major areas, or as narrow as many newspapers segmenting census tracts by buying power and customizing the newspaper advertising inserts by carrier route. Walgreens customizes the products each of their stores carries based on its geographic location and the consumers in that store's buying area.

One of the best applications of a geographic segmentation and targeting strategy is that of the Applebee's restaurant chain. Applebee's has been highly successful in locating new restaurants in small, rural towns that have no competitive casual dining

restaurants. These small towns, often with as few as 20,000 people, can just barely support one restaurant. Thus, competitors such as Chili's, Ruby Tuesday, and T.G.I. Friday's are reluctant to enter with a second restaurant and locate their new restaurants mostly in the suburbs of large cities. This leaves Applebee's with a captive audience in these small rural markets.

Potential Rating Index by Zip Markets (PRIZM) is a geographic segmentation performed by Claritas, Inc. It uses multiple attributes in a segmentation approach called *geo-clustering*. Geo-clustering results in richer descriptions of segments than traditional demographics because it captures the socioeconomic status as well as psychographics of neighborhoods in similar clusters. PRIZM classifies over 500,000 neighborhoods into one of sixty-two distinct segments called PRIZM Clusters. These clusters take into account affluence, education, family life cycle, degree of urbanization, race, ethnicity, and mobility. The PRIZM clustering is based upon the maxim that "birds of a feather flock together," meaning that people with similar interests and purchasing behavior will tend to live near each other. The PRIZM Clusters can be broken down to ZIP code, ZIP + 4 code and census tract and block, to allow precise targeting tools for direct mail marketers as well as for retailers interested in locating the best location for a new store.

The sixty-two PRIZM Clusters are given descriptive names to increase their utility and to make them easier to remember. Examples are **Blue Blood Estates, Rural Industria, Kids and Cul-de-Sacs, Latino America, Shotguns and Pickups,** and **Back Country Folks.** The Rural Industria cluster is described as follows:

"Young families in heartland offices and factories. Their lifestyle is typified by trucks, *True Story* magazine, Shake n' Bake, fishing trips, and tropical fish. Annual median household income is $22,900."

Marketers with databases of customers with addresses can analyze their sales by these sixty-two PRIZM Clusters to determine in which segments their sales are strongest and where market development opportunities may exist. These "microsegments" also allow marketers to more precisely target diverse segments and neighborhoods, especially with direct mail and newspaper advertising that can be directed to specific neighborhoods. These geographic segments are also very helpful for planning new store locations for national chains like McDonald's and Walgreens.

The Helene Curtis Company, in marketing its Suave shampoo brand, used PRIZM Clusters to identify neighborhoods with high concentrations of young working women. These women respond best to advertising messages that Suave is inexpensive yet will still make their hair "look like a million." Barnes and Noble, the bookstore chain, locates its stores where there are concentrations of *money and brain people,* because they buy a lot of books.[5]

---

[5] Kotler, *Kotler on Marketing,* 78.

Social Class Segments

Consumers can be segmented by their social class, which is determined by occupation and affluence of the household. Seven social classes commonly used are:[6]

- **Lower lower** – Poverty stricken and usually out of work. Dependent on public aid or charity. 7 percent of Americans.
- **Upper lower** – Working at unskilled jobs, with living standards near the poverty level. Often educationally deficient but striving toward a higher class. 9 percent of Americans.
- **Working class** – Average pay blue-collar workers. Depend heavily on relatives for economic and emotional support. Largest segment at 38 percent of Americans.
- **Middle class** – Average pay white-collar and blue-collar workers who live on "the better side of town." They buy popular products to keep up with trends. Aim their children to a college education. 32 percent of Americans.
- **Upper middles** – Career concerned; have attained positions as professionals, independent businesspersons, and corporate managers. Highly civic minded. Are a good market for quality homes, furniture, and fine clothes. Represent 12 percent of Americans.
- **Lower Uppers** – Earned high income or wealth through exceptional ability in the professions or business. Seek to buy the symbols of status for themselves and their children. 2 percent of Americans.
- **Upper uppers** – Social elite who lives on inherited wealth and have well-known families. The Jet Set. Maintain multiple homes and send their children to the finest schools. They are a prime market for jewelry, antiques, homes, and vacations. Less than 1 percent of Americans.

Many companies use this simple social class segmentation approach to choose target segments, including automobile companies, retailers, and leisure activity companies.

Family Life Cycle Segments

Families have gone through fairly predictable life cycles in the past, which changed their purchasing behavior dramatically in different stages:[7]

> **Young-single households** are consumers of vacations, high-end stereos, and home theaters.
> **Young-married-no children** households are consumers of cars and home furnishings.

---

[6] Richard P. Coleman, "The Continuing Significance of Social Class to Marketing," *Journal of Consumer Research* 10, no. 3, December 1983.

[7] William Wells and George Gubar, "Life-Cycle Concepts in Marketing Research," *Journal of Marketing Research,* November 1996.

Young-married-children under six households are consumers of washers, dryers, infant formula, baby food, disposable diapers, vitamins, and toys. **Young-married-youngest child six or over** households are consumers of orthodontia services, clothing, bicycles, pianos, and athletic equipment.

Older-married-with children households are consumers of college educations, tasteful furniture, auto travel, and boats.

Older-married-no children under eighteen are consumers of vacation travel, luxury items, pharmaceuticals, and lasik surgery.

However, the utility of these family life cycle segments has declined somewhat in recent years, due to the emergence of alternative family structures that have added a great deal of diversity to the American landscape. For example, a significant segment for McDonald's is **single parents with children,** who have restaurant needs that are significantly different from the young-married-with children segments.

A Priori Segmentation – Product Specific Variables

Key Decision:
Selecting Segmentation Variables

	GENERAL CUSTOMER VARIABLES	CUSTOMER and PRODUCT INTERACTION VARIABLES
DIRECTLY OBSERVABLE (a priori)		Usage Rate User Status Purchase Frequency Stage of Adoption
MEASURABLE THROUGH MARKETING RESEARCH (post hoc)		

Other information is usually readily available that can be used to segment customers in a very inexpensive manner. This product-specific data includes usage rate, user status, usage frequency, and stage of adoption.

Usage Rate

Virtually all companies segment their customers into light, medium, and heavy users. This is a basic but very important way to segment customers, because in many markets 20 percent of your customers represent 80 percent of your sales.

Unfortunately, since most of your competitors have segmented the market in a similar fashion, it is very difficult to gain any competitive advantage by using heavy users as your primary target market. It is likely that most competitors are focusing on them as well, with a fierce marketing battle for their loyalty waging.

User Status

It is often useful to classify target customers based on the product usage status, such as whether they never used your product, are current users, or are ex-users. To increase your sales, current users are usually the best targets, since it is often possible to obtain a larger "share of wallet" from current customers than it is to convince an ex-user to come back to you.

Toys 'R' Us has classified toy shoppers into four segments based on their frequency of shopping at Toys 'R' Us, how much they want to shop there, and how much they spend.[8] These segments are:

- **Loyals** – the best customers; spend the most; go out of their way to shop at Toys 'R' Us
- **Enthusiasts** – love your store but for reasons of convenience or necessity, still spend more at other stores
- **Marginals** – Shop at your store out of necessity, but would rather shop elsewhere
- **Non-shoppers** – neither shop at or like your store

This allows them to develop different marketing strategies to retain the loyals while growing share among the enthusiasts and the marginals.

Purchase Frequency

Purchase frequency refers to how often a customer purchases a product, regardless of their usage rate. For example, two B-to-B customers may buy the same amount of product annually, but one customer may order weekly while the other customer orders quarterly. It is usually easier and more profitable to deal with customers who buy infrequently in larger lots, due to lower costs in order processing and delivery.

---

[8] Toys 'R' Us Consumer Insights, *Strategic Planning and Business Development Department* (presentation at American Marketing Association Marketing Research Conference, Chicago, September, 2002).

Stage of Adoption

It is often useful to group customers into segments based on the timing of their adoption of innovations, as suggested by Everett Rogers[9] and applied to high technology markets by Geoffrey Moore:[10]

- **Innovators** – the first 2.5 percent to adopt; highly venturesome; risk takers; high tolerance of uncertainty and failure. In high technology markets, they are referred to as "technology enthusiasts" or "techies." They pursue new technology products aggressively, because technology is a central interest in their lives. They are not too concerned with "bugs" in the product, being more concerned with being among the first to use the new technology.
- **Early adopters** – the next 13.5 percent to adopt; judicious; well-respected opinion leaders; successfully use innovation. In high technology markets, they are referred to as "visionaries." They are not technologists, but outgoing people who find it easy to imagine, understand, and appreciate the benefits of a new technology. They derive value from the strategic leap forward that the new technology enables and expect to get a jump on the competition by being the first to implement the new technology in their industry.
- **Early majority** – the next 34 percent to adopt; deliberate; carefully assess the pros and cons. Referred to as "pragmatists," they are driven by a strong sense of practicality and productivity improvement to their existing operations. They are risk averse, recognizing that many innovations wind up as passing fads, and are content to wait and see how others make out before they buy in. They want to see well-established references from other pragmatists. The firms that "cross the chasm" and capture this segment find it is key to substantial growth and profits.
- **Late majority** – the next 34 percent to adopt; skeptical; low tolerance for uncertainty; responsive to social norms and economic necessity. Referred to as "conservatives," they fear high technology and are against discontinuous innovations. They believe in tradition, are not comfortable in their ability to handle high-tech products, and like to stick with things when they work well for them.
- **Laggards** – the last 16 percent to adopt; traditional; suspicious. Referred to as "skeptics," they simply do not want to have anything to do with high-tech products. The only time they ever buy a technology product is when it is embedded inside another product and they do not know it is there, such as a microprocessor within the brake system of a new car.

---

[9] Everett M. Rogers, *Diffusion of Innovations,* 4th ed. (New York: Free Press, 1995).
[10] Geoffrey A. Moore, *Crossing the Chasm: Marketing and Selling High-End Products to Mainstream Customers,* rev. ed. (New York: HarperBusiness, 1999).

For marketers of high-technology products, it is important to recognize that major psychographic differences exist across these five segments, and that these segments respond very differently to new technology products. High-tech marketers need to understand where their market is along the adoption process and make the required changes to their marketing mix to ensure their continued growth. Often, products are upgraded, debugged, made easier to use, bundled with complementary products, and offered at a lower price. Those marketers that stick with the same product and marketing mix that was popular with innovators and early adopters are not likely to "cross the chasm," finding that the early majority rejects their offering due to their different needs and psychographic makeup.

Many have criticized these adoption segments for their inconsistent nature across different product categories and the lack of correlation between the trait of innovativeness and other personality characteristics. Individuals can be innovators in one product category and laggards in another. Thus, caution should be used in generalizing these segments across industries.

Post Hoc Segmentation – General Variables

Key Decision: Selecting Segmentation Variables

	GENERAL CUSTOMER VARIABLES	CUSTOMER and PRODUCT INTERACTION VARIABLES
DIRECTLY OBSERVABLE (a priori)		
MEASURABLE THROUGH MARKETING RESEARCH (post hoc)	Values Lifestyle (Psychographics) Attitudes about Product Category Media Usage	

Powerful new insights on customer segments often arise after quantitative marketing research information is collected from customers and analyzed thoroughly. This process is called **post hoc** segmentation, meaning that customers are grouped into segments **after** marketing research information has been collected from them.

General variables in post hoc segmentation approaches include values, lifestyles, attitudes, and media usage.

Values and Lifestyles

Values and lifestyles segmentation, sometimes referred to as psychographic segmentation, attempts to group people into similar groups based on their activities, interests, and opinions. This segmentation approach reached its peak in popularity in consumer-packaged goods in the 1980s, when most major advertising agencies had their own version of psychographic segmentation. The mantra was: "The better you understand your target customer, the better you can communicate with them."

Values that lie at the core of consumer choices have been described as preferred end-states; as internal principles, standards, and courses of action; and as cognitive representations of social and interpersonal demands placed on people. A common theme among behavioral psychologists is that **values are a central component of the persona that guides consumer attitudes and behaviors.** Examples of values that will impact the banking industry are the degree of risk aversion, consumption versus saving, and debt propensity.[11]

Roper Starch Worldwide has looked at how sixty values vary across consumers in thirty major countries around the world, interviewing 30,000 respondents aged thirteen to sixty-five in their own homes in 2000. While the top ten values were covered in Chapter 1, we will report on the global value segments derived from all sixty values here.

After each respondent reacted to each of the sixty values, cluster analysis was used to group respondents with similar values together. This process resulted in six segments, which Roper Starch named and described as follows:

- **Creatives** are "Renaissance People" who are deeply involved in all areas of life. Their perfect day may involve playing tennis with a friend after work, researching a new car on the Internet, and finally settling down with some jazz music and a good book. Marketers need to challenge their minds and broaden their horizons.
- **Fun Seekers** are "Party People" who stress social and hedonistic pursuits. Their perfect day may involve going to the beach with friends, going to the park for a game of soccer, and then going out for drinks, dinner, and a movie in the evening. Marketers need to entertain them with fun, friends, and fantasy.
- **Intimates** are "People People" who value relationships above all else. Like fun seekers, they are social creatures, but their focus is more on family than friends and their pace more relaxed than energetic. Their perfect day may involve watching an afternoon soap opera on television, chatting with Mom on the phone, and playing a computer game with the kids in the evening. Marketers need to help them relax and enjoy life with those they love.
- **Strivers** are "Workaholics" driven by a desire for status and wealth. They care most about the things that the other segments care least about: ambition,

---

[11] James W. Peltier et al., "Interactive Psychographics: Cross-Selling in the Banking Industry," *Journal of Advertising Research,* March 2002.

power, wealth, and status. They don't have time to play; they are too busy getting ahead. Their perfect day is to work late, come home and watch the news, and check the Internet for stock tips. Marketers need to cut to the chase and tell them what's in it for them without wasting their time.
- **Devouts** are "Traditionalists" who have strong convictions about faith, modesty, duty, and respect for the past. Like Intimates, they are family-oriented, but for them it is more of a responsibility than a pleasure. Their perfect day may involve attending a religious service, preparing a good dinner for their family, and then watching a home improvement show on television. Marketers need to show respect for them and their families.
- **Altruists** are "Humanitarians" who place relatively higher value on social values and the world at large. Their perfect day may involve volunteering at a local nursing home, coming home to make a stir-fry family dinner with vegetables from their garden, then watching a nature show on public television. Marketers need to enrich their lives so they can contribute to the world around them.

Comprehending these segments helps explain actual consumer behavior across many different categories, such as liquor, financial services, technology, media, automotive, and others. For example, Creatives are leading-edge consumers in their enthusiasm for and use of technology, most notably personal computers.[12]

Further, understanding the varying proportions of these six segments on a country-by-country basis can help marketers better allocate their marketing resources to countries with high proportions of target segments.

The most well known approaches to lifestyle segmentation in the United States were developed by SRI International and are known as VALS (Values and Life Styles) and VALS 2. These typologies are based on motivational theories, such as Abraham Maslow's hierarchy of needs, consumers' self-identity, and consumers' financial status. Respondents answer batteries of questions on activities, interests, opinions, personality, and personal values, and then these respondents are grouped into segments with others who have responded to the questions in a similar fashion. The nine VALS segments derived from this approach are:

- *Survivors* – the economically, educationally, and socially disadvantaged. Tend to be older. Represent 4 percent of Americans.
- *Sustainers* – the very poor but hopeful in their outlook. 7 percent of Americans.
- *Belongers* – the conservative, conforming, conventional traditionalists. Their key drive is to fit in and belong. This largest VALS segment represents 39 percent of Americans.
- *Emulators* – the younger, upwardly mobile, ambitious, status conscious people. They emulate the Achiever lifestyle. 8 percent of Americans.

[12] Roper Starch Worldwide, "Re-Mapping the World of Consumers," *American Demographics,* October 2000.

- *Achievers* – the well-educated, well-to-do people who enjoy the material things that life has to offer. Competent and self-reliant. 20 percent of Americans.
- *I-Am-Me* – the young and individualistic experimenters. Tend to be dramatic and impulsive. Represent 3 percent of Americans.
- *Experiential* – the people who want to experience life to the fullest. Seek direct experience and vigorous involvement. Attracted to the exotic and strange. Artistic. 6 percent of Americans.
- *Societally Conscious* – the people whose focus in life is social responsibility. Support conservation and environmentalism. Do volunteer work. Seek to live frugal lives. Represent 11 percent of Americans.
- *Integrated* – the tolerant people who have put it all together and achieved a high degree of psychological maturity. Self-assured, self-actualizing, and self-expressive. This smallest VALS segment represents only 2 percent of Americans.

The VALS system was revised in 1989 to focus more explicitly on understanding and explaining consumer behavior. The VALS 2 framework consists of eight segments: **actualizers, fulfilleds, achievers, experiencers, believers, strivers, makers,** and **strugglers.** These segments continue to be derived by grouping consumers on their general personality traits but are refined using contemporary research on product diffusion.

While these VALS segments are very interesting to marketers, the key to their utility is how well these segments explain differences in product usage and brand preferences in your category. Many marketers have gotten away from off-the-shelf segmentation approaches, like VALS, because they did not differentiate consumers in terms of buyer behavior. Instead, these marketers have developed customized segmentation approaches that include needs and benefits specific to their product category, as well as attitudes toward brands in that category. These segmentation approaches often yield greater insight into customer segments that not only differ on lifestyles but on category and brand usage as well.

Attitudes about Product Category

Customer attitudes toward a specific product category are frequently used to create actionable segments of consumers. Attitude statements can be derived from previous research among category consumers as well as from focus groups or depth interviews. Usually, twenty to twenty-five attitude statements are sufficient in an attitude battery.

Respondents are asked if they agree strongly, agree somewhat, neither agree or disagree, disagree somewhat, or disagree strongly (Likert scale) with each of the attitude statements. Examples of attitude statements for the hair care product category[13] are:

- I know my hair is clean when it smells fresh.
- I refuse to go anywhere when my hair doesn't look right.

[13] James H. Myers, *Segmentation and Positioning for Strategic Marketing Decisions* (Chicago: American Marketing Association, 1996).

- I don't worry about my hair; I just wash it when I have time.
- I just use whatever hair care products are around the house.
- Shampoos with conditioners in them don't provide enough conditioning.

As you imagine how your family members and close friends may respond to these statements, some may agree strongly with many attributes, others might disagree strongly with many attributes, while others may be mixed. This variation from individual to individual is precisely the information used to identify and develop attitudinal segments.

Media Usage

Every segmentation study should include a thorough measurement of the media usage habits of the respondents, including frequently watched television programs, magazines and newspapers read, and favorite Internet websites. Understanding these media habits is critical to help the marketer effectively communicate with target consumers.

These media habits may be helpful as input to the analysis that creates market segments. More important, once market segments are identified and the target segment is selected, this media usage information can be analyzed at the market segment level. This will allow the marketer to select media that are effective in reaching the target customer.

Post Hoc Segmentation – Product Specific Variables

Key Decision: Selecting Segmentation Variables

	GENERAL CUSTOMER VARIABLES	CUSTOMER and PRODUCT INTERACTION VARIABLES
DIRECTLY OBSERVABLE (a priori)		
MEASURABLE THROUGH MARKETING RESEARCH (post hoc)		Needs Benefits Sought Loyalty Status Usage Occasions Attitudes about Brands Brand Preferences Price Sensitivity Reactions to New Concepts

Product specific variables can often provide the most powerful information in a market segmentation study. Understanding customer needs that the product satisfies, understanding benefits sought in the product, or understanding the needs at various usage occasions can often uncover unserved segments that represent a tremendous opportunity for the astute marketer. We will discuss these and other product-specific variables in this section and provide examples of how these segmentation studies have afforded powerful competitive advantages to the company conducting them.

Needs

Needs-based segmentation came into prominence in the 1980s, based on the work of Russ Haley of the University of New Hampshire. The fundamental principle of needs-based segmentation is that the needs people are seeking to satisfy are the basic reasons for the existence of true market segments.

In market segmentation research at Mobil Oil on gas station customers, five distinct customer segments were found, all representing 16-24 percent of gasoline dollar expenditures. These five segments had very different needs when it came to filling their car with gasoline and were named:

- Speedsters
- Soccer Moms
- Car Buffs
- Price Shoppers
- Loyalists

Understanding these five segments in-depth helped Mobil Oil develop effective marketing strategies for their target segments. For example, the Mobil SpeedPass, a small device that fits on a key chain and can be waved in front of the gas pump to charge gasoline, was developed to address the need for speed among the "Speedster" segment. This segment was also known as "3 Fs," since it valued Food, Fuel, and Fast.

Mobil had developed three product options for the Speedster segment: a credit card-shaped device that was carried in the wallet, the key chain device, and a device that could be mounted on the car visor and be read automatically by a sensor near the gas pump. Many top managers at Mobil wanted to proceed to market with the visor-mounted device, since it was passive and, once mounted on the visor, the customer could forget about it. These managers felt that this would be the most preferred option among customers and only reluctantly agreed to delay launch for a market research study to be conducted.

Many at Mobil were surprised when most target customers strongly preferred the key chain device to the other two devices. The credit card device offered few advantages over going into one's wallet for any credit card. The visor-mounted device caused concern among many customers, who worried that their credit card would be charged every time they drove by a Mobil station! These customer insights were only gained when Mobil took the time to get the input of target customers into the three options.

The Mobil SpeedPass has been very successful among the target market. Some McDonald's restaurants even allow customers to charge food using their SpeedPass. Another example of customers "not being rational" and doing something different from what business managers expected them to do!

Benefit Segmentation

A very powerful way to segment consumers is by the benefits sought from the product offering. This will often result in very different customer segments, requiring vastly different products and marketing mixes to compete effectively. The do-it-yourself paint market is a good example of the power of benefit segmentation.

Do-It-Yourself Paint

Companies selling paint to consumers in an undifferentiated manner have focused on generic benefits, such as one coat coverage, durability, ease of application, and color availability. As all paint marketers stressed these important but generic benefits, paint became a parity product category where the low-priced product usually got the business.

Other paint companies who took a more customer centric approach searched below the surface to understand if different segments existed within the do-it-yourself paint market. Perhaps segments that sought different benefits in the painting experience existed that could be targeted with different marketing mixes. To their delight, three highly distinctive segments emerged. Little overlap was found among the benefits sought by these three segments, so this market can be thought of as three distinct submarkets.

The three segments were named **Avoiders, Discriminating Decorators, and Economizers.** We'll describe these three segments briefly here.

- **Avoiders** hate to paint, and will buy the best quality paint to avoid painting again as long as possible. They want paint that is guaranteed to last a long time. An attitude statement that AVOIDERS agree with strongly is "When I paint, I always buy the paint that will last the longest."
- **Discriminating Decorators** are focused on looks, decorating, and styling. They want a wide variety of colors to choose from, custom mixing, and advice on combining colors. An attitude statement that DISCRIMINATING DECORATORS agree with strongly is "It's important that the color of my paint blends with my decorating."
- **Economizers** want a good deal on paint. They hate the expense of painting and will select a familiar brand that appears to be a good deal. An attitude statement that ECONOMIZERS agree with strongly is "I'm willing to buy a different color paint to save a little money."

This simple but neat market segmentation should make it clear how a marketing mix strategy focused clearly on one of these three segments will be more effective than the generic strategy addressing general category benefits.

A review of recent Benjamin Moore Paints advertising, both on television and in magazines, reveals that they clearly understand the DISCRIMINATING DECORATOR segment and are positioning their brand at this segment. Magazine ads show a female decorator in a beautifully decorated room, thanking the Benjamin Moore Color Preview Studio display. "It helped me choose a paint color I love and gave me great decorating solutions. I even found the perfect matching trim color. And my Benjamin Moore dealer gave me helpful hints about finding the right finish." This masterful marketing is an excellent example of strategic market segmentation in action. It is no surprise that Berkshire Hathaway acquired Benjamin Moore Paints for over one billion dollars in November of 2000. Warren Buffett, chairman of Berkshire Hathaway, Inc., said "We are extremely excited about the opportunity to add a company with such an outstanding reputation for quality and leadership in its industry to the Berkshire group." Identifying brands with strong brand equity and investing in them aggressively has made Warren Buffett very wealthy.

Marriott Hotels

Marriott Hotels has conducted thorough segmentation of the hotel market and has used it to serve different market segments and to position their different hotel brands effectively: Ritz-Carlton, Marriott, Courtyard, and Fairmont. These offerings are clearly targeted at different segments of the business and leisure traveler markets, which will minimize cannibalization among the Marriott brands.

An effective method of segmenting customers is based on the utility provided to them by different levels of product or service features and benefits. For example, some customers may be very responsive when the price of an automobile changes in a choice-based conjoint study, while other customers may be most responsive to change in the size of the car. These "feature level driven" segments will be described further in Chapter 6, when product optimization insights are covered and the example of "The Compelling Offer" is given.

Loyalty Status and Price Sensitivity

Many markets include customers who are extremely loyal to one brand in the market, with Harley-Davidson motorcycle owners being a good example. Most Harley riders would rather die than be caught riding a Honda or Suzuki bike. These same markets often include a segment at the other loyalty extreme, a variety-seeking segment, which has low loyalty to any brand because they value the experience of trying new brands continuously. This segment gets bored quickly and derives pleasure from the new experiences that different brands provide. A good example is found in the fast food market, where some customers tire quickly of their Whopper and fries lunch and seek alternative choices continuously.

Loyalty status and price sensitivity are closely related segmentation variables among U.S. beer drinkers. Three segments of consumers have been found among these beer drinkers, when their loyalty status and their price sensitivity are considered jointly. Each of these segments is about equal in size:

- **Brand Loyalists** – Have one favorite brand and usually buy it on all occasions; will switch if in a situation where their favorite brand is not available (e.g., a sporting event)
- **Shoppers** – Have a pool of acceptable brands and usually select a brand from their pool based on price, availability, and variety
- **Price Loyalists** – Like to buy beer at a low price and will stock up on almost any brand that is on sale

Beer marketers are competing feverishly to attract the profitable brand loyal drinkers to their major brands and have developed lower-priced, unadvertised brands for the price loyal segment. It should be noted that markets for most products and services will usually include a sizable price loyal segment.

Brand Attitudes and Preferences

Segments may be developed based on varying attitudes about brands and preferences among brands in a product category. One segment may be found that is loyal to the beer brands from the Miller Brewing Company, drinking mostly Miller Lite and Miller Genuine Draft. Another segment may be found that is loyal to light beers, and drinks only Miller Lite, Bud Light, and Coors Light. It is important to understand these segments, since the competitive set and the marketing tactics are very different for each.

Reaction to New Concepts

Often, the inclusion of new product concepts in a market segmentation study can help cluster consumers into more meaningful and useful segments. By having customers rate their interest in ten to fifteen different new products with varying product features, different segments often emerge, including one or two segments that are not interested in any of the new products, several segments that value different concepts, and one or two segments that are highly interested in many of the new concepts. When used with other variables in the cluster analysis, this segmentation approach often results in meaningful segments for new product development efforts.

Usage Occasions

For some product categories, the **needs and benefits sought** by users vary on different **usage occasions**, and brand usage may be dictated by the externalities of each occasion. For example, the hotel selected by business travelers may be quite different from the hotels selected by the same individuals when they are on vacation. Grouping people into segments only blurs your ability to detect meaningful segments, because the brand choice is often dictated by the occasion, rather than the individual's lifestyle, overall needs, or overall benefits sought.

For these product categories, **occasion-based** segmentation has proved to be quite useful. People are asked to recall one or two recent occasions and to describe

the situation, the benefits sought, the motivations at the occasion, the brand selected, and other key variables. Then these occasions are grouped to develop **occasion-based** segments, which can then be targeted with a marketing mix.

Consider the **import beer** market in the United States. Heineken had been the leading import brand of beer for most of the past century but was recently passed up by Corona. The Gambrinus Company, which imports Corona from Mexico, achieved this success by focusing on white-collar working profession-als, according to Don Mann of Gambrinus.[14] Critical to Corona's rapid growth was a deep knowledge of the needs at beer occasions when imported beers are consumed. Over the past several years, Corona has clearly and consistently positioned their beer as the beer that is perfect when **relaxing** on vacation at a beach and **escaping** the pressures of the everyday world. Relaxation and escape are strong emotional needs among drinkers of import beer, and Corona television commercials execute against these needs beautifully. In one commer-cial, a bottle of Corona and a cellular phone are on a small table on a secluded beach, with the blue ocean in the background. The relaxed arm of the beer drinker is shown throwing flat stones into the ocean so that they skip across the surface of the water. The cellular phone then rings, and without missing a beat, the arm picks up the phone instead of a rock and flings it into the blue ocean, skipping it along the surface. Despite the absence of words in this com-mercial, the images speak legions about how Corona is the perfect beer to have to relax and escape the pressures of your daily life, even if you are not sitting on a beach in the Caribbean.

Tiffany & Co., the high-end jewelry retailer, has effectively used occasion-based segmentation to reposition itself from the jewelry retailer for **special peo-ple**, to the jewelry retailer for everyone on **special occasions**. This strategic marketing shift has maintained a targeted strategy while increasing the number of buying opportunities dramatically.

Which Variables are Best to Use in Market Segmentation Studies?

The previous charts have identified nineteen possible variables that can be used individually or jointly to identify market segments. But it is impossible to include all nineteen variables in a single study and still collect reliable, valid information from respondents. Therefore, the following guidelines may be helpful:

- **Post hoc** segmentation variables are usually more powerful than **a priori** segmentation variables, since most competitors often are already using a priori variables in their marketing. Post hoc variables provide the company with the opportunity to gain valuable insight into the values, lifestyle, needs, and benefits sought by customers.

---

[14] Hillary Chura, "Corona Thirsts for Expansion: Gambrinus Push for 'Extra' Variety Targets African-Americans," *Advertising Age,* 20 August 2001.

- **Product-specific** segmentation variables are usually more powerful than **general** segmentation variables, since they often yield more actionable insights and segments that differ on brand preferences and usage. As mentioned earlier, a segmentation solution that lacks differences in brand usage across the segments is interesting but not particularly actionable.
- Therefore, **post hoc product-specific** variables (lower right-hand corner) are frequently the variables that provide the best **customer insights** and yield strong competitive advantages in the marketplace.

Ways to Segment Business-to-Business Markets

Apple Computer, Inc., has survived in the highly competitive personal computer market by focusing their marketing efforts on several B-to-B segments, such as the education market, graphic designers, and R and D scientists. While their share of the overall market is less than 5 percent, Apple holds strong positions in these target segments.

The major ways that Business-to-Business markets have been successfully segmented are shown in the following diagram.

Key B 2 B Decision: Selecting Segmentation Variables

	GENERAL CUSTOMER VARIABLES	CUSTOMER and PRODUCT INTERACTION VARIABLES
DIRECTLY OBSERVABLE (a priori)	Firm size Industry Location Size of Decision Making Group Centralization of Buying	Usage Rate User Status Order Size Stage of Adoption Length of Relationship
MEASURABLE THROUGH MARKETING RESEARCH (post hoc)	Personality of Decision Makers Customer Corporate Culture Motivations Goals	Needs Benefits Sought Loyalty Status Purchasing Criteria Price Sensitivity

Siemens recently developed a focused strategy on four industries: hospitals, airports, stadiums, and university campuses. Siemens has assigned a single senior-level

manager to each of these a priori industry segments.[15] Unfortunately, this a priori segmentation on general variables is likely to be quickly copied by competitors and neutralized.

B-to-B marketers are also likely to find the most powerful segmentation of business customers when using the **post hoc, product-specific variables:** needs, benefits sought, loyalty status, purchasing criteria, and price sensitivity.

Segmentation on Multiple Variables

It is rare to find a **single** variable that groups your target customers into segments that are meaningful from a marketing standpoint. Usually, the cluster analysis tools that are available can establish meaningful segments looking across multiple variables simultaneously. For example, segments of diabetics could be created by looking at their attitudes about having diabetes, combined with their reactions to new blood glucose-monitoring product concepts. Today's powerful computers combined with cluster analysis software can look for cluster solutions across thousands of respondents and across multiple variables in minutes, a task that was not possible just twenty-five years earlier.

Qualitative First, Then Quantitative

Prior to conducting a quantitative segmentation study, a company is well advised to spend at least one month conducting secondary data searches and performing qualitative research. Focus groups and customer visits often provide a richness of understanding of the customer that will greatly enhance the quality of the segmentation study and reveal new questioning areas to include in the segmentation survey.

Selecting which of the nineteen major segmentation variables to include in the study is a major challenge for marketers. Including too many will lead to respondent fatigue and data of questionable validity. Choosing too few variables may result in missing an important variable that could be a key variable in segmenting customers effectively.

The objectives of the segmentation study, as well as thorough qualitative research, can guide in the selection of the variables to include in the segmentation study. For example, if the segmentation study is being done to guide new product development, some of the key segmentation variables to include are needs, benefits sought, attitudes about product category, and reactions to new concepts.

It is not unusual to conduct ten to twelve focus groups to guide the design and development of the segmentation study questionnaire.

Cluster Analysis

Cluster analysis is the primary analytical tool used in market segmentation and seeks to classify consumers into relatively homogeneous groups based on a set of

---

[15] Kotler, *Marketing Insights from A to Z,* 131.

variables on these customers. Cluster analysis seeks to **maximize** the differences **between** the segments, while simultaneously **minimizing** the differences **within** the segments. Cluster analysis seeks to assign customers to segments so that there will be as much similarity within segments as possible and as much difference between segments as possible, while maintaining a reasonable number of segments to consider.

Most cluster analysis algorithms look for similar respondents to group together by calculating the Euclidean distance between all possible pairs of respondents, and looking for respondents with low levels of variation in their responses across the batteries of questions in the survey. The Euclidean distance between a pair of respondents is a straightforward, simple calculation; it is the square root of the sum of the squared differences in values given by the two respondents to a series of questions. Let's look at a simplified example, where we have asked three respondents to respond to a five-point agree/disagree scale.

	Question 1	Question 2	Question 3	Question 4
Respondent 1	5	3	5	3
Respondent 2	3	1	3	4
Respondent 3	2	1	2	2

The first step in cluster analysis is to look at the Euclidean distances across these three respondents. Let's start by calculating the differences in responses across these respondents.

Differences between R1 and R2 = 2, 2, 2, 1
Differences between R1 and R3 = 3, 2, 3, 1
Differences between R2 and R3 = 1, 0, 1, 2

The next step is to square these differences, because we want to give more weight to large differences in ratings between respondents.

Squared differences between R1 and R2 = 4, 4, 4, 1
Squared differences between R1 and R3 = 9, 4, 9, 1
Squared differences between R2 and R3 = 1, 0, 1, 4

The next step then is to sum these squared differences.

Sum of squared differences between R1 and R2 = 13
Sum of squared differences between R1 and R3 = 23
Sum of squared differences between R2 and R3 = 6

The final step in calculating the Euclidean distance is to take the square root of the sums of the squared differences between respondent's values.

Square root of the sum of squared differences between R1 and R2 = 3.6
Square root of the sum of squared differences between R1 and R3 = 4.8
Square root of the sum of squared differences between R2 and R3 = 2.4

Thus, the Euclidean distance between respondents 2 and 3 reveals that their responses were more similar than the other two pairs of respondents, and respondents 2 and 3 probably belong in the same segment.

While it is fairly easy to see that respondents 2 and 3 had similar answers from the simple example in the previous table, cluster analysis and powerful computers are required to detect these patterns when there are 500 respondents in a study and eighty questions or ratings from each respondent.

With a sample size of 500 respondents in a segmentation study, the solution that maximizes differences between segments and minimizes differences within segments is to create 500 segments of single individuals. With the exception of one-to-one marketers (direct mail), most marketers would find it very tenuous to develop marketing strategies for 500 distinct segments.

At the other extreme, developing one marketing strategy for the entire market based on the responses of all 500 respondents would be rather easy, but probably ineffective. So what is the best number of segments in an effective market segmentation study?

This answer involves both statistical as well as judgmental considerations. Statisticians can calculate the number of segments that explains the majority of variance across respondent's answers and where the point of diminishing returns occurs. For example, a seven-segment solution may explain the majority of variance across respondents, with an eight-segment solution explaining a negligible increase in variance. However, going to a six-segment solution would result in a measurable drop in the amount of variance explained in the respondents' answers. Therefore, the statistical vote is for **seven segments.**

The best statistical solution provides a good starting point for the marketer to examine that and other solutions. Experience has shown that the ability to retain and use segmentation studies diminishes when the number of segments exceeds five or six, so parsimony would suggest examining the best segmentation solutions involving four, five, or six segments. Years of experience and a thorough qualitative understanding of customers will help the marketer select the solution with the highest degree of consistency with what is currently known about the market. Additionally, brand behavior across segments should be carefully examined, because large variations in the brands used across segments reveals that the segmentation structure is "explaining" brand usage behavior. Segmentation studies that reveal constant market shares for all brands across the segments have limited strategic utility for the marketer.

Marketers who have no hypotheses on how the market may best be segmented may want to include many of the 19 variables shown in the first table of this chapter in their segmentation study questionnaire. Caution should be exercised, however,

to properly encourage respondents to provide quality responses to the survey and to keep the survey of reasonable length. Pre-tests of the questionnaire with three to four respondents should be conducted, and these pre-test questionnaires should be thoroughly reviewed to assure that valid, reliable information is being obtained. Respondents to these pre-test interviews should be thoroughly debriefed to understand areas of the questionnaire that were unclear or ambiguous to the respondent.

Cluster analysis should then be conducted using different groupings of questions, and cluster solutions can be examined for statistical soundness and marketing utility. It is not unusual to examine twenty-four different segmentation solutions, with four, five, and six segment solutions for eight combinations of variables included in the cluster analysis.

Which Segment Should Be Targeted?

When the segmentation study is completed and the best segment solution has been determined, the real enjoyment begins. The company then needs to decide which segment they will target; where they are going to focus their scarce resources. If the company has sufficient resources, more than one segment can be targeted. Distinct marketing mixes need to be developed for each targeted segment, however. The biggest mistake made by many companies is going after too many segments with an unfocused marketing mix and succeeding in none of the segments.

The segments need to be profiled on all the data from the survey and carefully analyzed. Only after careful deliberation can the target segment be selected and agreed to by all decision makers within the firm. The selection of the target segment is more art than science, even though much quantitative information is available on each of the segments. The **targeting criteria** to consider in selecting a target segment are:

- **Segment size**
- **Growth rate**
- **Price sensitivity**
- **Profitability**
- **Strategic fit to your company's strengths and image**
- **Operational ability to deliver benefits sought by segment**
- **Strength of your brand in segment**
- **Competitors' strength in segment**
- **Barriers to entry**

The first question upon the completion of a good segmentation study is "how **large** are each of the segments?" This should be expressed in **number of customers** as well as in **unit volume and revenue.** For example, the largest segment may represent 40 percent of customers, but because many in this segment are light users of inexpensive products, represents just 25 percent of the category sales volume and 20 percent of sales revenue. A smaller segment, with many heavy users buying premium-priced products, may represent just 10 percent of customers, but

represent 20 percent of the category sales volume and 25 percent of sales revenue. Thus, it may be a better decision to target the smaller customer segment, because each customer here consumes over three times the amount of a customer in the larger segment.

The second targeting criterion is the measured or estimated **growth rate** of each of the segments. Obviously, growing segments, with all other factors being equal, would be preferred to declining segments.

Segments that are highly **price sensitive** usually make poor targets, because it is difficult to build loyalty among consumers whose primary focus is price. They are likely to switch away quickly to any competitor that undercuts your company in price. However, some companies with operational cost advantages, such as Wal-Mart and Southwest Airlines, have successfully targeted these price sensitive customers.

The fourth criterion in selecting a target segment is the **profitability** of each segment, which combines the revenue represented in each segment less the cost of serving each segment. Occasionally, segments are found that are very expensive to serve. In the diagnostic testing industry, the volume of diagnostic blood testing done on automated instruments in the physician's office segment is large and attractive. Unfortunately, due to the high level of turnover of lab technicians in this segment, the customer service costs and operator training costs in this segment are staggering, making many of these customers unprofitable to have as customers.

A fifth criterion is the **strategic fit of the segment to your corporate strengths and weaknesses.** An ideal target segment will place high value on your strengths, and not care about your weaknesses. If you were Mercedes-Benz, you would want to avoid targeting a customer segment that is focused on an inexpensive automobile with few comfort features. If you are the maker of Sam Adams beer, you would want to focus on beer drinkers who are looking to reward themselves occasionally with a special, fuller-bodied beer.

The sixth criterion is your company's **operational ability to deliver the benefits sought** by the target segment. Wendy's faced a major challenge in the 1980s when drive-through windows created an increased expectation among many of their customers for quick service, since Wendy's restaurants had focused on most customers dining in on their cooked-to-order food.

The seventh criterion for selecting a target segment is the **strength of your brand and competitive brands** in each segment. An ideal segment to target would be one where your brand has a reasonable, established share position (10-20 percent), and no major competitor has a large, dominant share. This would be a segment where you don't face a strong, well-established competitor who is well entrenched. Rather, most users are often using the brand they selected for almost "random" reasons and are usually not loyal to it. Segments that would make poor targets would be ones where you do not have an established position to build on (less than a 5 percent market share), or where a major competitor has a dominant share (40 percent or more), indicating that this competitor is likely to be well positioned among loyal users in the segment.

The final criterion to examine in selecting a target segment is the existence of **barriers to entry** to a segment. Barriers to entry could include:

- The high cost that customers would have to bear to switch to your product, including the cost of the product and customer training
- A competitor locking up most customers in a segment with a five-year purchasing contract
- High brand equity and loyalty to a competitive brand in the segment

While low barriers to entry can be a positive factor when trying to enter a segment, it can turn into a negative factor when trying to defend a segment from competitors.

While many seek a mathematical formula to combine these eight criteria and come up with one "attractiveness" number for each segment, **targeting** defies mathematical summarization and remains an art form. A valuable tool to aid in segment targeting is the targeting matrix, which follows. Wherever possible, actual numbers should be included. For more subjective criteria, such as strategic fit, a +/- system is used, where ++ is very high, + is high, - is low, and - - is very low. A "0" can also be used for a neutral midpoint between high and low.

Segment Targeting Exercise
Which segment would you target?

	Segment 1	Segment 2	Segment 3	Segment 4	Segment 5
Segment Size	35%	25%	15%	15%	10%
Growth Rate	-	+	++	-	++
Price Elasticity	High	High	Low	Medium	Low
Profitability	-	-	+	+	++
Strategic Fit of our Brand	+	-	++	+	-
Our Brand Market Share	18%	4%	12%	8%	2%
Competitive Intensity	High	Medium	Medium	Low	Low
Barriers to Entry	High	Low	Low	Low	Low

Many marketers, focused only on segment size, would instinctively select Segment 1 in the previous example, since it represents over one-third of the market. However, upon closer consideration of all eight targeting criteria, many marketers feel Segment 3 is the best target, because of its high growth rate, the low price sensitivity of consumers in the segment, its high strategic fit, low barriers to entry, reasonable market share for our brand, and decent profitability.

However, the varying circumstances of each firm will dictate differing importance levels on each of the criteria and could result in the selection of a target market as those circumstances change.

Investment Cost

- Four focus groups, conducted by a skilled moderator, including analysis and report, will cost:

  - $20,000–$25,000 in the United States
  - $20,000–$22,000 in France and Japan
  - $17,000–$19,000 in the U.K. and Germany
  - $4,000–$6,000 in China and India

- Twenty depth interviews, conducted by a skilled moderator, including analysis and report, will cost approximately $15,000 – $20,000 in the United States and Japan and $12,000 – $15,000 in major European countries.
- A comprehensive Market Segmentation study of 1,000 target customers (B-to-C), done with a mail survey lasting one hour, with the proper respondent incentive to ensure a good response rate (25 percent or more), will cost approximately $125,000 – $175,000.
- A comprehensive Market Segmentation study of 300 business customers (B-to-B), done with telephone recruitment followed by a mail survey lasting one hour, with the proper respondent incentive to ensure a good response rate (25 percent or more), will cost approximately $80,000 – $100,000.

Market Segmentation Checklist

- Does your firm focus on target market segments or are you a "one size fits all" company?
- Is your company afraid to focus on a target segment for fear that you will be neglecting other customers?
- Does your company rely on the easily collected, a priori method of segmenting customers that is likely also used by all of your competitors?
- Does your company talk about segments consisting of products rather than consumers?
- How well does your company understand need-based and benefit-based market segments?

- Is occasion-based segmentation an approach your company should consider?
- If you are planning for a major market segmentation study, have you allowed time for and budgeted for a qualitative phase prior to the start of the quantitative study?
- Has your company reached agreement on the target segment and segment to serve?
- Did you utilize multiple criteria in selecting a target segment?
- Is your company trying to serve too many market segments?
- How widespread is the knowledge of your target segment(s) throughout the company?
- Are all elements of your mix (product, price, advertising, channels) focused on serving that target segment?

PERCEPTIONS AND DIFFERENTIATION

INSIGHT 5: Successful marketers create brand perceptions in the minds of target customers that differentiate their brand on a key benefit.

"There is no such thing as a commodity. All goods and services can be differentiated and usually are."

Theodore Levitt, in *The Marketing Imagination*[1]

Customer Insight Pyramid

Why Study Customer Perceptions?

While customer perceptions of brands can be hazy and are often less than totally accurate, they still deserve close study by marketers. Customer perceptions need to be studied carefully because these perceptions drive both brand preferences and purchase behavior. Proactive marketers track the image of their brand and attempt to carefully manage customer perceptions of their brand.

---

[1] Theodore Levitt, *The Marketing Imagination,* rev. ed. (New York: Free Press, 1986), 72.

This allows them to differentiate their brand from competitive brands and **position** their brand in the minds of their target customers on key benefits that impact purchase decisions.

Establishing a rich set of associations for a brand over time can produce positive results for the marketer. Philip Kotler illustrates this with clear examples: "We have a richer, more complex set of associations for 'Coca-Cola' and 'Jaguar' than we do for 'Cott' or 'Mitsubishi.' A richer set of associations can increase the ease with which we recall a brand, affect our feelings toward it and affect our price sensitivity. It is hard to justify a price premium for a brand about which we know little."[2]

Volvo is one of the best-positioned car brands, positioned on the SAFETY benefit that is very important to their target market. This differentiation from other car brands has allowed Volvo to avoid competing only on price, as undifferentiated car brands are often forced to compete. BMW has differentiated their "driving machines," being well positioned on the exceptional performance benefit. Michelin Tire ads that show a baby sitting in a tire clearly differentiate their brand on the safety benefit. Frank Perdue successfully differentiated his brand of chicken through a guarantee of tenderness and a brighter yellow color. Perdue brand chicken commands a 10 percent price premium over store brand chicken.

What is Positioning?

Positioning can be defined as *creating a place for your product relative to competitive products in the minds of target customers that meaningfully differentiates your product on a key benefit that impacts purchase decisions.* The key here is that the brand does not reside in the headquarters of the company, but exists in the mind of the customer. Differentiating a brand from competitive brands in the customer's mind is the fundamental task required to avoid becoming a commodity product that can only compete on price.

Unfortunately, recent evidence suggests that more brands are becoming commodities, than are commodities becoming differentiated brands. A recent study conducted by Copernicus and Market Facts revealed that only four of the fifty-one product and service categories studied were becoming more differentiated over time. Ninety percent were **declining** in the degree of differentiation, with banks, bookstores, bottled water, credit cards, and fast food restaurants leading the pack in becoming more similar and having the least brand differentiation.[3]

In this chapter, two major positioning tools will be covered:

- Perceptual maps
- Positioning triangles

---

[2] Philip Kotler and Gregory Carpenter, "Where Do We Go From Here? Changing the Rules of the Marketing Game," in *Mastering Marketing,* Tim Dickson, exec. ed. (London: FT Pitman, 1999), 8.

[3] Kevin Clancy and Peter Krieg, "Surviving Death Wish Research," *Marketing Research,* Winter 2001.

Before we get to the tools, however, let's explore the four levels of product attributes that can impact how consumers perceive our product or service.

The Four Levels of Product

Many authors, most notably Theodore Levitt in *The Marketing Imagination,* have described the consumers' view of the firm's product offering as consisting of four levels: the core (or generic) product, the tangible (or expected) product, the augmented product, and the potential product. These levels are important to understand because it is impossible to differentiate a generic product, although differentiation becomes easier and more effective as you move to the outer rings of the product.

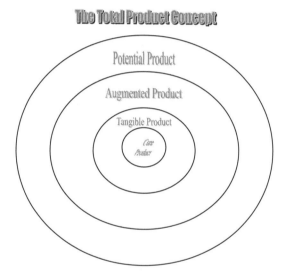

The core product is the basic need that the customer satisfies in buying the product. It is the "hole" rather than the drill bit. Satisfying the customer on the core product is the basic table stakes required to play the game for all competitors. For a car company, the core product is a vehicle that is able to transport people from one place to another. Little opportunity exists for a car company to differentiate itself based on this core product.

The tangible (or expected) product represents the minimal expectations of the target customer. It consists of features, brand name, price level, and quality level. The **expected** car for most customers delivers good gas mileage, has a fair price, has good acceleration, and has a good sound system.

The augmented product offers the customer more than his or her minimal expectations and offers the **strongest opportunity for differentiation**. The augmented product includes enhancements to the tangible product in the form of additional features and services to make the product more attractive versus competitive products,

such as customer training, delivery, warranty, and rapid customer service. Augmented features on a car can include heated seats, navigation systems, CD music players that hold multiple CDs, and DVD players to play movies for children in the back seat.

The potential product consists of everything that is feasible to attract, satisfy and retain customers. Innovative car manufacturers are continually exploring how new technologies can address customer dissatisfiers and problems, working on innovations like systems to slow cars down automatically as the distance from the car ahead reaches a dangerous threshold distance.

Sensation Transference

Consumer perceptions of products can be influenced by more than the physical product itself. Perceptions can also be impacted by marketing cues, such as advertising, brand name, packaging, smell, and the color of the product. When these marketing cues affect how the consumer reacts to the product, which is frequent, we can say that the external stimulus has transferred some sensation to the experience of the physical product itself. This phenomenon of **Sensation Transference** was popularized in the field of marketing by Dr. Louis Cheskin in the United States in the 1930s. In his research, Cheskin found that packaging design and color directly influences consumer perceptions of product performance. Cheskin's consulting work with major American companies helped produce the Gerber healthy baby symbol, McDonald's golden arches, and yellow margarine.

When margarine (also known then as "oleo") was first introduced in its natural white color, acceptance was very slow. Research conducted among margarine triers who had not made repeat purchases revealed that many consumers felt it "just didn't taste as good as butter." Cheskin found that the simple addition of a tasteless yellow food coloring to the white margarine significantly improved the perception of its flavor, moving its taste perception much closer to butter.

The national introduction of Crystal Pepsi in 1993 illustrates the phenomenon of Sensation Transference well. This clear cola had a taste so similar to regular Pepsi that it could not be distinguished from other colas in blind taste tests. However, when cola drinkers tasted Crystal Pepsi and could see the clear color of the liquid, most cola drinkers described the taste as similar to 7 Up and Sprite and different from colas. This conditioning of taste expectations based on the color of the product occurs for other food products as well, including beer. The dissonance created in the minds of soft drink consumers by the clear color of a cola ultimately led to its failure and withdrawal from the market.

Of course, car manufacturers are acutely aware of the impact of a car's color on perceptions and feelings of the car buyer. Red is a popular color among young car buyers looking for excitement and a fast car. Color also impacts perceptions of companies in the e-world. Recent research was conducted on the impact of the color of a company's web page on the imagery of the company and its products.[4] The research found that color is one of the most important design elements of a

---

[4] "Shades of Meaning," *The Wall Street Journal,* 15 April 2002.

web page, capable of conveying different messages and influencing customer perceptions substantially.

This research revealed that the color of the web page has a dramatic impact on customer perceptions of the company itself:

- **BLUE** – the safest and most understood color, favored by tradition-laden companies, such as Ford and American Express; conveys **stability**
- **GREEN** – overused in the early days of the Internet, now underused, its softer shades can produce a **calming effect**
- **RED** – creates attention; signifies **passion, celebration,** and **love**; often used as a call to action in buttons and hot links
- **WHITE** – represents **purity** and **innocence**; produces a cool and refreshing feeling; common in luxury websites
- **BLACK** – conveys dark and negative qualities but also symbolizes **strength** and **reliability**

Many are amazed to learn about the phenomenon of Sensation Transference, and some refuse to believe that something as simple as a color on a web page can impact how customers feel about a company. These skeptics feel that, as rational beings, our conscious mind deals only with concrete, rational stimuli to make judgments and decisions. These skeptics fear that if the Sensation Transference phenomenon is real, marketers can wield tremendous power over them by "manipulating" their thinking and behavior.

Beer marketers have used the color of their packaging to support and reinforce taste attributes for many years. Many major brands, such as Budweiser, have made use of white to reinforce the "cool and refreshing" feeling. Most brands of light beer, notably Coors Light and Bud Light, have made heavy use of silver to communicate cold, drinkable, and refreshing. Taste tests of Coors Light, with the package present and with the package absent, produce different results. With the "Silver Bullet" can in view, the brand is rated higher on attributes such as "light," "smooth," and "refreshing." Guinness Stout uses a black can to reinforce the strong, full-bodied taste of their product.

A major beer marketer has used this Sensation Transference phenomenon to measure the perceptions imparted to a new beer in development by alternative **brand names**. Consumers were recruited to taste three new beers in development, named Sebring, Scandia, and Kuhlbrau. Beer drinkers were asked to taste these three beers on a sequential monadic basis (one at a time in rotated order) and to rate them on a series of attributes and on overall preference. Large, significant differences were found across these three names in this taste test, despite the fact that all three "brands" were poured from the same beer bottle! Brand names can have a significant impact on the taste perceptions of a beer.

Brand imagery studies in Canada for cigarette brands have consistently found that brand names and package designs impact the sensory evaluation of cigarettes. A baseline assessment is developed through a masked evaluation of the test brands where the logos are covered with tape. This serves as the baseline measurement for the product alone. Then, sensory evaluations are obtained in the context of a

name, a package, or both. For example, the name "Du Maurier Special Mild" altered taste perceptions toward a milder product.

Can the Name of a Mutual Fund Affect the Perceptions of Rational Investors?

Mutual funds companies have also found that names of their various funds are critical to the positioning of their funds and to attracting investor money. A study conducted by Michael Cooper and P. Raghavendra Rau of Purdue University and Huseyin Gulen of Virginia Polytech Institute of 296 stock mutual funds between 1994 and 2001 found that funds that changed their name, adding words such as "growth" or "large," attracted 22 percent more money than similar funds that did not undergo a name change. This was found to be true even if the fund name change was purely "cosmetic," without any change at all to how the fund invested money![5]

This study points to the power of a brand name in influencing investor perceptions of the future prospects of a mutual fund. The name of a mutual fund may provide some investors with a shortcut way to invest without having to do their homework on the past performance and investment portfolio of the fund.

The smell of products can also trigger memories and feelings and influence our attitudes and behavior toward such products as ground coffee, shampoo, and new cars. Many coffee stores in shopping malls will actually blow their exhaust fans from their coffee grinders into the mall aisles, "capturing" the coffee drinker through positive memories from their youth and pulling them into the store to purchase their fresh ground coffee. Research has found that emotion is strongly linked to odor memory, and that the sense of smell is often a stronger cue for emotion than visual or verbal stimuli.[6]

The phenomenon of Sensation Transference has important implications to marketers who wish to keep their brand image aligned with the changing needs and preferences of their target consumers. As preferences evolve, changes to the physical product alone may not be as effective as changes to other elements of the marketing mix, such as brand name, package claims, and package color. As more beer drinkers have shifted to lighter tasting beers, most U. S. brewers have reduced the bitterness levels of their products. But they have also put their light beers in silver cans to reinforce, and enhance, the taste perceptions of lightness and smoothness.

Brand Imagery

It is critical that marketers understand how customers perceive their brands and track the **brand imagery** among their target consumers. As consumers connect positive associations to a brand, the brand can develop strong brand equity and command a premium price.

---

[5] "Shades of Meaning."
[6] Michael Bendig, "Fragrance — The Strongest Cue for Emotions," *Research World, ESOMAR,* May 2003.

Brand imagery has multiple dimensions, with **product imagery, user imagery,** and **occasion imagery** being three important components of brand imagery.

- Product imagery attributes describe consumer perceptions of the product experience and their reactions to using the product. Examples of beer product imagery attributes would be light tasting, full-bodied, heavy, and smooth tasting.
- User imagery attributes describe consumer perceptions of the type of person that uses the product. Examples of user imagery attributes for beer brands would be "for people like me," "is popular with my friends," "a brand for blue-collar beer drinkers," and "a brand for people who love to party."
- Occasion imagery attributes describe consumer perceptions of the appropriateness of a given brand for different usage occasions. Examples of beer occasion imagery attributes are "a brand that I would buy for friends in a bar," "a brand for special occasions," and "a brand to quench my thirst on a hot day."

By understanding the perception of a brand on these attributes, relative to key competitive brands, the marketer can fine-tune the image of the brand to be consistent with the expectations and preferences of the target consumer. But analyzing your brand on dozens of attributes relative to numerous competitors can get unwieldy and confusing. This is where **perceptual mapping** can help provide a clear, two-dimensional "map" of the market.

Tool One: Perceptual Mapping

The old proverb that a picture is worth a thousand words is definitely true in the field of Marketing. Perceptual maps are the major marketing tools used to show how brands are positioned in the minds of customers and to help marketers position their products more effectively. Perceptual maps can clearly show the relationships among a number of brands in a two-dimensional picture and help marketers to understand which brands are **perceived to be similar,** to determine which **dimensions** consumers use to differentiate brands, and to **identify gaps** in the market that may represent opportunities for new products. They are also very helpful to marketers who are attempting to reposition a mature, declining brand.

Perceptual maps utilize proximity measures among different brands, obtained through customer surveys, as input. To create a perceptual map, the marketer usually identifies ten to fifteen key attributes through qualitative research that impact brand perceptions in the product category. Customers are then asked to rate eight to ten brands on those attributes. Then, using multidimensional scaling (MDS) techniques, or factor analysis techniques, these ten to fifteen attributes and eight to ten brands are plotted in a two-dimensional space. These statistical programs operate by finding the "best fit" of the brands on several important dimensions,

where quality of fit is determined by how well the distance between the brands on the perceptual map matches the distances in the respondent's original ratings of brands on attributes. While some of the original distances are compressed, this disadvantage is offset by the advantage of being able to visualize a market in a two-dimensional space.

Let's take the U.S. beer market as an example. Beer drinkers were asked to rate a number of brands on product imagery attributes as well as user imagery attributes. Typically, a five-point scale is used, with a 5 representing "strongly agree" and a 1 representing "strongly disagree." The attributes included:

- Heavy
- High quality
- Smooth tasting
- Darker in color
- Good tasting
- Strong tasting
- Pleasant aftertaste
- Smooth tasting
- Full-bodied
- Would buy for friends at a bar
- Popular with my friends
- Can drink a lot of at one time
- A brand to drink anytime
- For someone like me
- A brand for special occasions

After obtaining ratings of all brands on these attributes, the statistical program looks for underlying factors or dimensions that can summarize these fifteen attributes in the two-dimensional space. Clearly, some of these attributes are similar and describe the same underlying phenomenon. For example, "darker," "strong tasting," and "heavy" were attributes that all rated similarly for a given brand. Therefore, the statistical program collapsed these individual attributes into a dimension that was named **"beeriness."**

A second dimension was also uncovered. Attributes like "popular with friends," "for someone like me," "can drink a lot of at one time," "smooth tasting," and "good tasting" were rated fairly similarly for a given brand. These attributes were collapsed into a factor that was named **"popularity/drinkability."** These two factors captured almost 80 percent of the variance in attribute ratings across brands. In nonstatistical language, this means that these two dimensions captured most of the differences that beer drinkers perceive across these brands.

The map with these two dimensions follows. The dimension that captures the most variance is usually shown horizontally, in this case, the "beeriness" attribute.

Perceptual Map of U.S. Beer Market

Two Dimensions Explain Most of the Differences Among Brands

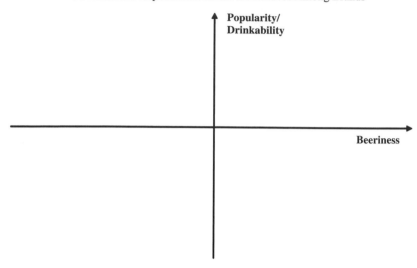

Prior to the introduction of light beers in the mid-1970s, the beer market looked like this:

Perceptual Map of U. S.Beer Market

Brand Positions Prior to Launch of Light Beers

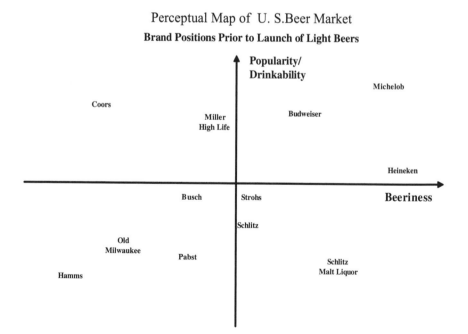

Michelob held a desirable position in the beer market, with no competitor in its "space." Michelob was perceived as the best American beer, highly popular, and having an excellent balance of beeriness and drinkability. Its position in the beer market became a target for imported beers, such as Heineken and Corona.

The fastest-growing beer brand in the early 1970s, however, was Coors, which had a unique position in the beer market and was well positioned among many new beer drinkers who wanted a less "beery," drinkable beer. The macro trends in beverages at that time were moving lighter, resulting in many beer drinkers shifting toward the Coors position in the beer space. Coors was delighted by this growing popularity, even though they weren't quite sure why it was happening. This strong position held by Coors became the target space for Miller Brewing Company as it developed Miller Lite.

The following map shows how successful Miller Lite was in positioning itself in beer drinkers' minds as similar to the fast-growing Coors brand. It achieved this not only through the taste of the beer itself but also by an excellent positioning strategy and outstanding advertising. The positioning strategy will be discussed later in this chapter.

Perceptual Map of U. S. Beer Market

Brand Positions AFTER the Launch of Light Beers

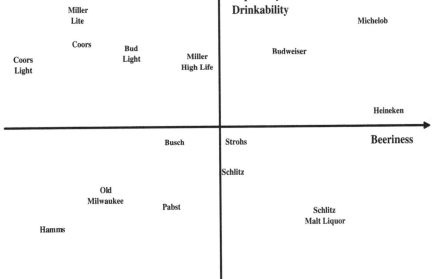

Note the interesting position of Coors Light, as the "lightest of the lights." This differentiated position has been a key to the strong growth of this brand, making the brand highly popular among beer drinkers who want to drink a good-tasting

beer but don't want a strong beer taste. Additionally, Coors Light is perceived as a beer that is lower in alcohol, which is a powerful benefit for beer drinkers, many of them female, who want to drink beer but remain "in control."

Another method of producing perceptual maps is multiple discriminant analysis, which produces multiple dimensions on the perceptual map. The following is a good example of a map with multiple dimensions, for pain relieving products. Dr. Marshall Rice, chief statistician of SurveySite (http://www.suverysite.com), recommends this technique over the others because it produces maps he feels are most easily interpreted.

In the vector map that follows, the length of each attribute vector indicates how well that attribute differentiates between the brands. The map shows that pain relievers are distinguished in two major ways: **gentleness** and **effectiveness.**

The angle between the lines provides important information as well. The size of the angle reflects how strongly correlated the attributes are to each other. "Long lasting" and "effective" have a small angle, meaning these attributes are highly related to each other. If attributes are at right angles, such as "gentle" and "reasonably priced," it means there is little relationship between them. If they are opposing, like "long lasting" and "reasonably priced," this means they have a negative correlation; as one increases, the other decreases.

Pain Reliever Perceptual Map

Multiple Discriminant Analysis Produced Six Dimensions
Source: www.surveysite.com

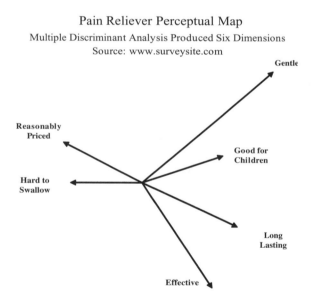

If we now look at the same map with the brands positioned on it, we can see how brands are perceived by consumers on the attributes. As a brand moves out on an attribute and away from the center, the perception of a brand possessing the attribute increases. For example, Tylenol is perceived as gentler than any other brand. Bayer is perceived as the most reasonably priced product.

You can also see which brands are perceived as similar and compete with each other, such as Tylenol and Motrin, which are very near each other on the map. There is likely to be a good deal of brand switching between these two brands, as the map shows them to be almost interchangeable in the mind of the customer.

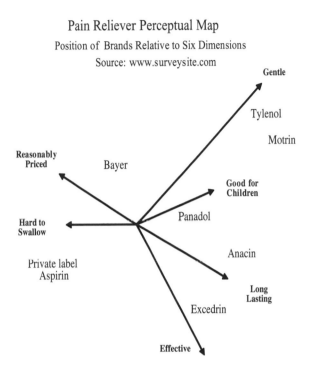

Pain Reliever Perceptual Map
Position of Brands Relative to Six Dimensions
Source: www.surveysite.com

While perceptual maps can be developed using all customers in a market, they are usually more useful when developed for one or more target customer segments. Interesting and meaningful differences are often found in brand perceptions across customer segments, which can allow the marketer to position the brand powerfully among consumers in the target segment.

Perceptions Among B-to-B Customers

Understanding the perceptions of target customers in the B-to-B environment is also very powerful for the strategic marketer. Perceptions should be collected from target customers for your company and all key competitors on the key attributes customers use to compare companies. Research has shown that B-to-B customers tend to evaluate their suppliers along four broad dimensions:

- **The product/service and its price**
- **The company and its policies**
- **The sales representative**
- **The service support**

The **product** (or **service**) itself and the **price** charged are very important in differentiating B-to-B products, but increasingly products are becoming more similar in the minds of customers, and the other three dimensions are playing a larger role in setting a company apart from its competitors. Take Caterpillar, a company that manufactures large earth-moving equipment. During the 1990s, Caterpillar faced strong competition from Japanese companies who were making products of similar quality but selling them for approximately 25 percent below the price charged by Caterpillar. Rather than joining in a price war with competitors, Caterpillar successfully differentiated itself with exceptional customer service, which included a service guarantee that was highly valued by customers who couldn't afford to have broken down equipment that delayed expensive projects. Caterpillar guaranteed parts delivery to any place in the world within twenty-four hours and has successfully defended its market position despite a significant price premium. Caterpillar understood the importance of the **augmented product** to its worldwide customers.

Characteristics of the **company and its policies** that result in strong ties with customers are familiarity, financial soundness, leadership competence, and corporate social responsibility. Financial soundness is important because customers do not want to go through the effort of developing a business relationship with a supplier that may be lost or undermined because of financial weakness.

Characteristics of the **sales representative** that contribute to a strong relationship are familiarity, expertise, customization capability, similarity, empathy, likeability, trust, and the salesperson's power within his or her organization. Many companies underestimate the importance of nurturing and maintaining strong relationships between their sales representatives and their customers, since this relationship can enhance customer loyalty to a company. Companies that frequently reorganize sales territories or move sales reps between territories often are weakening a key customer connection and many times see a decline in customer loyalty rates and sales. Enlightened marketers encourage those sales reps that want to remain in a familiar territory to do so and develop career paths for these sales reps that allow them to get promoted within the sales organization without having to say good-bye to valuable customers.

Tool Two: The Positioning Triangle

Of all the tools in the strategic marketer's toolbox, *positioning* often has the single largest influence on the consumer's buying decision. Positioning is the "art" of marketing, given that there are many ways to position a brand in the mind of the customer. Kotler has identified seven possible sources for positioning a brand: (1) attribute positioning, (2) benefit positioning, (3) application positioning, (4) user positioning, (5) competitor positioning, (6) category positioning, and (7) quality/price positioning.[7]

---

[7] Philip Kotler, *Kotler on Marketing: How to Create, Win, and Dominate Markets* (New York: Free Press, 1999).

Alice Tybout and Brian Sternthal of the Kellogg School of Management have done breakthrough work on the "art" of positioning. They have found that "successful positioning involves **affiliating** a brand with some category that consumers can readily grasp, and **differentiating** the brand from other products in the same category." They refer to this as **competition-based positioning.**[8] The positioning model of competition-based positioning follows.

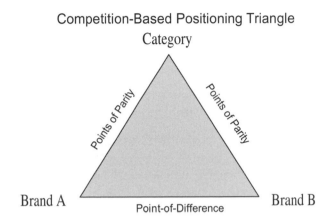

The preferred approach to positioning is to inform consumers of the brand's category membership before stating its point-of-difference relative to other brands in the category. For established brands, category membership is often obvious and may not require deliberation. The point-of-difference is often a benefit that is important to target customers, one that clearly distinguishes it from competitive brands.

Position on Customer Benefits, Not Product Attributes

Many companies mistakenly assume that if they position their brand on a **product attribute** rather than a **customer benefit,** rational customers will figure out the benefit for themselves. This naïve assumption reflects a product-focused orientation rather than a customer-focused orientation. Successful marketers make the differentiating benefit explicit to customers. Take FedEx as an example. Their current four-word slogan, "The World On Time," clearly communicates two important benefits to target customers: "global reach" and "on-time delivery." A product attribute positioning of "We Have More Planes Than Anyone" would have fallen well short of differentiating them on a benefit important to target consumers.

---

[8] Brian Sternthal and Alice Tybout, "Segmentation and Targeting," in *Kellogg on Marketing,* ed. Dawn Iacobucci (New York: John Wiley and Sons, 2001), 50.

Tybout and Sternthal point out that the strongest positions are ones in which a brand has a clear point-of-difference on a benefit that **prompts category use,** and recommend that category leaders utilize this key benefit and preempt competition by outshouting them on this benefit.[9]

Let's look at how Miller Lite utilized this positioning model at their launch in the mid–1970s.

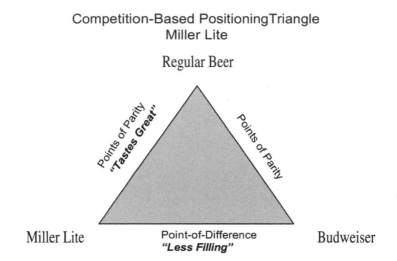

Competition-Based PositioningTriangle
Miller Lite

Regular Beer

Points of Parity
"Tastes Great"

Points of Parity

Miller Lite

Point-of-Difference
"Less Filling"

Budweiser

To **establish membership** in the regular beer category and distance itself from prior diet beers, which tasted awful, Miller Lite effectively used the "tastes great" point of parity benefit. Macho male ex-athletes supported this tastes great benefit by enjoying the beer in humorous situations. To **differentiate itself** from other established beer brands, such as Budweiser, Miller Lite effectively used the "less filling" point-of-difference benefit. This less-filling benefit was supported by the fact that the brand had "one-third fewer calories than our regular beer."

In many of their commercials in their first seventeen years with this campaign, two macho beer drinkers would argue over the reason that more people were drinking Miller Lite. One would argue "Tastes Great," while the other would argue "Less Filling." This successful campaign, grounded in a solid competition-based positioning strategy, is considered by many advertising experts as one of the most effective advertising campaigns of all time. Now, let's turn our attention to an example of weak positioning.

---

[9] Sternthal and Tybout, "Segmentation and Targeting."

ZIMA – What is it?

Coors Brewing Company launched Zima, a clear malt beverage, in the late 1980s. It was one of the first beverages in a product category that became known as "flavored malt beverages" among beverage marketers. But did customers understand Zima's category membership?

Zima was clear, came in a unique bottle, and had a unique taste described by some as a "lighter-tasting gin and tonic." The advertising campaign stressed that Zima was "Zomething different," and intentionally avoided establishing to which category of beverages Zima belonged. This curiosity building, teaser approach led to high rates of customer trial of Zima, as many consumers were anxious to try the new beverage and determine if it was like a beer, or like a wine cooler, or like a mixed alcoholic drink, or like "zomething" else. But because the taste was rather unique and Zima did not position itself properly, many consumers could not figure out what Zima was, became confused, and did not position Zima on any relevant dimensions in their mind. This lack of a position in the mind of the customer led to most of the Zima triers never buying Zima a second time and forgetting about it. Consumers simply didn't know how to position Zima on the beverage map in their minds, and it failed to establish a meaningful connection. Failure to establish category membership can be fatal.

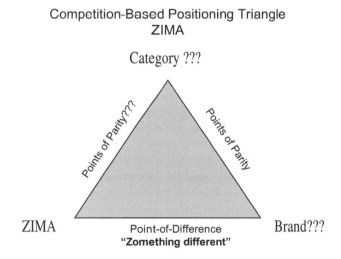

Competition-Based Positioning Triangle
ZIMA

Goal-Based Positioning

Tybout and Sternthal also point out that for sustained success, marketers need to link the brand to customer goals, which they refer to as **goal-based positioning.** Laddering is often used to associate attributes to functional benefits, then to emotional benefits, and finally to customer goals, or the **brand essence.** Tybout and Sternthal caution marketers to limit the number of benefits that are made **focal** in the positioning strategy and to avoid positioning by committee, on multiple

benefits. Processing a benefit of a brand requires substantial cognitive resources on the part of the target consumer. Further, claiming multiple benefits can confound consumers' efforts to define what the product is.[10]

Four "Ds" of Successful Positioning

Tybout and Sternthal have studied the successful positioning strategies of many brands and have proposed the four "Ds" of effective brand positioning.[11] The four Ds are:

- **Definition** – make it clear to your target market what your brand stands for and what category your brand is in.
- **Differentiation** – communicate a compelling point-of-difference.
- **Deepening** – over time, you must deepen the **connection** of your brand to the goals and values of target customers, with every element of your marketing mix designed to support your positioning efforts.
- **Disciplined Defense** – don't overreact to the actions of competitors by abandoning your positioning strategy; if you change your strategy too often, customers will become confused about what your brand stands for.

Successful brands carve out a strong space in the minds of their target customers and strengthen that position over time, not overreacting to the actions of competitors. Michelin Tires has a strong position as a quality tire that will keep your family safe and has continued to deepen this positioning over time.

Successful marketers use **perceptual maps** to understand how consumers perceive brands and to determine which attributes and benefits differentiate brands from one another. Successful marketers then develop **positioning strategies** with this knowledge to meaningfully differentiate their brand from competitive brands in the minds of target customers on benefits that drive category usage. Successful marketers deepen the connection of their brands with the goals and values of target customers. Successful marketers grow winning brands profitably.

Investment Cost

- Four focus groups, conducted by a skilled moderator, including analysis and report, will cost:

  - $20,000–$25,000 in the United States
  - $20,000–$22,000 in France and Japan
  - $17,000–$19,000 in the U.K. and Germany
  - $4,000–$6,000 in China and India

---

[10] Sternthal and Tybout, "Segmentation and Targeting."
[11] Sternthal and Tybout, "Segmentation and Targeting."

- A quantitative consumer perceptual mapping study, involving a nationally representative sample of 300 consumers, screened by telephone and then interviewed by a mail survey, will cost approximately:
  - ○ $35,000–$45,000 in the United States
  - ○ $30,000–$40,000 in Japan
  - ○ $25,000–$30,000 in the U. K. and France
  - ○ $20,000–$25,000 in Germany and Italy
  - ○ $5,000–$7,000 in China

- A Business-to-Business perceptual mapping study, involving a telephone survey lasting fifteen minutes, among 200 business executives, where the sampling list is provided to the research firm, would cost:

  - ○ $37,000–$43,000 in the United States
  - ○ $26,000–$30,000 in the U. K. and Japan
  - ○ $20,000–$25,000 in Germany
  - ○ $9,000–$12,000 in Italy

Perception and Differentiation Checklist

- Do you mistakenly believe your product is close to being a commodity where differentiation is almost impossible?
- Do you disregard customer perceptions because your customers are not as technically knowledgeable as your employees and because their perceptions are not precisely accurate?
- Do all elements of your marketing mix, including product, name, advertising, package color, and price, work together to deepen your positioning?
- Do target customers clearly understand the product category in which your brand is competing?
- Do you have a compelling point-of-difference from other brands in that category?
- Have you explored augmented product benefits and potential product benefits for meaningful points of differentiation?
- Have you limited the number of benefits you communicate to customers to keep your brand focused?
- Have you developed perceptual maps for each of the market segments you are targeting?
- Do you own a unique space on the perceptual map of your product category, or are you in a crowd with other undifferentiated brands?
- Is your location on the perceptual map a desirable one, or should you strive to reposition your brand over time?
- Are there holes in the perceptual map that may represent opportunities for new products?
- Do you remain committed to your successful positioning strategy, defending it from others in your company who want to change it frequently?

CRITICAL FEATURES

INSIGHT 6: The most successful product offerings are those that focus on delivering only those features that have the most impact on customer purchase decisions.

"The integration of marketing research into new product development and marketing is part of our hybrid culture at Nokia. The role of marketing research is to deliver foresight that is actionable."

John Markham, Director of Global Marketing Research,
Nokia Mobile Phones

Customer Insight Pyramid

Creating Better Products

Theodore Levitt, one of the thought leaders and pioneers in the field of marketing, offered this sound advice on the imagination required of effective marketers:

> The purpose of a business is to get and keep a customer. Without solvent customers, there is no business. Customers are constantly presented with lots of options to help them solve their problems. They don't buy things, they buy solutions to problems. The surviving and thriving business is a business

that constantly seeks better ways to help people solve their problems. To create betterness requires knowledge of what customers think betterness to be. This precedes all else in business. The imagination that figures out what it is, imaginatively figures out what should be done, and does it with imagination and high spirits will drive the enterprise forward.[1]

But how do companies determine how to **"create betterness"** in their products without over-featuring products? This chapter will explore methods for determining which are the key features that drive customer decisions and which are the "nice to have" features that customers really don't want to pay for.

Studies on new product development have shown that the single biggest factor in the failure of new products is poor product definition, which is directly related to the ability of the firm to discover and synthesize customer input. "The best companies are skilled at conducting more thorough, in-depth customer interviews and visiting customers at their sites, with more functions from their company involved. Other companies tend to define product attributes to match the company's core competencies, rather than providing what the customer really wants. The incontrovertible evidence demonstrates that, during the fuzzy front end of product development, the logical focus and starting point must be the consumer. The process of identifying customer value attributes for any product must be a disciplined one."[2] Thus, starting with a disciplined exploration of the overt AND latent needs and desires of target consumer can significantly increase the probability of new product success.

Philip Kotler proposes that there are only three ways that a company can deliver more value than its competitors: charge a lower price, help the customer reduce other costs, or add benefits that make the offer more attractive.[3] This chapter is all about the third option, **delivering the optimal feature and benefit package** to target customers to make your product preferred over competitive offerings. Top management commitment to providing superior value to target customers does not mean giving them everything that they want; it involves developing a "package" of features and benefits at an attractive price that is preferred by target customers over competitive "packages."

The Product Developer's Dilemma

In deciding how many and which features to include in a product, product developers face a challenge that the author has named the **product developers dilemma.** It is unwise to overload products with features that drive up prices, when they provide little value to customers. On the other hand, products that lack

---

[1] Theodore Levitt, *The Marketing Imagination,* rev ed. (New York: Free Press, 1986), xxii.

[2] Sheila Mello, *Customer-Centric Product Definition: The Key to Great Product Development* (New York: AMACOM, 2002), 18–19.

[3] Philip Kotler, *Kotler on Marketing: How to Create, Win, and Dominate Markets* (New York: Free Press, 1999).

important features will find few customers interested in purchasing them. Thus, the product developer's dilemma is as follows:

- If you optimize **all** product features to meet customer needs, you will have a product that few customers *can afford to buy.*
- If you optimize **few** product features to meet customer needs, you will have a product that few customers *will want to buy.*

The key is to identify and optimize those product features that have the strongest relationship to target customer purchase interest. Then the optimal "bundle of features and benefits" can be delivered to target customers. Enlightened marketers utilize indirect, trade-off techniques to identify these highly desired product and service features and launch products that their sales-people find to be very easy to sell in competitive markets.

The Kano Model

Professor Noriaki Kano developed a model in the early 1980s to help product developers understand the impact of different product features on customer satisfaction. This model has become known as the Kano model.[4]

The Kano model recognizes that the fulfillment of different customer requirements do not have the same impact on customer satisfaction. The Kano model conceptualizes the impact of fulfilling the product feature requirements on customer satisfaction as taking on one of three mutually exclusive types, as shown in the following model.

Kano Model

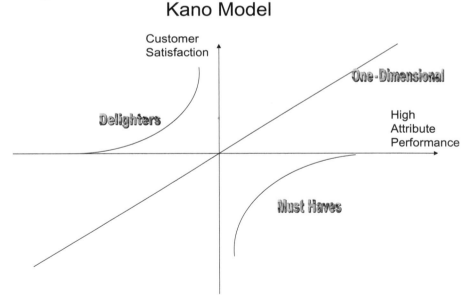

---

[4] Noriaki Kano, et al., "Attractive Quality and Must-Be Quality," *Quality* 14 no. 2, (Tokyo, Japan, Society for Quality Control, 1984).

"Must Haves" are features that represent the minimum requirements to participate in the market. If performance is low on these attributes, customer satisfaction drops dramatically. However, as performance meets and exceeds the threshold, increased performance does not further increase customer satisfaction. Think of the rear view mirrors on a car. Without any mirrors, customer satisfaction is likely to drop, since consumers have come to expect an interior mirror and two exterior mirrors on their car. However, putting six mirrors on the car is unlikely to increase satisfaction much beyond that found with three mirrors.

"One-dimensional" features are those that have a positive, linear impact on customer satisfaction. A good example of this is the gas mileage delivered by the car; the higher the miles per gallon, the higher the satisfaction.

"Delighters" are features that do not currently penalize companies that do not provide them, but can reward companies that introduce them and delight their customers. They are disproportionately powerful in impacting customer satisfaction for your product. They provide a window of opportunity for innovative companies that know how to anticipate, identify, and satisfy latent or undermet customer needs. An example of delighters is heated seats, especially in the northern regions of the United States.

The Kano model is a useful framework to help companies devise product strategies, because it helps them understand the "table stakes" of competing in a market as well as which features will allow them to add extra value to customers. This can allow them to assess how much of their developmental resources should be put behind different features. It helps firms understand which features can satisfy and delight customers, thereby allowing companies to offer a base model (bronze), premium models (silver), and super premium models (gold). Gold models will be innovative and include "delighter" features, allowing the company to charge a premium price above other products on the market.

Over time, however, these "delighters" will shift down the Kano chart and become "one-dimensional." Later, they will shift further and become minimum requirements. What delights customers today will be a minimum requirement tomorrow. Think of overnight package delivery. When FedEx introduced this service, it was delightful to be able to ship packages overnight to customers and have them arrive the next morning. This fantastic service really pleased customers, who raved about this rapid delivery service. Today, overnight package delivery has come to be expected performance by many customers for all deliveries.

In *Managing Customer Value*,[5] Bradley Gale takes this idea of attribute life cycles several steps further. Gale identifies seven stages in the life cycle of an attribute:

1. **Latent** – the need for the attributes is not yet apparent
2. **Desired** – the need for the attribute is known but not currently supplied
3. **Unique** – only one pioneer delivers the attribute well

---

[5] Bradley T. Gale, with Robert Chapman Wood, *Managing Customer Values: Creating Quality and Service that Customers Can See* (New York: Free Press, 1994).

4. **Pacing** – one provider is the clear leader on delivering the attribute but others chase
5. **Key** – differences in performance on the attribute determine competitiveness
6. **Fading** – all suppliers start to catch up
7. **Basic** – attribute is a minimum requirement

While attributes often took many years to progress through these stages in the past, the rapid pace of technology can now transform a latent attribute into a basic requirement in a much shorter time. An example is the ability to take a photograph with a cellular phone and send it to a friend. This once latent need is rapidly becoming a basic, minimum requirement for cellular phones; in 2004, half of all cell phones produced were expected to include this **key** feature.

Usability Testing

Usability testing is a powerful tool to collect customer input, usually during the early development phase of a new or upgraded product. It grew out of early human factors research that focused on how to best design instrument panels for Air Force fighter pilots.

Usability testing is different from other marketing research techniques in that it is the only technique focused on examining the interaction of the consumer and the product. Usability testing involves asking real customers, and not expert employees, to try out new products while they are being developed to assess their ease of use and user-friendliness. Usability testing is very effective in diagnosing exactly why a product is rated as hard to use and to evaluate several possible solutions to user difficulty problems.

Dr. Edward McQuarrie has found that usability testing is an excellent tool for software designers to test their "mental models" of how customers will use the software product. "Implicit in your design is a mental model of how users will interact with your software. Usability studies provide a way to test whether your model is correct by observing what happens when users actually attempt to use your product. Where do they make mistakes, and what kind of mistakes occur? Where do they get confused or become hesitant?"[6]

McQuarrie has found that usability testing is most beneficial for novel, complex products, and adds two corollaries:

• Any software-driven product is by definition complex.
• Novelty and complexity compound one another's effects.

Companies need to remember that their new products are not novel or complex to their internal product developers, but may be so to their target consumer, whose view of new technology products is "Oh no! Not another product to figure out!"

---

[6] Edward F. McQuarrie, *The Market Research Toolbox: A Concise Guide for Beginners* (Thousand Oaks, Calif.: Sage Publications, 1996), 132.

The Dental Products Division of 3M utilizes mannequins, with human-like mouth features, to test new products in development. Dentists are recruited to perform simulated procedures and dental operations on these mannequins to evaluate prototype hardware products and materials. This is one of several methods used by 3M Dental Products Division to gather customer input during the "fuzzy front end" of the new-product development process.

Beware of Creeping Featurism

Usability testing is also used heavily by computer software developers to test how consumers use new versions of software. Usability testing is also heavily used to test websites during their development. The product developer often sits next to the customer during the usability session, observing the customer using the product, detecting any problems the consumer may experience, and asking questions as needed. An excellent book on this topic was written by Donald Norman, called *The Design of Everyday Things*.[7] In this usability classic, Norman talks about how usability testing can help avoid one of the deadly temptations of the new product designer: **creeping featurism.**

Creeping featurism is a disease, fatal if not treated promptly. It is the tendency to add to the number of functions that a product can do, often extending the number of features beyond reason and adding high complexity to the operation of a product. With an overly large number of special-purpose features, there is no way that a product can remain usable and easily understandable to the typical customer. An example of a product that suffered from creeping featurism was the Iridium global satellite telephone, which came with an instruction manual 220 pages long when it was launched in November 1998. The Iridium system achieved just 1 percent of the target of one million customers in the first year before going bankrupt.

The best cures for creeping featurism are to practice preventative medicine, using great restraint to avoid overcomplexity, or to make any new features invisible to the average consumer. Usability testing, where the technical product designer can interact with typical nontechnical customers, is an excellent process to allow companies to practice this preventative medicine during the early stages of product design.

Dell Computer prides itself in its **customer experience** strategy, which puts the customer at the heart of everything the company does. Dell involves customers early and often in the new product development process, recording customers on video as they use computer products. Dell observes customers in their usability lab to determine how to make their computers easier for the consumer to assemble and use. Michael Dell credits the customer experience strategy as a key element in the phenomenal success of Dell Computer in the 1990s: "When you engage directly with your customers, you begin to develop an intimate

---

[7] Donald A. Norman, *The Design of Everyday Things* (New York: Doubleday, 1990).

understanding of their likes, needs and priorities. You find out what's working for them–and why."[8] Further, "The challenge in any business is finding a perfect match between what your customer wants and what you can produce. If you're constantly getting feedback from your customers about what they're buying, what their preferences are, what their needs are, and how well you're doing to meet those needs – and you're willing to listen – you can make the most of the opportunities implicit in those needs."[9]

Michael Dell, like many customer-focused leaders, spends about 40 percent of his time with key customers. When people ask him why he spends so much time with customers, his response reflects his classic marketing orientation: "I thought that was my job."[10]

Usability testing is a very helpful qualitative tool in the fuzzy front end of new product definition. But further on in the process, major decisions need to be made on the inclusion or exclusion of major, expensive product features. For these decisions, large samples of target customers are needed to conduct quantitative feature trade-off studies. The most widely used technique to gather quantitative input from customers on what trade-offs they will make with new products is **conjoint analysis.**

Conjoint Analysis

Conjoint analysis is a powerful quantitative marketing research technique used to measure the relative importance of different product features to customers. It was popularized in the marketing discipline by Paul E. Green of the Wharton School at the University of Pennsylvania, and it continues to have tremendous popularity among marketers who are facing the product developer's dilemma. According to Green, described by many as the father of conjoint analysis, "Virtually all of the Fortune 500 companies have used Conjoint Analysis in the development of new products, repositioning old products, and deciding prices."[11]

Often referred to as "trade-off analysis," conjoint analysis helps product developers select the mix of features to offer on a new or revised product or service. It estimates the customer's value system, which specifies how much value a customer places on each level of a number of features. The fundamental idea behind conjoint analysis is that the product or service offering can be broken down into a set of relevant, tangibles attributes and described by a set of attribute levels.

Conjoint analysis requires respondents to trade off one attribute versus another, thereby allowing the marketer to differentiate between critical attributes and "nice-to-have" attributes. This trade-off process among attributes closely mirrors customer

---

[8] Michael Dell with Catherine Fredman, *Direct from Dell: Strategies that Revolutionized an Industry* (New York: HarperBusiness, 1999), 140.

[9] Dell with Fredman, *Direct from Dell,* 145.

[10] Dell with Fredman, *Direct from Dell,* 168.

[11] Paul Green and Abba Krieger, "Slicing and Dicing the Market," in *Mastering Marketing,* Tim Dickson, exec. ed. (London: FT Pitman, 1999), 57.

decision making in the real world. Conjoint analysis also allows the marketer to assess the relative importance of different levels of each of the features to the customer. Conjoint analysis is powerful in that it can help the marketer identify optimal levels of each attribute to maximize customer preference in the new product under study.

Conjoint analysis works best for high involvement, thinking products, and has been successfully applied with computer workstations, telephone systems, photocopiers, computer printers, cars, cameras, credit cards, banking services, insurance policies, hotel facilities, theme parks, and even state lottery games.[12] Conjoint analysis should be used cautiously for other products, especially low involvement, feeling products. The following chart can be used as a guideline for determining the applicability of conjoint analysis for different products. (This model will be discussed in more depth in the following chapter.)

	Thinking (Rational)	Feeling (Emotional)
High Involvement	Conjoint works well (Digital camera)	Difficult to include emotional attributes (Sports car)
Low Involvement	Conjoint may give distorted attribute importance (Disposable razor)	Conjoint should be used very cautiously (Beer)

Some marketers who prefer simpler approaches often ask respondents to rate the importance of attributes from a list, using an importance scale. This approach is problematic for two reasons:

- Rating the importance of one attribute at a time is an unrealistic context for most consumers and does not reflect the typical purchase process where attributes are "**con**sidered **joint**ly." Customers typically make purchase decisions considering bundles of attributes simultaneously.
- When rating one attribute at a time, most consumers will tend to rate **all** of them as extremely important, but they are probably unlikely to pay for all of them when the product is introduced. Also, high importance ratings on all of the attributes do not provide the discrimination across attributes that can be obtained from trade-off techniques.

To illustrate how conjoint works, let's look at a simplified example where we are interested in understanding the trade-off customers make between brand and

---

[12] Paul Green and Abba Krieger, "Evaluating Demand for Innovative Products," in *Mastering Marketing,* Tim Dickson, exec. ed. (London: FT Pitman, 1999), 189.

price in the infant formula market. For each of these two attributes, we decide to use two levels, as shown in the following table:

	Similac	Store brand
$4.79 for 32-ounce can		
$5.49 for 32-ounce can		

Next, we create four conjoint cards, each showing one of the four possible combinations of these two attributes. We then randomize the cards and ask respondents to rank them by how much they prefer each "product bundle." These four conjoint cards would read:

- Similac, 32-ounce can, $4.79
- Store brand, 32-ounce can, $4.79
- Similac, 32-ounce can, $5.49
- Store brand, 32-ounce can, $5.49

In this simple example, it is likely that most respondents will rank the well-known brand at the lower price as their first choice, and the store brand at the higher price as their last choice. (We didn't need a conjoint study to tell us that!)

	Similac	Store brand
$4.79 for 32-ounce can	1	
$5.49 for 32-ounce can		4

Where conjoint analysis provides valuable insight is in what the consumer picks as the second choice:

- Similac at the higher price, revealing that brand is more important than price to this respondent, or
- Store brand at the lower price, revealing that price is more important than brand to this respondent

	Similac	Store brand
$4.79 for 32-ounce can	1	2?
$5.49 for 32-ounce can	2?	4

This **trade-off** the customer is making between brand and price is the *essence* of conjoint analysis, which forces consumers to choose between different levels of different attributes. Conjoint analysis avoids the problems created by asking customers to state how important an attribute is, and obtains more valid, predictive insights by having customers trade off one attribute against another. This trade-off procedure can discriminate between critical attributes, nice-to-have attributes, and irrelevant attributes.

There are many types of conjoint analysis, ranging in complexity from a simple card sorting exercise involving eighteen cards to fully computerized, interactive, adaptive trade-off tasks, where the computer software will present attribute level combinations based on the respondents' prior response patterns. A simple card sorting conjoint study can assess customer responses to six attributes, each having three levels. The more recently developed conjoint analysis software packages offer fully computerized, interactive, adaptive conjoint study methods that can assess customer responses to as many as thirty different attributes, with each attribute having two to five levels.

Qualitative Research is Always the First Step

Prior to conducting quantitative conjoint analysis, the marketing team needs to conduct thorough qualitative consumer research and work with other functions in the firm to:

1. Identify the key product features that **impact the customer purchase decision.** These product features should include the four levels of product, including the tangible product, the augmented product, and the potential product. These attributes need not be currently available, as conjoint can test the appeal of future attributes well, as long as they are clearly described to customers and the benefits of these features are understood by customers. This will permit the marketer to determine the impact of new features that are currently not available to customers. These tangible, augmented, and potential product features should be **actionable,** meaning that the firm can make changes to the level of these features based on the conjoint study results. These features need to be **clear** and **unambiguous.** These features need to be expressed in the **customers' language,** not the company's technical jargon, to obtain meaningful results from customers.
2. Develop several discrete levels of delivery for each product feature included in the conjoint study. These levels should capture the decision ranges relevant to the company and can be binary with two levels (feature present/feature not present) or continuous with multiple levels, such as price ($4, $5, $6, $7, $8). Attribute levels of competitors' current and future products should also be comprehended in the design to be able to assess preference of the company's current and future products relative to competitors' current and future products. Caution should be used to ensure that the range of the levels for each attribute is realistic and not

unusually large, because the size of the range for an attribute can impact the importance calculated for that attribute.

Once this table of attributes and levels has been developed, "product feature bundles" are developed utilizing combinations of attribute levels. Statisticians are usually involved in developing these combinations, using a fractional factorial design to systematically vary the levels of features within these bundles. It is rarely possible to use a full factorial design and present respondents with all possible combinations of attribute levels, since the number becomes gigantic quickly. For example, if you have six attributes, with each attribute having three levels, you have $3 \times 3 \times 3 \times 3 \times 3 \times 3$, or 729, possible combinations to show respondents. This is clearly not possible without conducting five-hour interviews, most of which would be random answers from burned out respondents. In this case, the statistician can utilize fractional factorial software to select eighteen of those 729 combinations, which will allow the statistician to estimate the response to the missing 711 combinations with a high degree of accuracy.

For the simpler card sort exercise of eighteen product feature "bundles," the data collection process is quite simple. The respondent can either **rate** each of the eighteen "products" on a likelihood-to-purchase scale or an overall preference scale, or the respondent can simply **rank** the cards based on preference for the eighteen "products." Both methods have been shown to produce good discrimination across attributes and actionable results.

The ranking method involves two steps; first, the eighteen product feature "bundles" are sorted into liked, neutral, and disliked piles; second, the respondent ranks the "bundles" within each pile by how much each is preferred by the respondent. This will result in a ranking of all eighteen "products," from the product liked most to the product liked least.

Conjoint Deliverables

The conjoint analysis mathematical model will then analyze these preference rankings against the feature levels provided in each of the eighteen "products," and estimate two important outputs:

1. **Attribute Importance Scores** – conjoint calculates the importance of each of the attributes included in the conjoint study; the importance scores usually add to 100 percent. These importance scores represent the relative impact of each attribute on the consumers' preference decisions.
2. **Attribute Level Utility Scores** – utility scores measure the relative "worth" of each level of a particular attribute. Each level of each attribute receives a utility score (often referred to as "part worth utilities"), representing the respondent's willingness to trade it off for something else. Utility scores are a standardized measure of value across attributes and allow comparisons across disparate attributes. For example, would a car

purchaser trade off an extended warranty for an increase of 3 miles per gallon?

Using these utility scores, simulation models can then be developed to estimate how changes in the levels of different attributes impact customer preferences for your product as well as your competitor's products. For example, if your competitors' product has a total utility of fifteen across its six attributes, and your product has a utility of thirteen, the conjoint simulator can provide insight into which features can be modified that will most quickly increase your utility above fifteen to allow you to surpass the preference level of your competitor.

Marriott Courtyard

In the past, the Marriott Corporation had been very successful with a strategy of locating full service hotels in good downtown locations. However, when it began to run out of good downtown locations in the 1980s, it wondered if there would be adequate demand for a new hotel concept located outside of downtown areas. This new line of hotels would be targeted at both economy-minded business travelers as well as economy-minded weekend leisure travelers. Marriott needed answers to the following questions:

- What features and amenities should the new chain have?
- What is the best location strategy?
- What is the best pricing strategy?
- What should the new hotels look like to clearly distinguish them from other hotels?
- What services are most important within the room?
- What trade-offs do customers make between these services and price?

Marriott conducted thorough marketing research in the development of the new chain, including **conjoint analysis** to optimize the hotel features to meet the needs of the target segments in an affordable manner. The newly designed **Courtyard by Marriott** chain became highly successful and now has over 300 hotels and revenue exceeding $1 billion.[13]

A major benefit of conjoint studies is the ability to assess the importance of price relative to other product features. It is common to find that price is **not** the most important feature to customers; it is often third or fourth in importance. Often a company will find that increasing the levels of delivery of the top two or three most important features results in customers' willingness to pay an amount well in excess of the company's cost of providing those enhancements. This is the essence of a value-added strategy, and results in a win-win solution for both the customer and the company.

---

[13] Green and Krieger, "Slicing and Dicing the Market," 55.

Perhaps the most comprehensive and well-conducted conjoint study that the author has ever seen was conducted in 1999 by the Corporate Executive Board of Washington, D.C., and involved the optimization of employment offers to high-potential employees. Despite the application to the human resource area, the conjoint study methodology used was identical to applications in the marketing area. The highlights of that study provide an excellent overview of the application of interactive conjoint methodology.[14]

THE COMPELLING OFFER – A Quantitative Analysis of the Career Preferences and Decisions of High Value Employees

In addition to attracting **customers** with compelling product offerings, companies also need to attract **quality employees** with compelling employment offers. The development of an attractive employment offer has strong parallels to the development of winning product offerings. Understanding which employment offer components have the greatest value to current employees also allows the firm to increase employee retention levels.

The Corporate Leadership Council of the Corporate Executive Board conducted this study for its membership of over 700 companies to help them engage and retain their top employees during the dot-com boom of the late 1990s.[15] High paying job offers from six-month-old dot-com companies were causing high turnover in many companies, and hard information was needed to determine which parts of the employment "package" were really important to their "high value" employees.

The objectives of the study were:

- Identify the preferences of high value employees and the most leveraged attributes of a compelling employment offer.
- Assess the satisfaction of high value employees with their current employment offers.
- Identify strategic opportunities for recrafting a compelling employment offer for high value talent.

Participating companies identified about one-fourth of their employees, which were named "high value" employees, to be surveyed. These high value employees had one or more of the following characteristics:

- Defined as top performers
- Hold a skill or competency that is highly valued by the company

---

[14] Corporate Leadership Council, *The Compelling Offer: A Quantitative Analysis of the Career Preferences and Decisions of High Value Employees* (Washington, D. C., Corporate Executive Board, 1999), 3–4, 12–15, 48–51, and 54–55. (This study is used with the permission of the Corporate Leadership Council of the Corporate Executive Board and is only available to members of the organization. Inquiries may be directed to the Corporate Leadership Council at 202-777-5000 or at www.corporateleadershipcouncil.com).

[15] Corporate Leadership Council, *The Compelling Offer,* 23.

- Have "high trajectory" within the corporation; that is, likely to be promoted rapidly to positions of greater responsibility

In total, 10,900 high value employees were identified in these nineteen member companies representative of the membership as a whole, and these employees were sent computerized surveys. 5,877 employees responded to the survey, for an unusually high response rate of 54 percent. This high response rate made the Corporate Leadership Council confident that the survey responders were representative of the overall population of high value employees.

Prior to finalizing the survey, qualitative research was conducted with high value employees to identify the attributes that were important to them in an employment offer. This research and subsequent brainstorming sessions resulted in the identification of thirty attributes for the study, which were grouped into four major categories: compensation and benefits, work environment, work-life balance, and organizational environment. The thirty attributes were broken down as follows:

- **Compensation and benefits (7)** – external salary equity, health benefits, internal salary equity, stock options, retirement benefits, base salary compared to current salary, and bonus as percent of base salary
- **Work environment (9)** – manager quality, coworker quality, recognition, cutting-edge work, empowerment, role clarity, work challenge, internal mobility, and project responsibility
- **Work-Life Balance (7)** – location, flextime, childcare, hours, telecommuting, travel, and vacation
- **Organizational environment (7)** – fit with company and industry, risk taking, company reputation, senior team reputation, company size, development reputation, and technology level

The Corporate Leadership Council could have had respondents simply rate each of these thirty attributes on an importance scale, with 10 = highly important to me and 1 = not at all important to me. Or the Corporate Leadership Council could have had respondents rank order the thirty attributes, from most important to least important. These two methods would have been easier to include in a research study but would have yielded results of questionable validity. Instead, the Corporate Leadership Council decided to utilize conjoint analysis because it felt that this well-tested marketing research tool would provide the needed discrimination across attributes in a more valid manner.

For each of these thirty attributes, various levels were identified, ranging from two levels for flextime (no flextime permitted; flextime schedules permitted as long as work goals are met) to a high of five levels for external **salary equity, base salary, hours,** and **vacation.** The five levels of these last four attributes are shown in the following table.

LEVEL ONE	LEVEL TWO	LEVEL THREE	LEVEL FOUR	LEVEL FIVE
Company pays about 30 percent below market for my position	Company pays about 15 percent below market for my position	Company pays "market rate" for my position	Company pays about 15 percent above market for my position	Company pays about 30 percent above market for my position
50 percent less than current salary	25 percent less than current salary	Same as current salary	25 percent more than current salary	50 percent more than current salary
Work about forty hours per week	Work about fifty hours per week	Work about sixty hours per week	Work about seventy hours per week	Work about eighty hours per week
Able to take two weeks of vacation per year	Able to take three weeks of vacation per year	Able to take four weeks of vacation per year	Able to take five weeks of vacation per year	Able to take six weeks of vacation per year

Notice how clearly and unambiguously these levels of the attributes are specified. Also notice the balanced symmetry of the first two attributes. Last, all attributes are specified at enough levels to capture the range of decision making for employment offers (i.e. it is unlikely to expect employment offers that include thirty hours or ninety hours of work in a week).

The next step was to expose respondents to combinations of levels of these thirty attributes to assess their choices when attributes varied in a systematic manner. If all possible combinations of these thirty attributes were developed, the respondent would have to be exposed to over 39 million billion combinations. Luckily, interactive conjoint software exists to measure the importance of thirty attributes and the utility of the levels of those thirty attributes in an accurate manner with exposure to twenty-five to thirty paired choices.

Rich Johnson, founder of Sawtooth Software in Sequim, Washington, was a pioneer in the area of interactive software for conjoint measurement, and his firm's ACA brand of conjoint software is the most widely used in the world. These software programs are used on a computer where the respondent is presented with a pair of employment offers, each containing different levels of six of the thirty attributes. The respondent is then asked to select the job offer that is

preferred. The computer screen showing the pair of options could look something like this:

Employment Offers: "Which job offer do you prefer?"

Attribute	Job Offer #1	Job Offer #2
Base Pay	50% increase in pay	25% increase in pay
Health Benefits	Company offers no benefits	Company offers full benefits
Manager Quality	Work for an average manager	Work for best manager in company
Work Challenge	Less challenging work	Same work challenge as now
Vacation	Two weeks of vacation per year	Four weeks of vacation per year
Telecommuting	Three to four days per week	No telecommuting available

Attributes and attribute levels are rotated through multiple screens like the previous example to allow the conjoint software to estimate the importance of each of the attributes, as well as estimate the utility of each of the levels of each attribute. Usually, twenty-five to thirty paired choices, taking the respondent about twenty minutes, are sufficient for the interactive conjoint model to estimate attribute importance and the utility of each of the levels of the attributes. Respondents in this study were given the survey on a computer disk, which they completed and returned by mail to the Corporate Leadership Council.

The results of the Compelling Offer Study were quite interesting, and surprised many human resource (HR) managers, who felt that they had a good handle on what is important to prospective employees. It turned out that the single most highly valued attribute to high value employees was **Manager Quality,** which was almost twice as important as the average attribute. HR managers had ranked this attribute in the bottom half of attributes when they ranked the attributes based on their judgment, prior to the study. Next in importance to these high value employees were:

- **Base Salary**
- **External Equity**
- **Health Benefits**
- **Business Travel**
- **Retirement Benefits**
- **Hours**

- **Company Reputation**
- **Recognition**
- **Internal Equity**

The five least important attributes to these high value employees were: child-care, company size, telecommuting, fit with company, and flextime.

Thus, the study identified the most-valued attributes to allow employers to develop compelling employment offers. It also allowed them to determine the utility of each of the levels of the attributes to help them assess the value of each level of the thirty attributes to employees, relative to their cost of providing each level. But the Corporate Leadership Council was not finished; they decided to dig deeper into the database of 5,877 respondents to see if there were segments within the total sample that valued different features.

Upon performing cluster analysis, using the feature level utilities of each respondent, four distinct segments emerged that clearly valued different attributes in their employment. These employee segments are very different from one another and need to be addressed with customized, distinct employment offers, since what one segment values may be of low interest to the other three segments. These four segments are shown.

Segment Name	"Work Oriented"	"Home & Family"	"Reward Oriented"	"Work to Live"
Segment Size	35 percent	30 percent	17 percent	18 percent
Place greater value on:	• Cutting-edge work • Challenging work • Risk-taking environment • High internal mobility • Empowerment • "World class" senior managers	• Location • Current company • Flexible work schedule • Low travel • On-site childcare • Role clarity	• Internal salary equity • Bonus • High base salary • Pay above market rate • Stock options • High quality manager	• Low level business travel • Low level work hours • Location • High base salary • High quality manager • Vacation
Place lesser value on:	• Location • Business travel • Work hours • Base salary • Pay above market rate • Vacation	• Internal salary equity • Base salary • Bonus • High quality manager • Pay above market rate • Cutting-edge work	• Location • Development • Work hours • Flexible work schedule • Current company • "World class" senior managers	• Bonus • Cutting edge work • Risk-taking environment • Challenging work • Internal salary equity • Empowerment

The **Work-Oriented** employee places higher value on work environment factors and is willing to sacrifice many work-life elements. The **Home & Family** employee places higher value on a stable work environment with added work-life benefits, and places lesser value on compensation and cutting-edge work. The **Reward-Oriented** employee places high value on compensation ("Show me the money!"). The **Work-to-Live** employee wants it all – both high compensation and vacation with low levels of work and travel! Companies may want to avoid extending salary offers to this employee segment.

Thus, a company needs to select the segment or segments that best match their employment needs, and then utilize a simulation model to customize their employment offer to be highly attractive to the target segment(s). (These simulation models can calculate the total utility of a specific job offer by adding the part worth utilities of each of the attribute levels.) These customized offers will have the greatest "traction" in affecting career decisions. This strategy will be much more successful than a generic employment offer to all prospective employees.

Conjoint analysis provides an additional method to segment markets, based on the varying utility placed upon different product features by employees, or customers. The Compelling Offer Study provides a powerful example of how these differences in feature utility can create heterogeneous segments with low overlap that are highly actionable to the enlightened human resources manager.

Utilizing Conjoint Results – The GMC Win-Focus-Parity Strategy

General Motors manufactures and sells large trucks for industrial markets through its GMC Division. This division makes heavy use of conjoint analysis to optimize its truck product line, interviewing both target segment truck drivers and purchasing agents to assess the importance of features. GMC then uses a **Win-Focus-Parity** strategy to develop products that succeed in the market:

- **WIN** – Identify two to three of the most important features and become world class on these features
- **FOCUS** – Identify other important features and match the best-in-class competitor on these features
- **PARITY** – On other features, select one competitor and match them on these features

GMC has found that this strategy has helped them develop and market appealing, affordable trucks in a very competitive market. This disciplined, customer-driven approach is a best practice from which all companies involved with high involvement, rational products can benefit.

Discrete Choice Modeling

While conjoint analysis is very helpful in understanding the importance of different product features to customers, as well as the worth customers place on different levels of those features, it does have its shortcomings. It does not directly

provide marketers with estimates of market shares that could be achieved by new products with different feature combinations; it is not a good tool for assessing price elasticity; and it does not provide a good measure of potential cannibalization of current products by the new product.

Discrete choice modeling (DCM) was developed to address these shortcomings of conjoint analysis, and is an advanced, evolved form of conjoint analysis. DCM utilizes multinomial LOGIT regression techniques to estimate purchase probabilities based on varying product features and to model consumer behavior. It predicts consumers' brand choices given different combinations of feature alternatives, for new or existing products, within dynamic competitive markets. It can be used to predict share of choices for each brand as well as to estimate the impact on the test brand if competitors were to change their marketing strategies.[16]

Discrete choice modeling presents customers with sixteen to twenty-four "buying scenarios," either on paper or on a computer. Within these sixteen to twenty-four scenarios, brands, features, and prices are varied, and respondents are asked to choose one of the product options shown. By asking customers to make a *discrete choice* from among a group of products with differing feature levels, market share models based on probabilities of brand choice can be built for new or existing products. Simulation models can then be used to estimate market share and cannibalization for alternative product configurations and marketing mixes. Discrete choice modeling has been used quite effectively to estimate the potential of new products and determine from which brands the new brand will draw market share.

Discrete choice modeling does not require an experimental design to pair up all attributes, as is required for most conjoint studies. Rather, selected attribute combinations can represent real world products. Discrete choice modeling was used heavily by many companies in the hotel industry, who were interested in determining the right attributes of a hotel and the hotel room to get the target customer to choose it over competitive offerings. It is also used by manufacturers of high definition television receivers, who are interested in providing key features to target customers at a price that will allow them to achieve their market share and profit objectives. A typical DCM study for high definition television receivers may require the customer to make twenty discrete choices from twenty purchase scenarios. One purchase scenario may look something like this:

---

[16] John Golanty, "Using Discrete Choice Modeling to Estimate Market Share," *Marketing Research* 7, no. 2, 1995.

Scenario 31

If you had the following wide screen (16 x 9 aspect ratio) high definition televisions to choose from, which, if any, would you choose to buy?

Brand	Hitachi	Panasonic	Philips	Sony	Some other brand	None of these
Type	Plasma	Rear Projection	LCD	Rear Projection		
Screen Size (Diagonal)	52 inch	53 inch	23 inch	57 inch		
Picture Quality Rating	Excellent	Very good	Very good	Very good		
Ease of Use	Very good	Good	Fair	Very good		
Warranty	12 months	12 months	12 months	24 months		
Depth	6 inches	30 inches	4 inches	27 inches		
Price	$6,000	$2,000	$1,800	$2,400		
Check one box:	☐	☐	☐	☐	☐	☐

The respondent would be shown approximately twenty of these scenarios and would make one choice on each scenario. Levels of selected features would be varied by the marketer, to be able to assess the impact of changes to those features on the consumer's choice behavior.

The design of discrete choice modeling studies requires a lot of homework on the part of the marketing team to understand the competitors' marketing mix and possible marketing strategies; this understanding will allow the products of competitors to be modeled more accurately and ensure that the right features are varied in the design to allow simulation modeling later. For example, if the price of the Sony TV is held at $2,400 on all 20 scenarios, it will not be possible to simulate the impact of a price decrease by Sony after the data is collected.

Note also that the consumer is not forced to pick one of the four televisions shown, but they can pick some other television, or pick nothing. This allows the statistician to do a more accurate job of estimating market shares based on these choices.

However, the "share of choices" from the discrete choice model is not the same as the brand share in the marketplace. This is because the model assumes the test conditions of 100 percent immediate awareness, 100 percent immediate distribution, and user expectations that are met exactly once the product is tried. To convert discrete choice shares to market shares, each of these assumptions must be adjusted to reflect more realistic circumstances. For new brands, the differences

between adjusted market shares and unadjusted choice shares tend to be much greater, leading to lower market shares and underscoring the need to be cautious when interpreting unadjusted discrete choice output.[17]

Discrete choice modeling is becoming as popular as traditional conjoint analysis because of its realistic choice context for customers and its capabilities to estimate shares and source of business. Many suppliers of conjoint analysis software have now introduced new versions of Choice-based conjoint to close the gap somewhat on the more powerful discrete choice models. (Choice-based conjoint was the method used in the Compelling Offer Study example presented earlier in this chapter.)

Traditional conjoint still has many fans, however, because it is easier to implement, relies on less complicated mathematical models, and is more appropriate than DCM at the earlier stages of new product development. "No marketing research technique comes close to offering either the managerial power or the economic efficiency of conjoint analysis."[18]

Investment Cost

- Four focus groups, conducted by a skilled moderator, including analysis and report, will cost:
  - $20,000–$25,000 in the United States
  - $20,000–$22,000 in France and Japan
  - $17,000–$19,000 in the U.K. and Germany
  - $4,000–$6,000 in China and India
- Twenty depth interviews, conducted by a skilled moderator, including analysis and report, will cost approximately $15,000–$20,000 in the United States and Japan and $12,000–$15,000 in major European countries.
- Usability testing usually involves inviting customers to your development labs to work on products at early stages of development. Firms should plan to begin with at least two to four employees involved in the usability lab full-time. Human factors engineers and market researchers are the mix of employees needed.
- A quantitative conjoint analysis study, involving a nationally representative sample of 200 consumers, screened by telephone and then interviewed personally for thirty minutes, will cost approximately $40,000–$50,000 in the United States. However, many firms have moved to Internet interviews in the United States and have cut this cost in half.
- A multinational conjoint analysis study, involving nationally representative samples of 200 consumers in each of three countries, screened by telephone and then interviewed personally for thirty minutes, will cost approximately $115,000–$130,000.

---

[17] Golanty, "Using Discrete Choice Modeling to Estimate Market Share."
[18] Dick McCullough, "A User's Guide to Conjoint Analysis," *Marketing Research* 14, no. 2, 2002.

- A Business-to-Business conjoint study, among 100 business executives interviewed in person, where the sampling list is provided to the research firm, would cost:
  - $37,000–$44,000 in the United States
  - $26,000–$32,000 in the U. K. and Japan
  - $21,000–$25,000 in Germany
  - $9,000–$12,000 in Italy
- A quantitative discrete choice modeling study, involving a nationally representative sample of 200 consumers, screened by telephone and then interviewed personally for thirty minutes, will cost approximately $55,000–$65,000 in the United States. However, many firms have moved to Internet interviews in the United States and have cut this cost in half.
- A multinational discrete choice modeling study, involving nationally representative samples of 200 consumers in each of three countries, screened by telephone and then interviewed personally for thirty minutes, will cost approximately $127,000–$140,000.

Product Feature Optimization Checklist

- Are your products over-featured and too complicated to use by anyone except your highly trained engineers?
- Are you clear on the three most important product attributes to your customers?
- Are you best in class on those three product attributes?
- Are you actively searching for the "delighters" to incorporate into your products of the future?
- Do you have an ongoing usability testing program to allow customers to find the "bugs" months before product launch?
- Have you conducted conjoint studies on your key markets to ensure that your products offer valued features that can command a premium price?
- Do you regularly conduct discrete choice modeling studies to optimize major products and to predict market share and source of business for those products once launched?

MARKETING COMMUNICATIONS

INSIGHT 7: The most effective marketing communications combine a rational benefit with an emotional need.

*"The aim of advertising is not to state the facts
about a product, but to sell a solution or a dream."*

Philip Kotler

Customer Insight Pyramid

Can Advertising Communications Break Through the Clutter?

Customers are bombarded with thousands of advertising messages each day. Through the process of selective perception, most of these messages never penetrate the conscious minds of customers. Yet, even though most messages never register in the conscious mind, some messages circumvent the conscious mind and have an impact on the unconscious mind. Much research has shown that people are typically on "autopilot" in their everyday lives, and that reactions to advertising are often intuitive rather than rational, and usually unconscious rather

than conscious. "Advertising provides 'secret attractions' and fascinations to the **unconscious** mind, which are enjoyable, compulsive and irrational to the **conscious** mind"[1]

Advertising that connects with the needs and dreams of the target customer can break through the clutter and have an effect. Enlightened marketers have developed sophisticated methods to create and test advertising messages that reach customers on the conscious and unconscious levels and create preferences for their brands. Brand equity is built through the cumulative impact of effective advertising that resonates with the target customer.

Understand the Target Market Before You Attempt to Communicate with Them

Having a clear understanding of the target market is an important prerequisite to effectively communicating with them. The author remembers being involved with focus groups of beer drinkers for a brewery that was hoping to penetrate the "super-premium" product segment. This high-end product segment was at the time dominated by Michelob, a special brand produced by Anheuser-Busch in St. Louis for over a century. Regular drinkers of Michelob (consumed the brand two or more times in the past month) were recruited for the focus group, and the brand director at the company came to observe the focus groups from behind the one-way mirror. The brand director was very disappointed as the Michelob beer drinkers arrived for the focus group. "These are Michelob drinkers?" he asked incredulously. He had expected clean-cut men in their 30s wearing sport jackets, instead of the younger men in T-shirts and jeans who were the frequent Michelob drinkers. His perceptions of the target market had been shaped by Madison Avenue advertising, rather than reality and experience in bars with Michelob drinkers. Some may argue that aspirational advertising is effective, but if the target beer drinker sees men in sport coats in beer advertising, he is likely to tune it out through the process of selective perception. Positioning a new beer brand requires showing beer drinkers that the target can relate to and aspire to be like, but not overshooting the target so badly that the beer drinkers portrayed in the advertising have no relevance to the target market. Needless to say, this new brand of beer was not successful, in large part due to advertising that did not resonate with target consumers.

Advertising Needs to Work on Both the Rational and the Emotional Levels

The power from understanding both rational and emotional reasons for consumer behavior lies in combining these in both the positioning strategies and in the advertising. "Truth is both rational and emotional. In case after case, the richest

---

[1] Neil Sharman, John Pawle, and Peter Cooper, "Quantifying the Emotional Effects of Advertising," *Research World, ESOMAR*, September 2003, 32.

level of communication comes from combining a rational brand benefit with an emotional need."[2] Powerful brands present a compelling benefit and support it with a believable product attribute. Consider Miller Lite, which made the bold boast that the brand was "less filling" when it was launched in 1974. This emotional benefit claim (less filling = I can enjoy more beer!) was believable because it was supported by the rational attribute of "fewer calories," which was subtly included in the advertising.

Brands and ideas that have an emotional meaning to us are more likely to be stored in memory and available for later recall. These connections are critical as we stand in front of a crowded store shelf, trying to make a choice from forty brands of breakfast cereal. Emotional memories in the unconscious mind play a key role in brand selection, even though we may feel we are being very rational in this purchase decision.

Gerald Zaltman offers further interesting insights about the role of memory in advertising in his excellent book *How Customers Think*.[3]

> Marketers do strive to create powerful memories for consumers for a product or service. Ad campaigns aim to facilitate a consumer's storage and recall of the feelings and thoughts associated with a product. Marketers play a central role in creating consumers' memories, thanks to memory's intricate association with metaphor.
>
> Memories manifest themselves physically as electrochemical etchings in our brain cells. Neuroscientists call these etchings *engrams*. As we encounter and absorb information, that information enters neutrons that represent *short-term* memory. There it may evaporate in seconds or be passed on and etched into other neutrons that represent *long-term* memory. Of course, not everything we encounter is recorded for later retrieval. But if a fact or event has **emotional significance** to us, we'll be more likely to store it in long term memory. Once stored, engrams are activated by *cues* or *stimuli*. Some cues are obvious. Others are quite subtle, working their magic in the shadows of the unconscious mind. Olfactory cues are hardwired into the brain's limbic system, the seat of emotion, and stimulate vivid recollections. Typically, we're not consciously aware of most cues. Yet these stimuli count among the most influential tools that marketing managers can use to incite the memories that will inspire consumers to buy. Managers can increase the likelihood of creating enduring memories by emphasizing unique product qualities that have personal significance for consumers. [Above emphasis added.]

---

[2] Lisa Fortini-Campbell, *Hitting the Sweet Spot: How Consumer Insights can Inspire Better Marketing and Advertising,* new ed. (Chicago: The Copy Workshop, a division of Bruce Bendinger Creative Communications, Inc., 2001). 100.

[3] Gerald Zaltman, *How Customers Think: Essential Insights into the Mind of the Market* (Boston: Harvard Business School Press, 2003), 166–168, 177.

Do the Golden Arches influence the unconscious mind as you drive along the highway? Do the red Budweiser signs influence the unconscious mind as you sit in a ballpark watching the Chicago Cubs? Does the smell of fresh ground coffee beans as you walk past the coffee store in the mall elicit a response from the unconscious mind? Does the blue "Intel inside" logo on your laptop computer make you feel differently about the quality of your IBM ThinkPad? If you're not convinced yet, read on.

In this chapter, we will review some fascinating research on how television advertising works, review the exposure effect, which states that a person can form preferences for a brand without any conscious thoughts occurring, review a leading advertising strategy model, review the advertising testing process that went into creating award-winning ads from Oreo cookies, Miracle Whip and the General Motors OnStar system, and cover the major methods for pre-testing advertising, as well the major measures to assess the effectiveness of advertising after it has been on the air.

How TV Advertising Works

Most elements of the marketing mix are measured to assess their effectiveness, with considerable rigor, precision, and confidence. The redemption rates and return on investment of coupons are monitored and evaluated. The impact of a small price promotion is closely monitored and measured. The impact of product enhancements is carefully tested using simulated test markets prior to national launch. It is quite surprising that the impact of the largest marketing expenditure, television advertising, has been neglected in many firms. One reason for this neglect may be the difficulty of measuring both the short-term and the long-term impact of advertising.

In 1995, Leonard Lodish of the Wharton School at the University of Pennsylvania and several of his colleagues completed a comprehensive analysis of the results of 389 real-world split-cable TV advertising experiments; they published the results of their breakthrough study in a leading marketing journal.[4] This study involved analysis of the 389 experiments in the Information Resources historical BehaviorScan database.

BehaviorScan is a real-world experimental laboratory, comprised of demographically representative households in purchasing panels in each of five geographically dispersed markets in the United States. The panel in each of the five medium-sized markets includes 3,000 households. Each household's supermarket purchases are recorded via supermarket checkout scanners so that supermarket purchasing behavior can be precisely measured. Purchases made in nonscanner stores are captured by hand-held scanners used in the home.

---

[4] Leonard M. Lodish et al., "How TV Advertising Works: A Meta Analysis of 389 Real-World Split-Cable TV Advertising Experiments," *Journal of Marketing Research* 32, no. 3, November 1995.

BehaviorScan households receive all of their television programs via cable TV, and advertising can be directed to or removed from individual households on a targeted basis. This has allowed the execution of many carefully controlled advertising experiments to test advertising copy and advertising weight.

This meta-analysis revealed that television advertising was indeed effective, but only under certain conditions. When effective, advertising produced considerable volume effects:

- A mean increase of 18 percent in unit sales
- An impact that emerged fast, typically within six months
- An impact that often lasted for more than two years

But Lodish found that many of the long-held television advertising "rules of thumb" were **false.** The tenets that were shown to have little support were:

1. To increase market share, television share of voice must be larger than your current market share.
2. At least three exposures of an ad per person are required to make a significant impact.
3. More television advertising is better than less.
4. Television advertising takes a long time to work.

Many in the advertising world were surprised by these findings that contradicted the advice they had been giving to valued clients for years. But the facts were in, and the skeptics had no other facts to dispute these solid findings.

Major Findings on How Television Advertising Works

The **major findings** from this breakthrough analysis were the following:

- Increased advertising weight relative to competition did not necessarily result in higher sales.
  - It was easier for **less well established** brands and **smaller** brands to effect a change with increased television advertising weight.
  - Brands in **growing product categories** and in categories with **more purchase opportunities** are more likely to be able to improve sales through increased television advertising weight.
  - **New brands** and **line extensions** tended to be more responsive to advertising.
- Effective advertising produced an 18 percent increase in sales.
  - Effects tended to be stronger when the advertising message was intended to change attitudes rather than reinforce them.
  - Effects tended to be stronger when the copy strategy had recently been changed. It is important to keep the message fresh in the minds of the target consumers. This research analysis showed that **the benefits of constant change in television advertising copy are likely to outweigh the risks.** Copy should change frequently and regularly; there is considerable danger in maintaining the status quo. Companies

need to avoid lulling their target consumers into boredom and complacency. Note that these frequent changes are to the advertising copy, not to the brand's positioning. The strategic positioning of the brand should remain stable for as long as possible, as Miller Lite did with their introductory positioning strategy that remained stable for seventeen years.

- The impact of effective advertising emerged within six months and often lasted for more than two years.
- Standard flighting of media plans, in which advertising is cycled "on" for several weeks and then "off" for several weeks, were relatively unlikely to increase sales. **Concentration** of advertising weight appears to offer more advantages than dispersion. This is especially true for new products, which need to advertise their products heavily early on to stimulate trial of the new product.
- For established brands, there was **not** a strong link between standard measures of advertising effectiveness, such as **television commercial recall** and **persuasion,** and the sales impact of the advertising in the market. This suggests that it may be more effective to test advertising in the market using an experimental approach rather than relying solely on pre-test measures such as recall and persuasion.

Because so many of the long-held rules of thumb about television advertising were shown to be false, Lodish suggests that television advertising should be tested and evaluated constantly to determine precisely what works.

Television Advertising Strategy at Frito-Lay

Frito-Lay applied many of these principles to their brands to test and validate the many new findings from this study.[5] For Frito-Lay, innovation and brand size were critical to differentiating effective advertising from ineffective advertising. Their experience confirmed many of the Lodish study findings, and Frito-Lay developed three new marketing guidelines from their research:

1. Advertise some form of "news" for lesser brands.
2. Advertising for larger brands is not likely to drive sales if it contains no "news."
3. Advertising effects occur quickly and tend to last if they occur at all.
   a. Once the most effective advertising has been identified, there is likely to be a bonus in the form of long-term impact that approximately doubles the short-term impact.
   b. If a television advertising campaign does not work in the short-term, it will not work in the long-term.

---

[5] Leonard Lodish, "When Do Commercials Boost Sales?" in *Mastering Marketing,* Tim Dickson, exec. ed. (London: FT Pitman, 1999).

Frito-Lay also found that the only way to determine if advertising was working was **to test constantly.** Frito-Lay found that the investment of several hundred thousands of dollars in testing television advertising was a good investment to evaluate the hundreds of millions spent on advertising.

The Exposure Effect

In a classic journal article entitled "Affective and Cognitive Factors in Preferences,"[6] Robert Zajonc and Hazel Markus present a remarkable psychological phenomenon named the **"exposure effect,"** in which affective processes (such as positive attitudes and preferences) can be formed independently of cognitive processes (such as advertising recall and advertising awareness). Preferences can be acquired through the repeated exposure to a brand stimulus without any awareness occurring on the part of the consumer. This sounds like marketing manipulation, doesn't it?

This exposure effect is supported by numerous research studies, including a fascinating experiment conducted by Zajonc and William Kunst-Wilson.[7] In that experiment, subjects were presented with visual stimuli – high contrast polygons – at viewing conditions that resulted in only chance recognition. The polygons were exposed a number of times each, under viewing conditions (duration of exposure and level of illumination) that did not result in recognition of these polygons above the level of chance.

During a subsequent second session, the subject was shown pairs of stimuli, now under perfectly optimal viewing conditions. In each pair, one item was an old stimulus, shown during the exposure series, and the other was a similar, new stimulus, never previously exposed. Subjects were asked which of the two polygons was new and which was old, and then which of the two polygons they preferred.

The results showed that the respondents could not recognize the old stimuli from the new stimuli at a level above chance (i.e. not significantly different from 50 percent). However, this was not the case for preference judgments. *Subjects liked the old stimuli more than the new ones, even though they were unable to recognize them!*

Cognitive participation is not necessary for the occurrence of an affective reaction. Put another way, we do not have to be attentive to be persuaded. Does this mean that marketers can manipulate us and get us to buy products we don't want? That is probably going too far. But it does mean that our feelings toward a brand can become more positive due solely to repeated exposures to that brand's logo or advertising.

---

[6] Robert B. Zajonc and Hazel Markus, "Affective and Cognitive Factors in Preferences," *Journal of Consumer Research* 9, September 1982.
[7] William Kunst-Wilson and Robert B. Zajonc, "Affective Discrimination of Stimuli that Cannot Be Recognized," *Science* 207, February 1980.

The implications of this finding on advertising and advertising testing are enormous.

- The advertising practitioners who believed in a universal **Learn–Feel–Do** reaction among consumers to advertising had to face hard evidence that other processes, such as **Feel–Learn–Do,** occurred among consumers in purchasing certain products.
- The beer drinker in the focus group that always states that "advertising doesn't affect me" reveals his enormous naïveté toward the exposure effect.
- The ubiquity of advertising symbols, such as the Nike swoosh, when connected to emotions by other advertising can be silently increasing preferences for the brand without our awareness and knowledge.
- Changing an attitude that has evolved primarily from affective sources, and therefore having considerable extracognitive support, may require different methods (and be much more difficult) from methods needed to change attitudes based on cognition. It may require an attack on the affective basis of the preference. In other words, a fact-based cognitive approach will probably be ineffective in changing attitudes toward a competitor who has built a strong image based on emotion-based affective advertising.

It is possible that a considerable amount of the advertising to which a person is exposed, which is not cognitively processed and which we conclude has no effect, may still be extremely important in forming habits, attitudes, and preferences. Brand loyalty purchases can result from the mere exposure to the brand and its logo. This is especially true for products where purchase choices are frequently repeated, where problems are few, and where the individual is not much concerned with a single choice.[8] Repeated exposures to a brand stimulus will often result in a more positive attitude toward that brand. Is it any wonder why Budweiser has its large logo in almost every major league baseball park in America?

This study has led to many other studies that have demonstrated that advertising need not be informative to be effective. Nor need advertising be verbal only; emotional and visual elements can also enhance preference for a brand. Further, brand attitudes are not formed exclusively on the basis of beliefs about the brand; brand attitudes can be based on emotions as well.[9] "For many products, the evaluation of the product is more likely to be controlled by **emotional appeals,** which can be established by having the product associated with positively loaded images, persons or situations."[10] This explains why many enlightened beer advertisers avoid telling beer drinkers about their grains, hops, and brewing process but

---

[8] Flemming Hansen, "Hemispheral Lateralization: Implications for Understanding Consumer Behavior," *Journal of Consumer Research* 8, no. 1, June 1981.

[9] Demetrios Vakratsas and Tim Ambler, "How Advertising Works: What Do we Really Know?" *Journal of Marketing* 63, January 1999.

[10] Hansen, "Hemispheral Lateralization," 31–32.

rather attempt to connect their brand to the more powerful emotions involved in many beer consumption occasions, such as male bonding and reward.

The Foote Cone and Belding (FCB) Advertising Planning Model

The Chicago-based advertising agency Foote Cone and Belding (FCB) proposed a planning model for developing advertising strategies for their clients' many different brands, based on two critical dimensions. The first dimension was whether the product is a "thinking" product, involving mostly rational benefits, or a "feeling" product, involving mostly emotional benefits. The second dimension was whether the product is "high involvement" or "low involvement."[11] Examples of types of products in each of the quadrants are shown in the following table.

	Thinking Products	Feeling Products
High Involvement Products	Informative (auto insurance, car battery, digital camera)	Affective (sports car, expensive watch, eyeglasses)
Low Involvement Products	Habitual (disposable razor, liquid bleach, insect repellent)	Satisfaction (beer, snacks, cigarettes)

High involvement products are characterized by:

- Much time spent on the decision
- Many alternatives considered
- High level of information search and processing
- Usually higher priced
- Usually longer purchase cycles

Low involvement products are characterized by:

- Little time spent on the decision; often impulse products
- Few alternatives considered; choice is based on the similarity of situation with those in the past
- Low level of information search
- Usually lower priced
- Usually frequently purchased goods

---

[11] Richard Vaughn, "How Advertising Works: A Planning Model," *Journal of Advertising Research* 20, no. 5, February/March 1980.

The role of advertising is very different for products across these four quadrants and is shown in the following table:

, *Role of Advertising*

	Thinking Products	**Feeling Products**
High Involvement Products	Informative Advertising needs to provide specific information and demonstrate product	Affective Advertising needs to be a high emotional impact execution
Low Involvement Products	Habitual Advertising serves as a reminder	Satisfaction Advertising needs to bring attention to the brand through executional elements, such as humor

Thus, advertising needs to play the traditional informative role for high involvement, thinking products, a role that economists feel is the primary role of advertising. But for the other three typologies of products, the role of advertising is very different. For these products, advertising must create emotional connections, or remind people to buy the brand on their next shopping trip, or simply bring attention to the brand. Understanding the role your advertising needs to play is critical to effectively measuring its impact in the marketplace. Ads intended to bring attention to a brand and ads serving as reminders may have top-of-mind brand awareness as a key metric of advertising effectiveness. Ads intended to create an emotional connection with the consumer may have attitude ratings toward the brand as a key metric of advertising effectiveness. Brands attempting to provide specific information about the brand to target consumers may have advertising copy playback as a key metric. The metrics used to assess the effectiveness of advertising must be closely aligned with the objectives and goals of the advertising.

Oreo Cookies Advertising Testing

The success of the Oreo cookie brand has been enhanced by a strong commitment on the part of Nabisco to the gathering of **customer insight** during the development of their advertising. In Chapter 3, the following positioning statement that guided the development of all Oreo advertising was shown:

Generations can twist open and unlock the possibilities and wonder of childhood experiences, teenage times, or hopes and dreams that have since

been forgotten. An Oreo is a magical door, which can transport us into a dimension of youth. Within seconds, we can reflect back on our own childhood when a simple pleasure like eating an Oreo was part of every fun-filled day.

This powerful statement revealed the depth of **customer insight** that Nabisco has into the cookie consumer. Doug Conant, senior vice president of marketing at Nabisco when it won the David Ogilvy Award in 1994, stated that Nabisco believes:

- Great advertising works in the marketplace by *involving, persuading, and motivating* consumers.
- Great advertising creates and reinforces brand preference by communicating a unique and relevant product-based point-of-difference and *establishing an emotional tie between the consumer and the brand.*
- Great advertising establishes and consistently *reinforces a distinctive image* for the brand and strengthens brand equities.
- Great advertising reflects a commitment to *truly understand the target consumer* and the brand.

Great advertising grows out of a *process focused on learning* and it rarely emerges fully formed.

This last point, a process focused on learning that rarely emerges fully formed, is pivotal and is the key objective of Nabisco's copy research process.[12] Nabisco continually tests and refines advertising ideas so that they resonate strongly with target consumers.

Advertising Development at Nabisco

The advertising development and testing process used by Nabisco for Oreo cookies in 1994 involved the following steps:

- Three benefit statements were developed to capture the full range of consumers' emotional attachment to Oreos.
- The advertising agency was asked to develop preliminary advertising concepts on storyboards (which look like large comic strips) to capture the essence of the three strategies.
- Storyboards were then shown to target consumers in one-on-one interviews as a communications check, and not as an evaluation of the concepts.
- After assessing the communication ability of each concept storyboard, enhancements were made to the storyboard commercials and "liveamatics"

---

[12] Norma Larkin, "Unlocking the Magic of Oreos," Case Number 1 in *Marketing Research That Pays Off: Case Histories of Marketing Research Leading to Success in the Marketplace,* Larry Percy, ed. (New York: The Haworth Press, 1997), 8.

were made, which are rough commercials that are inexpensively produced, usually using stock photographs and sound.

- Five commercials were pre-tested using the ASI Recall Plus methodology. ASI pre-recruited five samples of target customers to watch a pilot situation comedy in their homes on a cable station, during which one of the five test commercials is aired. Respondents were re-contacted twenty-four hours after the program to obtain recall levels and communication playback for each of the five commercials. Persuasion was assessed by comparing brand preferences to a sixth control group who was exposed to the program without a test commercial.

- Two strong commercials emerged from this quantitative copy testing, and comparisons across multiple measures were used (copy effect index, communication of "makes you feel like a kid" and "fun/enjoyment," net elements liked, and overall opinion of commercial) to select the final advertising campaign from which further commercials were "pooled out."

Miracle Whip Advertising Testing

Kraft Foods, and their advertising agency J. Walter Thompson, won a Gold Medallion Award in 1998 from the Advertising Research Foundation for excellent use of research in the "Don't Skip the Zip" advertising campaign for Miracle Whip dressing. The brand had been experiencing a decline in sales for about a decade due to decreased usage of both the brand and the category. Furthermore, the advertising campaigns for the previous decade had been inconsistent in the portrayal of the Miracle Whip brand, thereby diluting its image in the minds of target customers.

The first step was to better understand the consumer, to learn why usage was in decline and what strengths Miracle Whip had to offer that could bring customers back to the brand. According to customer insights and strategy director for Kraft Foods Jill Orum, "we needed to develop some **INSIGHTS** about how Miracle whip fits into the consumers' lives to create a message that would resonate strongly in our advertising and increase saliency of the brand [emphasis added]."[13] (Saliency involves the degree of recognition and connection of the brand to the consumer.)

Six rounds of focus groups were conducted in order to gain greater learning about the perceived advantages and uses of Miracle Whip, among heavy Miracle Whip users and heavy users of both mayonnaise and Miracle Whip. Creative projective techniques were used to get to the root of consumers' feelings, including writing a letter to Miracle Whip as though it were a person.

Heavy loyal users of Miracle Whip, who represented one-third of the users but 60 percent of Miracle Whip sales, were found to love Miracle Whip and had very personal feelings toward the brand. The product was a necessity for these moms that wanted to please their families with a tasty dish, as Miracle Whip was the

---

[13] "The ARF Names Ten Ogilvy Award Winning Campaigns," *Journal of Advertising Research* 38, no. 2, March/April 1998, 59–60.

product that allowed them to do so. The brand, therefore, was loaded emotionally for consumers with families, but past advertising had been focused on product attributes (tangy, zip, less fat). This new emotional insight appeared to be a meaningful way of refocusing the brand communication.

The resulting strategy was to create advertising that appealed to Mom's desire to please her family with the foods they love, while maintaining and reinforcing the message of Miracle Whip's taste and unique product benefits ("tangy zip"). Qualitative research was again conducted during the development of the advertising to ensure the ads resonated with the target market, and insights gained here were used in the development of several ad campaigns, including the "Don't Skip the Zip" campaign.

The campaigns were then put through a quantitative advertising pre-test to screen out all but the strongest campaigns for further development. The research revealed that the "Don't Skip the Zip" ad was the strongest performer on all measures, beating out even the benchmark ad from the last Miracle Whip campaign. The "Don't Skip the Zip" ad effectively communicated the intended message, was found to be highly enjoyable, and was among the highest-scoring ads in the Awareness Index for any Kraft Foods product. This highly effective advertising campaign increased brand awareness and improved brand imagery as well as increased sales substantially from the level before the introduction of the new campaign.

This structured, disciplined approach to gaining **customer insight** and using it to drive a brand positioning strategy worked very well for Kraft Miracle Whip, as it has for many other companies that are customer driven. Let's take a look at one more award-winning advertising campaign that was driven by **customer insight.**

General Motors OnStar System Advertising Testing

For drivers who fear that their car will break down on a lonely road in the middle of the night, General Motors (GM) has developed a "panic button" called the OnStar system. After installing the OnStar system in a new GM car, a monthly subscription fee and the press of a button gives customers access to a 24 hour/7 day a week call center staffed with highly trained advisors who can interpret glaring dashboard lights or dispatch emergency assistance if they detect that your air bag has been deployed. GM wanted to achieve sales of 4 million systems by 2003, after selling just 1 million in 2000, and decided to conduct marketing research to gain **CUSTOMER INSIGHT** into customers' needs for systems such as OnStar.[14]

The first step was to conduct qualitative research to explore consumer attitudes toward the OnStar system. A series of focus groups among subscribers and nonsubscribers to OnStar revealed the two customer emotional values that were addressed by the OnStar system that led to high interest in the system: **safety** and **security.** OnStar customers view the system as a form of **"empowerment,"**

[14] Joan Raymond, "Even Superheroes Need to Stop for Directions," *American Demographics,* March 2001.

allowing them to hit the open road knowing that they have help available to them at the push of the button.

Ethnographic research conducted in-home and in-car by a group of anthropologists from *Cultural Dynamics* revealed that the OnStar's advisors were extremely important to their subscribers.[15] In the cold, hard world of technology, OnStar's "real," friendly, and knowledgeable advisors were a welcome touch of humanity. Armed with this knowledge, OnStar and its advertising agency began to shape the creative strategy.

Additional focus groups during the advertising development process revealed very positive reactions to an advertising campaign featuring the comic book hero Batman. This superhero character was an excellent fit to the "personality" of the OnStar brand, being viewed as **trusted, caring, capable,** and **responsive.** The new campaign featuring the "Caped Crusader" for OnStar was launched in February 2000, with early technology adopters as the target market segment.

The Batman campaign boosted new service activations of OnStar systems from 100,000 per month in January of 2000 to nearly 300,000 per month in June of 2000. Subscriber renewal rates increased from 32 percent to 58 percent. The brand also experienced a 17-percentage point increase in unaided brand awareness and a whopping 42-percentage point increase in total brand awareness (unaided brand awareness added to aided brand awareness). Finally, the ad campaign was also successful in driving traffic to OnStar's website, with home page hits increasing by nearly 600 percent six months after the advertising campaign began.

David Ogilvy on Advertising Research

David Ogilvy, the marketing researcher who became a legendary advertising agency founder, has consistently stressed the productive role of marketing research in developing, evaluating, and improving great advertising. While affirming the link between superior research and superior advertising, Ogilvy has also shown where research can be used to make even greater contributions:[16]

> "Research has often led me to good ideas, such as the eye patch in the Hathaway shirt campaign."

> "I have seen ideas so wild that nobody in his senses would dare to use them — until research found that they worked."

> "Research has also saved me from making some horrendous mistakes."

> "The most important word in the vocabulary of advertising is to test. Never stop testing and your advertising will never stop improving."

Given Ogilvy's sound advice, let's move then to examining the methods used to test advertising.

---

[15] Raymond, "Even Superheroes Need to Stop for Directions."
[16] William A. Cook, "Ogilvy Winners Turn Research Into Creative Solutions," *Journal of Advertising Research* 39, no. 3, May 1999, 59.

Advertising Testing

Advertising strategy development needs to occur well before the advertising development process starts by having a deep understanding of the demographics, psychographics, feelings, attitudes, needs, and preferences of the target market. Only after the company has segmented the market effectively, selected an appropriate target segment, and developed a sound positioning strategy is it ready to develop and test advertising.

Advertising testing needs to occur both during the development of advertising as well as after the advertising is produced and aired. The goal is not to measure people's opinions about the advertising but to measure the impact of the advertising on the target consumers' awareness of the brand, attitudes toward the brand, preference of the brand, and purchasing behavior of the brand. Testing of advertising during the development stages is often called **pre-testing,** while attempting to measure the impact of advertising after it has been on the air is often called **post-testing.** The role of pre-testing is to make sure that only the strongest commercials get produced and aired, while the role of post-testing is to assess the effectiveness of an advertising campaign over time and determine when an advertising campaign may be "wearing out."

While there are many measures of "strong commercials" in assessing advertising effectiveness, many companies have historically utilized three measures to assess if their advertising is having an impact:

- **Intrusiveness** – Does the ad get noticed and involve the target customer?
- **Communication** – Does the ad communicate a message, either rational, emotional, or both, that is meaningful to the target customer?
- **Persuasion** – Does the ad make target customers more likely to buy the product?

Different levels of emphasis may be placed on these three measures, depending on the objectives and goals of the advertising.

However, many different approaches have been utilized to evaluate the effects of advertising, some with good success and others with mixed success. Let's examine five major quantitative testing methods that have been in widespread use over the past twenty years: recall testing, recognition testing, persuasion testing, purchase behavior testing, and likeability.

Five Categories of Advertising Testing Methods

Advertising copy-testing methods can be grouped into five major categories, depending on their primary measure of advertising effectiveness:

- **Recall** – these copy-testing methods typically recruit target consumers to watch a television program in their homes, during which the test commercial is embedded. Respondents are telephoned the following day to determine the percent of respondents that can recall seeing the commercial and how many can recall key copy points. Examples of recall testing methods

include Gallup & Robinson and Mapes & Ross. However, Brian Sternthal points to the problem of using explicit measures, such as recall of an advertising message, to assess advertising effectiveness: "Consumers often have **difficulty in tracing the origin of their knowledge.** People respond to advertising by relating what they know to the ad content. What is stored in memory is a combination of the message information and recipients' own thoughts. Free recall and other explicit measures of memory are likely to be poor indicators of advertising effectiveness."[17] The exposure effect, as well as Zaltman's seventh premise that most thought, emotion, and learning occur without our awareness, would make one suspect the validity of recall measures of advertising. Research studies have found that recall measures indeed do have weak correlations to purchasing behavior, and that recognition is almost always better than recall in the retrieval of information stored in the memory.[18] However, some marketers continue to use recall of advertising as their primary measure of advertising effectiveness.

- **Recognition** – these copy-testing methods involved showing respondents edited cues of advertising with the brand name masked. Those who can correctly identify the brand advertised in the commercial have been exposed to it. The brand imagery and brand preferences of this "exposed group" are then compared to the brand imagery and preferences of the group who did not correctly identify the brand in the ad. The difference between these groups is used to estimate the **"ad effect."** Recently, online surveys have been used effectively to test advertising using this recognition approach. Examples of recognition testing methods include Bruzzone Research Company (BRC) and Communicus.

- **Persuasion** – these copy-testing methods involve the forced exposure of advertising to target respondents in a theater-like environment or on-air, and utilize pre-test and post-test measures of brand preference (or simulated purchase) to estimate the ability of the ad to persuade target respondents to prefer the test brand over others. Diagnostic measures are also obtained, such as comprehension of message, perception of brand uniqueness or brand differentiation, and viewer involvement. Performance on these measures is compared to industry norms provided by the testing company to allow the comparison of the test ad to benchmarks compiled from thousands of ads tested previously. Examples of persuasion testing methods include McCollum/Spielman Worldwide, ASI, and ARS.

- **Purchase behavior** – copy-testing methods that use an experimental approach to measure the impact of advertising on purchase behavior directly are clearly the most valid approaches to measuring the impact of

---

[17] Brian Sternthal, "Advertising Strategy," in *Kellogg on Marketing*, ed. Dawn Iacobucci (New York: John Wiley and Sons, 2001), 240–241.
[18] John Lynch and Thomas Srull, "Memory and Attentional Factors in Consumer Choice: Concepts and Research Methods," *Journal of Consumer Research*, June 1982.

advertising. Unfortunately, these approaches require a great deal of time and are extremely expensive ways to test advertising. Advertising experiments conducted at the Campbell Soup Company in the 1970s tested the effects of increased advertising, shifts to different media (such as outdoor ads), shifts to different markets, and new creative approaches. A one-year long experiment for Chunky Soups evaluated the shift of 25 percent of the spot television budget to outdoor advertising in two test markets. An increase in sales of 8 percent was found after eight months, an increase that was attributed to new people reached by outdoor advertising that were not reached previously by television advertising. In five experiments of new advertising campaigns at Campbell, increased sales were found in three of the experiments.[19] Currently, the most popular experimental method for testing the impact of advertising on purchase behavior is BehaviorScan, offered by Information Resources, Inc. This electronic test marketing service offers an in-market laboratory that allows the marketer to isolate the effects of advertising from promotional and competitive effects. BehaviorScan allows different ads to be aired to different households within the same markets using split-cable TV testing in a number of carefully controlled cities throughout the United States. Within the same market, households on the BehaviorScan panel are assigned randomly to an A panel, B panel, or C panel. BehaviorScan has the ability to send different commercials into each of the three panels and can monitor the shopping habits of each household through supermarket scanners. Each household is given a "member discount card" to use in the supermarket, which allows BehaviorScan to identify purchases by individual household. In a typical copy test, Panel A may be exposed to new ad campaign 1; Panel B may be exposed to new ad campaign 2, while Panel C continues to see the current ad campaign. Over a three to six month period, small differences in supermarket sales across the three panels can be attributed to the differential impact of advertising, given that all other factors are controlled for in the experimental design. BehaviorScan has also been used effectively to test different levels of advertising (media weight tests) and to assess the impact of alternative couponing and sampling programs on household behavior.

• **Likeability of Ad** – More television advertisers today are relying heavily on entertainment value to capture the attention of target viewers and hope that viewers will pay some attention to it. Many advertisers are placing heavy emphasis on **likeability** of their ads, including the world's largest advertiser, Procter & Gamble (P&G). According to Jim Stengel, P&G's global marketing officer, the company weights its copy testing heavily on whether the consumers say they'd like to watch the ad again. "For each element of the marketing mix, we should ask ourselves, 'Would consumers

---

[19] J. Eastlack and Ambar Rao, "Conducting Advertising Experiments in the Real World: The Campbell Soup Company Experience," *Marketing Science*, Winter 1989.

choose to look at or listen to this?' Let that be the benchmark. All market-ing should be permission marketing."[20] Many advertising testing companies measure ad likeability, usually on a second-by-second basis, using hand-held "Perception Analyzers," which customers use to express their reactions to the advertising execution.

Which Advertising Testing Measure to Use

Recent research cited here casts doubt on the ability of measures of **ad recall** to predict advertising effectiveness, and this approach is likely to continue to decline in usage.

Persuasion measures remain in use by many marketers, even though the evidence suggests that these are poor measures of advertising effectiveness for established brands. It is likely that the intuitive appeal of this measure will keep it as a widely used measure of advertising effectiveness, especially for new products and products with predominantly rational reasons for purchase.

For large consumer brands, experimental approaches to measure the impact of advertising on actual **purchase behavior** (such as BehaviorScan) continue to be sound marketing investments.

Ad recognition measures, combined with measures of **ad likeability,** have grown in popularity, as these measures have shown a good relationship with consumer purchase choices. More and more evidence is being published that suggests that these measures are the most predictive of advertising that has a posi-tive impact on sales. For consumer products and services, **ad recognition** and **ad likeability** are the future of advertising assessment.

Implicit Measures of Advertising Effectiveness

After new advertising has been aired for a period of time, it is useful to assess the impact of the new advertising on target consumers (i.e. post-test) using implicit measures rather than the explicit measures used in many of the pre-tests discussed above. Sternthal and Angela Lee suggest four implicit measures that can be used to more accurately assess advertising effectiveness:[21]

- **Brand recall and knowledge** – people are asked to tell what they know about the brand rather than what they recall about the advertising. Tracked over time, effective advertising should deepen the relationship between the brand and the target customer.
- **Top-of-Mind Brand Awareness** – this is the percent of target customers who respond with your brand when prompted with a category

---

[20] AdAge.com, "P&G Marketing Boss Slams Ad Industry for Foot-Dragging," quoted in *Research World, ESOMAR*, March 2004, 5.
[21] Brian Sternthal and Angela Lee, "Putting Copy-Testers to the Test," in *Mastering Marketing*, Tim Dickson, exec. ed. (London: FT Pitman, 1999).

clue. For example, when asked, "When you think of beer, which brand comes to mind?" more people will respond with "Budweiser" than with any other brand, due largely to the cumulative impact of many years of effective, frequent Budweiser advertising. Research has shown that the brands that consumers recall first tend to be the brands that are used most often by those same consumers. Further, top-of-mind brand awareness will lag share of users for a brand that is in the growth phase and will exceed share of users for a declining brand.[22]

- **Attitudes toward the brand** – in addition to probing what people *know* about a brand, it is also important to assess how people *feel* about the brand.
- **Extent to which the advertising increases loyalty or boosts resistance to competitors' overtures** – these measures are perhaps the most important of the implicit measures, and they are also the most difficult to measure. An experimental approach, such as that offered by BehaviorScan, could assess brand-switching trends across household panels exposed to different levels of advertising. A robust experiment of this nature, however, could require twelve to eighteen months to execute.

All marketers should have consumer studies in place to track these implicit measures of advertising effectiveness, as they are critical in assessing the return on marketing dollars invested. Annual measures of brand knowledge, brand attitudes, and brand recall (not ad recall) can determine if advertising efforts have strengthened the relationship between target customers and the brand. If advertising hasn't had an impact on these implicit measures over time, the return on the advertising investment is questionable and the advertising strategy should be reassessed.

Testing Impact of Internet Banner Advertising

The Internet continues to attract a growing share of advertising dollars, as consumers are spending more time online and less time watching television. According to Nielsen/NetRatings, web advertising accounted for 3.3 percent of total advertising spending in the United States in 2003, up from 3.1 percent in 2002.

P&G, the world's leading spender on marketing, wanted to determine if banner ads appearing on many web pages on the Internet were an effective advertising medium for their target customers. They partnered with Information Resources, Inc., the large marketing research firm that provides syndicated supermarket scanner information, to test the impact of online banner advertising on off-line purchases of three P&G products.

Seven different banner ads were created for the three different products, and the ads were exposed to a test group during a sixteen-week test period. This Internet panel of 3,000 households agreed to allow their online activity to be

---

[22] Alin Gruber, "Top-of-Mind Awareness and Share of Families: An Observation," *Journal of Marketing Research* 6, no. 2, May 1969.

monitored. Utilizing sound experimental design principles, P&G selected a matched panel of 3,000 households to serve as the control group. The control group was analyzed to ensure that they matched the test group in aggregate on demographic characteristics as well as on off-line purchasing behavior. The control group's online activity was also monitored, but they were not exposed to the P&G banner ads. Purchase behavior among both the test and control panels was monitored via store scanners by Information Resources, Inc.

For two of the three products tested, banner ads did not significantly increase the purchases of the exposed group as compared to the control group. However, for the third product, an impulse brand, banner advertising did significantly increase the purchases of the exposed group as compared to the control group. It appears that banner ads may serve as an effective "reminder to buy" for well-known impulse brands.

The Ten Commandments of eAdvertising

Information Resources, Inc., expanded upon this work in partnership with Unilever in Greenwich, Connecticut, to measure the incremental volume impact from eAds for eight brands, controlling for other ads and in-store stimuli.[23]

Using DoubleClick's cookie-based targeting method, up to eight ads per week were served to test panelists in women-oriented sites for fifteen weeks. The research resulted in "10 Commandments" of consumer packaged goods eAdvertising:

1. Consumers **are** influenced by banner ads.
2. **eAds work for top-tier brands** and show potential for stronger results with smaller brands.
3. Online ads can effectively drive offline sales.
4. News drives ad impact.
5. Brands in expandable consumption categories (ones where larger inventories and package sizes in the home tend to lead to increased consumption, such as beer, soft drinks, and snacks) are likely to respond well.
6. TV-sensitive brands are likely to produce better eAd results.
7. Messages are key drivers of incremental sales.
8. Ad messaging should determine optimal ad units.
9. Frequency matters, but not at the expense of reach.
10. Return on investment is driven by improved media efficiency and impact.

Based on this research, the authors of the article concluded that the Internet should be an integral part of the marketing communications planning for any consumer packaged goods company.

[23] Patti Wakeling and Brian Murphy, "Evidence that eAds can be Effective," cited in *June 2002 Conference Report* (ARF Annual Convention and Research Infoplex New York, N. Y., April 2002).

Brain Waves and Electrical Brain Activity

A thought-provoking article appeared in *Forbes* magazine in 2003 covering current research on the tracking of brain activity and using these measures to assess if brand preferences were forming.[24] Electroencephalographs were used to pick up cognitive functions in twelve different regions of the brain, showing memory recall and the level of attention paid to visual and aural stimuli.

MRI machines were used to pick up 1,000 brain images while respondents were shown pictures of different cars. Among the companies looking into whether brain signals can supplement or replace traditional tests of consumer response to commercials are General Motors, Ford of Europe, and Camelot, the national lottery operator in the United Kingdom.

All of this research is moving toward the elusive goal of finding the "buy button" inside the consumer's head and to test products, advertising, and packaging for their ability to activate this "buy button." While initial results of this research look promising, it is unlikely that a consumer's "buy button" will be found. Rather, brain activity monitoring could prove to be an important supplemental test of marketing stimuli in the future, once the issues of high cost and testing effects of the equipment on the respondent are resolved.

Investment Cost

- Four focus groups, conducted by a skilled moderator, including analysis and report, will cost:
    - $20,000–$25,000 in the United States
    - $20,000–$22,000 in France and Japan
    - $17,000–$19,000 in the U.K. and Germany
    - $4,000–$6,000 in China and India
- A computer-assisted central location advertising pre-test among three representative samples of 100 consumers each, lasting ten minutes, would cost:
    - $33,000–$40,000 in Japan
    - $24,000–$30,000 in the United States, U.K., and Australia
    - $17,000–$22,000 in France and Germany
    - $8,000–$11,000 in Russia and China
- A tracking study to measure the implicit measures of advertising effectiveness, such as brand recall, brand knowledge, top-of-mind awareness, and attitudes toward brands, among a nationally representative sample of 1,000 consumers, conducted by telephone at a rate of fifty a week for twenty consecutive weeks, lasting fifteen minutes, would cost:
    - $62,000–$70,000 in Japan
    - $47,000–$53,000 in the United States and France
    - $38,000–$42,000 in the U.K. and Germany

---

[24] Melanie Wells, "In Search of the Buy Button," *Forbes,* 1 September 2003.

- ○ $17,000–$20,000 in Italy
- ○ $6,000–$8,000 in Russia
- A Business-to-Business telephone survey to track implicit measures of advertising effectiveness, lasting fifteen minutes, among 200 business executives, where the sampling list is provided to the research firm, would cost:
  - ○ $30,000–$35,000 in the United States
  - ○ $22,000–$26,000 in the U. K. and Japan
  - ○ $18,000–$21,000 in Germany
  - ○ $7,000–$9,000 in Italy
- On-air recall copy tests, utilizing 150 target consumers and a telephone survey, typically cost about $25,000–$30,000 per commercial.
- Recognition-based copy tests, conducted online with 150 target consumers, typically cost about $30,000–$35,000 per commercial.
- Forced exposure persuasion copy tests, conducted in a theater setting with 150 target consumers, typically cost about $30,000–$35,000 per commercial.
- Test market experiments, utilizing systems like the BehaviorScan system, typically cost $200,000–$275,000 for exclusive category testing in several markets.

Communication Message Checklist

- What emotional significance does your brand hold with your target customers?
- Does your advertising address these emotional needs of your target customers?
- Into which of the FCB quadrants does our product best fit?
- Are your advertising objectives consistent with the role of advertising in that quadrant?
- Does your advertising present the product's functional and emotional benefits closely together?
- Does your advertising present new information to customers that has personal relevance to them and has some connection to what they already know?
- Do you keep your positioning stable while keeping your advertising new and fresh?
- Do you have a rigorous system in place to test your advertising regularly, and do you constantly improve your advertising based on the results?
- Do you rely on verbatim recall of advertising as your primary measure of advertising effectiveness, or do you utilize broader measures, such as top-of-mind brand awareness, brand knowledge, brand preference, and actual brand purchases?

PRICE SENSITIVITY

INSIGHT 8: Your customers will be more willing to pay a premium price when you help them understand the value of the benefits of your product offering.

Pricing is both a science and an art. Theory will get you some way in understanding the science; but only by practice will you learn the art.

Lakshman Krishnamurthi, Kellogg School of Management

Customer Insight Pyramid

The High Impact of Price Sensitivity

No marketing decision has more immediate impact on bottom-line profitability than does the pricing decision. On high volume products, a few pennies more per unit can mean millions of dollars of increased revenue and profit. Gaining customer insight on price sensitivity is critical to ensure that the price level is consistent with the *value* of the product or service in the mind of the target customer.

The Three Pricing Decisions

When making pricing decisions, marketers can make two wrong decisions and one right decision:

- **WRONG**: Set the price **above** the value perceived by customers. The result will be that few customers will buy and the warehouses will remain full of inventory.
- **WRONG**: Set the price **below** the value perceived by customers. The result will be that many customers will eagerly buy, inventories will run out, and back orders will occur.
- **RIGHT**: Set the price **at** the value perceived by customers. The result will be satisfied customers who feel that they are getting a fair price, a predictable stream of products in inventory, and higher profits than in either of the other two cases.

The Three Cs of Pricing Determination

There are many ways companies determine what price to charge for their product. The simplest is basing the pricing decision on **cost,** using a cost-plus calculation. While this approach may result in some profit for the firm, it is unlikely to maximize profits because money may be "left on the table" in cases where the firm is providing high value to customers and is only marking up the product slightly.

Other firms determine their price by setting them at or near **competitors'** prices. For undifferentiated products, this indeed may be the only appropriate option. In most cases, this is a poor strategy because it assumes that your product and competitors' products provide identical value to customers.

The extent to which competitors should affect your price depends on four factors:[1]

- What is your brand equity?
- How loyal are your customers?
- How substitutable are the products?
- What is the extent of market concentration?

Thus, your competitors will be able to impact your pricing when your brand equity is low, when your customer loyalty is low, when products are perceived as substitutes, and when markets are highly concentrated, with many brands chasing scarce customers. When your brand is effectively differentiated, has high brand equity, has loyal customers, and is not in a concentrated market, price cuts by competitors will have minimal impact on purchasing of your brand.

Enlightened firms base their pricing decision on **customer value,** which is usually a win-win situation for the company and the customer. If the firm provides

---

[1] Lakshman Krishnamurthi, "Pricing: Part Art, Part Science," in *Mastering Marketing,* Tim Dickson, exec. ed. (London: FT Pitman, 1999), 81–87.

more value to customers than competitors do, customers are often willing to pay more for this offering, and the firm is rewarded with increased revenues and profits to invest in the future of the business. This is the essence of the capitalist system of government; provide more value and you will be rewarded for it.

Differentiating advantages based solely upon functional innovation, however, can be short lived. "But a psychological advantage, properly nurtured, can live on for a long time. It is brand equity that makes cross-price elasticities asymmetric and favorable to you. The smart marketer builds in differentiation, real or perceived, to try to make comparisons across products more difficult. The smart marketer also finds the market segment that will value these differentiating features."[2]

Understanding Customer Value

Prior to measuring a customer's willingness to pay for a product or service, the pricing strategist must understand what drives customer value. According to two highly regarded pricing experts:[3]

> Value is the objective worth to a customer of satisfying the benefits they seek from a product or service. It's the potential level to which willingness-to-pay can be raised, and revenue captured, with an effective strategy for managing value perception, and the prices charged. **Willingness-to-pay will fall short of value if customers don't understand the benefits of a product** [emphasis added].

Thus, it is critical that the marketer understand the potential value that could be created by the product or service for the customer and communicate this value creation prominently in its advertising strategy. Making the mistake of assuming that the value of new features will be "obvious" to all customers dilutes the customer's willingness-to-pay for those new features. The marketer needs to measure the value created (or not created) carefully by the product/service offering to target customers.

> Measuring value is concerned primarily with understanding the system of value delivery – determining how the integration of a new product or service into a buyer's business creates incremental value and then measuring or estimating the monetary worth of this incremental value.
>
> Usually features by themselves are insufficient to produce benefits or value. Thus, an objective of values research is to identify the value creation system of which your product or service is an integral part – the system of features and benefits. This helps make sure features will produce the benefits to justify the price that reflects the value. Understanding value is a consultative in-depth process, with open-ended inquiry and exploration of customer problems, solutions, and consequent outcomes.[4]

---

[2] Krishnamurthi, "Pricing: Part Art, Part Science", 86.

[3] Gerald E. Smith and Thomas T. Nagle, "How Much are Customers Willing to Pay?" *Marketing Research*, Winter 2002, 20–25.

[4] Smith and Nagle, "How Much are Customers Willing to Pay?" 20–25.

An example of understanding customer value involves a software company that develops laboratory information systems (L.I.S.) for hospitals. This L.I.S. company developed a highly reliable information system to collect patient blood test results from different blood analyzer instruments in the hospital laboratory. The system then incorporated these results into the library information system, which interfaced easily with the hospital information system for billing and archiving purposes, compared the results to the patients previous test results, and reported the results to the nurses station on each floor on computer terminals in time for the physicians who were doing morning rounds to act upon. Prior to this product's launch, most of this test result collation was done manually.

To understand the additional value created for the hospital by this new laboratory information system, depth interviews were conducted among doctors, nurses, hospital administrators, and laboratory staff to understand the benefits provided by the new L.I.S. fully and into what monetary value those benefits might translate.

Clear customer benefits were discovered in this "value research" that allowed the manufacturer to position the product successfully and justify the high price of the system. Among the customer benefits found that were worth a lot of money to the customers were:

- Fewer errors in the reporting of lab test results, which could be lethal if patient results were mixed up
- A saving of several hours per week per nurse in tracking down blood test results, which previously involved phoning the lab and waiting while the lab supervisor tried to track down the latest patient test results. This saving in nurse time is easily translated into dollars and cents
- Improved patient recovery time, as most physicians would now have timely, accurate blood work results to adjust patient medication and treatment regimens. This increase in quality of care had significant impact on patient satisfaction as well as physician satisfaction

By going beyond the technical features of the new L.I.S. system and understanding how its use would create value within the customer's environment, this company was able to communicate this value effectively to customers as they launched the system, and to execute a premium price strategy successfully. The success enjoyed by this company allowed it to invest further resources into continual improvements of this successful product line.

Thus, understanding the value created for customers by your product offering is the critical first step in developing a pricing strategy. Only when your product is framed in this "value positioning" can you expect customers to realistically respond to purchase likelihood questions on your "value proposition." If technical features alone describe your product, you can expect few customers to be willing to pay a premium price for the product. Remember, customers buy solutions, not products. They are uninterested in your new, latest technical features; they are very interested in how your product can make their life less stressful or more enjoyable.

Let's look at an example of a company that set prices based on competition rather than customer value and the penalty that was paid as a result.

Coors Pricing Strategy in Expansion Markets

During the 1970s, the Coors Brewing Company was still a regional brewery, serving only eleven states in the Western United States. Its single brewery in the foothills of the Rocky Mountains in Golden, Colorado, was at maximum capacity. Even though beer distributors outside of the eleven-state area were begging for the rights to distribute Coors beer, the brewery could barely supply the loyal customers they had within their current eleven-state marketing area. In the country's biggest beer-consuming state, California, Coors market share reached 55 percent.

Coors beer had become tremendously popular in the 1970s for a number of reasons, including:

- Americans' taste preferences moved to lighter beverages, such as bottled water, white wine, and lighter-tasting beers like Coors.
- The demand created by the limited distribution made Coors tremendously popular in the thirty-nine states where it wasn't available. Skiers returning from great vacations in Colorado remember drinking this beer during their vacation and began smuggling cases of Coors back to their home states and charging exorbitant prices for it. This scarcity created high value in the minds of many beer drinkers nationally.
- A popular movie, starring Burt Reynolds, called *Smokey and the Bandit,* was about the adventures of a trucker who was attempting to smuggle an entire truckload of Coors beer to east of the Mississippi.
- The "Rocky Mountain" imagery of cold, clean water, surrounding the Coors brewery, was effective in communicating powerful emotional cues to beers drinkers, such as "smooth," "light," and "refreshing."

It seemed that Coors was in the right place at the right time with a lighter, refreshing beer for which more and more young beer drinkers were looking. Coors was enjoying tremendous success, with very modest investments in marketing and advertising. It seemed that nothing could go wrong for this Rocky Mountain legend.

Things changed in 1976, when the AFL–CIO labor organization was unsuccessful in organizing a union among the Coors Brewery workers and called for a national boycott of Coors beer. The Coors family felt that a union would get in the way of their relationship with their loyal brewery workers, some of whom were second and third generation brewery employees. But the boycott hit sales of Coors hard. Sales in the eleven-state marketing area dropped dramatically, as loyal union workers pressured their friends as well as strangers in bars not to drink that "scab" beer, a derogatory term for products made by companies that were being boycotted by unions.

But Coors had an out. As sales dropped in California, Colorado, and Washington, they could easily expand their marketing area and select distributors in nearby states

that had been extremely eager in the past to distribute the golden beer from the Rockies and get rich quick.

A plan was developed to expand to three to six states every other year, and this expanded distribution strategy was successful in returning the brewery to near-full capacity and high profitability. As new states were opened, distributors were brought on board, and heavy television advertising announced the arrival of the "taste of the Rockies." However, the marketing group was uncertain on the pricing strategy for Coors in these expansion states, since Coors still enjoyed a "highly special" image in these states where Coors had never been available, except from "bootleggers" who had smuggled it back from Colorado and charged several multiples over the price of Budweiser for it.

Several options were available for pricing Coors beer in these expansion markets:

- **Customer value** pricing strategy, where the price would be at a moderate to large premium over mainstream beers, such as Budweiser
- **Customer value** pricing strategy, where the price would be at a small to moderate premium over mainstream beers, such as Budweiser
- **Competitor-based** pricing strategy, where Coors would be priced similarly to Budweiser, which was its major competitor in its eleven-state marketing area

To make a good pricing decision that would price the product at the value that customers place upon Coors beer in these expansion states, a marketing research study was conducted. The study involved exposing a Coors introductory television commercial to target beer drinkers in these expansion states and obtaining their purchase interest in Coors and the expected share of their beer consumption that Coors might capture. However, the study involved three separate groups of consumers, each exposed to a different price for Coors, reflecting the three previously stated pricing options.

The results of this marketing research study were very encouraging, in that many customers expected to pay more for Coors than for Budweiser because of the special image that Coors enjoyed in these expansion states. In fact, beer drinkers expected to pay a moderate to large premium over mainstream brands for the newly available Coors. This was the marketer's dream, because this price premium could:

- Go to offset the increased shipping costs as the beer was delivered to markets farther from Golden, Colorado
- Go to fund investments in marketing and advertising, since Miller Brewing in Milwaukee seemed to be increasing the "table stakes" required to compete in the beer business
- Return more profit to the shareholders

Marketing management was delighted by these marketing research results and recommended a pricing strategy that would be above Budweiser beer, consistent with the expectations and value perceptions of customers.

President Bill Coors, however, vetoed the idea of charging more for Coors in these new markets. He felt it would be "unethical" to price Coors above Budweiser

in Illinois, when it was priced similarly to Budweiser in the eleven states in the Western United States. He cared little about the value that customers placed upon his grandfather's creation and felt that Budweiser was the pricing reference for Coors beer. Despite numerous discussions on pricing and the profit impact of a premium price, Bill held to his decision to follow Budweiser in price regardless of what customers thought Coors beer was worth.

This misguided pricing strategy created perceptual problems among many beer drinkers during the launch in the new states. Beer drinkers, delighted by the press reports and new advertising for Coors beer coming to their state, eagerly went to their local store to buy a case of this new, special Coors beer from Golden, Colorado. Most were expecting to pay a premium for this elixir from the Rockies that had been unavailable to them previously and hoped it wouldn't be so expensive that they couldn't afford it. When they saw Coors beer in the store at the same price as Budweiser, many experienced "cognitive dissonance" and wondered what was wrong with this Coors beer. Was it old Coors beer that they couldn't sell in California? Was it a different, lower-quality version of the "real" stuff sold in Colorado?

This lack of alignment of the elements of the marketing mix can create a great deal of confusion among consumers. When the product, advertising, and image all lead a consumer to expect something special, the pricing strategy also needs to support that premium strategy and work synergistically with the other marketing mix elements. When the pricing strategy is inconsistent with the other marketing mix strategies and does not work synergistically within the marketing mix, customer confusion is the result. Rather than achieving the forecasted double-digit market shares at a premium price, Coors achieved single-digit market shares in many expansion states at a lower, mainstream beer price. The low success of Coors beer in many expansion markets has kept Coors a distant third to Budweiser and Miller in the beer wars, despite the addition of a major Coors facility in Virginia to finish and package beer.

Price Promotional Strategy

Setting the everyday price is the first major decision facing the marketer. But a second pricing decision is almost equally important: how frequently to conduct price promotions, where the price of the product is reduced temporarily to induce channel members to display your product at a reduced price in their stores and to induce target customers to switch to your brand. "Sales promotions work poorest in markets of high brand similarity, attracting brand switchers who are looking for low price and who won't be loyal to the brand. Sales promotions should be used sparingly, because incessant prices off, coupons and deals can devalue a brand in the consumers' mind."[5]

Let's examine the impact of a major change in price promotion strategy by the world's largest marketing spender, Procter & Gamble (P&G), which began in 1991.

---

[5] Philip Kotler, *Marketing Insights from A to Z: 80 Concepts Every Manager Needs to Know* (Hoboken, NJ: John Wiley and Sons, 2003), 161.

P&G Everyday Low Pricing Strategy

Procter and Gamble, maker of such well-known brands as Crest toothpaste, Tide detergent, Pampers diapers, Folgers coffee, Bounty paper towels, and Pantene shampoo, is the world's largest marketing spender, with 2002 expenditures of 4.5 billion U.S. dollars. This expenditure level is over $1.2 billion more than second place Unilever.[6]

Beginning in 1991, P&G decided to make major changes in its marketing mix strategy in an attempt to reduce its operating costs and strengthen brand loyalty. These changes involved:

- Substantial reductions in the number of temporary price promotions
- Substantial reductions in coupons
- Introduction of "Everyday Low Prices" in their place
- Increases in advertising expenditures

These marketing changes ran counter to the general trend of promotion increases at the expense of advertising that prevailed in the packaged goods industry during the 1980s and early 1990s. However, P&G found that retailers tended to stockpile products when promotional allowances were offered, which impacted P&G profitability, disrupted P&G production schedules, and strained the warehouses of both P&G and the retailers. P&G initiated the "Everyday Low Pricing" strategy to address these operational and profitability issues.

P&G also hoped that the low everyday price strategy would keep deal prone customers from switching to competitors, and that the increased advertising expenditures would build stronger brand equity for its brands over time.

The effects of these major policy changes were recently reported in a leading journal.[7] This comprehensive analysis looked at 118 brands in twenty-four different product categories in the consumer packaged goods industry over a seven-year period beginning in 1990.

During that period, P&G policy changes resulted in:

- 16 percent decline in price deal frequency for P&G brands
- 53 percent decline in P&G coupons
- 20 percent **increase** in the net price paid by consumers for P&G brands
- 20 percent increase in advertising expenditures behind P&G brands

Competitors' response to these changes in P&G marketing tactics was mixed. For advertising and coupons, competitors followed P&G directionally but not completely. For price deals, competitors did not follow P&G at all and continued to offer temporary special price promotions to retailers to induce newspaper features, store displays, and temporary consumer price reductions. The net price paid by consumers for

---

[6] Source: *Advertising Age* magazine, cited in "Marketing News," American Marketing Association.

[7] Kusum Ailawadi, Donald Lehmann, and Scott Neslin, "Market Response to a Major Policy Change in the Marketing Mix: Learning from Procter & Gamble's Value Pricing Strategy," *Journal of Marketing* 65, no. 1, January 2001.

competitors' brands **increased only 8 percent** over the period, less than half of the increase in the P&G prices. Thus, P&G's relative value to the customer decreased.

Many consumers reacted negatively and quickly to the elimination of coupons by Procter & Gamble. Some consumers boycotted P&G products; others held public hearings to "fight for their right to save." Many of these coupon users turned to competitors' brands, with these competitors seeing the redemption rate of their coupons increase by as much as 48 percent. The New York state attorney general took P&G to court in 1997 over the elimination of coupons, accusing P&G of colluding with competitors to eliminate coupons. P&G, without admitting any wrongdoing, agreed to settle these antitrust charges by paying $4.2 million.

The P&G strategy resulted in serious market share losses for most of its brands, with the average brand across the twenty-four categories losing about one-fifth of its market share over the seven-year period. The decrease in share was due primarily to **decreased penetration**, meaning a loss of users, rather than decreased **share-of-requirements** among users who continued to use P&G brands. Thus, it appears that P&G lost a segment of consumers who respond well to deals and coupons, but maintained their business with other customers. The effects of P&G's increased advertising expenditures during this period were difficult to measure.

But this strategy cannot be judged as a success or failure without looking at the impact upon P&G profitability, since many firms have found it healthy to shed unprofitable customers, lose market share, and enhance their overall profitability. The following chart shows a significant drop in P&G profits in 1993, during the early stages of the strategy. This significant profit loss was a strong signal to P&G that their reduction in price deals and coupons was too extreme and forced them to rethink their pricing and "couponing" strategy. Fortunately, profits recovered thereafter as adjustments were made to the marketing mix strategy.

Procter and Gamble
Earnings Per Share 1989–1999
Source: Mergent Online

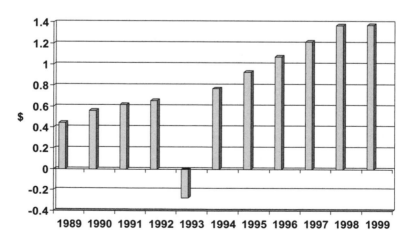

The authors of the study concluded that cuts in promotion, even if coupled with increases in advertising, would not grow market share for the average established brand in mature consumer goods categories. In this case, P&G competitors refused to match the moves made by P&G fully and gained significant market share due to their competitive advantage among the coupon sensitive segment. Further, these changes in marketing tactics by P&G resulted in price increases for P&G products that were two and a half times larger than the price increases of competitors. P&G may have been well served by conducting limited area test markets of these strategies prior to their national implementation.

Pricing Issues

Developing an effective pricing strategy requires a consideration of many factors, both internal to the company as well as external factors. Lakshman Krishnamurthi has identified seven issues that must be considered to have an effective pricing strategy:[8]

- Pricing should reflect strategic objectives (profits or market share).
- Pricing should reflect the customer target.
- Pricing should reflect product positioning.
- Pricing should reflect competitive position.
- Pricing should take costs into account, noting that **variable cost is the floor** and **customer value is the ceiling.**
- Pricing should take channel considerations into account.
- Pricing should understand the product life cycle (growing brand or mature brand?).

Companies should strive to understand the value their product offering provides to customers so that they can set prices based on customer value rather than on the other extreme of variable cost.

Krishnamurthi also suggests nine possible methods to assess consumer responses to pricing, which will be discussed next.[9]

Methods for Testing Pricing

The nine methods identified by Krishnamurthi for determining consumers' price sensitivity range from simple and subjective, to the complex and objective. They involve managerial judgment, use of analogous products, benchmarking, the analysis of historical data, economic value, focus groups, surveys using a monadic split-cell design, conjoint analysis, and experimentation. We'll begin with the simple and proceed to the complex.

- **Managerial judgment** – This method involves assembling a group of decision makers, including product managers, salespeople, engineering, and

---

[8] Lakshman Krishnamurthi, "Pricing Strategy and Tactics," in *Kellogg on Marketing*, ed. Dawn Iacobucci (New York: John Wiley and Sons, 2001), 270.
[9] Krishnamurthi, "Pricing Strategy and Tactics," 283–286.

so forth, and having each estimate the percent change in sales to various price increases and price decreases. These estimates are then aggregated to provide an internally generated demand curve.

- **Use of analogous products** – This method involves pricing the current generation of the product based on previous generations. It assumes that consumers will assess the "fairness" of pricing based on the improvements in the new product as compared to previous generations of the product.
- **Benchmarking** – This method involves an analysis of price response of competitive products; if a competitor raised price by 5 percent but only lost 2 percent in unit sales, we may decide that we also have an opportunity to increase total revenue through a price increase
- **Analysis of historical data** – Many firms have access to high quality historical sales and pricing data, either from internal records or from syndicated sources. This past data can be analyzed to understand the change in volume that followed a change in price to allow estimation of a demand curve for their products.
- **Economic value** – Economic value modeling involves using a currently used product for a reference price, adding an incremental monetary amount that represents the additional value provided by your product, then subtracting an amount that represents the cost to the customer of switching to your product (e.g., training costs).
- **Focus groups** – Broad price expectations and perceptions of value across brands can be obtained from customers in focus groups. However, this approach should not be used when a specific price point needs to be determined, as many consumers tend to understate the price they are willing to pay when asked directly.
- **Surveys using a monadic split-cell design** – Purchase intention surveys can be used to obtain likelihood of purchase of a product, with different groups of customers exposed to the same product but at different prices. A demand curve can be generated by using the different prices with different random samples of target customers. For example, five random samples of 100 customers each are selected, with each sample exposed to the product offering at a different price. The first sample responds to the product offering at a price of $50, the second sample responds to the identical product offering except at the price of $65, and so on for prices of $80, $95, and $110. Having a single respondent respond to a product using multiple price points causes confusion on the customer's part and will usually result in an understatement of what customers are actually willing to pay for the product. By having separate cells for each of the price levels, you are keeping the respondent *naïve* as to the purpose of the research study, thereby avoiding biased data from respondents who may catch on to the game if you were to show them the same product at different price levels.
- **Conjoint analysis** – Conjoint analysis can be used to calibrate trade-offs customers make between price and various levels of product attributes. Simulation models can be used to model the preference for and value

placed upon competitive products as well as your product under various pricing strategies. Advanced forms of conjoint analysis, namely choice-based conjoint and discrete choice modeling, can begin to measure the price elasticities of the numerous brands in a market.

- **Experimentation** – Controlled field experiments, such as controlled store tests, are excellent methods of assessing price response. Matched groups of test and control stores are selected, with the price varied in test stores for a period of time and sales results compared to those in control stores. When conducted properly, experiments provide reliable measures of consumer price sensitivity. However, live experiments can be costly, time consuming, and difficult to implement with retailers.

Direct Approach or Indirect Approach?

Direct questioning approaches, such as asking customers what they would pay for a product, are problematic and should be avoided whenever possible in pricing research. These direct approaches are rarely predictive of what actually happens in the marketplace and therefore often produce misleading results. With direct questioning approaches to pricing, you are focusing the respondent on only one part of the marketing mix and putting the respondent in an "expert" role, rather than keeping the respondent in the role of a consumer.

There are two reasons for the poor validity of direct questioning approaches in pricing research:

- Many consumers assume that businesses take a cost-focused approach to pricing their products, with manufacturers adding a "fair profit" to their costs; these consumers are puzzled and confused when manufacturers survey them on the price they should charge for their products.
- Some consumers, when asked what price a product should be, catch on to the intent of the research and will usually answer with a price that is below the price that they would actually pay.

Indirect approaches, which keep the respondent naïve as to the purpose of the research, are needed to provide external validity for the pricing research. Otherwise, shrewd respondents will play along with the game and provide answers that are not only useless but also misleading. Indirect approaches simply work better to determine the price that matches the value that customers place on the product or service.

Three Recommended Approaches for Testing Pricing

Of the nine methods for testing pricing, only three indirect approaches are recommended. They are:

- **Surveys using a monadic split–cell design**
- **Conjoint analysis**
- **Experimentation**

These three methods will now be examined in more depth.

Surveys Using Monadic Split-Cell Design

Monadic approaches to pricing research using a survey approach split the sample into several separate cells and ask a purchase interest question, with a different price in each of the cells. "Well executed monadic tests are the least biased way to measure price sensitivity in a survey context. No respondent ever knows that other prices are being tested or that price is the object of the research."[10]

The most frequently used purchase interest question uses a symmetrical, balanced five-point scale:

- Definitely will buy
- Probably will buy
- Might or might not buy
- Probably will not buy
- Definitely will not buy

To estimate the percentage of consumers who will eventually buy the product, customer responses from the previous scale need to be adjusted for overstatement. For most consumer packaged goods products, many marketers use the 75-25-10 adjustment technique. That is, 75 percent of those who respond "definitely will buy" are expected to actually buy the product in the first year; 25 percent of those who respond "probably will buy" are expected to actually buy the product in the first year; and 10 percent of those who respond "might or might not buy" are expected to actually buy the product in the first year. (It is assumed that **none** of those who gave the bottom two responses will buy the product in the first year.)

Let's look at an example for a product where five price levels were tested:

Estimated Trial Rates at Five Price Points
Based Upon Five Cell Monadic Purchase Interest Survey

Survey Results						Estimated Trial %					
	$50	$65	$80	$95	$110		$50	$65	$80	$95	$110
DEF. WILL BUY	22%	20%	20%	17%	9%	DEF. WILL BUY	16.5	15.0	15.0	12.8	6.8
PROB. WILL BUY	31	30	27	30	22	PROB. WILL BUY	7.8	7.5	6.8	7.5	5.5
MIGHT OR MIGHT NOT BUY	22	20	21	24	24	MIGHT OR MIGHT NOT BUY	2.2	2.0	2.1	2.4	2.4
PROB. WILL NOT BUY	17	20	17	18	25	PROB. WILL NOT BUY	0	0	0	0	0
DEF. WILL NOT BUY	8	10	15	11	20	DEF. WILL NOT BUY	0	0	0	0	0
TOTAL	100%	100%	100%	100%	100%	TOTAL	26.5%	24.5%	23.9%	22.7%	14.7%

[10] David Lyons, "The Price is Right (or is it?)" *Marketing Research*, Winter 2002, 8.

The left half of the table shows the responses to the purchase interest question from the five separate groups of customers, and the right half of the table shows the estimated trial rates.

Note that trial, as expected, declines slowly as price increases up to an inflection point above $100, where trial drops significantly.

The demand curve looks as follows:

% Trial at Five Price Points

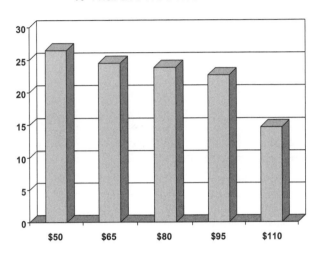

If our objective is to maximize revenue and there are 100,000 potential buyers in the market, we would set the price at $95, since this price produces the highest revenue of the five prices tested (100,000 × 23% × $95 = $2,185,000).

Revenue at Five Price Points
Thousands of Dollars

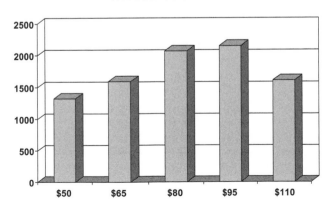

If our objective were to maximize profits, we would then extend the calculations by including product cost.

Strengths and Weaknesses of Monadic Split-Cell Research

Monadic pricing tests are simple, defensible, and widely used, but their precision suffers from the sampling variance that arises from having independent samples for each price point. It's tempting to avoid these variance problems by abandoning the monadic framework and asking each respondent a series of purchase likelihood questions, each about the same product but at different prices. This approach, however, produces an overwhelming response bias based on price and should be avoided if valid purchase likelihood estimates are sought.

Conjoint Analysis (and Discrete Choice Modeling)

Conjoint analysis and discrete choice modeling are attractive options for testing pricing because they can measure the price–demand response for multiple competitors in a market. These models can also model a wide variety of pricing scenarios across several brands, as opposed to just measuring the effects of a single product's price as in a typical monadic test.[11]

Let's return to the Compelling Offer conjoint study from Chapter 6 and look at the two most important variables in an employment offer: **manager quality** and **base salary. Base salary** is the price charged by employees to work for us. The part-worth utility of each level of these two attributes is shown on the following graph.

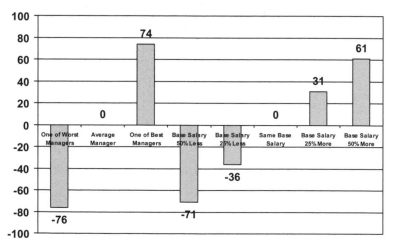

Part-Worth Utility of Levels of
Manager Quality and Base Salary

---

[11] Lyons, "The Price is Right (or is it?)" 8–13.

Considering just these two attributes, the simulation model would show that an employment offer with one of the best managers in the company at a base salary 50 percent higher than the current salary would be overwhelmingly preferred (utility of + 74 + 61 = 135) over an employment offer with one of the worst managers in the company at a base salary 50 percent lower than the current salary (utility of −76 −71 = −147).

A more interesting insight is the modeled preference for an employment offer with one of the best managers at a 50 percent **lower** salary (utility of 74 − 71 = 3) over an employment offer with one of the worst managers at a 50 percent higher salary (utility of −76 + 61 = −15). It appears that these high-value employees are taking a long-term view in an employment offer, willing to sacrifice current salary to work with and learn from one of the best managers in the company.

One can also use these part-worth utilities to "dollarize" the worth of a utility point for each attribute, as follows:

- Assume that the average current base salary of these high performers is $100,000.
- Therefore, the end points for the base salary scale can be expressed in actual dollars: $50,000 and $150,000.
- This range is $100,000.
- The range of utility points for this base salary attribute is 132; which is the range between −71 and 61.
- The dollar range of $100,000 is divided by the utility point range of 132, resulting in an estimate of each utility point being worth about $758 in base salary.

Therefore, we can determine that an average manager is worth about $58,000 ($758 × 76 utility points) more in an employment offer than one of the worst managers. Further, one of the best managers is worth about $56,000 ($758 × 74 utility points) more in an employment offer than an average manager.

Whether using conjoint analysis or discrete choice modeling to estimate price sensitivity, one should vary more than just the pricing variable to avoid the respondent learning that the study is only about price. This awareness on the part of some respondents may bias the data that is collected and result in an overstatement of price sensitivity.

Many marketers prefer discrete choice modeling (DCM) to conjoint analysis to estimate price sensitivity of customers, because DCM presents specific, realistic branded products to respondents in simulated buying scenarios, while conjoint presents simulated products to respondents by combining attribute levels using a fractional factorial design. DCM deals with actual products with actual prices and provides better estimates of price sensitivity, and the impact of various prices on market share, than does conjoint analysis. Conjoint is the preferred tool upstream in the development process, during the early stages of product development, when products can be described primarily in terms of tangible product features.

Experimentation

Controlled field experiments offer the best opportunity to measure the response of customers to changes in price accurately and validly, since they occur in the "real world" of the marketplace. In a price experiment, conditions are controlled so that the impact of the independent variable (price) can be manipulated to test its impact on a dependent variable, usually sales volume. Conditions are controlled through the use of "control" markets, where the independent variable is not manipulated. Results of the test markets are compared to the results of the control markets to estimate the impact of the price variable on sales volume.

If thirty stores are used to test four new price levels versus the current price, it is important to randomly assign the thirty stores to the five treatment levels (current price plus four new prices). Then the five groups of six stores should be looked at in aggregate and compared to each other to make sure that they match closely on key characteristics. For example, if one group of six stores includes all stores in high-income neighborhoods, while the other groups of six stores include no stores in high-income neighborhoods, the randomization of the thirty stores to the five treatment levels should be repeated and checked again on key characteristics.

While controlled field experiments have high external validity if properly controlled, they do have several serious limitations:

- Convincing retailers to allow you to manipulate prices within their stores can be challenging, and in many cases, expensive to implement.
- The effect of small changes in price on sales volume or market share could take a long period of time to measure accurately, depending on the purchase cycle of the product being measured.
- Usually a large sample of stores is required to conduct an effective experiment, with at least five test units assigned to each treatment level.

Despite these limitations, experimentation remains a popular and highly effective method to test consumer response to price. Many marketing research firms offer "controlled store testing" as a full service product, managing retailer relationships, implementing price changes at the appropriate stores, and monitoring the experiment as it runs its course to ensure that external events do not contaminate any stores.

Some firms, notably Kraft Foods, have shifted their emphasis from experimentation to **marketing mix modeling** of retail store scanner data. Marketing mix modeling helps firms like Kraft understand the impact of price changes by Kraft and competitors on market share. Including in-store observational data on product displays and coupon redemption, as well as data on newspaper and television advertising, allows these models to sort out the short-term and long-term effects of these marketing mix variables.

Pricing for Lifetime Revenues – "Give Away the Razor and Sell the Blades"

Many firms that sell expensive products, which have a "disposal" trail of follow-up products that are purchased, have found that it is often profitable to accept low or no profit on the "razor" and slightly up-charge the "razor blades." Companies that make computer printers have found this pricing practice to be highly useful and earn high margins on ink printer cartridges.

When a customer is viewed on a lifetime revenue basis, it is often a good pricing strategy to provide the initial product free, when the customer can only use your company's products as the disposable trail in the product. Legal issues should be investigated carefully before partaking in a "give away" strategy, however, because there have been cases where courts in some countries, such as Italy, have interpreted these giveaway products as bribes.

This strategy can be easily tested through the use of trade-off techniques, such as discrete choice modeling. Some product offerings tested could include high cost razors with low cost blades; others could include medium cost razors with medium cost blades; while still others could include low cost razors with high cost blades. The model could estimate market shares and lifetime customer revenues for these alternatives based on the choices customer make, allowing the marketer to choose the strategy that maximizes the lifetime profitability of the customer franchise.

Investment Cost

- Four focus groups to understand the customer value of your product offering, conducted by a skilled moderator, including analysis and report, will cost:
  - $20,000–$25,000 in the United States
  - $20,000–$22,000 in France and Japan
  - $17,000–$19,000 in the U.K. and Germany
  - $4,000–$6,000 in China and India
- A computer-assisted central location pricing survey, among five representative samples of 100 consumers each, lasting ten minutes, would cost approximately $40,000–$45,000.
- A Business-to-Business telephone pricing survey lasting fifteen minutes, among 200 business executives, where the sampling list is provided to the research firm, would cost:
  - $34,000–$39,000 in the United States
  - $24,000–$28,000 in the U.K. and Japan
  - $19,000–$22,000 in Germany
  - $8,000–$10,000 in Italy
- A quantitative conjoint study, involving a nationally representative sample of 200 consumers, screened by telephone and then interviewed personally for thirty minutes, will cost approximately $40,000–$50,000. However, many firms have moved to Internet interviews in the United States and have cut this cost in half.

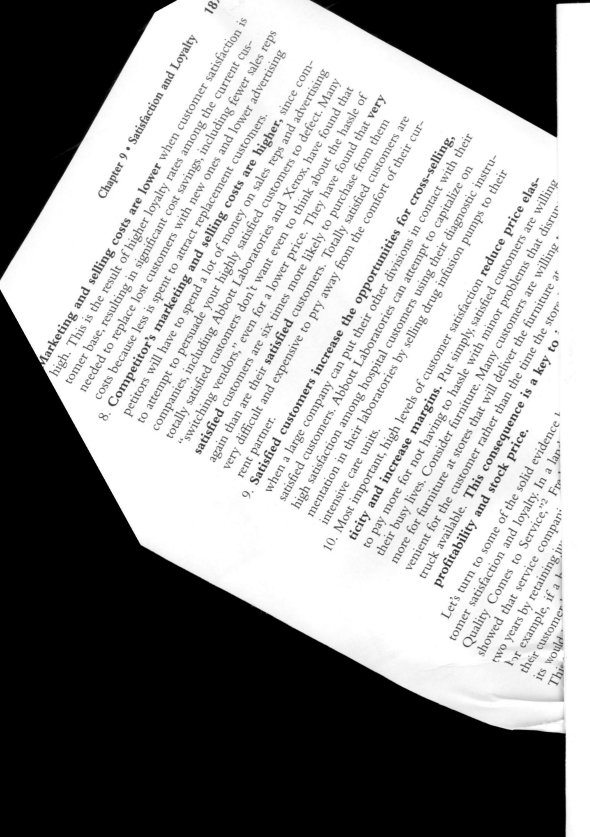

Marketing and selling costs are lower when customer satisfaction is high. This is the result of higher loyalty rates among the current customer base, resulting in significant cost savings, including fewer sales reps needed to replace lost customers with new ones and lower advertising costs because less is spent to attract replacement customers.

Competitor's marketing and selling costs are higher, since competitors will have to spend a lot of money on sales reps and advertising to attempt to persuade your highly satisfied customers to defect. Many companies, including Abbott Laboratories and Xerox, have found that totally satisfied customers don't want even to think about the hassle of "switching vendors", even for a lower price. They have found that **very satisfied** customers are six times more likely to purchase from them again than are their **satisfied** customers. Totally satisfied customers are very difficult and expensive to pry away from the comfort of their current partner.

9. **Satisfied customers increase the opportunities for cross-selling,** when a large company can put their other divisions in contact with their satisfied customers. Abbott Laboratories can attempt to capitalize on high satisfaction among hospital customers using their diagnostic instrumentation in their laboratories by selling drug infusion pumps to their intensive care units.

10. Most important, high levels of customer satisfaction **reduce price elasticity and increase margins.** Put simply, satisfied customers are willing to pay more for not having to hassle with minor problems that disrup... their busy lives. Consider furniture at stores that will deliver the furniture at ... more for the customer rather than the time the store ... venient for the customer. **This consequence is a key to ... profitability and stock price.**

Let's turn to some of the solid evidence ... tomer satisfaction and loyalty. In a lan... Quality Comes to Service,"[2] Fra... showed that service compani... two years by retaining ... For example, if a ... its customer ... its would ... This ...

- A quantitative discrete choice modeling study, involving a nationally representative sample of 200 consumers, screened by telephone and then interviewed personally for thirty minutes, will cost approximately $55,000–$65,000 in the United States. However, many firms have moved to Internet interviews in the United States and have cut this cost in half.
- A multinational Discrete Choice Modeling study, involving nationally representative samples of 200 consumers in each of three countries, screened by telephone and then interviewed personally for thirty minutes, will cost approximately $127,000–$140,000.
- A controlled store experiment, conducted by a full service outside research firm, will cost approximately $25,000–$30,000 for a six-month test.

Price Sensitivity Checklist

- Is **customer value** your focal point for setting prices?
- Do you create unique value and differentiate your product from competitors to earn a price premium?
- Does your pricing capture the full customer value, or are you leaving money on the table?
- Does your pricing strategy reflect your company's strategic objectives?
- Can you differentiate your offering at the augmented product level, like Caterpillar does with customer service?
- Have you focused on a market segment that really values your point of difference?
- Is your pricing strategy consistent with your product positioning?
- Does your pricing strategy work synergistically with all of the elements in your marketing mix?
- Are your price promotions so frequent that they are weakening your brand equity?
- Do you utilize quantitative marketing research and experimentation to test pricing alternatives?
- Do you avoid asking direct pricing questions of your target customers?

Attempting to delight **all** customers is an unwise strategy and can lead to weak financial results. Companies need to focus on potentially profitable customers in their target market and encourage customers who have a negative lifetime value to defect to competitors. Many B-to-B firms are developing information systems to understand their costs for serving each customer and calculating profitability on a customer-by-customer basis. This allows them to allocate their value-added services to their most profitable customers.

Philip Kotler has stated that the main thrust and skill of marketing is **buil** **demand**. "Demand building consists of three processes: getting custom— ing customers, and growing customers."[1] The focus of this chapte— ter two processes: **keeping** and **growing customers.**

Positive Consequences of Satisfied Custom—

Just what are the positive consequences of ¹ that focus on delighting their custom— pen as a result:

1. Customer **goodw'** enhanced. Ther— tomers about bad —

2. Satisfied customers — word-of-mouth adver— place high credibility o—

3. Satisfied customers stay w— **time customer value** to

4. Satisfied customers have **hig**. company's product. In many p— shop across different companies, Repeat rates for any one compan— spread their purchases across five c— tomer satisfaction can increase the re— percent fair share level with five comp.

5. Satisfied customers will often **increase** pany's product. Consider Six Flags amuse— a wonderful time will come back several ti— don't may come only every other year.

6. Companies with highly satisfied customers can **of the customer wallet."** For example, Ameri— like their highly satisfied customers to fly less frequ— competitors.

The Commerce Department's National Institute of Standards and Technology has continued this analysis of Baldrige winners relative to the S & P 500 and has found similar consistent results between 1995 and 2001. Note on the following char— that the Baldrige winners outperformed the S & P 500 by more than sixfold in 199—

3 B. Ray Helton, "The Baldie Play", Quality Progress 28, no.2, February 1995.

[1] Philip Kotler, *Kotler on Marketing: How to Create, Win, and Dominate Marke*— Free Press, 1999), 46.

The Baldie Play

Further evidence appeared in a quality management journal in 1995. Baldie Play", examined the trends in stock prices of recipients of the Mal— Baldrige National Quality Award relative to the trends in the stock market general. The Baldrige award is presented annually by the U.S. Commerc— Department to companies that demonstrate a dedication to quality processes and general. Clearly, firms that win this award have put customer focus. The largest weighting in the judging criteria (30 percent of the weight) involves processes used by the firm to understand customer requirements and measure customer satisfaction.

This article compared the return of $1,000 invested in the eleven publicly traded Baldrige winners and the S & P 500, between 1988 and 1993. Dow Jones Industrial firms and the return of a similar $1,000 invested in the thirty While the S & P investment grew 34 percent over the same five years! That is a three-to-one percent over that five-year period, the **investment in the Baldrige winners** **grew a spectacular 99** percent and the Dow investment grew 42 ratio relative to the S & P 500! The author is surprised that more mutual funds haven't started "Customer Focused Firm" funds.

Stock Performance of Baldridge Award Winners ($1,988 – 1993)
$1,000 Invested in 11 Winners ($1,988 – 1993)

Source: "The Baldie Play", Ray Helton, Quality Progress, February, 1995

Stock Performance of Baldridge Award Winners
Ratio of Return on Investment Relative to S & P 500
Source: U. S. Commerce Department National Institute of Standards and Technology

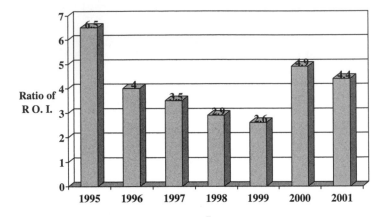

Other studies have expanded upon these results by looking at other measures of success among quality winners. A joint study between the Georgia Institute of Technology and the University of Western Ontario found that a broader sampling of winners of quality awards (including the Baldrige award) experienced a 44 percent higher stock price return, a 48 percent higher growth in operating income, and a 37 percent higher growth in sales when compared to a control group of companies of similar size and in similar industries.

At the risk of boring the already persuaded reader, one further example must be included.

The American Customer Satisfaction Index and Stock Prices

The American Customer Satisfaction Index (ACSI) is a quarterly measure of customer satisfaction, derived from a survey conducted by the National Quality Research Center at the University of Michigan Business School. Customers are surveyed about their satisfaction with more than 190 companies and fifty government agencies. Each quarter, one-fourth of these companies and agencies are included in the survey so that each year all are covered. Telephone surveys are conducted with a random sample of 16,000 customers each quarter, and customers are asked questions regarding expectations, value perceptions, and quality perceptions for the relevant companies. Responses are then translated, by a complex statistical model, into a customer satisfaction index, which ranges from 0 to 100. This score is reported for each of the sixty or so companies and agencies each quarter and compared to peer companies as well as to the rating the company received in the previous year.

This index is closely watched by Wall Street analysts, because research has found that companies with high customer satisfaction scores tended to have shares

that performed above average in stock price performance. University of Michigan Professor Claes Fornell, the director of the National Quality Research Center and one of the designers of the ACSI, has published research in the *Harvard Business Review* (March 2001) that showed that a 1 percentage-point rise in his customer satisfaction index translated into a 3 percent rise in the stock price of the respective company.[4]

The *Wall Street Journal* reported on the stock trading activity of Fornell,[5] noting that he took out short positions in Home Depot and McDonald's, two firms that had seen declines in their satisfaction scores. At the same time, Fornell purchased shares in Costco Wholesale Corp. and Yum Brands, Inc., two firms that had seen increases in customer satisfaction scores. While Fornell's ACSI-based portfolio was down about 6 percent between April 2000 and February 2003, the Dow Jones Industrial Average was down about 30 percent over the same period. A ratio of five-to-one between the two bundles of stocks! Doesn't this ratio sound familiar?

Stock Performance of Claes Fornell Portfolio

Trades Based Upon Company Ratings on American Customer Satisfaction Index

Source: "Researcher Uses Index to Buy, Short Stocks", WSJ, February 18, 2003

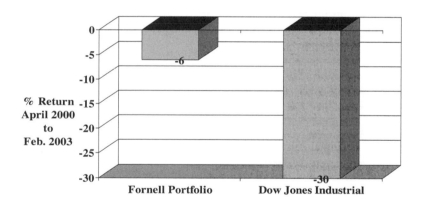

By now it should be evident that focusing on delivering customer-defined quality products and fully satisfying your customers often have positive financial benefits for the long-term value of the firm. But should a firm drive financial performance through **externally focused** customer satisfaction programs, through **internally focused** quality improvement programs, or both?

---

[4] Cited in Jon E. Hilsenrath, "Satisfaction Theory: Mixed Yield," *Wall Street Journal,* 19 February 2003.

[5] Jon E. Hilsenrath, "Researcher Uses Index to Buy, Short Stocks," *Wall Street Journal,* 18 February 2003; Hilsenrath, "Satisfaction Theory: Mixed Yield."

Results of a research study on this issue were published recently in the *Journal of Marketing*.[6] In this breakthrough study, the authors looked at firm profitability and stock returns of firms over time and analyzed these measures across:

- Firms that focused **externally** on customer satisfaction and retention
- Firms that focused **internally** on quality improvement and cost reduction programs, such as TQM and six sigma
- Firms that attempted to do both

Although it is clear that no firm can neglect either revenue expansion or cost reduction, this study showed that firms that adopted a revenue expansion/customer satisfaction emphasis performed best. Firms that focused internally on quality and cost reduction and firms that tried to emphasize both strategies simultaneously lagged behind the performance of externally focused firms by a significant margin.

Need for Measurement of Customer Satisfaction

The need to keep target customers fully satisfied is clearly established. So how does a firm put the processes in place to understand what their target customers require to remain fully satisfied and loyal?

The first step is to gain agreement and commitment from the management team to a continuous process of customer satisfaction measurement. This is a race with no finish line; there are no quick fixes here. Keeping customers fully satisfied is a continuous improvement process, and metrics need to be in place to understand if your process is moving the needle at all, and in which direction. Vince Lombardi, legendary coach of the Green Bay Packers, once stated, "If you're not keeping score, you're only practicing."

Kotler has called market share a backward-looking metric and customer satisfaction a forward-looking metric. I agree. The author has used customer satisfaction scores to predict market share three months forward with a high degree of accuracy.

The author has found five key points to keep management supportive of customer satisfaction measurement programs, which are often the target of cost reduction pressures in tight budget times:

- **Over 90 percent of unsatisfied customers don't complain**. Firms that rely only on complaint tracking to monitor satisfaction and dissatisfaction issues are burying their heads in the sand. Most customers find it too much of a hassle to complain about the majority of product problems; rather, they take their business to your competitors because you haven't asked them how you were doing. Many dissatisfied customers want to stay with their current vendor, but expect the firm to make the effort to initiate two-way communication and build the relationship.

---

[6] Roland T. Rust, Christine Moorman, and Peter R. Dickson, "Getting Return on Quality: Revenue Expansion, Cost Reduction, or Both?" *Journal of Marketing* 66, no. 4, October 2002.

- **It costs five times more to get a new customer than it does to keep a current customer.** This often-quoted statistic from the TARP organization in Washington, D.C., is dramatic, and the author is amazed at the disproportionate level of resources many companies spend to gain new customers relative to the resources spent to retain and grow current customers. Kotler estimates that companies spend as much as 70 percent of their marketing budget to attract new customers, while 90 percent of their revenue comes from current customers.[7] This spending focus on getting new customers is somewhat like a marital relationship; during the dating process, the couple pays close attention to every need and desire of the partner, but this fervor tends to diminish after the couple has exchanged vows. Married couples that work hard at their relationship stay together for a long time; companies need to work on their relationships with their current customers to earn their loyalty.
- **Companies can almost double their profits within two years by retaining just 5 percent more of their customers.** (Thank you, Reichheld and Sasser for your excellent work.) Companies can also benefit by calculating the lifetime customer value of their customers, which will highlight the importance of investing in the retention of profitable customers.
- **Satisfied customers are more willing to pay premium prices.** In today's competitive markets, more and more downward pressure is exerted on prices. Reactive companies will succumb to this pressure by lowering prices, thinking that this is their only option to compete. While this results in lower prices for consumers, it does not provide enough profit for many firms to survive. The U.S. airline industry has fallen into this trap, and many airlines have been forced into bankruptcy in recent years. Smaller airlines, focused on satisfying target customers, have done surprisingly well (Southwest Airlines, Jet Blue, Midwest Express). Satisfying a clear target segment of customers at a profit seems to be a simple business model that is missed by the larger airlines.
- **Satisfied customers have a strong relationship to customer loyalty, firm profitability, and stock price.** The studies cited previously provide rock hard evidence for these claims.

Management needs to be continuously reminded of these benefits to maintain commitment to the measurement of customer satisfaction, since positive survey results can often lag process changes by six to twelve months. However, if a firm was to have a quality issue with a key product that was not detected prior to being shipped to customers, the dissatisfaction can show up in the measurement results almost immediately, allowing the firm to respond quickly and hopefully recover before customer satisfaction is permanently damaged. Your customers are your

---

[7] Philip Kotler, *Marketing Insights From A to Z: 80 Concepts Every Manager Needs to Know* (Hoboken, NJ: John Wiley and Sons, 2003).

ultimate quality control department. While most CEOs think that this could never happen in their firm, their actions are frequently encouraging it. Setting cost reduction targets for their manufacturing operations often forces manufacturing management to purchase cheaper raw materials, cut back on key processes, and ship products that no longer meet the minimum needs of customers.

Quality Problems and the Demise of the Schlitz Brewing Company

The classic example of a quality meltdown is the Joseph Schlitz Brewing Company, founded in Milwaukee in 1849. When the author joined this firm in 1973, it was the number two brewery in America and was putting plans in place to surpass Anheuser-Busch as the number one brewery. The untimely death of their CEO, Robert Uihlein, to leukemia in the late 1980s resulted in the vice president of finance taking over the reins of the brewery. Significant cost reduction programs were instituted, which resulted in raw ingredient changes and a shortening of the brewing process. Several brew masters resigned in protest rather than be responsible for the Schlitz beer that was now being produced. Product quality problems ensued, and Schlitz beer that spent too much time on retail shelves developed flakes from secondary fermentation. Imagine the beer drinker that pours a Schlitz beer proudly for a friend into a tall beer glass, only to see flakes swirling through the beer! A cynical marketing manager suggested the beer could be used in small plastic paperweights to create Christmas scenes with swirling snow when inverted!

Obviously, this quality problem destroyed the Schlitz quality image nurtured by the brewery for over 120 years. The brand dropped from being number two behind Budweiser to almost nothing in several years. The brewery limped along for several years on the strength of lower-priced Old Milwaukee before being acquired by the Stroh Brewing Company of Detroit in 1982.

While a customer satisfaction program may not have saved Schlitz, the lesson is clear: abusing customer trust and falling below minimal customer quality expectations can have immediate disastrous results. Staying constantly focused on customer requirements is a minimum requirement for business survival. Kotler put it well in *Marketing Insights from A to Z*:

> If your people are not thinking customer, they are not thinking. If they are not directly serving the customer, they'd better serve someone who is. If they don't take care of your customers, someone else will.[8]

Sometimes "Obvious" Customer Requirements aren't that Obvious

Many firms feel that they know their customers well and don't invest in listening to their customers in a systematic manner. They feel that theirs is a simple business, and they focus internally on product and technical issues. They figure out customer requirements themselves, sitting around conference tables and drinking

---

[8] Kotler, *Marketing Insights From A to Z,* 36-37.

coffee. These firms also frequently underestimate the knowledge and skills of their competitors, with disastrous results.

Even obvious customer requirements can be tricky to get right. The author was presenting results of a customer satisfaction study to a management team at Abbott Laboratories and was challenged when results showed that Abbott lagged a best-in-class competitor on **"fast, responsive field service."** The service manager shared internal metrics on how service response time to customer problems had been reduced from seventy hours to seven hours over the past five years. He was quite proud of this performance and didn't believe the results of the large, quantitative telephone survey were accurate. He felt his service team was doing a great job and was getting to customer sites as quickly as they could.

It was decided to dig deeper into this "fast, responsive field service" issue, and to conduct several focus groups with hospital laboratory managers to further understand their requirements for field repair service on their blood testing instruments. These instruments performed automated blood testing to detect diseases and measure thyroid hormone levels and therapeutic drug levels. The service manager had to be sold on the idea of spending his money on focus groups on this issue, since he thought the requirement was obvious and easy to understand: **get there quick, fix the instrument as quickly as possible, and get to the next service call quickly.**

Everyone was surprised when none of the twenty customers in the two focus groups said anything similar to "get there as quickly as possible!" These busy, stressed-out laboratory managers described the ideal service call this way:

1. Return my phone call within thirty minutes to let me know that you are aware of my service problem.
2. Make an appointment to fix my instrument at a time that is convenient for me (the morning rush is very hectic in the lab, since blood tests need to be completed on hospital in-patients as early as possible so doctors will have blood test results when they do their late morning rounds).
3. Show up at the agreed upon time.
4. When the instrument repair is completed, stop by my office and inform me of what went wrong and how it was fixed.
5. Call me on the telephone the next day to double-check on the quality of the repair.

The service manager was flabbergasted after the focus groups, since he had been driving his large service organization using faulty internal metrics. The service incentive system that had been in place, based on minimizing the service response time, was actually working against what customers wanted! The service manager, grateful that the focus groups had been conducted, was open to acting on these **customer insights** and changed the service incentive system to focus upon how closely the service rep arrived to the agreed upon appointment time. With this change, wonderful things happened:

• Customers were more satisfied with the company and the service effort.

- Service reps were more efficient in their travel, since they could cluster service calls in the same city rather than chase across their large territories in a reactive manner.
- Service reps traveled fewer miles and cut their gasoline bills and "windshield time" by more than 20 percent.
- Service reps enjoyed their personal interactions with the lab managers, feeling more like consultants and less like repair people.

Even a requirement as obvious as "fast, responsive field service" is not as obvious as one might think. Life would be so much simpler if customers just acted in ways we want them to act. Which customer requirements have you defined yourself that may be off as far as this one?

The Service Recovery Paradox

While customers don't expect firms to be perfect, they do expect firms to acknowledge a problem and make it right. Surprisingly, some firms tend to deny problems when customers complain, or worse, suggest the problem was the result of customer misuse or ignorance.

Service recovery can have a positive impact on customer satisfaction, if handled correctly. However, there are dramatic differences in customer response to service recovery after the **first failure** compared to customer response to service recovery after the **second failure**.

In an article in the *Journal of Marketing,* James G. Maxham III and Richard G. Netemeyer presented their fascinating findings on the "recovery paradox."[9] They show that for a **single** failure **with satisfactory recovery** by the company, customers rated the firm paradoxically **higher** on satisfaction and repurchase intentions than before the service failure!

So should a firm create problems just so they can recover and achieve these benefits? Definitely not, since customers penalized companies on these measures after the **second failure**, regardless of how well the company recovered. Obviously, customers are willing to give companies one chance to make it right. But after the second failure, most customers are no longer forgiving. Customers do not want companies to be "recovery experts," but expect companies to take corrective and preventative actions to keep their products from needing service.

The service recovery paradox makes it imperative for companies to track service history carefully on customers. It needs to pay careful attention to identify profitable customers who have had **one** service problem and provide high levels of attention and preventative maintenance to minimize the chance that a second service problem will occur. Thus, an ongoing complaint tracking system can both drive process improvements as well as maintain strong customer relationships.

---

[9] James G. Maxham III and Richard G. Netemeyer, "A Longitudinal Study of Complaining Customers' Evaluations of Multiple Service Failures and Recovery Efforts," *Journal of Marketing* 66, no. 4, October 2002.

The Four Customer Typologies

In a classic *Harvard Business Review* article, Thomas Jones and Sasser offer excellent thoughts on "Why Satisfied Customers Defect."[10] They suggest that there are four customer types, based on how satisfied the customers are with the company and how loyal the customers are to the company. The following table shows this typology.

	High Loyalty	Low Loyalty
High Satisfaction	*APOSTLES*	*MERCENARIES*
Low Satisfaction	*HOSTAGES*	*TERRORISTS*

The **apostle** is the bedrock of the company; this customer is fully satisfied and keeps returning to purchase from the company. Companies should strive to have as many of their target customers become apostles, since they are usually very profitable and provide positive word-of-mouth advertising.

The **mercenary** is fully satisfied with the firm's offering but tends to chase low prices and buy on impulse. They are usually not profitable, since they are expensive to acquire and are quick to depart for a lower-priced deal. There is little a firm can do to build a profitable business with mercenaries, and they can be expected to be there when your deal is the best at that time.

The **hostage** is an interesting customer, currently loyal to you even though not fully satisfied with your offering. This customer is usually unable to switch to a competitor because an alternative to your product offering is not available. This customer is trapped and stuck with buying from you. This is a very volatile situation, since you could lose as much as a third of your business overnight if the competitive landscape were to shift. The hostage would gleefully take his business elsewhere without a second thought. Businesses with a large portion of hostages in their customer base need to place high priority on understanding the needs of their hostages and devoting sufficient resources into turning them into apostles.

The **terrorists** are the most dangerous customers, since they are very unhappy with your product offering and can't wait to tell other customers about their bad experiences with your firm. You probably shouldn't have made them a customer in the first place, since it is usually very difficult and expensive to meet their high demands. Firms should fire these customers and hope that they take their unprofitable business to one of your lucky competitors.

So, how does a firm measure customer satisfaction and loyalty levels to allow it to classify customers into these four quadrants? Customer satisfaction data is usually collected from customers using a survey, while customer loyalty data can be collected using a survey, by using actual customer purchase information, or a combination of the two. Let's get into more depth in the next section.

---

[10] Thomas O. Jones and W. Earl Sasser, Jr., "Why Satisfied Customers Defect," *Harvard Business Review*, November 1995.

Measures of Customer Satisfaction and Customer Loyalty

Many companies utilize a five-point symmetrical scale to measure the satisfaction of their customers: very satisfied, satisfied, neither satisfied or dissatisfied, dissatisfied, very dissatisfied. These and other scales of satisfaction tend to measure customer **attitudes,** which may not be a perfect predictor of future behavior.

Common **attitudinal** measures of loyalty are the likelihood of the customer to repurchase from the firm and the likelihood of the customer to recommend the firm to others. When actual behavior cannot be obtained, these attitudinal measures usually have to suffice.

The ultimate measure of loyalty, of course, is actual behavior, measured by the share of purchases in the product category that the customer made with your company. On products with a long purchase cycle, retention rates can be a useful metric. This requires information on customer purchases of competitor's products as well as products from your firm. This information can be acquired on a syndicated basis from large marketing research firms, such as A.C.Nielsen, Information Resources, and I.M.S., or from an industry trade association.

Many firms find it useful to conduct **brand-switching** studies to understand competitive dynamics in their product category. These involve a longitudinal survey design, where a panel of the same customers is interviewed at different points in time, usually annually. The customers are asked a number of questions, including which brand they use most often. Retention rates can then be determined as well as measuring switching behavior among brands across time.

Comprehensive Customer Satisfaction Measurement Program

Given the high impact of customer satisfaction on profits and stock price, it is important for firms to develop a comprehensive measurement program to measure the needs and satisfaction levels of target customers continually. There are three major requirements of a comprehensive program:

- The program needs to include both **qualitative** and **quantitative** components. It must include tools for listening in-depth to small groups of target customers, as well as tools for collecting "hard data" from large samples of target customers.
- The program needs to collect customer perceptions of your company and your **key competitors** on key performance **attributes**. Collecting feedback on only your company can lead you into a false sense of security. Customers judge your company's performance more on a relative basis to competitors rather than on an absolute basis.
- The program contains components that are conducted on a **regular basis** (annually) as well as components that are triggered by **transactions,** such as a new purchase or a service call.

A comprehensive measurement program will include multiple components (or modules) to measure customer satisfaction and loyalty. Five frequently used components are shown in the following chart:

Module 1 Customer Focus Groups	Module 2 Competitive Bench- marking	Module 3 Customer Satisfaction Tracking	Module 4 New Purchase Follow-Up	Module 5 Service Call Follow-Up
Groups of Target Customers	Sample of Target Customers	Census or Sample of Current Customers	Customers Who Pur- chased in Past Thirty Days	Customers Who Had Service Call in Past Seven Days
Anonymous Group Interviews	Anonymous Surveys	Company Identified Surveys	Company Identified Surveys	Company Identified Surveys
Timing: Ongoing	Timing: Annually usually sufficient	Timing: Ongoing rolling interviews	Transaction- based	Transaction- based

Let's now investigate these five modules in more detail.

Module 1: Customer Focus Groups and Customer Visits (Qualitative)

This is the starting point for any new customer satisfaction measurement pro-gram. Just what exactly is important to target customers? With what are they dis-satisfied? Which attributes are important to them? How do they go about purchasing products in your category?

These depth questions can only be answered adequately by spending time listen-ing to your customers. While focus groups are the most commonly used tool for this qualitative research, **other types of qualitative research** are also effective.

- **Customer visits** by management have proved very beneficial for many firms to help senior executives experience the world from the vantage point of the customer. In some cases, these customer visits by management have produced transformational changes in how a company conducts its business. It is important that this interaction take place at the customer site, to allow the executive to observe and experience the context in which the product is used. It is also important that executives conduct ten to twelve interviews annually across different customer segments to avoid getting a narrow view of the customer base. Many executives, especially those with engineering or R and D backgrounds, resist this process because they feel uncomfortable meeting with customers. The author has overcome this issue in the past by arming executives with the **"three simple questions"**:
  - **"What do we do well?"** (Since they are buying from you now, you want to hear the positives about your performance to begin the interview.)

- ○ **"What can we improve?"** (Here, you are giving your customer the chance to tell you the areas where you may not be precisely meeting their expectations. It is amazing how many customers have been waiting eagerly for an executive from a company to ask them this question.)
- ○ **"How can we keep you as a satisfied customer?"** (This powerful question sends a very important **emotional** message to your customer: "your business is important to me and I have taken the time to come to your site and hear it personally." The author has been amazed at the impact of this question on customer loyalty.)

These three questions are usually enough to provide a quality one-hour interview with the customer. Experience has shown, however, that the timing of these interviews can vary significantly, depending on the type of customer involved. For example:

Interviews with **terrorists** tend to be shorter with low customer involvement, since they have already given up on your firm and will be an ex-customer shortly.

Interviews with **mercenaries** are also short, with these customers usually trying to persuade you to lower your prices.

Interviews with **apostles** tend to be of average length and very gratifying, with these customers often singing the praises of your firm. A mistake made by many salespeople when the "suits" want to go out and see customers is to take their management to all apostles in the hope of creating the impression that all of the customers in this territory are fully satisfied. The danger here, of course, is that management will leave with the false impression that "all is well" with all customers, when that is rarely the case. **Apostles** should be included in a customer visit program but should not dominate the customer mix.

Interviews with **hostages** tend to be the longest but usually provide the most useful **customer insights.** These customers are using your product because no adequate alternative exists currently, but they are not fully satisfied with your performance. They wish you would get your act together, since they usually don't like the work of finding and working with a new vendor. They can easily provide many key insights into areas for improvement, and proactive firms can use these insights to convert many of these hostages into apostles. This is an area of high payout.

Managers doing customer visits need to spend most of their time listening, clarifying, and probing and avoiding selling or arguing with customers or telling customers why their needs are difficult to meet. Probing questions such as "why is that important?" and "will you tell me more about that?" work very well to get below surface answers like "your quality is only average."

There is an important point to be made about the phenomena of raised customer expectations that result from these customer interviews. The simple process of listening to customers will raise their expectations that you will **act** on some or all of their suggestions. It is important that the company be committed to utilize resources to improve their product and service offering and to communicate these changes back to customers. If customers spend their time giving your

company their honest ideas and see no change, they can become cynical and actually become less loyal to your company.

- **Mystery shoppers** are used by many service companies to obtain feedback on how well their frontline employees are treating customers. Restaurants and hotels make frequent use of mystery shoppers, who are hired to play the role of the customer and report back to the company on their experiences. McDonald's utilizes mystery shoppers to observe the hospitality, speed of service, and cleanliness of their restaurants as well as competitor's restaurants. Each McDonald's restaurant receives twelve to twenty mystery visits per year. Taco Bell also utilizes mystery shoppers to spy on its 6,700 restaurants.[11] In addition to observing the restaurant and timing service with a hidden stopwatch, these mystery shoppers utilize thermometers and scales in their cars to take the temperature of burritos and weigh them to insure they measure up to Taco Bell standards.

Module 2: Competitive Benchmarking (Quantitative)

As customer feedback is obtained from customers, it is critical to understand how customers assess the performance of your company **relative to your competitors.** This is done by having customers provide attribute ratings on your firm as well as relevant competitors and comparing your performance to your competitors, especially your best-in-class competitor.

Attribute ratings obtained in a vacuum can be misleading. Let's assume that you asked a sample of 100 target customers to rate your performance on twenty-five attributes using an anonymous Internet survey. You've used a five-point semantic differential scale, where 5 represents a rating of *excellent,* and 1 represents a rating of *poor.* You've received mean ratings of 4.5 on product reliability and 4.1 on knowledge of sales force. It would be easy to conclude that additional resources to improve customer satisfaction should be spent on sales force training.

However, let's assume you used a benchmarking methodology and had those 100 target customers rate your four key competitors as well. You've now found that these four competitors all received mean ratings of 4.7 on product quality and mean ratings of 3.5 on knowledge of sales force. All of the sudden an area that you thought was an area of strength (reliability) is a glaring competitive weakness.

It is important to compare your company's rating to your competitor with the highest rating on each attribute, rather than to the average of your competitor's ratings. This is because most customers will see your performance on an attribute as deficient if it lags any competitor, even though your performance is above the category average. The "category average" does not exist in your customers' minds and is a meaningless notion to customers.

It is usually possible, with a well-constructed survey and the proper incentives, to get valid rating information from customers on five companies/brands across

---

[11] Ameet Sachdev, "Mystery Shoppers Work for Change in the Fast Food Industry," *Chicago Tribune,* 26 December 2001.

twenty attributes. Beyond 100 customer judgments, respondent fatigue can result in poor data. The attributes are usually rotated across interviews to avoid order bias.

While competitive benchmarking studies provide the critical competitive dimension, their major weakness is the limit on the number of attributes that can be included. Because many companies want to track their performance on more than twenty attributes, benchmarking studies are complemented with more detailed, one company, company identified tracking studies.

Module 3: Customer Satisfaction Tracking (Quantitative)

Tracking studies are usually company identified, since customers are only rating your company and identification often provides positive public relations value. These surveys frequently include a short letter from the company president urging the customer to provide frank feedback to allow the company to satisfy target customers fully.

Many businesses have reasonably small-sized customer base sizes to allow surveys to be sent to all customers annually (a census). Abbott Laboratories used an inexpensive mail survey in twenty-eight languages to survey all of their 50,000 laboratory customers in forty-six countries every year. Response rates for a well-constructed mail survey can reach 25 percent, which is adequate to track changes over time. Companies with very large customer bases can draw a random sample of customers rather than conduct a census.

Abbott Laboratories decided to split its customers into four random groups of 12,500 and to survey these four groups in a different quarter of each year. These quarterly random samples provided more timely results on progress of their continuous improvement program. Abbott processed these worldwide surveys in Atlanta, Georgia, allowing a central, consistent database to be built. This centralized database allowed management to quickly access customer survey results for any of the forty-six countries, for geographic area subtotals, or for a worldwide total.

Abbott closely tracked those countries that were achieving significant increases in customer satisfaction, looked for the attribute increases that were driving those increases, and benchmarked the internal process improvements that were impacting the higher attribute ratings. In one medium-sized country, customer satisfaction had increased dramatically as a result of increased ratings on "customer service" attributes. Service processes were examined, and the increased ratings appeared to be the result of responding to customer comments on previous surveys and making improvements to address the service issues:

- providing field service engineers with cellular phones
- increasing the number of hotline service people at headquarters from four people to eight people

These investments in customer-driven process improvements paid for themselves many-fold in the first year, as both customer loyalty and sales increased substantially. These specific, successful process improvements were shared with all forty-six countries quarterly to allow the sharing of winning ideas with other countries with similar issues.

IBM conducts 40,000 customer interviews in seventy-one countries each year, in twenty-six different languages. A central database catalogs the data and makes it available to a team of managers who generate company-wide initiatives. The database contains every known problem that IBM has ever encountered and allows them to go in, respond, and fix the customer's problem quickly.[12]

Module 4: New Purchase Follow-Up

Virtually every car company invests in customer surveys of their new buyers, conducted within the first month of ownership. This is because most car problems tend to show up within the first thirty days, and the customer feedback allows the car company to fix any problems proactively that the customer has detected. These surveys also allow companies to assess performance of its channel partners, such as dealers and retailers, who may provide training, installation, and other services outside of the company's direct control.

Module 5: Service Call Follow-Up

In this chapter, we have talked about the concept of *satisfactory* service recovery, which after the first failure can actually improve customer satisfaction. But many companies allow their service people to define when the service problem of a customer is resolved satisfactorily. **This is a mistake made by an internally focused company.**

It is important to contact customers after a service call to determine if they feel the company has adequately resolved their service problem to their satisfaction. Firms have found as many as one-third of "closed customer service tickets" have not resolved the service concerns of these unhappy customers. Interviewing these customers on the phone, preferably the day after the service call, can keep these apostles from becoming hostages.

Prioritizing Customer Satisfaction Modules

Since most firms will lack the time and resources to launch all five modules of this satisfaction and loyalty measurement program simultaneously, the following suggestions are offered:

1. Always start with Module 1 – Qualitative Research to obtain an in-depth understanding of customer requirements. Focus groups (or customer visits) among key customer segments are often a modest investment relative to the insight provided. These efforts will usually move a company about halfway up the customer learning curve and put them in a good position to benefit fully from future modules.
2. Next, a company should invest in quantitative research, with Module 3 – Customer Satisfaction Tracking the next best investment. These

---

[12] Robert Hiebeler, Thomas B, Kelly, and Charles Ketteman, *Best Practices: Building Your Business with Customer-Focused Solutions* (New York: Simon and Schuster, 1998).

..ny-identified surveys of current customers can quickly uncover
..eas of customer "aggravation" that are unknown inside the company,
many of which can be fixed with inexpensive process improvements. For
example, some customers calling your company's telephone service hotline may prefer leaving a message and phone number rather than staying
on hold, after being assured that their call will be returned quickly, in the
order it was received, by a service representative knowledgeable of the
customer's service history.

3. Next, a company should invest in Modules 4 and 5 – New Purchase
   Follow-up and Service Call Follow-up, as these surveys are relatively
   inexpensive and can often become a key part of a larger, customer relationship management effort.

4. Last, a firm should invest in Module 2 – Competitive Benchmarking. It is
   here that the performance of the company can be judged in the competitive context. Average performance on an attribute may be acceptable to
   customers, if your best-in-class competitor is also delivering at an average
   level. Good performance on a different attribute may be unacceptable to
   customers, if your best-in-class competitor is delivering at very good performance levels. Thus, it is not your absolute performance that customers
   react to, but your performance **gaps** relative to your best-in-class competitor on each performance attribute.

It may take your firm several years to implement all of the modules of this program, but the payout will be huge. As the information from these five modules is
shared with all employees throughout the company, and as employees are given
monetary incentives to work cross-functionally to improve key measures, employees begin to develop creative, low-cost methods to delight customers. As more
and more customers become **apostles,** the firm begins to make more money.
This increase in profits can then be used to continue to reward employees for
delighting customers. It is a process that works wonderfully. Just ask any winner
of the Malcolm Baldrige Award.

Do *Lost Customer* Surveys Add Insight?

Some companies have begun to survey lost customers to understand the reasons
for the customer defections. But why wait until a customer has defected before
trying to understand how to delight them?

To use a medical analogy, this is like conducting an *autopsy* to determine the
cause of death. In the author's experience, lost customer surveys rarely provided
new insights, but pointed to the same reasons that benchmarking and tracking
studies revealed for customer dissatisfaction. Thus, lost customer surveys are often
a duplicative waste of resources.

To return to our medical analogy, benchmarking and tracking studies are the
diagnostic blood tests done while the patient is still alive to determine the cause of
the disease before it proves fatal for the patient. Don't let the patient die to determine the cause of death via an autopsy.

Best Practices Example – Dow Chemical

Dow Chemical Company has developed a very sophisticated model to under-stand the factors that impact the loyalty of their customers. In a presentation to the American Marketing Association in Chicago in September of 2002, six factors were identified that had been found to have a statistically significant impact on customer loyalty over time:

- Perceived value provided by Dow
- Satisfaction with Dow
- Image of Dow
- Business relationship with Dow
- Positive experience/positive problem resolution
- Customer characteristics

Dow Chemical has quantified the impact of these factors, as well as identified key attributes driving several of these factors:

- Perceived value is driven by perceptions on six key attributes: product quality, cost, customer service, technical support, availability, and delivery.
- Business relationship is driven by perceptions of the ease of doing business with Dow as well as overall satisfaction.

Following is the Dow Loyalty Model, shown graphically.

Dow Chemical Loyalty Model

American Marketing Association Conference Presentation, September, 2002

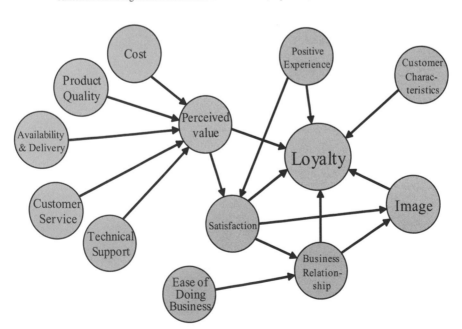

Dow Chemical has also modeled the impact of increasing the level of customer loyalty on its share of each customers chemical business and has found it to be direct and significant. On average, a 1 percent increase in customer loyalty is estimated to generate a 1.2 percent increase in account share. Given this relationship, it is then possible to estimate the profitability of increased resources placed behind customer satisfaction initiatives.

Creating customer-based models of what drives the business, as shown here in the Dow Chemical model, is the key to a successful business strategy. A simple, elegant, and accurate model can help the company create a clear understanding of customer needs, which can focus the organization at all levels on effectively meeting those needs. Organizational focus, needed changes, resources, and success measures should all be derived from this business success model.

Investment Cost

A comprehensive customer satisfaction program, conducted globally, can cost several million dollars. Many firms find this investment hard to undertake at one time, and will begin with Modules 1 and 2 in their key countries and add other countries and modules as resources become available.

The following estimates are from the ESOMAR 2003 Prices Survey:

- Four focus groups, including analysis and report, will cost:
  - $20,000–$25,000 in the United States
  - $20,000–$22,000 in France and Japan
  - $17,000–$19,000 in the U.K. and Germany
  - $4,000–$6,000 in China and India
- Competitive benchmark telephone survey of 200 target customers, lasting thirty minutes, including analysis and report, will cost:
  - $32,000–$36,000 in the United States
  - $23,000–$25,000 in the U.K. and Japan
  - $14,000–$15,000 in Hong Kong and France
  - $5,000–$9,000 in China and India
- Customer satisfaction web surveys of 200 current customers, including analysis and report, will cost:
  - $15,000–$19,000 in the United States and Japan
  - $10,000–$13,000 in the U.K., Germany and France
  - $6,000–$9,000 in China and Russia
- Costs for New Customer Follow-Up studies and Service Call Follow-Up are similar to the customer satisfaction web surveys.
- Costs can be lowered by "piggy-backing" studies; that is, having a research firm with global capabilities conduct the same survey across multiple countries at the same time.
- Translating non-U.S. focus group tapes into English will increase the cost of these groups by approximately 25 percent.

Customer Satisfaction Checklist

- Are customers viewed as one-time transactions?
- How are you building long-term relationships with customers?
- Has your management team had direct contact with key customers within the past six months?
- Do you understand how customers rate your performance on key attributes (company, product, price, service, sales force) relative to your key competitors?
- Do you conduct frequent identified surveys with customers to find out if your continuous improvement activities are impacting customer perceptions, satisfaction, and loyalty?
- Is a portion of your employee monetary incentive system tied to customer satisfaction results, so that employees will know you are serious about customer satisfaction?
- Do you use mystery shoppers to see how employees treat customers?
- Is the focus of all employees to delight customers, or to help frontline employees delight customers?
- Are all employees clear on the areas of customer satisfaction that the firm is focused on improving?

NEW PRODUCTS

INSIGHT 10: The development of successful new products requires the continuous participation of target customers.

"When we listen to the voice of the market, we need to remember that customers are not going to give us all the solutions to their needs and wants. That means we also have to listen to the voice of General Motors. You have to work at the balance between the market pull and the technology push."

Lloyd Reuss, former General Motors president, in a 1989 speech.

Customer Insight Pyramid

Customer Insight Pyramid

- New Product Success
- Satisfaction and Loyalty
- Perceptions And Positioning
- Critical Features
- Communication Messages
- Price Sensitivity
- Customer Segmentation and Targeting
- Unmet Needs
- Emotional and Rational Reasons
- Macro Trends

Why is New Product Success So Important?

New products are the lifeblood of any successful company; they help ensure that the company can compete in new and growing market segments. Successful new products reduce the reliance on older products that compete in declining market segments. New products are critical to achieving long-term growth in sales and profits.

Despite this, the new product failure rate still exceeds 80 percent. Discontinuous innovations, such as videoconferencing, DVDs, and the electric car, are especially challenging for marketers since they require a great deal of customer education and persuasion. Reasons that have been offered for the high rate of new product failure include:

- Lack of product differentiation from current products
- Poor screening of ideas generated
- Poor test marketing
- Communication and promotion not executed well
- Competing against a strong brand
- Saturated target market

While there are many reasons for this high failure rate, leading marketing thinkers suggest, "a possible explanation for this relatively poor success rate and the difficulties in developing truly innovative new products may be the poor utilization of appropriate marketing research and models."[1]

New technology can create "enablers" that form new markets and products quickly. Understanding the customer needs that will drive these markets is a challenging process, according to David Bakken: "The key to finding the emerging market for a new technology lies in thinking creatively, but realistically, about what the new technology will allow potential users to do that they couldn't do before. The less restrictive our initial scan, the more likely we are to uncover customers with a critical need for the benefits offered by this technology. We may identify several different need segments through this kind of activity."[2]

"New customer needs originate upstream of the marketplace in changing customer circumstances."[3] Insight into these changing customer circumstances – combined with the knowledge of technological possibilities – is the critical starting point for successful new product development. Staying close to the customer and having them participate in the new product development process will enable companies to see and anticipate these changing customer circumstances and be prepared with new products that meet those needs when they "float downstream to them."

Innovation requires direct human interaction between target customers and the cross-functional development team. Companies need to understand that the participation of customers is critical to new product success, especially at the early stages, often called the "fuzzy front end." However, relying on customers to **initiate** the new product development process by continuously suggesting ideas for

---

[1] Jerry Wind and Vijay Mahajan, "Issues and Opportunities in New Product Development: An Introduction to the Special Issue," *Journal of Marketing Research* 34, no. 1, February 1997, 1–12.

[2] David G. Bakken, "The Quest for Emerging Customer Needs," *Marketing Research* 13, no. 4, Winter 2001, 33.

[3] Bakken, "The Quest for Emerging Customer Needs," 30.

new products is ludicrous and will lead to disappointment. Most customers aren't expert or informed enough to lead in initiating new product ideas; that's the job of your R and D team who has stayed close to the customer.

Many managers have become disillusioned with all market research because they have had poor results when they asked customers directly to identify the products they need in the future. Customers are simply too busy with their own problems to worry about doing your idea generation job for you. Involving them in an iterative process is the key to continuously improving the value you can profitably provide to them in the future. It has been estimated that a typical customer spends fifteen minutes per week thinking about your products, while a typical new product developer spends over 2,400 minutes per week thinking about those products. Given this, the **initiation** of new product ideas should remain the responsibility of the well-informed product development team that clearly understands the desired outcomes and solutions sought by the target consumer.

The New Product Development Funnel

Many firms have had success in new product development by utilizing a good balance of *customer needs understanding* and *technological possibilities* at the start of the product development "funnel." They then use marketing research tools throughout the process to test, refine, and sometimes kill new products in development. A good illustration of this funnel follows and was developed by Ellen Stein, then a research associate at the Harvard Business School.[4]

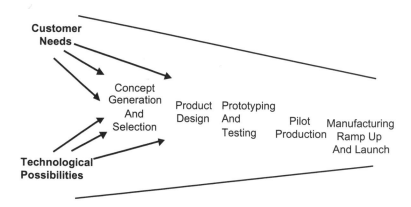

The Product Development Funnel

This model is a powerful way to visualize the participation of customers in the new product development process, with heavy involvement being most critical

[4] Marco Iansiti, Thomas J. Kosnik, and Ellen Stein, "Product Development: A Customer-Driven Approach," *Harvard Business School Case 9-695-016*, November 1994, 1996.

during the "fuzzy front end" of the process. Constant monitoring of the macroenvironment, market trends, and customer needs will continue throughout the new product development process to ensure that the value proposition will still meet dynamic customer needs.

New Product Development at Hershey's

Anthony Pingitore, who was new product director at Hershey's when Hershey's Chocolate Milk won a major new product award in 1985, described the new product development funnel at Hershey as follows:

> I think the key to our success in new products is having a lot of concepts in what we call a funnel. Our goal is to have many new products in development – in research, in concept development, and in prototype development – at the same time so we can pick the one or two best ones and then take them further along the research chain. We have an on-going process in which thousands of ideas turn into hundreds of concepts that turn into 50 ideas that are brought to prototypes and maybe one or two or three make it to the marketplace.[5]

Customer participation in this narrowing funnel is critical to identify those several products that go to market each year from the thousands of new product ideas generated at Hershey.

Marketing research throughout the funnel can help identify the products with high potential that should keep moving through the funnel, as well as the "dogs" that need to get killed. Products that fail to generate purchase interest among target consumers, which the author has labeled "dogs," drain scarce resources from the potential stars in the company's product portfolio. Corporate and Strategic Insights Manager at Ford Motor Company Wayne McCullough states that marketing research can assist in each of the seven core stages of new product development:

1. Ideation
2. Screening
3. Product development
4. Pre-testing
5. Product testing
6. Post-testing
7. Product rollout

During ideation, marketing research aids in the idea flow because it understands the consumer thoughts that prompted the new product idea. During screening, marketing research can weed out bad ideas, evaluate strengths and weaknesses of

---

[5] Kevin J. Clancy and Peter C. Krieg, *Counterintuitive Marketing: Achieve Great Results Using Uncommon Sense* (New York: Free Press, 2000), 42.

good ideas, assess the uniqueness of an idea, and explore reasons for interest (or lack thereof) in the idea. During product testing, marketing research can assess performance against clearly defined goals, watch and listen to customers, and check that the message that customers want to hear is the same as Ford wants them to hear.

To optimize the use of marketing research, the research manager should get involved early and stay involved, clearly capture and represent the voice of the customer, reduce or eliminate assumptions decision makers make, and manage knowledge by tracking assumptions and hypothesis testing.[6] These best practices can minimize the chance of an "escalation of commitment" by management behind a car model that does not generate any excitement among the target consumer segment.

Who Needs Customer Involvement?!?!

However, there are still those who disdain the involvement of the customer in the new product development process, feeling it is a waste of valuable time and money. They feel product development is a creative process, which will only be stifled by involving those noncreative customers.

An early critic of customer participation in new product development was Henry Ford, whose mass production of the black Model T made him very successful before large competitors entered the automobile market. Ford was quoted to say, "If I'd asked people what they wanted, they'd have said a faster horse." Had Ford avoided the direct questioning approach and probed into customer dissatisfaction with traveling, his family might still be running the leading car company in the world, as Ford did over 100 years ago.

Among the most vocal contemporary critics is Bill Mitchell, who headed General Motors styling for nearly twenty years. Mitchell's work encompassed the Buick Riviera in the 1960s through the Corvettes of the early 1980s. He was described as someone who fought everyone who attempted to tamper with his car designs, especially the design of the Corvette. He railed against design committees and market researchers and felt car designers **should be left alone.**

> Frank Lloyd Wright did not go around ringing doorbells asking people what kind of houses they wanted! There is not one good-looking car I designed that market research had anything to do with![7]

This genius car designer clearly did not appreciate the distinction between abdicating design responsibility to consumers, which is threatening and impractical, and having customers participate in the new product development process, which is a best practice now at most car companies. There is simply too much at risk to trust the genius of a great car designer blindly and not obtain customer feedback on new car designs.

---

[6] Wayne McCullough, "Best Practices in Marketing Research" Conference, quoted in "Research Conference Report," January 2002, RFL Communications, Inc.
[7] Jason Stein, "Bill Mitchell Profile," *Wheelbase Communications,* February 2002, from the Pioneer Press, February 2002, 8 of Automotive Section.

This **lack of customer involvement** in new product development is also common among some pharmaceutical companies, such as Amgen, that take a strict technology-driven view rather than a customer-driven view. Amgen has had a fair degree of success in the past starting with brilliant science and then finding unique uses for it. "Customer benefits are dictated by the technology, with only secondary input from customers as the development process proceeds. Testing with end-users is highly valued, but the emphasis is on technical feasibility and acceptance. This is very different from a market-driven development process that combines an understanding of the market situation and technological possibilities with deep insights into customer problems and requirements, and then seeks new opportunities to deliver superior customer value."[8]

The Evidence for a Balanced Approach at the Start of the Funnel

The argument made by Amgen is compelling and many technology-focused executives buy into it. But is there evidence to support the inclusion of customer insight in the early stages of new product development?

Studies have found that high-technology firms win more often when they adopt a balanced approach, rejecting the market-driven versus the technology-driven dichotomy. One study of six high-technology firms, including Hewlett-Packard, Motorola, and General Electric, found that **successful projects:**

- Exploited the organizations core competencies
- Were closely aligned with the competitive strategy
- Were continually immersed in timely, reliable information about customer and user preferences or requirements.

By contrast, when the development team didn't collect and use extensive market information, the projects rarely succeeded.[9]

Technology leadership was a necessary condition for success but was not sufficient; a technology orientation needs to be combined with a market orientation if the opportunity is to be fully realized.

George S. Day[10] also identified an in-depth, long-term study of a large computer systems firm that identified three major impediments to a market orientation.[11] These three **impediments** were:

- An *engineering-driven culture* that encouraged beliefs that "customers don't know what they want," and that marketing inputs just reflect what the

---

[8] George S. Day, "Misconceptions about Market Orientation," *Journal of Market-Focused Management* 4, no. 1, June 1999, 5–16.

[9] Glenn Bacon et al., "Managing Product Definition in High-Technology Industries: A Pilot Study," *California Management Review* 36, no. 3, Spring 1994.

[10] Day, "Misconceptions about Market Orientation," 5–16.

[11] "Marketing's Limited Role in New Product Development in One Computer Systems Firm," John P. Workman, Jr., *Journal of Marketing Research* 30, no. 4, 1993, 405–421.

competition is doing. Marketing people are widely believed to lack technical expertise in this culture

- An *organizational structure* where most marketing tasks, such as product
management and strategy development, were done within the engineering
group
- Unrelenting *time-to-market pressure,* which puts enormous pressure on
design teams to make decisions quickly

Firms striving to succeed by balancing a market-driven approach within a
technology-driven approach need to address these three impediments, less the best
intentions get compromised in the heat of the new product development battle.

Escalation of Commitment

Firms developing new products need to avoid the *escalation of commitment* until
they have identified the winners and killed the dogs. The escalation of commitment occurs when executives, desperate for any new product success, prematurely
commit their loyalty to a new product whose potential has not yet been fully evaluated among target customers. These executives often tell Wall Street analysts
about these new products prematurely in an attempt to generate excitement and
increase the price of the company's stock.

If these premature new products progress successfully through the funnel,
everything is fine. But few do, if you recall the mortality rate of new product ideas
that proceed through the Hershey funnel. Many early ideas turn out to be "dogs"
that are hard to kill once the company has gone public with their "next big breakthrough." This happened with Motorola and their ill-fated global satellite phone
spin-off, Iridium LLC. Management was blindly committed to the idea of providing global satellite communications, despite growing evidence throughout the
eleven-year development process that the communication market and customer
needs had evolved dramatically.

Once the "train leaves the station" and begins to pick up speed, it is hard to
stop it, back it up into the station, and get it on the right track. A key issue in new
product development is to discourage spiraling executive commitment on a new
product until market research among target customers has shown that the product has met its minimum performance targets.

Mohanbir Sawhney and Philip Kotler suggest that in the information-rich
regime of the new century, market sensing and responding processes are becoming simultaneous, not sequential. Instead of playing a role at the beginning and at
the end of the design process, persistent connectivity with customers throughout
the product development process allows customers to play an active role in
designing, creating, and adapting new offerings. In a networked enterprise, every
functional area can potentially interact directly with customers.[12]

---

[12] Mohanbir Sawhney and Philip Kotler, "The Age of Information Technology," in Kellogg
on Marketing, Dawn Iacobucci, ed. (New York: John Wiley and Sons, 2001), 403.

The Hallmark Cards Customer Panel

One of the leaders in inviting customers to participate in the new product development process is Hallmark Cards of Kansas City, Missouri, a leader in the greeting card market. Hallmark developed a computerized idea exchange process and invited target customers to become "consumer consultants" in developing new greeting card products.

In a speech at the American Marketing Association Conference in Chicago in September of 2002, Tom Brailsford described the customer Internet panels used by Hallmark to:

- Get closer to customers
- Help customers articulate their unmet needs
- Improve the flow of knowledge between customers and Hallmark product developers.

Hallmark's "Idea Exchange" online community has facilitated valuable knowledge creation, sharing, and learning in real time.

Hallmark launched their first "Customer Community" in November of 2000 by inviting 250 female target consumers to be "consumer consultants" and to participate in product and promotional development over the Internet. Hallmark has given each member access to the other members so that the community can communicate and share ideas with each other as well as with Hallmark. Each member has posted a picture and details about herself on the Internet. Hallmark was surprised by the degree that their panelists bonded as a community and the candidness of the panelists in giving Hallmark an unprecedented view into their lives. This Internet-based customer community has helped Hallmark by evaluating products, providing input into key strategic issues, and has come up with a couple of potentially big new product ideas for Hallmark.

The first customer community was so successful that Hallmark launched three additional communities in 2001 and 2002:

- Grandparents
- Latinas
- Women over 40 – No Kids at Home

Hallmark now has interactive access to over 800 consumers twenty-four hours a day, seven days a week.

This qualitative tool to achieve **customer insight** has allowed Hallmark to stay very close to their target customers. Artists and Hallmark product managers can easily interact with the customer community, and do so frequently. But the real measure of the success of the idea exchange has been that the CEO of Hallmark has also interacted directly with members of this customer community.

Need for Global Input in New Product Development

Firms that market globally need to avoid the temptation of conducting thorough marketing research on a new product in only their home country, and then

launching the product globally, hoping that there will be a common need for their product offering in other countries. Many companies in the United States, for example, conduct their development marketing research only in the United States; it is a rare occasion that multicountry studies are conducted as part of the development of new products.[13] Yet, the evidence suggests that products with global design marketed at world and nearest neighbor export markets achieve market shares that are almost **double** the shares earned by products with domestic design aimed at the same export markets.[14]

Further evidence of the critical importance of conducting marketing research as products are launched globally was presented by Kamran Kashani in the *Harvard Business Review*. Kashani identified the major errors made by firms in marketing products globally, with the most frequent error that led to lack of success being **"lack of adequate marketing research."** Of the products that **utilized marketing research** in the global launch, **two-thirds succeeded.** Of the products that **did not utilize marketing research** in the global launch, only **one-third succeeded**. Thus, in this study, the utilization of marketing research in global marketing **doubled** the probability of success.[15]

Tools for Developing Successful New Products

Seven tools for increasing the probability of new product success will be discussed in this chapter:

- Problem Detection
- Customer Advisory Panels
- Lead User Process
- Information Acceleration
- ZMET and Qualitative Techniques
- Concept Screening
- Simulated Test Markets

Problem Detection Methods

A straightforward method to generate ideas for future products is to ask consumers who have used the product to talk about any disappointments they have experienced or problems they have had with the product. This can be done effectively in focus groups, with depth interviews and during customer visits at the customer site. Diaries can be given to customers to record their negative experiences with a product and collected several weeks later and analyzed. Kotler has

---

[13] Wind and Mahajan, "Issues and Opportunities in New Product Development," 1–12.

[14] Elko J. Kleinschmidt and Robert G. Cooper, "The Performance Impact of International Orientation on Product Innovation," *European Journal of Marketing* 22, 1988.

[15] Kamran Kashani, "Beware the Pitfalls of Global Marketing," *Harvard Business Review*, September 1, 1989.

cautioned, however, that this approach tends to produce product and service *improvements* rather than product and service *innovations.*

Customer Advisory Panels

Recruiting a group of customers to serve on an "advisory panel" has paid big dividends for many firms, especially those in B-to-B markets. This advisory panel of eight to twelve customers should include knowledgeable customers who have been vocal and critical in the past about your company's need to change strategies or tactics. Dissatisfied customers should be included, since they often have the most valuable input. The panel should meet with the key decision makers at the company at least once a year, with twice per year being the most effective frequency. Typically, panel meetings convene for dinner and spend the entire following day in the panel meeting.

These customers should be reminded that the company wants to hear "the good, the bad, and the ugly" from them. They need to resist the temptation of getting too close to the company, because they will then tend to avoid telling the company about their "warts," shortcomings, and bad practices. New customers should be rotated on to the panel over time to replace those who no longer desire to stay engaged.

These panelists can be an excellent source of competitive intelligence. If they attend trade shows, they can observe new product offerings and report back to your company on the competitive products that represent the biggest threats to your firm in the future. They can also serve as "mystery shoppers" and provide feedback on the strengths and weaknesses of the sales people in your booth at the trade show.

A key benefit of a customer advisory panel is the increased loyalty that often develops among advisory panel members to the sponsoring company. They feel good to be listened to by one of their vendors and have a vested interest in the success of your firm because they have been asked to contribute to the strategic direction your firm will take in the future.

But perhaps the greatest benefits of developing partnerships with customers through advisory panels are in developing and launching new products. They can keep your new product ship steered in the right direction through the early stages of new product definition. They can help you develop effective marketing strategies for the new product prior to the launch. But most important, they become **customer advocates** for the product that they were personally involved in developing. Many of these advisory panel members are proud to be partners in the birth of the new product and are often early adopters of it. They are eager to advocate "the product that they created" to their peers.

Customer advisory panels have also been used effectively in the B-to-C world, as well. Hallmark's customer panels that can be accessed in real time through the Internet are clearly a best practice. Marketing Research Director for Levi Strauss Europe Flemming Thygesen has utilized customer advisory panels to develop rich insights into the needs and preferences of their target apparel customers.

These youth panels were developed among core target customers to better understand lifestyles, habits, values, category engagement, and brand engagement and are convened several times over a six-month period. These customer panels "gave us access to rich insights for our core customer groups across Europe," according to Thygesen.

The entire marketing team is encouraged to participate in these panels. "Brand groups, sales people and the advertising creative departments came to watch the workshops. And we took a huge step by creating a Consumer Insight Day – a full day of workshops and debriefings – so that the entire brand and creative teams were grounded in consumer insights prior to writing product briefs."[16]

Many customers are delighted to partner with companies on an "advisory panel." If your firm is a large market leader, many customers will be delighted to give you several days of their time each year for a modest honorarium. Travel, meal, lodging costs, and this modest honorarium are often sufficient to engage customers to come to your headquarters and provide their expert input to the future success of your company. Occasionally, customers from the advisory panel are hired by companies because of their empathy for and strong knowledge of the world of the customer.

Lead User Process

Lead users are customers who have adapted your current product to meet needs not foreseen by your product developers. The needs of these lead users may represent latent needs that exist in the broader market. In many B-to-B markets, lead user customers have thought up and even prototyped the majority of new products. It is just a matter of finding them and encouraging them to share their insights and ideas with your company. Of course, they also need to be compensated for their time and ideas.

The *lead user process* is a method for developing breakthrough products and is based on two major findings by innovation researchers at 3M:

- Many commercially important products are initially thought of and even prototyped by users rather than manufacturers.
- These products tend to be developed by "**lead users,**" who are well ahead of market trends and have needs that go far beyond those of the average user.[17]

These discoveries helped many B-to-B firms transform their process for creating breakthrough products from scratching their heads and brainstorming to a process of systematically identifying, observing, interviewing, and learning from

---

[16] Flemming Thygesen, "Proving Research's Value in a Company Where No One Really Cared to Know," quoted in "Research Department Report," July 2002, RFL Communications, Inc, 2.

[17] Eric Von Hippel, Stefan Thomke, and Mary Sonnack, "Creating Breakthroughs at 3M," *Harvard Business Review,* September 1999, 4.

lead users. For example, an automobile manufacturer may look to auto-racing teams to find lead users for developing innovative car braking systems. Companies that claim that they cannot anticipate what the market will buy in the future have probably not been able to identify and exploit the insights of their most advanced customers.

Kotler put his ideas on lead users well in a recent book:

> The truth is that the future is already here; it has already happened. The task is to find and study what the small percentage of future-defining customers want. The future is already here but is unevenly distributed to different companies, industries and countries.[18]

But how does a firm identify lead users? "Development teams assume that savvy users outside the company have already generated innovations; their job is to track down especially promising lead users and adapt their ideas to the business needs. **True lead users are rare**. To track them down most efficiently, project teams use telephone interviews to network their way into contact with experts on the leading edge of the target market."[19]

These lead users are then invited to a two to three-day workshop where the assembled group shares their individual insights and experience with each other, as well as cross-functional teams from the sponsoring firm.

While the lead user process does not guarantee success with new products, it has been effective in providing many companies with a systematic method of finding customers on the leading edge of markets. The lead user process usually opens up new avenues for the company to explore in directions that they hadn't imagined in their hectic world of meetings, deadlines, and phone calls.

While organizations should involve innovators and lead users in the initial stages of the new product development process, input on the market potential of the new product should not be limited to these small groups. There is increasing evidence that the characteristics and needs of innovators are very different from segments that may adopt the product at later stages in the product life cycle.[20] Marketing research also needs to be done among the early majority and the late majority as the product moves through its life cycle.

Information Acceleration

Many skeptics feel that marketing research is useless for markets or products that do not currently exist. They feel it is impossible for consumers to provide good input on something they have never seen, experienced, or for which they know of no use or role. Yet, good forecasts have been developed for nonexistent products

---

[18] Philip Kotler, *Marketing Insights from A to Z: 80 Concepts Every Manager Needs to Know* (Hoboken, NJ: John Wiley & Sons, 2003), 68.

[19] Von Hippel, Thomke, and Sonnack, "Creating Breakthroughs at 3M," 5.

[20] Geoffrey A. Moore, *Crossing the Chasm: Marketing and Selling Technology Products to Mainstream Customers* (New York: HarperBusiness, 1991).

by using new, creative processes that can simulate the benefits of that product in a future environment.

Information Acceleration is a process that was developed by Glen Urban of the Massachusetts Institute of Technology to provide customers with a fuller experience of products that currently do not exist and that may be marketed in the future. The use of virtual reality (multimedia computer representation) capabilities in Information Acceleration allows marketers to enhance the customer experience of new products by "creating the future environment" and to place consumers in the future scenario implied by the breakthrough innovation. In many cases, realistic estimates of the market potential of new products that have not yet been prototyped can be obtained.

This approach has strong interest among management in firms where the cost of product prototyping is high, where products are risky, and where the products will eventually require huge financial outlays, as is the case of the electric automobile.

Information Acceleration and the Electric Car

General Motors worked with Urban to obtain customer feedback on an electric car by simulating the experience using virtual reality. The consumer was "accelerated" to the future environment with full information and the ability to control the product search. The new infrastructure of recharging stations for electric vehicles was also simulated.

> A virtual showroom for an electric vehicle was created, in which the potential customer could "walk" around the car, "climb in" the car, and discuss the car with a salesperson. The customer could access television advertising and consumer magazine articles, read prices in a virtual newspaper, and even get advice from fellow consumers – all simulated on a multimedia computer.[21]

This application of information acceleration with electric cars resulted in an accurate market forecast and a key insight:

- The sales forecast was for sales of only 1,000 electric cars in 1998 through 2000
- The identification of a high level of latent demand for an economy car with a *hybrid power system* (electric and gasoline) for reliability

When General Motors launched custom-built electric cars in 1999, only 700 were sold in the first year, very close to the forecast provided by Urban. It appears that the larger market opportunity is for the hybrid car, as many major automobile manufacturers are now pursuing the hybrid (electric and gasoline) power system.

Other validations of the Information Acceleration process have proved promising. Urban has applied the process to the Buick Reatta sports car and to a B-to-B product, a blood cell analyzer that was targeted to physician's offices.

---

[21] Glen Urban et al., "Information Acceleration: Validation and Lessons From the Field," *Journal of Marketing Research* 34, February 1997, 143–153.

Based on these studies, Urban is confident that simulated information sources can be created to approximate physical environments and human interaction, and that Information Acceleration has the potential to forecast actual sales.[22]

ZMET and Qualitative Research

The Zaltman Metaphor Elicitation Technique is also very useful in developing new products, especially discontinuous innovations. Gerald Zaltman states that "understanding consumers' metaphors enables managers to imagine the nature of consumers' needs with respect to discontinuous innovations outside of consumer experience and beyond the reach of more conventional, literally oriented research tools. *Metaphors are the primary means by which companies and consumers engage one another's attention and imagination.* Understanding these deep or core metaphors can help marketers identify some of the most important but hidden drivers of consumer behavior."[23]

A recent qualitative study using focus groups was conducted among type I diabetics, those who typically develop the disease during their teenage years. These middle-aged diabetics were asked to prepare a collage using pictures from magazines that described their feelings about being diabetic and to bring these collages to a focus group the following week.

It was startling to see the darkness and sad images across most of these collages. Most diabetics had taped used insulin syringes to their collages to communicate their daily struggle with injections. Dark colors were used on many collages, and respondents talked about how their diabetes makes them feel more mortal and how they know that their disease could be slowly killing them. One respondent included a photograph of Jesus Christ on the cross to communicate her feelings about her "suffering" with this disease for the rest of her life. These incredible images about life with diabetes would not have been uncovered without the use of collages in this qualitative research.[24]

Concept Screening

Many companies that have developed good processes to generate many new product ideas have also developed processes to screen these ideas with customers. This concept screening process can weed out the bad ideas and identify good ideas that are of interest to target consumers. Concepts are typically screened first in focus groups to eliminate confusing ideas and sharpen good ideas. The strongest concepts are then exposed to large numbers of target customers who are on prerecruited panels, who are sent these concepts through the mail or, increasingly,

---

[22] Urban et al., "Information Acceleration: Validation and Lessons From the Field," 143–153.

[23] Gerald Zaltman, *How Customers Think: Essential Insights into the Mind of the Market* (Boston: Harvard Business School Press, 2003), 92–93.

[24] Unpublished marketing research study, based on the author's personal experience.

over the Internet. Target consumers rate their level of like or dislike of each concept, rate the uniqueness of each concept, and state how likely they are to buy the product described in each concept on a standard five-point purchase interest scale. Concepts that exceed a target "hurdle rate" (such as 40 percent of target customers say that they definitely will buy) then proceed to further development.

Simulated Test Markets

Enlightened companies launch products with a well-researched assessment of the opportunity for the new product. These companies utilize quantitative marketing research tools to simulate their market prior to launch and forecast demand for their new products well before they reach the market.

Surveys among target customers, using concept statements, are done well before product launch to measure purchase intentions and estimate the consumer trial rate. In addition, product use tests are often done as part of the simulated test market process to estimate repeat rates among consumers who try the product. These enlightened companies avoid nasty surprises during market launch by thinking through the best-case scenario, the expected scenario, and the worst-case scenario prior to market launch.

Simulated test markets utilize primary market research in which the buying process for a given product category is simulated. Mathematical models are used to forecast sales volumes based on the results of the primary marketing research, where refined concepts are tested with the actual product to refine trial rate estimates, estimate repeat rates, and estimate depth of usage rates. For example, a simulated test market for Plasma televisions would involve prototype televisions in a simulated retail store with competitive products available and a salesperson present to answer questions.

Simulated test market models have been developed that can accurately estimate first-year and second-year sales for new products, using five critical model inputs:

- **Trial rate** (the percent of target customers who buy at least once)
- **Repeat rate** (the percent of triers who buy a second time)
- **Depth of usage** (the amount of product used)
- **Marketing expenditures** (used to estimate the percent of target consumers who become **aware** of the new product)
- **Distribution rate** (needed to measure the availability of the product to the customer when he or she is purchasing)

The trial rate is usually estimated from the standard five-point purchase interest question, which has five closed-end responses:

- Definitely will buy
- Probably will buy
- Might or might not buy
- Probably will not buy
- Definitely will not buy

Research companies that conduct simulated test markets and forecast new products have extensive experience with many new products, and they are able to use their large databases of previously tested products to convert consumer responses into estimated trial rates. A major challenge is to adjust for the overstatement in consumer responses to the preceding purchase interest question; some customers never purchase a product even though they responded "definitely would buy" or "probably would buy" in the survey. The degree of adjustment for overstatement is impacted by a number of factors, including:

- The absolute price of the product
- Price/value perceptions
- Need fulfillment
- The uniqueness of the product
- The degree of liking of the product

Let's look at a simple example of how a simulated test market may forecast the market for DVD movies. Let's assume that we are forecasting the future market for DVD movies prior to their launch, and we define the target market as innovator households that are likely to own a DVD player in the next year, which we estimate to be 25 million households. From our primary market research survey, we have found good trial interest for DVDs at $10 each in the responses to the purchase interest question, and we estimate that the trial rate will be 60 percent in the first year. Our simulated test market also allowed customers to view prototypes of the DVD movies, and we estimate that 80 percent of those that tried the DVD movies will make a repeat purchase. Further, the research has helped us to identify that those not making a repeat purchase buy an average of 1.5 DVD movies on that first trial purchase, while those making repeat purchases buy an average of 5 DVD movies per year. We have analyzed our marketing expenditures against past product launches and estimate that the dollars we are spending will result in 80 percent awareness among the target market in the first year. Last, our distribution strategy and tactics will result in 90 percent of our target market being able to find DVD movies in the neighborhood retail outlets where they normally shop.

Thus, the first year dollar sales volume can be estimated through simple multiplication, as follows:

- **SALES FROM THOSE WHO NEVER BUY (40 percent of target households) =**
  - 10 million households × 0 movies = $0
- **SALES FROM THOSE WHO ONLY BUY ONCE (12 percent of target households) =**
  - 3 million households × 1.5 movies × $10 = $45 million
  - However, 20 percent of these households never become aware of the new DVD movies and 10 percent can not find them in retail stores, so the number of households is reduced from 3 million to 2.16 million
  - 2.16 million households × 1.5 movies × $10 = $32.4 million

- **SALES FROM THOSE WHO REPEAT (48 percent of target households) =**
  - 12 million target households × 5 movies × $10 = $600 million
  - However, 20 percent of these households never become aware of the new DVD movies and 10 percent can not find them in retail stores, so the number of households is reduced from 12 million to 8.64 million
  - 8.64 million households × 5 movies × $10 = $432 million
- **TOTAL SALES =** $0 + $32.4 million + $432 million = $464.4 million

While this calculation is somewhat simplified, it provides an illustration of how many simulated test market models forecast first-year sales for a new product category.

Many simulated test-marketing models are available commercially, with BASES being the most frequently used for consumer-packaged goods, and IPSOS/VANTIS being most frequently used for durable consumer goods, such as DVD players, Plasma TVs, digital satellite TV, and cell phones.

Simulated test markets also offer the benefit of confidentiality, compared to actual test markets. Competitors can quickly copy products that they see in live test markets, minimizing or even stealing the critical first mover advantages experienced by many innovative companies.

Recommended Tools for Developing Successful New Products

The utility of these new product development tools will vary by the stage of the new product development process, as shown in the following table.

Utility of New Product Development Tools by Development Stage

	Ideation Stage	Screening Stage	Development and Refinement	Market Testing
Problem Detection	++		+	
Customer Advisory Panels	++	+	++	
Lead User Process	++		+	
Information Acceleration			++	+
ZMET and Qualitative	++		++	
Concept Screening		++	+	
Simulated Test Markets			+	++

During the early ideation stage, the most effective tools are problem detection methods, customer advisory panels, the lead user process, and ZMET and qualitative tools. As many ideas are generated in this first stage, a process to screen the concepts among target customers in a quantitative research study is the important second stage. Customer advisory panels, information acceleration, and qualitative approaches facilitate further development and refinement of the strongest ideas in the third stage. Last, simulated test markets can be used to estimate sales for the new product in the marketplace. The final stage is market launch, with a probability of success that increases as more of the new product development tools are utilized.

Investment Cost

- A customer advisory panel of ten customers who meet at your headquarters twice per year can be conducted for approximately $150,000 to $200,000 per year, which includes travel and accommodations for the panelists, as well as an honorarium equal to two days salary for your customer.
- A lead user program to identify and personally interview ten lead users will cost a minimum of $40,000 per year.
- Information acceleration programs can be very expensive, with most of the cost in developing the virtual reality product and market. These studies, which could cost over one million dollars, should only be pursued by firms with large investment decisions facing them.
- Twenty depth interviews, conducted by a skilled moderator using ZMET or similar techniques, will cost approximately $40,000–$45,000, including analysis and report.
- Concept screening can now be done using customer panels that respond quickly to surveys over the Internet. A concept screening study of 200 target consumers can be as inexpensive as $15,000 for widely used products.
- Simulated test markets can be expensive, but they can provide valuable insight into the size of market opportunities and how to modify the product or the marketing mix to meet market share objectives. A simulated test market for a consumer packaged goods product will cost approximately $100,000–$125,000; a simulated test market for a consumer durable product will cost approximately $125,000–$150,000.

New Products Checklist

- Is your company continually striving to find new, better solutions to customers' problems?
- Does your company have a "funnel" system to encourage the generation of numerous customer-focused new product ideas?
- Are your new product concepts innovative or are they mostly me-too line extensions?

- Does your firm use a balance of customer needs understanding and knowledge of technological possibilities throughout the new product development process?
- Does your firm have difficulty in "killing the dogs," especially when the dog is the CEO's "pet" project?
- Does your firm have an engineering-driven culture that believes that customers don't know what they want in the future?
- Does time-to-market pressure encourage design teams to make critical decisions too quickly?
- Are customer information systems in place to allow all managers to access comprehensive and timely information easily on the target segment?
- Is customer information fully integrated throughout the new product development process?
- Does your firm have a culture that supports innovation and risk-taking?
- Does your culture support the sharing of discoveries across development groups?
- Is your firm totally committed to innovation?
- Does your new product development process have a balance between "executive foresight" and **customer insight**?
- Does your development process involve the early collection of customer input before the investment of significant R and D funds and before escalation of commitment occurs among management?
- Do you regularly generate new product ideas and screen them with customers?
- Do you collect customer input from all major countries around the globe during product development?
- Do you have a customer advisory panel that can serve as a "sounding board" for new strategies and new product ideas?
- Do you seek out lead users and learn from them?
- Do you use simulated test markets to quantify new product opportunities before "rolling the dice"?

ACTION PLANS AND METRICS

"Marketing Research is the first step and the foundation for effective marketing decision making."

Philip Kotler[1]

All functions within the firm need to be involved in the creation of superior value for customers. Customer insights need to be the language that breaks down functional silos and allows firms to make good decisions interfunctionally that create superior customer value. **Customer insight** must be at the forefront of all employees' minds as they make decisions that will impact the future of the organization.

Customer insights must not reside solely in the marketing department in the firm, but must be shared throughout the organization to allow decisions to be made interfunctionally. Firms need to establish a knowledge management system to permeate the organization with customer insights, to allow all decision makers to hear the voice of the customer clearly and make decisions through this viewing lens. All functions within the firm need to take responsibility for the creation of satisfied, loyal customers.

Transformation to a Customer Insight-Driven Organization

Five critical conditions or competencies must be developed within an organization to enhance its ability to achieve significant competitive advantages by transformation into a customer insight-driven organization:

1. **Top management dedication to and leadership on providing superior value to customers**
2. **Creation of chief marketing officer and vice-president of customer insight positions**
3. **Inter-functional cooperation and incentives**
4. **Dedicated marketing research expertise**
5. **Shared, easy to access and interesting customer insight intranet**

Putting in place action plans to develop these competencies will accelerate the rate at which a firm gains competitive advantages; advantages that will be hard for competitors to identify and copy. Once these competencies are in place, the

---

[1] Philip Kotler, *Marketing Insights from A to Z: 80 Concepts Every Manager Needs to Know* (Hoboken, NJ: John Wiley & Sons, 2003), 118.

company can then utilize the **CUSTOMER INSIGHT PYRAMID** to implement the customer insight program.

Let's look into each of these five competencies further.

Top management dedication to and leadership on providing superior value to customers

The starting point for the transformation of an organization is top management, which has to establish and consistently communicate the customer value vision and reflect that vision in all decisions and actions. "Building an organization's culture and shaping its evolution is the **unique and essential function of leadership.**"[2]

Top management must engage not just the minds but also the hearts of the entire organization. "Unless the desired customer-value commitments and behaviors emanate from the organization's culture, the commitments and behaviors will not endure, not to mention command the attention and allegiance of all functions in the organization. Only in an organization whose *core value* is the *continuous creation of superior value for customers* will there be the requisite leadership, incentives, learning, and skills to enable the continuous attraction, retention and growth of the most profitable customers in each target market [emphasis added]."[3]

There must be a firm belief among all employees that every interaction they have with customers is important to keeping that customer loyal to the company. Jan Carlson of SAS Airlines referred to these interactions as "the million moments of truth" that determine a company's success in the marketplace.[4]

The CEO needs to take personal responsibility for defining customer value as the driving force behind the strategy of the organization. The three most potent mechanisms for transmitting and embedding this **customer value culture** are all manifestations of leadership:[5]

- Deliberate role modeling, teaching, and coaching by leaders
- What leaders pay attention to, measure, and control
- Leaders reactions to critical incidents and organizational crises

Role modeling should begin with the CEO announcing that he or she is spending the entire next week meeting with the company's top ten customers. The CEO should meet with the appropriate management at each of these ten

---

[2] Peter M. Senge, "The Leader's New Work: Building Learning Organizations," *Sloan Management Review* 32 no.1, Fall 1990, 7–23.

[3] John Narver, Stanley Slater, and Brian Tietje, "Creating a Market Orientation," *Journal of Market-Focused Management 2,* 1998, 241–255.

[4] Kotler, *Marketing Insights from A to Z,* 32.

[5] E. H. Schein, "The Role of the Founder in Creating Organizational Culture," *Organizational Dynamics 12,* Summer 1983.

customer sites. The salesperson responsible for each of these customers should have no trouble identifying the key people to meet with; if they are not able to identify the key decision makers, they are not doing their job. Most customers are very happy to meet with senior management from one of their "vendors"; in fact, many of your customers have likely wished for a long time that you would take a more active interest in understanding their business and their needs.

The CEO should use the three simple questions suggested in Chapter 9 during these customer visits:

"What do we do well?"

"What can we improve?"

"How can we keep you as a satisfied customer?"

These simple questions work magically, if asked sincerely with active listening. The customer will greatly appreciate your effort in coming to her or his place of business to enhance your relationship.

These customer visits can turn into win-win, relationship-building interactions, especially if the following conditions are met:

- The CEO starts the interaction by thanking the customer for their business and letting the customer know that the purpose of the visit is to allow top management to learn firsthand about the needs of the company's most important customers.
- The CEO and any others present from the vendor firm need to spend over 80 percent of the time listening, only speaking to ask clarifying or probing questions (What do you mean by that? Can you tell me more about that?).
- No effort is made during this interaction to sell anything. This is very difficult for many ex-salespeople, not to try to sell products during this learning interaction. The truth is that the relationship you are building by deep listening to your customer will make that customer much more likely to consider your company's products actively in the future.
- No effort is made to "correct" inaccurate customer perceptions about your products during this meeting. In the worst example experienced by the author, one customer visit deteriorated into an argument between the customer and the salesperson over the benefits of our product versus a key competitor's product. This clearly set the relationship back. Misperceptions by the customer need to be noted and addressed in subsequent customer communications.
- The CEO assures the customer that this is not a one-time cameo appearance, but asks the customer if he or she can come back again in six months to stay on top of the changing needs of this important customer.
- The CEO thanks the customer at the end of the interaction and assures the customer that their input will be considered in future decisions made by the company.
- The CEO takes action on some of the customer suggestions and communicates those customer-driven changes to all customers.

This process can not only make these top ten customers more loyal and heavier buyers of your products (apostles) but can make them customer advocates who will tell their peers what a great customer-driven company yours is.

Perhaps the best example of top management leading the customer insight process through role modeling is Jeffrey Bleustein, chairman and CEO of **Harley-Davidson** in Milwaukee, Wisconsin. One of thirteen employees who led a leveraged buyout of the company from AMF in 1981, Bleustein has turned the company around from near bankruptcy in 1985 to eighteen consecutive years of record sales and profits. Early in the turnaround, Harley executives mounted motorcycles and reached out to customers through road trips and rallies. The road trips were partly influenced by the fact that Harley-Davidson was nearly broke and didn't have sufficient resources to invest heavily in marketing and advertising.

A key element in Harley's success has been the intimate relationship developed with customers on these trips, as well as a deep understanding of what a Harley-Davidson motorcycle means to these owners. According to Bleustein, "Harley is about **freedom, individuality** and **affiliation** with a community." This depth understanding came not just from formal marketing research studies but also from Harley-Davidson executives immersing themselves in the world of the Harley rider through participation in the Harley Owners Group, also known as **H.O.G.** Much of the collective wisdom of Harley executives has come from hours on the road with Harley riders who have shared their biking stories with company senior management. According to Bleustein, "We were doing 'close to the customer' marketing before it ever had a name."[6]

Harley-Davidson established H.O.G. in 1983 in response to a growing desire by Harley riders for an organized way to share their passion and show their pride. By 1985, forty-nine local chapters had sprouted around the country, with a total membership of 60,000 riders. Today, more than 800,000 members belong to one of the 1,300 chapters worldwide, making H.O.G. the largest factory-sponsored motorcycle organization in the world.

"Harley has a time-intensive method of keeping up with what customers want: Half of its 8,000 employees ride a Harley-Davidson. Everyone, including Bleustein, has to go through a dealer to get one, if only to see what a customer's experience is like. Hundreds also hit rallies around the United States. They pick up ideas there by seeing how riders customize their bikes."[7]

Harley's production of motorcycles has grown at an average rate of 13 percent per year over the past fifteen years. Its share of the heavyweight motorcycle market has reached 48 percent. Its customer base has reached over 2 million riders. And Harley-Davidson is the only brand in the world that loyalists regularly tattoo on their bodies.

---

[6] Rick Barrett, "Company Aims to Keep Its Wheels Turning," *Milwaukee Journal Sentinel,* 24 August 2003.

[7] Jonathan Fahey, "Love into Money," *Forbes,* 7 January 2002.

Creation of Chief Marketing Officer and Vice-President of Customer Insight Positions

This visible leadership of the CEO will provide a great jump-start to the transformation process, but the commitment to customer value creation then needs to be developed throughout the organization. The company needs to establish a position of chief marketing officer, to put the marketing function on the same level as other senior executives in the company, such as the chief financial officer. Enlightened companies committed to understanding customer insights, such as Frito-Lay and McDonald's, have established the chief marketing officer position. Without this organizational parity for the marketing function, a customer insight focus can be lost during tough economic or financial times. It is during these tight times where **customer insights** can provide the greatest competitive advantage, since many of your competitors may have tightened their marketing budgets significantly.

The chief marketing officer needs to establish an ongoing customer visit program for the president and for all of the vice-presidents throughout the company. These can be done in teams of two or three; larger groups of senior executives tend to overwhelm customers. When the vice presidents of manufacturing, finance, R and D, marketing, and operations all have experienced the world of the customer "out there in the real world," there is a greater likelihood that decisions will be made with the needs of the customer in the foreground rather than in the background.

The strategic planning processes used by the company must be built around customer insights to provide superior value to customers, and they must set a clear course to achieve the aim of providing superior customer value. At Harley-Davidson, executives fresh from a H.O.G. rally are likely to understand deeply the external opportunities and threats as well as fairly assess Harley's strength and weaknesses. This will result in strategies that are grounded in fact, not in hopes and dreams. The strategic planning function should report into the chief marketing officer if the company truly wants to become customer driven.

The position of **vice president of customer insight (VPCI)** should be established to own the process of developing and disseminating customer insights and to implement the Customer Insight Pyramid described later in this chapter. This VPCI should be skilled in many of the tools described throughout this book, with strengths in qualitative marketing research, quantitative marketing research, and market intelligence. Most important, this VPCI must have strong empathy for the needs of target customers and be the untiring, shouting voice of these customers within the company.

Interfunctional Cooperation and Incentives

Once management has clearly established the vision of creating superior value for customers and the chief marketing officer and vice president of customer insight positions have been established, it needs to strive to reduce interdepartmental conflict, increase interdepartmental connections, and push decision making down into the organization. Only then can employees begin to work in harmony toward the common goal of providing superior customer value, and transform the organization, rather than working in independent silos toward disjointed departmental goals.

This interfunctional coordination is essential to the transformation of organizations, with customer insights serving as the common understanding to help coordinate interfunctional activities. "Everyone's job is defined in terms of how it helps to create and deliver value for the customer, and internal processes are designed and managed to ensure responsiveness to customer needs and maximum efficiency in value delivery."[8]

Critical to keeping employees focused on providing superior value to customers is a reward system that reflects progress toward that goal. Incentives, including salary bonuses and promotions, need to be based on external customer measures, such as customer satisfaction levels, customer's perceptions of value provided by the company, and customer retention rates. It is amazing how employees focus on those activities that impact their wallet.

Dedicated Marketing Research Expertise

Companies serious about using customer insights to achieve competitive advantages will establish formal processes to monitor continuously their macroenvironments and the perceptions, needs, preferences, and satisfaction of their customers. They will establish dedicated departments, such as marketing research, whose primary function is to be the **customer advocate** within the firm, channeling the needs of the customer into all decisions the firm makes and making sure that decisions are made that continue to provide added value to target customers. The voice of the customer needs to be heard in the company boardroom, as well as by the company's service engineer in Anchorage, Alaska. Director of Global Marketing Research for Mobile Phones at Nokia John Markham has established the following mission for his department:

> Enable better-informed decision making, through delivering world-class understanding of markets, customers, and their product requirements.

He sees the role of marketing research as **delivering foresight that is actionable.** Thus, marketing research at Nokia not only delivers the voice of the customer but also helps Nokia identify new strategic opportunities.

Marketing researchers within the corporation need to be good business thinkers first, and good communicators second. Members of the marketing research department need to have the requisite analytical skills but also be able to understand the business decisions involved and persuasively communicate with all levels of management. MBAs tend to be well suited for this consultative and analytical function in the firm. Technical specialists often have trouble communicating with management in their language of earnings per share, return on investment, and payback period. Technical specialists are readily accessible within external marketing research firms.

Most firms do not find it affordable to create a large internal marketing research function unless they have a large, constant volume of marketing research

---

[8] Frederick Webster, *Market-Driven Management: Using the New Marketing Concept to Create a Customer-Oriented Company* (New York: Wiley, 1994).

studies, as can be found at firms the size of Procter & Gamble. Many firms hire marketing researchers to take responsibility for: 1) the formulation of the marketing problem or opportunity to be studied, 2) the decision as to whether to consider outside marketing research expertise, 3) the identification of the appropriate external resources, and 4) the communication of the research findings and recommendations to company management. The following chart can provide guidance as to which marketing research functions can be handled with internal staff and which functions should be contracted to outside consultants.

Marketing Research Resources
Internal versus External

	Internal Resources Can Be Utilized	Consider External Resources
Secondary Data	Government and SEC sources Marketresearch.com Esomar.org directory Competitive Web Page Monitoring	Competitive Intelligence
Exploratory Approaches	Customer Visit Program Customer Advisory Panels Observation Ethnography	Focus Groups Depth Interviews Projective Techniques Laddering
Descriptive Approaches	Usability testing Internet surveys Internet customer panels	Segmentation Studies Perceptual Mapping Trade-off studies Pricing studies Advertising testing
Causal Approaches	Test Marketing	Simulated Test Markets

Increasingly, more marketing research surveys are being conducted electronically over the Internet, replacing the prior approaches of telephone interviews, personal interviews, and mail interviews. Many sources report that over half of all consumer interviews in the United States were conducted over the Internet in 2003, and that this trend will continue to grow. Voice mail, answering machines, and caller I.D. have made it very difficult to reach a representative sample of target consumers via the telephone, and nonresponse rates continue to increase. Many market researchers have called this the second technology revolution to impact the marketing research industry, with the first being the introduction of UPC codes and store scanners in the 1970s to measure product movement accurately and continuously through retail outlets.

Shared, Easy to Access, and Interesting Customer Insight Intranet

The discovery and dissemination of customer insights is critical to sustaining a focus on delivering superior value to customers and ensuring that activities are evaluated in terms of their contribution to customer value. For a customer insight-driven culture to grow in the organization, customer insights need to be disseminated by formal as well as informal communication channels, and must easily flow both laterally and vertically through the organization.

At the Dental Products Division of 3M, a Customer Information System (CIS) is in place that includes results of all customer surveys, focus groups, and product evaluations. In addition, virtually all customer contacts – from visits by field representatives to customer calls into the telephone hotline – are also entered into the CIS to allow anyone to assess how well specific products and services are meeting customer satisfaction goals and to spot opportunities for new products.

In 2001, the Toys "R" Us Marketing Research Department created an intranet to provide broader dissemination of consumer insights throughout the company. The intranet site includes a digital marketing research library. The intranet site is accessible to the entire organization and includes the latest consumer trends. Monica Woods, the vice president of Consumer Insights at Toys "R" Us, takes pride in the role of the Marketing Research Department in designing, engineering, and implementing the intranet site from scratch, at zero cost, which is now getting critical customer information out to the entire organization.[9]

This customer insight intranet must also be interesting to encourage users to return on a regular basis. Stories of customer experiences with the company's products and service often are of more interest than tables of numbers and charts. Making examples of company "heroes," who went the extra mile to provide superior customer value, and rewarding them with shares of stock in the company are very effective in setting examples for all employees.

Firms that want to benefit from **customer insights** need to create this shared knowledge base that is easily accessible by all employees. George S. Day in *The Market Driven Organization: Understanding, Attracting, and Keeping Valuable Customers* argues:

> The knowledge base of a market driven organization is arguably its most valuable asset. What distinguishes a market driven firm is the depth and timeliness of market knowledge that enables it to anticipate market opportunities and respond faster than its rivals.[10]

Market-driven organizations need to build knowledge management systems for synergistic information distribution that are accessible throughout the organization

---

[9] Monica Wood, "Creativity, Enthusiasm and Risk Taking 'R' Keys to Marketing Research Department's Growing Success," quoted in "Research Department Report," March 2003, RFL Communications, Inc.

[10] George S. Day, *The Market Driven Organization: Understanding, Attracting, and Keeping Valuable Customers* (New York: Free Press, 1999), 102.

to assure that the relevant information and insights are available when and where they are needed. Market-driven organizations have found that a marketing intranet within their company can provide a great impetus to this **customer insight** sharing, allowing them to add significant value to their customers.

One danger of this decentralized information sharing approach is that new customer insights may not be interpreted in the context of past knowledge of the target customer, and marketing tactics may be developed that react to one new marketing research study rather than the totality of what is known about target customers. Larry Chandler, former vice president of business research for McDonald's, suggests that "knowledge synthesis be used to link any new information to prior information, to create useful, actionable, and focused information." This function is usually best performed by a stable, knowledgeable staff of strategists in the Marketing Research Department.[11]

Measuring Marketing Progress

The ultimate measure of successful marketing programs is their impact on the profitability of the company and, therefore, on the company's stock price. But this impact is hard to isolate from the many other factors impacting a company's profitability. How, then, can the effectiveness of marketing programs be assessed? Some key marketing metrics exist within internal company records, while other key marketing metrics can be measured externally by collecting information from the marketplace and customers. It is useful to categorize these metrics as **Company Focused, Market Focused,** or **Customer Focused,** as shown in the following table.

KEY MARKETING METRICS

	Company Focused	Market Focused	Customer Focused
Observable Internally	• Unit sales growth • $ sales growth • Profitability of business • $ profit growth • New products as a percent of total sales	• Profitability of market segment	• Customer retention rate • Length of relationship • Profitability by customer
Measurable Externally	• Customer perceptions of and attitudes toward company • Customer satisfaction with company • Willingness to recommend company • Likelihood to repurchase from company	• Unit market share • $ market share • Percent ACV Distribution • Share of advertising voice	• Trial rate • Repeat rate • Share of wallet • Top-of-mind awareness • Unaided awareness • Total awareness (unaided plus aided)

---

[11] Larry Chandler, personal communication with author, 2 December 2004.

Company-Focused Metrics

A focus of many top executives is the impact that marketing programs are having on the growth in unit sales, dollar sales, and profitability. While some marketing programs can be measured in the short-term (e.g. coupons), other marketing programs may not impact these financial metrics in the short-term (e.g. advertising). Sales of new products as a percentage of total company product sales are a good measure of the ability of the company to launch and grow successful new products. In rapidly growing markets, it is not unusual for this target to be as high as 35 to 45 percent of sales.

However, companies can fall into the trap of driving sales and profit growth at the expense of growing relationships with their target customers. Over the long-term, this could lead to high customer turnover and declining market share. Therefore, it is important to have a "balanced scorecard" and measure the perceptions of and attitudes of customers toward the company. Further, many firms measure the satisfaction of customers with the company, their willingness to recommend their company, and their likelihood to purchase from the company in the future.

Market-Focused Metrics

Many marketers are able to assess the profitability of each target market segment and use this information in their strategic targeting decisions. Equally important is the trend in their market share over time, since high internal growth could simply reflect a rapidly growing market. Consumer packaged goods firms play close attention to their All Commodity Share (ACV) distribution, which is the share of outlets that carry the brand on their shelves, weighted by the ACV of each store. Also important is the share of voice a firm commands, which is the percentage of the company's advertising expenditures relative to the total advertising expenditures for the relevant product category.

Customer-Focused Metrics

Many firms focus on customer metrics to assess the effectiveness of their marketing efforts, as these metrics often have the most immediate response to marketing programs and are easiest to isolate. Internal records on customer retention rates, lengths of relationship, and profitability can provide hard, accurate information on how well marketing programs are working. For new products, it is critical to assess the share of customers who are aware of them, have tried them once, and have repeat purchased the new products.

For key company products, it is important to measure continually their top-of-mind awareness among target customers. (Top-of-mind awareness is the percentage of customers that mention your brand **first** when asked an unaided awareness question, such as: "When you think of beer, which brands come to mind?") Studies have shown that top-of-mind awareness levels higher than a brand's market share are common for growing brands, and that top-of-mind awareness levels

lower than a brand's market share are common for declining brands. Total awareness levels combine all brands mentioned on an unaided basis, with those mentioned on an aided basis. (An example of an aided awareness question is: "Are you aware of Michelob Ultra?")

Every major marketing program should be measured against the objectives of the program, using the appropriate marketing metrics from the previous table. The metrics should include both internal and external metrics to maintain a balanced scorecard of financial and customer metrics. If the marketing program is a broad, company level effort, company level metrics may be most appropriate. If the marketing program is a brand-focused effort, then customer level metrics may be most important. The key point is to understand the customer response that is expected in the relevant time frame and measure whether the marketing effort is having the intended impact. If it is, additional investment may be called for. If the desired impact is not observed, it is probably time to cut your losses.

Implementing the Customer Insight Pyramid

Companies new to the concept of gathering customer insight are encouraged to proceed slowly and focus on several of the insights in this book rather than trying to address too many initially and failing. It is suggested that the process start at the bottom of the Customer Insight Pyramid and work upward. Assuming that the company is starting from scratch but plans to dedicate the resources to reach the top of the pyramid, a time horizon of two to three years should be the minimum planning horizon.

Customer Insight Pyramid

Appendix A

Summary of Customer Insight Tools

1. Macro Trends
   a. Environmental scanning
   b. Secondary data acquisition
   c. SWOT analysis
   d. Scenario planning
   e. Data Mining
2. Unmet Needs
   a. Observation
   b. Ethnography
   c. Focus groups
   d. Depth interviews
   e. Archetype research
   f. Customer visits
3. Emotional and Rational Motivations
   a. Projective interviewing techniques
   b. Zaltman Metaphor Elicitation Technique
   c. Laddering
4. Segmentation and Targeting
   a. Cluster analysis
   b. Targeting matrix
5. Perceptions and Differentiation
   a. Perceptual mapping
   b. Positioning triangle
6. Critical Features
   a. Kano model
   b. Usability testing
   c. Conjoint analysis
   d. Discrete choice modeling
7. Marketing Communications
   a. Advertising testing – explicit methods
   b. Advertising testing – implicit methods
8. Price Sensitivity
   a. Monadic surveys
   b. Conjoint analysis and discrete choice modeling
   c. Experimentation
9. Satisfaction and Loyalty
   a. Customer visits and mystery shoppers
   b. Competitive benchmarking
   c. Customer satisfaction tracking
   d. New purchase follow-up surveys
   e. Service call follow-up surveys

10. New Products
    a. Problem detection methods
    b. Customer advisory panels
    c. Lead user process
    d. Information acceleration
    e. ZMET and qualitative methods
    f. Concept screening
    g. Simulated test markets

INDEX

A

Abbott Laboratories, 30
Achievers, 86
ACNielsen Company, 24
Activities, interests and opinions information
    (AIO), 8
ACV chain, 64
Advertising development
    five categories in testing methods, 157–160
    General Motors OnStar System, 155–156
    implicit measures of effectiveness, 160–161
    Miracle Whip, 154–155
    Nabisco, 153–154
    testing, 157
    testing measures, 160
Affiliating
    in successful positioning, 116
Age group dynamics—2010 *vs.* 2000, 6f
Aging, 4–5
All commodity share (ACV) distribution, 236
Altruists, 85
American Customer Satisfaction Index (ACSI)
    stock prices and, 189–193
Analogous products
    use in testing pricing, 175
Anheuser-Busch, 19, 71
Apostle customer, 196, 199
Applebee's, 77
Apple Computer, Inc., 93
Application positioning, 115
A priori segmentation, 75, 77
    general variables, 76f
    product specific variables, 80f
Archetype research, 42–45
    customer unmet needs, 33
    investment cost, 49
    PT Cruiser and, 44–45
Attribute importance scores, 131
Attribute level utility scores, 131
Attribute positioning, 115
Attributes, 64
    seven stages in life cycle of, 124–125
AT&T Wireless Services, 14
Augmented product, 115

B

Bakken, David, 208
Baldie Play, 188
Barnes and Noble, 78
Bath in a box, 36
Beecher, H. K., 56

Beer brand choice
    emotional or rational, 53–54
    product imagery, 110
Beer industry
    import market, 92
    market segmentation, 72–73
Beeriness, 110
Beer market, U.S.
    perceptual map, 111f, 112f
BehaviorScan, 146–147
Belongers, 85
Benchmarking
    in customer satisfaction measurement
        programs, 200–201
    in testing pricing, 175
Benefit positioning, 115
Benefit segmentation, 89
Best Buy, 59
Best practice model
    Dow Chemical Company, 204–205, 204f
"Be there now" addiction, 10
Black, Carol, 77
Bleustein, Jeffrey, 230
Boiled frog analogy, 1–4
Bounded rationality, 52
Brain activity
    advertising and, 163
Brand analogies, 60
Brand essence, 118–119
Brand imagery, 108–109
Brand loyalists, 91
Brand loyalty
    market segmentation, 72
Brand perceptions, 103–120
Brand recall, 160
Brand-switching studies, 197
Bud Light, 59
Budweiser beer, 59, 71
Building demand, 186
Business-to-business markets
    focus groups, 41–42
    perceptions among, 114–115

C

Calder, Bob, 38
Candice group, 8–9
Cartoon caption completion, 59
Cashing-out, 9
Category positioning, 115
Caterpillar, 115
Cathy group, 8–9
Central Intelligence Agency, 22

Changing customer behavior, 6
Cheskin, Louis, 106
Chief Marketing Officer, 231
Chili's, 78
Claritas, Inc, 78
Clinical approach
    focus group research, 38
Cluster analysis, 94–97
Coca-Cola Company, 52
Cocooning, 9
Collages
    in qualitative research, 54
Combat Insecticide Disks, 59
Commercial secondary information, 24
Common threads, 3
Communication
    in advertising, 157
Company focused metrics, 235–236
Compatibility, 17
Compelling offer, 133–138
Competition-based positioning, 116
    triangle, 116f, 117f, 118f
Competitive intelligence, 20
Competitive trends, 19–20
Competitor positioning, 115
Competitors' pricing
    Coors' pricing strategy, 170
    marketing and selling costs, 187
    in pricing determination, 166–167
Complexity, 17
Conant, Doug, 153
Concept screening
    developing successful new products, 220–221
Confidence trend, 10
Conjoint analysis, 127–130, 132
    and discrete choice modeling, 179–180
    in testing pricing, 175–176
Conjoint deliverables, 131–132
Conscious mind, 143–164
Consensus maps, 63
Consequences, 64
Consumer behavior, 22
    emotional and rational behavior, 51–67, 240
Consumer drawings, 59
Consumer rights, 63
Contextual inquiry, 34
Continuous innovations, 16
Cooper, Michael, 108
Coors Brewing Company, 1–2, 17, 112, 118
    strategy in expansion markets, 169–171
Corporate Leadership Council, 133–138
Cost
    in pricing determination, 166–167
Creating betterness, 122
Creatives, 84
Creeping featurism, 126–127
Critical features, 121–142, 240
    investment cost, 141
    optimization checklist, 142

Cross-selling
    opportunities for, 187
Crystal Pepsi, 106
Cultural unconscious, 43
Customer advisory panels
    developing successful new products, 216
Customer advocates
    marketing research department, 232
    new products, 216
Customer benefits, 116
Customer focused metrics, 235–237
Customer goodwill, 186
Customer insight, 2, 24, 26
    action plan and metrics, 227–241
    beer brand choice, 53–54
    Coca-Cola Company, 52
    creation of vice-president for, 231
    during development of advertising, 152–153
    disciplined approach to, 155
    Harley-Davidson, 56
    intranet, 234–235
    market driven or self-centered, 239
    Oreo cookies, 54–55
    summary of tools, 240–241
    unmet needs, 31–49, 240
    ZMET, 63
Customer insight-driven organization
    transformation to, 227–228
Customer insight pyramid, 1f, 31f, 51f, 69f, 103f,
        121f, 143f, 165f, 185f, 207f
    implementing, 237f
Customer panel
    Hallmark Cards, 214
Customer perceptions, 103–104
    satisfaction and loyalty, 185–206
Customer requirements
    obvious, 193–194
Customer satisfaction programs
    attitudinal measures, 197
    comprehensive measurement programs,
        197–198
    externally or internally focused, 190–191
    four typologies, 196
    lost customer surveys, 203
    measurement, 191–193
    prioritizing modules, 202–203
    quantitative tracking studies, 201–202
Customer's language, 130–131
Customer unmet needs, 31–49
    checklist, 40
Customer value
    Coors' pricing strategy, 170
    culture, 228
    in pricing determination, 166–167
    understanding, 167–169
Customer visits, 45–47
    customer satisfaction measurement program,
        198–199
    customer unmet needs, 33

investment cost, 49
practical guide, 46
success of HP and, 47

D

Daimler–Chrysler, 44–45
Data mining, 20, 28–29
David Ogilvy Award, 15, 54
Day, George S., 14, 212, 234
Deepening
  in positioning, 119
Definition
  in positioning, 119
Delighters, 124
Dell Computer, 70, 126
Demographics
  market segmentation, 72
Demographic segmentation, 77
Demographic trends, 4–8
Depth interviews, 42
  investment cost, 48
Depth of usage, 221
Devouts, 85
Differentiation
  declining, 104
  in positioning, 119
  strongest opportunity for, 105
  in successful positioning, 116
Diffusion rate, 17–18
Digital and traditional camera sales, U.S., 17f
Dimensions of products, 109
Disciplined defense
  in positioning, 119
Discontinuous innovations, 16
Discrete choice modeling (DCM), 138–139,
    179–180
Distribution rate, 221
Divide and conquer
  strategy for success, 71
Do-it-yourself paint market, 89
Donovan, Jim, 44
DoubleClick, 162
Dow Chemical Company, 204–205, 204f
Down-aging, 9
Driving needed change, 3
Dynamically continuous innovations, 16

E

eAdvertising
  ten commandments of, 162
Early adopters, 82
Early majority, 82
Economic trends, 12–14
Economic value
  in testing pricing, 175
Eleanor group, 8–9
Emotional appeals, 159
Emotional motivations, 51–67

checklist, 67
  investment cost, 67
  marketing communications for, 143–144
  marketing tools for uncovering, 57–67
Emotional significance, 145
Employees, high-value
  attraction of, 133–138
  attributes important to, 134, 135f, 137f
Employment offers, 136f
Empowerment, 155–156
Emulators, 85
Engineering-driven culture
  in new product development, 212–213
Environmental scanning, 20–22
Escalation of commitment
  in new product development, 213
ESOMAR 2003 Prices Survey, 48
Ethnography
  customer unmet needs, 33, 35–37
  investment cost, 48
Everyday low pricing strategy
  P&G, 172–174
Experience, 3
Experiential, 86
Experimentation
  in testing pricing, 176, 181
Exploratory approach, 47, 48f
  focus group research, 38
Exposure effect, 149–151
External sources
  customer information, 37

F

Family life cycle segments, 79–80
Federal Reserve Board's Survey of Consumer
    Finances, 12–13
Feel-learn-do, 159
Flexible life stages trend, 11
Focus groups, 37–42
  advantages, 40
  approaches for, 38–30
  appropriate business issues for, 39–40
  B-to-B markets, 41–42
  customer satisfaction measurement program,
    198–200
  customer unmet needs, 33
  disadvantages, 40–41
  experiential benefit, 40
  investment cost, 48
  moderator skills, 40
  in testing pricing, 175
Foote Cone and Belding (FCB) Advertising
    Planning Model, 151
Ford Motor Company, 239
Fornell, Claes, 190
  portfolio performance, 190f
Four levels of product, 104–105
Frequency of purchase, 28

Freshness, 63
Frito-Lay, 148–149
Fun seekers, 84

G

Gale, Bradley: *Managing Customer Value,* 124
Gallup & Robinson, 158
Galvin, Christopher, 14
General Motors (GM), 35, 70, 74, 138, 211, 219
    advertising testing, 155–156
Geo-clustering segmentation approach, 78
Geographic segmentation, 77–78
Gerstner, Lou, 45
Global Business Network, 27
Goal-based positioning, 118–119
Goldman, Alfred, 38
Google, 23
Green, Paul E., 127
Group interaction, 40
Gulen, Huseyin, 108

H

Haley, Russ, 88
Hallmark Cards, Inc., 3, 10, 21
    customer panel, 214
Harley-Davidson Motorcycles
    customer insight process, 230
    marketing research by, 55–56, 90–91
Hartley, Jeffrey, 35
Helene Curtis Company, 78
Hershey's, 210–211
Hewlett-Packard (HP)
    customer visits, 47
    Medical Products Division, 34
Hierarchical value map
    Mitsubishi Eclipse Automobile, 65f
Historical data
    analysis in testing pricing, 175
Home & family employee, 138
Hostage customer, 196, 199
Household income trends, 1f, 12–14
Household trends by type 1980-2000, 7f
Hughes, Arthur, 28
    Strategic Database Marketing, 28–29
Hunkering down trend, 10

I

I-Am-Me, 86
Ideation
    new products, 210
Immigration
    growth into the U. S., 7
    into U.S. by country of birth 1990-2000, 8f
Import beer market, 92
Indirect techniques, 32
Information acceleration
    developing successful new products, 218–219
    electric car and, 219
Information Resources, Inc., 24, 161

Innovators, 82
Integrated, 86
Interfunctional cooperation and incentives,
    231–232
Internal sources
    customer information, 34
Internet sites
    for secondary data acquisition, 23
    testing impact of banner advertising, 161–162
Intimates, 84
Intrusiveness
    in advertising, 157
Investment costs, 29–30, 48–49, 67, 100, 119, 141,
    163, 182–183, 205, 224
Ipsos-Insight, 23
Iridium, 32

J

Johnson, Rich, 135
Jones, Thomas, 196
Jump Associates, 36

K

Kano, Noriaki, 123
Kano Model, 123–125, 123f
Kastenholz, John, 35
Kellogg School of Management, 38
Kitchen in a box, 36
Kodak, 17
Kotler, Philip, 45, 69, 115, 143, 186, 193, 213
Krishnamurthi, Lakshman, 165
Kuester, Sabine, 15
Kunst-Wilson, William, 149

L

Laddering, 64–66
Laggards, 82
Langer, Judith: *The Mirrored Window: Focus Groups
    from a Moderator's Point of View,* 11
Late majority, 82
Latent needs
    vs. overt needs, 32–33
Lazar Group, 39
Leadership
    superior value to customers, 228
Lead user process
    developing successful new products, 217–218
Learn-feel-do, 159
Leo Burnett Advertising, 63
Levitt, Theodore: *The Marketing Imagination,* 103,
    105, 121
LexisNexis, 24
Lifestyles, 9
Lifetime customer value, 186
Lifetime Entertainment Services, 77
Likeability of ad, 159–160
Lodish, Leonard, 146
Longing for bygone days trend, 10
Lost customer surveys, 203

M

Macro trends, 1–4, 238, 240
  brand perceptions, 103–120
  checklist, 30
  critical features, 121–142
  emotional and rational motivations, 51–67
  focus, 20
  marketing communications, 143–164
  new products, 207–225
  pricing sensitivity, 165–183
  satisfaction and loyalty, 185–206
  segmentation and targeting, 69–101
  tools, 20, 21f, 22f, 25f, 26f, 27f
  typology, 3
Malcolm Baldrige National Quality Award, 21, 188
  stock performance of winners, 188f, 189f
Managerial judgment
  testing pricing, 174–175
Mapes & Ross, 158
Market-driven organization, 239
Market focused metrics, 235–236
Market gaps, 109
Marketing communications, 143–164, 240
  communication message checklist, 164
  investment cost, 163
  understanding the target market, 144
Marketing expenditures, 221
Marketing metrics, 235f
Marketing mix modeling, 181
Marketing progress
  measurement, 235
Marketing tools
  uncovering emotional motivations, 57–67
  which tools to use when, 66–67
Market intelligence, 29
Market research
  dedicated expertise, 232–233, 233f
  expense or investment?, 238
  internal vs. external, 233f
Market segments, 73–74. see also Segmentation
  benefits sought, 75
  brand preferences, 75
  lifestyles, 75
  media usage, 75
  needs, 75
  price sensitivity, 75
  product and service features, 75
  reaction to new concepts, 75
  usage occasion, 75
  which variables to use in studies, 92–93
Markham, John, 121
Markus, Hazel, 149
Marriott International, Inc, 21, 90, 132
McCann-Erickson Advertising Agency, 59
McCollum/Spielman Worldwide, 158
McCullough, Wayne, 210
McDonald's, 2–3, 30, 58, 80
  wireless networks in, 18–19

McQuarrie, Edward F.: *Customer Visits: Building Better Market Focus,* 46, 125
3M Dental Products Division, 126, 234
Means-End theory, 64–66
Mediamark Research, 24
Mercenary customer, 196, 199
Mildred group, 8–9
Miller Brewing Company, 19, 112
Miracle Whip
  advertising testing, 154–155
Mitchell, Bill, 211
Mobil Oil, 88
  SpeedPass, 89
Moderator
  focus groups, 40
Monadic split-cell design
  strengths and weaknesses, 179
  surveys using, 175, 177–179
Monetary value of purchase, 28
Montaguti, E, 15
Moore, Geoffrey, 82
Mother archetype, 43
Motorola, 14, 32
MTV, 33, 37, 42
Must haves, 124
Mutual Fund
  naming effects, 108
Mystery shoppers
  in customer satisfaction measurement programs, 200

N

Nabisco, 54
  advertising development, 153–154
Netnography, 37
Net population growth, 5
New products, 207–225, 240
  checklist, 224–225
  development funnel, 209–210, 209f, 212–213
  escalation of commitment, 213
  Hershey's, 210–211
  importance of success, 207–209
  initiation of ideas, 208–209
  investment costs, 224
New purchase follow-up
  in customer satisfaction programs, 202
New technology acceptance
  five factors inhibiting, 15
Nielsen/NetRatings, 161
Nokia, 121
Norman, Donald: *The Design of Everyday Things,* 126
Nostalgia trend, 11, 44
Not the old 9-to-5 trend, 11–12

O

Obituaries
  in qualitative research, 54
Observability, 17

Observation
    customer unmet needs, 33–35
    investment cost, 48
Occasion-based segmentation, 91–92
Occasion imagery, 109
Ogilvy, David, 156
One-dimensional features, 124
One-on-one interviews, 42
Operational excellence
    strategy for success, 71
Oreo cookies
    advertising testing, 152–153
    emotional or rational, 54–55
Organizational structure
    in new product development, 213
Overt needs
    vs. latent needs, 32–33
Oxygen Network, 77

P

Pain relievers
    perceptual map, 113f
Perceptions and differentiation, 103–120, 240
    checklist, 120
    investment cost, 119
Perceptual maps, 104, 109
    beer, 111f, 112f
    pain relievers, 113f, 114f
    use by marketers, 119
Persuasion
    in advertising, 157, 158
Peterson, Don, 185, 239
Phenomenological approach
    focus group research, 38–39
Photo sort
    in qualitative research, 54, 60
Picture interpretation, 59
Pingitore, Anthony, 210
Placebo effect, 56–57
Popcorn, Faith, 9
Popularity/drinkability, 110
Positioning, 104–105
    definition, 72
    four "Ds," 119
    strategies, 119
Positioning triangles, 104, 115–116
Post hoc segmentation, 75
    general variables, 83f
    product specific variables, 87f
Post-testing
    new products, 210
Potential Rating Index by Zip Markets (PRIZM), 78
Pre-testing
    new products, 210
Price elasticity, 187
Price loyalists, 91
Price promotional strategy, 171
Price sensitivity, 165–183, 240
Pricing decisions, 166

Pricing determination
    three Cs, 166–167
    three recommended approaches for testing, 176–177
Pricing issues, 174
    checklist, 183
    direct approach to customers, 176
    indirect approach to customers, 176
    for lifetime revenues, 182
    testing methods, 174–176
Pring, David, 23
Problem detection methods
    developing successful new products, 215–216
Procter & Gamble (P&G), 19, 33, 159
    earnings per share 1989-1999, 173f
    everyday low pricing strategy, 172–174
Product attribute, 116
Product development
    alternative strategies, 70f
    customer involvement, 211–212
    dilemma, 122–123
    global input for, 214–215
    new products, 210
    tools for successful new products, 215–224, 223f
Product imagery, 109
Product rollout
    new products, 210
Product segments, 74–75
Projective interviewing techniques
    uncovering emotional motivations, 57–60
Protocol Research Solutions, 23
Psycho-drawings
    in qualitative research, 54
Psychographics
    lifestyle trends, 8–9
    market segmentation, 73
PT Cruiser
    archetype research and, 44–45
Purchase behavior, 158–159
Purchasing behavior, 1–30

Q

Qualitative research, 130–131
Quality/price positioning, 115
Quality problems
    Schlitz Brewing Company, 193

R

Raid Roach Spray, 59
Rapaille, Clotaire, 43
Rational motivation, 51–67
    checklist, 67
    investment cost, 67
    marketing communications for, 143–144
Rau, P. Raghavendra, 108
Recall, 157–158
Recognition, 158
Refusing to age trend, 10
Regency of purchase, 28

Reichheld, Frederick F., 187
Relative advantage, 17
Repeat purchasing, 186
Repeat rate, 221
Reptilian instinct, 43
Resilience trend, 10
Reuss, Lloyd, 207
Reward-oriented employee, 138
Rice, Marshall, 113
Ritz-Carlton Hotel Company, LLC, 21, 445
Robertson, Thomas S., 15
Rogers, Everett M: *Diffusion of Innovations,* 17, 82
Role-playing, 59–60
Roper Starch Worldwide, Inc, 12
Royal Dutch Shell, 26
Ruby Tuesday, 78

S

Safety and security needs, 44
Sales representative, 115
Sasser, W. Earl, Jr., 187, 196
Satisfaction and loyalty, 185–206, 240
  checklist, 206
  investment cost, 205
Satisfied customers
  importance of, 185–186
  positive consequences of, 186
Sawhney, Mohanbir, 213
Sawtooth Software, 135
Scenario planning, 20, 25–27
Schlitz Brewing Company
  quality problems, 193
Schwartz, Peter: *The Art of the Long View,* 25–26
Screening
  new products, 210
Secondary data acquisition, 20, 22–23
Segmentation. *see also* A priori segmentation;
    Market segments; Post hoc segmentation
  attitudes about product category, 86–87
  beer industry, 72–73
  benefit segmentation, 89
  brand attitudes and preferences, 91
  business-to-business markets, 93–94
  checklist, 100–101
  cluster analysis in, 94–97
  customer and product interaction variables, 75
  definition, 72
  demographic, 77
  general variables, 75
  geo-clustering, 78
  geographic, 77–78
  investment costs, 100
  loyalty status and price sensitivity, 90–91
  media usage, 87
  multiple variables, 94
  s, 88
  se frequency, 81
  to new concepts, 91
  variables, 76f, 80f, 83f, 87f, 93f
  ption, 82

targeting and, 69–101, 240
targeting criteria, 97
targeting exercise, 99f
usage occasions, 91–92
usage status, 81
user status, 81
values and lifestyles, 84–86
Self-centered organization, 239
Sensation transference, 106–108
Sentence completion, 58
Service call follow-up
  in customer satisfaction programs, 202
Service recovery paradox, 195–197
Sex appeal, 64
Share of the customer wallet, 186
Shoppers, 91
Simmons Market Research Bureau, 24
Simon, H. A., 52
Simulated test markets
  developing successful new products, 221–223
Single most important set of consumer insights, 63
Single-person households, 6
Sloan, Alfred, 74
Social class segments, 79
Societally conscious, 86
Spouse acceptance factor, 37
Sprite, 106
SRI International, 85
Starbucks
  wireless networks in, 18–19
Stengel, 159
Sternthal, Brian, 116, 158
Story completion, 58
Strategic marketing process (STP), 72
Strategic planning, 29
Strivers, 84–85
Survivors, 85
Sustainers, 85
SWOT analysis, 20, 24–25

T

Tacit experience, 34
Target, 36
Targeting, 97–101
  criteria, 97
  definition, 72
Technological innovations
  customer participation, 16
  typology of, 16–17
Technology adoption trends, 14
Television commercial recall, 148
Terrorist customer, 196, 199
Testing
  new products, 210
T.G.I. Friday, 78
Thelma group, 8–9
Third person techniques, 58–59
Time-to-market pressure
  in new product development, 213
Top-of-Mind brand awareness, 160–161

Total product concept, 105f
TOWS analysis, 25
Trade-off analysis, 127–130
Trial ability, 17
Trial rate, 221
TV advertising
  how it works, 145–149
  major findings, 147–148
TV Guide, 60
Tybout, Alice, 116

U

U. S. Census Bureau, 22
U. S. Population aged 21-27, 4f
U. S. Population by age groups, 1980-2020, 5f
Unconscious mind, 143–164
Unilever, 35
7-Up, 106
Usability testing, 125–126
Usage occasions
  market segmentation, 73
Usage rate
  market segmentation, 72
User imagery, 109
User positioning, 115
User status
  market segmentation, 72

V

Value, 64, 165
Values and Life Styles (VALS), 85
Verbal exercises
  in qualitative research, 54

Vice-President of Customer Insight, 231
Vivísimo, 23

W

Web page
  color effects on customer perception, 107
Welch, Jack, 45
Wesely-Clough, Marita, 3, 10
WI-FI networks, 18–19
Willingness-to-pay, 167
Win-focus-parity strategy, 138
Wireless fidelity adoption, 18–19
Women's Entertainment (WE), 77
Word association, 58
Work-oriented employee, 138
Work-to-live employee, 138
World's Top Ten Values, Roper Starch, 12

Y

Yankelovich social monitor, 10–12

Z

Zajonc, Robert, 149
Zaltman, Gerald: *How Customers Think: Essential
    Insights into the Mind of the Market,* 60, 145,
    220
Zaltman Metaphor Elicitation Technique
    (ZMET), 60–64
  qualitative research and, 220
Zigzagging women trend, 11
ZIMA, 118